Richard Woodman was born in London in 1944 and crewed in a Tall Ships race before becoming an indentured midshipman in cargo-liners at the age of sixteen. He has sailed in a variety of ships, including weather ships, lighthouse traders and trawlers, serving from apprentice to captain. He is the author of twenty-three works of fiction and non-fiction, a member of the Royal Historical Society, the Society for Nautical Research, the Navy Records Society and the Square Rigger Club. In his spare time he sails an elderly gaff cutter with his wife and two children.

'This author has quietly stolen the weather-gauge from most of his rivals in the Hornblower stakes' *Observer*

'Packed with exciting incident, worthy of wide appeal to those who love thrilling nautical encounters and the sea' *Nautical Magazine*

'It is in the technical detail of ship handling, sails, rigging and myriad other details that Richard Woodman excells' Philip Wake, *Seaways*

Also by Richard Woodman

Nathaniel Drinkwater Series

AN EYE OF THE FLEET
A KING'S CUTTER
A BRIG OF WAR
THE BOMB VESSEL
THE CORVETTE
1805
BALTIC MISSION
IN DISTANT WATERS
A PRIVATE REVENGE
THE SHADOW OF THE EAGLE
EBB TIDE

WAGER
THE DARKENING SEA
ENDANGERED SPECIES
WATERFRONT
UNDER SAIL

THE FIRST NATHANIEL DRINKWATER OMNIBUS
THE SECOND NATHANIEL DRINKWATER OMNIBUS
BLAZE OF GLORY!

Death or Damnation

The Fourth Nathaniel Drinkwater Omnibus

Under False Colours
The Flying Squadron
Beneath the Aurora

RICHARD WOODMAN

A *Time Warner* Paperback

This omnibus edition first published in Great Britain by Time Warner Paperbacks in 2002

Previously published separately:

Under False Colours
First published in Great Britain in 1991 by John Murray (Publishers) Ltd
This edition published by Warner Books in 1992
Reprinted 1996, 2000

The Flying Squadron
First published in Great Britain in 1992 by John Murray (Publishers) Ltd
This edition published by Warner Books in 1993
Reprinted 1994, 1996, 2000

Beneath the Aurora
First published in Great Britain in 1995 by John Murray (Publishers) Ltd
This edition published by Warner Books 1996
Reprinted 1999

A CIP catalogue record for this book is available from the British Library.

ISBN 0 7515 3190 1

Typeset in Palatino by M Rules
Printed and bound in Great Britain by Clays Ltd, St Ives plc

Time Warner Paperbacks
An imprint of
Time Warner Books UK
Brettenham House
Lancaster Place
London WC2E 7EN

wwwTimeWarnerBooks.co.uk

Under False Colours

For my father, who first mentioned the Northampton boots.

Contents

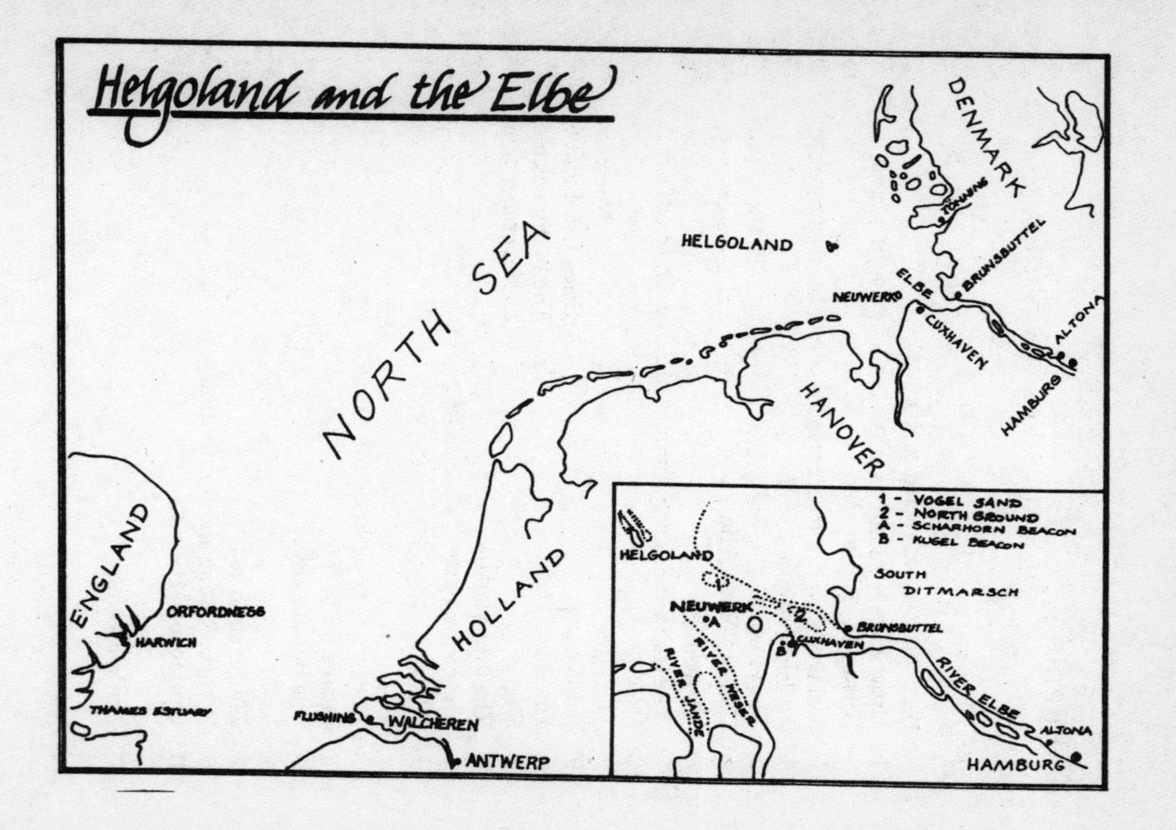
Helgoland and the Elbe
NORTH SEA
DENMARK
TÖNNING
BRUNSBUTTEL
HELGOLAND
ELBE
NEUWERK
CUXHAVEN
ALTONA
HAMBURG
HANOVER
HOLLAND
ENGLAND
ORFORDNESS
HARWICH
THAMES ESTUARY
FLUSHING
WALCHEREN
ANTWERP
1 - VOGEL SAND
2 - NORTH GROUND
A - SCHARHORN BEACON
B - KUGEL BEACON
HELGOLAND
SOUTH
DITMARSCH
NEUWERK
A
2
B
BRUNSBUTTEL
CUXHAVEN
RIVER WESER
RIVER JANDE
RIVER ELBE
ALTONA
HAMBURG

PART ONE

The Baiting of the Eagle

'The British Islands are declared to be in a state of blockade.
All commerce and all correspondence with the British Isles are prohibited.
Every . . . English subject . . . found in countries occupied by our troops . . . shall be made prisoners of war.
The trade in English commodities is prohibited . . .'

NAPOLEON
Articles 1, 2, 4 and 6,
The Berlin Decree,
21 November 1806

Chapter One

August 1809

Upon a Secret Service

'God's bones!'

Nathaniel Drinkwater swallowed the watered gin with a shudder of revulsion. His disgust was not entirely attributable to the loathsome drink: it had become his sole consolation in the weary week he had just passed. Apart from making the water palatable the gin was intended as an anodyne, pressed into service to combat the black depression of his spirits, but instead of soothing, it had had the effect of rousing a maddeningly futile anger.

He pressed his face against the begrimed glass of the window, deriving a small comfort from its coolness on his flushed forehead and unshaven cheek. The first floor window commanded a view of the filthy alley below. From the grey overcast sky – but making no impression upon the dirty glass – a slanting rain drove down, turning the unpaved ginnel into a quagmire of runnels and slime which gave off a foul stench. Opposite, across the narrow gutway between the smoke-blackened brick walls, a pie shop confronted him.

'God's bones,' Drinkwater swore again. Never in all his long years of sea service had an attack of the megrims afflicted him so damnably; but never before had he been so idle, waiting, as he was, above a ship's chandler's store in an obscure and foetid alley off Wapping's Ratcliffe Highway.

Waiting . . .

And constantly nagging away at the back of his mind was the knowledge that he had so little time, that the summer was nearly past, had *already* passed, judging by the wind that drove the sleet and smoke back down the chimney pots of the surrounding huddled buildings.

Yet still he was compelled to wait, a God-forsaken week of it now, stuck in this squalid room with its spartan truckle bed and soiled, damp linen. He glared angrily round the place. A few days, he had been told, at the most . . . He had been gulled, by God!

He had brought only a single change of small clothes, stuffed into a borrowed valise with his shaving tackle; and that was not all that was borrowed. There were the boots and his coat, a plain, dark grey broadcloth. He had refused the proffered hat. He was damned if he would be seen dead in a beaver!

'You should cut your hair, Drinkwater, the queue is no longer *de rigueur*.'

He had avoided *that* humiliation, at least.

He turned from the window and sat down, both elbows on the none-too-clean deal table. Before him, beside the jug and tumbler of watered gin, lay a heavy pistol. Staring at the cold gleam of its double barrels he reflected that he could be out of this mess in an instant, for the thing was primed and loaded. He shied bitterly away from the thought. He had traversed that bleak road once before. He would have to endure the gristle-filled pies, the cheap gin and the choked privy until he had done his duty. He swung back to the window.

The rain had almost emptied the alley. He watched an old woman, a pure-finder, her head covered by a shawl, her black skirt dragging on the ground where amid the slime, she sought dog turds to fill the sack she bore. Two urchins ran past her, throwing a ball playfully between them, apparently oblivious of the rain. Drinkwater was not deceived; he had observed the ruse many times in the past week. He could see their victim now, a plainly dressed man with obvious pretensions to gentility, picking his way with the delicacy of the unfamiliar, and searching the signs that jutted out from the adjacent walls. He might be something to do with the shipping lying in the Thames, Drinkwater mused, for his like did not patronize the establishment next door until after dark. He was certainly not the man for whom Drinkwater was waiting.

'You'll recognize him well enough,' Lord Dungarth had said, 'he has the look of a pugilist, a tall man, dark and well set up, though his larboard lug is a trifle curled.'

There had been some odd coves in the alley below, but no one to answer that description.

Drinkwater watched the two boys jostle the stranger from opposite sides, saw one pocket the ball and thumb his nose, saw the stranger raise his cane, and watched as the second boy drew out the man's handkerchief with consummate skill, so that the white flutter of its purloining was so sudden and so swift that it had vanished almost before the senses had registered the act. The two petty felons, their snot-hauling successful, capered away with a gleeful dido, the proceeds of their robbery sufficient to buy them a beef pie or a jigger of gin. The stranger stared after them, tapped his wallet and looked relieved. As the man cast a glance back at the trade signs, Drinkwater withdrew his face. A moment later the bell on the ship's chandler's door jangled and the stranger was lost to view. In the narrow ginnel a vicious squall lashed the scavenging pure-finder, finally driving her into shelter.

Drinkwater tossed off the last of the gin and water, shuddered again and contemplated the pistol. He picked it up, his thumb drawing back each of the two hammers to half cock. The click echoed in the bare room, a small but deliberately malevolent sound. He swung the barrels round towards him and stared at the twin muzzles. The dark orifices seemed like close-set and accusing eyes. His hand shook and the heavy, blued steel jarred against his lower teeth. He jerked his thumb, drawing back the right hammer to full cock. Its frizzen lifted in mechanical response. It would be *so* easy, so very easy, a gentle squeezing of the trigger, perhaps a momentary sensation, then the repose of eternal oblivion.

He sat thus for a long time. His hand no longer shook and the twin muzzles warmed in his breath. He could taste the vestiges of gunpowder on his tongue. But he did not squeeze the trigger, and would ever afterwards debate with himself if it was cowardice or courage that made him desist, for he had become a man who could not live with himself.

In the months since the terrible events in the rain forest of Borneo, his duty had kept him busy. The passage home from Penang had been happily uneventful, blessed with fair winds and something of a sense of purpose, for Lord Dungarth had written especially to Admiral Pellew – then commanding the East Indies station – that Captain Drinkwater and his frigate were to be sent home the moment they made their appearance in the China Sea. The importance of such an instruction seemed impressive at a distance. His Britannic Majesty's frigate *Patrician* had arrived at Plymouth ten days earlier and Drinkwater had been met with an order to turn his ship over to a stranger and come ashore at once. Taking post, he had reported to the Admiralty. Lord Dungarth, head of the Secret Department, had not been available and Drinkwater's reception had been disappointingly frosty. The urgency and importance with which his imagination had invested his return to England proved mistaken. Captain Drinkwater's report and books were received, he was given receipts and told to wait upon their Lordships 'on a more convenient occasion'.

Angry and dejected he had walked to Lord North Street to remonstrate with Dungarth. He had long ago angered the authorities – in the person of John Barrow, the powerful Second Secretary – but had hoped that his destruction of the Russian line-of-battle ship *Suvorou* with a mere frigate would have mollified his detractor. Apparently he remained in bad odour.

There had been more to fuel Captain Drinkwater's ire than official disapprobation. In a sense he had been relieved to have been summoned so peremptorily to London. He did not want to go home to Petersfield, though he was longing to see his children and to hold his wife Elizabeth in his arms again. To go home meant confronting Susan Tregembo, and admitting to her the awful fact that in the distant jungle of Borneo he had been compelled to dispatch his loyal coxswain Tregembo, whose tortured body had been past all aid, with the very pistol that he now held. The fact that the killing of the old Cornishman had been an act of mercy brought no relief to Drinkwater's tormented spirit. He remained inconsolable, aware that the event would haunt him to his own death, and that in the meantime he could not burden his wife with either himself or his confession.*

In such a state of turmoil and self-loathing, Drinkwater had arrived at Lord Dungarth's London house. A servant had shown him into a room he remembered, a room adorned with Romney's full length portrait of Dungarth's long-dead countess. The image of the beautiful young woman's cool gaze seemed full of omniscient accusation and he turned sharply away.

'Nathaniel, my dear fellow, a delight, a delight . . .'

His obsessive preoccupation had been interrupted by the entry of Lord Dungarth. Drinkwater had thought himself ready for the altered appearance of his lordship, for Admiral Pellew, sending him home from Penang, had told him Dungarth had lost a leg after

*See *A Private Revenge*.

an attempt had been made to assassinate him. But Dungarth had been changed by more than the loss of a limb. He swung into the room through the double doors on a crutch and peg-leg, monstrously fat, his head wigless and almost bald. The few wisps of hair remaining to him conferred an unkempt air, emphasized by the disarray and untidiness of his dress. Caught unprepared, shock was evident on Drinkwater's face.

'I know, I know,' Dungarth said wearily, lowering himself into a winged armchair, 'I am an unprepossessing hulk, damn it, a dropsical pilgarlic of a cove; my only consolation that obesity is considered by the *ton* a most distinguished accomplishment.'

'My Lord . . .?' Drinkwater's embarrassment was compounded by incomprehension.

'The Prince of Wales, Nathaniel, the Prince of Wales; a somewhat portly adornment to the Court of St James.'

'I see, my Lord, I had not meant to . . .'

'Sit down, my dear fellow, sit down.' Dungarth motioned to a second chair and regarded the drawn features, the shadowed eyes and the thin seam of the old sword cut down Drinkwater's hollow cheek. 'You are altered yourself; we can none of us escape the ravages of time.' He pointed to the Romney portrait: 'I sometimes think the dead are more fortunate. Now, come sir, a drink? Be a good fellow and help yourself, I find it confounded awkward.'

'Of course.' Drinkwater turned to the side table and filled two glasses.

'At least our imbroglio in the Peninsula has assured a regular supply of *oporto*,' Dungarth said, raising his glass and regarding Drinkwater over its rim, his hazel eyes as keen as they ever were. 'Your health, Nathaniel.'

'And yours, my Lord.'

'Ah, mine is pretty well done in, I fear, though the brain ain't as distempered as the belly, which brings me in an orotund way,' Dungarth chuckled, 'to my reasons for sending for you.' His lordship heaved his bulk upright. 'I'll come directly to the point, Nathaniel, and the point is Antwerp.

'We've forty thousand men on Walcheren investing Flushing; forty thousand men intended to take Antwerp, but bogged down under the command of that dilatory fellow Chatham.'

'The *late* earl,' Drinkwater joked bleakly, referring to Chatham's well-known indolence.

'You've heard the jest.' Dungarth smiled as he rang for his servant. 'Where are your traps? We'll have them brought round here. And William,' he said as he turned to his valet, 'send word to Mr Solomon that he is expected to dine with us tonight.'

'The point is,' Dungarth went on when the man had withdrawn, 'we are no nearer securing Antwerp than when we went to war over it back in 'ninety three, unless I am much mistaken. The expedition seems set to miscarry! We have expended millions on our allies and it has gained us nothing. We bungle affairs everywhere – I will not bore you with details, for their recounting does no one credit, but our fat prince is but a symptom of the disease . . .'

Dungarth's tone of exasperation, even desperation, touched Drinkwater. He had sensed in the earl's voice a war weariness, and the fear that all his services were to come to nothing.

'Between us, Nathaniel, I am driven almost mad by blunders and folly. Furthermore, Canning holds the purse for my work at the Secret Department, and I fear to cross Canning at this delicate juncture.' Dungarth paused.

'And this delicate juncture touches me, my Lord?'

'Yes, most assuredly. D'you command a following on that frigate of yours? A lieutenant who can be trusted?'

'I have a lieutenant who is dependent upon me, and a midshipman with an acting commission whom I would see advanced.'

'You can depend upon the lieutenant, utterly?'

'I can depend upon them both.'

'Who are they?'

'Lieutenant Quilhampton . . .'

'The cove with a wooden hand?'

'The same, my Lord, and a man recently displaced by my removal from the ship.'

'And the other?'

'Mr Frey, an able fellow, well enough used to doing his duty now.'

'How would they fare doing duty in a gun-brig on special service?'

'Admirably, I shouldn't wonder.'

Dungarth seemed to consider some secret design, then he looked up. 'Very well, since there seems no impediment . . .'

'Ah,' Drinkwater broke in, 'there is one matter to be taken into account: Mr Quilhampton is anxious to marry. The affair has been deferred before and I doubt his *fianc*ée will consent to further delay.'

Dungarth frowned. 'Then let him marry at once, or wait . . .'

'Wait, my Lord, for how long?'

'How long is a rat's tail? Be assured this service will not last long. It must be accomplished before the ice forms in the Baltic –'

'The Baltic . . .?' Drinkwater interrupted, but a distant bell diverted Dungarth's attention.

'That will be Solomon, Nathaniel,' he said, ponderously drawing himself to his feet. 'He is to be trusted, despite appearances.'

Dungarth's man announced the visitor and Dungarth performed the introductions. 'My dear Solomon, may I present Captain Nathaniel Drinkwater, lately arrived from the Pacific; Nathaniel, Mr Isaac Solomon, of Solomon and Dyer.'

'Y'r servant, Mr Solomon,' Drinkwater said, taking the Jew's hand. He wore the shawl and skull cap of Orthodoxy and had a fine-boned, palely handsome face framed by long, dark hair.

'Yours, Captain Drinkwater,' Solomon said, bowing slightly and regarding Drinkwater with an appraising eye.

'You will not refuse a slice or two of cold mutton, Isaac?' Wielding his crutch, Dungarth led them into an adjacent room and they settled before the earl resumed. 'What we propose,' Dungarth said, drawing Drinkwater into the web of intrigue and indicating that the mysterious Jew was party to the plot, 'is to send you to Russia.'

'To Russia!' Drinkwater frowned. ' 'Tis late in the year, my Lord . . .' He began to protest but Dungarth leaned forward, his knife pointedly silencing the criticism.

'A single cargo, Nathaniel,' he began, then threw himself back in his creaking chair, 'but Isaac, you elucidate the matter.'

'I have no need to extol the effects of the blockade of the European coastline by our naval forces, Captain,' Solomon said in a low, cultured voice, 'it is our chief weapon. But to oppose it the Emperor Napoleon has proclaimed a "Continental System", an economic interdiction of any British imports upon the mainland of Europe and Russia. Such a declaration was first thought to have been the phantasm of a disordered mind; alas it has proved remarkably successful.'

Drinkwater watched the eloquent gestures of the Jew's hands, accurately guessing the man belonged to that international mercantile confraternity that overcame political boundaries and evaded belligerent obstacles whenever possible.

'Two years ago we took Helgoland, both as a listening post with its ear close to the old independent Hanse city of Hamburg, and as an entrepôt for our trade . . .'

'But a wider breach must be cut in Napoleon's wall of *douaniers*, Nathaniel,' Dungarth broke in suddenly, 'something that does more than merely discredit his policy but *destroys* it! A cargo to Russia, a cargo to Russia as one of many cargoes! Such a cargo, widely advertised in Paris, could not fail to sow seeds of mistrust between Napoleon and his vacillating ally, Tsar Alexander.'

'You seek, if I understand aright,' Drinkwater said, 'to detach the Russian Tsar from his present alliance and reunite him with Great Britain?'

'Exactly! And it is our only chance, Nathaniel, before we are ruined, our last chance.'

'And this cargo, my Lord, has something to do with me, and Lieutenant Quilhampton?'

'It does.'

'Well, what is this cargo?'

'A quantity of Northampton boots, Nathaniel.'

'*Boots*?' Drinkwater's astonishment was unfeigned.

Dungarth nodded, his face a mask of serious intent, adding, 'and yourself, of course, to be employed upon a most secret service.'

Chapter Two *August 1809*

Baiting the Eagle

Below him the jangle of the chandler's door bell recalled Drinkwater to the present. The stranger emerged, settling his tricorne hat on his head and holding it there against the wind. The man turned away with his coat tails flapping, leaving the alley to the sleet and a solitary mongrel, which urinated purposefully against the wall of the pie shop opposite. The grey overcast was drawing the day to a premature close, but still Drinkwater sat on, recalling the twilight of that dawn, eight days earlier, when at the end of a night of planning he had sat at Lord Dungarth's escritoire. Apart from the servants, Drinkwater had been alone in the house, Isaac Solomon having departed an hour earlier, his lordship following, bound in his coach for the Admiralty.

'Do you write to your protéges, Nathaniel,' he ordered, 'and I will have orders drawn up for the expeditious preparation of a gun-brig for your escort. Deliver your letters by seven and I will have them carried by Admiralty messenger.' He had been about to depart then added, as an afterthought, 'If you wish to leave word for your wife, I will have it sent after your departure. It would be best if few people know your whereabouts.'

Few people, Drinkwater ruminated savagely, would think of looking for him here, even if they knew him to be in London; and the fact that his Lordship's proposal fell in with his private desires did nothing to assuage his sense of guilt. To this was added an extreme distaste for his task. It was perfectly logical when expounded in Lord Dungarth's withdrawing room, but it was a far cry from his proper occupation, commanding one of His Britannic Majesty's ships of war.

'You will assume the character of a shipmaster of the merchant marine,' Dungarth had instructed. 'Here are a coat and *surtout*,' he had said as his servant brought the garments in, 'and a pair of hessian boots.'

Drinkwater regarded them now; they had once been elegant boots, a tassel adorning the scalloped tops of their dark green leather.

'I don't need more than one at a time, these days,' he recalled Dungarth joking with bitter irony. 'I'll have your sea kit shipped aboard Quilhampton's brig . . .'

Drinkwater had slipped into Wapping feeling like a spy.

And he felt worse now, worn by the tedious days of idle waiting, trying to sustain his spirits with the assurances of Dungarth and Solomon that his part in lying low in Wapping was crucial to the success of the mission, but unable to stop worrying whether or not Elizabeth knew of *Patrician's* arrival home, or how Quilhampton, the matter of his marriage pressing, had viewed his secret orders.

But over and over again, as he waited interminably, it seemed, his thoughts came round to the secret service to which he was now irrevocably committed.

'Isaac has provided the capital and made arrangements for a large consignment of boots and greatcoats to be loaded aboard a barque lying in the Pool of London. To all outward appearances the whole transaction is a commercial one, a speculative venture that contents the manufacturers,' Dungarth had explained.

That much Drinkwater had guessed. Mr Solomon was clearly a cut above the Jewish usurers, slop-sellers and hawkers who supplied credit, cash and personal necessities to His Majesty's fleet. Solomon had alluded to a considerable illicit trade run through Helgoland and Hamburg, actively encouraged by Bourrienne, once Napoleon's private secretary, but then the Governor of Hamburg.

'M'sieur Bourrienne,' Solomon had explained, 'suffered from a sense of grievance at the loss of his influential position with the Emperor; his co-operation was not difficult to secure.' Solomon had smiled. 'And, of course, Captain, every cargo sold to Hamburg or Russia is of benefit to England . . .'

Staring down into the rain-lashed ginnel, Drinkwater thought of the snatches of rumour and news he had gleaned in his brief period back on English soil. There were scandals in both the army and the navy, in addition to the fiasco that seemed inevitable at Walcheren. More disturbing were the riots in the north and the increasingly desperate need for markets for manufactured goods. Doubtless Solomon would profit privately from this venture, for Dungarth's remarks concerning Canning suggested his alliance with the Jew was a bold stroke, but if a trade could be opened with Russia, it might ameliorate the sufferings of the labouring poor as well as achieve the object Dungarth had in view.

But would a consignment of boots succeed in disrupting a solemn alliance between the two most powerful individuals on earth? True, there were a few other titbits. 'A few hundred stand of arms,' Dungarth had enthused, 'and a brace or two of horse pistols in the consignment, sufficient to equip a squadron or two of cavalry. Given the usual cupidity of the tier-rangers and the other waterside thieves, word of the nature of the consignment will become common knowledge along the Wapping waterfront.'

And that was the crux of the affair, that was why he, Captain Nathaniel Drinkwater of the Royal Navy, was detached upon a secret service, why he occupied this squalid, rented room and played the character of a merchant shipmaster, perpetually drunk, cantankerous and misanthropic. Sadly, it was all too easy in his present state of mind.

'Among that waterside riff-raff, you have only to find Fagan,' Lord Dungarth had finally said, 'and spread this tittle-tattle to him. He's a man known to us, d'you see, Nathaniel, a courier who passes regularly between London and Paris carrying gossip and the odd, planted message. You have merely to indicate the value, content and destination of your cargo, for its departure to be reported to Paris. We are expecting Fagan daily; he keeps rooms above a pie shop in Wapping . . .'

Drinkwater peered across the alley. It was almost dark. He struck flint on steel and coaxed a stump of candle into life.

'We want you to bait the eagle,' Dungarth had said as they rose to disperse, 'see that the Emperor takes the lure . . .'

It was not quite that easy, of course, his instructions went much further. He had to ship with the cargo, to play the charade to the last scene, to see that it reached Russia safely.

Drinkwater stood stiffly and stretched. If Fagan did not arrive soon the enterprise would have to be scrapped. Perhaps he had already arrived, and was engaged elsewhere; how did one trust or predict the movements of a double agent?

Drinkwater threw himself on the narrow bed and considered

Dungarth's warning of the burden of the war, his consuming conviction that only an alliance with Russia would break the stalemate between Great Britain's superiority at sea and France's hold on the continent of Europe.

Drinkwater remembered the Russian army in its bivouacs around Tilsit. The sheer size of that patient multitude was impressive and the cogent fact that the Tsar's ill-trained levies had inflicted upon Napoleon's veterans the near defeat of Eylau and the Pyrrhic victory of Friedland argued in favour of Dungarth's ambitious policy.

'We *must* have Russia as a continental reinforcement,' Dungarth had reiterated with characteristically single-minded vehemence. 'Without her almost inexhaustible resources of manpower, there is nothing on earth to oppose France . . .'

That was true. Prussia had long ago succumbed, Austria was beaten, Germans, Poles and Danes all bowed to the imperial will. Apart from the British, only the isolated Swedes and the erratic Spaniards defied Paris . . .

'And it's such a fragile thing, Nathaniel,' Dungarth's voice echoed in Drinkwater's memory, 'this alliance between Alexander and Napoleon, so flimsy, based as it is upon a mutual regard by two vain and selfish men. The one is utterly unreliable, the other determined, wilful, but fickle . . . we have only to interpose a *doubt*, the one about the other and . . .'

He woke with a start, aware that he had dozed off. It was quite dark in the room, for the candle had gone out. From the alley came the noise of a few passers-by, seamen bound for the neighbouring knocking shop, he guessed, noting the rain had stopped. From within the house came the dull buzz of conversation and domestic activity. The ship's chandler had shut up his store to take his evening meal with his wife and mother-in-law. Later, when he had finished, he would come and attend to his uninvited guest. He was in the pay of the government, a gleaner of news who talked freely to masters and mates in want of necessaries for their ships, seamen requiring outfits and slops and all those associated with the huge volume of merchant trade which flourished despite Napoleon's Continental System.

The gin had left Drinkwater thirsty and with a foul taste in his mouth. He got up and peered into the jug. The stale smell revolted him and he found he was in want of the privy.

'God's bones,' he swore, putting off the distasteful moment and standing by the window scratching the bites of the vermin which infested his mattress. Overhead the cloud was shredding itself to leeward. 'Wind veered nor' west,' he muttered to himself. Neither the westerly gale nor the veering wind would allow a boat to slip across the Strait of Dover. Fagan would not come tonight, nor tomorrow. Not unless he was a man of uncommon energy and sailed from Cherbourg, or some other port well to the westward.

Drinkwater went back to the bed and, hands behind his head, stared up at the pale rectangle of the ceiling. Where were Quilhampton and Frey now? Had James Quilhampton caught the mail coach and raced to Edinburgh to marry Mistress MacEwan? Drinkwater had sent him a draught to be drawn on his own prize agent to finance the wedding; but there was the troublesome person of the girl's aunt and the matter of the banns.

And had Frey done as instructed, and seen the bulk of Captain Drinkwater's personal effects into safe-keeping aboard his gun-brig?

The thoughts chased themselves round and round Drinkwater's brain. He longed for a book to read, but Solomon's clerk had conducted him to the vacant room above Mr Davey's chandlery with such circumspection that Drinkwater, eager not to lose a moment and expecting the mysterious Fagan to appear within hours of his taking post, had not thought of it for himself. Mr Davey's store had yielded up a copy of Hamilton Moore, but Drinkwater had spent too many hours conning its diagrams of the celestial spheroid in his youth to derive much satisfaction from it now.

Lying still, the urge to defecate subsided. How long would he have to wait before he confronted Fagan? And how would he accomplish that most subtle of tasks, the giving away of the game in a manner calculated to inform without raising the slightest suspicion?

A scratching at the door roused him from his lethargy. He opened the door upon Mr Davey's rubicund face.

'A bite to eat, Cap'n?'

'Aye, thank you, Mr Davey, and I'd be obliged for a new candle.'

'Of course . . . if you'll bide a moment . . .'

Davey slipped away to return a few moments later. 'Here you are, sir. There's no news I'm afraid, Cap'n . . .'

'And not likely to be with this wind,' Drinkwater said morosely as Davey struggled with flint and steel.

'I wouldn't say that, Cap'n. Mr Fagan has a way of poppin' up, as it were. Like jack-in-the-box, if you take my meaning.'

'D'you know him well, then?'

'Well enough, Cap'n,' replied Davey, coaxing the candle into life. 'He takes his lodging in the room yonder. When I gets word I tell the one-legged gennelman.'

'I see. And the customer you received late this afternoon? What was his business?'

Davey winked and tapped the side of his nose. 'A gennelman in a spot o' trouble, Cap'n Waters,' he said, using Drinkwater's assumed name. 'Word gets round, d'ye see, that I sell paregoric elixir . . .' Davey enunciated the words with a certain proprietorial hauteur. 'He's afeared o' visiting a quack or a 'pothecary, but mostly o' Job's Dock.'

'*Who's* dock?' asked Drinkwater, biting into the gristle that seemed the chief constituent of the meat pie Davey had brought him.

'Job's Dock, Cap'n, the venereal ward at St Bartholomew's. He's got himself burnt, d'ye see . . .'

'Yes, yes . . .' Drinkwater was losing his appetite.

'I stock a supply for the benefit of the seamen . . .'

'I understand, Mr Davey, though I did not know tincture of opium was effective against the pox.'

'Ah, but it clears the distemper of the mind, Cap'n, it relieves the conscience . . .'

When a man has a bad conscience, Drinkwater thought, the most trivial remarks and events serve to remind him of it. Perhaps Davey's paregoric elixir would remove the distemper of his own mind. He visited the privy and turned instead to the replenished jug of gin. An hour later he fell asleep.

He had no idea how long he had slept when he felt himself being shaken violently.

'Cap'n, sir! Cap'n! Wake ye up, d'ye hear! Wake up!'

Snatched from the depths of slumber Drinkwater was at first uncertain of his whereabouts, but then, suddenly alarmed, he thrust Davey aside to reach for his pistol. 'What the devil is it, Davey? Damn it, take your hands off me!'

' 'Tis him, sir, Fagan . . .!'

Drinkwater was on his feet in an instant and had crossed the room to stare out over the dark gutway of the alley. No light betrayed any new arrival over the pie shop opposite. There were noises from the ginnel below, but there always were as the patrons of the adjacent bordello came and went.

'He's next door, sir, in Mrs Hockley's establishment, Cap'n.'

'How the deuce d'you know?' asked Drinkwater, drawing on the borrowed boots.

'She sent word, Cap'n. She keeps her ears and eyes open when I asks her.'

'You didn't mention me?' Drinkwater asked, relieved when Davey shook his head.

He wondered how many other people knew that Fagan was expected in the Alsatia of Wapping. It was too late for speculation now. His moment had come and he must act without hesitation. He pulled on his coat and took a swig of the watered gin, swilling it round his mouth and spitting it out again, allowing some of it to dribble on to his soiled neckcloth.

'I wouldn't take your pistol, Cap'n, Ma Hockley don't allow even the gentry to carry arms in her house . . . here, take the cane.'

Drinkwater took the proffered malacca, twisted the silver knob to check the blade was loose inside, clapped his hat on his head and left the darkened room. 'Obliged to you, Mr Davey,' he said over his shoulder as he clattered down the stairs with Davey behind him. Davey pushed past him at their foot and led him through the store, opening the street door with a jangle of keys and tumbling of locks.

To Drinkwater, even the air of the alley smelled sweet after the stifling confinement of his room. Despite the slime beneath his feet and the sulphurous stink of sea-coal smoke, the wind brought with it a tang of salt, blown from the exposed mudflats of the Thames. He caught himself from marching along the alley and walked slowly towards the door of Mrs Hockley's. It was open, and spilled a lozenge of welcoming yellow lamplight on to the ground.

He turned into the doorway to be confronted by a tall ugly man.

'Yeah? What d'you want then?'

Drinkwater leaned heavily on his cane. He hoped his nervousness gave some credibility to his attempt to act drunk. He chose to speak with deliberate care rather than risk exposure by a poor attempt to slur his words.

'A little pleasure . . . a little escape . . . a desire to make the acquaintance of Mistress Hockley . . .' He eased his weight against the wall.

''Eard of 'er, 'ave you?'

'In the most favourable terms.' Drinkwater leaned against the wall while Mrs Hockley's pimp and protector half turned and thrust his head through a door leading off the hall.

'Got a nob here, Dolly, a-wishin' to make your hacquaintance . . .'

Mrs Hockley appeared and Drinkwater doffed his hat and, still leaning on the wall, made a bow.

'Madam . . . at your service . . .' He straightened up. She was a voluptuously blowsy woman in her forties, her soiled gown cut low to reveal an ample bosom which she animated by shrugging her shoulders forward. 'Charmed, Madam,' Drinkwater added for good effect, admittedly stirred by the unrestrained flesh after so long an abstinence. 'I am in search of a little convivial company, Madam . . .'

'Oh, you 'ave come to the right place, Mr . . .?'

'Waters, Madam, Captain Waters . . . in the Baltic trade . . .'

'Oh, ain't that nice. Let the Captain in, Jem.' She smiled, an insincere stretching of her carmined lips, and took his arm. 'What does the Captain fancy, then? I 'ave a new mulatto girl an' a peachy little virgin as might have just bin specially ordered for your very pleasure.'

Drinkwater followed her into a brightly lit room. It was newly papered and an India carpet covered the floor. Over the fireplace hung a large oil painting, an obscene rendering of the Judgement of Paris.

Four of Mrs Hockley's 'girls' lounged in various states of erotic undress on *chaises-longues* and sofas with which the room seemed overcrowded. The light was provided by an incongruously elaborate candelabra which threw a cunningly contrived side-light upon the bodies and faces of the waiting whores. Of the mysterious Fagan there was no sign.

'A little drink for the Captain,' Mrs Hockley ordered, 'while he makes his choice.'

Drinkwater grinned. 'No, thank you, I did not come here to drink, Mrs Hockley . . .'

'My, the Captain's a wit, to be sure, ain't 'e girls?'

The whores stared back or smiled joylessly, according to their inclination. Drinkwater swiftly cast an eye over them. He was going to have to choose damned carefully and he was aware that his knowledge of the female character was wanting.

'This is Chloë, Captain, the mulatto girl of whom I spoke.' She had been handsome once, if you had a taste for the negro, Drinkwater thought, her dark eyes still contained a fire that suggested a real passion might be stirred by even the most routine of couplings. She would be dangerous for his purpose, a view confirmed by her sullen pout as he turned his attention away.

'And this is Clorinda . . .' Bored and tired, Clorinda stared back at him through lacklustre eyes, her pseudo-classical trade name sitting ill upon her naked shoulders. 'And this is Zenobia . . .'

Mixed blood had produced a skin the colour of *café au lait* and a luxurious profusion of raven hair. Zenobia was not handsome, her face was heavily pocked, but she had a lasciviously small waist and she met his stare with a steady gaze. She held his eyes a moment longer than prudence dictated, but the twitch of pure lust that ran through Drinkwater was masked mercifully by a heavy thud from the floor above. It prompted a self-conscious giggle from Chloë and the fourth girl as Mrs Hockley, growing impatient with her vacillating customer, played her ace. 'And this, Captain, offered to you at a special price, is Psyche.' Mrs Hockley drew the girl forward and, like a trained bear, the giggling bawd assumed a demure, downcast pose, as though reluctantly offering herself. 'A virgin, Captain . . . certified so by Mr Gosse, the chirurgeon.'

Psyche's shoulders twitched and Drinkwater caught the inelegant snort of a suppressed laugh. The means by which Mr Gosse established Psyche's intact status were not in doubt.

'Really?' he said, trying to show interest while he made up his mind. There was a strong reek of gin on Psyche's breath. Clorinda was poking an index finger between the bare toes of her right foot and Chloë had turned away. Only Zenobia watched him, a look of hunger in her eyes. She turned slightly, cocking a hip at him in a small, intimate gesture of invitation. He looked again at her waist and the riot of black hair that tumbled over her shoulders and down her back, curling over the breasts elevated by her tight corsage. From overhead, the bumps indicated someone was having a riotous time. He hoped its originator was Mr Fagan.

'How much, Mrs Hockley, are you asking for this quartern of bliss?' He gestured to Psyche with the head of his cane.

'Two guineas, Captain,' Mrs Hockley said, placing an intimate hand on Drinkwater's arm as if implying some kind of guarantee.

'And she is truly a virgin?'

'Would I lie, sir?' she asked, her hand abruptly transferred to her bosom, her red lips an outraged circle and her false lashes fluttering. 'She is fresh as a daisy, Captain, as I live and breathe . . .'

'As she lives and breathes, Madam, there is an excess of gin! I'll take Zenobia.'

'Oh, sir, you *are* a wit, Zenobia is two guineas . . .'

'Ten shillings, Madam, and for as long as I want pleasuring.' He was sickening of the charade, eager to be out of the heavily perfumed stink of the room.

'In advance, Captain, if you please.'

He drew the coins from his waistcoat pocket, dropped them into Mrs Hockley's eager palm and abruptly gestured Zenobia to lead him to her chamber. Upstairs, the false luxury of Mrs Hockley's *salon* gave way to a bare-boarded landing with half a dozen unpainted deal doors leading from it.

Zenobia, whose given name was more certainly Meg or Polly, entered one of them and closed the door behind them. The room had a small square of carpet, an upright chair and a bed. The sheets were stained and rumpled. The window had been bricked up, Drinkwater noticed, as Zenobia went round the room, lighting a trio of candle stumps from the single one she had brought upstairs. The air was filled with the strong scent of urine as Zenobia pulled a drab screen to one side. Instead of a commode a cracked china jordan stood on a stool.

''Ave a piss. Capt'in. I'll get undressed.'

'No, wait . . . how much will you be paid for this, Zenobia?' 'Five shillin' plus me board and lodgin', why?' She had paused and was looking at him.

'Because I want you to do something special for me.'

She turned away and made to unhook her stays, her face uninterested. 'You'll still have to piss . . . I'm a clean girl . . .'

Drinkwater blushed, aware that, for all his bravado, he was not used to this sort of thing, was unfamiliar with the rituals of what passed for love, and of what exotic treats might be available to him.

'You don't understand, I'll give you two guineas . . .'

The woman looked up sharply, throwing her skirt over the back of the chair and drawing her stays from her body. Her breasts, still tip-tilted, swung free, catching the light of the candles.

'You pay me what you like. I'll do what you want, but no beating. If you beat me, I'll scream for Jem. An' I wants to see yer 'and-spike . . .'

'For God's sake, *be quiet*. Here . . .' Drinkwater fished the coins from his pocket and held them out to her. She seized them and bit them.

'Is a man called Fagan in the house?' he asked, before she could say more.

She looked at him through narrowed eyes. Her hand reached out for her skirt and she drew it to cover her breasts as though he had asked her a most improper question. 'What's yer game?' She backed towards the door.

'It's all right Zenobia, I mean you no harm. Just tell me if a man called Fagan is in the house. If you help me I'll pay you another guinea.' He knew it was a mistake, the moment the words were out of his mouth. He saw the quick movement of her eyes to his waistcoat pocket, gauging how many more guineas reposed there. If she summoned Jem they might roll him for the contents of his pockets and that would be disastrous. He took a small step forward and she fell back towards the door.

'You ain't 'ere for a fuck, are you?' she asked, edging towards the door, her voice rising wildly. He raised his cane and stabbed its point into the door, preventing her from opening it. His left hand reached out and caught her black tresses. He gave a quick tug and pulled the wig from her head. With a sharp whimper she shrunk back into the room, crouching in her humiliation. He knelt quickly beside her, putting an arm about her shoulders. Strands of hair clung to her skull and suddenly he felt sorry for her.

'Please, Zenobia,' he hissed insistently into her ear, '*trust* me. You will come to no harm and I will not forget you. Is the man Fagan here, now? A big man, like a prize fighter, with a thick left ear? Tell me.'

She looked up. 'You won't tell Mrs Hockley?' Her eyes were imploring.

'What? That I didn't bed you?'

'No, about my 'air. If she knows about my 'air, she'll chuck me out. I've a boy to feed, a good boy . . .'

'No, of course not. I'll give you something for the boy if you help me . . .'

'Will ya? Honest?'

'Yes, now come, I haven't much time . . .' He stood and held out his hand. She took it and gave him a shy smile, sitting herself on the bed.

' 'E's 'ere,' she jerked her head, 'next door, wiv Annie, I means Lucinda. It was 'im, the pig, as was making all the bleedin' noise.'

'Will he stay all night?'

'No, not 'im. 'E'll be at it for an hour or so, then 'e'll sleep orf 'is drunkenness, then 'e'll give 'er another turkin' afore he leaves. 'E likes 'is money's worth, does Mr Fagan.'

'Does he just leave? He doesn't stop below, for a drink or a chat with Mrs Hockley?'

'What you askin' all these questions for? Are you a runner, or a magistrate's man or somefink?'

'No . . .' He fell silent, trying to think out his next move. He had to come upon Fagan in a situation of the most contrived casualness . . .

'Have you ever been with him?'

'Fagan? No. 'E's the kind who gives a girl a rough time.'

'How d'you know?' Drinkwater asked.

'We talk, Mister,' Zenobia said, a note of contempt in her voice. 'We don't spend all our lives on our bleedin' backs. Annie, I means Lu, told me.'

'You mean you don't offer yourself to him because of . . .' He picked up the wig and held it out to her.

'Yeah, 'e'd soon find out, then 'e'd tell Ma Hockley and I'd be in the gutter.'

'D'you have a bottle of gin or anything here?'

'I got a bit.' She held up her skirt questioningly. 'You ain't going to . . .?'

He shook his head and said, 'Where's the bottle?'

Fastening her skirt she reached on to a shelf. The bottle was only a quarter full. 'It ain't free.'

'I'll give you tuppence for it. Now listen,' he dug for the pennies, 'I want you to be a very good girl. I want you to tell me the moment Mr Fagan comes out of the room next door . . .'

'You ain't going to . . .' she made a lunging and twisting movement with her right hand, 'give 'im one wiv that rum degen of yours, are ya?' She nodded at the sword-stick. 'I don't want nuffink to do wiv you –'

'I only want to talk to him.'

She stared at him, weighing him up, her head cocked on one side. ''E's a dangerous bugger. If 'e gets wind I helped you . . .'

'Look,' said Drinkwater urgently, exasperation creeping into his voice, 'if you do exactly what I ask, I'll leave another two guineas with the chandler next door. For your boy . . .'

'How do I know . . .?'

He did not blame her for her suspicions, but he could now hear the noise of voices from the adjacent room. All the indications were that Fagan had finished with the obliging Annie. He had no time to lose. 'Do as I say,' he said sharply, keeping his voice low, 'or I'll have that wig off again and I'll be on that landing screaming for Mrs Hockley that you've poxed me!'

The words struck her like a whip. Her face blanched. She turned and put her hand out to a framed print on the wall. Lifting it off its hook she jerked her head at the hole hidden behind it. 'See for yerself.'

He put an eye to the hole and peered through into the next room. The white body of a voluptuous girl lay spread in total abandonment on the bed. Her hands were tucked behind her head, her tawny hair fanned out across the pillow. She was laughing at some remark her companion was making. Then the bulk of a man came into view. He was almost dressed, his hands busy with his neckcloth. Drinkwater needed to see no more. He turned back into the room, took the print from Zenobia's hand and replaced it.

''E gets a bit rough sometimes,' she said, nodding at the erotic print, 'Ma Hockley sometimes keeps an eye on 'im. All the rough ones get that room.'

Her tone suggested a pathetic attempt to palliate what she had taken for anger on Drinkwater's part. The poor creature must be desperate for money.

'Get into bed, pull the sheets up . . .'

She did as she was bid while he pulled off his coat and tugged at his own neckcloth until it hung loosely about his neck. He threw his coat over his arm and picked up his hat and cane. Hoping to look as if he had just risen from a bed of illicit love he stood beside the door, his right hand on the knob. He turned to Zenobia. 'I'll leave the money with Mr Davey next door. I've some business to transact with him.'

He opened the door a crack. Outside the landing was lit by a single lantern. From below came loud male laughter, more customers, Drinkwater guessed, which might make his task easier. He strove to catch the noise of the latch of the adjacent door, but Zenobia was saying something.

Angrily he turned. 'Quiet,' he hissed.

'Don't ya want it then?' She was holding out the nearly empty gin bottle.

'Damn!' he muttered, crossed to the bed and grabbed it from her. As he reached the door again he saw the light from Annie's opening door, and the shadow of a man's figure. The sound of his voice rolled along the bare passage.

'Let me go, you wanton bitch.'

On tip-toe, Drinkwater stepped out on to the landing, closing the door behind him. Fagan stood in the adjacent doorway. Annie was clinging to him, stark naked. Fagan was pulling her arms from about his neck.

'Upon my soul, you've been riding a fine horse, sir,' Drinkwater said in a loud voice. Fagan looked round at him and finally disengaged himself as Annie slipped back into her room. 'Heard you thrown a few times as you went over the fences.'

'What's it to you?' Fagan turned, his expression darkly belligerent.

'Nothing sir, nothing, except it puts a fellow off his own gallop. Have a drink,' Drinkwater held out the bottle. 'Cool yourself . . .'

Fagan stared at Drinkwater, frowning. 'Who the hell are you?'

'Captain Waters at your service, sir. Master of a barque lying in the stream. Waiting for a wind.' Drinkwater stepped towards Fagan, putting up his left arm with its coat, cane and hat to catch Fagan's elbow in a gesture of assumed friendship. 'Got a damned good rate for my freight, if I can run it,' he rattled on. 'If I can persuade those jacks-in-office of the Custom House that it's for Sweden.' He threw back his head and laughed, feeling the resistance in Fagan's demeanour relax. They made their way to the head of the stairs.

Fagan paused at the top and turned to his accoster. Drinkwater smiled to cover his anxiety; Fagan's next remark would show Drinkwater whether he had the slightest chance of success in this mad enterprise.

Fagan's irritation at the untimely encounter appeared to have gone. He affected a degree of casual interest in Drinkwater's drunken gossip.

'But it ain't for Sweden, eh, Cap'n? That your drift?' There was the trace of a brogue there, Drinkwater noted as he nodded. He held out the gin bottle again. 'Here,' he said, 'drink to my good fortune,' and he finished the sentence with a laugh.

'So where are you taking it? Somewhere the Custom House men wouldn't like, eh?'

'Drink,' Drinkwater repeated, boldly banging the bottle into Fagan's barrel chest. The big Irishman continued to regard him through shrewd eyes. 'Go on, drink, wash that woman out of your mouth . . . Customs Officers? God damn you, no, I'm on to bigger game than running a cargo to the damned French or the Dutch.' Drinkwater stopped suddenly and stared hard at Fagan, as though recovering his wits and regretting his free tongue.

'So where would you be taking your cargo, Cap'n, if not to the French?'

Drinkwater made to push past Fagan. He drew his mouth into a mirthless grin, as though suddenly nervously anxious. 'Ah, that'd be telling. 'Tis a secret . . . a damned good secret . . .' He was almost past Fagan, had his right foot on the top stair when he delivered the Parthian shot. 'And one the damned French would love to know . . .'

Fagan's paw shot out and jerked Drinkwater's left shoulder back so that he struck the bannisters. 'Hey, damn you!'

'Don't push, Cap'n . . . I'll have the drink you were kind enough to offer me, and then we should take a bite to eat. Rogering makes a man hungry, eh?' Fagan began to descend the stairs, his powerful fist digging into the scarred muscle of Drinkwater's right shoulder. Drinkwater felt himself propelled downwards. At the foot of the stairs he twisted free. 'I have a boat to catch . . .'

'And what ship would you be going to?'

'That's my business, sir.'

'Oh, come now, Cap'n. All men are brothers in a house of pleasure. I'm only after a little light conversation. You were civil enough to be sure, when that wench upstairs had left you in a good humour. You're not mean enough to deny a fellow a companion over his breakfast.'

Fagan slapped him amiably on the back and Drinkwater was ironically aware that they had exactly reversed roles.

'I can easily find out your ship. I know your name and I can soon bribe a Customs man to show me your inward jerque note . . . if I had a mind for such foolishness. But d'you see I'm a trifle out o' luck myself at the moment and, taking you for a man o' spirit, I was wondering if we might strike a deal. An investment in your cargo, perhaps, with a decent return on it, might set me up and save you a guinea or two of your own.' Fagan paused and Drinkwater pretended to consider the matter. Hearing their voices, Mrs Hockley had emerged from her salon to see if her customers were satisfied.

'I didn't know you gennelmen was acquainted,' she said, but Fagan took no notice and with his arm across Drinkwater's shoulders, thrust him out of the street door. 'Come,' he said, 'we'll discuss the matter over a bottle of porter and a decent beef pie.'

They had crossed the alley and Fagan was hammering on the locked door of the pie shop. Drinkwater looked up at the narrow strip of starlit sky above their heads. The wind was dying to a breeze.

A boy, woken by the noise, let them in and Fagan sent him back to his bed with a cuff. Moving with the ease of familiarity, Fagan led Drinkwater into a back kitchen where a large table and a black iron stove stood. The stove had a banked fire and Fagan, kicking it open, soon had a stump of candle guttering on the table. Then he drew half a pie from a meat-safe and cut two slices with a pocket knife. Turning aside he found two horn beakers and set them down.

'Come now, Cap'n, sit yerself down. Where's that bottle o' yours?'

Drinkwater meekly did as he was bid. 'How much were you thinking of risking, Mr . . .?'

'Gorman, Cap'n, Michael Gorman . . . well now, how would, say, two hundred pound do; say at a five per cent return on completion o' the voyage, to be remitted by . . . when would it be remitted?'

'It would be a single voyage, Mr Gorman. I'm not expecting a homeward freight. That depreciates my chance of profit, and there are risks, Mr Gorman, very great risks, and five per cent on two hundred, well . . .' Drinkwater broke off and shrugged. Affecting lack of interest he took a bite at his slice of pie.

'Well, just supposing, and I'm not saying I will, but think of what it means to reducing your own capital risk . . . you are risking your own capital in the venture, ain't you?'

'Would I take such risks for another?' Drinkwater asked, his mouth full.

'No, no, of course not. But just supposing I was to invest *four* hundred pounds, could I expect a return of five per cent?' Fagan leaned forward and Drinkwater met his eyes. 'I'm not saying I can raise the money, but if I could, would you shake on the deal?'

'I might.'

'Well what is the cargo? I must know . . .'

'Of course, Mr Gorman,' Drinkwater said reasonably. 'A few stand of arms, greatcoats and military boots . . .' Drinkwater watched the tiny, reactive muscles round Fagan's eyes. Leaning forward over the candle they showed clearly, twitching even as Fagan lowered his eyes in dissimulation.

'You'd be wanting something on account?' Fagan did not wait for an answer. 'I'll give you ten guineas now, against your written receipt, I've pen and paper to hand . . .' Fagan rose and disappeared up a narrow staircase hidden behind a door. In a few minutes he was back. He threw the guineas on to the table and produced a pen and inkwell. The gold gleamed dully in the candle light. Drinkwater stared at it. It was a bribe, designed to disarm him for the next question. He took up the pen and dipped it.

'And where would these military boots be bound, Cap'n Waters?'

Drinkwater did not look up as he carefully wrote the receipt. 'To Russia, Mr Gorman. There's a great demand for English armaments and military stores in Russia.' He passed the receipt across the table and laid down the pen, looking directly at Fagan. 'I shouldn't wonder if the Tsar ain't considering some trouble, but that's no concern for the likes of us, is it now, Mr Gorman?' He stood and took up his cane. 'Do you bring the balance to Davey's chandlery at noon and I'll have a deed made out in your favour.' He put his hat on and held out his hand. 'I hope you profit from the venture, Mr Gorman.'

Fagan rose and took Drinkwater's hand. The Irishman seemed withdrawn, as though inwardly meditating. 'Until noon then . . .'

In the alley Drinkwater gave his cane a half-twist, ensuring the blade was ready for use against footpads; then he turned and made his way past Davey's chandlery. Fagan would be watching him, and he must not betray his intimacy with the chandler, though to use his premises as a rendezvous would not excite suspicion. He had until noon and before then he had to meet Solomon.

Again the air in the alley was wonderfully fresh, and he walked with a lighter step. He was not gratified merely at being out of doors again, nor of having, as Dungarth had eloquently put it, baited the eagle, but because he no longer had to dissimulate. Nathaniel Drinkwater was not cut out to play games in brothels, nor to be a spy.

Chapter Three *August 1809*

The Jew

It was not, Drinkwater reflected as he waited for an answer, a duty normally expected of a senior post-captain, to be waking up Jewish merchants in the middle of the night, notwithstanding the usefulness of the race both to the officers and the men of His Majesty's navy, or, in the matter of high finance, to His Majesty's government. However, in the event, there were mitigating and somewhat personal circumstances that encouraged him.

He had made the journey from Wapping to Spitalfields without mishap or interference, if one excepted the invitations of the score or so of raddled drabs too caried to work under the roof of a respectable house. He had passed a few roistering jacks, a brace of kill-bucks slumming it down from St James's, two decrepit parish Charlies and the sentinels outside the Royal Mint.

Drinkwater heard the heavy bolts withdrawn and the door opened a trifle.

'Captain Waters, Mr Solomon.'

'Come in, come in. ' Drinkwater felt the Jew pluck his sleeve. A lamp illuminated the hall and a faint odour of unfamiliar cooking filled the air.

'I apologize for the lateness of the hour, Mr Solomon.'

'There is no need, Captain, it is as arranged. Pray follow me.'

Solomon's study lay off the hall, a comfortable, book lined room, with a large desk on which sat piles of ledgers, and an exotic landscape in oils above a fire of sea-coal.

'As you see,' Solomon said, indicating a chair, 'I was working. Please be seated. You will find a glass and decanter beside you.' He held up his pale hand at Drinkwater's query. 'No, I do not indulge.'

Drinkwater sipped the claret. After the raw rasp of gin, the rich Bordeaux was revivifying. 'You have no idea how excellent this is, Mr Solomon,' he said.

'Would you like a bath, Captain? It will not take long to arrange. You will want hot water for a shave and his lordship has sent fresh clothes for you.'

'I fear I stink a trifle.'

'A trifle, Captain, but you have been successful, yes?'

'Indeed. The bait was well swallowed. If I mistake not, the news will be in Paris within the week. And you and the ship?'

'They expect you to arrive at any moment. You are to sail as a supercargo, sent, I have told the master, by the consigners. He is aware that certain high placed individuals have an interest in his cargo,' Solomon smiled. 'So prevalent is the practice of revenue evasion that the matter was easily arranged, as was your assumed status. The master, Captain Littlewood, has accepted the fact that the ship is cleared outwards at the Custom House in your name. You may make such private arrangements as you require once at sea.'

'That seems satisfactory. What news of the gun-brig?'

'Your man joined her at Harwich two days ago. She will be at the rendezvous by now. Will you sleep an hour while the water heats?'

'A moment more of your time, Mr Solomon . . .'

'Of course, how can I be of service?'

Drinkwater stood and undid his waistcoat. 'Forgive me a moment . . .' He turned away and drew from within his breeches a small baize bundle. 'I would appreciate your opinion, Mr Solomon, as to the value of this.'

He rolled the heavy nuggets of unrefined gold on to Solomon's desk where the light sparkled on the gritty irregularities of their surfaces. Drinkwater watched the Jew as he bent over the gold. His sensitive fingers reached out and he cupped them speculatively in one hand.

'Where did you acquire these?'

'From a dead man in California.'*

'California?'

'A province of Spanish America.'

'What is your title to it, Captain?'

'A spoil of war, I imagine, though doubtless a law-broker would

*See *In Distant Waters*.

argue differently. It was found by an American citizen in a land claimed by Spain, Russia and Great Britain, somewhere beyond the rule of all but the most natural law – that of possession. I am not a greedy man, Mr Solomon, but I have obligations beyond my means, dependants I have collected in the course of my duties and for which the state bears the moral burden but which it has abandoned to my ingenuity. I offer you ten per cent of the value if you can dispose of them without fuss.'

From a drawer Solomon drew a small box and lifted out a set of hand held scales. He weighed the nuggets, nodding with quiet satisfaction.

'I think this *avoirdupois* will make your burden considerably lighter, Captain,' Solomon said wryly. 'It would be premature of me to mislead you, but upwards of two thousand pounds would seem possible. I see that surprises you, well, well.'

Drinkwater shut his foolishly gaping mouth. Solomon smiled.

'Now, an hour's rest, and then a bath.'

Drinkwater slept well, luxuriating in clean linen and down pillows. Later he broke his fast in Solomon's study. The Jew's quiet manner gave the impression that while his guest slept he had been busy, and, even as Drinkwater drank his fourth cup of coffee, Solomon bent industriously over papers and ledgers on his desk. From within the house came the noise of a banging door, a snatch of children's laughter and the sound of a family. The noises shocked Drinkwater with the pain of nostalgia and he tore his mind from the contemplation of such things. Beyond the windows, the raucous bedlam of Spitalfields market intruded. Drinkwater watched Solomon. He was deeply touched by the man's solicitude, the clean linen for his soiled body, the hip bath, warm towels and an apparently copious supply of hot water. Dungarth might have suggested the clean underdrawers, the starched shirt, breeches and stockings, but Solomon had attended to the details and Drinkwater was vaguely ashamed of his suspicion of the Jew.

From time to time a confidential clerk, a Hebrew like his master, came and went upon errands concerned with Solomon's business interests. After one of these Solomon looked up and, seeing Drinkwater had finished his breakfast, smiled and removed the spectacles from his nose.

'I trust you have had sufficient, Captain?'

'To the point of over-indulgence, Mr Solomon, but I think the bath the kinder thought on your part.'

Solomon inclined his head, then pulled out his watch. 'You will be wanting to leave shortly . . .'

'There is one small matter that has just occurred to me.'

'Please . . .?'

'Would you be kind enough to advance a small sum against the gold?'

'Of course, but I have yet to advance you the money for contingent expenses.'

'No, this is a private request. Say twenty sovereigns?'

'Of course, Captain.' Solomon rose and from a fold in his robe, produced a ring of keys. Bending to a safe behind his desk, he drew out two purses. From the larger he took a handful of coins and placed twenty pounds on the table. The other he held out to Drinkwater. 'Two hundred and fifty Maria Theresa *thalers*, Captain, on account.'

Drinkwater took the purse and pocketed the coins.

'They have not the value of your specimen, Captain, but they are more readily negotiable.'

'Indeed they make me the more apprehensive, though I confess to a fit of nerves when confronted with the pimp last night. He would have had rich pickings even if he undervalued the sale. You wish me to sign a receipt?'

Solomon shook his head. 'It is better there is no record of such a transaction, Captain. A nosy clerk, a ledger left open carelessly . . .' Solomon shrugged and waved his hand, 'you understand?'

'I think so.' Drinkwater paused, then asked, 'The man Fagan, he took the bait well enough. Will he report to Talleyrand?'

Solomon nodded. 'Yes, and Fouché too, that is why your disguise was necessary. Fouché might have smelt a rat had we not dissembled, now he will bring the matter to the Emperor's notice if Talleyrand does not.'

'So Fouché is also betraying his master?'

Solomon smiled again, a curiously knowing smile, like an adult distantly watching the tantrums of children. 'Napoleon has taught them all that ambition knows no boundaries. Do you recall Aristotle's epigram on the state of mind of revolutionaries? That inferiors revolt in order that they may be equal, but equals that they may be superior.'

'He had a point,' Drinkwater agreed. 'So Lord Dungarth concludes Napoleon himself ordered the attempt on his life in which he lost his leg, and that this was intended not merely to destroy his lordship and to damage our Secret Service, but to serve as a warning to Talleyrand and perhaps Fouché?'

Solomon shrugged, spreading his hands palms upwards. 'To *discourage les autres*, perhaps . . . but you are inclined to doubt the assumption, yes?'

Drinkwater's mouth twisted in a wry expression. 'I am not convinced. We blame Napoleon as the head of the body, but the cause may be elsewhere. Mayhap the heart . . .'

Solomon's intelligent eyes watched his guest, though he did not press the point. Drinkwater's grey eyes were introspective.

'Well,' Solomon broke in on Drinkwater's thoughts, 'it is true that men are not always moved by logic in these matters, Captain, though the French can generally be expected to employ reason more than most; but passions and desires, even distempers, are powerful motives in all human activities. Napoleon is, after all, a Corsican.'

Drinkwater gave a short laugh. 'A follower of the vendetta, yes! So Dungarth *did* go into France to arrange for some such "accident" to befall the Emperor; well, well . . .' Drinkwater recalled earlier attempts to dislodge Bonaparte. He remembered picking up the mysterious and half-mad Lord Camelford from a French fishing boat in the wake of the Pichegru conspiracy. A *quid pro quo* might also account for Dungarth's detached lack of vindictiveness.

'Who can say, Captain? I am not in his lordship's full confidence, but many things are possible among these shadows.'

The metaphor, intended by Solomon to turn the conversation away from speculation, failed in its purpose. Instead, it uncannily echoed Drinkwater's own theory, developed in the long months since he had first heard of the explosion of the fougasse beneath the earl's carriage.

'It is the shadow world to which I allude, Mr Solomon. That the Emperor himself, with all his preoccupations, made so clumsy and obvious an attack is unlikely, but perhaps it was done by someone wishing to incriminate Bonaparte.' He paused, catching Solomon's interest again. 'Like you, I flatter myself that I enjoy a measure of his lordship's esteem and confidence. Like you I see some corner of the affair. But unlike you here in London, I have been at a more personal risk, and if I am correct, the matter touches me.' Drinkwater caught the Jew's eyes. Solomon showed no reaction to the oblique and gentle goading. 'Did his lordship never mention a woman?'

Solomon's narrowed eyes betrayed the whetting of his interest. His stock in trade was not simply gold, nor bills of exchange, to say nothing of Northampton boots. Isaac Solomon traded as much in news, gossip and informed opinion; his was a business that turned on channels of intercourse denied to others, more obscure than those of diplomacy, but they were far more robust. They withstood the blasts of war, the impostures of envoys and the imposition of military frontiers with their *douaniers* and tariffs.

'You imply *dux femina facti*, Captain? That a woman was leader of the deed?'

Drinkwater smiled and nodded. 'Just so. 'Tis a theory, no more.' He did not admit that after the past week's almost unendurably squalid inactivity he felt himself electrified by the speed and stimulation of events overnight; nor that his theory, viewed objectively, was insubstantial as air. He too was as devoid of logic as Solomon's hypothetical protagonists. Besides, how did one explain to a man of Solomon's obvious intelligence, a hunch that had matured to conviction?

'Tell his lordship, when next you speak, that I am of the opinion that he fell victim to the malignance of a widow.'

Solomon raised his dark eyebrows. 'Whose widow?' he asked softly.

'The widow of Edouard Santhonax, Mr Solomon, née Hortense de Montholon; Dungarth is acquainted with the lady.' He held out his hand. 'Good day to you, sir. I am much obliged to you for your kindness and courtesy, and hope we meet again.'

They shook hands. The Jew's grip was firm and strong. Drinkwater felt a strange kinship with the man that was as hard to explain as it was to deny; rather like his belief that it had been Hortense Santhonax who had been influential in the placing of the infernal device beneath Dungarth's carriage, he thought.

'I will tell his lordship what you have said, Captain. He has never mentioned her in my hearing.'

'She was an *emigrée* we rescued after the revolution, but she had her head turned by Edouard Santhonax and soon afterwards turned her coat. She was in this country during the naval mutinies of 'ninety-seven. In a fit of weakness Lord Dungarth let her return to France, where she married. Her husband was one of the Emperor's personal aides-de-camp . . . he fell in an action with the frigate *Antigone*.'

'Which was under your command?'

'Yes. That was just over two years ago. It was our fate to cross swords several times and I earned his wife's displeasure long before I made her a widow. So did Dungarth. The last I heard she was sharing Talleyrand's bed.'

Solomon nodded gravely, as though lodging the facts precisely in his astute mind. 'I will tell his lordship what you say '

'Obliged sir. Now I must be off.'

Drinkwater was back in Davey's chandlery by noon. He still wore the borrowed hessian boots and the soiled waistcoat, but clean breeches, shirt and neckcloth combined with a dark blue coat with plain gilt buttons to proclaim him a shipmaster. Davey produced his valise from the room above and shook his head when asked if Fagan had been enquiring after Captain Waters.

'I saw him leave this morning,' Davey said, nodding in the direction of the pie shop opposite, 'but I ain't seen him since.'

'It don't surprise me,' said Drinkwater turning his attention to another matter. 'There is something personal I would be obliged to you for attending to, something entirely unconnected with this affair. There is a woman next door in Mrs Hockley's establishment who hawks herself under the name of Zenobia . . .'

Davey frowned with concern. 'I know her; the black-haired trull.'

'Just so, but 'tis a wig . . .'

'Did ye make that discovery before or after you . . .?'

'A fool could see it at pistol shot, Mr Davey!'

'You've saved yourself . . .'

'Job's Dock, I know it, but do you persuade her to get herself to a physician. She wants none of your paregoric elixir. Take her boy on as an apprentice and here is twenty pounds to see to the matter. You would oblige me greatly, Mr Davey.'

'You be careful of a soft heart in your line o' work, Cap'n. She will lose her living . . .'

'She will lose her life else. Just oblige me, sir,' he said curtly.

Davey took the money reluctantly and Drinkwater had turned

for the door when a scruffy boy burst into the shop with a jangle of the bell, thrust a piece of paper on the counter and ran out again, being gathered up by a gang of ne'er-do-wells who promptly ran off. Davey caught the paper from fluttering to the floor, cast an eye over it and handed it to Drinkwater.

Mr Gorman regrets he is unable to raise the necessary funds for the transaction with Capn. Waters, but begs the Capn. leave his deposit with Mr Davey.

'I thought as much,' Drinkwater said, adding Fagan's guineas to the money laid out for Zenobia. 'There Mr Davey, you are become a banker *and* a philanthropist in a single forenoon.'

Drinkwater had no difficulty hailing a waterman's boat at Wapping Stairs and having himself pulled off to the barque *Galliwasp*, whose name Solomon had given him. He noted as the waterman's skiff rounded her stern that she was pierced for eighteen guns. He wondered how many she actually mounted. More gratifying, given the frustrating week of delay he had suffered, was the fact that her topsails and courses hung ready in their buntlines, lifting and billowing in the westerly breeze. A young ebb bubbled around her creaking rudder stock and, as he looked upward before seizing the manropes and ascending her rounded side, he sighted a welcoming party that gave every appearance of wishing to be away.

'Captain Littlewood at your service, sir . . .' The master was a small, rubicund man with a mop of white hair tied under his cocked hat in an unruly queue. He had, despite a regal paunch, a restless energy that soon became apparent the moment the formalities of welcome were over. 'I had word from Solomon and Dyer that you would want to leave the moment the ebb was away; my boy will see you below,' and he turned, speaking trumpet to his mouth, bellowing to let the topsails fall and to sheet home. Drinkwater was hardly below before, through the stern windows, he saw the distant prospect of London bridge receding as they slipped downstream. Mr Solomon had arranged things to a most efficient nicety.

'Built for the West India trade, sir,' Littlewood explained when Drinkwater joined him on the deck. 'Gives her the look of a sloop o' war. Hellum down a point . . . 'midships . . . meet her . . . steady . . . steer so . . . Mind you she don't mount so many guns . . . Lee braces there, look lively now! Only a dozen carronades . . . Haul taut that fore-tack, Mister, God! What's the matter with you? Had your brains dished up in a whore's bedpan? You'll have us spliced to the King's Yard at Deptford and the whole damned crew of you pressed before you can say "Lucifer", deuce take you! Mind you we've a quaker or two to fill the empty ports . . .'

Drinkwater noticed the dummy gun barrels just then being dismounted and rolled out of the way.

'. . . And she's been doubled round her cut-water, though I apprehend the ice will be late in the Baltic this year. Stand by the braces! Make a show of it passing their Lordships' palace now. Let 'em see what fine jacks the press missed . . . Easy larboard wheel now . . .'

They slid past Greenwich Hospital and Littlewood kept up the commentary, goading and cajoling his crew, dodging sprit-sailed barges, a post office packet and a large East Indiaman off Gravesend. His crew, few in number compared to a naval complement, seemed agile and able enough. Drinkwater was content to relax for the first time in weeks. He realized, as someone else accepted the responsibility for a ship's navigation, that he enjoyed the freedom of merely overseeing which, with a man of Littlewood's stamp to hand, would be an easy task. He realized, too, that the mental fencing with Fagan and Solomon had driven all thoughts of his obsessive guilt from his mind.

He watched a red kite wheel back over the marshes below Tilbury, and a flight of avocets stream in to settle on the emerging mudflats of the Lower Hope. Soon, he thought, staring down river, the pelagic gannets would glide past them, for already the air was sharp with the salt tang of open water.

'Captain Littlewood . . .'

'Captain Waters.'

'A word with you, sir.'

Littlewood took a look at the set of the sails and crossed the slightly heeling deck. 'I don't know what orders your charter party gave you, Captain, but are you aware we have to rendezvous with a naval escort?' Drinkwater asked.

'I was instructed, sir, to wait upon your pleasure and that you would acquaint me with such instructions as were necessary.'

Dungarth or Solomon had done their work well. It was damnably unusual to find a master in the merchant service so willing to relinquish his much cherished independence.

'I was told you were a seafaring man, Captain Waters,' Littlewood went on, partially explaining his acquiescence, 'and that our cargo is for Riga. I command, but under your direction as the charter party's supercargo.'

'Quite so, Captain Littlewood; you seem to understand the situation thoroughly. I trust that you are satisfied with your own remuneration?'

Littlewood laughed. 'Tolerably well,' he admitted. 'The ship had been taken up for the Walcheren business but, thank the Lord, this other matter came up . . .'

'Ah, yes,' Drinkwater hedged, wondering how much Littlewood already knew, and trying to recall what Solomon had told him. It was probable, he concluded, that having been requisitioned by the Transport Board, Littlewood guessed the authorities were behind the present charter. When he better knew the man, Drinkwater resolved, he would be frank with him, but not yet.

'Don't worry, Captain Waters,' Littlewood said as if divining Drinkwater's train of thought, 'honest men never profit. Who am I to query one transport engaged in a little trading on the side, eh? In the last war I was once master's mate and I know there ain't an admiral, nor a post-captain neither, that don't keep a few widows' men on his books to feather his own nest! Why, love a duck, what's one old barque missing from two or three hundred sail o' transports, eh?' Littlewood grinned and edged closer to Drinkwater who was wondering whether the allusion to naval graft was a sly reference to himself. 'Lord love you, Captain,' Littlewood added with a nudge and a wink, ''tis to most Englishmen's inclination to sacrifice their principles to profit, and, when a *lord* tosses the purse, why damn me, sir, 'tis a *command*!'

Chapter Four *August–September 1809*

The Gun-brig

'Pray mind your head, sir. Take a seat . . . perhaps a glass?' Bent double under the deck beams in the cramped cabin, Drinkwater eased himself into a rickety chair. Opposite him, across the table, Lieutenant James Quilhampton seated his tall, spare frame on to a second chair, splayed his legs and propelled himself dextrously across the cabin to a side shelf where a trio of glasses and a chipped decanter nestled in fiddles.

The small, one-hundred-ton vessel lifted easily to a low swell rolling down from the northward. With just sufficient wind to give them steerage, James Quilhampton's twelve-gun command in company with the *Galliwasp*, stemmed the flood tide sweeping south round Orfordness.

'Welcome to His Britannic Majesty's gun-brig *Tracker*, sir,' Quilhampton said as he poured two glasses of blackstrap with his sound hand. 'My predecessor was a tall fellow. He had this chair fitted with castors.' He swivelled round and propelled himself back towards the table whose once-polished top bore the stains of ancient wine rings, assorted blemishes and idly carved notches in its rim. 'A becket allows me half a fathom traverse centrical upon the ring bolt below.'

Quilhampton leaned forward with a full glass held in his wooden fist. Drinkwater disengaged it from the painted fingers, conscious that the young man's awkwardness was due to more than his old disability.

Drinkwater raised the glass of what looked like a villainous concoction. 'Your good health, my dear James, and to that of your wife.' Drinkwater sipped and suppressed the strong instinct to wince at the acidulous wine. 'I am sorry to be the cause of you having to part so soon.'

Drinkwater saw the flush of embarrassment mount to Quilhampton's face.

'I am . . . that is to say, I am not . . .' Quilhampton spluttered, 'damn it, sir, she is not my wife. In short, I'm not married!'

Drinkwater frowned, staring at his friend with unconcealed concern. 'Is it the odious aunt?'

Quilhampton shook his head vigorously.

'She refused you?'

'No, damn it, she did not refuse me.' Quilhampton tossed off his glass, suddenly shot sideways with a rumble of castors, refilled it and trundled back to the table. He took a mouthful of the second glass and slammed it, slopping, down on the table. A blood-red drop of spilled wine reflected the light from the skylight above them.

'I put it off, sir, delayed the thing . . . it didn't seem fair . . .'

Quilhampton stared at the spilled wine, his expression one of extreme anguish. He dabbed at the escaped droplet with his forefinger, dragged it so that its form became elongated round his fingertip and formed the shape used in the tangent tables to express infinity; then it broke and Quilhampton raised his finger and looked up. Two separate droplets of wine now gleamed on the neglected polish of the table top.

'It was better, sir . . .'

'But you regret it now, eh?'

Their eyes met. 'Of course I do.'

'Is the situation irreversible?'

'I expect so, by now.'

'Damn it James, the poor young woman has waited six years! What has she done to be spurned?' Drinkwater bit his lip. He wanted James Quilhampton's mind uncluttered by such preoccupations, and was aware that he was increasing the young man's misery. 'I'm sorry James, 'tis none of my affair. I assume she was otherwise attached?'

'I wish she had been,' interrupted Quilhampton hastily. 'It is my fault, my fault entirely. The fact is I came up all standing and jibbed it.' The swiftly swallowed wine began to unlock Quilhampton's tongue. 'I've no money, sir . . . oh, I'm deeply grateful for your influence in securing this command, but I've little in the way of expectations and my mother . . .'

'But you do still feel something in the way of affection for

Mistress MacEwan?' Drinkwater asked sharply, a trifle exasperated and anxious to get on to the reason for his visit.

'More than ever.'

'And she for you?' Quilhampton's dejected nod revealed the true state of affairs.

'For God's sake, man, write to her, hail a fishing boat and get a letter to the post-master at Harwich. I need your undivided attention on our service, James; I cannot support a bleeding heart.'

'Of course not, sir. I'm sorry. Had you not pressed me . . .'

'Very well. Let the matter rest. Assure the young woman of your affections and that I shall have you home again before the ice forms in the Baltic.'

'Thank you, sir. I am indebted to you. Another glass?'

Drinkwater stared down at the half-finished blackstrap. 'Thank you, no. Now, James, to the business in hand . . .'

He outlined their task, amplifying Quilhampton's orders and explaining the reason for his own disguised appearance, already intimated in Quilhampton's instructions.

'I fear it is an open secret now, sir. I have several of the old Patricians aboard, Derrick, for instance.'

The news that a few hands from their former ship had been transferred with Quilhampton and Frey did not surprise Drinkwater. Quilhampton went on to explain that the brig had been undermanned, his predecessor being frequently compelled to relinquish hands to frigates and sloops desperate for men and under orders for foreign service. The dry-docking of the old *Patrician* at Plymouth had released her company and Drinkwater was rather pleased that the eccentric Quaker who had served as his own clerk was aboard.

'He's rated servant,' Quilhampton said, 'though I employ him as a purser's clerk.'

'If I ever command again, I should not be sorry to have him back.' Drinkwater smiled at Quilhampton's look of surprise. 'I am not entirely in good odour at the Admiralty, James. I once crossed Mr Barrow. That is why I wanted you to have this command: I cannot guarantee you preferment by your personal attachment to my person.'

'But this special service, sir, surely 'tis important enough to warrant some recognition?'

'It is precisely because it must only be recognized by the

intended party that it is unlikely to merit attention elsewhere. It is inimical to secret operations that they should be trumpeted. For your own part an efficient execution of your duty will earn my warmest approbation, and therefore,' Drinkwater was about to say 'Lord Dungarth's', but thought better of it. His Lordship's department was not commonly known about in the sea service. It was sufficient for Quilhampton to know he sailed under secret Admiralty orders.

They were just then interrupted by a knock at the cabin door. Mr Frey's head peered round.

'Beg pardon, sir, but the wind's freshening and the merchantman's jolly boat crew are a trifle anxious about the delay.'

'Don't disparage a merchant seaman, Mr Frey,' said Drinkwater rising cautiously. 'Captain Littlewood would only man his boat on my strictest promise that you would not press any of them.'

Frey grinned. 'The thought did occur to me, sir.'

'I'm sure it did.' Drinkwater picked up his hat and went on deck. The tiny ship with her stumpy carronades ranged along her deck was neat and well ordered, even if she did show all the signs of hard service and lack of fresh paint. Drinkwater had exaggerated Quilhampton's chances of preferment. It was frequently the fate of lieutenants-in-command to discover that being posted into a gun-brig was a cul-de-sac to ambition.

'Why is Captain Drinkwater incognito, sir?' Frey asked Quilhampton, alluding to Drinkwater's plain coat, as they watched their former captain being pulled away from *Tracker*'s side in the *Galliwasp*'s boat. 'And why is he aboard that barque?'

Quilhampton turned abruptly. 'I'll explain later, Mr Frey. At the moment I would be obliged if you'd lay me a course to intercept that bawley. I've a letter to write.'

From the deck of the *Galliwasp* Drinkwater watched Quilhampton's little brig run down towards a fishing bawley, heave-to and pass the fateful letter. He sighed with relief and hoped the affair, if not settled, would cease to weigh on Quilhampton's mind. As for himself, he felt depressed by the interview with his friend, not so much on account of James Quilhampton's amorous miscarriage, as by the wider implications of their meeting. In the stinking room above Davey's chandlery, fortified by gin and a sense of purpose inculcated by Lord Dungarth, and afterwards – misgivings soothed by

Solomon's confident assurance – the mission assumed a vital character. As long as he remained detached from the Service it was possible to maintain this assumption; but the sight of Quilhampton's puny little gun-brig with its dozen bird-scaring carronades made him doubt the wisdom or importance of Dungarth's cherished plan. On the one hand the sight and smells of even so small a man o' war were powerfully nostalgic to a sea-officer, on the other the very size of the brig seemed totally inadequate as an instrument of defiance to the French Empire. Moreover, the sight of his old friends had awakened other, more personal memories; the dark preoccupations he had managed to shake off for a while. Frey's report that he had Drinkwater's personal effects aboard *Galliwasp* for safe-keeping, reminded Drinkwater of the painful reasons why he could not have them conveyed home. The death of Tregembo hung over him like a spectre, and continued to do so in the subsequent days as they headed for the Skaw. The ambivalence of his position aboard the *Galliwasp* confined him to his cabin and denied him the occupations he was used to, though Littlewood was an amiable host and allowed him the freedom of his deck. But at that moment of parting from Quilhampton, as he watched *Tracker* swing and her sails fill as she sought to catch up with her consort, Drinkwater's gaze stretched beyond the filling canvas of the gun-brig, taking in the long shingle spit and the twin lighthouses at Orfordness. It was hereabouts that he had fought the Dutch frigate *Zaandam* whose magazine had been blown up by the intrepidity of James Quilhampton while he himself had given the death wound to Edouard Santhonax. It was odd, if not fateful, the way his path had crossed that of the French officer. Providential, he admitted privately, a manifestation of what he held to be a spiritual truth. It had been a desperate fight as Drinkwater sought to bring out of Russia a state secret, and Santhonax attempted to thwart him.

Now Drinkwater was going back, and the thought struck him that perhaps he was still bound to Santhonax, even in death, for the moment of his fall from grace at the Admiralty had concerned the preservation of the secret, and its consequences continued to affect him and those close to him.*

*See *Baltic Mission*

*

'Damn this wind!' bellowed Littlewood, clapping a hand over his hat. 'Why don't it back a point, or even fly to the sou'west.'

It was not a question, merely an explosion of frustration as the northerly wind forced them to lay a course to the eastward of their intended track, driving them towards the Bight of Helgoland rather than north east for the Skagerrak. They had already made a long board to avoid the Texel, and reached the latitude of Whitby with every prospect of fetching the Skagerrak, but the wind had veered a point and obliged them to lay a course of east-north-east, directly for the Horns Reef.

'The season for the equinoctials will be upon us soon,' Drinkwater said consolingly, though he no more liked the delay than Littlewood, for both men were worried about the cold northerly wind hastening the formation of ice in the Baltic.

' 'Tis too much to ask for a fair wind,' Littlewood said irritably, turning to follow Drinkwater's stare. Astern of them *Tracker* buried her bow, then lifted it, the water streaming from her knightheads and the spray tearing to leeward in a cloud.

'She's about as weatherly as my hat!'

Drinkwater grunted agreement. Even in this wind, which was no more than a near gale, conditions on the gun-brig would be appalling. He recalled his own service in a cutter: it had been wet and gruelling, but at least they had had the satisfaction of going to windward like a witch. Poor Quilhampton was going to have to exert himself to the utmost to carry out his orders. The thought made Drinkwater smile grimly.

'You are amused, Captain?' Littlewood asked.

Drinkwater nodded. 'A little,' he admitted. 'The young fellow in command over there had his head filled with romantic notions the other day. I daresay he has other things on his mind just now.'

Littlewood laughed. 'I'll shorten down for him, if you wish; there's no point in outrunning him.'

'I'd be obliged to you, Captain Littlewood,' Drinkwater nodded, acutely conscious that it was the gun-brig that was to afford them protection, rather than the reverse.

'It's bound to back soon,' said Littlewood, turning away to give orders to his crew, 'bound to . . .'

But Littlewood's optimism was misplaced. Nightfall found them shortened to triple reefed topsails and the clew of a brailed spanker as the wind increased to gale force.

Chapter Five *September 1809*

The Storm

Drinkwater was unable to sleep. Although *Galliwasp* was not his personal responsibility the habits of command were too deeply ingrained to be swept easily aside. Besides, the moral burden for the former West Indiaman and her mission were laid squarely upon his lop-sided shoulders, so at midnight, wrapped in a tarpaulin, he sought Littlewood and found him at his post on deck.

'There are times, Captain Waters, when the temptation to suck on a bottle in one's bunk and leave the deck to one's mates and the devil are well-nigh irresistible,' Littlewood shouted, staggering across his wildly lurching poop to grab a backstay somewhere behind Drinkwater's right shoulder.

'You don't fool me, sir,' Drinkwater shouted back, grinning in the darkness despite his discomfort. Littlewood's black humour suggested he would be a good man in a tight corner. 'Though I imagine a snug anchorage in the Scheldt seems more attractive than our present position.'

Littlewood leaned towards Drinkwater. 'It's getting no better, Captain,' he said, the confidence imparted in a loud voice to sound above the mounting roar of the rising wind. 'By my reckoning we can let her go 'til morning, but at first light we will have to put about . . .'

'You'll have to wear ship . . .'

'Aye,' Littlewood agreed, 'she'll not tack in this . . .'

Both men stared to windward thinking the same thoughts simultaneously. The *Galliwasp* heeled under the wind's weight, rolling further to starboard as grey seas-reared out of the darkness to larboard and bore down upon her. Some broke to windward and the spray from their collapsing crests streamed across their exposed deck with a sibilant hiss. Some she rode over, groaning and creaking in protest as the roaring gale plucked new, higher pitched notes from the strained weather stays and a curious resonant vibration from the slacker, leeward rigging. Others broke on board, sluicing with a roar across the deck and filling the scuppers and waterways of the starboard waist, while some broke against the hull with Titanic hammer blows that shook the *Galliwasp* from keel to truck. Then the thwarted wave threw itself into the air where, level with the rail, the wind caught it and drove it downwind with the force of buckshot; an icy assault that struck exposed cheeks with a painful impact and left the wet skin to the worse agony of the wind-ache that followed.

The duty watch huddled from the hazard in odd corners, only the mate on watch and the helmsmen weathering it behind a scrap of canvas dodger. Even Drinkwater and the bare-headed Littlewood could not avoid the stinging, lancing spume bursting upon them out of the black and howling darkness.

Ineffectively dodging one such explosion, Drinkwater recovered his balance and dashed the streaming water from his eyes, to stare astern and to leeward.

'What the devil's that?' he asked.

'Bengal fire?' queried Littlewood beside him.

The thrust of the wind sent both men down the deck to leeward. They cannoned into the lee rail, aware that the deep red flare had gone, either extinguished or obscured by an intervening wave crest.

'There's another!' Littlewood pointed, though Drinkwater had already marked the sudden glow.

'Signal of distress from the brig, sir.' The *Galliwasp*'s second mate staggered from handhold to handhold to make his report.

'We see it, Mr Munsden, thank you.'

'It'll be the brig, sir.'

'So we apprehend,' replied Littlewood, turning to Drinkwater. 'That young fellow in command, the lovesick one, what stamp of man is he, Captain?'

'Not one to prove craven,' snapped Drinkwater with mounting anxiety. Straining his eyes into the impenetrable darkness that followed the dousing of the second flare, his brain raced as he thought of Quilhampton and Frey struggling, perhaps for their very lives, less than a mile away.

'Captain Littlewood! You'd oblige me if you'd put up your helm and wear ship now, sir! We should fall off sufficiently to catch a sight of the *Tracker* and you've enough men on deck to see to it.'

Drinkwater sensed Littlewood hesitate, then with relief saw his white head nod agreement and heard his shout. 'Mr Munsden . . .!'

But from above their heads came a thunderous crack and then the whole ship shook violently as the main topsail blew out.

Littlewood spun round and with a bull-roar galvanized his crew. 'Away aloft there you lubbers, and secure that raffle! Call all hands, Mr Munsden!'

Drinkwater swore with frustration, turning from the flogging canvas to stare again into the darkness on the starboard quarter, praying that on the beleaguered deck of the *Tracker* they would light another Bengal fire. But there was no sign of the flare of red orpiment and Drinkwater succumbed to a sensation of blazing anger as another stinging deluge swept the *Galliwasp*'s deck.

'By your leave, sir,' he shouted at Littlewood, shoving past the captain and climbing into the main shrouds, suddenly glad to do something, even if the work in hand was not what was expected of a post-captain in His Majesty's Navy.

He reached the futtock shrouds before he felt the folly of his action come with a shortness of breath and a weakness in the knotted muscles of his mangled shoulder. The power of the wind aloft was frightening. Gritting his teeth, the tail of his tarpaulin blowing half way up his back, he struggled into the top. Here, he found himself face to face with one of the *Galliwasp's* men who recognized him and made no secret of his astonishment.

'Jesus, what the bloody hell . . .?'

'Up . . . you . . . go . . . man,' Drinkwater gasped, 'there's work to be done.'

The mast trembled and the flailing of the torn canvas lashed about them. The air was filled with the taste of salt spray and the noise of the wind was deafening, a terrifying howl that was compounded of shrieks and roars as the gale played on the differing thickness of standing and running rigging, plucking from them notes that varied according to their tension. Each responded with its own beat, whipping and thrumming, tattooing the mast timbers and their ironwork in sympathy, while the indisciplined, random thunder of the rent canvas beat about them.

The men of *Galliwasp*'s duty watch scrambled up beside

Drinkwater, huddling in the top until they saw their moment to lay out on the trembling yard. Drinkwater found himself shuddering shamefully, regretting the foolhardy impulse that had driven him aloft. It had been a complex nervous reaction prompted initially by the need to do *something* for Quilhampton and his brig. Denied of the familiar catharsis of bawling orders to achieve results, he had sought to influence the *Galliwasp*'s small civilian crew by this foolhardy gesture. There had also been the realization that from aloft he might obtain a better view, might indeed be able to see the *Tracker* and direct some means of alleviating his friend's plight from such a vantage point. But neither of these rational if extreme reasons were what truly motivated him: what he sought in the wildness of that night was the oblivion of action, the overwhelming desire to court death or to cheat it, to invite fate to deal with him as it saw fit, to submit himself to the jurisprudence of providence, for the truth of the matter was that he could no longer bear the burden of his guilt for the death of old Tregembo.

The folly of his ill-considered action came to him now as he panted in the gyrating top, dinging with difficulty to the mast as his body was flung backwards and forwards and the thudding of his heart failed to arrest the pitiful weakness that made jelly of his leg muscles, so that he quivered from within as he was buffeted from without.

Littlewood was shouting from below, 'Lay out, lay out!' and Drinkwater realized the master had ordered the barque's helm put up so that she eased off the wind and ran before it, taking the flogging remnants of the topsail clear of the yard. The men around him were suddenly gone, their feet scrabbling for the footrope, one hand dinging to the robands, the other reaching for the stinging lashes of the wild strips of canvas. Now they were mere ghosts, grey and insubstantial shapes in the gloom, laying out along the yard that seemed to lead into the very heart of the gale.

Drinkwater stood immobilized, unaware that he was the victim of mental and physical exhaustion. Not since the day more than two years earlier, when he had hidden in an attic in Tilsit observing the meeting of Tsar Alexander and the Emperor of the French, had he known a moment to call his own. The strain of bringing home the secret intelligence; the fight with the *Zaandam*; the killing of Santhonax, and the damage to *Antigone*; the row with Barrow at the Admiralty; the hanging of a seaman and the blight it had thrown on the outward voyage of His Majesty's frigate *Patrician*; the killing of the deserters beneath the waterfall on the island of Más-a-Fuera; the loss and recovery of his ship and the consequences of their finally reaching Canton to make the fateful rendezvous with Morris – all seemed to have led inexorably to the terrifying necessity of murdering his oldest and most loyal friend. And to add to his guilt was the knowledge that Tregembo had sacrificed everything out of a sense of obligation to himself, Nathaniel Drinkwater.

While he could drown in gin the memory of what had happened, and play the agent at Lord Dungarth's behest; while he could avoid confronting the truth by dicing fortunes with Fagan or veil his soul with the mercantile intrigues of Isaac Solomon, his self-esteem dung to this outward appearance from habit. But now the gale had laid his nerves bare and drawn him up into the top by playing upon his anxiety, pride and weakness. Now it held him fast, exhausted, robbed of the energy or courage to lay out upon the yard and serve as an exemplar to the merchant seamen even now pummelling the torn topsail into bundles and passing gaskets to secure it. He wondered if they could guess at his fearful inertia as he clung to the reeling mast for his very life.

Why had he not reached the yard before this torpor overcame him? Why had he not dropped into the sea and the death he longed for? Why did some instinct keep his hands clenched to the cold ironwork of the doubling?

Quilhampton . . .

The thought came to him dully, so that afterwards he thought that he must have swooned and lost consciousness for a few seconds, saved only by the seaman's habit of holding fast in moments of overwhelming crisis. Quilhampton's plight and his own deeply engrained and ineluctable sense of duty brought him from the brink of what was both a physical and a spiritual nadir.

Reeling, Drinkwater stared out to starboard where he thought *Tracker* might be seen, and he was suddenly no longer the supine victim of his own fears. The wind that had desolated him now returned to him his vigour, for he was abruptly recalled to the present with the sinister change in the wind's note. As he sought some sign of the gun-brig he became aware of the changed condition of the sea. It was no longer a dark mass delineated by streaks of spume and the roar of breaking crests tumbling to leeward. No longer did the sea rise to the force of the gale. Now it was beaten; the white breakers were shorn as the sound of the wind grew from the scream of a gale to the booming of a storm.

Beside him the mast creaked and with a sound like a gunshot the foretopsail blew out and the flogging of canvas began again, transmitted to the mainmast via the stays, a shuddering that seemed fair to bring all three of the barque's masts down. Below him Littlewood was bawling more orders and his men were laying in from the main topsail yard. Their faces, what he could see of them, were wild, fierce with desperation, excoriated by anxiety and the onslaught of salt spray which scoured the flesh and made looking to windward impossible. For an indecisive moment Drinkwater cast about him, conscious only of the vast power of the storm and the strain on the *Galliwasp*, but as Littlewood's men struggled over the edge of the top to go forward and try and secure the foretopsail, he recalled Quilhampton and tried again to make out the gunbrig in the surrounding darkness.

Littlewood was keeping his ship's head before the wind but Drinkwater was unable to see anything more than a small circular welter of seething white water, a tiny circumscribed world in which only they existed. He was aware too, that he was having difficulty breathing, that he could no longer cling to his perilous perch and retain the strength to descend the mast. Fearful of his own weakness as much as the wind's violence, he fought his way over the edge of the top, pressed into the futtock shrouds and impeded by the updraught of the wind. Like a fly in a web he struggled until he regained the comparative safety of the deck.

Littlewood had all hands mustered now, transformed by the catalyst of crisis into an inferno of energy. Unlike the complex arrangements on a man-of-war, with its chains of command extending from the quarterdeck into the nethermost regions of the ship, a merchantman's master was at once in supreme command but on an occasion such as this, driven of necessity to perform many duties himself. His mates and petty officers were also strained in the extremity of their situation, tailing on to ropes, heaving and belaying as they fought to subdue the flogging foretopsail and to brace the yards. Littlewood himself was struggling at the helm and Drinkwater crossed the deck to grab the opposite spokes and help him.

'Obliged,' shouted Littlewood. 'We've three feet of water in the well . . . Did you see . . . ease her a point, Captain . . . did you see anything of the brig?'

'Nothing.'

For a while they struggled in silence, Littlewood ducking and staring aloft, and bellowing out the occasional word to his mate who at the foot of the foremast stood holding a halliard ready to render it on its pin. From time to time, with a look over his shoulder, Littlewood eased a spoke to keep *Galliwasp* off before the wind, but no words were necessary since Drinkwater understood instinctively. There was no danger of their being pooped, for the wind prevented the high-breaking seas from rearing over the ship's stern. Their greatest worry was the strain being imposed on the gear aloft.

Drinkwater, still shaken from his own exertions, was content for a moment to let Littlewood fret over the *Galliwasp*. He stared dully at the swinging compass card, still lit by the guttering flame of the binnacle oil lamp. He felt Littlewood's tug on the wheel and responded. Then, suddenly realizing that something was wrong he looked up.

'What the devil . . .?' Littlewood craned round anxiously.

There was a sudden, unexpected lull, the booming of the wind ceased and dropped in register, and Drinkwater shot another look at the compass card.

'We've swung her head three points in the last few –' he began, but the explanation was already upon them.

'Up helm!' roared Littlewood, thrusting the wheel over. Then the backing wind was upon them, striking them with the violence of an axe blow to the skull, stopping the ship dead, catching her aback and tearing the half furled canvas of the reefed foretopsail out of its gaskets and hurling the frayed mess at the men who sought to tame it.

The first casualty was a topman, an able seaman flung from the yard, who vanished into the sea with a scream. It seemed to Drinkwater that the shriek lasted until after the dismasting, that the renewed boom of the wind reasserted itself only after the scream had finished, and it was the falling of a man who, as a last act, tore at the stays and plucked the masts out of the *Galliwasp* in a gigantic act of protest. It was a stupid fancy, confounded by the facts that confronted them an instant later: the man lost and the barque's three masts lying in ruins around them.

There was a hiatus of shock, and then came the voices of men, some shouting in pain, others bawling for assistance, a few asserting their authority. Drinkwater fought his way through a tangle of rigging, aware that the wheel was smashed by a falling spar and that Captain Littlewood had been less fortunate than himself and was trapped by the yard that had dashed the wheel to pieces. Beneath their feet the barque began to roll as the tangle of wreckage, much of it falling over the side, dragged them beam-on to the wind. And its sudden shift now threw up a confused sea, buffeting the disabled ship and increasing the difficulties of her company.

'Captain Littlewood,' Drinkwater called, as he struggled to free the master, 'are you hurt, sir?'

'Only a trifle . . . but I cannot move . . .'

Drinkwater stood up and bellowed 'Mr Munsden!' and was relieved to hear the second mate's voice in reply. 'Can you lay your hands on a handspike or a capstan bar. Captain Littlewood is held fast here!'

They eased the weight on Littlewood after a struggle, raising the fallen yard from across his belly and dragging him out. Periodically seas crashed aboard, sluicing through the chaotic raffle of ropes, spars and torn sails like a river in spate choked by fallen trees. Elsewhere about the littered deck, other groups of men were helping to free their comrades. As Littlewood struggled to his feet they were aware that they no longer had to shout in each other's ears to make themselves heard: the storm, having done its worst, was content to subside to a mere gale again. Littlewood ordered a muster of his crew; in addition to the lost topman, two others were found dead, one was missing and three were badly injured. A dozen others had cuts, bruises and scratches of a less serious nature.

Soaked to the skin, they took stock of their situation. The backing wind was no longer so cold and they began to sweat with the effort of clearing the *Galliwasp*'s deck in an attempt to get her under command again.

When it came, the dawn found them lying helplessly a-hull, rolling constantly in the trough of the sea and making leeway. The wrecked top-hamper overside laid a wide, smooth slick to windward which prevented the waves breaking aboard. The wind continued to drop during the forenoon. With a vigorous plying of axes and knives they cut away the wreckage, salvaging what they could. Captain Littlewood proved as energetic in adversity as when things progressed well. Drinkwater, stripped to his shirt in his efforts to help, recalled Littlewood's personal stake in the ship and her cargo, content for the moment to throw himself into the urgent task of saving themselves.

It was after noon before they had brought a semblance of order to the ship, leaving her trailing downwind of her wrecked jib-boom to act as a sea-anchor and hold her head to wind and sea. The cook relit the galley range and served a steaming burgoo laced with rum and molasses that tasted delicious to the famished and exhausted men.

His mouth full, Littlewood beckoned Drinkwater aft and the two men conferred over their bowls.

'I don't like our situation, Captain Waters. There is four feet of water in the well, and as for our reckoning, well . . .' With the back of his right hand, his spoon still clutched in his fist, Littlewood rasped at his unshaven chin. A smear of burgoo remained behind.

'I have been giving that some consideration myself,' said Drinkwater, 'but with this overcast . . .' he cast a glance at the lowering grey sky, 'we have little to go on beyond our wits. Let us adjourn below and look at the chart.'

In the stern cabin Littlewood poured them both a glass of rum and unrolled a chart. The nail of the stumpy index finger he laid on their last observed position was torn and bleeding. He drew his finger tip south.

'We'll have made leeway towards the Frisians, then, with the shift of wind, east, towards the estuaries.'

Drinkwater looked from the long curve of islands that fringed the coast of north Holland and Hanover to the extensive shoals that stretched for miles offshore, littering the wide mouths of the Jahde, Weser and Elbe. How far away were those lethal sands with their harsh and forbidding names; the Vogel, the Knecht, the Hogenhorn and the Scharhorn? How far away were the fringe of breakers that would pound them mercilessly to pieces if their keel once struck the miles and miles of shoal they thundered upon?

'We have enough gear salvaged to jury rig her and run before it. With luck we might reach to the norrard.'

Littlewood's torn finger moved north, away from its resting place on the flat island of Neuwerk lying athwart the entrance to the Elbe.

'It offers us our best chance if we avoid the Horn's Reef and

Danish letters-of-marque. Of course it's a risk . . .' the master drowned his incomplete sentence in a mouthful of rum.

Beyond the island of Sylt lay the port of Esbjerg from which Danish privateers would swoop on the *Galliwasp* with alacrity. The Danes had not forgiven Great Britain the abduction of their fleet two years earlier, nor the bombardment of their capital, Copenhagen. A British ship falling into their hands could expect little mercy: a British naval officer none whatsoever. One caught in disguise would almost certainly be hanged or shot; Drinkwater had seen such a man, strung up by the Dutch above a battery at Kirkduin.

'D'you have a larger scale chart?' Drinkwater asked, shying away from the hideous image.

'Aye.' Littlewood turned and pulled a chart tube from a locker. From it he drew a roll of charts. Drinkwater waited, feeling the rum warm his belly. 'You are thinking of Helgoland?'

'Yes.'

They spread out the second chart and Drinkwater noted it was an English copy of a survey commissioned by the Hamburg Chamber of Commerce.

'Too risky,' Littlewood said, shaking his head. 'If we are out in our reckoning, or if we miscalculate and are swept past, then our fate is sealed.'

'We could anchor and make a signal of distress. There is often a cutter or a sloop stationed near the island.'

'There is as often as not a damned French custom-house lugger, or worse, a Dutch coastguard cutter; that damned island attracts them like a candle does moths. The fact is, Helgoland is too much of a hazard. I'd rather take my chance to the norrard and hope for the sight of a British cruiser than poke my head into that noose!'

Littlewood's voice rang with the conviction of a man who had made up his mind and would brook no interference. His eyes met those of the still uncommitted Drinkwater and he summoned a final argument to ram home his conviction.

'What would the French garrison in Hamburg say when they seized our cargo, Captain, eh? Mercy bow-coup, damn them, and all I'll get in receipt is board and lodging in a cell! You know well enough I *have* to think of my ship. We'll take our chance to the norrard.'

Littlewood let go his end of the chart and it rolled up like a coiled spring against Drinkwater's hand which held down the opposite margin. The sensation of a tiny wounding, a reminder of Littlewood's ultimate responsibility struck him. Drinkwater was not a naval officer in Littlewood's mind but an encumbrance, and Drinkwater faced a situation over which he had no real control. Matters had gone too far for him to contemplate casting aside his disguise in order to usurp Littlewood's command of the *Galliwasp*. Besides, his authority to do even that was difficult to prove and impossible to enforce. The first intimation of naval command would reek so strongly of the press in the nostrils of *Galliwasp*'s people that he would very likely be in fear of his life.

Littlewood's assessment was the truth and his solution the only practical one. Clawing their way to the north bought them sea room, time, and the chance of an encounter with a British man-of-war; running to leeward, for all that the British-occupied island lay downwind, was too much like clutching at a straw.

'Very well. I agree.' Drinkwater nodded.

'Pity about that gun-brig . . .'

Drinkwater lingered in the cabin after Littlewood returned to the deck. He could be heard exhorting his crew to further exertions as *Galliwasp* rolled and pitched sluggishly – what remained of the dead burden of her wrecked top-hamper lying over her bow – holding her head to wind. Her buffeted hull creaked in protest and Drinkwater heard the monotonous thump-thump of her pumps starting again as Littlewood sought to prevent his precious cargo being spoiled by bilge water.

'God's bones!' Drinkwater blasphemed venomously and struck his clenched fist on Littlewood's table. What in hell's name was he doing here, presiding ineffectually over the shambles of Dungarth's grand design?

The thing was a failure, a fiasco . . .

The matter was finished and Quilhampton was lost, for it was inconceivable that his little brig could have withstood the onslaught of the night's tempest. The mission – if that was what Dungarth's insane idea to force the war to a climax could be called – had foundered with the *Tracker*. Littlewood was right and there was nothing more they could do except preserve themselves and their cargo. Perhaps, if they regained the English coast, the ruse might be attempted again after the spring thaw. It was something to hope for.

But the loss of Quilhampton, Frey and their people brought an inconsolable grief and Drinkwater felt it weigh upon him, adding to the depression of his spirits. It was then that the idle and selfish thought insinuated itself: with the loss of *Tracker* had gone his sea-chest and all his personal effects.

Chapter Six *October 1809*

Coals to Newcastle

Drinkwater woke with a start, his heart hammering with a nameless fear. For a moment he lay still, thinking his anxiety and grief had dragged him from sleep, but the next moment he was struggling upright. Shouts came from other parts of the ship, shouts of alarm as other men were woken from the sleep of utter fatigue. *Galliwasp* struck for a third time, her hull shuddering, a living thing in her death throes.

He reached the deck as the cry was raised of a light to leeward.

'*Where* away?' roared Littlewood, struggling into a coat, his face a pale, anxious blur in the gloom.

'To loo'ard, Cap'n! There!'

Both Drinkwater and Littlewood stared into the darkness as *Galliwasp* pounded upon the reef for the fourth time and the hiss and seething of the sea welled up about her and then fell away in the unmistakable rhythm of breakers.

Then they saw the light, a steady red glow which might have been taken for a glimpse of the rising moon seen through a rent in the overcast except that it suddenly flared into yellow flames and they were close enough to see clouds of sparks leap upwards.

' 'Tis a lighthouse . . . Helgoland lighthouse!' Littlewood called, then bellowed, 'In the waist there! A sounding!'

Drinkwater felt Littlewood's hand grip his arm. 'Cap'n Waters,' he said, his voice strained and urgent. 'They must have been asleep,' – referring to the watch of exhausted men who had laboured throughout the preceding day to prepare *Galliwasp*'s jury rig – 'and we've drifted . . .'

'By the mark seven, sir!'

'She's come off!' snapped Drinkwater, watching the bearing of the light and feeling the change in the motion of the *Galliwasp*.

'By the deep nine!' confirmed the cry from forward.

'They may not have been asleep,' Drinkwater said consolingly, as Littlewood, in his agitation, still clung to Drinkwater's sleeve. 'That light was badly tended.' Both men stared at the now flaming chauffer which seemed to loom above them.

'Do you anchor, upon the instant, sir!'

At Drinkwater's imperative tone Littlewood shook off his catalepsy.

'Yes, yes, of course. Stand by the shank painter and cat stopper!'

It was a matter of good fortune that they had had the foresightedness to bend a cable on to the best bower the afternoon before. Indeed they had mooted anchoring, but decided against it, believing they had sufficient sea room to remain hove-to overnight and able to get sail of the barque before the following noon.

'By the deep eleven!'

The anchor dropped from the cat-head with a splash and the cable rumbled out through the hawse-pipe. Littlewood was roused fully from his momentary lapse of initiative. Drinkwater heard him calling for the carpenter to sound the well and the hands to man the pumps. The pounding that the *Galliwasp* had taken on the reef must surely have started a plank or dislodged some of her sheathing and caulking. Littlewood must be dog-tired, Drinkwater thought, feeling useless and unable to contribute much beyond feeling for Littlewood a surrogate anxiety. He turned to the flames of the lighthouse as he felt *Galliwasp*'s anchor dig its flukes into the sea bed and the ship jerk round to her cable.

Carefully Drinkwater observed the bearing of the light steady.

Littlewood stumped breathlessly aft. 'He *was* asleep . . . the mate I mean . . . God damn his lights . . .'

'The bearing's steady . . . she's brought up to her anchor.'

'Thank God the wind's dropping.'

'Amen to that,' murmured Drinkwater.

'She's making water, sir.' The carpenter came aft and made his report at which Littlewood grunted. 'We'll have to keep the men at the pumps until daylight.' He raised his voice. 'Mr Watts!'

The mate came aft, a shuffling figure whose shame at having fallen asleep was perceptible even in the darkness. As Drinkwater overheard Littlewood passing orders to keep men at the pumps he reflected on the situation. The *Galliwasp*'s hands had laboured like Trojans, Watts among them. There were too few of them, far fewer than would have been borne by a naval vessel of comparable size.

Detached, Drinkwater could almost condone their failure. Littlewood turned towards him with a massive shrug as Watts went disconsolately forward.

'I'll stand your anchor watch for you,' Drinkwater said. 'You have all been pushed too hard.' Littlewood stood beside him for a moment, looked forward, where the thudding of the pumps were beginning their monotonous beat, and then stared aft, above the taffrail, where the flaring coals of Helgoland light burned.

'Obliged to 'ee,' he said shortly, and went below.

Dawn revealed their position. To the south east the cliffs and high flat tableland of the island dominated the horizon. Their concern at the difficulties of fetching the flyspeck of rock had been confounded by a providence that had landed them on the very reefs which ran out to the north-west of Helgoland itself and which, just to seaward of them, now lay beneath a seething white flurry of breaking swells, the last vestiges of the tempest.

Drinkwater could see dearly the column of the lighthouse, together with the roofs of some buildings and the spire of a church. To the left of Helgoland lay a narrow strait of water in which several merchant ships lay at anchor. Beyond them the strait was bounded by a low sandy isle on which a pair of beacons could be clearly seen against the pale yellow dawn. Drinkwater found the battered watchglass that nestled in a rack below the *Galliwasp*'s rail, focused and swept the cliff top. The rock rose precipitously, fissured and eroded by countless gales and the battering of the sea. Tufts of thrift and grass, patches of lichens, and the streaked droppings of seabirds speckled the grim and overhanging mass. Floating like a cloud above the cliff edge, hundreds of gulls hung on motionless wings, ridge-soaring on the updrafts of wind. Then Drinkwater saw the men, two of them, conspicuous in British scarlet. He lowered the telescope and stowed it. Striding aft he found *Galliwasp*'s ensign and took it forward. Their situation must have been obvious, even to the pair of lobsters regarding them from the cliff, but there was no harm in underlining their predicament, or in declaring their nationality.

Walking forward past the tired men labouring half-heartedly at the pump handles, he caught hold of a halliard rigged on a spar raised and fished to the stump of the foremast. Bending on the ensign he ran it up, union down in the signal of distress.

'D'you reckon on any help from the shore, Cap'n?' asked one of the party at the pumps, an American, by his accent.

'We've been seen by two soldiers on the cliff top,' Drinkwater answered confidently as he belayed the flag halliard, 'and I see no reason why those vessels at anchor shouldn't lend us a hand.'

He pointed and the men, grey faced with fatigue, looked up and saw the anchored ships for the first time.

'Say, Cap'n Waters, what is this place?'

Drinkwater grasped the reason for their anxiety. They had no idea where they were, and probably considered his act of hoisting a British ensign a piece of folly.

'It's all right, lads,' he said, 'this is Helgoland. It's British occupied; those soldiers ain't Frenchmen.'

He could see the relief in their faces as they spat on their hands and resumed the monotonous duty of keeping the *Galliwasp* afloat until help arrived.

Help arrived in the form of Mr Browne and two naval launches. The heavy boats crabbed slowly towards them, rounding the eastern point of Helgoland under oars. They were full of men and followed by several smaller boats from the merchant ships.

Mr Browne, a heavily built man with a florid face and white side-whiskers, was dressed in a plain blue coat secured with gilt buttons. On these Drinkwater noticed the anchor of the naval pattern. Mr Browne, he correctly deduced – together with his two launches – was a servant of the crown.

'Browne,' the man announced, staring about him as he clambered over the *Galliwasp*'s rail. 'King's harbour-master.'

'Litttlewood, Master of the *Galliwasp* of London, bound for the Baltic from the London River. This is Captain Waters, supercargo.'

Browne nodded perfunctorily at Drinkwater.

'You're in a pickle, to be sure,' said Browne, pushing a tarred canvas hat back from his forehead and scratching his skull.

'I've a valuable cargo, Mr Browne,' said Littlewood with a show of tired dignity, 'and I've every intention of saving it.'

Browne cast a ruminative eye on the fat shipmaster.

'We've a great deal of valuable cargo hereabouts, Mister,' he said in an equally weary tone, 'but we'll see what can be done.' He sniffed, as though the noise signified his taking charge of the situation, then turned to the ship's side, cupping two massive hands about his mouth and shouting instructions to the boats assembling round the wallowing *Galliwasp*.

'We'll tow her in, boys . . .' He turned to Littlewood, 'Is she taking much water?'

'Enough, but the pumps are just holding their own,' Littlewood replied, throwing Drinkwater a quick glance to silence him. Watts had just reported the water to be gaining on them.

'If she looks like foundering,' the harbour-master bellowed to his boat coxswains, 'we'll beach her on the spit by the new beacon.'

Browne turned inboard again, fished in a pocket, brought out a quid of tobacco and thrust it into his mouth. 'We'll buoy-off your anchor, Cap'n, save a bit o' time and miss the worst of the ebb against us in the road. Can your men get a rope ready for'ard?'

By noon, having set a scrap of sail on the jury foremast and submitted to the efforts of the boats orchestrated by Mr Browne, the *Galliwasp* lay anchored to her second bower just off the new beacon, where she would take the bottom at low water.

To the east the low sandy isle protected them from easterly winds. Extending north-west and south-east, reefs like the one they had struck twelve hours earlier protected them from the north and south.

To the west, the direction of the prevailing wind, the island of Helgoland formed a welcome bulwark. Less forbidding from this eastern aspect, the tableland inclined slightly towards them. Along the beach were situated a row of wooden buildings, some under construction. From among them a road climbed the rising land to a neat village surrounding the church spire whose cruciform finial Drinkwater had spotted from the far side of the island. On the beach, fronting the row of wooden buildings, a beacon with a conical topmark was in transit with the lighthouse beyond.

'Well, sir,' said Browne after dismissing the boats, 'you could show your appreciation in the usual way.'

Littlewood nodded as Browne rubbed a giant paw across his lips.

'Come below, Mr Browne,' said Littlewood, relief plain on his face, 'and you as well, Cap'n Waters, you've been on your pins since the alarm was raised.'

They went below and Browne's eyes gleamed when he saw the mellow glow of rum.

'Good Jamaica rumbullion, Mr Browne,' said Littlewood, handing the harbour-master a brimming glass.

'The best, sir,' said Browne expansively now that the job was done. 'You will have to clear your cargo, Cap'n Littlewood. I will take you ashore later,' he went on, indicating there was no hurry and edging his empty glass forward across the table with the fingers of his huge hands.

'I should be obliged, Mr Browne, if you would favour me by arranging an interview with the Governor,' put in Drinkwater. Browne turned his gaze upon Littlewood's supercargo.

'The Governor's only concerned with military affairs, Cap'n . . .'

'Waters.'

'Cap'n Waters, if either of you have commercial matters to discuss, Mr Ellerman, chairman of the Committee of Trade will be able to assist.' He turned back to Littlewood. 'If you want to discharge your cargo, Cap'n Littlewood, he's the man to consult.'

'But where can we store it?'

'Them wooden shacks they're puttin' up all along the foreshore,' Browne said, draining his second tumbler of rum, 'they call warehouses. Most are empty . . . speculation,' Browne said the word with a certain disdain. 'Someone'll *rent* you sufficient space, I'm sure.'

'I'd still appreciate your arranging an interview with the Governor, Mr Browne,' Drinkwater said with quiet insistence.

Browne looked at Littlewood who nodded. 'Oblige Cap'n Waters, Mr Browne, if you please.'

'God's strewth,' growled the King's harbour-master, 'this ain't another cargo on the bleeding secret service, is it?'

'Well sir?'

The officer seated behind the desk looked up from a sheaf of papers and regarded Drinkwater over a pair of pince-nez. From the expression on his face Drinkwater expected an intolerant reception. He had been led to believe, during the stiff climb up through the village to the old Danish barracks in the company of Mr Browne, that the Governor was plagued by the merchant fraternity who seemed to regard the island as more a large warehouse than a military outpost. Some of this disdain had rubbed off on Browne, who railed against the ever-increasing number of 'commercial gennelmen' who were littering his foreshore with their hastily erected warehouses. By the time Drinkwater was shown into the Governor's presence by a young adjutant, he was more than a little irritable himself.

'You are Colonel Hamilton, the Governor?' Drinkwater asked, pointedly ignoring the fidgeting adjutant at his elbow who had just told him the Governor's name. Hamilton's face darkened.

'You sir!' he snapped. 'Who the deuce are you?'

'This is Captain Waters, sir, supercargo aboard the barque *Galliwasp* – the disabled vessel I reported to you earlier, sir,' the subaltern explained.

'I wish to see you alone, Colonel,' Drinkwater said, ignoring the two soldiers who exchanged glances.

'Do you now,' said Hamilton, leaning back in his chair so that the light from the windows glittered on the gilt buttons of his undress scarlet, 'and upon what business, pray?'

'Business of so pressing a nature that it is of the utmost privacy.'

Drinkwater turned a withering eye on the junior officer, unconsciously assuming his most forbidding quarterdeck manner.

'Captain Waters,' drawled Hamilton as he removed the pince-nez and laid them on the papers before him. 'Every confounded ship, and every confounded master, and every confounded supercargo, agent, merchant and countin' house clerk, comes here bleatin' about *private business*. I am a busy man and Mr Browne will do all he can to assist your ship and her cargo . . .' Hamilton leaned forward, picked up and repositioned the pince-nez on his nose and bent over his paperwork.

'No, Colonel. *You* will assist me . . .'

'Come sir.' Drinkwater felt the adjutant's hand on his arm but he pressed on.

'You will assist me by obliging me with a private interview at once.' As Hamilton looked up, his face as red as his coat, Drinkwater turned to the adjutant. 'And you will wait outside.'

'Damn it, sir,' said the young man, 'have a care . . .'

'OUT!' Drinkwater roared, suddenly furiously glad to cast off the mantle of pretence. 'I demand you obey me, damn you!'

The adjutant put his hand to his hanger and Hamilton leapt to his feet. 'By God . . .'

'By God, sir, get this boy out of here. I've a matter to discuss with you in private, sir, and you will hear me out.' Hamilton hesitated, and Drinkwater pressed on. 'After which, Colonel, you may do as you please, but you are a witness that your adjutant laid a hand upon me. On a quarterdeck, that would be a grave offence.'

Hamilton's mouth shut like a trap. As Drinkwater caught and held his eyes a glimmer of comprehension showed through the outrage. Still standing he nodded a dismissal to the fuming adjutant.

'Well, sir,' Hamilton said once again, his voice strained with the effort of self-control, 'perhaps you will give me an explanation?'

'My name is not Waters, Colonel Hamilton, but Drinkwater, Captain Drinkwater, to be precise, of the Royal Navy. I am employed upon a secret service with a cargo destined elsewhere than Helgoland, and I am in need of your assistance.'

Hamilton eased himself down into his chair, made a tent of his fingers and put them to his lips.

'And what proof do you have for this claim?'

'None, Colonel, apart from my vehemence just now, but if it sets your mind at rest, the name of Dungarth may not be unknown to you. It is Lord Dungarth's orders that I am executing; or at least, I *was* until overcome by the recent tempestuous weather.'

'I see.' Hamilton beat his finger tips gently together, considering. Lord Dungarth's name was not well known except to officers in positions of trust, and Hamilton, for all the obscurity of his half-colonelcy in the 8th Battalion of Royal Veterans, was among such men in his capacity as Governor of Helgoland.

Hamilton appeared to make up his mind. He leant forward, picked up a pen, dipped it and wrote a note. Sanding the note he sealed it with a wafer, scribbled a superscription and sat back, tapping his lips with the folded paper. For a moment longer he regarded Drinkwater, then he called out: 'Dowling!'

The adjutant flew through the door, 'Sir?'

'Take this to Nicholas.'

The junior officer's tone was crestfallen. It was clear he would rather have leapt to the rescue of his beleagured commander.

'Take a seat, Captain,' said Hamilton after Dowling had gone.

'Obliged.'

The two men sat in absolute silence for a while, then Hamilton asked, 'Are you personally acquainted with his Lordship, Captain Drinkwater?'

'I have that honour, Colonel Hamilton.'

'For a long while?'

'He was first lieutenant when I was a midshipman aboard the *Cyclops*.'

A desultory small-talk dragged on while they waited. Hamilton sought to draw personal details out of Drinkwater who gave them graciously. At last a knock on the door announced the arrival of Mr Nicholas.

'Mr Edward Nicholas, Captain Drinkwater, is in the Foreign Service.'

Drinkwater rose and the two men exchanged bows. Nicholas, a younger man than Hamilton, with quick, intelligent dark eyes, exchanged glances with the Governor, then studied Drinkwater.

'He says he's under Dungarth's orders, Ned. Got a cargo intended for a secret destination. Rather think he's your department – if he ain't a fake.'

Nicholas's eyes darted from suspect to suspector and back again. Then the slight figure in its sober grey suit sat down on the edge of Hamilton's desk and dangled one leg nonchalantly.

'What is your Christian name, Captain Drinkwater?'

'Nathaniel.'

'And what ship did you command in the summer of the year seven?'

'The frigate *Antigone*. Upon a special service . . .'

'Where? In what theatre?'

'That is none of your concern.'

'It would greatly help our present impasse if you would tell me,' Nicholas smiled. 'Come, sir, be frank. Otherwise these matters become so tedious.'

'The Baltic.'

'Good. You knew my predecessor here, Mr Mackenzie . . .'

'Colin Mackenzie?'

'The same. He was with you in the – Baltic, was he not?' There was just the merest hint of a pause before Nicholas said 'Baltic', implying the proper name was a vague reference and that both men knew more than they were saying.

'I was employed at Downing Street, Captain Drinkwater, in the drafting of the special orders prior to Lord Gambier's expedition leaving for the reduction of Copenhagen and the seizure of the Danish fleet. I recall your name being mentioned by Mr Canning in the most flattering terms.'

Drinkwater inclined his head. It was odd how pivotal that Baltic mission had been. Before it, all had been hope and aspiration; afterwards, following the approbation of Government and the meteor strike at an unsuspecting Denmark in a pre-emptive move to foil the French, fate had discarded him. It was Hamilton who interrupted Drinkwater's metaphysical gloom.

'None o' that proves he's who he says he is.' Hamilton spoke as though Drinkwater was not there. Nicholas ignored the Governor. Drinkwater guessed they did not get on.

'If you want our assistance, Captain Drinkwater, you will have to be more frank with us. Where is your cargo destined for? I assure you, both Colonel Hamilton and I are used to matters of state secrecy.'

'It is intended for Russia, and I require it to be removed from the *Galliwasp* and stored securely in requisitioned space. I will then attempt to arrange for another vessel to relieve the *Galliwasp* if she proves too damaged to re-rig.'

'*You require*, do you, sir?' Hamilton spoke in a tone of low sarcasm.

'For what purpose is your cargo going to Russia, Captain?' Nicholas persisted.

'To break the blockade.'

'We do that from here,' put in Hamilton sourly. 'One would think it the only purpose for holding the island.'

'But you do not implicate the Tsar by such a transaction,' said Drinkwater quietly, and now his words engaged the attention of both men.

'How so?'

'The purpose of my mission, gentlemen, the reason why a post-captain of the Royal Navy is obliged to submit himself to sundry humiliations, is that this cargo is designed to draw attention to itself, to shout all the way to Paris the single fact that Alexander, faithful ally of the Emperor of the French, is trading with his friend's sworn enemies.'

'And break the accord between Paris and Petersburg,' said Nicholas, his eyes bright with comprehension. 'Brilliant!'

'And what is this cargo?' asked Hamilton.

'Military stores, Colonel. Greatcoats, boots, muskets . . .' Drinkwater began, sensing victory. Hamilton only laughed.

'Devil take you, sir, you jest. We've the *Delia*, the *Hanna*, the *Anne*, the *Ocean*, the *Egbert* and the *Free Briton* lying in the roads right now, their holds stuffed with ordnance stores, clothing, ball and cartridges. Captain Gilham of the *Ocean* has been languishing here since last May! They too were intended for a secret service! I'm afraid, Captain Drinkwater, you've brought coals to Newcastle!'

Hamilton's laughter was revenge for Drinkwater's *lèse-majesté*, an assertion of superiority that pricked Drinkwater's pride. Yet the Governor had missed the point.

'Whatever the purpose of these other ships, Colonel Hamilton, the *Galliwasp* was not intended to end up at Helgoland.'

'We will write to London for instructions, Captain Drinkwater,' Hamilton said coolly. 'Besides, even a lobster knows the Baltic will be closed to navigation in a week or two. You must perforce become a guest of the mess. I am sure that Lieutenant Dowling will be only too happy to look after you.'

'You are placing me under constraint, sir?'

'Only as a precaution, Captain,' Hamilton went on happily, 'until Mr Nicholas here has received instructions from His Majesty's Government. We are not far distant from an enemy coast, you know.'

'And Captain Littlewood and his cargo?'

'Captain Littlewood may make arrangements among the mercantile fraternity and repair his ship if he is able to. Browne will give what assistance he can, no doubt. Be a good fellow, Ned, and call Dowling in again. Good day to you, Captain.'

Chapter Seven *October–November 1809*

Helgoland

The weeks that succeeded this unpromising interview were tedious in the extreme. Drinkwater's sole positive act was to write to Dungarth explaining his predicament and whereabouts. Of necessity, his words were terse and he carried round in his head the sentence admitting the failure of his mission: *It is with regret that I inform you that due to the tempestuous weather we have been cast up on the island of Helgoland at so late a season as to render the continuation of the voyage impracticable until the spring . . .* Diplomatic affairs, Drinkwater knew, might be entirely upset by so delayed an arrival of his cargo.

Pending word from London, Drinkwater had taken Littlewood into his confidence to the extent of allowing the *Galliwasp*'s master to give out that their cargo was intended for a secret service to Sweden. It was an open secret that the situation in that country was unstable and a shipment of military stores would raise no eyebrows, particularly as so many of the other ships in Helgoland Road seemed destined for a similar purpose.

Littlewood agreed to this proposal. He had much on his mind and Drinkwater left him to the supervision of the discharge and storing of *Galliwasp*'s cargo and the survey of his damaged ship.

For his own part, Drinkwater was allowed a small room in the former Danish barracks and the freedom of the garrison officers' mess, but he was not a welcome guest. The officers regarded him with a suspicion fostered by Hamilton and confirmed by Dowling, while Nicholas, to whom Drinkwater felt a natural attraction, maintained a polite, uncommunicative distance. Although not exactly a prisoner, Drinkwater felt he was afforded the hospitality of the Royal Veterans in order that they might the better keep an eye on him. He took to walking on the wild western escarpment of the island, losing himself among the rocks and the sparse grass in the company of the wheeling seabirds whose skirling cries seemed to echo the bleakness of his mood.

In the frustration of his situation, Drinkwater felt himself utterly bowed by the overwhelming dead weight of a hostile providence. His lonely, introspective thoughts followed a predictable and gloomy circle that bordered on the obsessive. Intensified by his isolation they threatened to unhinge him and in other circumstances could have led him to succumb to the oblivion of opium or the bottle. From his involvement in Russia to the loss of Quilhampton, the train of his tortured thoughts drove him to seek out the lonely parts of the island, to curse and fulminate and regret in equal measure, only returning to what normality was allowed him during his nightly visits to the bleak mess.

Here he found some mitigation of his misery. Lieutenant McCullock of the Transport Service, an elderly naval officer with a lifetime's service to his credit, was not unfriendly in a gruff way; nor was Mr Thomson, agent of the Victualling Board, and from these men he gleaned a little information about the island and its inhabitants.

Perhaps McCullock was cordial only because it was rumoured that the irritable grey-eyed man with the scarred cheek, the old-fashioned queue and the lop-sided shoulders was a post-captain in the Royal Navy. If it was true, it behove McCullock to mind his manners. Mr Browne seemed impervious to such a suggestion, though he was sufficiently expansive to explain that the native Helgolanders subsisted from fishing.

'They long-line for cod and 'addock from open boats in companies of a dozen or so men,' he said, 'and every one is licensed to sell liquor by hancient privilege.' Browne wiped the back of a huge hand across his mouth and grinned. 'Gives our noble Governor a parcel o' trouble.' Browne grinned and nodded in the direction of the two sentinels at the beach guardhouse.

The 8th Battalion of Royal Veterans who, with a handful of Invalid Artillery made up the island's garrison, were largely elderly or pensioned soldiers, re-enlisted for the duration of the war with France and her allies. One or two were younger men considered unfit for service with a regular line battalion in Spain.

'Weak in the arm and weak in the head,' Browne muttered, as they passed the two lounging sentries. ' 'Hain't worth a musket, rum nor bread,' he intoned. 'It's them young, useless buggers that give the Governor his problems.'

It was clear that Mr Browne considered his own drinking, evident from his complexion and the reek of him, to be beyond gubernatorial judgement.

'Weak 'eads can't 'old their liquor, d'ye see.'

They walked down through the village with its neat, brightly painted cottages and fantastically spired church. The helices and finial reminded Drinkwater of those in Copenhagen. Pigs and chickens ran about the cottages, each of which had its own vegetable garden set behind walls of whitewashed stone.

'Then there's the women,' Browne went on. 'Most of 'em are married, and that pastor fellow keeps an eye on 'em when their menfolk are away fishing, but we've got a spot o' bother wiv one or two.'

They watched a buxom, middle-aged woman with flaxen hair and a ruddy face peg a pair of wet breeches on a line of gaily dancing washing. She gave them a shy smile.

'*Guten tag*,' said Browne with the proprietorial hauteur of a seigneur.

'*Guten tag*, Herr Browne.'

'I observe it is the women who carry the coals to the lighthouse,' remarked Drinkwater.

'It earns 'em a few shillings,' Browne said as they reached the boat landing. Here Browne took his leave and Drinkwater, as had become his daily habit, inspected the progress Littlewood and his party were making on the refitting of the *Galliwasp*.

Emptied of her cargo, they had hauled her down and careened her, exposing the torn sheathing and a hole stove in her planking by a rock. She had escaped serious damage to her keel, though much of her false keel had been torn off in the grounding. They had replaced the damaged planks, doubled them and recaulked her strained seams until, by the end of October, Littlewood had pronounced her hull sound and they set to work on the foreshore, making new spars.

They had been fortunate in finding a quantity of timber on the island, brought by several prudent shipmasters, and they were able to make a number of purchases to facilitate the repair work.

Littlewood daily expressed his satisfaction and Drinkwater acknowledged his report with assumed gratification. In his heart he thought Littlewood would end up the loser, for they daily expected the packet boat with orders from London which would put an end to the Russian mission.

The packet *King George* left Helgoland with Hamilton's letter and Drinkwater's report in mid-October, bound for Harwich. By the end of the month, Hamilton estimated, they should have the instructions that would end Drinkwater's equivocal status, but this proved not to be the case. A breezy October turned into a grey, chill and misty November, when the wind swung east and fell light.

Such conditions, though delaying the mails from England, increased the activity of the smugglers. Fishing boats and *schuyts* of up to thirty tons burthen sailed into Helgoland Road to trade for the luxuries dealt-in by the two dozen merchant houses whose wooden stores crowded the foreshore. They came out from Brunsbuttel and Cuxhaven on the Elbe, Blexen and Geestendorf on the Weser and Hocksiel on the Jahde to smuggle the luxuries Napoleon's Continental System denied the wealthier inhabitants of his reluctant empire. Tea, coffee, spices, Oporto and Madeira wines, silk and cotton, and above all, sugar, were in demand by the new bourgeoisie created by the success of French arms. In small quantities, slipped ashore on lonely landings on the featureless coasts of Kniphausen, Bremen, Oldenburg and South Ditmarsch, these goods found their way across Europe, a reciprocal trade to the brandy, lace and claret which came across the Channel to the English coast.

Frequently the smugglers brought news: either gossip or copies of the Hamburg papers, giving the island its military justification as a 'listening post'. Occasionally they brought intelligence of a graver sort with the arrival of an agent. One such gentleman appeared on an evening in November. Lieutenant Maimburg's arrival coincided with that of His Majesty's gun-brig *Bruizer* which had returned from a patrol along the Danish coast in quest of Danish gun-boats reported to have been sighted off Syllt. The appearance of Lieutenant Smithies of the *Bruizer* and Lieutenant Maimburg of the King's German Legion, was the excuse for a riotous evening in the officers' mess.

Maimburg, whose duties were more that of a spy than a soldier, had brought with him fifteen Hanoverian lads, recruited for the Legion then serving in Spain; he had also brought news of a

Turkish victory over the Russians at a place called Siliskia, and a rumour that Napoleon had ordered areas of Hanover ceded to his puppet kingdom of Westphalia, while a matching Eastphalia was to be created as a kingdom for his stepson, Eugene de Beauharnais. Such gossip had the mess buzzing with speculation, and amid the chink of bottle and glass the chatter rose. Sitting quietly, Drinkwater learned also that a week or two earlier, news of peace between France and Austria had been augmented by rumours of joint action by the Emperor of the French and the Austrian Kaiser in support of the Tsar against the Turks.

But these social occasions were infrequent. The life of the colony beat to the slow, intermittent rhythm of news from the Continent and news from England. The delay to the Harwich packet was reflected in the irritability of the garrison officers. For Drinkwater, the long wait became a purgatory.

Hamilton's continuing dislike and Nicholas's cautious indifference made his situation profoundly depressing. He could assume the character of a merchant shipmaster in the line of duty, but to be cast out into a limbo of suspicion was almost more than he could bear.

One afternoon, inspecting the decayed grate of the lighthouse, he caught sight of a sail to the westward. The Harwich packet doubled the buoy marking the Steen Rock and fetched an anchorage in the road. Too agitated to rush down to the barracks, Drinkwater maintained a stoic isolation on the western bluff, where Dowling, thundering up on Hamilton's charger, found him.

Hope leapt into Drinkwater's heart as he watched Dowling coax the beautiful dun hunter over the tussocked grass. The charger was the only horse on the island and the news must have been important for Hamilton to have allowed Dowling the use of it.

'The Governor summons your presence upon the instant, sir,' Dowling called, reining in his mount twenty yards short of Drinkwater. 'Upon the instant, d'you hear?' he added, then wheeling the horse, cantered away.

Drinkwater watched him go; there had been too much of a smirk on Dowling's chops to augur well. He made his way to the barracks as near instantly as his legs would allow and was ushered in to Hamilton's presence. Nicholas was already there.

'Sit down, Captain,' Nicholas said smoothly. Hamilton rose and stood staring out of the window on to the parade ground. It was clear that he was leaving matters to the younger man.

'I'll stand, if you've no objection,' said Drinkwater coldly.

'None whatsoever.' Nicholas picked up a letter which lay before him on Hamilton's desk. 'I'm afraid, Captain, that it appears your situation is more confused than ever. Lord Dungarth has not favoured us with a reply.'

'Not replied?' Drinkwater was taken aback. 'I don't understand . . .'

'It seems,' Nicholas went on, 'that there has been a duel in the Government. Lord Castlereagh and Mr Canning have been at pistol-point on Putney Heath.'

'Go on, sir,' said Drinkwater incredulously.

'Mr Canning has, we understand, been wounded, though not mortally. The incident has brought down the Government . . .'

'But Lord Dungarth,' Drinkwater began, only to be interrupted by Hamilton turning from the window.

'Has not written, Mr Whatever-your-name-is.'

Drinkwater met the Governor's triumphant gaze with an expression of continuing disbelief.

'I have already spoken with Captain Littlewood,' Hamilton continued, 'he reports his ship will be ready to reload in a day or two. He will return to England as soon as he is able. As for yourself, you will embark in the *King George* and are free to leave aboard her. She will depart in a couple of days. Was I not waiting for a courier from Hamburg, I should order her master to leave at once.'

The implication in Hamilton's words was clear: his disdain, surely unmerited no matter what the misunderstanding that had arisen on their first acquaintance, had developed into a passion. The shock of realization struck Drinkwater with sudden force. It dislodged him angrily from his long wallow in despair. Hamilton's overt prejudice goaded him to a reaction from which all his subsequent actions sprang.

'Sir,' he said, 'I hope fervently to meet you again in circumstances which accord me greater satisfaction.' Then, not trusting himself further, he stalked from the room.

He did not stop walking until he had regained the lonely bluff on the western extremity of Helgoland. Hamilton's perverse attitude, rooted in God-knew-what pettiness, had sent his mind into a spin. There was undoubtedly a good reason why Dungarth had not written. Whatever it was – and it most certainly had nothing to do with the duel fought between Castlereagh and Canning – it was inconceivable that it should result in Dungarth abandoning Drinkwater or his own position at the head of the Admiralty's Secret Department.

Drinkwater wished now he had been more explicit in his letter, at least intimated that Governor Hamilton did not believe he was a naval officer. If Dungarth knew he was at Helgoland, he doubtless assumed Drinkwater would make the best of a bad job. But if he did not . . .

Drinkwater recalled Dungarth's own warning that trouble was brewing between Canning and Castlereagh. The consequent ructions, he had guessed, would affect British foreign policy.

Drinkwater paused and stared at the grey sea below him. The swell broke against the rampart of the island, a filigree of white foam rolled back from the rocks, harmless-looking from this height. In the west, behind rolls of dark cumulus, the sunset was pallid. Drinkwater sniffed the air and stared about him. There were fewer birds about than earlier, most were already roosting on the cliff. He looked again at the swell and barked a short laugh.

There would be a westerly gale by morning. He would go when the packet sailed, but that would be when God decided, not Colonel Bloody Hamilton! He turned, intending to walk back by way of the lighthouse. He would achieve something following his visit to Helgoland, send a letter of censure to the Elder Brethren of the Trinity House for allowing so archaic a system as the chauffer to continue in service, when a parabolic reflector and Argand lights would provide a reliable light on the island!

With such consoling and indignant thoughts he began the return journey. He had not gone a hundred yards before he almost fell over the seaman.

The man was asleep, but woke with a start as Drinkwater stumbled and swore.

'God damn it, man, what the devil are you doing here?'

'I beg pardon, Cap'n Waters. Guess I must have fallen asleep. I came up here more or less like yourself, fixing to get some peace and quiet.'

Drinkwater recognized the American seaman he had last spoken to at the *Galliwasp*'s pumps.

'Sullivan, ain't it?'

'That's correct, sir,' Sullivan replied, brushing himself down.

'You're an American, aren't you?'

'A *Loyalist* American, Cap'n. I hail from New Brunswick now, though I was born in Georgia. My paw was with Colonel Kruger at Fort Ninety-Six.'

'Ah yes, the American War. You're a long way from home, Sullivan.'

'Aye, Cap'n, and a damned fool for it, and if I wanna get home I have to keep clear o' Lootenant Smithies. He's made threats to press some o' the boys from the *Galliwasp*. That's why I spends my liberty hours up here, away from the grog shops.'

'I see. Well, good luck to you. The sooner you get that barque refitted, the sooner you'll see New Brunswick again.'

He walked on, unaware that the encounter with Sullivan was the second event of consequence that day.

Drinkwater avoided the company of the garrison officers that night. He went, without dinner, directly to his room. There seemed little point in disobliging Hamilton. He would happily leave on the *King George*, when the packet sailed. He had begun making up an account to settle with Littlewood when a knock came at his door. It was Nicholas.

'May I speak with you, Captain Drinkwater?'

'Why the change of tack, sir?' said Drinkwater coolly. 'I thought all that was necessary had already been said.'

'Not quite, sir. May I . . .?'

Drinkwater lit a second candle and motioned Nicholas to sit on the bed. He sat himself on the single rickety upright chair that served all other offices in the bare room. 'I shall not be sorry to leave this place,' he said, looking round him.

'Sir,' said Nicholas urgently, 'I must apologize for Colonel Hamilton's attitude as well as my own. He is a harassed man, sir, under pressure from many quarters and, if you will forgive the metaphor, you were a timely whipping-boy. The fact is, sir, that if you are who you say you are – damn it, this is difficult – but put bluntly, sir, as a post-captain you were seen as a threat . . .'

'Damn it, Mr Nicholas, I only wanted a degree of cooperation.'

'I think, sir, that you are a man of more decisiveness than the Governor. He is a trifle jealous of those whose, er, energy threatens to compromise his authority.'

'Which is why you yourself so assiduously toe his line,' said Drinkwater wryly.

'Er, quite so, sir. I have to endure a long posting here.'

Drinkwater smiled. 'Well, as for my decisiveness, Mr Nicholas, it has not been much exercised lately. In fact – well, no matter. To what do I owe your present visit?'

'A word with you privately, sir. I have given much thought to what you have told us. I have also consulted Captain Littlewood who told me that he was secretly informed in London that you were a naval officer of distinction.'

'Who told him that?' Drinkwater asked, recalling Littlewood's occasional sly 'jibes'.

'His charter-party, I understand. A Mr Solomon . . .'

'I see. Why then if you knew that, did you not intercede with Hamilton?'

'It only occurred to me to ask three days ago and since then, with the arrival of Lieutenant Maimburg, I have been much occupied with despatches. Besides . . .'

'Your relationship with Hamilton is not always easy.'

'Quite so, sir, quite so.'

'But you could have said something today.'

'I did not make the connection until dinner this evening, sir. It did not occur to me earlier and besides, there are certain matters that are exclusively my concern, as agent for the Foreign Service.'

'I see.'

'But before I can go any further, sir, before I can act on my own initiative, I have to satisfy myself that you are indeed the officer of whom I have heard.'

'And how do you propose to do that?' Drinkwater asked drily.

'You mentioned your acquaintance with Colin Mackenzie. What was it you jointly achieved in the, er, Baltic?' There were good reasons why he should remain silent, but there were equally good reasons for not doing so.

'What have you in mind, Mr Nicholas, if I prove to be who I claim? I am after all, about to be repatriated. Do you just wish to satisfy your curiosity?'

'You might yet achieve your objective, sir. You might yet convince the French that your cargo *was* bound for Russia, that the Russians *are* buying quantities of arms and that it suggests a secret accord between St Petersburg and London.'

'And how do you propose I, or should I say "we" are to accomplish this, Mr Nicholas?'

'Wait, sir. I beg you be patient. I can at present only conceive the grand design. Ever since I heard of Lord Dungarth's idea, I was struck by the subtlety of it. It understands exactly the circumstances likely to directly attract Napoleon's attention. But first, sir, answer my question: what was it you and Colin Mackenzie jointly achieved?'

It was as if a lock had been picked in Drinkwater's soul. As the candles guttered in the fervid breath of the eager Nicholas and the shadows of their figures leapt on the peeling limewashed walls of the barrack room, it seemed that his visitor was a providential messenger, sent to release him from his purgatory. Fate had decided upon a reprieve, and he felt his spirits rise with the enthusiasm of the younger man.

'Well, sir, if I hear you have breathed a word of this to anyone, I shall shoot you.' He said it without meaning it, but the flat tone of voice menaced Nicholas so that he caught his breath and nodded.

Drinkwater smiled. 'We are like conspirators, are we not, Mr Nicholas?'

'I hope not quite that, sir.'

'Lord Dungarth once said to me that he imagined himself as a puppet-master, pulling strings that made others jump. A rum fancy, but not inaccurate. Very well. Mackenzie and I were at Tilsit. There were two other men involved, one of whom is dead and neither of whom need concern us now, and what we achieved was the theft by eavesdropping of the secret compact made verbally between the Tsar and Napoleon Bonaparte. Now do you believe I am Nathaniel Drinkwater, sir?'

'I do, sir, and I am most regretful that I did not from the start. I can only say that it may be providential that I made the discovery this evening, for only today have circumstances conspired to make my new proposal possible.'

'It is pointless to engage in mutual recrimination,' Drinkwater agreed. 'Please proceed.'

'Well, Captain Drinkwater, I have already expressed my admiration for Lord Dungarth's idea. It is highly probable that he has taken other measures to augment the plan . . .'

'How do you mean?'

'Well, it would not work unless the enemy heard about it . . .'

'You are very astute, Mr Nicholas,' said Drinkwater, thinking of his success in the whore-house, 'that is indeed quite true. You think his Lordship even now might be absent from London on some such task?'

'I think it most likely, sir. If all had gone well your cargo would have been delivered by now and the veracity of his claim, wherever laid, could have been checked.'

Drinkwater's heart was thumping with excitement. It was unlikely that Nicholas was right, for Dungarth was no longer fit to risk his life in France, but the thought that he could have been absent from London for a prolonged period had simply not occurred to Drinkwater. Hamilton would not have written to Dungarth personally, and Nicholas would have written to Canning. Canning would not have had time to deal with the correspondence before his pointless duel; and Dungarth's absence, even on so innocent an excuse as taking the waters at Bath, would explain why no answer had been forthcoming.

'You may have a point, Mr Nicholas, pray go on.'

'Well, as I believe you know, there are transports lying in the road that were destined for a secret service.'

'I have met Gilham of the *Ocean*, yes . . .'

'It was intended that a rebellion was raised in Hanover in favour of King George, the legitimate sovereign.'

'But the plan misfired?'

'Yes, the troops intended for it were sent instead to Spain and we have had to content ourselves with recruiting for the King's German Legion. By the same packet that failed to bring your accreditment, I received a *Most Secret* despatch, one whose contents I am not necessarily obliged to make known to Colonel Hamilton.' Nicholas paused, as if to add emphasis to the drama.

'By which I take it you are about to strain the exact nature of the, er, obligation in my favour, eh?'

'Quite so, sir,' Nicholas said. 'The point is, that the Ordnance Board have written off the entire convoy. This was the news that arrived today. The cost is transferred to Mr Canning's Secret Service budget and Mr Canning is . . .'

'Out of office!'

'Exactly so!'

'And in the absence of Mr Canning, *you* are going to take it upon yourself to dispose of those cargoes to me in order that I may exceed my own instructions and devise a means by which the whole are delivered to Russia? No, no, Mr Nicholas, at least not until the spring. The Baltic will be frozen and by then . . .'

'The Elbe is still open.'

'The Elbe?' Drinkwater sat back in astonishment, making his chair creak. 'You are suggesting we land those cargoes in the Elbe?'

'It is only necessary that Paris believes they were *consigned* to Russia.'

'But what you are suggesting is the disposal of Crown property to the enemy!'

'Think what we would gain. The success of Lord Dungarth's mission with the enemy swallowing the bait in the belief that they had won the advantage while at the same time we should have disposed of the goods at a profit.'

'But . . .'

'The Government, Captain Drinkwater, has already written off those stores to the disposal of the Secret Service,' Nicholas repeated persuasively.

'Do we have some trusty person in Hamburg capable of acting as agent for the sale?'

'Indeed we do!' Nicholas said grinning, and Drinkwater found it impossible not to smile in response.

PART TWO
The Luring of the Eagle

Engand is a nation of shopkeepers.

NAPOLEON,
Emperor of the French

Chapter Eight *November–December 1809*

The Lure

For a long while Drinkwater sat in silence and Nicholas watched anxiously. The longer the silence persisted, the less Nicholas thought he had convinced his listener. He began reciting a catalogue of reasons why the mission could not possibly be misjudged.

'If you have any misgivings, Captain Drinkwater, consider the facts. The funds of the Secret Service have been worse spent. We have squandered thousands on the Chouans . . . we have wasted huge amounts on fomenting the *émigrés* in Switzerland . . . the Comte D'Antraigues and Mr Wickham have gobbled up fantastic sums, all to no effect . . .'

But Drinkwater was not listening. Nicholas's words had acted like a drum beat to his tired heart. First the anger roused by Hamilton's rudeness had made him receptive to Nicholas's proposal; then the chance meeting with Sullivan, the *ci-devant* American, who had sown the seed of an idea . . .

He got up and began pacing up and down the spartan room: three paces to the wall, three paces to the bed, up and down, up and down.

'We have already enjoyed one brilliant success, sir, from this very island when Mr Mackenzie was here and superintended the mission of Father Robertson . . .'

Drinkwater stopped pacing and held up his hand. 'Stop, Mr Nicholas, you are being indiscreet. Whatever Mr Mackenzie's achievements, beware of seeking a reputation imprudently. Your case has much to recommend it; now I desire that you listen to me.'

Drinkwater began to walk back and forth again, though at a slower pace, his head down and his forehead creased in concentration.

'There will be a gale by morning and the packet will be delayed.

We must use this time to bring the Governor round. He has only to arrest and deport me for this scheme of yours to be stillborn. That I must leave to you, but I will give you some cogent reasons for pressing the point.

'To enable us to deliver a convoy would necessitate the co-operation of too many men and I doubt the fellows on those merchant ships will agree. However, we might mount an operation with two vessels. It will be known in Hamburg that these ships have been idling here for months; it would not be difficult to persuade the authorities there that their crews are disaffected, or threatened with the naval press. The Emperor Napoleon has inveighed against the application of the press against the hapless seamen of Great Britain . . .

'Apart from these two vessels, the remaining ships may be deployed as decoys in such a way as to give the impression of our sincerity, without committing them. Is there a rendezvous with the mainland that would not admit too great a risk to our people?'

'Yes, Neuwerk, an island ten leagues to the east and three from Cuxhaven.'

'Ah, yes, I recollect it from the chart. Well then, under the strictest discipline I think we might achieve something. Holding back most of the ships will perhaps serve to salve Colonel Hamilton's conscience, but he must put it about publicly that now the Ordnance Department have relinquished responsibility for the vessels, he wants them out of his charge.'

'I have no doubt but that he'd oblige you there.'

'He has no love of the mercantile lobby. Can we guarantee such an attitude will be made known ashore?'

'Gilham and company have rumbled with discontent for nigh on six or seven months, sir. The smugglers who buy from the warehouses report the movements of ships to and from the island. It cannot have escaped the notice of the authorities in Hamburg that some of them have been choking the anchorage for a long time.'

'And that they bear the distinctive marks of troop transports,' added Drinkwater, thinking of the large 'DA' painted on the bows of Gilham's *Ocean*.

'Quite so, sir, and if you make much of the disaffection of the crews when you are obliged to confront the *douaniers* . . .'

'Yes, Mr Nicholas,' Drinkwater broke in, 'but such a claim needs to be corroborated by whatever gossip precedes us. You say you have a trusted contact in Hamburg; I shall need also a German linguist. I know you to speak the language, do you know a person of such calibre that would accompany us?'

'Yes, I do. You recollect Colonel Hamilton spoke of delaying the packet until a message arrived?' Drinkwater nodded. 'And you recall me saying that it was only tonight that events conspired to make this present proposal possible?'

'I recollect.'

'There is a merchant house whose head is a man called Liepmann, a Jew, resident at Altona and master of a considerable business chiefly connected with the import of sugar. He is adept at maintaining this trade notwithstanding the present blockade and we are sympathetic to his needs. He is known to the French, having opened up a lucrative communication with the city's former Governor, M'sieur Bourrienne. He is a go-between, a broker . . .'

'And will handle the commercial aspects of this transaction of ours, eh?' Drinkwater asked, jumping to the obvious conclusion.

'Quite so. We, I mean, the Governor, is awaiting news as to how matters are to be conducted in the wake of Bourrienne's departure and under the rule of Reinhardt, the new French minister. The man who brings this, Herr Reinke, is surveyor to the Chamber of Commerce, continually mapping the shifting sandbanks of the Elbe, a man whose absence is not missed for a few days and who can be relied upon as an expert pilot and linguist. It is his arrival the Colonel anticipates.'

'I see. And Liepmann, can you communicate a matter of this complexity with him directly, or must we wait for Herr Reinke to return to Hamburg?'

Nicholas shook his head. 'I can send him a cryptogram by way of a fishing boat.'

Very well.

Drinkwater stopped pacing up and down and stood over Nicholas. He was resolved now, convinced that they had a chance of success.

'You will explain our intention in full to London, Mr Nicholas, is that clearly understood?' He did not want his motives misunderstood if the affair *did* miscarry, or he himself failed to return. 'Encode the message and do your best to reassure Colonel Hamilton that what we intend is a bold stroke.'

'A decisive stroke, wouldn't you say, sir?'

Drinkwater caught the twinkle of humour in the younger man's eyes.

'Indeed.' He smiled, then added, 'it would be even better managed if you could persuade him the idea was his own.'

Nicholas's eyebrows shot up. 'I could try, but I doubt that I possess sufficient tact for that.'

They laughed, just like conspirators, Drinkwater thought afterwards.

'And the communication with Herr Liepmann . . .'

'If you draft it, I will code it.' Nicholas hesitated then said, 'I think, Captain Drinkwater, that it would be to our advantage if you also knew the method of communication with Herr Liepmann. It might, after all, be useful to you in the event of any problems that might arise.'

'I see you are well cut out to be a diplomat, Mr Nicholas,' Drinkwater said wryly. 'This code is known to you and the Colonel . . .'

'And Herr Liepmann.'

'Very well. I agree. Now, Mr Nicholas, paper and ink, if you please. I will see you tomorrow when I hope to have spoken with Littlewood and, I think Gilham. In the mean time, oblige me by seeing if there is sufficient bunting on this God-forsaken island to manufacture a dozen Yankee ensigns.'

'*Yankee* ensigns, Captain, you mean *American* ensigns?'

'That is precisely what I mean, Mr Nicholas.'

'May I ask why?'

'No, you may not. I shall tell you tomorrow evening, when I have decided whether or not this lunatic proposal of yours has the least chance of success. Now, sir, pen and ink, and then leave me alone.'

The gale came with the dawn and Drinkwater went out to revel in the rising wind that so accorded with his mood. Unshaven, his stock loosened and his eyes gritty from lack of sleep, Drinkwater felt again the electrifying thrill he had last experienced when talking to the Jew Solomon after his night of dissipation in the Wapping stew.

It seemed now a pity to waste that night of seedily shameful labour, and it was a consoling thought that the success of the resuscitated mission might avenge the loss of Quilhampton and all the brave fellows aboard the *Tracker*.

He was convinced that, given the right conditions, they could deceive the French. If neglectful providence chose to favour their endeavours they might achieve a great deal more, for the detachment of the Tsar from his alliance with Napoleon was too grand a design to baulk at for the loss of a few muskets and pairs of boots . . .

Drinkwater stretched and sniffed the damp air as it rolled a grey cloud over the heights of the island, obscuring the lighthouse tower and the church spire. It reminded him of the squadrons of His Britannic Majesty's Fleet keeping watch and ward off Ushant and La Rochelle, off L'Orient and Toulon, the Scheldt and the Texel.

Just suppose there was a rupture between St Petersburg and Paris; just suppose for a second time the Grand Army was drawn off to the east where it had narrowly missed defeat at the hands of the Russians at Eylau . . .

Just suppose the apparently senseless deaths of Quilhampton and Frey, and even of poor Tregembo, were transformed into so rich a prize as a lasting peace . . .

Then the storm-battered ships of the western squadrons and the Mediterranean fleet could be withdrawn; their people could go home to their families; he himself could go home to Elizabeth and their children.

He shivered, suddenly chilled in the damp air. Flights of such improbable fancy were inimical to the grim, omnipresent business of war. He went inside again, in search of hot shaving water and a solution to the greatest obstacle he foresaw to the enterprise.

The compliance of Captain Littlewood was essential to the success of Nicholas's idea. A second ship in support would add credibility to Drinkwater's appearance in the Elbe while the remainder could, at little risk, play their part without being committed. But without the *Galliwasp*'s cargo, nothing could be attempted, let alone achieved.

Littlewood was, therefore, the first person with whom he discussed the plan that morning. He found the shipmaster on the foreshore talking to Watts and Munsden, his two mates. Seeing Drinkwater approach, Littlewood extended his arms then dropped them disconsolately by his side. Beyond the trio, *Galliwasp* had been hauled off to a mooring buoy, one of a trot laid by Browne and his seamen to enable ships to ride out bad weather. A pair of sheerlegs rose from the barque's waist and most of her company hung about the water's edge, where a pair of boats lay drawn up on the beach.

'I'd hoped to get the main mast in her this morning,' bemoaned Littlewood, 'but this damned gale . . .'

He left the sentence unfinished.

'Well, Captain Littlewood, count your blessings,' said Drinkwater cheerfully, 'at least you have her off the shoal.'

'Just what I were sayin', Cap'n Waters,' said Watts. 'She'd not take another poundin'.'

'Perhaps, Captain Littlewood, you'd take a turn along the foreshore with me,' Drinkwater said.

They walked south in silence. To their left lay the road with its crowd of anchored ships and the sandy island beyond. To their right the steep cliffs of the island rose from the sand and rock pools of the narrowing littoral strip. Waders ran about on the tideline of bladder wrack left by the last high-water. A pair of pied oystercatchers took flight, their brilliant orange bills shrieking a piping cry of alarm as the two men disturbed them.

'I was wondering when you'd be along, Cap'n Waters,' said Littlewood as the beach narrowed beneath the beetling rock face of the cliff.

'I've passed the time of day with you most mornings, Captain Littlewood,' Drinkwater said cautiously, wondering how best to approach the subject he wished to broach.

'That's not what I mean.' Littlewood cocked a shrewd eye at Drinkwater.

'What exactly is it that you *do* mean then?'

'I'm not a fool, Captain Waters. I don't need a supercargo to deliver a cargo anywhere in the world. I know *what* you are, if not *who* you are.'

'Mr Solomon was indiscreet . . .'

'Mr Solomon was protecting his investment, Captain,' Littlewood said, according Drinkwater's rank a less than casual ring. 'I knew you'd be up in them barracks a-thinkin'. You see, I *know* my cargo's valuable, and I ain't just talking pounds, shillin's and pence.'

'Solomon told you *that*?' Drinkwater's expression betrayed his surprise.

Littlewood laughed. 'No, he ain't that indiscreet, but I knew a lot was ridin' on the sale and I wouldn't have had a shipmate like yourself, Captain, if the matter didn't stink o' Government. Besides, you don't get withdrawn from the Scheldt expedition without a deal of influence in high places.' Littlewood paused, then added, 'And I've some cargo aboard on my own account.'

Drinkwater stopped and looked at Littlewood. It occurred to him that he had been too much taken up with his own preoccupations, too morbidly bemoaning his fate to have paid sufficient attention to others whose lives were as much at hazard in the affair as his own.

'What sort of cargo, Captain Littlewood?' Drinkwater asked.

'Why sugar loaves, Captain Drinkwater, sugar loaves.'

'May I ask you then what you would now do, left to your own devices?'

'I live by profit. No Government pay supports me or my family. Doubtless I'd discharge my cargo in a Swedish port; you'd have little objection to that?'

'Only that it fails in its objective.'

'We've already failed in that. Besides, though the objective, as you call it, was set by the Government, the cargo was consigned at the expense of Solomon and Dyer. Whatever the outcome, they and your humble servant are entitled to a modest profit, Captain.'

'Very well, Captain Littlewood, suppose I was to ask you a second question: do you, or Solomon and Dyer, have an agent either here,' he paused as Littlewood's eyes narrowed, 'or in Hamburg?'

Drinkwater watched the other man's face with interest. He sucked in his cheeks and raised his eyebrows but his eyes remained fixed on Drinkwater. It was clear the idea of selling his cargo to a nearer market than Gothenburg had already occurred to him, for when he blew out his cheeks he asked, 'And if my men won't sail for Hamburg, Captain?'

'I should requisition your ship and man her with Mr Browne's ratings,' Drinkwater said, advancing a contingent argument he had discovered during the small hours of the previous night.

'Is Mr Browne now amenable to your discipline, then?' Littlewood said, alluding to the equivocal status the whole island must have known Drinkwater had been accorded.

'Mr Browne knows his duty . . .' Drinkwater bluffed, 'perhaps we managed our deception better with others than with you.'

Littlewood chuckled and looked at the horizon. 'If we pay 'em, Captain, I'll answer for ten – a dozen men.'

Drinkwater caught the significance of the first person plural and grinned as Littlewood swung round and faced him. 'How well d'you know Captain Gilham? Could we persuade him to join us?' Drinkwater asked.

Comprehension dawned large in Littlewood's eyes. 'My God, Captain, you are going way beyond a modest profit and a new gown for Mistress Littlewood.'

'I'm going for very high stakes, Captain Littlewood. With luck Mistress Littlewood will be able to take the air with four in hand.'

'Damn it, sir. If Gilham ain't game *I'll* guarantee his ship. What about the others?'

'I have plans for them, but the affair will depend upon the reliability of those that take part. Too many might lay us open to disaster; those that come must be volunteers, volunteers for a dangerous service. Only when you have those men game enough should you advertise extra payment. *Then* you can promise gold.'

'You have thought of everything, Captain, I congratulate you.'

'Thank you,' said Drinkwater ironically. 'We enter the Elbe under American colours, though ultimately there's no attempt to claim American nationality. We have been lying at Helgoland for months, our crews are unpaid and disaffected . . .'

'Where Gilham's concerned that ain't so far from the truth.'

'Then you must moot it thus among the masters. Do not reveal my part until you have sounded their opinion. When they realize they can get out of this place at little risk and with a profit, they'll fall in with my plan.'

'And you'll not risk more than the two ships, the *Galliwasp* and the *Ocean?*'

'Not if I can avoid it, though I may want the others to proceed to Neuwerk in due course. Do I recollect you mentioning to me that *Galliwasp* carried a consignment of sugar on your own account?' Drinkwater asked.

'Aye, loaf sugar.'

'I think you may find a good market for the stuff, Captain, in which case Mrs Littlewood's carriage is assured.' Littlewood chuckled and Drinkwater went on. 'I think we will have the services of a competent pilot and an agent able and willing to purchase the cargoes.'

'Would that be Herr Liepmann, Captain?' Littlewood asked.

'Damn me, yes, how the deuce . . .?'

'He is Solomon and Dyer's agent.'

'Is he now,' Drinkwater said, one eyebrow raised quizzically. 'How very curious.'

Odd how things came together as though drawn inexorably by fate, Drinkwater thought.

'Better not make too much of our leave-taking,' he said as they approached the landing place. 'Get *Galliwasp* refitted and your cargo reloaded. We can do nothing until you are ready. Sound out the other masters and let me know in due course what their attitude is.'

'Aye, I'll see to it. As for this morning, what shall I give out as the nature of our conversation?'

Drinkwater considered the matter for a moment. 'Why, that I've overheard talk in the mess that the Ordnance Board is abandoning the convoy.'

'That should set the cat among the pigeons,' Littlewood rumbled.

'It just happens to be true, Captain Littlewood.'

He found Nicholas waiting for him when he returned to the barracks.

'Is your despatch ready, Captain?' Nicholas asked, a trifle impatiently, drawing from his breast a small octavo volume bound in brown calf. 'Dante, Captain, The Reverend Cary's translation.' Nicholas turned a few pages. 'Canto the second. You must commit these lines to memory.' Nicholas dipped the pen he had leant Drinkwater and began to scratch on a sheet of paper, quoting as he wrote:

Thy soul is by vile fear assail'd which oft
So overcasts a man, that he recoils
From noblest resolution, like a beast
At some false semblance in the twilight gloom.

Nicholas finished scrawling and looked up. 'Now, sir, 'tis perfectly simple: write the letters of the alphabet beneath each letter of the verse, omitting those already used, thus: *Thy soul is . . . a* to *h*, leaving the *s* of *is* blank, for you have used it in *soul*, and so on to the end. *I* and *j* are synonymous and those letters not found in the verse, *j*, *p* and *q* substitute for *x*, *y* and *z*. Cary's translation is new and not much known on the continent, though Liepmann has a copy. You have only to learn the verse.'

After Nicholas had gone, Drinkwater read the lines again as he committed them to memory. It struck him first that they uncannily described his own situation and the realization made the hairs on the nape of his neck crawl with a strange, primeval fear. And then, as he strove to remember the verse he realized that he no longer felt the oppression of spirit so acutely, that the mental activity of the last hours had roused him from his torpor.

This lift in his mood was sustained during the three days that the gale blew, three days during which he worked over and over his plan and committed Dante's lines and the information of Gilham's charts (which Littlewood had surreptitiously obtained for him) to memory. By the light of guttering candles he pored over and over them and finally burnt the blotchy copy of Cary's rendering of the Florentine poet's words in the candle flame. The plan to carry the cargoes into Hamburg had gained a powerful grip on his imagination and he eagerly awaited Nicholas's assurance that he had won Hamilton over to the plot.

He knew he could no longer dwell on the loss of his friends, only grasp the promises and seductions of tomorrow. That much, and that much alone, was allowed him. 'Hope,' he muttered to himself, '*must* spring eternal.'

Then, in the wake of the gale, as it blew itself out in glorious sunshine and a spanking breeze from the west-north-west, His Britannic Majesty's Sloop *Combatant*, carrying additional cannon for the defence of the island and confidential mail for the Governor, put an end to the dallying.

'It is providential, my dear sir, quite providential don't you know,' Nicholas said, hardly able to contain himself. 'Colonel Hamilton has received instructions from Lord Dungarth regarding yourself, Captain Drinkwater: combined with the arrival of the cannon it has quite put the backbone into him.'

'Lord Dungarth's instructions don't run contrary to our intentions then?'

'Quite the reverse . . . and here are letters for yourself.'

Nicholas pulled two letters from the breast pocket of his coat. Taking them Drinkwater tore open the first. It was from Dungarth.

London, Nov. 26

My Dear Nathaniel,

I am sorry to hear of your Misfortune. The Venture has Miscarried in common with the Affair in the Scheldt. Your Failure is Insignificant beside this. You may also have heard of Rupture in Government. All, alas, is True. Take Counsel with Ed. Nicholas and Act as you see fit. Solomon and Dyer have Accepted Heavy Losses.

Yours, & Co

Dungarth.

There was precious little sympathy for the Jew, Drinkwater thought as he opened the second letter. Its superscription was in a vaguely familiar hand. The letter was cautiously undated.

London

Honoured Sir,

I am Privy to Matters closely related to your Circumstances. Your Personal Credit stands Highly here and you will Increase the Indebtedness of Your Humble Servant if you are able to Release my Agent and his Vessel to make those provisions necessary for a Small Profit to be Realized on all our Capital at Stake.

I have the Honour to be, Sir,

Isaac Solomon.

Drinkwater could not resist a rueful smile; it was a masterpiece. As Dungarth passed the cost of the failed mission to Solomon, the wily Jew inferred that, while the gold Drinkwater had lodged with him in good faith was of considerable value, its possession and sale guaranteed Solomon and Dyer's losses were handsomely underwritten! In short he, Nathaniel Drinkwater, would finance the expedition!

Drinkwater looked up at Nicholas. It could not have escaped either Dungarth's or Solomon's notice that Helgoland's occupation was chiefly to facilitate trade with the rest of Europe.

'I feel the strings of the puppet-master manipulating me, Mr Nicholas,' he said. 'Pray do you have any instructions regarding myself?'

'Indeed sir, his Lordship's letter to the Governor advised him to allow us to confer. But I am to take you to Colonel Hamilton forthwith.'

Drinkwater reached for his hat and both men stepped out into the passageway. 'Did you receive any further instructions about the other ships – Gilham's and the rest?' Drinkwater asked as they made their way to Hamilton's quarters.

Nicholas shook his head. 'No. I fear Government is still too disorganized as a result of Canning's disgrace . . . come, sir, here we are . . .'

Hamilton was standing with his back to them, staring out of the window. Behind him a gentle slope of grassland cropped by a handful of sheep rose to the tower of the lighthouse. Wisely, Drinkwater broke the silence.

'I am pleased to hear that matters have been happily cleared up, Colonel Hamilton. Will ye give me your hand?'

Hamilton turned and Drinkwater saw he was holding a letter. He seemed lost for words, embarrassed at the position in which he found himself.

'Come, Colonel, my hand, sir. Let us bury the hatchet . . . perhaps over a glass?' At Drinkwater's hint Hamilton unbent, took his hand and muttered something about 'spies everywhere' and 'havin' to be damned careful'.

'Perhaps, sir, you would show Captain Drinkwater the letter,' Nicholas suggested, 'while I . . .'

'Yes, yes, pour us a glass, for God's sake.' Hamilton handed over Dungarth's letter and threw himself down in his chair.

Admiralty, London
26 November 1809

Lt. Col. Hamilton,
Governor,
Helgoland.

Sir,

I am in Receipt of your Letter of the 2d. Ultimo. The Officer You have Apprehended aboard the Galliwasp, barque, Jno. Littlewood, Master, is in the Employ of my Department on a Special Service. It is not Necessary to make known his Name to you, but you will know him by the following Characteristics, Viz: Engrained Powder Burns about one Eye; an Ancient Scar from a Sword Cut on the Check and a Severe Wounding of the Right Shoulder causing it to be much Lower than the Left.

You will greatly Oblige me by affording Him your utmost Hospitality and free congress with Mr Nicholas. This Officer knows my Mind and His Directions may be assumed as Congruent with my own.

I have the honour to be, sir, & Co
Dungarth.

It was the most perfect *carte blanche* Drinkwater could have wished for, not to say the most perfect humiliation for poor Hamilton.

Drinkwater laid the letter down on Hamilton's desk and their eyes met.

'It is perhaps as well that his Lordship's letter arrived no earlier, Colonel,' Drinkwater said.

'How so . . .?' Hamilton frowned.

'I was in damnably low spirits and had nothing of much sense to communicate. Now, Colonel, I have a proposition to make that will advance the service of our country . . .'

'A glass gentlemen,' Nicholas interposed. 'Schnapps, Captain Drinkwater.' Then he added, 'From Hamburg.'

Chapter Nine *December 1809–January 1810*

Santa Claus

Staring astern from the taffrail of *Galliwasp* Drinkwater watched Helgoland dip beneath the western horizon. He wondered if he would ever see it again and the thought brought in its train the multiple regrets and self-recriminations that had become a part of him in recent years. He had written to Elizabeth and the task, long postponed, had wrenched him from his deep and complex involvement with his secret mission. Nicholas would post the letter if he had not returned in two months. It told Elizabeth everything. He had left her the burden of writing to Quilhampton's fiancée and Frey's family, giving her a form of words to use.

It was no use looking back, he thought resolutely, and smacked the oak rail with the flat of his hand. He turned forward. Gilham's *Ocean* was wallowing sluggishly on their larboard beam, her bottom foul with grass despite the efforts to scrape it clean. *Galliwasp* ghosted along under topsails, keeping station on her slower sister in the light, westerly wind. Drinkwater looked up to judge the wind from the big American ensign. The stars and bars flaunted lazily above his head.

'There's Neuwerk on the starboard bow, Captain,' Littlewood pointed with his glass, then handed it to Drinkwater.

Behind the yellow scar of the Scharhorn sand which was visible at this low state of the tide, the flat surface of the island of Neuwerk was dominated by the great stone tower erected upon it.

Drinkwater studied it with interest as the young flood tide carried them into the mouth of the River Elbe. The island was to be, as it were, the sleeve from which he intended playing his ace. He handed the telescope back to Littlewood.

'Let us hope it is not long before we see it on the other bow,' Drinkwater said with assumed cheerfulness. He wished they had left Helgoland a day earlier, before the arrival of the depressing news. It cast a cloud over the enterprise, though Drinkwater, Nicholas and Hamilton had kept the intelligence to themselves.

In the period of waiting for *Galliwasp* and the other vessels to be made ready, their crews sounded and appointed and the secret messages sent to Liepmann in Hamburg, Drinkwater had been daily closeted with Hamilton and Nicholas.

On the occasion when Drinkwater had first broached the idea with Hamilton and the Governor had grasped the olive-branch thus held out to him, Nicholas had judiciously kept Hamilton's glass full of schnapps. Between them Nicholas and Drinkwater had boxed the Colonel into a corner from which his naturally cautious nature could not extricate him. In some measure a degree of bellicosity had been engendered by the arrival of *Combatant* and her cargo of cannon, and Drinkwater had insisted that the seamen of all the ships help to land and site them. This thoughtfulness on Drinkwater's part earned him Hamilton's grudging gratitude, for he himself had shown too great a prejudice against the merchant shipmasters and trading-post agents to rely on any willing co-operation from them. For his own part, Drinkwater's act was not disinterested. Requesting such assistance was a ready means of measuring his command over the odd collection of merchant seamen and naval volunteers that he would shortly lead into the enemy heartland. The fact that after months of inactivity *something* was afoot proved a powerful influence.

As a mark of their improved relationship Hamilton, Nicholas and Drinkwater got into the habit of dining together, partly to keep up Hamilton's enthusiasm and partly to discuss the progress of the preparations.

Over the dessert wine one evening Hamilton became expansive and Drinkwater learned of Helgoland's real importance as a 'listening post' on the doorstep of the French Empire.

'Hamburg has always been important,' Hamilton said. 'We nabbed Napper Tandy there after the Irish Rebellion. The place was full of United Irishmen for years.'

'They say Lord Edward Fitzgerald's wife is still resident there,' added Nicholas.

'She's supposed to be French, ain't she?' asked Drinkwater, 'though I believe her sister's married to Sir Thomas Foley. I recall *him* at Copenhagen.'

'Were you in Nelson's action, Captain Drinkwater, or Gambier's?'

'Nelson's, Colonel, just before the last peace.'

'It was after Gambier's scrap that we took this place from the Danes.'

'Yes. I was bound for the Pacific by then.'

'And after *that* Colin Mackenzie carried into effect a master-stroke,' added Nicholas.

'Ah, yes, you mentioned some such affair, a Father Robinson . . .'

'Robertson. A Jesuit who was sent from here via Hamburg to contact the Spanish forces Napoleon had isolated as a garrison on the island of Zealand – for Napoleon occupied Denmark as soon as we had seized the Danish fleet, all the while inveighing against British perfidy!'

'That would be about the time of the Spanish revolt, then?'

'Quite so. The object was to inform the Spaniards of their countrymen's uprising against the French and, if possible, repatriate them.' Nicholas refilled his glass, then went on. 'Robertson posed as a cigar and chocolate salesman and made contact with their commander, the Marquis of Romana. As a result the entire corps was withdrawn aboard the squadron of Rear-Admiral Keats then cruising in the offing.'

'Almost all, Ned, a few of the poor devils were unable to escape. They say squadrons of riderless horses were left charging up and down the beach in perfect formation!' Hamilton amplified.

'What of Robertson?' Drinkwater asked.

'I believe he got back to England eventually. He was multilingual, don't you know, a remarkable fellow . . .' Nicholas's admiration was obvious and not for the first time Drinkwater found himself wondering how much the young man might want his own reputation enhanced by a similar *coup de main*.

'Boney was reported to be hoppin' mad, when he heard of the loss of the Spanish corps,' Hamilton said, 'Romana's troops were considered to be the best in the Spanish army.'

The story and its outcome were satisfying to men planning their own foray and added to Drinkwater's high hopes, but on the eve of their departure news of a more sinister kind reached the island, borne by Herr Reinke, whose long awaited arrival signalled the end of their preparations.

On receipt of the news Nicholas had withdrawn to write to Lord

Bathurst that his nephew, lately employed on diplomatic service in Vienna, had mysteriously disappeared at Perleberg and was presumed dead.

He confided as much to Drinkwater, warning him of the dangers he ran, as a naval officer out of uniform, in going to Hamburg. 'I beg you to be careful,' he said. 'I am sure that Napoleon has taken this revenge in part for the successes Robertson and others have enjoyed at his expense. He would be especially glad to seize anyone connected with the betrayal of the Tilsit agreement.'

'I understand,' Drinkwater had said, 'there is no need to labour the point.'

'Schar buoy, Kapitan,' Herr Reinke, the pilot pointed ahead. 'You make good course a little more to ze east.'

Drinkwater nodded at Munsden, standing by the helmsman. 'Bring her round a point, Mr Munsden, if you please.'

He exchanged glances with Littlewood. To facilitate the negotiations shortly to be opened with the authorities at Hamburg, Drinkwater was to assume the character of *Galliwasp*'s master, leaving Littlewood free to deal with matters of trade with which Drinkwater had no experience.

It was refinements of this nature which had occupied Drinkwater in recent weeks, refinements designed to make plausible the defection of several British master mariners in the cause of profit.

To these had been added another. Both *Combatant* and *Bruizer* had been ordered on cruises, so that reports that there were no men-of-war in Helgoland Road would encourage belief in the merchant masters' decision to dispose of their cargoes. In a day or two, whenever they might return, either or both *Combatant* and *Bruizer* would be sent into the mouth of the Elbe, as though seeking out the whereabouts of the missing transports.

To emphasize the anxiety of the Governor to recall his cruisers, Bengal fires would be thrown up from the lighthouse at two hourly intervals during the coming night.

Referring to the chart spread on the companionway cover, Drinkwater monitored Herr Reinke's directions. They passed between the Scharhorn and the Vogel sands and left Neuwerk Island astern, raising the Kugel beacon and the flat mainland on which the town of Cuxhaven nestled behind its sea wall. They passed the familiar fishing boats, any one of which might have been a visitor to Helgoland, and doubled the North Ground where the river narrowed. Small villages appeared, each cluster of houses nestling close to its church: Groden, with its wind-pump, Altenbruch and Otterndorf. The South Ditmarsch shore closed from the north and, with the tide now ebbing and the sun setting at the end of the short, mid-winter day, they anchored off Brunsbuttel.

'We shall have visitors soon,' said Littlewood, pointing to a boat putting off from a large, heavily sparred cutter that lay anchored inshore of them. 'She's a Dutch-manned hooker of the Imperial Customs. They're smart as mustard in these waters, those square-heads,' Littlewood said in reluctant admiration.

Drinkwater studied the cutter. The massive mainmast, exaggerated tumblehome and huge leeboards marked her as a formidable craft amid the shallow waters of the adjacent coast. He remembered such a cutter with which he had fought at the battle of Camperdown. Whether it was the recollection, a sense of foreboding, or the cold of the December twilight, Drinkwater could not tell, but suddenly he shivered.

It was almost dark when the customs boat pulled alongside. Two officers in cocked hats and boatcloaks were followed up the ship's side by four armed seamen, one carrying a lantern.

'You are Americans, *Ja*?'

'*Nein, mynheer,* we are English!' Littlewood stepped forward. Drinkwater watched a second boat go alongside the *Ocean.* He hoped Gilham would play his part and then jettisoned the thought. It was too late to worry now, they were committed and Captain Gilham, for all his unprepossessing appearance, did not seem averse to his task. A thin man with spectacles on a long nose, his face was a mass of broken veins, suggesting he was a toper. Drinkwater had learned, however, that Captain Gilham never touched liquor, held Sunday services aboard his ship and spent much of his time recording what he termed 'the marvels of atmosphereology'. The result, Drinkwater had been told, was a meticulous log of weather observations taken every six hours, day and night for the past sixteen years.

'You are *English*?' the astonished Dutch customs officer was asking. 'Den vy do you come into ze Elbe, mit your scheeps?'

Littlewood explained. 'We have been tricked by our Government. We have been kept at Helgoland too long,' he gestured at the *Ocean*'s riding light. 'Captain Gilham has been seven months waiting for orders. We have received no pay, no provisions; my charter has expired. Now we wish to discharge our cargoes. If the British Government don't want them, perhaps we may find a market in Hamburg.'

The two Dutch officers looked at each other and the older one shrugged, saying something to the other which inferred the English speaker was the junior.

'Vat is your cargo?'

'Boots,' Littlewood said, raising one foot and waving his hand at it, 'coats, big coats, some muskets, flints, powder and shot.'

The junior *douanier*'s eyes opened wide and he translated for the benefit of his colleague. The senior muttered something, then strode to the rail and cupped his hands about his mouth, bellowing across to their friends aboard *Ocean*.

'He's asking what cargo the *Ocean* has,' Littlewood murmured.

A hail came from the other boarding party. For a few moments a shouted dialogue echoed back and forth between the two anchored ships, breaking the silence that had followed sunset and the dropping of the wind. At last the senior officer turned back to the waiting men and issued some orders. The other translated.

'You must here stay at Brunsbuttel. I vill here stay mit my men,' he gestured at the seamen with him, then accompanied his superior to the ship's side and saw him safely into the boat. As it pulled away the departing *douanier* shouted something.

'He say I am to shoot anyone who make trouble.'

'We ain't going to make trouble. Is he coming back in the morning?'

'*Ja*. He vill make zis arrival telled to Hamburg.'

'That is very good.'

'Dat is ver' good, *ja*.'

Drinkwater made a small movement of his head in *Ocean*'s direction and Littlewood took the hint.

'Captain Gilham!' he hailed, 'is everything well with you?'

'Perfectly well, sir, the temperature is falling and we'll have a touch of seasmoke on the water at dawn.'

The laughter that greeted this weather report eased the tension. Having set their own anchor watch, the crew of the *Galliwasp*, including her putative master, drifted below in search of food and sleep.

*

'You were right, Captain Gilham,' Drinkwater said, welcoming the master of the *Ocean* aboard the next morning. A low fog lay like smoke over the surface of the river so that the two ships seemed to float-upon cloud, and in pulling across, Gilham's disembodied head and shoulders had drifted eerily, the boat beneath him invisible.

'It's not a matter of judgement, Captain Waters, but simply the appreciation of an immutable natural law.' He looked up at the cloudless sky. ' 'Tis a raw morning, but the sun will soon burn this off.'

'Did your guests make any objection to your paying us a visit?' Drinkwater asked, nodding towards the Dutch customs officer who stood warily watching them.

'Oh, they made a fuss, but . . .' Gilham shrugged and disdained to finish the sentence. Drinkwater smiled.

'Are your men still game?'

'Certainly. Why should they not be? They are being well paid for a little inconvenience. They were more discontented lying at anchor in that detestable anchorage.'

Drinkwater envied Gilham the cold, unemotional approach of a man whose life was guided by the simplistic principles of profit and loss.

'Every man has his price, they say,' Drinkwater said.

'And it is a very accurate saw, sir,' added Gilham, cocking an appraising eye at the mysterious 'captain' Littlewood had informed him was a personage of some importance.

'You sound as though you have done this sort of thing before, Captain.'

'I am told,' Gilham replied obliquely, 'that best Bohea is available for guests at the Tuileries and Malmaison.'

'As is cognac at the Court of St James . . . hullo, our friend stirs.'

Both men watched the uncanny sight of a large gaffed mainsail hauled aloft from an unseen deck as the Dutch customs cutter got under way. The long masthead pendant with its Imperial device trailed out in the light north-westerly wind. Littlewood joined them and in silence they observed the manoeuvre. After a few minutes they heard the splash of an anchor and the rumble of cable, then the mainsail disappeared again. The Dutch cutter was anchored closer to the two British merchant ships.

'When this seasmoke burns off,' Gilham said, 'you'll see her guns run out.'

'That ain't a matter of immutable law, Captain Gilham,' Drinkwater remarked lightly, 'but it's a damned sound judgement.'

A few minutes later, arriving as weirdly as Gilham had done, the senior Dutch customs officer clambered back over the *Galliwasp*'s rail. Seeing Gilham he frowned and addressed a few curt words to the tired junior he had left to stand guard the previous night. The younger man said something in reply, then shrugged.

The senior officer crossed the deck, his face angry. He asked Gilham a question and the younger officer translated.

'He say vy do you come this scheep?'

'To talk with my friends,' said Gilham, his expression truculent. 'How do we know you won't cheat us?'

The junior of the two Dutchmen shrugged again and relayed the message. The exchange reversed itself.

'It is *verboten* you make talk.'

It was Gilham's turn to shrug. 'I do not understand.'

Again the pantomime of translation. This time there was a longer exchange, then: 'Vy do you come here to Brunsbuttel?'

'We told you last night,' Gilham said sharply, his self-appointment as spokesman lent force by his very real frustration. 'Because I have been waiting at Helgoland for seven months to discharge my cargo.' He held up his fingers to emphasize the period. 'Now the British Government tell me it is not wanted. I have no money. I must pay my crew. I have the expenses of my ship. I have a wife. I have sons.' He punched the air with his index finger, advancing on the unfortunate Dutchman until his fingertip tapped the blue-coated breast, physically ramming at him the cogency of the simple sentences. 'Now I come to sell to the Hamburgers what the British Government does not want. Tell that to your chief, and tell him that he does not tell me what I must and must not do. I am master of the *Ocean* and by heaven, I'll not be pushed around by you, or him!'

Drinkwater watched the Dutchmen; one quailed visibly under Gilham's onslaught, the other's face darkened as he understood the import of Gilham's speech. As his junior turned to explain, he was brushed aside. Gilham found himself under attack. The senior officer exploded into a tirade of invective in which God, swine and the English were recognizably called upon.

The senior *douanier* did not wait for this to be translated for his audience, but turned on his heel and went over the *Galliwasp*'s rail in a swirl of his cloak. His colleague began to stammer out an explanation but ceased as Gilham touched his arm.

'Never mind, my friend,' he said, impishly smiling, 'we understand.'

The customs officer stood nonplussed, then shrugging dismissively shouted something to his seamen and followed his commander over the side. A moment later another young officer climbed aboard.

'The king is dead, long live the king,' Gilham said drily.

'Well, I suppose we'll just have to wait and see what happens now,' Littlewood remarked. 'I wonder if there's fog in the outer estuary?'

By noon the visibility had improved and in the crisp, cold air, they could see the light tower at Cuxhaven and beyond it, the gaunt outline of the Kugelbacke beacon. Closer, the green river bank to the north and the white painted houses and spired kirk of Brunsbuttel spread out along the Ditmarsch shore. Closer still, the low, black hull of the Dutch cutter swum out of the dissipating mist.

'Looks as innocent as a swimhead barge, don't she,' said Littlewood as they studied her sharply raked bow.

'Not with those black muzzles pointing at us,' said Gilham.

'How d'you rate your own people if it came to a fire fight?' asked Drinkwater in a low voice.

'They don't have any practice,' replied Littlewood, 'though they'd be game enough.'

'Well, gentlemen,' said Gilham resolutely, 'if you're contemplating a private war, I'm returning to the *Ocean*. As I said to that squarehead, I've an interest in survival, never having rated glory very highly. Besides,' he added as he whistled for his boat's crew, 'it's dinner time.'

Littlewood and Drinkwater, who dined later, stood in silence for a while, curiously sweeping their glasses along the shoreline. The pastoral tranquillity of the scene was far from the blasts of war they were discussing. Cattle grazed the water-meadows and they could see the red flash of a shawl where a girl was tending poultry on the foreshore.

'Boat putting off from the Dutchman.' Munsden's report made

them turn their telescopes on the cutter. Both of their recent visitors were leaving, bound for the beach where a horseman rode down to meet them.

In the sunshine they could see a green uniform topped by a plumed shako.

'French officer of *chasseurs*,' said Drinkwater, holding the figure in his Dollond pocket-glass.

'I can see some more of them, look, behind the large cottage to the left of the church . . .'

Drinkwater swung his glass to where Littlewood was indicating. He could see mounting figures pulling out of what he presumed were their horse-lines.

'I wonder why he never asked for our papers,' pondered Littlewood as the two men watched the Dutchmen leap ashore and confer with the French officer.

'I think we annoyed him too much and he was frustrated by not being able to speak to us directly. Gilham upset him and I suspect he's reporting us to his superiors. He's got us under his guns and he may be under some constraint, being a Dutchman.'

'There are some fiercely republican Dutchmen,' Littlewood said.

'Yes, I know.'

'I wonder what lingo they speak between each other?' Littlewood mused as they watched the French officer jerk his horse's head round.

'God knows,' said Drinkwater.

The French officer apparently shouted an order and four troopers, the men that had just mounted up, broke away from the horse-lines and rode after him as he set off eastwards at a canter.

'Odd that he needs an escort,' said Littlewood, lowering his glass and wiping his eye. 'Matter of waiting now,' he added.

They were compelled to wait two days before they learned of my reaction in Hamburg. Early on the morning of the first of these, however, a cloudy morning with the wind backed into the southwest, the horizon beyond the yellow scars of the exposed sandbanks to seaward was broken by the grey topsails of two ships.

In silence the observers on the decks of the *Galliwasp* and *Ocean* watched their approach with anxiety. This anxiety was real enough, for the first event of that day had been the arrival at Brunsbuttel of a jingling battery of horse artillery. The unlimbered field guns now pointed directly at them and, with the cannon of the Dutch cutter, neatly enfiladed them. Until the appearance of the distant topsails, the curious aboard *Galliwasp* and *Ocean* had occupied their enforced idleness by studying the artillerymen who, having established themselves, lounged about their pieces.

Despite the protests of their guard, Littlewood had sent Munsden aloft with the watch-glass to call down a commentary on events to seaward of them which was eagerly attended by those below.

'They are the *Combatant* and the *Bruizer*, right enough, and they're just clewin' up their main an' fores'ls.'

'Where are they?'

'Comin' up abeam of Cuxhaven . . . aye, *Combatant*'s roundin' up into the tide . . .'

'Anchoring or taking a tack inshore?' Littlewood asked anxiously, for whatever he did, *Combatant*'s commander *must* look as though he was making a determined effort to retake the truant merchant ships.

'She's opening fire!'

They could see the yellow flashes from the deck now, and the sloop's yards braced sharp up as she crabbed across the young flood tide.

'There won't be much resistance at Cuxhaven,' said Littlewood, 'if the last reports were correct.'

'No,' said Drinkwater, staring through his glass, his heart beating for those two distant ships. The thunder of that opening broadside rolled dully over the water even as *Combatant* loosed off a second and a third.

'*Bruizer*'s standin' on,' reported Munsden, unconsciously betraying the plan, the gun-brig making directly for them while the heavier sloop occupied whatever might be at Cuxhaven in the way of artillery. And then they knew. Six yellow pin points of muzzle flashes were followed by another six.

'My God, they've got two batteries of horse-artillery there! They weren't evident the other day when we passed.'

'Moved in this morning, like our friends yonder,' Littlewood said, jerking his head at the nearer shore without lowering his glass.

'*Bruizer* comes too far to the north, Kapitan,' said Herr Reinke, the pilot and surveyor. 'He must be careful.'

Drinkwater transferred his attention to the gun-brig. Unaware that any resistance would be forthcoming from Cuxhaven, a pretext for the withdrawal of the two men-of-war had to be invented. To achieve this, Smithies had been ordered to incline his course so as to take the bottom on the North Ground, the sandbank opposite Cuxhaven. The resulting confusion would offer the commander of the *Combatant* a pretext for breaking off the action. In fact there was little risk to the shallow draft gun-brig. The tide was rising and with her anchor down, she would float off in an hour or two.

But with the *Combatant* engaging artillery ashore and Smithies acting over-zealously, the ruse looked as though it might be more realistic than was intended.

'If anything miscarries, Captain,' Littlewood muttered beside him, aware of Drinkwater's apprehension for the naval ships, 'don't forget to look cheerful!'

Drinkwater grunted, his throat dry. Of course, Reinke could be wrong. At this distance it was notoriously difficult to judge angles of aspect.

'*Bruizer*'s struck sir!' Munsden called. 'And lost her foretopmast!'

Littlewood burst into a cheer and slapped Drinkwater heartily on the back. Drinkwater staggered under the impact of the blow and coughed on his chagrin. Over the water the rolling concussions of the *Combatant*'s guns duelling with the batteries at Cuxhaven echoed the thumping of his heart.

An answering cheer came from the men ranged on the customs cutter's deck. Littlewood rounded on the Dutch officer aboard *Galliwasp*, 'Why you not weigh your anchor and go and fight?' he urged. The *douanier* shook his head.

'Cuxhaven guns make stop your scheeps.' And so it proved. *Combatant* broke off the action and tacked across the stream as the tide slackened. *Bruizer* refloated and swung her head seaward. A boat was seen between the two ships, then, as *Combatant* went about again, she drew *Bruizer* in her wake on an unseen towline. As she tacked back towards the Cuxhaven shore she laid a few last broadsides at the enemy. Apart from holes in her sails, she appeared unscathed.

'As neat a piece of seamanship as I've seen in a long while,' said Littlewood from the corner of his mouth.

'If she had lost a mast, then things might have turned out differently,' breathed a relieved Drinkwater. He already had cause to regret the loss of one gun-brig.

'Oh, he kept out of range of those nine-pounders . . . but I'm glad to see *you* looking a little more cheerful at that spectacular British defeat.'

Littlewood grinned at Drinkwater, and this time Drinkwater smiled back.

'Russia? You are saying, Captain, that your cargo was consigned to *Russia*?'

'Yes,' said Drinkwater, staring levelly at the dark and handsome Frenchman in the sober black suit. His plain, elegant clothes reminded him of Nicholas and it was clear the two had more in common than the unaffected good taste of their dress; both were the diplomatic, and therefore the political, emissaries of their respective masters. Monsieur Thiebault had arrived from Hamburg to carry out an examination on behalf of Monsieur Reinhard, the Emperor's minister in that city. Upon Monsieur Thiebault's appraisal of the curious submission of the two British shipmasters depended the success, or otherwise, of the grand deception. And incidentally, Drinkwater thought, driving the underlying fear from the forefront of his mind, ultimately their own survival.

'But why?'

'It is a market, M'sieur. With the continent closed to us by the decree of your Emperor, we must sell wherever we can. Had I not been driven by bad weather to Helgoland, I would not be suing for purchase by you . . .'

'Yes, yes, we have been over that,' Thiebault said testily, his command of English impeccable, 'but Russia is also under an embargo.'

Drinkwater laughed and Littlewood beside him smiled knowingly.

'We are able to trade with Russia, M'sieur, quite easily. As you see . . .' Drinkwater nodded at the three grey greatcoats and the two pairs of hobnailed boots on the table between them. 'Samples to whet their greedy appetites' Littlewood had called them when he suggested exhibiting their cargo.

'And your consignee was the Russian Government?'

'That is clear from the papers before you, sir,' said Littlewood.

'And on the papers before me it states that Captain Waters here is the master of this ship,' Thiebault said suspiciously.

'Captain Waters,' Littlewood said, brushing the matter aside, 'is new to the trade. I am acting on his behalf and as agent for the consignors.'

'And who *are* the consignors, Captain Littlewood?'

'You can see from the manifest, sir, Solomon and Dyer.'

Thiebault listened to something whispered in his ear by the senior Dutch officer. He nodded and consulted a second *douanier* on his right, a very senior French officer of the Imperial Customs Service.

'Mynheer Roos tells me this merchant house is known in Hamburg. Is that why you have chosen to offer your cargo here, despite the embargo?'

'M'sieur, Mynheer Roos knows well that a regular trade has been opened for some time between us. The Governor of Hamburg, M'sieur Bourrienne, encouraged it as a form of relief for the citizens . . .'

'That is not quite the case,' said Thiebault hurriedly. Bourrienne had been recalled by the omnipotent Napoleon, to whom he had once been confidential secretary, on the grounds of corruption and disobedience.

'Perhaps not *quite* the case, M'sieur, but certainly the facts behind it,' Littlewood said mischievously.

'Tell me, gentlemen, as a matter of perhaps mutual interest, are Solomon and Dyer the *only* London house trading with Russia?'

'I shouldn't think so,' laughed Littlewood insouciantly, to Drinkwater's admiration. It was clear that Littlewood relished the cut and thrust of mercantile bargaining and had imbibed every detail of his assiduous coaching on Helgoland. He was proving his weight in gold, Drinkwater thought wryly.

Thiebault rubbed his chin in thought, his eyes never leaving the faces of the four men ranged in front of him.

'And you, Captain,' he referred to the report of Mynheer Roos. 'Gilham. Your cargo was under contract to the British Government?'

'As I've already explained, M'sieur, I've been buzznacking . . .'

'I do not understand that word, Captain Gilham,' Thiebault said sharply. 'Confine yourself to the question.'

'Yes, I was on a Government charter.'

'And you chose a treasonable course of action . . .'

'We were told in Helgoland that the operation was not now to be undertaken. We were told that the Government had written off our cargoes. Experience tells me that I will be extremely fortunate to recover my expenses.'

'What was this operation?' Thiebault asked.

'Oh, an attempt to raise the population of Hanover against the French and Prussian interference. It was common knowledge.'

'Was it?' Thiebault said archly. 'And why do you suppose your Government decided, how do you say, to call it off, eh?'

Gilham chuckled and worked himself forward on his chair. 'Because, M'sieur, they are embroiled in a grand fiasco off Walcheren, that much we know both from your Hamburg newspapers and from the scuttlebutt at Helgoland.'

'*Scuttlebutt*?'

'Gossip . . . tittle-tattle . . . news by word of mouth . . .'

'Ah, yes.' Thiebault swivelled his eyes to the fourth of his interviewees. 'And you, Herr Reinke. You are a surveyor are you not? You have produced surveys for the Chamber of Commerce at Hamburg, yes? You speak excellent English, I hear.'

Reinke nodded gravely.

'It is not good to find you on an English ship.'

'I was making a survey off Neuwerk, M'sieur Thiebault, when I was captured by fishermen. They took me to Helgoland where they were rewarded. The English stole my survey and paid the fishermen for me.' Drinkwater heard the story delivered in Reinke's dead-pan accent.

'We received no report of this incident, Herr Reinke.'

'It only happened five days ago. I am gone for many days sometimes, on my work.'

'And these gentlemen obliged you by setting you free.'

'You could say his arrival made up our minds for us, M'sieur,' Littlewood said.

Thiebault looked at Littlewood. 'You mean it was providential?' he said, and something of doubt in his tone alarmed Drinkwater.

'No, I merely meant that what we had been discussing amongst ourselves was made possible by Mr Reinke's capture.'

Drinkwater's eyes met those of Thiebault and they were like two fencers, each watching for the almost imperceptible facial movement that communicated more than words, but spoke of truth and resolution.

'And how, Captain, er, Waters, do you know you can trust us? Suppose we promise you payment, then take your cargoes and throw you into gaol?'

'Because you are a man of honour and will give us a *laissez-passer*,' Drinkwater leaned forward, 'and because there are three other ships waiting at Helgoland under orders to return to England which, if they receive favourable reports from Hamburg by means which you know to exist, will also deliver up their cargoes, cargoes of ball, cartridge, clothing and small arms.'

'And how do you know we would not let this message go and lock *all* of you up?'

'Because it would put a stop to *all* British shipments . . .'

'Not for long, your countrymen are too greedy for that.'

'Of course,' smiled Drinkwater, 'they would ship their trade to Russia in expectation of a greater profit than you can offer.

Thiebault looked at him through narrowed eyes. All the men in the *Galliwasp*'s cabin knew that illegal trade flourished in spite of the Emperor's proscription. Indeed it was connived at on every level of Imperial legislation and Hamburg was notorious for being the chief channel for this illegal traffic.

'If we agree to your proposition, gentlemen, and reach a satisfactory conclusion that is beneficial to us all,' Thiebault gestured round the table, hinting that all, though opposed in theory, shared a common interest, 'how will you explain your action to your owners?'

'There are six ships involved, M'sieur. The misfortunes of war might be invoked to explain their loss. They are of course insured . . .'

Littlewood's explanation had been devised by Drinkwater, but not its masterly embellishment. He had not considered the loss to the insurers, but clearly the thought of this additional damage to the economy of Great Britain appealed to Thiebault. Moreover, Littlewood was about to give greater proof of his fitness for the task.

'By the way, did we mention the sugar?' he asked innocently.

'Sugar?' Thiebault and his colleagues stiffened perceptibly.

'Yes, the best, we have a small amount in addition to these,' Littlewood gestured at the boots.

'Well,' said Thiebault, recovering, 'it is a most attractive offer gentlemen, assuming, of course, that we can afford it.' He conferred again with his flanking *douaniers*, then rose to his feet. 'Very well, gentlemen. I must, naturally, report this affair to Hamburg. I am sure they will be interested to know that Saint Nicholas has arrived from so unexpected a quarter . . .'

'Saint Nicholas?' quizzed Littlewood.

'Ask Herr Reinke. It is a German custom, is it not Herr Reinke? Happy Christmas, gentlemen.'

Chapter Ten *January 1810*

Hamburg

'It is good, Kapitan,' Herr Reinke said in his flat, humourless English, 'everything is arranged.'

'There are no problems?' Drinkwater enquired, hardly able to believe what Reinke, Littlewood and Gilham accepted without apparent misgiving.

'No.' The ghost of a smile now played about Reinke's face. 'You have not been many times in this trade?' he asked, though he seemed to be merely confirming an impression rather than seeking a fact. 'You are surprised it is easy, yes?'

'Yes, I am.' Drinkwater poured two glasses of Littlewood's blackstrap, handing one to the German surveyor.

'*Prosit*. Things are a little different now. When Bourrienne was Governor it was more easy.'

Drinkwater knew of the corruption, if corruption it was, that had flourished under the city of Hamburg's disgraced Governor. Bourrienne's hand had been light on the helm, but deep in the pockets of his unwilling subjects, for he had connived at flouting the proscriptive decrees of his Imperial master on the pretext that too severe an imposition of trading embargoes would produce indigence and destitution among the inhabitants of the Hanseatic towns. Such disaffection, Bourrienne had argued, could fester and then erupt as open rebellion. It was rumoured to be happening in Prussia and other German states unhappy with their vassal status. Bourrienne's recall and subsequent disgrace was a measure of Napoleon's displeasure, and a gauge too, Drinkwater thought, of the Emperor's likely reaction to news of similar irregularities with Russia.

'In fact, Kapitan, more than one thousand English ships already discharge their cargo here, in Hamburg, every year since you take Helgoland.'

'I see. Then there is a ready supply of capital in the city?' Drinkwater persisted. Such details he had left to Nicholas, assured by him that they would encounter no obstacles and which, preoccupied as he had been by the planning and writing of orders concerning the logistic and military side of the operation, he had been content to ignore. Now, in the very heart of the great city, as he waited for the hatches to be opened and the contraband cargo discharged, he found his curiosity aroused.

'*Ja*,' said Reinke. 'Mainly Jews, like your Herr Liepmann, but also good German merchants. Herr Liepmann is knowing that the Governor must provide some stores for the Grand Army. Some things, like these boots you have, the Governor will sell to Paris. Herr Liepmann will buy from you, the Governor's agents will buy from Liepmann. Paris is happy it has boots; the Governor is happy: he has a profit because he sell at more than Herr Liepmann sell to him; and Liepmann is happy because he also has a profit when he buy from you and sell to the French. And *you* are happy because without Liepmann buy your cargo, you have nothing.'

'But how,' Drinkwater asked, feeling far from happy, 'did Herr Liepmann reach this accommodation with the Governor? And how does he preserve it when Bourrienne leaves and Reinhard arrives with new orders to enforce the embargo more strictly?'

'Ach, you don't understand *that*! Well, that is most easy.' A smile of pure worldly cynicism lit up Reinke's sober face. 'We are not barbarians. The French take Hamburg and we must live, *nein*? We must, what is word . . .?'

'Adapt?'

'*Ja*, to adapt. Hamburg must adapt. There are ways of doing things. Herr Thiebault, he is *un homme d'affaires*, he understands . . .'

'And has a taste for sugar?'

'*Ja*! You understand Kapitan, but also, I think, he is much interested by these boots.'

The seasmoke they had experienced at Brunsbuttel became a daily phenomenon as they lay at buoys off the city of Hamburg. The ships had worked their way slowly upstream, catching the wind and tide when they served, anchoring when they became foul and hampered progress. Reinke piloted them skilfully, for the channel wound between a vast expanse of salt marsh and shoals. The flat wilderness of reed beds where the mighty Elbe swirled and eddied over the shallows was the haunt of heron and harrier, of a myriad species of ducks and geese. Alders and willows crowded the banks and midstream aits, and cattle stood hock deep in the water-meadows near the scattered villages past which they had slipped under their false, American colours.

At Blankenese the land began to rise in a series of low hills until, beyond the village of Altona, they could see the smoke and spires of the great city that lay on the Elbe's northern bank. Here, in accordance with Thiebault's instructions, they were directed to secure to midstream mooring buoys. Their Dutch escorts departed and French soldiers, grizzled infantry of a line battalion recruiting its strength in the 'soft' posting of garrison duty, took over as their guards. The contrast they made with Hamilton's men struck Drinkwater, for these were veterans in the real sense of the word, men whose entire lives had been spent in bivouac, men used to scraping a bare subsistence from the country they found themselves in, men of almost infinite resource, easy in their demeanour like his own seamen, yet possessed of the intelligent eye, the keen weapon and that invisible yet detectable *esprit* that marked them as invincible. Their proximity increased Drinkwater's unease.

On their arrival Littlewood was escorted ashore. When he returned he reported he had met the mysterious Herr Liepmann. He expressed himself satisfied with the transaction and said that Liepmann had undertaken to transmit a secret message through his own channels to Isaac Solomon in London. Three days into the new year lighters arrived alongside, each with a gang of workmen and more guards.

'They,' said Littlewood nodding at the blue uniforms of a platoon of *voltigeurs*, 'are proof that the French authorities themselves are taking this little lot into safe-keeping.' Here Littlewood shifted his nodding head to the first bales of greatcoats that swung up and out of *Galliwasp*'s hold.

Drinkwater was aware that he ought to have shared the obvious euphoria of Littlewood and Gilham, but he could not shake off the thought that matters had gone too well and that the plan had worked almost too faultlessly. In his mind he reviewed the interviews, Thiebault's reactions and Reinke's laboured explanations. There could be no doubt that a cargo had been shipped from London for Russia, and that the French knew about it, for if Fagan had not alerted them, Thiebault had most certainly done so and had made no attempt to disguise the fact that he had digested the information with interest.

Drinkwater ought, he knew, to have enjoyed a sense of relief far greater than that of his companions for, against the odds, he had carried out his orders. The enemy had been baited and taken the lure, and this appeared to have been confirmed by the account of the 'naval battle' off Cuxhaven in the Hamburg newspapers, for it was too preposterous a story not to have originated in Paris, a reprint of *Le Moniteur*'s account of 'two British frigates trying to force a passage into the Elbe in pursuit of neutral, American shipping. They had been engaged and driven off by horse-artillery detachments, one having been dismasted.'

It was only after Reinke had translated this mendacious account that Drinkwater realized that the 'neutral, American shipping' referred to *Galliwasp* and *Ocean*, and that the report was virtual confirmation that the French had been deceived.

There was, he realized, no absolute guarantee that the men of the *Galliwasp* and the *Ocean* would be released, though Reinke assured him he had nothing to worry about. It was of little advantage to the French to hold merchant seamen, for they were outside the normal cartel arrangements for the exchange of prisoners and merely an expense, though their confinement did deprive the British of their services as pressed men. At a local level the pragmatic realization that their detention would deter others from bringing the desired luxuries through the blockade was a more persuasive argument in favour of letting them continue their voyaging.

'If Thiebault makes trouble,' Reinke promised, 'we will make trouble also.'

It was clearly in the interests of the Chamber of Commerce to ensure the freedom of the Britons in their midst, an action facilitated for all the parties concerned by the fiction that they were American, though it was difficult to imagine what form this 'trouble' might take.

As he leaned on *Galliwasp*'s rail and watched the beefy German lightermen swinging out the ground tier of bales with their heavy grey greatcoats hidden under the dull burlap, Drinkwater told himself he was becoming old and jittery, apprehensive that as a disguised sea-officer in enemy territory, he ran the risk of being shot as a spy.

Reinke left them that forenoon, removed now that the services of neither a pilot nor an interpreter were required. The authorities, having permitted the discharge of the cargo to commence, were content to keep the crews of the two ships in mid-stream quarantine. The work progressed slowly. Only one lighter per ship was allowed them, clear proof, Littlewood asserted, that the stores were being carefully housed under lock and key in some well-guarded warehouse.

Drinkwater waited impatiently, pacing *Galliwasp*'s poop. Pancakes of ice began floating sluggishly past them as the weather turned bitterly cold, the copper cupola of St Michelskirche standing green against the dark grey of a sky pregnant with snow. The first fall occurred on the second day of their discharging and Drinkwater woke next morning to a changed scene, the roofs of the city white and the hum of the quays and bustle of the river muted under the mantle of snow. At first he thought the lack of activity due to the snowfall, but then he marked a restiveness among their guards and noticed a propensity for the French soldiers to huddle and gossip quietly amongst themselves with more animation than was usual. Again, this too might have been attributable to the change in the weather, except that he was conscious of something else, a total lack of movement on the river. It was true there was more ice than there had been, but the Elbe was a great highway and a fishing ground, and he knew from long experience that men who earned their livelihood from trade and fishing do not cease at the first flurry of snow, rather they increase their activity before the severity of the weather stops them altogether.

'There's something amiss ashore,' Littlewood said, lowering the glass with which he had been scanning the adjacent quay.

'You've noticed it too,' said Drinkwater. 'It can't be another religious holiday, the churches are silent.'

'No, but there are soldiers on the quay there.' Littlewood pointed and offered Drinkwater his glass.

Drinkwater scanned the wharves. A troop of dragoons trotted past, their long carbines tucked in stirrup-holsters.

'Can't have anything to do with us,' Littlewood remarked, though his tone lacked conviction.

'Garrison reinforcements?' Drinkwater said. 'Perhaps the arrival of a French bigwig?'

'That might explain the stoppage of work, I suppose,' said

Littlewood disconsolately, 'I hope it won't detain us for long, I don't like this ice.' He gestured over the side, where larger floes, flat glistening sheets, revolved slowly in the stream, occasionally jamming athwart their hawse before tearing free and continuing their passage to the North Sea.

The following night, during the early hours, Drinkwater was shaken hurriedly awake. Littlewood, still wearing nightcap and gown and holding a lantern, stood over him.

'Cap'n Waters, get up! There's a summons from the shore! Thiebault's come aboard and he wants you and Gilham.'

'What o'clock is it?' asked Drinkwater, but Littlewood was not listening.

'Something's afoot! Two lighters will be here within the hour. That should take the remains of our cargo. Thiebault wants us and the *Ocean* under weigh by daylight.'

Littlewood left as hurriedly as he had come, leaving a confused Drinkwater to dress and follow him. On deck he found the French customs officer muffled in a cloak.

'Captain Waters?' Thiebault's voice was tense and his tone urgent.

'Yes? What is the meaning of this?'

'Please prepare yourself for an absence from the ship.'

'But I understand you wish us to be under weigh by dawn . . .' Drinkwater protested. Thiebault interrupted him.

'I can give you five minutes, Captain, but no more.'

'I demand an explanation . . .'

'I have loaded pistols which will persuade you to do as I ask,' Thiebault hissed. 'I do not wish to summon the guards, but I give you five minutes to attire yourself.'

Drinkwater spun on his heel and returned to his cabin, his mind a whirl. The dull, persistent foreboding was proved right, he thought, as he forced his feet into Dungarth's hessian boots, rolled up his shaving tackle and stuffed small clothes into a leather valise. For a moment he thought of leaping from the stern window, then dismissed the idea as stupid. He would freeze within minutes, his wracked shoulder no aid to such heroics. Wrapping himself in his boatcloak and jamming the plain tricorne on his head, he returned to the *Galliwasp*'s poop. Thiebault was impatient to be gone.

'You are quite safe, Captain Waters, but I am under the painful necessity of securing your person, and that of Captain Gilham, as guarantors.'

'*Guarantors!* What the devil d'you mean?' snapped an increasingly angry Drinkwater.

'Against the compliant behaviour of the other ships whose cargoes you have promised . . . come sir, I will explain, but you *must* attend me at once, we have not a moment to lose!'

Drinkwater turned to Littlewood, an unpleasant suspicion forming in his mind. 'Littlewood, are you a party to this knavery?'

'No sir! I shall do everything possible to expedite the arrival of the remaining ships, believe me!'

'I am compelled to, sir!' snapped Drinkwater.

'Come Captain. . .' Drinkwater felt Thiebault's hand at his elbow. He shook it off angrily, then Thiebault called out in a low but authoritative voice, '*M'aider, mes amis!*'

The grim infantrymen of their guard suddenly surrounded Drinkwater. He was hustled unceremoniously to the rail and down into the waiting boat. Collapsing, half-trodden on by the descending Thiebault, he found an indignant Gilham held at pistol point.

'What in God's name . . .?' Drinkwater began, but he felt himself seized from behind and a hand clapped firmly over his mouth. As the boat shoved off from the side of the *Galliwasp*, Thiebault leaned over the two Britons.

'Not a word, gentlemen, I insist. In a moment I will explain.'

And with that they had, perforce, to be content. With a regular dip and splash, the boat was pulled obliquely across the river, dodging the ice floes and bumping gently at the foot of a flight of steps set in a stone quay. They were bundled up these and into a carriage. Its blinds were drawn and Thiebault entered after them. He set a lantern in the sconce, then turned and took a pistol from one of his assistants. The door slammed shut and the carriage jerked forward with Gilham and Drinkwater staring down the barrel of Thiebault's pistol. From time to time the Frenchman cautiously lifted the edge of the adjacent window blind and peered out. In the lantern light Drinkwater noticed an unseasonal perspiration on Thiebault's forehead.

Less than half an hour had passed since Littlewood had woken Drinkwater, and in the confusion he had felt only an angry perplexity. But it was anger tempered with the odd feeling that he had expected some such event, and now that it had occurred and he was compelled to sit and wait upon events, he noticed Thiebault's anxiety with interest. Beside him Gilham was less philosophical.

'Well,' he demanded, 'what about this confounded explanation you promised?'

Thiebault let the blind drop for the third or fourth time and lowered the pistol, his thumb and forefinger easing the hammer so that the gun was no longer cocked and the frizzen clicked shut over the priming pan.

'Gentlemen,' he said with what Drinkwater thought was an effort to assume his customary urbanity, 'there has been a development in our affairs that was unforeseen. I assure you there is nothing sinister in your predicament. It is merely a precaution.'

'I do beg to differ, M'sieur Thiebault,' said Gilham sarcastically, 'it is hard to view midnight abduction at pistol point as anything other than sinister.' Gilham leaned forward and Drinkwater shot out a hand to restrain him.

'I think M'sieur Thiebault has problems of his own, Gilham. I think we are taken not merely as guarantors against the arrival of the other ships, but as hostages . . .'

'*Hostages*, by God!'

'Hold hard, sir!'

Thiebault, clearly compromised and, judging by his obvious anxiety, preoccupied with plans of his own that took precedence over any consideration, real or pretended, shot Drinkwater an unguarded look of pure astonishment.

Drinkwater seized upon his obvious advantage. 'Who has arrived in Hamburg, M'sieur Thiebault, to compel you to take this extreme action, eh?'

Thiebault's mouth opened, then closed. He offered no explanation, and Drinkwater knew his question had found its mark.

'You see, Gilham,' he went on, never taking his eyes off the French official, 'I believe that we are hostages to be delivered up to this person if M'sieur Thiebault here has to clear his name from any charge of trafficking with the British. Is that not so, M'sieur?'

Thiebault let his breath out with an audible hiss.

'Well?' Gilham persisted, 'what d'you say to that?'

'Yesterday,' said Thiebault resignedly, 'the Prince of Eckmühl arrived in Hamburg.'

'And who in the name of Beelzebub might *he* be? asked Gilham sharply.

'Marshal Davout, gentlemen,' said Thiebault, adding under his breath, '*le marechal le fer . . .*'

Chapter Eleven *January 1810*

Sugar

Captain Gilham had never heard of Davout, and the muttered soubriquet – evidence of Thiebault's fear of the marshal made no impression upon him. Instead he raged against the Frenchman's perfidy, subjecting Thiebault to a tirade of abuse until Drinkwater silenced him, to Thiebault's obvious relief.

'Where are you taking us?' he asked.

'To a property of Herr Liepmann's, Captain Waters, where you will be quite safe.'

Drinkwater suppressed a smile. It was clear to him that Thiebault's action was on his own account, or at least on the account of those engaged in illegal trade. Drinkwater knew little about Marshal Davout, but what he did know was enough to make him sympathetic to Thiebault's plight. Davout's Third Army Corps had held the main body of the Prussian army at bay at Auerstädt while Napoleon thrashed the remainder at Jena, accomplishing in a single day the destruction of the Prussian army. He was reputed to be unswervingly loyal to the Emperor, incorruptible and humourless, a man of ruthless severity and no private weaknesses. It was no surprise that Thiebault had been driven to the extremity of seizing the two masters of the British ships just then lying in the Elbe. It was bitterly ironic, Drinkwater thought, that by exchanging positions with Littlewood, he had thus compromised himself.

'I did not wish to disturb the safe despatch of your ships, gentlemen,' said Thiebault, 'that is why I left Captain Littlewood in charge as your – what do you say? Comprador?'

'Supercargo,' offered Drinkwater.

'Ah, yes . . .'

The carriage jerked to a halt and rocked on its springs for a moment before the door was opened. Thiebault hoisted himself from his seat. 'No trouble, gentlemen, I beg you.'

They descended into a dark, cobbled alley, barely wider than the coach. On either hand tall buildings rose and the air was filled with strange, exotic smells. Drinkwater knew at once that they were among warehouses.

In the Stygian gloom a blackness opened beside them with a creak and they were ushered into a cavernous space filled with a sweet, sickly smell. Then followed the crash of the closing door, the click and tumble of catch and lock, and the knock of a heavy cross-timber being put in place. A moment later the snick of flint on steel, and a flicker of light.

'Follow me, gentlemen,' Thiebault commanded, holding up the lantern.

As they made for a ladder between stacks of bales and cases, Drinkwater looked in vain for evidence of the boots or greatcoats that had come from either the *Galliwasp* or the *Ocean*. At length they ascended several flights of wooden stairs and found themselves in a small room, boarded with tongue-and-groove deals in the manner of a magazine.

'There is water here, gentlemen, and food will be brought to you twice daily. I will return soon. I do not think that you will be compelled to remain here above a week or ten days.' Thiebault gestured at the straw-filled palliasses that presumably furnished accommodation for a watchman. 'I regret, however, to tell you that escape is impossible. Herr Liepmann maintains a pair of hounds to guard against intruders. They were removed during our arrival. When I leave, they will be returned.' Thiebault paused. 'Also, I should advise you that there are many troops in the city.'

Thiebault made to leave them, but Drinkwater said, 'One thing I do not understand, M'sieur Thiebault.'

'What is that, Captain?'

'If you are so anxious to discharge the cargoes of the *Ocean* and the *Galliwasp* and want them to drop downstream by dawn for fear of discovery by Marshal Davout, why are you so anxious that the other ships come in?'

'That is no concern of yours!'

'What the deuce d'you make of all that?' rasped Gilham as the door closed behind Thiebault. 'I hope to heaven Littlewood's been paid.'

Drinkwater flung himself down on the nearer palliasse.

'I must say you seem damnably cool about this predicament, Waters. Ain't you worried about your cargo, man?'

'To be frank, sir, no.' Drinkwater propped himself up on one elbow. 'I don't think that Herr Liepmann will leave us here unattended, Gilham, so pray simmer down and let us do some thinking.'

'Or some praying,' said Gilham seriously.

'As you wish.'

Whatever the arrangements that Thiebault had made with Liepmann, it was inconceivable that the Jew should ignore the two British shipmasters held in his warehouse. Further ramifications of the affair occurred to Drinkwater as he lay in the cold and nursed the ache in his shoulder.

Thiebault was clearly heavily implicated in the illegal traffic passing through Hamburg. As a senior officer of the Imperial Customs Service he would be in an incomparable position to feather his own nest. But he would need to distance himself from his contacts, the merchants with whom he dealt, men like Liepmann who must never be left in any doubt that if Thiebault himself was ever threatened with Imperial retribution, he would strike them down first before they were able to lay evidence against him.

The presence, therefore, of his hostages in Liepmann's property, fully implicated the Jewish merchant. If Davout gave the slightest hint that he suspected Thiebault of collusion, Thiebault only had to order his own officers to apprehend Liepmann, together with two British shipmasters, to ingratiate himself with the marshal and prove his own zeal, efficiency and trustworthiness.

'If we can but make contact with Herr Liepmann,' Drinkwater reassured Gilham, 'I do not think we have much to worry about.'

'I hope you are right.'

Shortly after dark they heard the snarling bark of dogs below. The sound faded to whimpering and was followed by the noise of feet upon the stairs. A moment or two later a young man entered the watchman's hutch bearing a basket of food. Laying out cold sausages, bread and a bottle of wine on a napkin, he smiled and withdrew. As the two Britons bent to help themselves to the food they were aware of a tall man in the doorway. Drinkwater rose to his feet.

'Herr Liepmann?'

The man bowed gravely. Like Isaac Solomon he wore the long hair of Orthodox Jewry. '*Ja*, mein English ist not goot. You are Kapitan Waters, *ja*?'

'At your service, sir.'

'Goot. I know somet'ing of you from Herr Solomon . . .'

Drinkwater turned slightly so that his back was towards Gilham, and making a negative gesture with his right index finger held close to his breast, he then pointed it at his chest, indicating Gilham's ignorance.

'Ach . . .' Liepmann's head inclined in an imperceptible nod of understanding.

'Herr Thiebault is a very clever man, Herr Liepmann,' Drinkwater said slowly. ' I understand he must hold us hostage against your good behaviour.' Drinkwater accompanied this speech with a deal of gesturing and was rewarded by more nodding from Liepmann.

'*Ja, ja*.'

'Why does he want to bring in more English ships, the ships now at Helgoland? We know he is frightened of Marshal Davout . . .'

Liepmann looked from one to the other. His tongue flickered over his lips and a faint smile followed.

'Ze scheeps at Helgoland have guns, no?'

Drinkwater nodded.

'Marshal Davout he like guns. Herr Thiebault vill get guns. Make money and pleez Marshal Davout. You understand?'

Drinkwater nodded. 'Yes.'

'Damned if I do.'

'It is ver' dangerous for you here. You must not stay . . .'

Liepmann had his own game to play, Drinkwater thought, but it was essential that *Galliwasp* and *Ocean* escaped from the river before Drinkwater or Gilham made an attempt at getting out of Hamburg.

'We must wait, Herr Liepmann, until we hear from Helgoland that our ships are safe.'

'*Ja, ja*,' the Jew nodded. 'It will be ver' dangerous for you stay here. Zis is best place. When time come we take you out of Hamburg *mit* ze sugar.'

'Can you send a message to Helgoland,' Drinkwater asked, 'if I write it?' Liepmann nodded. 'Herr Nicholas has told me . . .'

'*Ja*,' Herr Nicholas tells me also.' Liepmann threw a glance in Gilham's direction and pointed at a ledger lying on a shelf. Inkpot and pen stood close by.

'In English, Kapitan . . .'

Drinkwater exchanged glances with Liepmann.

'It is safe?'

'*Ja*.'

Drinkwater took up the pen and wrote carefully in capitals:

G AND W TAKEN OUT OF THEIR SHIPS BY FORCE BUT PRESENTLY SAFE ENJOYING HOSPITALITY OF OUR MUTUAL FRIEND. ARRANGEMENTS SET AWRY BY ARRIVAL OF MARSHAL DAVOUT. SHIPS DISCHARGED OUTWARD BOUND.

He paused a moment, wondering how to sign himself, and then added: BALTIC.

Straightening up he handed the torn-out page to Liepmann. The Jew took the pen, dipped it in the inkpot and on another piece of paper began to write a jumble of letters, having memorized the crazy alphabet from Canto II of Dante. When he had finished the transliteration he opened the lantern and held Drinkwater's draft in the candle flame. The incinerated ash floated lazily about the table.

'There is one more thing, Herr Liepmann. You should understand that it was never intended that more ships would come, only that they would pretend to come. Do you understand?'

'They not come?' Liepmann regarded Drinkwater with surprise.

'No. They were to have gone only to Neuwerk . . . to look as if they were coming into the Elbe.'

'You do not wish to sell ze guns, *nein*?'

'No, only the greatcoats and boots.'

'Ach . . . and ze sugar, *ja*?'

'Yes,' Drinkwater said, matching the Jew's smile, 'and the sugar.'

Liepmann had turned to go when Gilham, his mouth full of the food which he had been busy eating during this exchange, asked, 'Herr Liepmann, did you pay Littlewood?'

Liepmann turned to Gilham, a look of mild surprise on his face. '*Ja*. I pay him goot . . . also for your scheep, ze *Ocean*, two thousand thalers . . .'

In the wake of Liepmann's departure Gilham grunted his satisfaction. With a wry look at his compatriot, Drinkwater helped himself to what was left of the sausages and bread.

He felt better with food inside him, aware that the winter's day, short though it had been, had passed slowly and been full of the uncertainties that kept a man from feeling hungry until actually confronted with food.

With a little luck they would be all right. A day or two lying low and then, when *Galliwasp* and *Ocean* were clear, Liepmann would smuggle them out of the city. Drinkwater was content to leave the details to the Jewish merchant. Davout would be settling in, receiving reports from the French officials and administrators, all of whom would be wary, and it would take even so dynamic a soldier as the marshal was reputed to be, a few days to decide upon what course of action to settle. There was no doubt that he had been sent to shut the gaping door that Hamburg had become in his master's Continental System.

'You seem to know a deal of what's going on,' Gilham said, suddenly jerking Drinkwater from his complacency and reminding him that if his real identity or position were known, then capture meant certain death.

He shrugged. 'It is not so very difficult to deduce,' he said with affected nonchalance, undecided as to whether to take Gilham into his confidence. 'D'you trust Littlewood?' he asked, deliberately changing the subject.

'I don't have much choice, do I?'

It was bitterly cold in the watchman's room and Drinkwater slept fitfully, waking frequently, the knotted muscles of his wounded shoulder aching painfully. Beside him Gilham snored under a blanket with a full belly and the sailor's facility for sleeping anywhere.

Drinkwater envied Gilham. He himself was desperately tired, tired of the burden Dungarth had laid upon him and tired of the interminable war. He had done his best and was no longer a young man. Now his shoulder pained him abominably.

He thought of his wife, Elizabeth, and their children, Charlotte Amelia and Richard. He had not seen them for so very long that they seemed to inhabit another age when he was another person. He found it difficult to remember exactly what they looked like, and found all he could call to mind were the immobile images of the little portraits that used to hang in his cabin when he was in command of a frigate and not cowering under borrowed blankets in a Hamburg garret.

Where were those imperfect portraits now? Lost with his other personal effects when the *Tracker* foundered and poor Quilhampton died, together with Frey and Derrick.

He tore his exhausted mind from horrible visions of his friends drowning, deliberately trying to recall the items of clothing, the books, charts and equipment he must have lost along with his sea-chest and the pictures of his family.

There was his sword and sextant, his journals and the little drawing case Elizabeth had given him, pretending it came from the children . . .

Mentally he rummaged down through the layers of clothing in the chest. The polar bear skin, presented by the officers of His Britannic Majesty's sloop-of-war *Melusine* and there, at the very bottom, cut from its wooden stretcher, the paint cracked and flaking, another portrait, found when he captured the *Antigone* in the Red Sea, ten, eleven years earlier.

Odd how he could recall *that* portrait in all its detail: the beautiful French woman, her shoulders bare, her breasts suggestively rendered beneath a filmy wrap of gauze, her hair *à la mode*, piled up on her head and entwined with a string of pearls. Hortense Santhonax, now widowed, though an unmarried woman when he had first seen her . . .

He closed his aching eyes against the moonlight that flooded in through the lozenge shaped window set high in the apex of the gable-end. It was all so long ago, part of another life . . .

Somewhere below him Liepmann's dogs stirred. Johannes, the young man who brought them their food and served as the Jew's watchman, was probably doing his rounds.

The whining suddenly rose to a bark of alarm. Once, twice, the hounds yapped before shots rang out. The barking ended in a mewling whine.

For a moment Drinkwater lay still, unable or unwilling to comprehend what was happening, then a muffled shout was followed by a curt, monosyllabic command.

Drinkwater threw off his blankets and reached for his boots.

'Gilham! Wake up!'

He kicked the recumbent figure into consciousness.

'What's the matter?' Gilham asked sleepily.

'The bloody French are here!'

Drinkwater pulled on his coat and kicked his blankets into the shadows. Feet pounded on the wooden ladders, the floor of their hideout shook. Gilham was on his feet, picking up the empty wine bottle from the table.

'Get in the shadows, man, and keep quiet!' Drinkwater hissed, though his own heart was pounding loud enough to be heard.

The door to the watchman's room was flung open. Three dragoons, clumsy in their high jackboots, burst into the room. For a moment they froze, staring about them, the moonlight gleaming on the bronze of their high, crested helmets and the steel of their bayonetted carbines. Then a fourth, a sergeant holding up a lantern, shoved past them. Drinkwater was aware of more men on the landing outside and the terrified whimper of a young prisoner. They had already seized Johannes.

The sergeant's lantern light swept the room, falling on the absurd gilt tassels on Drinkwater's hessian boots. A second later it played full in his face.

'Qu'est ce que vous foutez là?'

The lantern's light found Gilham, then the basket and utensils used to bring their supper, the pen and ink, the extinguished lamp and the torn pages of the ledger. A few black wisps of ash stirred in the air.

The dragoons stepped forward and Gilham shattered the wine bottle and raised its broken neck with a defiant cry. The noise terminated in a grunt as he doubled up in pain. The nearest dragoon's toecap struck him in the groin and vomit splashed on to the floor.

The dragoons secured their prisoners in a silence broken only by the rasp of Gilham's tortured breath. The sharp reek of spew filled the stuffy air. With cords about their wrists both Drinkwater and Gilham were pushed forward to join Johannes on the wooden catwalk that served as a landing from the topmost ladder.

They stumbled downwards, the sergeant and his lantern ahead of them, the shadows of themselves and their escort leaping fantastically on the stacks of baled and cased goods piled on all sides. At ground level the sergeant paused, ordering his patrol into rough formation. The circle of lamplight illuminated his boots and the long tails of his green coat with the brass eagles securing the yellow facing of the turn-backs. It fell also on the corpse of one of Liepmann's watchdogs, the pink tongue lolling from its gaping jaw. The sergeant kicked it aside.

'Ouvrez!' he ordered, and a blast of cold air struck them as the

door was swung open. The sergeant lifted the lantern and walked down the line of his men, peering at the three prisoners pinioned between the double files. He said something in a low voice which made his men snigger, then he swung round and Drinkwater saw the sabre in his right hand. Holding up the lantern in his left, he let the beam play on the stack of bulging sacks beside them.

'Hippolyte,' he commanded, *'allez . . . votre casque, mon ami.'*

The dragoon who had thrown open the warehouse door trotted obediently up and doffed his helmet. He held it upside down as the sergeant lifted his sword arm.

'Qu'est que ce?' he asked mockingly, slashing at a sack. Sugar loaves tumbled into Hippolyte's helmet and the dragoons roared with laughter.

'Voila!' cried the sergeant with a flourish. *'Nom de Dieu! Sucre!'*

And the patrol lurched forward into the dark cobbled alleyway in high spirits, locking the warehouse door behind them.

Chapter Twelve *January 1810*

The Iron Marshal

They were not long in the custody of the sergeant and his troopers. At the end of the alley they found a mounted officer whose helmet, scabbard and horse furniture gleamed in the flaring light of a torch held by an orderly on foot. The leaping flame, lighting his face from below, gave it a demonic cast as he stared down at the prisoners, listening to the sergeant's report. The officer's bay mount shifted uneasily beside the flickering brand, tossing its head and throwing off flecks of foam from curling lips. The officer soothed its arched neck with a gloved hand.

With the stately clip-clop of the charger bringing up the rear they marched off, crossing a moonlit, cobbled square, to halt in the high shadow of the Rathaus. Despite the midnight hour, messengers came and went, clattering up to the waiting orderlies who grabbed flung reins as the aides dashed into the lit archway, the flanking sentries snapping to attention and receiving the most perfunctory of salutes from the young officers.

Drinkwater, Gilham and Johannes were marched off to a side door, entering a stone flagged passage that opened out into an arched chamber guarded by two shakoed sentinels and containing a staff officer who sat writing at a desk. The escort of dragoons was dismissed, infantry took over and the dragoon officer made a *sotto voce* report to the staff captain. The latter barely looked up, though his pen scribbled busily across the uppermost of a small pile of papers. These formalities over, the three prisoners were taken through an ironbound door and locked into a small chamber which had clearly been used as a storeroom.

Gilham and Drinkwater exchanged glances but their silence did nothing to reassure the young German. Johannes was agitated to the point of visible distress and would have broken down completely had not their incarceration ended suddenly. A tall corporal of fusiliers, his shako plume raking the lintel of the door as he ducked into the makeshift cell, called them out.

'*Allez!*'

They trooped out and followed the corporal; two soldiers with bayonets fixed to their muskets fell in behind them. At the staff officer's desk they were motioned to pass, and climbed a flight of stone steps to halt outside impressive double doors guarded by two further sentries.

'The holy of holies,' muttered Gilham and in the silence that followed Drinkwater could hear the chatter of Johannes's teeth. When the doors opened it startled the three of them.

Monsieur Thiebault advanced towards them. His face was pale and he wrung his hands with a nervous compulsiveness.

'Gentlemen . . .' he said, attempting a reassuring smile, stepping aside and ushering them forward, 'His Excellency will see you now . . .' He nodded at the guards.

Drinkwater and Gilham started forward with Johannes in their wake, but Thiebault, Drinkwater noticed, made a sharp gesture with his hand and turning his head Drinkwater saw the boy's arm seized by one of the soldiers. He caught Thiebault's eye and the customs officer raised his shoulders with a fatalistic shrug.

Drinkwater's heart was pounding. If he let slip the slightest hint of his real identity, he would be shot as a spy. Though Gilham did not know of his status as a sea officer, he might make some indiscreet reference . . .

'Leave the talking to me, Gilham,' he snapped in a low voice as they were ushered into a high chamber, lit by a dozen candelabrae. A fire blazed in a grate and above the mantelpiece hung the mounted heads of a pair of tusked boars. Between them were emblazoned the castellated arms of the Hanseatic City of Hamburg. More hunting trophies were displayed on the dark panelling of the burghers' council chamber that was now occupied by the commander-in-chief of the Army of Germany.

Louis Nicholas Davout, Prince of Eckmühl, Duke of Auerstadt and Marshal of France, sat at a desk in the centre of the room, his balding head bent over a pile of papers, his polished boots reflecting the fire and his gold-laced blue coat tight over powerful shoulders. Beside him, in a similar though less splendid uniform, a plumed bicorne tucked neatly under his elbow, an aide-de-camp stood in a respectful attitude.

The marshal said something in a low voice, the aide bent attentively, replied as the marshal dashed off a signature, took the document with a click of his heels and left the room. The jingle of the aide's spurs ceased as the double doors closed behind him and Drinkwater, Gilham and Thiebault were left in a silence broken only by the crackle of the fire.

Slowly the marshal lifted his head and stared at them. The firelight reflected off his pince-nez hid his eyes, but Drinkwater was conscious of a firm mouth and round, regular features. When Davout removed the spectacles his expression was intimidating. The light danced on the coils of oak leaves embroidered upon his breast as he sighed and leaned back in his chair.

'M'sieur Thiebault . . .' he murmured, looking at the two Britons before him. Thiebault launched into a speech punctuated by ingratiating *'Monseigneurs'*.

Whatever the content of Thiebault's discourse, Drinkwater was conscious of the unwavering gaze of Davout, the man the French themselves called 'the iron marshal', the archangel of the Emperor Napoleon. He tried at first to meet Davout's eyes, then, finding the scrutiny too unnerving and with the thought that such a wordless challenge was dangerous, Drinkwater tried to make out the gist of Thiebault's explanation while his eyes roved about the chamber with the affected gaucherie of a man aroused by curiosity. He hoped his apprehension was not obvious.

He heard, or thought he heard, Thiebault mention the word *'Russie'* but could not bring himself to look at the marshal. Then Thiebault said it again and Drinkwater, conscious that Davout was still staring at him, dropped his own gaze. At the marshal's feet, amid a small heap of dispatch boxes, a leather wallet and a travelling valise, lay a frayed roll of canvas. It had been kept tight-rolled but now untied, it had sprung open enough for Drinkwater to see its inner surface.

The shock of recognition brought a wave of nausea so strong that for a moment he thought he might faint. Instead he moved, shifting his weight forward before recovering himself with a cough. He was better placed to see now the familiar portrait.

Looking down beside Davout's shining black boot heels Drinkwater saw the crown of the woman's head, the coils of auburn hair wound with pearls and the arch of a single eyebrow set against the eau-de-nil background that the artist had painted.

He saw too the star shaped flaking where the unstretched canvas had shed the slight impasto of the flaming hair and the white gesso ground showed through. The position and shape of that bare patch confirmed what Drinkwater had already guessed, that the rolled canvas beneath the desk of Marshal Davout was the portrait of Hortense Santhonax that once hung in the cabin of the *Antigone* and which had, until very lately, rested at the bottom of his sea-chest.

He felt the flesh on the back of his neck crawl and brought his incredulously staring eyes up to meet those of the marshal.

'M'sieur Thiebault speaks that you had cargo for Russia, *oui*?'

Recovering himself, Drinkwater nodded. 'Yes, Excellency, military stores . . .'

'*Et sucre, n'est-ce pas?* And sugar . . .?' Davout's accent was thick, his English uncertain. 'Why come to Hamburg, not Russia?'

'My ship was damaged in a storm, sir. We,' Drinkwater gestured vaguely at Gilham who had the presence of mind to nod, suggesting their circumstances had been identical, 'put into Helgoland. Then the winter, the ice in the Baltic . . .' he made a helpless gesture of resignation, 'we could not go on to Russia. At Helgoland the Government told us they had abandoned us and we decided to sell our cargo here, in Hamburg.'

Drinkwater paused. Without taking his eyes off the two Britons, Davout queried something with Thiebault who appeared, by his nodding, to be confirming what Drinkwater had said. Drinkwater decided to press his advantage, mindful of the rolled and damaged portrait at Davout's feet.

'We had an escort of the British navy, but we became separated . . .'

'What name this ship . . . this escort?' Davout's poor English, learned during a brief period as a prisoner of the Royal Navy when a young man, could not disguise the keenness of his question.

Tracker,' said Drinkwater, noticing the exchange of glances between Davout and Thiebault and the half-smile that crossed the marshal's face.

'You have news of her?' Drinkwater asked quickly. Davout's eyes were cold and he made no answer, while Thiebault was clearly unnerved by Drinkwater's effrontery in asking such a question.

'You sold your cargo, *Capitaine*?'

'Yes . . .'

'The sugar?'

'Yes.' Drinkwater looked at Thiebault. Perspiration was pouring from the customs officer's forehead and it was clear that Thiebault's future, as much as that of Drinkwater and Gilham, rested upon this interview. Such anxiety argued that Davout's hostility must be at least in part aimed at Thiebault. This consideration persuaded Drinkwater to press his question again.

'Do you have news of *Tracker*, Excellency?'

Behind Davout Thiebault, his face twisted with supplication, made a gesture of suppression. Davout ignored the question.

'P*eut-être* . . . perhaps you not go to Russia . . . perhaps you only make these papers.' Davout struck the desk and Drinkwater saw the *Galliwasp*'s confiscated documents with the crown stamp of the London Customs House upon them, among those on his desk. The pince-nez were lifted to the bridge of the marshal's nose, then lowered as Davout got to his feet and came round the table to confront Drinkwater.

'You come to Hamburg as a spy?'

'*Monseigneur, l'explication* . . .' began Thiebault despairingly.

'*Assez!*' snapped Davout, turning away from Drinkwater with a contemptuous wave of his hand. He returned to his desk and picked up the pince-nez he had left there. Casting a baleful look at Thiebault he spoke a few words.

'Was the *Tracker* coming to Hamburg?' Thiebault translated.

'The *Tracker*?' Drinkwater said with unfeigned surprise, 'No, of course not.' He turned towards Davout, an alarming thought forming in his mind. 'No, Excellency, the *Tracker* was under orders for Russia . . .'

Drinkwater was unable to gauge whether or not the marshal believed him, for a knock at the door was followed by the reappearance of the aide-de-camp. It was clear that he was expected and that the matter was of greater importance than the interrogation of two British shipmasters caught breaking the Emperor's Continental System. Davout returned to his desk and curtly dismissed Thiebault and the prisoners. He did no more than nod at the young French officer, who left the doorway immediately.

Thiebault accompanied them to the foot of the steps where a weary glance from the staff officer still shuffling paper was followed by a bellow for their guard.

'What in God's name was all that about?' asked Gilham unable to remain silent.

'Oblige me a moment longer,' muttered Drinkwater motioning him towards Thiebault who was addressing the staff officer. Thiebault turned towards them, his expression one of relief. His tone was suddenly preternaturally light, the manner an attempt to recover his former insouciance. He had clearly suffered an ordeal.

'Well, gentlemen, I think His Excellency is satisfied with the, er, arrangements . . .'

'You mean the boots?' said Gilham sarcastically.

'Indeed, Captain . . .'

'What the devil was all that about the *Tracker*, M'sieur?' Drinkwater asked, frowning.

'Are our ships clear of the river?' Gilham added.

'Gentlemen, gentlemen, please; His Excellency has ordered that you be taken to Altona, to the military hospital there, just for a few days. It is a mere formality, I assure you.' Thiebault lowered his voice, 'His Excellency is due to inspect the defences of Lubeck shortly. I will send you word . . . now, if you will excuse me . . .'

Thiebault turned to go as two fusiliers approached. At the same moment the door at the far end of the room opened, admitting a blast of cold air which set the flames of the candles on the staff officer's desk guttering. A French officer escorted a cloaked figure towards them. The officer was resplendent in the campaign dress of a lieutenant in the horse chasseurs of the Imperial Guard. His scarlet pelisse was not draped, *à la hussard*, from his left shoulder, but worn over the dolman, the gold frogging buttoned to his neck against the cold. His overalls were mud spattered, evidence of a long, hard ride, and his face, below the fur rim of his busby, was fiercely mustachioed. He drew the cloaked person after him, reached down to the sabretache that trailed over the flagstones with his scabbard and drew out a sealed document.

'Lieutenant Dieudonné à votre service,' he said, holding out the letter. *'Pour le Maréchal . . .'* He nodded at the cloaked figure, his green and red plume throwing a fantastic shadow on the wall.

The momentary distraction had provided Thiebault with an opportunity to escape, and though Gilham protested, more questions on his lips, Drinkwater was rooted to the spot, overcome by a moment of premonition that prepared him for the shock as the cloaked figure threw off its hood.

As she shook her head the auburn hair fell about her shoulders, and although he could not see the woman's full face, there was no doubt about that profile, at almost the same angle as she had assumed for the artist Jacques Louis David. He knew the face so well, for David's portrait – painted for her dead husband and later captured by Drinkwater – now inexplicably lay rolled under the desk of the Prince of Eckmühl.

In his distraction Drinkwater resisted the tug of his guard so that the soldier became angry, stepped behind him and thrust his ported musket into the small of his prisoner's back with a sharp exclamation. Drinkwater stumbled forward, losing his balance and attracting the attention of Lieutenant Dieudonné and the woman. Gilham caught Drinkwater's arm; recovering himself, Drinkwater looked back. Beyond the menacing guard the woman was staring after him, her face in the full light of the leaping candles on the staff officer's desk.

There was no doubt about her identity: she was Hortense Santhonax and she knew Nathaniel Drinkwater to be an officer in the Royal Navy of Great Britain.

Chapter Thirteen *January 1810*

The Firing Party

Outside stood the carriage that had brought Madame Santhonax, its door still open. A dozen chasseurs sat on their horses round it, exchanging remarks. Drinkwater moved forward in a daze. He was tired, cold and hungry, and the night's events had become unreal. For months – since the terrible events in the jungle of Borneo – he had been deprived of all energy, overcome by a mental and physical lethargy impossible to throw off. There had been brief moments when he felt he was recovering, when Dungarth had inspired him to take on the mission to Russia, when Solomon had entertained him that morning after his night of filth and subterfuge, and when young Nicholas had revived the failed project at Helgoland.

But these had been brief and faltering revivals and, he could see now, merely fatal circumstances conspiring to bring him to this strange encounter. He was deep in blood, the killer of Edouard Santhonax, the executioner of Morris and murderer of poor Tregembo. Now he was to be called to account, to die in his turn, shot as a spy on the denunciation of a French woman within the Rathaus. He was convinced she had recognized him, for their eyes had met and she could have read nothing but fear in his expression. Nausea rose in his gorge, he missed his footing again and again Gilham caught him.

'Are you all right?'

'Aye,' gasped Drinkwater, feeling a cold sweat chill his brow in the icy air.

'I think they want us in the carriage,' Gilham said, his hand under Drinkwater's elbow.

Not *her* carriage, surely, he thought, that was too ironic a twist of fate. In any case, at any moment . . .

'Arrête!'

This was it. The denunciation had been made, the staff officer was running out after them and he was about to be arrested, unmasked as a spy and on the summary orders of Marshal Davout, shot like a dog.

But Drinkwater was wrong.

The staff officer called something to the chasseurs, one of whom was a non-commissioned officer. They were bundled into the carriage and Drinkwater caught the elusive scent of the widow Santhonax. He sank shivering into the deep buttoned leather of the seat and closed his eyes as the carriage jerked forward.

'Are you well, Waters?' Gilham asked again.

'Well enough. Just a little tired and hungry . . .' No denunciation had come; perhaps she had not recognized him. Why should she? It had been a long time; they had changed, though age seemed to have enhanced rather than diminished her beauty. Nor did she possess a portrait of him to remind her of his features . . .

Drinkwater's relief was short-lived. The carriage swung round a corner and jerked to an abrupt halt. The door was flung open and they were ordered out.

'Regardez-là, messieurs,' the non-commissioned officer said, leaning from his creaking saddle.

They stood at the entrance of a courtyard. It was lit by flaring torches set in sconces and seemed to be full of soldiers, infantrymen under the command of an elderly, white haired captain who was tucking a written order inside his shako before putting it on.

'What the devil . . .?' Gilham began, but Drinkwater cut him short, his heart thumping painfully in his chest. Far from feeling faint, the greatest fear of all had seized him and he felt a strong impulse to run.

'It's a firing party!' he hissed in Gilham's ear. A word of command and the milling rabble of soldiers lined up in two files. A moment later a man was led out from an adjacent doorway. It was Johannes.

'God's bones!' Drinkwater swore. He wanted to move, to do something, but his legs would not respond and he watched helplessly as a bag was pulled down over Johannes's wildly staring eyes. He saw the young man's legs buckle, heard the muffled screams as he was dragged to the wall. With the ease of practice Johannes's trussed hands were tied to a ring bolt in the masonry and the boy fell forward in a faint. The double file of fusiliers raised their loaded muskets on the captain's command and a volley rang out, echoing round and round the courtyard as the body of Johannes slumped downwards. Pulling a torch from a sconce the white haired captain walked forward and leaned over the boy's shattered body. Casually he emptied a pistol into the left ear. A surgeon came forward; Drinkwater and Gilham were ushered back to the carriage. As they climbed in and the door was shut, Gilham echoed Drinkwater's own thoughts.

'Poor fellow. For a moment I thought that was for us.'

They sat in silence for a while, the death of Johannes and their part in it weighing heavily upon them.

'That was because of the sugar, wasn't it?' remarked Gilham, seeking some quieting justification for his conscience.

'Yes, I believe so,' muttered Drinkwater.

'It allowed that bugger Thiebault to clear his own yardarm,' Gilham went on. 'Which was what he was doing with all that jabbering to Monseigneur What's-his-name, eh?'

'Yes, I imagine so . . .'

'Sacrificed that poor young devil to save his own skin.'

'I do not think,' said Drinkwater, slowly recovering himself, 'that whilst Marshal Davout would turn a blind eye to the military stores, he could countenance the sugar. It was too blatant a breach of the Emperor's proscription of British imports.' He paused. Gilham's face was no more than a pale blur in the darkness that had come with moonset and an overcast sky promising more snow. 'I am surprised a man of Davout's stamp did not have us shot out of hand too. I think Thiebault must have pleaded for us . . .'

'You think we are out of danger, then?'

'I think you are, Captain, but as for myself, I am not so sure.'

'Why ever not?'

'It is probably best that you do not ask that question. I will answer it only by saying that your association with me places you in the greatest danger.'

'What on earth are you talking about?'

'I sincerely wish I could tell you, Gilham, but prudence dictates that I hold my tongue at least for a little longer. What you are ignorant of cannot be held against you. The example of Johannes might have been intended to warn the people of Hamburg against obtaining sugar, but we were made to witness it as a warning to ourselves. No doubt His Excellency the Marshal considers his act magnanimous . . .'

'But I . . . oh, very well,' Gilham said before lapsing into a perplexed silence.

Opposite him, Drinkwater strove to order the chaos of his thoughts. There was no doubt about the accuracy of Gilham's assessment of Thiebault's conduct. He had indeed 'cleared his own yardarm' and sacrificed Johannes to satisfy the Marshal's notion of loyalty to the Emperor's edicts. Davout's clemency to both himself and the British shipmasters had been purchased along with the Northampton boots. The profit and loss of that account was a matter between Littlewood, Liepmann, Thiebault and the minister of war in Paris, but possibly Davout had retained his reputation for incorruptibility. What ought to have brought Drinkwater a measure of satisfaction was the clear indication that so unimpeachable and elevated a servant of the Empire as Davout was convinced that the original destination of the boots had been Russia. It made the desperate charade Drinkwater had endured in Mrs Hockley's brothel an unnecessary farce.

But he derived no consolation from these considerations, for far more disturbing were the appearances of the portrait and its subject. It was an inescapable fact that the former had come from his very own sea-chest, taken aboard His Britannic Majesty's gun-brig *Tracker* for safe-keeping. Its survival argued a case for the survival of the brig, for had the brig foundered, the chest – stowed in her hold – would have sunk with her. The only possible explanation was that *Tracker* had been captured, probably disabled in the tempest and driven ashore as *Galliwasp* had been, but on less hospitable shores.

Perhaps then, Quilhampton and Frey, Derrick and the others were still alive! He felt a surge of hope, of revitalization, kindle in his heart. If only it were true, how much of the burden would it lift from his shoulders! Surely, in a world that could disinter the portrait of Hortense Santhonax, so small a miracle was possible?

And what of her; had she recognized him? And if so, had she denounced him to Davout?

He tried to recall the strange encounter in the Rathaus. She had undoubtedly seen him, as he had seen her. He had known her not merely because he had kept her hidden likeness for years, but because he had met her, rescued her from revolutionaries and carried her safe to England, an *emigrée* refugee.

She had been exquisitely beautiful then, a proud young aristocrat, Hortense de Montholon, whose association with the equally proud republican, Edouard Santhonax, had led to their eventual marriage and the turning of her coat. She had gone back to France at the end of the Terror and been landed on the beach at Criel by Lord Dungarth and an unknown master's mate called Nathaniel Drinkwater. He thought her more beautiful in her maturity, grown stately as Republic had given way to Empire and the *parvenu* crown had need of a new aristocracy.

And now their paths had crossed again; the widow Santhonax was in Hamburg, and their eyes had met!

But she had been a prisoner!

The realization hit him like a pistol ball, so that he exclaimed out loud.

'Damn it, Waters, are you unwell?'

'I have just recalled something. Tell me Gilham, did you notice the cavalry officer who came in as we were leaving?'

'The hussar fellow with the lady? Yes, of course I did, striking pair.'

'What did you make of 'em?'

'What d'you mean?'

'How did you interpret their relationship?'

'Their relationship?' Gilham asked in astonishment.

'Was there *anything* that struck you about it?'

'Well, she was brought in under constraint, like us . . .'

'Precisely!' said Drinkwater, relieved the impression had not been the work of his highly charged imagination. 'She was a detainee.'

'Is that what you wanted me to say?'

'It was what I hoped you would think. She was brought under escort, and an escort of Guard chasseurs is no ordinary escort, in this very carriage . . .'

'But what in heaven's name has this woman to do with us? Look, Waters, there's something damned fishy going on.' Gilham's tone of voice had changed, become guarded, suspicious. 'Why did you insist on doing all the talking back there? You were accustomed to taking a back seat, letting Littlewood jabber. I think you owe me an explanation.'

Drinkwater sighed, staring at the pale oval of Gilham's face as he leaned forward in the gloom.

'Very well,' he said resignedly. It was perhaps better to level with Gilham. There might be no time for explanations later, and Gilham seemed a cool enough fellow in his way.

'My name is not Waters, Captain Gilham. I will not worry you with such details; suffice it to know that I am a post-captain in the navy . . .'

'Dear God!' Gilham fell back in his seat.

'You need not worry. Your treasonable act of selling military stores to the enemy was only achieved with the assistance of both His Majesty's navy and His diplomatic service.'

'I have been duped.'

'I suspect we have all been duped a little, in one way or another. Hardly anyone in this affair is precisely what he seems, but to keep to the point . . .'

There was considerable relief in confessing things to Gilham. He felt better for the confession, felt that speaking aloud conferred a kind of existence upon his theories, delivered them from the dark womb of his turbulent mind to the harsh reality of this bitterly cold winter's night.

'It was intended to ship *Galliwasp*'s cargo to Russia; you may have realized from Davout's reaction that it would have been contrary to French interests, casting suspicion on the Tsar's reliability as their ally.'

'And having failed to do that, a shipment into Hamburg in so public a manner achieved the same objective.'

'Exactly, except that the French profited from the boots.'

'But at a cost,' added Gilham, and Drinkwater could almost hear the smile in his voice.

'Aye, at a cost. You may recall Littlewood speaking of the loss of our escort.'

'The brig *Tracker* that you mentioned tonight? I wondered why that came up.'

'We thought she had foundered, but I now know her to have fallen into enemy hands.'

'How the deuce d'you know that?'

'Because beneath Davout's desk was a rolled canvas portrait. That portrait was my property, held aboard the brig with the rest of my personal effects.'

'Your wife?'

'No.' Drinkwater shifted uneasily, glad of the darkness, aware that the relief of confession came at a price. 'It was captured aboard a French frigate, the *Antigone*, years ago, when it was cut-out by the people of the brig *Hellebore*. I brought her home and subsequently commanded her. I kept the portrait as a curiosity; you see I knew the lady in my youth . . . I was much struck by her. . .'

'And she was the woman brought in tonight by M'sieur Moustache, eh?'

'Yes.'

'So she knows you are the spy that Davout suspected.'

'I think that is the gist of it,' Drinkwater said slowly. 'She has no reason to think well of me, though I once did her a small service.'

'She will denounce you then, if she was under detention, perhaps to gain her own freedom.' Gilham's tone was confidently matter-of-fact, as though the thing was a *fait accompli*.

'Did the marshal strike you as a man to be swayed that easily?'

'He was certainly not a man who would compromise his position for a woman's blandishments, no, but if he had already made some connection between a captured portrait, a portrait in the possession of the enemy . . .'

'D'you think that the finding of an old, damaged portrait would have aroused any suspicion unless the lady was well known to the discoverer, and under some suspicion already? If I told you that she was the mistress of a highly placed but disgraced French official all of whose intimates might have fallen under suspicion, would you not think the matter took a different turn and might be seen in another light?'

'It would depend on how eminent this fellow was.'

'The Emperor's former minister for Foreign Affairs?'

'*Tallyrand*?'

'Just so.'

'Whew! Then it is a coincidence she's in Hamburg?'

'No, I don't think so. The lady is here on her own or Talleyrand's account, perhaps to contact London through Helgoland. The coincidence is that *we* are in Hamburg . . .'

'D'you think she will hold her tongue? About your identity?' Gilham asked anxiously.

'I think she will keep her own counsel until it suits her, which does not mean I may rely upon her silence. I imagine she might be tempted to seek a private squaring of accounts *after* she has contacted Helgoland.'

'So we must wait upon our friend Thiebault?'

'Altona is on the Elbe, Gilham, and we are both seamen.'

Gilham chuckled in the darkness and shortly afterwards the carriage drew up at the military hospital at Altona.

Drinkwater had thought the night could spring no more surprises on him, but he was wrong. The military hospital at Altona was a complex of long, low wooden buildings surrounding a snow covered parade ground. It was almost dawn when they arrived and a few figures were about, dark visaged men in tattered fatigues.

'Who the devil are they?' asked Gilham of nobody as they stood shivering while the chasseurs handed them over to more of the ubiquitous blue-coated infantry Napoleon had planted across the face of Europe.

A soberly dressed man hurrying past with a small bag stopped beside them.

'English, yes?'

'Yes, we are English,' announced Gilham. 'You are not French?'

'I am Spanish, *Señor*. *My* name is Castenada, Doctor Enrico Castenada, before in the service of the Marquis de la Romana.'

Comprehension dawned on Drinkwater. 'You were left behind when the Marquis's army was withdrawn from the Danish coast by the Royal Navy.'

'*Si, señor*, that is correct.' He switched to French and said something to the guards. They shrugged and closed the gates behind the departing chasseurs.

'Come, I will take you to the English quarters,' Castenada said beckoning them to follow.

'There are other Englishmen here?'

'*Si, señor*, I practise my English with them.'

They crossed the parade ground as a bugler started to blow reveille. More men appeared, most in worn, darned clothing, some wearing bandages, a few on crutches. There was something familiar about them . . .

'Sir? Is it you? Captain Drinkwater, sir?'

The speaker's carious teeth grinned from an unshaven jaw, his breath stank of poor diet and personal neglect. He swung round and called out, 'Hey, lads, it's the Cap'n!'

'You're from *Tracker*, ain't you?' Drinkwater asked grinning. 'How's Mr Quilhampton?'

The man turned and shook his head. ''E ain't so good, sir, but 'e put up an 'ell of a fight, bless yer!'

'What about Mr Frey?'

'I'm all right, sir!' said Frey running up and seizing Drinkwater's outstretched hand. His eyes were full of tears and the two men clasped each other with relief.

'Why, I'm damned glad to see you, sir, damned glad!'

Chapter Fourteen *January 1810*

Altona

'How many of you are there?' asked Drinkwater eagerly, his mood transformed by the meeting with Frey. 'No, wait.' He turned to the grinning seaman who had first recognized him. 'I'd be obliged if you'd warn the men not to use my name.' He lowered his voice. 'I'm here incognito, d'you see.'

The man laid a finger beside his nose, winked and grinned lopsidedly, exposing his foul teeth. 'Aye aye, sir, I understands, we'll hold our tongues, don't you worry.'

'Very well then, be off and see to it!'

'Aye, aye, sir.'

Drinkwater turned his attention back to Frey. 'So, how many of you are there?'

Frey looked away. 'Eleven.'

'*Eleven?* God's bones, is that all?'

'That excludes the badly wounded, sir; there are seven of them, plus the Captain, Lieutenant Quilhampton. They took him to Hamburg last night.'

'Last night?' Drinkwater frowned. Had Quilhampton been somewhere within the Rathaus at the same time as he and Gilham? Had Davout summoned him for questioning in connection with the discovery of that damned portrait?

'He's badly wounded, sir,' Frey said, breaking his train of thought.

'How badly?'

'He took a sword thrust, sir, in his left arm, above the stump. It was gangrenous when we arrived here and Doctor Castenada had to perform a second amputation. Mr Quilhampton was in a high fever when they took him last night.'

'God damn!' Drinkwater blasphemed impotently. For a moment his thoughts were with his friend, lying delirious in the hands of the French, then he mastered himself. 'Is there somewhere less exposed that we can talk? This is Captain Gilham, by the way, the master of the *Ocean*, transport. Mr Gilham, a protégé of mine, Mr Frey.'

The two men shook hands perfunctorily.

'They are very lax here, sir. There is talk about a new Governor having arrived . . .'

'We know,' Drinkwater cut Frey short, 'but somewhere to talk, for the love of God, it's too cold here . . .'

Frey led them into a barrack hut that appeared to be a sort of officers' mess. It was full of Spaniards, the remnants of Romana's Army Corps, left behind when Rear-Admiral Keats evacuated the bulk of the Spanish forces from Denmark.

Frey indicated a table and two benches reserved for the *Tracker*'s pitifully small number of surviving officers.

'You had better make your verbal report, Mr Frey.'

Frey nodded, rubbing his hands over his pinched face. Drinkwater noted the grime of his cuffs and neck linen. His hollow cheeks had not been shaved for several days and his eyes were red rimmed and sunken.

'You recall the night of the tempest, sir?'

'Yes, very well.'

'We lost our foretopmast within the first hour. It was badly sprung and the stays slipped at the cap. As we strove to clear the wreckage we were continually swept by the sea and lost several men in the confusion, both aloft and from the deck. We burnt bengal fires for assistance, but were not certain of your whereabouts by then . . .'

'We saw them and put about, but were unable to find you. Soon afterwards we were in like condition and drove ashore on Helgoland, but pray go on.'

'We were less fortunate, sir. By daylight we had three feet of water below and in so small a vessel it damned near had us foundering. We had precious little freeboard and were wallowing abominably. Mr Q., sir, was a tower of strength. Though we had lost a deal of our company, including both the bosun and carpenter, we got sail on her and strove to make northing . . .'

'But the wind backed and drove you east.'

'Aye sir, you were in like case no doubt?'

'Aye.'

'We fetched upon a bank, drove over it and anchored in its lee. When the gale abated we began to set things to rights. We had men at the pumps three hours out of every four and one fell dead from the labour. But Mr Q. drove us near as hard as he drove himself; we found the leak, clapped a fothered sail over it and began to gain on the water in the hold. We planned to empty half our water casks and wing 'em out in the hold for buoyancy, but the Danes came out in their confounded gunboats. They lay off and simply shot us to pieces with long twenty four pounders. We didn't stand a chance until they boarded us. Then we gave them cold steel, for there was scarce a grain of dry powder in the ship and that had been spent in the carronades. I think there were about forty of us when the action began . . .'

'And James was wounded when the Danes boarded?' Drinkwater prompted.

Frey nodded. 'Aye, sir. He did his damndest . . .'

'Mr Frey,' Drinkwater said after a moment, drawing Frey from the introspection he had lapsed into on recounting the fate of the *Tracker*. 'I would not have you think I ask this question from meanness of spirit, but what became of my personal effects?'

'We took some care of those, sir. Mr Q. had your chest sown into canvas and the whole tarred over. They weren't in the hold, d'you see, Mr Q. had 'em stowed in his cabin. When the Danes took the *Tracker*, they looted her of anything moveable. I'm afraid, sir,' Frey admitted, lowering his eyes, 'your chest was seized along with the ship's orders, sir.' He paused and looked Drinkwater full in the face. 'That was my fault, sir. I had forgotten about them in the heat of the action, sir, after Mr Q. was wounded . . .'

Drinkwater looked at the crestfallen Frey. After Quilhampton had fallen the command of *Tracker* would have devolved to him, and in the bitter moment of surrender Frey had forgotten to destroy the brig's secret orders.

'So the enemy know we were bound for Russia?'

'Yes sir, and the private signals for the . . .'

'Yes, yes, I realize that!' said Drinkwater sharply, aware of the irony.

'I'm mortified, sir, there's no excuse . . .'

'I'm sorry, I spoke hastily, I implied no reproach, it's just that . . . well, never mind. You will have to admit these things in your written report, but I do not think you need concern yourself over much.'

'Sir?' Frey looked puzzled.

'No court martial will condemn an officer who has been through what you went through, Mr Frey and, by your account, gallantly defended his ship. You must submit to the court's judgement, of course.'

'I have already written my report, sir,' Frey said gloomily.

'Well, no matter of that now,' Drinkwater said. He was impatient to reassure Frey and though both he and Quilhampton – if he survived – would have to appear before a court martial, such considerations were in the future and Drinkwater was more urgently pressed by the present.

'Just one thing more, Mr Frey, before we decide what is to be done.' He noticed Frey's expression change, responding to the positive note in Drinkwater's voice. 'What happened after you submitted to the Danes? By what authority were you brought to Altona?'

'Oh, the French appear to control the Danes, sir. As soon as we got ashore, after the *Tracker* was looted and burned for she was hulled and aground by the time we struck – we were turned over to the French garrison at a place called Tonning. The Danes, though willing to fight us at sea – for revenge on our attack on Copenhagen three years ago I reckon – seem to lack independence ashore. There are French troops quartered upon them. It was the French that finally took the ship's orders . . . and your effects, sir,' Frey added as an apologetic afterthought. But what of you, sir?'

Drinkwater looked at Frey. He had been wondering about the precise circumstances in which the portrait had come to light and compromised Hortense. He would never know, of course, and there were far more immediate things to consider.

'Me? Oh, I will tell you one day, Mr Frey, when we are in better spirits and have put these present misfortunes behind us. Come, sir, tell me something about this place. You spoke – ah, Gilham, you have found something with which to break your fast.' Drinkwater looked up at the merchant shipmaster.

'This is for you: burgoo, though a thin stuff compared with our usual British fare, but 'twill warm you.'

'I'm obliged to you.'

'I will get some for your young friend if you'll hatch some way out of this damnable place.'

'You'll take your turn with us, not wait for Thiebault?'

'I don't trust that lizard, damn him, not now he's under the thumb of Marshal What's-his-name.'

Drinkwater could not resist a grin. 'Very well, now Mr Frey . . .'

'Well, 'tis a hospital really, as you doubtless guessed. We were brought here because so many of us were wounded.'

'Were you one of them?'

'Only a trifle, sir, a scratch, that's all. Several men have died since we arrived, but we have been tolerably well treated, allowed to bury our dead, and the commissioned officers permitted, on parole, to walk on the river bank.'

'Ah, that's good. Have you given your parole?'

'I wouldn't, sir.'

'Why not?'

'Mr Quilhampton forbade it, sir. He said 'twas enough to lose his ship, but he would not surrender his honour.'

'A Quixotic notion, but I apprehend he had ideas of escape, eh?'

'He did not know how ill he was.'

'I see,' Drinkwater paused, 'and are visits permitted to Altona itself?'

'Oh yes, we sent a man in to purchase foodstuffs . . . before we ran out of money.'

'D'you think it possible to send a message to Altona? Do any of the villagers enter the hospital at all?'

Frey's brow creased in a frown. 'Well there is a boy that comes up with fresh bread and the Commandant has some intercourse with the place for his table . . . Doctor Castenada would be the man to ask, sir. He is a remarkable fellow.'

'Is he to be trusted?'

'Aye, sir, as far as I can judge. He professes a dislike of the French.'

Drinkwater grunted and rubbed a hand across his stubbled chin. 'I used,' he said, 'to have some sneaking regard for 'em – unpatriotic, don't you know – but it seems to me that the Rights of Man was a not entirely dishonourable banner to fight under. Then last night Gilham and I saw a boy shot for hoardin' sugar . . .'

'We hang smugglers, sir,' Frey said.

'That's rather why I had a sneakin' regard for the Frogs,'

grinned Drinkwater. 'Now tell me, if I asked you to plan the seizure of a boat large enough to take two dozen men down stream, what would you say?'

Frey's face was transformed by sudden enthusiasm. 'I've thought about it, sir! There is little time, for the ice is already forming along the reed beds, but there's a ballast bed just below the village and they bring barges down from Hamburg and fill 'em there. They've sails and sweeps, a dozen of us could easily . . .'

'How the devil d'you know all this if you refused your parole?'

'I didn't say I hadn't had a walk along the river bank, sir!'

'I think, Captain Gilham,' Drinkwater said, 'that we may have discovered an exit from our impasse.'

'I hope to heaven you're right, my dear fellow, for if your friend chooses to denounce you, well . . . I don't think we have much time.'

Drinkwater needed no reminding that time was pressing. For all he knew Davout might have despatched a galloper that very morning with a message to Altona to have a certain 'Captain Waters' placed under close arrest.

Even if Hortense had not recognized him – and he was certain in his heart that his face had stirred some memory it was likely that when confronted with the portrait and the story of its being found aboard a British man-of-war, the connection was inevitable.

Seeking a quiet corner, Frey took him to consult Castenada. The worthy surgeon provided ink and paper, nodding when Frey explained the new prisoner wished to communicate with someone in Altona.

For his own part, Drinkwater carefully wrote out the lines of Dante and encoded his message to Liepmann. It told briefly of their seizure in the warehouse, the interview with Davout and the suspected duplicity of Thiebault. Drinkwater also informed him of the fate of Johannes. Finally he made his request: *I ask that you find the whereabouts of Lieutenant Quilhampton, commander of the British ship seized at Tonning.*

'Do you know of a Herr Liepmann, Doctor Castenada?' Drinkwater asked, 'I believe he lives in Altona.'

'*Si* . . . yes, yes. He is well known. You want that I, er, convey that message?' Castenada pointed at the final draft Drinkwater had copied out.

'Yes, is it possible, without risk?'

'Yes . . . I will take it myself,' Castenada held out his hand and took the paper and stared at it. 'This is not English?'

'No . . .' said Drinkwater cautiously, unsure of the Spaniard's trustworthiness.

'It is like the pharmacopoeia, eh?' Castenada smiled and folded the paper. 'Fortunately, Herr Liepmann is supplying me sometimes, my, er,' he frowned and scratched his head, failing to find the right word and ending his unfinished sentence with a shrug.

'Ah, medicines!' offered Frey.

'Yes, yes, of course, medicines.' Castenada smiled with satisfaction.

'How soon can you go into Altona?' Drinkwater asked.

'Today, I go today. In hospital like this I always want more of the, er, medicines, no?'

Drinkwater nodded. 'Very well . . .'

He and Frey walked back across the parade ground where the snow was falling again. 'If he brings me a reply I shall know I can trust him, but it is better that I am not seen talking to him, for his sake as much as mine. Do you watch him, Mr Frey, and when he returns question him. This man Liepmann knows me and will reply in code. If Castenada plays his part, you may offer to get him and the twelve fittest Spaniards out of this place in your barge. Promise them that they will be repatriated to Spain at the expense of the British Government, d'you understand?'

'Perfectly, sir.'

'Now, have you given any thought as to how to get out of this place?'

'The main gate is locked at sunset, early at this time of year, after which a general curfew is imposed upon us all. It is never broken – there has been no need to break it . . .'

'Did you not think of escape before now?' Drinkwater broke in.

'I have thought of little else, sir, as I told you,' said Frey in an aggrieved tone and looking askance at Drinkwater, 'but I did not contemplate it without Mr Quilhampton, sir.'

'Of course, my dear fellow, forgive me, I have a lot on my mind. Pray go on, do.'

'The party to leave will break out on a given signal. When the guards shut the gates they invariably congregate in the guardhouse for a hot drink – chocolate if they can get it after which they take up their night duties. They are very slack, most of them, being invalids themselves recuperating from wounds or sickness. Castenada tells me several have a disgusting and intractable disease, others are malingerers. If we secured them, I estimate we have an hour before the alarm is raised, time enough to get to the river and seize a barge.'

'And the keys of the gates are kept in the guardroom?'

'The corporal of the guard has them.'

'What of the officers? Don't they make rounds?'

'The Commandant has a German mistress in Hamburg, Captain Chatrian is fond of the bottle and Lieutenant Blanchard is not known for his zeal. They make their rounds before turning in, but we have at least an hour. Immediately after curfew has been sounded the officers go to dinner.'

'The virtues of military routine, eh?' said Drinkwater drily. 'I think you can rely on some revision of this regime if Marshal Davout hears of it.'

'I don't think anyone was perturbed, sir, as long as it was only the Spanish that were held here.'

'Well, Davout may be a new arrival in Hamburg, but he ain't ignorant of the fact that a British brig was taken; my personal effects were in his possession.'

'*What?*' Frey was incredulous, but Drinkwater hurried on without amplifying the statement. 'I want you to leave tonight, Mr Frey.'

'*Tonight*, sir?'

'Yes, tonight, that is what I said. You have objections?'

'Only insofar as Mr Q. is concerned, sir.'

'I shall attend to James, Mr Frey. I am not coming with you. You will take Captain Gilham as pilot and make for Helgoland. Keep your eyes open for a Dutch cutter of the Imperial Customs Service, otherwise drop downstream by night if possible. On arrival at Helgoland you will deliver a message to the Foreign Service agent, Mr Nicholas, and report to the senior British naval officer. Is that clear?'

'Yes, sir . . . but what about you, sir?'

'*Exactly* what happens to me rather depends on the news Castenada brings from Herr Liepmann. One thing is certain, however, I have no intention of staying here a moment longer than you. I have had my fill of hanging around waiting upon events. I shall break out with you and require only that when you secure the guards you seize a pistol, some ball, flints and powder. A sword would be useful . . .'

Drinkwater wished he had the sword cane with which he had terrified the frightful whore in Ma Hockley's flop-house. 'A French sword bayonet will do.' He smiled at Frey. 'Very well, Mr Frey, any questions?'

'No sir.'

'Until tonight then. I leave you to make all arrangements, muster your men, and so forth. Let us say our farewells now and as inconspicuously as possible. Good luck my dear young fellow.'

Drinkwater nodded abruptly at Frey, then turned on his heel. It was going to be a damnably long day and at any moment, he thought, glancing at the sentries lounging at the gate, Lieutenant Dieudonné, or the overworked staff officer, or, God forbid, Hortense Santhonax herself, might appear at the entrance, demanding his further presence in Hamburg.

Castenada proved as good as his word; nor did Liepmann abandon him. His message was both coded and cryptic; translated it read: *This thing already known. I am your servant.*

Drinkwater frowned over the last sentence, recalling Liepmann's competence as an English speaker. Was it a mere awkward formality, or did he imply a more sincere and pragmatic attachment? Castenada, in whose quarters Drinkwater had deciphered the message, caught his eye.

'I speak with Herr Liepmann, Captain. Your friend Mr Frey he tells me he is to leave this place tonight; he asks me to find some of my men to go with him. I ask him how he is to escape and, after him not telling me, I, er, persuade him that my men will not make a foolish try. He tells me by barge. I know all the barges belong to Herr Liepmann . . .'

'Yes . . . go on.'

'I told Herr Liepmann . . .'

'You *what*?' Drinkwater snapped.

'Of course, Herr Liepmann say you must take. He will not report the barge missing.' Castenada smiled. 'You understand? Herr Liepmann is your friend.'

For a moment Drinkwater felt an ungracious, xenophobic suspicion, but the value of Castenada's helpful intervention could not be denied. Besides, he had no time to waste.

'I am indebted to you, Doctor Castenada, perhaps in happier times I will be permitted the honour of repaying you.' Drinkwater felt the stiff formality of the stilted phrases sounded insincere, but Castenada bowed with equal courtesy.

'There is one other thing, sir,' Castenada said. 'Herr Liepmann suggested a possibility of helping you, *señor*, if you made your way to his house.'

Drinkwater tried to recall if he had said anything in front of Castenada to indicate whether or not he himself intended to escape with the others – and decided he had not. Perhaps Liepmann guessed from the question in the note that Drinkwater would remain behind; perhaps it was a simple offer, an expansion of that coded phrase, *I am your servant*. Drinkwater had no way of knowing, but Liepmann was one of the confraternity of Isaac Solomon, and, oddly, he inspired in Drinkwater the same confidence. He nodded at Castenada. 'Thank you.'

Castenada told him the whereabouts of Liepmann's house. 'You will find the house, it is not difficult.'

'I am most grateful.' Drinkwater paused, then added, 'Doctor Castenada, I am aware that things may be made very difficult for you after we have escaped.'

Castenada shrugged. 'After the Marquis de la Romana escaped it was difficult, but I live. A doctor can always live, especially in war.'

'Is there anything I can do for you, after I return to England. Do you have a wife to whom I can pass a message? If you do not already know, there is a British army in Spain now . . .'

'I know, Captain, and it marches into Spain and out again, and just now it is marching out again. Like Spanish armies, Captain, eh? You have a piece of song they tell to me when I am speaking English for the first time: The Grand Old Duke of York, yes? He had ten thousand men, he march them up to the top of the hill, eh, Captain? And he march them down again.'

Castenada began to laugh and Drinkwater found it impossible not to laugh with him.

'Well Gilham, are you ready?'

'As much as I ever will be. I think you're mad to stay, but good luck.'

They shook hands and took a look round the bare room with its crude wooden beds. 'I have to admit that I am not keen to sleep here,' Drinkwater said, adding, 'you will be able to take your atmosphereological observations again soon.

A gleam showed in Gilham's eye and he drew a small notebook from his pocket.

'I have not stopped, Captain.' He smiled, then asked, 'By-the-by, what *is* your name?'

Drinkwater grinned. 'Ask Frey when you get to Helgoland. He'll tell you.'

'It's Drinkwater, isn't it? That fellow called you Drinkwater.'

'Maybe. Now let us see if the others are ready?'

They peered across the parade ground. A thick fall of snow obscured the far side and they could see nothing. Curfew had already been sounded and the 'patients' had all been locked in their wooden billets. They did not have long to wait. The stolen pick, a trophy of latrine digging, split hasp and staple from the pine planks of the building.

'You're the last,' hissed Frey.

'Privilege of rank,' murmured Drinkwater, feeling the old, almost forgotten thrill of action. Outside he and Gilham joined the crouching column of silent men sheltering in the lee of the hospital wards.

'I'd be obliged if you'd bring up the rear, sir. That's where the Spanish are.' Frey whispered in his ear then motioned his men on. Even in the snow and darkness Drinkwater recognized faces. Men he had flogged, men he had sailed with round Cape Horn and into the Pacific, men who had fought the Russian line-of-battle ship *Suvorov* to a standstill. Some of them saw him and grinned. With a pang of conscience he realized his clerk Derrick was not among them. He had not asked after Derrick and the omission bothered him. Then Gilham was tapping him on the shoulder and the faces passing him were no longer familiar. Drinkwater and Gilham fell in at the rear of the column.

Like a snake they moved round the perimeter of the parade ground. By the gate they could see a yellow loom in the snow where the guardroom door stood open. It was suddenly cut out and a man's silhouette appeared. With wonderful unity, the crouching, loping column froze, every man watching the guard pitch a cigar to the ground. A faint hiss came to their straining ears and the guard turned back amid the sound of laughter. The yellow light shone out illuminating the snow again.

From the rear Drinkwater could see Frey massing his men about the door. They appeared like dark sacks until, at a signal, they moved forward amid a few shouts.

Suddenly the gates were open and Drinkwater caught a glimpse of the guardroom and half a dozen trussed and gagged men. He began to run.

Beyond the gate the road swung to the right and Drinkwater almost collided with Frey.

'Good luck, sir. Two cables down this road there is a junction. It is the road between Hamburg, Altona and Blankenese. We turn right for the river, you must go left for Hamburg.'

'I know, Castenada told me. Good luck.'

'I could only find you a sword bayonet.' Frey thrust the weapon at him. The steel was bitterly cold to the touch. When he looked up he was alone. In the snow he could hear no sound of the retreating men, nor of the struggling guards. The loom of the hospital wall threw a dark shadow and he experienced a pang of intense fear and loneliness. A moment later he was walking swiftly south to the junction with the main road.

He had no trouble locating Herr Liepmann's house. It was set back off the road behind a brick wall, but the iron gates were open and the light in the porch beyond the formal garden gave the impression that it had been illuminated for his benefit. It was, he thought as he felt the scrunch of gravel below the snow, a welcoming sight.

There were signs of wheel tracks in the snow, a recent arrival or departure, he judged, for they had not yet been covered. Perhaps the generous lighting was for the carriage, not for him. The thought made him pause. Should he simply walk up to the front door?

At his tentative knock it was opened, and guiltily he flung aside the sword bayonet.

'*Kapitan, Wilcomm* . . . please . . . you come . . .'

Liepmann held out his hand and drew Drinkwater inside. The warmth and opulence of Liepmann's house seemed like the fairyland pictures of his children's books. He had not realized how cold he had been, nor, now that the heat made him perspire and his flesh crawl, how filthy he was.

'I have clothes and *wasser*, come . . .'

It was ironic, he thought, that he should again clean himself in the house of a Jew, but he did not object. Liepmann led him to a side chamber where a servant waited upon him, standing impassively while, casting dignity aside in the sheer delight of washing off the past, Drinkwater donned a clean shirt and underdrawers. Silk breeches and stockings were produced, together with an embroidered waistcoat. Finally, the man servant held out a low-collared grey coat of a now unfashionable cut which reminded him of the old undress uniform coat of the British naval officer. As he threw his newly beribboned queue over the collar and caught sight of himself in the mirror, he caught the eye of the servant.

The man made a small, subservient gesture of approval, stood aside and opened the door. Ushering Drinkwater back into the hall, he scuttled round him and reaching the door of a withdrawing room leading from it, threw it open.

Drinkwater was disoriented by the luxury of his surroundings and entered the room seeking Liepmann to thank him for the splendour of his reception. But Liepmann was not in the room. As the door was opened a woman rose from a chair set before a blazing fire. She turned.

He was confronted by Hortense Santhonax.

PART THREE
The Snaring of the Eagle

'Napoleon went to Moscow in pursuit of the ghost of Tilsit'

NAPOLEON,
J. Bainville

Chapter Fifteen *January 1810*

Beauté du Diable

In the shock of encounter Drinkwater's mind was filled with suspicion. He felt again the overwhelming dead weight of a hostile providence with sickening desperation. Suddenly Castenada's obligingness and Liepmann's absence seemed harbingers of this entrapment. He regretted the sword bayonet cast aside in the box hedge and felt foolish in borrowed finery before this breathtakingly handsome woman.

She wore travelling clothes, a dark blue riding habit and scuffed boots, about her throat a grey silk cravat was secured with a jewelled pin that reflected the green of her eyes. Hat and cloak lay beside her chair and she held nothing more threatening than a glass of Rhenish hock.

'We have met before,' she said, tilting her head slightly to one side so that a heavy lock of auburn hair fell loose from the coils on her head. She spoke perfect English in a low and thrilling timbre.

'Indeed, Madame,' Drinkwater said guardedly, acutely aware that this woman possessed in abundance those qualities of grace and beauty for which men threw away their lives. He footed a bow, wondering at her motives.

'Will you take a glass of wine, sir?' Her cool courtliness was seductive and she turned aside, sure her offer would not be rejected.

The hock was refreshing. 'I am obliged, Madame,' he said, maintaining a fragile formality despite his inward turmoil.

'You rescued me from the *sans-culottes* on the beach at Carteret, do you remember?' she went on, watching him over the rim of her glass, 'and you were with Lord Dungarth the night I was left ashore on the beach at Criel . . .'*

*See *A King's Cutter.*

He did not respond. She had turned her coat by then, having met Edouard Santhonax and thrown her lot in with the Republicans. He let her lead the conversation to wherever it was going, wondering if she knew he had given her husband his death thrust.

'But that was a long time ago, when we were young and *impetueux*, was it not?'

She stepped closer to him so that he could smell the scent of her. She was undeniably lovely with a voluptuously mature beauty made more potent by the confidence of experience. He felt the male hunger stir him, mixed with something else: for years that damned portrait had symbolized for him the essence of a ruthless enemy, battening on the unsatisfied passions of his young manhood. Its power lay in both its imagery and association with her, a synthesis of wickedness, of desire denied, of lust . . .

'It was no coincidence that you were with Marshal Davout, was it? No coincidence that my portrait had come into his possession?'

There was an edge in her voice now, keen enough to abort his concupiscent longing.

'You are deceived as to that, Madame,' he replied. 'It is true the portrait was once my property, but Marshal Davout acquired it from a British brig wrecked on the Jutland coast. I was not aboard the brig, Madame, you have my word on it.'

'Your word? And what reliance may I put on that? You are a British naval officer, you are in the territory of the French Empire and,' she looked him archly up and down, '*that* is not a uniform, M'sieur Drinkwater.'

Oddly, he felt no apprehension at the unveiled threat, rather that cool resignation, that surrender to circumstances he had experienced in action after the fearful period of waiting was over. He knew they were nearing the crux of this strange encounter and the knowledge exhilarated him. He smiled. 'You remember my name.'

'As I remember Lord Dungarth's.' She turned away to refill her glass.

'You have met him, have you not,' probed Drinkwater, 'since the business on the beach at Criel?' He did not wait for a reply, but asked, watching her keenly, 'Did you have him blown up?'

She swung round angrily. 'No!'

'I must perforce believe you,' he said, unmoved by the violence of her denial, 'and you must believe me when I tell you it was indeed coincidence that we met in Marshal Davout's antechamber. As to your portrait, I acquired it many years ago when I captured the French National Frigate *Antigone* in the Red Sea. She was commanded by your husband, Edouard Santhonax. It was among my belongings aboard the *Tracker* when she was herself taken a fortnight or so past.'

'Why did you keep it for so long, M'sieur?' She seemed calmer, as though his explanation satisfied her, and extended her hand for his empty glass. He gave it her, but did not immediately relinquish his own hold.

'I was struck by your beauty, Madame. You had already made an impression upon me.'

She could not doubt his sincerity, but his serious tone betrayed no sudden flare of passion.

'A lasting impression?' she asked mockingly, her eyes sparkling and a smile playing about the corners of her lovely mouth.

'So it would seem, Madame, though your husband had a more palpable effect . . .' He let the glass go.

'Your wounds?' she asked as she replenished the hock. She turned and held out the refilled glass. A coquettish gleam lingered in her eyes. 'Did you know I am a widow now?'

'Yes, Hortense,' he replied, his voice suddenly harsh, 'it was I who killed your husband.'

The words escaped him, driven by a subconscious desire to hurt her, to hide nothing from so bewitching a woman with whom this extraordinary intimacy existed.

Her face turned deathly pale, her eyes searched his face and her outstretched hand trembled. 'It is not possible,' she murmured in French. He took the glass and with his left hand steadied her, but she drew back, frowning. *'Mais non . . . l'Empereur . . .'*

She seemed to be considering something, seeking the answer to some personal riddle. 'I was told he was lost in Poland . . . then the disgrace . . .'

'There was no disgrace, Madame. He was a man of uncommon zeal. He was killed at sea aboard the Dutch frigate *Zaandam*.'*

'*A Dutch* frigate? I do not understand . . .'

'Madame,' he said with sudden intensity, 'I had obtained some

*See *Baltic Mission*.

information of considerable importance to London. I believe it was acquired at your husband's expense. He was attempting to stop me reaching England . . .'

She was no longer listening. It was as though he had struck her. Two spots of high colour appeared on her cheeks and her eyes blazed. '*Diable!*'

If Drinkwater felt he had wrested the initiative from her he realized now he had made a misjudgement. She seemed suddenly to contract, not out of fear or weakness, but with the latent energy of a coiled spring.

'So, *that* is why . . .!'

And then he saw that the hatred he had kindled was introspective, for when she spoke to him again her voice was flat, explicatory, rationalizing things to herself, but in English for his benefit.

'Then you also killed Hortense Santhonax, M'sieur Drinkwater, for my husband is numbered among criminals, a man disgraced in the service of the Emperor.'

'I can assure you,' he said quietly, 'your husband did his duty to the utmost. It was his death or mine; your widowhood or my own wife's.'

She sighed and shook off her abstraction. 'Since Edouard's disgrace I have received no pension, nor a *sou* of his due pay. I was abandoned by the Emperor, left destitute.'

'I believe the manner in which I harmed your husband was of very great importance to your Emperor,' Drinkwater said. He could not tell her the enormity of the secret he had brought home, that it was nothing less than the seduction of Tsar Alexander from his alliance with Great Britain and the intention of the two autocrats to partition Europe. Nor could he tell her it was that very alliance that his present mission sought to undermine. 'He was not alone in paying a price. I have not seen my wife since the event.'

She regained her composure and raised her glass. 'Do we drink to the misfortunes of war then?'

'It seems that we must, though I suspect your motives in doing so.'

'You thought I would denounce you to Davout and you do not trust me now?'

'I am not certain of anything, though in Hamburg you seemed to be under some constraint.'

'Le bon Dieudonné?' she smiled beguilingly. 'He is a man, M'sieur Drinkwater, and like *most* men,' she went on, 'predictable. Perhaps now you understand why so loyal a servant of Napoleon Bonaparte as the Prince of Eckmühl wished to question me when my portrait was found on a British ship.'

'Then your presence in Hamburg . . .'

'Was a coincidence as much as yours.' She seemed oddly relaxed. Could she so easily forgive the author of her downfall, or was she about to manipulate him as she intimated she had Dieudonné? Her next remark gave him no cause to think otherwise.

'Shall we sit down?'

Drinkwater's reply betrayed his unease. 'Where is our host?'

'Herr Liepmann?' she shrugged. 'I asked him to leave us alone for a few moments.' She had seated herself so that she was half turned towards him in the chair beside the fire. 'Pray sit. You have all the advantage standing, and that is unfair.'

'You forgive your enemies easily.'

She laughed. 'No. You are not my enemy, M'sieur Drinkwater, you are an agent of providence. Do you believe in providence?'

'Implicitly.' He sat himself opposite her. 'So why, when providence so neatly delivered me into your power, did you not denounce me in order to rehabilitate yourself with Davout and the Emperor? And why have you come here to Liepmann's house at Altona seeking this interview with me?'

'M'sieur Drinkwater, why have *you* come here? Or to Hamburg, eh? To sell boots to the French?' She laughed, a low chuckle that vibrated in her long throat. 'La, sir, it is common gossip in Hamburg, probably in Paris by now, that two British ships, cheated of a Russian market, sought their contemptible profit elsewhere.' She paused to sip her wine, then added, 'But that would not concern a naval officer, would it?'

'Quite so,' Drinkwater said, suppressing the satisfaction that the news gave him and ignoring the sarcasm in her voice.

'I will not press you for an explanation of your presence here,' she said after a pause, studying him. 'But you should know I did not make the attempt on Lord Dungarth's life. You must lay that at the feet of Fouché, or perhaps even the Emperor himself, who knows? But I have made his acquaintance, in France twice, and once in England.' She sighed. 'Edouard was my life; without him I would be an embittered *emigrée* living on charity in an English town. But he is dead and I must live; I have friends . . .' She caught his eye and then looked quickly away. She was discomfitted and he recalled Dungarth alleging an intimacy with Talleyrand. 'They are powerful friends and I am here in Hamburg on their behalf . . .'

'Go on,' he prompted, for she seemed suddenly indecisive.

'Will you do a service for me?' she asked, looking him full in the face.

'If it does not compromise my honour.'

'Will you take a message to London, to Lord Dungarth?'

Drinkwater sat back in his chair. 'Is that the coincidence that brought you to Hamburg?'

'More, it is the coincidence that brought me here to Altona. Lord Dungarth informed me that the Jew Liepmann, a merchant of Hamburg, was in touch with the British agent on Helgoland.'

Drinkwater wanted to laugh. The tension in his belly seemed to unwind, tugging at his reactive responses.

'You are not laughing at me?'

'No, Madame,' said Drinkwater with an effort, leaning forward and holding out his glass. 'Is there a little more wine with which to toast this alliance of ours. 'Tis a pity too much lies between us to be friends.'

'You have a wife, M'sieur.' She had become serious again he poured, paying him back in his own, barbed coin. He felt again the strong animal attraction of her. For a foolish moment he persuaded himself that it was, perhaps, not unrequited

'Touché, Madame,' he murmured, dismissing the fancy as conceit. 'Yes, I will take your message, but after another matter has been attended to.'

'What is that?'

The release of a British sea officer; he is badly wounded and has a lady awaiting news of him.'

'I know, Herr Liepmann has told me.'

'He was indiscreet . . .'

'No, no, he knew I could help. He knows both you and I are dangerous; I think he would be pleased to see us both satisfied and gone.' She paused, adding, 'This is *trés domestique, n'est-ce pas*, M'sieur?'

Drinkwater looked at her across the fire, returning her conspiratorial smile.

'Very.'

'I think we should call the Jew now.'

She rose and he stood while she rang the bell-pull. Letting the braided cord fall she turned to him and took a step closer. Looking him full in the face she raised her hand and touched his cheek with the tips of her fingers.

'Providence, M'sieur Drinkwater, providence. Perhaps it has not yet finished with us.'

And reaching into the breast of her riding habit she drew out a sealed packet and handed it to him.

Chapter Sixteen *January–February 1810*

The Burial Party

Long after she had gone and Liepmann had shown him to a small bedroom beneath the attic, Drinkwater sat by the open window, the quilt from the bed about his shoulders. It was impossible to sleep, for his wounded shoulder ached and his head spun with an endless train of thought.

The mood of intimacy had been broken after Liepmann's arrival. He came with news of the church bells ringing a tocsin to alert the countryside to the breakout from the hospital. They stood in silence to listen as the Jewish merchant drew aside the heavy brocade curtains and opened the tall French windows a little. Muffled by the falling snow, they could faintly hear men shouting and dogs barking.

'They go to the Elbe,' Liepmann said, closing the windows. He turned to Hortense and asked, 'You have told the Captain about the British officer, Madame?'

'Not yet.' She turned to Drinkwater. 'I knew of the ship wreck,' she said, 'and that my portrait was taken there. It was when I knew you were not a prisoner that I thought – that I decided to seek you out. As for the wounded officer from the wrecked ship, he was too ill to be questioned. *M'sieur le marechal* will have to be content with my own explanation. They said the Englishman was dying.'

Anxiety for Quilhampton must have been plain upon Drinkwater's tired face, for Liepmann added, 'Doctor Castenada is to travel to Hamburg tomorrow to return him to Altona.' The news brought Drinkwater little relief and Liepmann had his own worries. He drew a watch from his waistcoat pocket. 'Madame, it is late . . .'

Hortense bent and retrieved her hat and cloak. Liepmann helped her.

'Do not concern yourself, Herr Liepmann,' she said in her perfect English, darting a glance at Drinkwater. 'A woman seeking an assignation may pass freely anywhere. *À bientôt* Captain Drinkwater.'

'Madame.' He bowed as she swept out, leaving him prey to misgivings as to her motives. He heard the faint crunch of her conveyance on the snow covered gravel and then Liepmann came back into the room.

'She drives herself?' he asked.

'*Ja*, she is dangerous, that one – but I think . . .' he paused, 'she gave you papers for London?' Drinkwater nodded. 'Good. I can tell you that your two ships passed Brunsbuttel this morning.'

'Excellent,' said Drinkwater. 'Herr Liepmann, the British officer of whom we spoke earlier, he is a friend. I must get him out.'

The long-suffering Liepmann nodded slowly. 'We must talk . . .'

He was dog-tired when they at last retired. He had eaten nothing since the thin burgoo Gilham had obtained for him that morning. The hock had left him with a headache but he could not compose his mind for sleep and sat at the open window listening to the distant sounds of the search parties.

The night yielded no secrets. The dying away of the shouting proved nothing. Drinkwater thought of Frey and his men drifting slowly downstream amid the ice-floes, desperately hoping they had evaded their pursuers on the river bank. He thought, too, of James Quilhampton lying delirious a few leagues away, and of Elizabeth alone in her distant bed. But again and again his thoughts returned to Hortense with a fierce mixture of desire and suspicion.

Outside the snow had stopped. A few stars appeared, and then the moon. By its light he turned over and over the sealed packet she had given him. Was it for London? Or was it a piece of incriminating evidence deliberately planted on him? And was the 'assignation' to which she claimed she was going, a meeting to denounce him, a British naval officer out of uniform in the house of a well-known Jewish merchant? Marshal Davout would delight in seizing a British spy caught red-handed in Hamburg whilst at the same time destroying the centre of the apparatus by which his master's Continental System was being cheated. In self-preservation Thiebault would corroborate the suspect Madame Santhonax's story and they could expect cavalry in Altona by dawn!

What had Hortense to lose? By so simple a denunciation she could secure the Emperor's gratitude; Santhonax's backpay and her pension would be assured. He had not only confessed to having murdered her husband, but also provided her with a reasonable explanation which, made into a deposition before an advocate or a notary in Paris, would restore her husband's reputation at a stroke.

How could she not adopt such a course of action?

And yet . . .

And yet he would still have rather spent that sleepless night in her bed than anywhere else on earth.

Drinkwater woke to the alarming jingle of harnesses. He had fallen asleep across the bed fully clothed, as he might have done at sea. He had left the window open and was chilled to the bone. On leaping up and staring from the window, his worst fears were realized. A troop of brass helmeted dragoons, their grey cloaks thrown back to reveal their green coats, stood about the drive holding their tossing horses' heads. Immediately below, where the tracks of Hortense's chaise could still be seen, Herr Liepmann stood talking to a beplumed officer. A maid emerged bearing a tray of steaming *steins* and was made much of by the cavalrymen.

At almost the same instant, or so it seemed, the manservant who had attended him the previous evening entered Drinkwater's room after a perfunctory knock. Balanced on one hand bore a tray, with the other, its index finger at his lips, he commanded Drinkwater to silence.

The aroma of coffee, bread and sausages filled the cold air and Drinkwater relaxed. The appearance of breakfast and the raised finger did not, he judged, signal betrayal. To divert himself from being caught at the window, and compelled by hunger, he settled to the welcome food.

From time to time he rose, cautiously peering down to the driveway and was finally rewarded by the sight of the troopers mounting up. A few moments later Liepmann entered the room.

'I have news.' He held up a note. 'M'sieur Thiebault writes to tell me that trade is to stop . . . for a little while, you understand.' Liepmann smiled wryly.

'Thiebault sent the message by that officer of dragoons?'

'Lieutenant Boumeester is a Dutchman; they were Dutch

dragoons. Their loyalty is, er, not good.' Liepmann shrugged. 'It is not only fat burghers who like to sugar their coffee, Captain. I have other news: Boumeester tells me more soldiers come to guard the hospital. Marshal Davout is angry.'

'So we do not have much time.'

'I go to Hamburg today. My carriage and Doctor Castenada's will –' Liepmann held out his hands, palms flat towards him and brought his finger tips together, seeking the English

'They will meet?' offered Drinkwater.

'*Ja*, and I will speak. You must stay here. If I am not come back, do not worry. Go to the place we talk about last night.'

Drinkwater nodded, yawning. 'Your servants can be trusted?'

'They are paid by me, Captain. I will tell them what you need. *Auf weidersehen*.'

They shook hands. When Liepmann had left Drinkwater lay back on the bed. A moment later he was fast asleep.

It was almost dark when he awoke. The manservant was gently shaking him and indicating a tray of food, some rough, workman's clothes and a pile of furs. Drinkwater threw his legs out of the bed and rubbed his eyes. The manservant drew back a corner of the furs. A large horse pistol, a bag of balls and a flask of powder lay exposed. The weapon reminded Drinkwater with a shock of what the night held in store. He felt his heart thump as the lethargy of sleep was driven away.

'Herr Liepmann,' he asked, 'is he returned from Hamburg?'

'Eh?' The servant frowned and shrugged.

Drinkwater tried again. 'Herr Liepmann, is-he-come-from Hamburg?'

'*Ach! Nein, nein*.' The servant shook his head, smiled and backed out.

After eating, Drinkwater changed his clothes. Over woollen undergarments he drew a coarse pair of trousers and a fisherman's smock. Two of the furs he rolled tightly and secured across one shoulder, the rest he bundled up with his cloak. Liepmann had provided a pair of sabots, but instead he drew on Dungarth's worn, green hessian boots, for they were comfortable and he had formed an attachment to them as a talisman. Pausing a moment, he shoved Liepmann's borrowed silk stockings in a pocket. Loading the pistol he stuck it in his belt. Then he picked up the sealed packet given him by Hortense. Perhaps after all he had misjudged her. Drawing a pillow-slip from the bed he improvised a bag and lanyard, pulled the latter over his head and tucked the bag inside his smock. Finally he pulled his queue from its ribbon and shook his tousled hair so that it fell about his unshaven cheeks.

By the time he had finished it was quite dark. He heard the curfew sounded at the hospital and made his way downstairs. The manservant was waiting for him and beckoned him to follow. The heat of the kitchen made Drinkwater sweat. Lantern light was reflected from rows of copper pans and a large joint of meat lay half butchered on a large scrubbed table. But apart from Drinkwater and the servant, the stone flagged room was empty, cleared of cooks and scullions by the trusted manservant who now handed Drinkwater a heavy leather satchel. A glance within revealed cheese, bread, wine, schnapps and sausage. A door from the kitchen led directly from the house and the servant lifted the latch for him. Nodding gratefully, Drinkwater slipped out into the night; it was snowing again.

Lieutenant James Quilhampton drifted in and out of consciousness. The sound of hoof beats and the swaying of his narrow stretcher seemed to have accompanied half his lifetime. Periodically, familiar faces swam before him: his mother, Captain Drinkwater, young Frey, and Derrick the Quaker clerk he had inherited from Drinkwater. There were others too: Catriona MacEwan, elusive as always, and laughing at him as she ran perpetually away. He kept trying to follow her, but every time he tripped and fell, amid the terrible crashing of breakers and hideous thunder of cannon that made the abyss into which he descended shake in some mysterious way which he did not understand. Here *they* were waiting for him. The dark man with the saw and the knife whose kindly voice spoke in a foreign language and who thrust the knife into his arm so that he felt the white fire of amputation as he had done years ago during the bombardment of Kosseir.

When the man with the knife had finished another foreigner would appear. A man with spectacles and ice-cold eyes whose bald skull seemed too large for his shoulders and who took only a single look at him before uttering a curse. The bald man was God, of course, consigning him to the pit of hell, because Catriona was laughing at him and he fell again further and further, to where the dark man with the knife reappeared, pushing his hands into Quilhampton's very flesh. He knew the dark man was the devil and that he had been judged a great sinner.

Sometimes he heard himself shouting, for words echoed in his head and once another demon peered at him, a pale face with coiled hair that framed a face lit by the light from a lantern.

He felt better when the demon had withdrawn, cooler, as if he had been reprieved from the most extreme regions of hell, though the swaying rhythm of his body went on and on.

He must have slept, for when he was next aware of anything he was quite still, lying on his back in total darkness. There was a great throbbing in his left shoulder, as though all the pain of his punishment were being applied there. He found it difficult to breathe and, with growing consciousness, felt no longer the supine, indifferent acceptance of the feverish but the horror of the trapped. He tried to move: his right arm was pinned to his side. He raised his head: his forehead met obstruction. The sweat of fear, not hypothermia, broke from his body. The crisis of his amputation had passed but they had taken him for dead.

He was in his coffin.

Drinkwater found the boat quite easily, where the road from Altona to Blankenese dipped down to the very bank of the Elbe and a shingle strand marked the ballast bed. It must have been here that Frey had first seen Liepmann's barge, for large stakes had been driven into the ground as mooring posts. The fisherman's punt was drawn up in the centre of the little beach, a light craft such as a wild-fowler or an eel-fisherman might have used. Inside was a quant and a pair of oars, and he found it fitted with nocks intended for the latter cut in the low coaming.

Ice had formed at the water's edge but he could make out the darker unfrozen water beyond the shallow bay. Carefully he stowed the satchel and the spare furs, his boots crunching on the shingle. Once he stood stock-still when a dog barked, but it was only a mongrel in the village close by. When he was satisfied with the boat he moved up the beach, wrapped himself in the cloak and settled down to wait. A low bank some five feet high gave him a little protection from the snow and he squatted down, drawing his knees up to his chin.

He had slept too well during the day to doze, and the time

passed slowly. He took his mind off the cold and the pain in his shoulder by trying to calculate long multiplication sums in his head, forcing himself to go over the working until he was confident of the answer. Faintly, borne on the lightest of breezes, he heard the chimes of a distant clock and realized it was that of the Michaelskirche in Hamburg. For him to hear it so far downstream meant that the snow was easing. When he heard ten strike, as if by magic, the sky cleared. He got up and moved cautiously about to restore his circulation; it was getting colder.

Then he heard the stumbling feet and rasping breath of men carrying something. Drinkwater crouched until he could see them, four men bearing a coffin and a fifth bringing up the rear. His heart thumping, Drinkwater rose and showed himself.

Who the four men were he had no idea beyond knowing that Liepmann would pay them well for their work and their silence, but the fifth was Castenada, bag in hand. He came forward as the mysterious bearers lowered the coffin on to the shingle beside the punt.

'Captain . . .?'

'All is quiet, Doctor.'

Both men bent anxiously over the coffin and Castenada began to lever up the lid. Drinkwater waited. He wanted to ask after Quilhampton's condition and, at the same time, to warn his friend to keep silent.

With a grunt, Castenada pulled the lid aside. In the starlight the pale blur of Quilhampton's face was suddenly revealed, his mouth agape as he fought for air.

Castenada swiftly produced a bottle of smelling salts from the bag he had brought with him. He handed it to Drinkwater.

'Under his nose!' he ordered and Drinkwater did as he was bid while the surgeon chafed his patient's cheeks. Quilhampton groaned and Castenada transferred his attention to Quilhampton's shoulder, feeling the heat of the wound through the dressing and the sleeve of his coat.

'It is God's will, Captain,' he said, 'he is past the crisis, but he will have suffered from the shock.' Castenada put a hand on Quilhampton's forehead and clicked his tongue. Quilhampton groaned again.

'James . . . James, it is me, Drinkwater. D'you understand? You are among friends now, James. D'you understand?'

'Sir? Is that you?' Quilhampton raised his right hand and

Drinkwater seized it, squeezing it harder than he had intended in the intensity of the moment.

'Yes, James, it's me. We're going for a boat ride. Be a good fellow and lie quiet.'

'Aye, aye, sir,' Quilhampton whispered, his fever-bright eyes searching the blur that he could not really believe was Drinkwater's face.

Drinkwater stood up. 'Come.' he said, motioning with his hand, 'into the boat.'

They lifted him as gently as they could, laying him on the furs Drinkwater had prepared and covering him with more furs and the blankets Castenada had packed in the coffin.

The four Germans helped Drinkwater drag the punt out over the ice, until it gave way and the boat floated.

'*Danke*,' he gasped, his breath coming out in clouds that were already freezing on the stubble about his mouth. He lifted one foot to steady the punt and half turned towards Castenada.

'Thank you, Doctor,' he hissed at the grey shape standing at the edge of the ice.

'Wait!' Castenada bent and picked up his bag and handed something to the four men. Then he was plunging awkwardly through the broken ice and, teetering uncertainly alongside Drinkwater, grabbed his arm for support.

'I come with you. He will not live without a doctor, not in this cold!'

Drinkwater looked doubtfully at the narrow punt, then patted Castenada.

'Very well! Get in!'

Drinkwater tried to steady the narrow punt as Castenada climbed clumsily aboard, but it rocked dangerously. When the surgeon had settled down Drinkwater followed, seating himself amidships on the single thwart and shipping the oars. He looked briefly ashore. The four men had already gone, taking the coffin with them. They would fill it with earth and it would be buried in the morning.

Leaning forward he could see in the stern Quilhampton's face. 'Shall we go home, Mr Q.?'

'If you please, sir,' came the uncertain, whispered reply.

'Drinkwater turned his head and murmured over his shoulder, 'Are you ready, Doctor?'

Drinkwater dipped his oars and pulled out into the stream, feeling the mighty tug of the great river. He could just make out the skyline broken by the roofs of Blankenese and the spire of its little kirk. Tugging at the oars he watched their bearing draw astern as the Elbe bore them towards the sea.

Chapter Seventeen *February 1810*

Ice

At the first brightening of the sky Drinkwater sought shelter for the hours of daylight. Helped by the river's ebb they had dropped well downstream to where the Elbe widened, spreading itself among the shallows of shingle beds and islets towards its southern bank. Drinkwater pulled them up to a small reef of gravel which extended above the flood level far enough to support a sparse growth of low alder and willow bushes. Along the northern margin of this ait the stream ran deep enough to keep it ice-free, since a shallow bend in the main channel scoured its shore.

With his hands protected by the purloined stockings, Drinkwater was warm enough from the steady exertion of pulling and Quilhampton gallantly professed he felt warm enough, wrapped as he was in furs and blankets. Castenada was rigid with cold, so that, having run the punt aground, it was only with difficulty Drinkwater managed to assist first Quilhampton and then the Spanish surgeon into the shelter of the alder grove.

It was clear that the cramps of immobility as much as the cold were affecting Castenada, and watching him, Drinkwater concluded he suffered also from a heavy conscience; in his impetuous desire to assist Quilhampton he had abandoned his other charges.

Drinkwater busied himself gathering all the dry driftwood he could find, supplementing it with dead alder and willow branches. Paring a heap of kindling with the kitchen knife given him for cutting the sausage, and catching a spark from the horse pistol, he contrived to get a fire burning.

'This wood is dry enough not to make much smoke,' he observed, fanning the crackling flames as they flickered up through the sticks.

Quilhampton stared about them. 'The air is marvellously dry,' he said, and Drinkwater looked up from his task. The light easterly wind they had experienced during the night had died away. The sun was rising as a red ball and the Elbe reflected the perfect blue of a cloudless sky. The distant river banks seemed deserted as Drinkwater painstakingly surveyed them. He had no idea how far downstream they had dropped, but by the width of the river he guessed they had made good progress.

'If the weather stays this fair,' Quilhampton said as Castenada kneeled beside him to change his dressing, 'there will be little wind to worry us.'

'True,' said Drinkwater, and both sea officers looked at the low freeboard of the punt and thought of the long, exposed stretch offshore, beyond Cuxhaven.

'Perhaps we can lay our hands on another boat,' said Drinkwater with feigned cheerfulness, though both knew the risks such a course of action entailed.

'I expect we could do something to make her more weatherly,' Quilhampton said, the perspiration breaking on his face as Castenada tried to draw the ligatures from his stump after sniffing the wound.

'Do you use the lead acetate dressing, Doctor?' Drinkwater asked, hardly able to bear the pain on Quilhampton's drawn features.

Castenada looked up. 'Ah, you know the French method, eh, Captain? The method of Larrey, yes?'

Drinkwater shrugged. 'It was shown me by a French surgeon on the *Bucentaure* during the action off Cape Trafalgar.'

Castenada frowned and rewound the bandage over Quilhampton's hot stump. 'The *Bucentaure* . . . I thought . . .' he motioned Drinkwater to help him draw on Quilhampton's coat again.

'She was French? Yes, she was. I was a prisoner.'

'Ahhh.' Castenada sat back on his haunches and stared unhappily at Drinkwater.

'Doctor, I understand something of what you are feeling. When we are a prisoner we dream of freedom: when we are free we mourn for those left behind. Is that not the case?'

'Si, si . . . yes.'

'You should not judge yourself too harshly. Left to my tender ministrations, Mr Q. here would probably be dead by now.'

Drinkwater leaned forward and patted Castenada's shoulder. 'You are an agent of providence,' he said, aware that he had borrowed the phrase from Hortense Santhonax.

Towards sunset on that short winter's day, the cooling air laid a low mist over the Elbe and Drinkwater determined on an early start. He had spent part of the day asleep, but having first eaten from the scanty stock of supplies provided by Liepmann, he had observed the build-up of ice about them, certain it would encroach further during the following night. Having taken the precaution of placing the largest stones he could find on the islet in the fire, he raked them out and with Castenada's help, succeeded in rolling them in a blanket and placing them in the punt between Quilhampton's legs.

'Insurance against freezing my assets, eh, sir?' joked Quilhampton as the boat bobbed with its forefoot still aground on the shingle beach.

After each gulping a slug of schnapps, Drinkwater and Castenada shoved off and clambered in, settling themselves for the long night ahead.

'Very well gentlemen,' Drinkwater said, leaning forward with his oar blades just above the water, 'are we ready to proceed towards England?'

'I am ready to go to España,' chuckled Castenada from the bow and Drinkwater exchanged glances of amusement with Quilhampton.

Drinkwater set himself an easy pace, knowing it was not difficult to row for many hours with a favourable current, but the cold attacked his legs at once, for they were not subject to the constant movement of his upper body. Quilhampton kicked his blankets aside below the extended furs and shared the warmth of the stones.

'I'm obliged to you, James.'

They could hear Castenada's teeth chattering and invited the surgeon to sample more schnapps until all that could be heard from the bow of the punt was a light snore.

'I'm sorry about your arm, James,' he said, tugging an oar clear of a pancake of ice that spun, ghostly, on the dark water.

'Having already lost half, the remainder don't come as so much of a shock,' Quilhampton jested feebly. They fell silent and Drinkwater knew Quilhampton was thinking of Catriona.

'How did you lose it?' he asked, seeking to divert his friend's tortured mind. 'I know it was in defence of the *Tracker*, but specifically?'

'Foolishness,' Quilhampton said, a grim chuckle in his voice. 'Like most precipitate acts, it was one of pure folly. I had engaged a big tow-headed Danish officer, hand-to-hand. The fellow had the reach of an octopus and I had to get inside his guard, and damned quickly. He came at me like the devil and thinking I had a subtle advantage, I put up my timber hand and parried his low thrust, at the same time twisting my trunk to extend my own sword. The fellow was quicker than I thought: he disengaged, cut under my false hand and ran his blade to the hilt, clean through my elbow.'

'What happened to him?' Drinkwater asked, curiously.

'He took Frey's sword at the end,' Quilhampton said miserably, relapsing into silence. After a while he too slept.

Drinkwater pulled steadily at the oars, looking over his shoulder from time to time. By now his night vision was acute and he could make out the odd feature on the nearer bank. At last he sensed the ebb ease, then the slack water and the first opposing thrust of the flood. He pulled closer to the shore, seeking the counter-current, determined not to seek a resting place until dawn.

The rhythmic exertion of his body lulled him and he allowed his mind to wander. He felt a surge of confidence in himself. Now that the outcome depended solely upon his own efforts he felt a greater ease than he had enjoyed at the mercy of Thiebault and Liepmann, and even Captain Littlewood.

As for Hortense, he was certain now that she had not betrayed him. The papers that he felt stiff against his breast were genuine enough, and he recollected other facts to buttress her claims. He remembered Lord Dungarth telling him he had been in France twice, the same number of times Hortense had said she had met his lordship there. Moreover, Hortense had added that she had also seen Dungarth in England, a fact that might indicate she spoke the truth, for her English was flawless and she had lived there as an *emigrée* during the nineties.

It seemed that Dungarth had been right, all those years ago, in setting her free on the beach at Criel. If he had thought that having turned her coat once, she might do the same thing again, he had been proved correct.

Despite the desperation of their position, there were other considerations that gave him a ridiculous pleasure as he listened to the snores emanating from both ends of the punt. The squalid and shameful subterfuge he had embarked upon in Ma Hockley's whore-house in order to sow the seed in the informing ear of Mr Fagan, and the consequences of the Russian convoy and its near disastrous end on the island of Helgoland had at least achieved more than he had expected. The tale of British trade with Russia had been successfully carried to Custom House officers and a Prince-Marshal of the French Empire. That Hortense had joked about it was evidence enough that it would likely reach the ears of the Emperor Napoleon. He had, he thought, as he stared up at the star-spangled arch of the sky, every reason to be modestly pleased with himself . . .

The ice-floe was heavy and spun the punt round so that Drinkwater almost lost his starboard oar.

As he grabbed for it his arm was soaked to the elbow and the freezing water chilled him enough to make him gasp. A moment later the wildly rocking punt grounded and his passengers woke.

'God damn,' Drinkwater swore and easing a booted leg over the coaming, he tested the depth of the water. It took him twenty full, laborious minutes to work the punt back into navigable water, twenty minutes during which he discovered that Lord Dungarth's cast-off hessian boots, though of a fashionable style, let water damnably.

'I wonder,' he said in an attempt to restore the morale of his party after the incident, 'whether our Northampton manufactures are entirely waterproof?'

They holed up for the second day on a larger, lower islet than the first. It did not yield the same amount of dry wood and they spent a miserable day. Their only high spot was in getting Quilhampton on to his feet and making him dance about a little, supported between Drinkwater and Castenada.

'Who looks a damn fool now?' Drinkwater asked as, puffing and blowing, they eased the invalid back on to his furs. As the sun westered they plundered the diminishing stock of food in Liepmann's satchel.

As the time for departure approached, Drinkwater tried to search the river ahead, but he had no vantage point and, apart from discovering the main stream appeared to swing a little to the north-west, he gleaned little information.

They set out an hour before sunset. The ice in mid-river was more noticeable, and Drinkwater had frequent trouble with floes impeding the oars as he waited for the ebb tide. The punt bumped and spun violently at times, so that stifled grunts of pain came from Quilhampton. Castenada became increasingly silent as the desperation of their plight dawned upon his landsman's perception.

In the small hours they ran aground for the sixth or seventh time. Drinkwater got out and paddled, splashing round the punt, aware that as much ice as water lay underfoot.

It seemed colder than ever, the river running over a vast area of shallows which had frozen solid where pools had formed between the gravel ridges. Walking in a circle about the boat to the limit of the painter, Drinkwater discovered a section of shingle that rose two or three feet above the water. Returning to the punt he ordered Castenada on to his feet and between them they manhandled first Quilhampton and then the punt out of immediate danger.

Casting about they discovered the ubiquitous supply of driftwood which proved sufficient to light a fire, though the effort expended with flint and steel tested Drinkwater's patience to the utmost.

'We must shield the fire glow from observation,' he said, indicating Castenada's cloak, 'I have no idea where we are, though the villages about Cuxhaven cannot be too far away now.'

In blankets, cloaks and furs they lay as dose to the fire as they could. Shivering and miserable the three of them fell into a light sleep so that, after their exertions, dawn found them still unconscious.

The nightmare assailed Drinkwater shortly before dawn. It was an old dream, filled with the noise of clanking chains that might have been the sound of a ship's chain pump, or the fetters of the damned in hell. There was a woman's face in the dream, pallid and horrible, and she chanted dreadful words that he heard as clearly as if they were being whispered in his ear:

Thy soul is by vile fear assail'd which oft
So overcasts a man, that he recoils
From noblest resolution, like a beast
At some false semblance in the twilight gloom.

He could not make out whether or not it was the face of Hortense or Elizabeth, or some harpy come to warn him, but he woke to her scream and knew the dream for an old foreboding

He was bathed in perspiration and felt a constriction in his throat presaging the onset of a quinsy.

The long scream dissolved into the unimagined reality of a distant trumpet note.

Drinkwater was on his feet in an instant, hobbling with cramp. He looked about them.

'God's bones!'

During the night they had become separated from the main stream of the river and he had pulled them unwittingly into an extensive area of shallows bordering the southern shore. The sand and gravel banks here gave way to marsh and reed bed, a landscape frozen solid, as was the water about them. Here were no comforting deep runs of moving water, instead the petrified glitter of acres of thick ice, of brittle, frosted reeds and ice-hardened, snow-covered samphire.

Beyond the marsh, not a mile away on rising ground that commanded a view of the river, stood a village, its church spire clearly visible. Drinkwater scanned the lie of the land further west. Roughly equidistant with the village a broad sweep of the Elbe ran inshore, separated from their present resting place by the ice.

Crouching low, his leg muscles tortured with the pain of cramp, he returned to the encampment.

'Wake up,' he hissed, shaking Castenada and Quilhampton. 'There are troops in a village not a mile away. Wake up!'

Drinkwater slung the satchel over Quilhampton's good shoulder and helped him to his feet. Then he and Castenada gathered up their coverings and the three of them hurried towards the punt. Stowing their belongings Drinkwater bent to the task.

'James, I want you to walk very slowly, testing the ice, ahead of us. Doctor, lift that damned bow . . . the boat, man, the boat . . .'

They broke the punt out of its bed of ice and began to slide it over the ice, negotiating the frozen reeds and finding the going easier as they moved away from the bank. They were within half a mile of open water when Quilhampton, tottering uncertainly, looked back. Drinkwater saw his jaw fall as he stared over their struggling shoulders. He turned his head, almost losing his footing on the ice.

'God's bones!'

'Dios!' Castenada crossed himself, an unconscious, instinctive gesture.

The cavalryman sat on his mount just below the village and watched them. Their suddenly increased exertion confirmed his suspicions. He wheeled his horse and cantered up the snow-covered incline, jerking the animal's head round again as he broke the skyline. Turning in his saddle, one hand on the rump of his horse, he appeared to be shouting to someone behind him, then he was facing them, and kicking his horse forward.

As he spurred towards them they saw the sunlight glint on the curved blade of his sabre.

Chapter Eighteen *February 1810*

The Scharhorn

'James! Can you help?'

Quilhampton, pale from the effort of walking, nodded and took the painter in his right hand. Drinkwater motioned Castenada to the stern and fiddled with the toggled beckets that retained the quant pole alongside the coaming of the punt. Hefting it at its centre he pulled it clear and swung clumsily round, wheeling it as Castenada and Quilhampton ducked.

'Get moving!' he ordered, turning to face the horseman. In the wake of his struggling companions he backed along the scored ice with the painful slowness of retreat. The cavalryman was urging his nervous horse on to the ice. Somewhere behind him the shrill rapid notes of the alert cut through the bitter morning air. Letting one end of the long quant drop on to the ice, Drinkwater drew the pistol from his waistband, throwing his cloak back over his shoulders to leave his arms free.

The cavalryman had succeeded in getting his horse on to the ice and it skittered nervously, throwing up its reined-in head so that flecks of bloody foam flew from its mouth. Drinkwater waited, the advancing man clearly visible, the scarlet pelisse hooked to the neck, the overalls and the tall-plumed busby marking him as an officer of the horse chasseurs of the Imperial Guard. Drinkwater knew in his gut that it was Lieutenant Dieudonné.

At fifty paces Drinkwater lifted his pistol. The misfire clicked impotently in the clear air and he thrust the weapon back in his belt.

'Pox!'

He gripped the quant and lifted it across his body like a quarterstaff. The uneven weight of the thing made him unsteady on the ice and he slithered, recovering his balance with difficulty. He looked back. Quilhampton and Castenada seemed a long way away from him, but so did the water. With a dry mouth he confronted Dieudonné.

'Ah! Capitaine Boire l'eau, eh?' The man was grinning beneath the fierce moustaches as he kicked his reluctant mount forwards. The horse was angled in his approach, apprehensively rolling its eyes. Dieudonné's left hand held both reins tight and the poor beast's neck was arched by the restraint. Drinkwater saw Dieudonné was trying to pull the animal's head round in order to clear his sword arm for the line of attack.

Cautiously Drinkwater slid his feet forward. He knew he had one chance, and one only, for his weapon was too cumbersome to retrieve after a first thrust.

Dieudonné succeeded in getting the horse's head swung long before Drinkwater's improvised lance was within striking distance, but his cautious advance had closed the distance a little more than the Frenchman had reckoned on.

The charger, mouth foaming and teeth bared as it fretted on the bit, loomed over him. Drinkwater foreshortened his weapon and allowing himself to be carried by the inertia of its swing, flung himself forward, thrusting the lance not at Dieudonné, but at the animal's legs. At the same time Dieudonné leaned forward, cutting down over the crupper, the sabre whistling past Drinkwater's head as he slipped and fell headlong. The charger reared with a screeching neigh, lifting its front hooves clear of the ice.

For a moment it pawed the air in a furious attempt to keep its balance but its weight, bearing now on its hind legs, was too much for the ice. The sudden and ominous crack provided Drinkwater with the stimulus he needed to galvanize his aching muscles. As he rolled clear of the horse it reared still further. Caught off balance Dieudonné slipped sideways, lost his left stirrup and lurched towards Drinkwater. He attempted to recover his sword, which dangled from its martingale, but Drinkwater seized his wrist and pulled back with all his weight. With a crash, the ice gave way beneath the horse and it was plunging up and down, neighing frantically and tossing its head as the cold water struck its loins. The turmoil broke the ice further. Dieudonné floundered half in the water, desperately trying to keep in the saddle and recover the sword that had slipped from his wrist. Drinkwater retreated on to firm ice, then saw the chasseur's sabre lying between them, on the edge of the hole the plunging horse was enlarging every second in its terror. Drinkwater edged forward; with the toe of a hessian boot he caught the sabre and drew it from Dieudonné's reach.

'Sir! Sir!'

As he bent to pick up the gilt-mounted sabre, Quilhampton's voice impinged on his consciousness. He looked round. Castenada and Quilhampton had the punt poised on the ice-edge. Quilhampton was waving frantically for him to follow. Beyond Dieudonné's desperately struggling mount more men, on foot and carrying carbines or muskets, were advancing across the frozen salt marsh.

He looked again at Dieudonné. The man was up to his breast in water. The terrible shock of the cold was plain on his face.

'M'aider! M'aider, M'sieur, j'implore . . .!'

Drinkwater thrust the long quant pole across the hole. *'Votre amis attendez-vous,'* he managed in his best French and turned away.

The ice grew dangerously thin at the water's edge, but Quilhampton and Castenada, by luck or foresight, had found a ridge of gravel and launched the punt from its farther limit.

'Get in!' Drinkwater gasped as he slipped and slithered towards them.

Quilhampton lay in the stern as he reached them. 'Give the Doctor your pistol!' he called and Drinkwater did as he was bid, tumbling into the punt and collapsing breathlessly on the single, centre thwart. He felt the punt lurch and roll as Castenada clambered in, the big horse pistol in one hand, the powder flask in the other. A musket ball buzzed past them, then another, and they heard the sharp cracks bite the still air.

'You have to row, sir,' Quilhampton was saying, rousing him. 'Neither I nor the Doctor can do it, sir! You *have* to row!'

Still gasping, Drinkwater realized that he had stupidly considered himself safe once he reached the boat, so great had been his concentration in dismounting Dieudonné.

He shipped the oars and spun the boat round. What he saw when he was facing the shore spurred him to sudden, back-breaking effort. Twenty or thirty dismounted hussars, some kneeling, some standing, were aiming their carbines at the retreating boat and he could see the innocent puffs of smoke as they fired, and then the skilful manipulation of cartridge and ramrod. Little spurts of water jumped up all round the boat and a section of the coaming disintegrated in a shower of splinters, one of which struck Castenada in the face. He let out a yelp and the punt was struck again while several balls leapfrogged across the river's surface like stones thrown by boys playing ducks and drakes.

Mercifully the tide was ebbing and swept them swiftly out of range. As he pulled away, Drinkwater could see a group of men go to the assistance of Lieutenant Dieudonné and the last he saw was his charger being hauled from the broken ice.

'Are we making water, James?' Drinkwater asked anxiously.

'No, I don't think so. We've one hole near the waterline, but we can plug that.'

'With what?'

'We'll try a piece of sausage, sir.'

And looking at his friend leaning outboard, his one good hand thrusting a long slice of Liepmann's *wurst* into a shot hole, he began to laugh with relief.

They ate the rest of the sausage by way of breakfast and Castenada dressed his own wound. He also expressed his anxiety about Quilhampton and the delay in drawing the ligatures from blood vessels, pointing to the high colour forming on the young man's cheeks.

'I'm all right, sir,' Quilhampton protested, 'never felt better.'

'You are light-headed, James, Doctor Castenada is right. You have lost a lot of blood and these present trials must be placing a strain upon you.'

'Fiddlesticks, sir, er, beggin' your pardon,' he added, and Drinkwater nodded silent agreement with Castenada. They did not have any time to lose.

The skirmish with Lieutenant Dieudonné had thoroughly alarmed Drinkwater, for Dieudonné had made a jest of his real name and it was impossible not to ascribe that knowledge to any source other than Hortense.

To divert his mind from the agony he felt in his arms and especially his shoulder, he tried to reason out her actions. Had she really betrayed him?

If she had done so immediately on her return to Hamburg, Dieudonné would have caught him napping in the bed at Liepmann's where, had she acted with malice aforethought, she could have had him bound and trussed as a spy.

Or had she given him time to get away and *then* denounced him, as though suddenly recollecting the identity of the man she had seen when brought before Davout? If so she played a bold game of double bluff.

To deceive the Marshal she could have pretended to fret and puzzle over the origin of that battered portrait. Having at last recognized the stranger in the Marshal's antechamber, what would be more natural than to seek an interview with him? She could then share her recollection and suggest the Englishman Drinkwater had come to Hamburg for almost any nefarious purpose she liked to fabricate!

Such an action would clear her own name and might restore her to the Emperor's favour and her husband's withheld pension.

Dieudonné catching up with them on the river bank was sheer bad luck, for Hortense had no way of knowing how long it took to drop a boat down the Elbe, while the fact that it was Dieudonné – an officer of an élite unit employed on missions of delicacy and daring – who was poking about the marshes east of Cuxhaven, argued strongly for the accuracy of Drinkwater's guesswork.

'Town ahead.' Quilhampton struggled into a sitting position, pointing. His words jerked Drinkwater back to the present. A single glance over his shoulder told him the place was Brunsbuttel, and the tortuously slow way in which features on the bank were passing them told its own tale: they would pass the town in broad daylight against a flood tide.

For a moment Drinkwater rested on his oars.

'Flood tide's away,' remarked Quilhampton.

'Aye.' Drinkwater thought for a moment, then said, 'That officer, I know who he is, James – no time to explain, but he wasn't just on the lookout for escaped prisoners like Frey and his men. He was looking for us. For me to be precise.' He began to tug on his oars again, inclining the bow of the punt inshore.

'I daresay the alarm's been raised on both banks, but word may not have reached Brunsbuttel yet that they are after three men in a duck punt. D'you see?'

'Because that scrap was on the south side of the river?'

'*Si, si*, that is right,' exclaimed Castenada from the bow.

'So we will pull boldly past Brunsbuttel and you, James, will lie down while you, Doctor, will wave if you see someone ashore taking an interest.'

'*Wave*, Captain, I do not understand . . .'

'Like this,' snapped Quilhampton, waving his only hand with frantic exasperation.

'Ah, yes, I understand, *wave*,' and he tried it out so that, despite themselves, Drinkwater grinned and Quilhampton rolled his eyes to heaven.

There was less ice now, the salt inflow from the sea inhibiting its formation, although there were pancakes of the stuff to negotiate close to the shore.

Drinkwater pulled them boldly past the town. In the corner of a snow-covered field a group of cows stood expectantly while a girl tossed fodder for them. A pair of fishing boats lay out in the river half a cable's length apart, a gill net streamed between them. Their occupants looked up and watched the punt pull slowly past them. One of them shouted something and Castenada waved enthusiastically. The man shouted again and Castenada shouted back, revealing unguessed-at talents as a German speaker, for the fishermen laughed.

'What did you say?' Drinkwater asked anxiously.

'They ask where we go and I tell them to Helgoland for some food!'

'The truth is no deception, eh?' Drinkwater grunted, tugging at the oar looms. 'I did not know you spoke German.'

'In Altona it is of help to speak German and I speak already some English. When these men come from the English ship, I make my English better. I speak French too . . .'

They were almost past Brunsbuttel when Drinkwater caught sight of the sentry. The bell-topped shako of a French line regiment was familiar to him by now. Perhaps he stared too long at the fellow, or perhaps the soldier had been attentive during his pre-duty briefing, but Drinkwater saw him straighten up and stare with interest at the boat.

'Hey! *Arrête! Halte!*' The sentry's voice carried clearly over the water, but Drinkwater pulled on as the man unslung his musket and aimed it at them. He seemed to have second thoughts, his head lifting, then lowering again as he sighted along the barrel. Just then an officer ran up and the man raised his gun barrel to point at the escaping punt. When he at last fired they were out of range and the ball plopped harmlessly into their wake.

'*Dios!*' said Castenada crossing himself.

'James,' asked Drinkwater when he was certain they were clear, 'about south-west of us, somewhere on the larboard bow, can you see the Kugel beacon at Cuxhaven?'

'I see it!' said Castenada, pointing ahead.

Quilhampton raised himself and nodded. He seemed flushed again. 'Yes, yes, it's there all right.' He slumped back amid the furs.

'Very well,' Drinkwater went on, suppressing his anxiety over Quilhampton's deteriorating condition. 'That is where they will intercept us. Dieudonné – that officer – is bound to raise the alarm there. There ain't a black-hulled Dutch cutter in sight, is there? She's a big Revenue Cruiser . . .'

He stopped rowing and looked round himself, for Quilhampton appeared to be asleep. Castenada was staring at the horizon. 'I do not see any ships, Captain . . .'

Drinkwater touched his arm and pointed anxiously at Quilhampton in the stern.

The doctor frowned and shook his head. 'He is not good.' Castenada made a move as though to rise and pass Drinkwater, but Drinkwater shook his head.

'No, no, Doctor, you will have us over . . . listen, I think I may have an idea . . .'

He rowed on, occasionally glancing over his shoulder. After a while Castenada asked, 'Where is this idea, Captain?'

'Ahead of us, Doctor, a secondary channel I recall from the chart, to the north of the Vogel Sand. We do not have to pass close to Cuxhaven and it is not many hours until dark now.'

'You would like more food?'

'Yes, and the last of that wine unless you want it for him,' he nodded at Quilhampton.

'No, it is better for you now. We are near the ocean, yes?'

'Yes.'

'And Helgoland is not far?'

'Far enough,' said Drinkwater grimly.

The end of the short winter's day came prematurely with an overcast that edged down from the north. Once the sun was obscured the leaden cheerlessness circumscribed their visible horizon. More snow began to fall. Their only consolation was that they were safe from pursuit, but this had its corollary in that they could see nothing.

The ebb came away at last and Drinkwater and his companions devoured the last of the food. All they had left was a mouthful of schnapps each, which they determined to preserve. The question of where their next meal was coming from no one mentioned.

Drinkwater was reasonably certain that they had entered the secondary channel north of the New Ground which led past the Vogel Sand, but beyond that he had no idea where they were in the darkness.

They had been nearly ten hours in the punt without being able to stretch their cramped limbs and this, combined with the cold, the aches of old wounds and general fearfulness reduced their spirits to rock bottom.

To make matters worse Quilhampton was sliding in and out of consciousness and relapsing into fever. Castenada was silent, a man of undoubted courage, thought Drinkwater, but nonetheless profoundly regretting his impetuous action in joining them.

For his own part Drinkwater was suffering from a severe quinsy, the chronic pain in his distorted shoulder and the debilitating effects of having plied the oars for three days. He had no real idea where they were and, worn out with worry and exertion, he dozed off.

He woke with Castenada shaking him. The punt was aground, the pale loom of a sand hummock seemed almost totally to surround them.

'It must be low water,' he muttered, dragging himself with difficulty from the seductive desire to sleep. He had a faint notion that to sleep was to be warm . . .

'Is this Helgoland?' Castenada asked, and the ridiculous question finally dragged an unwilling Drinkwater back to his responsibilities.

'No . . . no, it ain't Helgoland, though I'm damned if I know where it is.'

With a tremendous effort he drew back the furs over his legs and forced himself to crouch. The silk stockings he wore as gloves were barely adequate to keep the cold from paralysing his hands, but somehow he levered himself so that he could swing his feet over the side.

The hessian boots leaked immediately and the freezing sand gave beneath him. He knew that at the tideline, where the water still drained from the recently uncovered sand, it was not dense enough to support any weight. Higher up though, where the sand had dried, it would bear and he floundered as quickly as he could through the dragging quicksand, taking the painter with him. He found firmer footing and dragged the punt as high as he was able, until Castenada joined him and, with Quilhampton's weight in the stern, they got it higher still.

The bare sandbank yielded no fuel but the movement restored their circulation. The pain of returning feeling was intense, beyond imagination, so that they both crouched apart on the sand, sobbing uncontrollably until it eased and they were able to act together again.

'*Dios*,' muttered Castenada speaking for both of them. 'Never, not the pain of the stone, nor sear of the brand can compare with that!'

When they had recovered, Drinkwater said, 'We must leave Quilhampton his furs, Doctor, but you and I must give up two of ours.'

'I do not understand.'

'We have fifteen leagues yet to go, across the open sea. The boat is not suitable: she is too low. If there is any wind the water will come in . . .'

'Ah, yes, I understand. You need furs to cover . . .' Castenada made draping gestures over the well of the boat with his hands.

'Yes, like an Eskimo's *kayak*, then we have a good chance. You will have shelter underneath.'

They found a long eel-line stowed in the forepart of the boat and with this and the skilleting knife they fashioned covers and passed lashing beneath the hull. Despite the risk of incoming breakers, Drinkwater decided to brave the rising tide. He knew that the tides were neap and hoped the bank they had landed on might not cover at all. If it looked like doing so they might have to make a portage to its eastern side and launch from there. Besides, he thought to himself, accepting the cogent argument of the only certainty, he was lost and he needed daylight to get his bearings.

He was certain afterwards that had they spent that night in the Elbe, fire or no, they would have perished. Their bodily reserves were almost exhausted and the cold of a land frost would undoubtedly have killed them. As it was the surrounding sea mitigated the temperature and this helped sustain them until they faced another bleak dawn.

The tide was already rising and they had to drag the punt higher and higher several times. The eel-line did not part and they decided prudence dictated they launch on the side of the bank away from the incoming breakers. They were low enough, but both men were anxious to avoid getting wetter than was absolutely necessary.

At the first light Castenada peeled off Quilhampton's dressing and sniffed the stump. Drinkwater waited for his diagnosis. He knew the slightest whiff of putrefaction signalled Quilhampton's inevitable death. His heart beating, Drinkwater bent over the exposed wound, shielding it from the cold as Castenada tugged the ligatures. Quilhampton stirred, opened his eyes and grunted as Castenada, with an appreciative hiss, drew the ligatures cleanly.

'I think his fever is not so much from this,' said the surgeon, replacing the lead acetate dressing, 'as from this . . .' He nodded about them. Quilhampton was asleep again. 'He is strong but,' Castenada clicked his tongue and shook his head, 'one more night . . . I don't know.'

The wind came up with the sun, a northerly breeze that kicked up vicious little waves and produced the low grumble of surf on the shoal.

Drinkwater knew the advancing tide would shortly cover their retreat and told Castenada they would have to make a move. Crossing himself the Spaniard nodded. They pushed the punt into the water and, wet to the knees, struggled aboard. Immediately the difference in their circumstances was obvious. They were no longer borne on the smooth, dark bosom of the Elbe; now they faced the open sea. It was more difficult to row and they realized very soon that they would make little progress under oars.

Drinkwater caught a glimpse of a distant beacon. He was certain that it was not the Kugelbacke at Cuxhaven, but could not remember how many beacons there were in the outer estuary, and though he recalled some on Neuwerk he could see no sign of the island. The beacon lay to the southward of them, and it seemed that during the early part of the night, just before they had grounded again, the ebb had carried them through one of the gullies that cut into the Vogel Sand, so that they had travelled south instead of west.

All that grey forenoon Drinkwater kept the frail craft hove-to with the northerly wind on the starboard bow and the flood tide setting them back into the Elbe.

They were too low in the water to see anything beyond the wave caps lifting on a horizon less than two miles away. Once they saw a buoy and Drinkwater tried desperately to reach it so that they could secure to it and await the ebb but the strength of the tide was against him and he was compelled to give up and it was soon lost to view. Then, some time towards noon, the sky began to clear again and the wind backed into the north-west and freshened, cutting up a rough sea that threatened, with the turn of the tide in their favour, to get far worse.

Two hours later Drinkwater lost an oar. Stupidly he watched it drift away, unable to do anything about it. Castenada said nothing. He was prostrated with sea-sickness, vomiting helplessly over the fur cover so that the wind bore the sharp stench to even Drinkwater's stupefied senses.

The punt lay a-hull, rolling its way to windward and at the same time being blown south. Darkness found them aground again, no more than a few miles from their starting-off point, having made good a course of west-south-west.

Castenada and Drinkwater floundered carelessly ashore. Their only thought was for Quilhampton and it occurred to Drinkwater in a brief moment of lucidity that they were wasting their time: Quilhampton was going to die because they were incapable of saving him.

They sat shivering on the punt listening to the delirious ramblings of their charge whilst they shared the last of the schnapps.

'In the bull-fight,' Castenada said, 'they watch to see if the bull makes a good death.'

Drinkwater nodded sagely and said, 'Scharhorn . . . this is the Scharhorn sand. . .'

He was pleased with himself for remembering the chart, and grinned into the darkness.

'That is not a good name,' said Castenada.

Drinkwater never had any recollection of the succeeding hours until waking to the grim thunder of breakers. The noise reverberated through the very sand upon which he lay and it was perhaps this appeal to his seaman's instinct that roused him from a slumber intended by nature to be his last. But this may not have been the only cause of his awakening, for a large, predatory herring gull had already drawn blood from his cheek and his sudden movement sent the bird screeching into disgruntled flight.

He sat up. It took him several minutes to fathom out his whereabouts and how he came to be lying exposed on the Scharhorn Sand. He cast about him and spotted Castenada, some distance off, and Quilhampton lying as though dead in the punt. Just beyond his friend, the white mist of spume rising over incoming breakers finally goaded him to action. The sudden fear of drowning overcame the pain of movement. He got to his feet and began to hobble towards Castenada. He tried shouting, but his quinsy and the schnapps he had drunk before his collapse made his throat dry. He began to feel the first tortures of severe thirst.

And then he saw it: not half a furlong distant, rising from the sand on a framework of massive timbers, the Scharhorn beacon.

Chapter Nineteen *February–April 1810*

Refuge, Rescue and Retribution

Acting Lieutenant Frey stood beside Lieutenant O'Neal on the heeling deck of the twelve-gun cutter *Alert*. From time to time he went forward, levelled a battered telescope and scanned the horizon. It was broken at two points: by the Vogel sand to the north and the Scharhorn to the south. Beyond the Scharhorn lay the low island of Neuwerk with its stone tower and beacons. The crew of the alarm vessel marking the entrance of the River Elbe – technically the enemy – waved cheerfully as the heavily sparred cutter with its huge gaff mainsail carried the wind and tide on her daily reconnaissance into the estuary. The deck-watch on the *Alert* waved back.

Frey walked aft again and shook his head.

'Nothing?' asked O'Neal in his Ulster accent.

'Nothing,' said Frey disconsolately.

'We'll take the tide up as far as Cuxhaven,' O'Neal said encouragingly.

The incoming tide had covered the Scharhorn Sand by the time Drinkwater had got Castenada and Quilhampton up on to the massive beacon. The heavy baulks of timber tapered to a platform halfway up, access being provided by a ladder so that during the summer months carpenters from Cuxhaven could repair the ravages of the winter gales. Above the platform the structure rose further, culminating in a vertical beam of oak about which, in the form of a vast cage, the distinctive topmark was constructed.

The effort of gaining the safety of the beacon cost them all dear. The three of them lay about the platform as though dead, and it was more than an hour before coherent thoughts began to stir Drinkwater's fuddled brain from the lethargy of relief at having found a refuge. He began to contemplate the bleak acceptance of eventual defeat. He knew death was now inevitable and thirst more than cold and exposure was to be its agent. They were still reasonably well provided for against the cold, having salvaged all the furs and blankets from the punt. Damp though they were, the furs provided a windbreak and some means of conserving their body heat. They were already thirsty and the task of dragging Quilhampton and their own unwilling bodies up the beacon made it worse.

It was not long before Drinkwater could think of nothing other than slaking his burning throat. His tongue began to feel thick and leathery, and his head ached. The more the desire for water increased, the more fidgety he found he became, fretting irritably, moving about and eventually standing up, clinging shakily to an upright and staring wildly round about them. He could see to the east the low island of Neuwerk with its tower and beacons, and beyond it the masts and yards of two or three anchored ships. Slowly, almost uncomprehendingly, he swung his red-rimmed eyes to the north.

The cutter was about two miles away, its mainsail boomed out as it ran east into the mouth of the Elbe. With despairing recognition he took it for the Dutch customs cruiser. Only after a few minutes did he realize the cutter had no lee boards, that the stem was ramrod straight, not curved, and the long running bowsprit was of an unmistakably English rig. He had been deceived! The foreshortened mainsail had given the impression of having the short narrow head of Dutch fashion, but this was no Netherlander, this was a British naval cutter, and now he could see the blue ensign at her peak as she passed on her way upstream toward Cuxhaven.

Hope beat again in his breast.

'They haven't gone up river yet, then,' said O'Neal, standing beside the two men leaning on the *Alert*'s tiller and nodding at the three ships anchored in Neuwerk Road.

'No,' said Frey, 'and that bodes no good for Captain Drinkwater.'

It was common knowledge at Helgoland, now that Littlewood had brought back the *Ocean* and the *Galliwasp* and Frey and his men had arrived in a stolen sailing barge, that a grand deception had been carried out against the French. It had never been

Drinkwater's intention that all the ships of the abandoned convoy should be used to deceive the enemy. Under the terms of the agreement with Thiebault, they were to have gone only as far as Neuwerk, there to await the release of *Ocean* and *Galliwasp*, a tempting surety for the good behaviour of the French.

Drinkwater's failure to appear; the complications arising from the appearance of *Tracker*'s survivors and unbeknown to Nicholas; Hamilton and Littlewood at Helgoland, the temporary interdiction on trade imposed by Thiebault as a result of Davout's arrival, meant that the ships had remained anchored off Neuwerk under enemy guns.

O'Neal studied them through his glass. 'The Yankee colours are all flying hauled close-up,' he observed, the precaution of having them-fly their American colours on slack halliards having been adopted as a secret signal that things were not well on board.

A tiny puff of white smoke appeared on the island and a ball plunged into the sea two cables on their starboard bow. The ritual shot had been fired at them every time they sailed into the estuary, but providing the cutter's reconnoitring sorties did no more than establish the emptiness of the river, they were otherwise unopposed. After an hour when they were well within sight of the Kugel beacon and the lighthouse at Cuxhaven, O'Neal shook his head. 'Damn all!'

'Aye . . .'

O'Neal raised his voice. 'Stand by to put about! Heads'l sheets there! Mainsheet! Bosun, stand by the running backstays!' He waited for his crew to run to their stations, then ordered, 'Down helm.'

With a brief thunder of flogging canvas the *Alert* came round to larboard, passed her bowsprit through the wind and paid off on the starboard tack.

'Now she'll feel the wind,' said O'Neal as the course was steadied and the sheets were hove down hard. Regular showers of spray rose over the weather bow and O'Neal studied a shore transit he had noted.

'She's lee bowing it,' he remarked, 'ebb's away already.'

Drinkwater never took his eyes off the distant cutter and the moment he saw her turn he descended to the platform from the upper part of the beacon from which he had been watching her.

Ignoring Castenada's half-witted protests Drinkwater gathered up the blankets. He wished he had the means of making a fire, but all thought of coaxing a spark from the sodden horse pistol lock was, he knew, a waste of time.

Laboriously climbing the beacon he sat and joined the blankets, corner to corner, then streamed the improvised flag from as high as he could reach, managing to catch a knotted corner of his extempore hoist in a crack in the timber topmark. The distress signal flew out to leeward, a stained patchwork of irregular shape.

Drinkwater leaned his hot and aching head on the weathered oak of the Scharhorn beacon, closed his eyes and hoped.

Frey saw the signal, staring at the beacon for a few seconds before he realized the distortion to its topmark. His heart skipped as he raised the glass and caught in its leaping lens the flutter of the blankets.

'D'ye see there?' he pointed. 'Distress signal! Port Beam!'

'Down helm! Luff her, haul the stays'l sheet a'weather!' O'Neal responded instantly to Frey's shout. 'Where away?' he asked, as soon as the *Alert* had come up into the wind, lost way and fallen off again, neatly hove-to and edging slowly to leeward.

'There, sir! On that damned beacon!'

'Very well. Get the stern boat away. You take her Frey, and mind the ebb o' the tide over that bank!'

Drinkwater saw the boat bobbing across the water towards the beacon. For a moment he stood stupidly inactive, his eyes misting with relief. With an effort he pulled himself together and stiffly descended again to the platform dragging the lowered blankets after him.

He tried waking the others but his throat was swollen and the noise he made was no more than an ineffectual croak. His head hurt and he found he could do little except watch the boat approach, his body wracked by shuddering sobs.

He had mastered his nervous reaction by the time Frey reached him, but it took him some time to recognize his former midshipman.

'Mr Frey? Is that you? You succeeded then, eh?' Drinkwater's voice was barely more than a whisper.

'Are you all right, sir?' Frey asked, his face showing deep concern at Captain Drinkwater's appearance. He waved for reinforcements from the boat and by degrees Quilhampton was lowered into it, bruised by further buffeting to his battered frame. Awkward and stumbling, Castenada and Drinkwater finally succeeded in getting aboard, and they began the journey back to the cutter.

The sea ran smooth over the bank, but where the retreating tide flowed into the channel a line of vicious little breakers briefly threatened them. At Frey's order the oarsmen doubled their efforts and they broke through the barrier to the open water beyond. Shortly afterwards they bumped alongside *Alert*'s black tumble-home. Hands reached down and dragged Drinkwater and Castenada up on to the cutter's neatly ordered deck. A strange officer confronted Drinkwater, his hand to the forecock of his bicorne hat.

' 'Tis good to be seein' you at last, sir,' he said smiling. 'We've been beatin' up and down for days now, lookin' for you. O'Neal's the name, sir.'

'I'm very much obliged to you, Mr O'Neal, very much obliged,' Drinkwater croaked. 'Mr Quilhampton here needs a masthead whip to get him aboard . . .'

Drinkwater could remember nothing after that, nothing at least beyond slaking his inordinate thirst and finally sinking into the sleep of utter exhaustion.

Lieutenant James Quilhampton woke to the sound of the wind. Above his head he could see exposed rafters and the underside of rattling tiles. The wind played among the cobwebs that strung about the rough, worm-eaten timbers, giving them a dolourous life of their own, an effect heightened by the leaping shadows thrown by a pair of candles that guttered somewhere in the room.

Quilhampton shifted his head. The walls were whitewashed, or had been a long time ago. Now flakes of the distemper curled from the damp walls and patches of grey mould disfigured the crude attempt at disguising the stone masonry. He located the candles on a table at the foot of his narrow bed. A man was asleep at it, head on hands, his face turned away. A long queue lay over the arm upon which his head rested. The hair was dark brown, shot with grey, and tied with a black ribbon.

Quilhampton frowned. 'Sir? Is that you?'

Drinkwater stirred and looked up, his face gaunt, the old scar and the powder burns about his left eye prominent against the pale skin.

'Aye, it's me.' Drinkwater smiled, yawned, stretched and hauled himself to his feet. He kicked back his chair and came and stood beside Quilhampton.

'More to the point, James, is that you?'

'I'm sorry . . .?' Quilhampton frowned.

'You've been talking a lot of drivel these last few days, I wondered – we all wondered – whether you were lost to us.'

'Where am I?' Quilhampton's eyes roved about the room again.

'Safe. You're on Helgoland, in the old Danish barracks . . . No, no, don't fret yourself, they ain't Danish anymore. They're the property of His Majesty King George . . .'

'King George . . . yes, yes, of course, foolish of me.'

'And you ain't to worry about that court martial, my dear fellow. I've been taking sworn affidavits from Frey and your people.'

Quilhampton nodded. 'That's most kind of you, sir.' He managed a wan smile. 'It's a pity you made me write to Mistress MacEwan pressing my suit.'

'Why?'

'I'll have to write again . . . she'll not want a man who hasn't –'

'I can't answer for Mistress MacEwan, James,' Drinkwater broke in, unwilling to allow his friend to subject himself to such morbid thoughts, 'but I'm damned if I'll have you considerin' such things until you're up and about. Castenada said if you got over the secondary fever, you had a fair chance of walking within a month. We'll make all our decisions then, eh?'

'You'll stay here for a month, sir?'

'Just at the moment, James. There's a March gale roaring its confounded head off out there, so we have precious little choice!'

Hearing the reassuring words, Quilhampton nodded and closed his eyes. He did not hear the note of impatience in Drinkwater's voice.

'I do not think I shall have any difficulty in persuading the Governor, my dear sir,' said Nicholas smiling at Drinkwater, 'none at all.'

'Very well. We need to conclude the matter, and as long as those three ships lie in limbo off Neuwerk . . .'

'Quite so, quite so,' Nicholas eyed the glass and its contents before passing Drinkwater the glass of oporto. 'Despatched by the Marquis of Wellesley, Canning's replacement at the Foreign Department,' he said with evident satisfaction, 'doubtless a tribute to his brother's successes in the peninsula . . .'

'And of his approbation at your, or am I permitted to say *our*, little achievement?' asked Drinkwater, raising the glass.

'Ah, sir, you mock me.'

'A little, perhaps.'

'Your good health, Captain.'

'And yours, Mr Nicholas.'

They sipped the port in unembarrassed silence, Drinkwater still studying the chart spread out before them, and in particular the Scharhorn Sand surrounding the island of Neuwerk. He wanted to return, to lay the ghosts of the Elbe that still haunted his dreams and to release the three transports from their anchorage under the French guns before Davout's proposed absence from Hamburg encouraged M. Thiebault to order them up the Elbe.

They were the ships that were to have stood surety for Thiebault's bond, the guarantee that he and Gilham and Littlewood would retire downstream, paid and unmolested. They and their crews had waited patiently until Drinkwater's release, expecting their 'recapture' daily, but a series of strong westerly winds and vicious gales had postponed the operation until the end of March.

'Of course you may not find things as easy as you assume, Captain,' Nicholas said guardedly.

'What d'you mean, sir?'

'While you were ill, two boats got off. One brought a secret despatch from Liepmann. He had it on good authority . . .'

'Thiebault?' enquired Drinkwater quickly.

Nicholas shrugged. 'Presumably, but there were what he called *inexplicable* rumours of a rift between Paris and Petersburg that were of a sufficiently serious nature as to suggest war was being contemplated, at least in Paris.'

'Good Lord! Then we succeeded better than I imagined; but how does this affect the meditated attack?' He flipped the back of his hand on the chart.

'It is also reported, Captain, that reinforcements have arrived in Hamburg, to wit, Molitor's Division, about nine thousand strong. Cuxhaven has received a reinforcement, so has Brunsbuttel . . .'

'The westerlies will have kept reinforcements from Neuwerk as surely as they have mewed us up here, I'm sure of it.'

'I trust you are correct, Captain, but I would be guilty of a dereliction of duty if I did not appraise you of the facts.' Nicholas held out the decanter. 'Another glass, and then we'll go and see Colonel Hamilton.'

'Very well, Mr O'Neal,' Drinkwater called to the dark figure looming expectantly at the *Alert*'s taffrail, 'you may cast us off!'

The huge, quadrilateral mainsail of the cutter, black against the first light of the April dawn, began to diminish in size as the *Alert* drew away from the four boats she had been towing. They bobbed in her wake while their crews settled themselves at their pulling stations.

'Mr Browne?' Drinkwater called.

'All ready, sir,' replied the old harbour-master.

'Mr McCullock?'

'Ready, sir,' the transport officer called back.

'Mr Frey?'

'Ready, sir.'

'Line ahead, give way in order of sailing.' Drinkwater nodded to the midshipman beside him. 'Very well, Mr Martin, give way.'

'Give way toooo-gether!'

The oar looms came forward and then strong arms tugged at them; the blades bit the water, lifted clear, flew forward and dipped again. Soon the rhythmic knocking of the oars in the pins grew steady and hypnotic.

Involuntarily Drinkwater shivered. He would never again watch men pulling an oar without the return of that nightmare of pain and cold, of ceaseless leaning and pulling, leaning and pulling. He recalled very little detail of their flight down the Elbe, almost nothing of the desperate skirmish with Dieudonné on the ice or the struggle to get Quilhampton into the comparative shelter of the Scharhorn beacon. What was indelibly etched into his memory was his remorseless task at the oars, which culminated in his stupidly losing one and nearly rendering all their efforts useless.

He kept telling himself the nightmare was over now, that he

had paid off the debt he owed fate and that he had received a private absolution in receiving Quilhampton back from the grave. But he could not throw off the final shadows of his megrims until he had released the three transports and all their people were safely back in an English anchorage.

He turned and looked astern. In the growing light he could see the other three boats. Two – McCullock's and Browne's – were the large harbour barges, one of which had welcomed them to Helgoland when *Galliwasp* had run on the reef, the third was the *Alert*'s longboat and the fourth a boat supplied by the merchant traders, commanded by Frey and manned by the vengeful remnants of *Tracker*'s crew. A handful of volunteers from the Royal Veterans commanded by Lieutenant Dowling were deployed among the boats.

Drinkwater led the column in *Alert*'s longboat. Wrapped in his cloak, Drinkwater stared ahead, leaving the business of working inshore to Mr Midshipman Martin, a young protégé of Lieutenant O'Neal's. He was aware of O'Neal's anger at being displaced from the chief command of the boat expedition, pleading that the matter was not properly the duty of a post-captain. But Drinkwater had silenced the Orangeman with a curt order that his talents were better employed standing off and on in support.

'You can run up the channel in our wake, Mr O'Neal, and blood your guns, provided you fire over our heads and distract the enemy from our intentions,' he said. Remembering this conversation he turned again. The big cutter had gone about and was now working round from the position at which she let go the boats and ran up towards Cuxhaven. O'Neal had brought her back downstream and would soon shift his sheets and scandalize his mainsail, ready to creep up in the wake of the boats, into the anchorage off Neuwerk.

'See 'em ahead, sir!'

The lookout reported the sighting from the longboat's bow in a low voice and Drinkwater nodded as Martin repeated the report.

He could see them himself now, their masts and yards clear against the pale yellow sky. They lay at anchor in line.

'Lay us alongside the headmost ship, Mr Martin if you please.'

'Aye, aye, sir.'

Drinkwater felt a worm of fear writhe in his belly. He was almost glad to feel again the qualms that beset every man before action, the fear of death and loneliness, no matter what his situation, how exalted his rank, or how many of his confederates crowded about him. It was a familiar feeling and brought a curious, lop-sided contentment, infinitely preferable to the anxieties of a spy. He eased his shoulders under the cloak and plain, borrowed coat. He was still not in uniform, but there was no longer any doubt about who and what he was.

They were seen by an alert guard aboard the transport *Anne*, a French guard put aboard by order from Hamburg with the object of securing the defecting British ships against the moment when Marshal Davout either relaxed his embargo on trade or decided to inspect a distant corps. His shout stirred an already wakening anchorage and the bugler on Neuwerk, about to sound reveille, blew instead the sharp notes of the alarm.

'Put your backs into it!' roared Drinkwater, exhorting his men; they might yet arrive with some of the advantage of surprise. He swung round at Martin as the midshipman put his tiller over to take a wide sweep around the *Anne*. 'Keep straight on, damn it!'

They heeled as Martin corrected his course and pulled past the first of the anchored ships. A single musket ball struck the boat's gunwhale, but they were past before the sentry had a chance to reload.

There was more activity aboard the *Hannah* but she too was astern before damage could be done to them. The *Delia* lay ahead now, already swinging to the wind as the flood tide that had brought them reached the brief hiatus of high water.

Suddenly pinpoints of yellow fire sparkled along the *Delia*'s rail. Musket balls struck the longboat and sent up the spurts of near misses all about them. In the centre of the boat a man was struck in the chest. He let go his oar and upset the stroke. His convulsion of agony came with gasps of pain and with thrashing legs he fell from his thwart. There was a moment's confusion as his trailing oar was disentangled, then order was restored.

'A steady pull, lads,' called Drinkwater, relieved now the action had started. 'Five more good strokes and we'll be alongside.'

With the exception of the centre thwart where the mortally wounded man lay cradled in his mate's arms, the men plied their oars vigorously, knowing they had a few seconds before the French reloaded.

'Stand-by forrard! ' shouted Midshipman Martin. 'Hook on!'

The *Alert*'s longboat bumped against the side of the transport *Delia*.

'Boarders away!' Drinkwater bawled, standing in the wildly rocking boat as most of her crew leapt up and reached for the main chains. He heaved himself up with cracking arm muscles, kicked his feet until he found a foothold, then drew himself up on to the platform of the chainwhale. He saw the dull gleam of a bayonet, got one foot on to the *Delia*'s rail and drew the hanger Hamilton had lent him. The infantry officer's weapon was light as a foil, but the clash with the heavy bayonet jarred him. He was clutching a shroud with his left hand and he let his body swing, absorbing the impact of the sentry's lunge. Disengaging his blade, he jabbed at the man's face. Instinctively the soldier drew back and Drinkwater flung himself over the rail and down on to the deck.

He was still weak from the ague he had succumbed to after the rigours of his escape and he landed awkwardly, his legs buckling beneath him, but others were about him now and the guard retreated aft, looking round for support from his confederates who were tumbling up from below in disordered dress. There were less than a dozen of them, but they were led by an officer, an elderly man with a bayonet scar sliced deep into his cheek. He gave a curt order and the muskets came up to the present.

'Charge!' Drinkwater bellowed, recovering his footing and running aft amid the fire of muskets and pistols. As his men came over the rail they discharged their firearms simultaneously with the enemy. There was a moment of flashes, cracks and buzzing, the cries of wounded men and then the two sides clashed together in hand-to-hand fighting.

The grizzled infantry lieutenant shuffled forward with the cautious confidence of the old warrior. He feinted with his heavy sword and Drinkwater felt the weight of it with a foolish, unnecessary parry. The Frenchman whipped his blade away, cut over Drinkwater's sword and lunged, at the same time slicing the blade of his weapon.

Had Drinkwater not held Hamilton's hanger his recovery would have been too late, but he was cool now, he had passed through the veil of fighting madness that had drawn from him the superfluous parry. He half turned, cannoned into another body, and in the second's respite had shortened his sword arm and jabbed the hanger with all his strength.

The French officer fell against him with a terrible gasp and Drinkwater recoiled, the man's body smell, mixed with the warm reek of blood, filling his nostrils. The French officer's sword clattered to the deck, the man dropped to his knees, then fell full length. Hamilton's hanger blade snapped off and Drinkwater was left stupidly holding the hilt and three inches of the *forte.*

Somebody lurched into him, he swung, confronted Martin and realized the thing was accomplished. The handful of Frenchmen remaining on their feet threw their muskets on the deck in token of surrender. Five of their fellow infantrymen lay dead or severely wounded, sprawled across the hatch and deck, and although one of their attackers writhed in noisy agony and three lay dead from their first volley, it was the death of their officer which persuaded them that further resistance was useless.

'Where are the crew?' Drinkwater snarled. *'Ou est les matelots Americaines?'* The Frenchmen pointed at the gratings covering the after hatchway.

'Get 'em out, Mr Martin!'

One of the sentries stepped forward and began to speak rapidly. Drinkwater could not understand a word but the meaning of the man's request was clear: to be left on Neuwerk, not taken prisoner.

'Put 'em under guard, Mr Martin!' He turned to the men scrambling out of the 'tween deck. 'Where's the master?'

'He's hostage ashore, sir.'

'God's bones! What about the mate?'

'Here, sir!'

'Get her under way. Cut your cable and make sail, the tide's just on the turn and the *Alert* cutter is in the offing! Mr Martin, get those prisoners in the boat, then –'

Drinkwater's order was lost in the boom of a cannon and a crash amidships where the ball struck home. Drinkwater ran to the rail, raised his hands and shouted at the adjacent vessel, *'Hannah* ahoy! Have you taken the ship?'

'Aye, sir, an' we've eight prisoners!' That was Browne's voice.

'Send 'em over in your boat, d'ye hear?'

A second and third crash came from the battery ashore but Drinkwater doggedly continued his conversation. 'Have you word from the *Anne*?'

'A moment, Cap'n!'

Browne turned away so that Drinkwater could not hear what he said, but a faint call from the farthest ship was, he thought, Frey's voice. It was almost full daylight now and he could see a man standing in the *Anne*'s rigging.

'That you there, sir?' Browne too was visible at the *Hannah*'s rail.

'Aye?'

'She's taken. They've eight men too.'

'Where's McCullock's boat?'

'Here sir, just come from the *Anne* to confirm Browne's report. We've the three o' them in the bag, sir.'

'Not yet we haven't. I'm not leavin' those Masters ashore. Do you pick up all the prisoners and follow me. All your men load their pieces. I'm going in to parley.' He turned and shouted orders at Martin then, seeing the mate of the *Delia* had a man hacking at the anchor cable with an axe and had the transport's main topsail in its clewlines he scrambled after Martin down into the longboat. A ball plunged into the water close to Browne's barge into which his prisoners were being forced and which still lay alongside the *Hannah*.

In the longboat, facing the downcast French guard from the *Delia* with musket and fixed bayonet, sat a private of the Royal Veterans.

'Be so kind as to lend me your ramrod,' Drinkwater requested, holding out his hand, fishing with the other beneath his own coat-tails. Drawing a white handkerchief from his pocket, Drinkwater knotted it about the private's ramrod.

Having gathered together the three boats loaded with the disarmed French, Drinkwater waved his improvised flag of truce and ordered Martin to pull inshore. From a low breastwork the flash and smoke of cannon fire continued, the scream of the shot passing overhead was followed by the thunder of the discharge rolling across the water. The noise of the shots hitting or falling short came from astern, only to be answered by the crack of *Alert*'s light six-pounders.

Drinkwater turned in alarm. O'Neal had worked his little ship well into the anchorage and already the *Anne* had escaped past the cutter which was drawing up towards the *Hannah* and the *Delia*. Both vessels had hoisted their false, American colours, a shrewd though quite useless attempt to deter the artillerymen ashore. But

Drinkwater had observed from the fall of O'Neal's shot that having mistaken their purpose, that zealous officer was directing his own cannon at the three boats pulling quickly towards the island.

'God's bones!' Drinkwater blasphemed, turning to Martin, 'Stand up, man, he might recognize you if he's looking, and wave this damned flag!'

The next moment the three boats were lost amongst a welter of splashes as shot from both sides plunged into the sea around them. An oar was shivered with an explosion of splinters and then, as if comprehension dawned simultaneously upon the opposing gunners, fire ceased and the boats emerged, miraculously unscathed, except for the loss of the single oar.

A few moments later, as with canvas flogging O'Neal tacked the *Alert* and stood slowly seaward again, Drinkwater's boat led close inshore.

'Here,' he said, seizing the flag of truce from the shaken Martin, 'I'll take that now.'

Drinkwater stood up and braced himself. 'Very well, Mr Martin, that'll do.'

'Oars!' ordered the midshipman. The tired seamen brought their oars horizontal and bent over the looms, leaning on their arms and gasping for breath. The other boats followed suit and the three of them glided closer to the beach. Drinkwater could see the shakoed heads of artillerymen above the island's defences.

'Messieurs,' Drinkwater cried in his appalling French, *'donnez moi les maitres des vaisseaux Americaines. J'ai votre soldats . . . votre amis pour . . .'* he faltered, and added 'exchange!'

A discontented murmur rose momentarily among the prisoners before Drinkwater snuffed it out with a harsh, 'Silence!' For a minute nothing happened, then an officer scrambled over the low parapet of the breastwork. They watched him walk, ungainly and bowlegged, through the sand of the foreshore towards the tide-line.

Drinkwater nodded at the man who had disclosed the whereabouts of the *Delia*'s crew. *'Vous parlez, m'sieur . . .'* he commanded.

After a few moments of animated conversation between the two men, in which several other prisoners attempted to intervene until Martin suppressed them, the officer tramped back up the beach, leaning in through an embrasure. A further wait ensued. Looking seawards, Drinkwater saw that O'Neal had brought the *Alert* round and the cutter's large bowsprit again pointed at Neuwerk as she stood inshore once more.

'I hope Mr O'Neal has a man in the chains, Mr Martin,' Drinkwater observed, indicating the approaching cutter, 'we can't afford to have him aground now the tide's fallin'.'

Martin screwed up his eyes and stared at his ship. 'I can see a leadsman, sir.'

Drinkwater grunted. 'Your eyes are better than mine.' He turned his attention back to the beach; the artillery officer was returning. At the water's edge he stopped and nodded, the plume of his shako bobbing.

'*D'accord . . .*'

'Run her ashore, Mr Martin,' Drinkwater said, sitting down as he saw the first of the British masters emerging through the embrasure. 'Not a bad morning's work, eh? Squares our account, in a manner of speakin'.'

Chapter Twenty *April–August 1810*

Outrageous Fortune

'So,' said Lord Dungarth, drawing the stoppers, 'we somewhat gilded the lily did we not? Oporto or Madeira?'

Drinkwater poured the *bual* and passed the decanters to Solomon. The Jew gracefully declined and returned them to their host.

'Insofar as my sojourn amongst the stews of Wapping was concerned,' said Drinkwater, pausing to sip the rich amber wine, 'yes.'

'It was essential to contact Fagan,' Dungarth said, 'though your interview with Marshal Davout clinched the matter. There was no harm in dissembling at the lowest level . . .'

'It was without doubt the very nadir of my self-esteem, my Lord. I'd be obliged if future commissions were of a less clandestine nature. A ship, perhaps . . .' Drinkwater deliberately left the sentence unfinished.

'A ship you shall have, my dear fellow, without a doubt, but first a month or two of the furlough you have undoubtedly earned by your exertions.'

'I shall hold you to that, my Lord, with Mr Solomon here as witness.'

They smiled and Dungarth sent the Madeira round again. 'I have taught you the business of intrigue too well.'

'It is not a type of service I warm to,' Drinkwater said pointedly. 'However, from what Nicholas reported was said at Hamburg, we succeeded.'

'Oh, *you* succeeded, Nathaniel, beyond my wildest hopes.' Dungarth's hazel eyes twinkled in the candlelight and it was clear he was withholding something. Drinkwater felt mildly irritated by his Lordship's condescension. He was not sure he had endured the ice of the Elbe to be toyed with, cat and mouse.

'May I enquire how, my Lord?' he asked drily. 'I presume from the papers Madame Santhonax . . .'

'I shall come to those in a moment. But now we have heard your story there is much we have to relate to you. Pray be patient, my dear fellow.' Dungarth's arch tone was full of wry amusement and Drinkwater, made indulgent by a third glass of *bual*, submitted resignedly.

'Your chief and most immediate success,' Dungarth resumed, 'lies with Fagan. His office as a go-between was discovered by Napoleon and used to compromise Fouché. The ignoble Duke of Otranto, by his bold initiative in raising an army to confront us on the Scheldt, has ably demonstrated that the French Empire may easily be usurped. Alarmed, his Imperial Majesty, having discovered Fouché had sent an agent to London, took Draconian action. The agent was Fagan. He arrived here last week. Before the week was out Fouché had been dismissed!'

'A malicious and fitting move by the Emperor,' said Solomon raising his eyebrows and nodding slowly. 'Almost proof that Bonaparte knew it was Fagan who first reported a trade opening between London and St Petersburg.'

Dungarth barked a short laugh. 'An engaging fancy,' he said, 'and knowing Nathaniel has a misplaced belief in these things, there is something else I should tell him, something more closely concerning his person.'

'My Lord . . .?'

'You mentioned the widow Santhonax . . .' Dungarth said pausing, 'and Isaac says you spoke of her at his house, intimating she might be behind my, er, accident . . .'

'*Dux femina facti*,' prompted Solomon.

'What of her, my Lord?' Drinkwater asked impatiently, suddenly uncomfortable at this mention of Hortense. 'I have related all that passed between us at Hamburg and Altona. Whether or not she finally informed on me, I have no way of knowing. Why else was Dieudonné so placed to intercept us?' He sighed. 'But I am also of the opinion that she gave me what she considered was time enough to make good my escape.

'I incline to your conjoint theory, Nathaniel,' Dungarth said, suddenly serious, his bantering tone dismissed. 'It is almost certain that she now enjoys some measure of the Emperor's favour, perhaps because Napoleon has divorced Josephine and married the Austrian Archduchess Marie-Louise. Doubtless he wishes pliable Frenchwomen to surround the new Empress, for the beautiful widow has been appointed to the Empress's household.'

'No doubt Talleyrand approves of the arrangement,' Drinkwater observed, 'but what of the papers she passed to me? If we are correct she took an enormous risk. Were they false?'

'Not at all! She is a bold woman and clearly placed great reliance on your own character. In fact they were proposals from Talleyrand himself, concerning the future constitution and government of France, proposals that he wishes me to lay before the cabinet *and* M'sieur Le Comte de Provence,* on the assumption that the days of Napoleon are numbered . . .'

'And that if Fouché can achieve what almost amounts to a *coup d'etat*, then others can too.' Drinkwater completed Dungarth's exposition.

Dungarth smiled. 'Yes. Either with an assassin's dagger or another campaign.'

'A Russian campaign, for instance,' added Solomon, drawing a folded and sealed paper from his breast.

It surprised Captain Drinkwater that St Peter's church was so full. The good people of Petersfield had certainly turned out *en masse* for the occasion. They shuffled and stared at him as he led Elizabeth and their children up the aisle.

Pausing to usher his children into the pew he cast his eyes over the congregation. Curious faces disappeared behind unstudied prayer books and mouths gossiped in whispers under the tilted brims of Sunday bonnets. He suppressed a smile. Many of the assembly had come out of devotion to his wife and her friend, Louise Quilhampton, whose efforts in starting a school for the children of the townsfolk and farm labourers had finally earned the formal approval of the Church of England.

Drinkwater nodded at the gentry settled on their rented benches and followed young Richard into the pew. A woman opposite in an extravagant hat smiled amiably at him and, after a moment, he recalled her as the bride's aunt with whom he had once shared a journey in a mail coach. Richard, the down of adolescence forming

*Later Louis XVIII after the Bourbon restoration and at this time resident in England.

on his upper lip, wriggled beside him and he put a restraining hand on the boy's knee. His son looked up and smiled. He had forgotten Richard had Elizabeth's eyes. Beyond him, Charlotte Amelia was nudging her brother, handing him a hymn book in which she indicated the number of the first hymn.

'I know,' the boy whispered, picking up his own copy. Drinkwater looked over their heads and caught his wife's eye. She looked radiantly happy, smiling at him, her eyes misty.

He smiled back, his mind suddenly – disloyally – filled with a vision of Hortense looking at him in the intimacy of Herr Liepmann's withdrawing room. Was he the same man? Had that event *really* occurred? He could no longer be sure, knowing only that he had thought of her intermittently ever since the conversation at Lord Dungarth's when his lordship had imparted the knowledge that the widow Santhonax was a lady-in-waiting to the Empress Marie-Louise. Nor did circumstances allow him to forget her, for had not the newspapers made much of the fire at the Austrian Ambassador's grand ball? Held by Prince Schwarzenberg in honour of the Imperial wedding, the festivities had been ruined by a disastrous fire in which the prince had lost his sister-in-law and others had been killed or maimed.

He found himself unable to shake off the conviction that Hortense had had some part to play in the dreadful event.

He was rudely recalled to the present by the viols and the cello screeching and groaning at one another as the orchestra tuned up. Then the general muttering swelled and heads turned as the groom and best man marched in. A satisfied murmur greeted Quilhampton and Frey who were resplendent in the blue, white and gold of full dress and strode in step, the muted click of sword hangings accompanying their progress to the chancel. The left cuff of Quilhampton's dress coat was stitched across his breast. He exchanged glances with his mother, Louise, who sniffled worthily into a cambric handkerchief. Drinkwater thought of tying a white handkerchief to a ramrod and waving it above his head.

The rector made his appearance and slowly the noise from the congregation subsided as they waited for the bride.

Quilhampton looked back towards the porch and Drinkwater marked the pallor of his face. He still bore the marks of his ordeal and appeared as drawn as he had during his court martial. Mercifully, it had been a brief affair held aboard the *Royal William* at Portsmouth. Drinkwater had occupied his time on Helgoland in securing sworn statements about the handling of His Majesty's brig *Tracker* and had drawn up a defence for the judge-advocate to read to the court. He had prevailed too, upon Lord Dungarth, to minute the Admiralty to note on the court's papers that the brig had been employed upon a 'special service'.

Quilhampton's surrendered sword had been returned to him with the court's warmest approbation, but James's smile of relief had been wan, as though other matters weighed more heavily upon his mind. Perhaps it was the verdict of his bride he most dreaded, Drinkwater thought, watching him turn anxiously towards the porch.

Catriona MacEwan entered on the arm of her uncle. She was a tall, striking young woman with a mane of red-gold hair piled under her flat bonnet and a dusting of not unbecoming freckles over her nose. The necks of the congregation craned as one, and the sigh of satisfaction was audible as she caught sight of the thin, awkward man at the far end of the aisle and smiled.

The orchestra sawed its way into sudden life, joined by the congregation. 'Rejoice, the Lord is King . . .' they boomed, 'Your Lord and King adore . . .!'

'Dearly beloved,' the rector intoned, 'we are gathered together in the sight of God, and in the face of this congregation, to join together this man and this woman in Holy Matrimony . . .'

'I hope they will be happy.'

'Yes.'

'They deserve it, after so long a time.'

'Yes.'

'It has been a long time for us too, my dear, far too long.'

'I know . . . I . . .' Drinkwater faltered, looking at Elizabeth as she sat on her side of the bed. She waited for him to finish his sentence, but he shook his head. He had been home a week but they were finding great difficulty in renewing their intimacy; both of them were guarded and uncertain, wrapped in their own diverse worlds and avoiding each other by pleading the unspoken excuse of preparations for Quilhampton's wedding. There was so much to say that Drinkwater felt the task quite beyond him.

'I keep thinking we are different people now.' she whispered, holding out her hand to him and drawing him down beside her.

'Yes, I know. So do I . . .'

Perhaps that was a starting point; they had that much in common . . .

He *had* to tell her, had to tell her everything; about all that had happened in the forests of Borneo; of his dark forebodings and the impossibility of seeing her when he had returned from the Indies; about the pathetic eagerness with which he had embraced Dungarth's secret mission and how it had misfired; how the *Tracker* was surrendered and Quilhampton lost his arm; of the whore Zenobia and the Jews, Liepmann and Solomon. He wanted to tell her of the meeting with Davout and the execution of Johannes; but most of all he wanted to tell her about Hortense . . .

Long after they had found each other again he lay awake while Elizabeth slept beside him. He knew he could never share all of these things, that they were his own soul's burden and that he must bear them silently until his death.

Listening to his wife's gentle breathing, he thought perhaps it did not greatly matter. In time, providence balanced all accounts.

Tomorrow he could share with her what he knew would please her. It struck him as perversely ridiculous that he had delayed telling her, but the moment had never seemed right. Besides, it had taken him some time to grasp the significance of the contents of Isaac Solomon's document, the paper passed to him after dinner the night he and the Jewish merchant had dined with Lord Dungarth.

It was an outrageous quirk of fortune that the gold should have realized so much. Sold and shrewdly invested by Solomon in a mysterious speculation, it had realized almost three thousand pounds. He had become, if not a rich man, a person of some independence.

The strange parcel arrived by the hand of an Admiralty messenger. Drinkwater thought at first it was a chart and, for fear of upsetting Elizabeth with so early a receipt of orders, took it aside and opened it privately. The oiled wrapping peeled back to reveal a familiar roll of canvas, the edges of which were frayed. He recognized it instantly. With a beating heart he unrolled it. The paint crackled and flakes lifted from its abused surface.

Its appearance shocked him from a far greater disfigurement than mere neglect: down the side of the painted cheek, from ear to chin, the beautiful face was ruined by a deliberately applied brown stain.

With a shaking hand Drinkwater picked up a small sheet of paper that fell from the centre of the roll. It was in Lord Dungarth's hand and was undated.

My Dear Nathaniel,
The Enclosed comes from Paris via Fagan. It seems the Lady was Disfigured in the Fire at the Austrian Ambassador's Rout. He was Asked to Ensure you Received it.
Dungarth

Drinkwater stared at the smeared mark. It was dried blood.

'God's bones,' he whispered, placing the roll of canvas in the grate. Fetching flint and steel he lit a candle and, squatting down, applied the flame to the corner of the portrait. The oil locked in the paint ignited and crackled with a volley of tiny explosions as the flames licked up the frayed strands, laying a smear of soot over the poor, ruined face. Standing, Drinkwater watched it burn until only a charred heap of ash lay at his feet.

Author's Note

The years 1809–1811 mark the turning point in what, until 1914, was called the Great War. Trafalgar and Austerlitz matched the sea power of Great Britain against the land power of the Napoleonic French Empire. With Russia allied to France and the Continental System in place, Napoleon was in a commanding position. By 1809 Britain had begun the long slog of the Peninsular War in support of the Spanish insurrection and was also attempting to liberate Antwerp whose occupation by the French had been the cause of war in 1793. The resulting Walcheren expedition was a disaster: it formed the prime cause of Castlereagh's notorious duel with Canning and brought down the Portland ministry. By 1811, Napoleon's restlessness drove him out of this stalemate. Russia had been disregarding the embargo of trade with Britain, and the Tsar, his country's economy in ruins, finally formalized his intention to leave the Continental System by *ukase* on the last day of 1810. Worse, Napoleon's brother Louis, King of Holland, connived at its evasion and the Emperor annexed his kingdom in mid-1810.

On the other side of the Channel there had been bad harvests in 1809 and 1810, there were numerous bankruptcies and the Luddites were destroying industrial machinery. Both sides suffered from an unprecedented economic crisis in 1811.

However a confident Napoleon, who had secured his succession through his divorce of Josephine and subsequent Austrian marriage, thought his marshals able to deal with Spain, and had already decided to invade Russia. These events were monitored by the British on Helgoland.

This former Danish island was used as a diplomatic 'listening post' (from which access to Hamburg does not appear to have been difficult). The best known secret mission connected with Helgoland was that of the priest James Robertson whose extrication of

Romana's Corps in 1808, left a detachment of sick hospitalized at Altona.

The island was also stuffed with British traders who bombarded the Foreign Office with petitions to build warehouses there. A number of facts suggest a secret mission had been under way at the time of Drinkwater's arrival and ended in failure. Captain Gilham and the *Ocean* were part of a convoy destined for a 'secret service' and the ships lay in Helgoland Road for months until the Ordnance Board wrote off their cargoes of military stores to Canning's Secret Service budget. The final fate of these ships is vague; they were either lost at sea 'or captured by the French near Calais'.

There are several intriguing references to the fact that the Grand Army, or part of it, supposedly marched to Moscow in Northampton boots, and it is highly likely that consignments of this nature passed through Hamburg or into Hanover, from whence came recruits for the King's German Legion.

Like Gilham, Colonel Hamilton and Edward Nicholas lived, and there is evidence that their relationship was sometimes strained. Reinke's charts still exist and McCullock, Browne and O'Neal are based on real people. At this time too, a report on the inadequacy of the Helgoland lighthouse was forwarded to London.

Fagan was an agent of Fouché's and a known go-between. Dieudonné of the *Chasseurs-à-Cheval*, provided the artist Gericault with a model for his spirited painting of *An Officer of the Imperial Guard*. He was destined to die in the Russian Campaign.

The rumours that passed through Helgoland in the winter of 1809, especially the news of Benjamin Bathurst, are all a matter of fact, as are the gale at the end of September, the west winds in the following March and the attack on Neuwerk in April 1810, when 'several American vessels were taken'.

Marshal Davout arrived at Hamburg in command of the Army of Germany in January 1810 and shortly afterwards shot a young man for the illegal possession of sugar loaves. The occupying forces were increased in March by stationing Molitor's Division in the outlying villages. This failed to stem the influx of imports and a furious Napoleon ordered the burning of all British goods discovered in the Hanse towns. The wily Hamburgers took to carrying luxuries past their guards in coffins. Herr Liepmann is my own invention but Nicholas refers to an influential person 'well-disposed to us', resident in, or near Hamburg, with whom a regular communication was maintained.

The fragility of Napoleon's Empire, exposed by Fouché's bold action in deploying an army to oppose the British invasion of Walcheren, was even more dramatically exploited by the republican General Malet who briefly took over the government in Paris during the Emperor's absence in Russia.

Lord Dungarth was not alone in perceiving it was the opposing might of the Russian army that was required to break the land power of Napoleon. Talleyrand had whispered as much to the Tsar at Erfurt.

It was Napoleon's claim that Tsar Alexander failed to exclude British trade which provided him with his excuse to invade Russia in 1812. He had long harboured the idea. The 'inexplicable rumour' of intended war between France and Russia reached Helgoland on 19 February 1810 and was reported to London by Edward Nicholas. Since the new ministry might consider Nicholas had exceeded his instructions, is it to be wondered at if he expressed an official doubt as to its truth and concealed his own part in its origin?

The Flying Squadron

For the crew of the cutter *Grace O'Malley* in gratitude

Contents

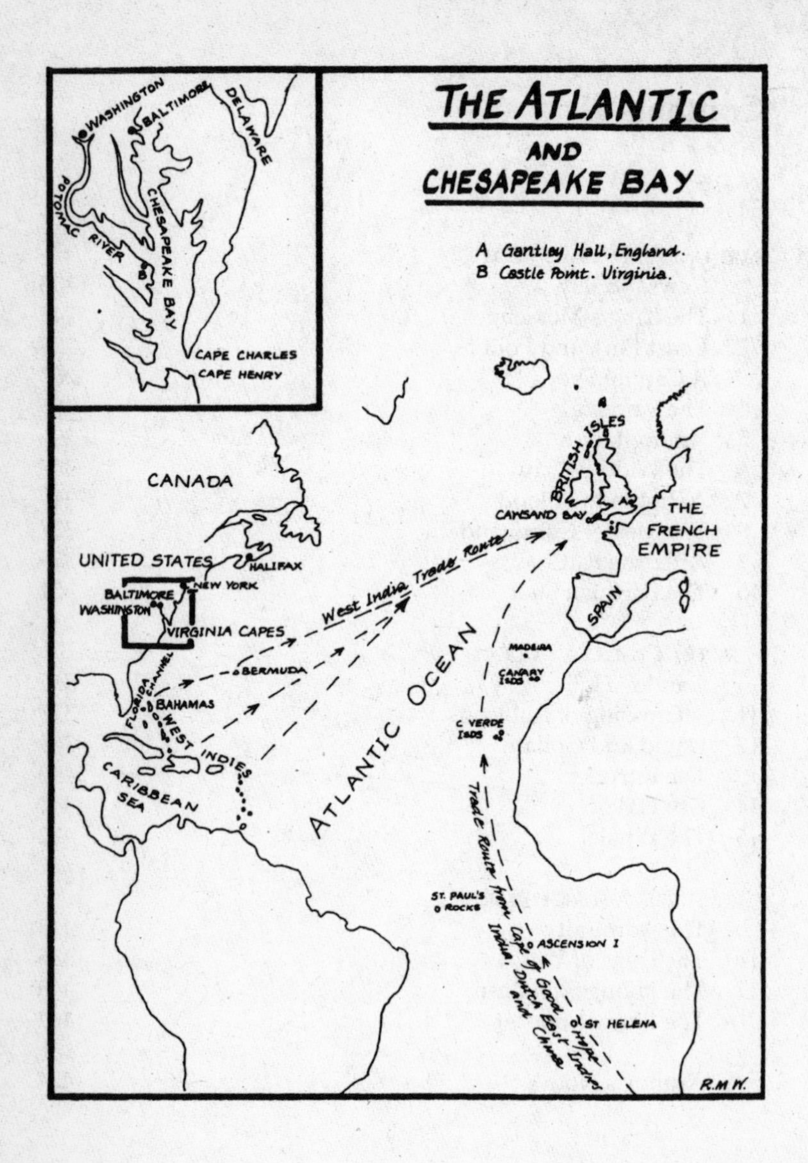
THE ATLANTIC
AND
CHESAPEAKE BAY
A Gantley Hall, England.
B Castle Point. Virginia.
WASHINGTON
BALTIMORE
DELAWARE
POTOMAC RIVER
CHESAPEAKE BAY
CAPE CHARLES
CAPE HENRY
CANADA
UNITED STATES
HALIFAX
NEW YORK
BALTIMORE
WASHINGTON
VIRGINIA CAPES
BERMUDA
FLORIDA CHANNEL
BAHAMAS
WEST INDIES
CARIBBEAN SEA
West India Trade Route
ATLANTIC OCEAN
BRITISH ISLES
CAWSAND BAY
THE FRENCH EMPIRE
SPAIN
MADEIRA
CANARY ISDS
C VERDE ISDS
ST. PAUL'S ROCKS
ASCENSION I
ST HELENA
Trade Route from Cape of Good Hope India, Dutch East Indies and China
R.M.W.

PART ONE
Hawks and Doves

'You will have to fight the English again . . .'

NAPOLEON

Cawsand Bay *August 1811*

The knock at the door woke Lieutenant Frey with a start. His neglected book slid to the deck with a thud. The air in the wardroom was stiflingly soporific and he had dozed off, only to be woken moments later with a headache and a foul taste in his mouth.

'Yes?' Frey's tone was querulous, he was irritated by the indifference of his messmates, especially that of Mr Metcalfe.

'Beg pardon, sir.' Midshipman Belchambers peered into the candle-lit gloom and fixed his eyes on the copy of *The Times* behind which Mr Metcalfe, the first lieutenant, was presumed to be. He coughed to gain Mr Metcalfe's attention, but no flicker of life came from the newspaper, despite the two hands clearly holding it up before the senior officer's face.

Frey rubbed his eyes and sought vainly for a drop of wine in his glass to rinse his mouth.

'Sir . . .', Belchambers persisted urgently, continuing to address the impassive presence of Mr Metcalfe.

'What the devil is it?' snapped Frey, running a finger round the inside of his stock.

Relieved, Belchambers shifted his attention to the third lieutenant. 'Cap'n's gig's approaching, sir.'

Glaring at the newspaper, Frey rose, his fingers settling his neck linen. He kicked back his chair so that it scraped the deck with an intrusive noise, though it failed to stir the indifference of his colleagues. Piqued, he reached for coat and hat.

'Very well,' he said, dismissing Belchambers, 'I'll be up directly.'

From the doorway, as he drew on his coat, Frey regarded his colleagues in their post-prandial disorder.

Despite the bull's eyes, the skylight shaft and the yellow glow of the table candelabra, the wardroom was as ill-lit as it was stuffy. At the head of the long table, leaning back against the rudder trunking, Mr Metcalfe remained inscrutable behind his newspaper. Mr Moncrieff, the marine officer, was slumped in his chair, his pomaded head thrown back, his mouth open and his eyes shut in an uncharacteristically inelegant posture.

Ignoring the midshipman's intrusion, the master, his clay pipe adding to the foul air, continued playing cards with the surgeon. He laid a card with a snap and scooped the trick.

'Trumps, by God,' grumbled Mr Pym, staring down at his own meagre hand.

Wyatt, the master, grinned diabolically through wreaths of puffed smoke.

Frey looked in vain for Mr Gordon, but the second lieutenant had retired to his cabin and only Wagstaff, the mess-servant, reacted to Frey's exasperated surveillance pausing expectantly in his slovenly shuffling as though awaiting rebuke or instruction. Frey noticed that there was little to choose between his filthy apron and the stained drapery which adorned the table. With an expression of mild disgust Mr Frey abandoned this scene of genteel squalor with something like relief, and retreated to the deck, acknowledging the perfunctory salutes of the marine sentries *en route*.

Emerging into the fresh air he cast a quick look about him. His Britannic Majesty's frigate *Patrician* lay at anchor in Cawsand Bay. The high blue arch of the sky was gradually darkening in the east behind the jagged, listing outline of the Mewstone. The last rays of the setting sun fanned out over the high land behind Cawsand village. Already the stone houses and the fish-drying sheds were indistinct as the shadow of the land crept out across the water. The still depths of the bay turned a mysterious green, disturbed only by the occasional plop of a jumping mullet and a low swell which rolled round Penlee Point, forming an eddy about the Draystone.

In contrast to the stifling air below, the deck was already touched with the chill of the coming night and Frey paused a moment, drinking in the pure tranquillity of the evening.

'Boat 'hoy!'

The bellow of the quarterdeck sentry recalled him to his duty. He settled his hat on his head and walked to the ship's side.

'Patrician!'

The answering hail brought some measure of satisfaction to Mr Frey. The stark, shouted syllables of the ship's name meant the captain was aboard the gig and, in Frey's opinion, the captain's presence could not occur soon enough.

More marines, the side-boys and duty bosun's mates were running aft to take their stations. Tweaking the sennit-covered man-ropes so they hung handily down the frigate's ample tumblehome on either side of the steps, Belchambers raised two fingers to his hat-brim.

'Ship's side manned, sir; Cap'n coming aboard.'

'Very well, Mr Belchambers.'

Frey watched the distinctive blue and white paintwork of the gig; the oars rose and fell in perfect unison. As the oarsmen leaned back, the bow of the boat lifted a trifle and Frey caught sight of Captain Drinkwater alongside the coxswain. There was another figure too, a civilian by the look of his garb. Was this the mysterious passenger for whom, it had been intimated, they were waiting?

A second boat crabbed out in the gig's wake. She was larger, with an untidy clutter of gear in her waist and a consequently less synchronous movement of her oars. Midshipman Porter had a less sure hand upon the tiller of the overloaded launch as it visibly struggled towards them. Frey rightly concluded it had left Dock Town hard well in advance of the gig and had been overtaken.

He stood back in his place as the gig ran alongside and a moment later, as the shrilling of the pipes pierced the peaceful stillness, Frey touched the fore-cock of his hat and Captain Drinkwater hove himself to the deck.

For a moment, as the pipes completed their ritual shrieking, Drinkwater stood at the salute, his eyes swiftly taking in the details of the deck. At last the tremulous echoes waned and faded.

'Evenin', Mr Frey.'

'Evening, sir.'

Drinkwater stood aside and put out a hand.

'Come, sir,' he called back to the civilian in the boat who stared apprehensively upwards. 'Clasp the ropes and walk up the ship's side. 'Tis quite simple.'

Frey suppressed a smile as Drinkwater raised his left eyebrow a trifle. The side party waited patiently while the man-ropes jerked and a young man, elegantly dressed in grey, finally hauled himself breathlessly on to the deck. Frey regarded the stranger with interest and a little wonder. The cut of the coat was so obviously fashionable that it was difficult not to assume the newcomer was a fop. Aware of the curiosity aroused by the contrast between the somewhat grubby informality of Frey's undress uniform coat and the attire of his companion, Drinkwater gave his guest a moment to recover his wind and gape about. Turning to the third lieutenant, Drinkwater asked, 'First Lieutenant aboard, Mr Frey?'

'Here, sir.'

Metcalfe materialized by magic, as if he had been there all along but chose that precise moment to forsake invisibility.

'We'll get under weigh the moment the wind serves.'

Metcalfe cast his eyes aloft and turned nonchalantly on his heels, his whole demeanour indicating the fact that it was a flat calm. 'Aye, aye, sir . . . when the wind serves.'

Frey, already irritated by the first lieutenant's idiosyncratic detachment, watched Captain Drinkwater's reaction to this piece of studied insolence with interest and anxiety.

'You take my meaning, Mr Metcalfe?' There was the hint of an edge to Drinkwater's voice.

Metcalfe completed his slow gyration and met the cool appraisal of his new commander with an inclination of his head.

'Perfectly, sir. May I remind you the ship still wants thirty-seven men to complete her establishment. The watch-bill . . .'

'Then, sir,' snapped Drinkwater with a false formality, 'you may take a party ashore when the launch is discharged and see what the stews of Dock Town will yield up.'

Frey noted the irritation in Drinkwater's tone as he turned back to the young man in grey.

'Mr Vansittart, please allow me to conduct you below, your dunnage and servants will come aboard from the launch directly . . .'

Frey nodded dismissal to the side party and exchanged glances with Midshipman Belchambers. They were, with Mr Comley the boatswain and Mr Maggs the gunner, the only officers remaining from *Patrician*'s last commission. Despite the drafts from the guardships at Plymouth and Portsmouth, the pickings of the Impress Service sent them by the Regulating Officers in the West Country and the sweepings of their own hot-press, they remained short of men.

Patrician had been swinging at a buoy in the Hamoaze when Captain Drinkwater had first come aboard and read his commission to the assembled ship's company. Her officers had regarded with distaste the mixture of hedge-sleeping vagrants, pallid gaol-birds, lumpish yokels and under-nourished quota-men who formed too large a proportion of the people. Afterwards Lieutenant Gordon had spoken for them all: ' 'Tis hands of ability we want, seamen, for God's sake,' Gordon had continued despairingly, 'not mere numbers to fill slots in a watch-bill.'

'That's all you're going to get,' said Pym the surgeon, having inspected them for lice, the lues, ruptures and lesser horrors, adding with some relish, 'a first lieutenant who slept in the ship would be an advantage . . .'

It was not, Frey thought, as Drinkwater and the grey-coated gentleman disappeared below, a very propitious start to the new commission. An absentee first luff, a crew of farm hands and footpads, with what looked like a diplomatic mission, did not augur well for the future. Mr Metcalfe had appeared eventually, in time to throw his weight about while they had completed rigging, warped alongside the hulk and taken in powder and shot. He had a talent, Frey had observed as they dropped down to the anchorage at Cawsand, for a dangerous inconsistency which threatened to set the ship on its ears and kept its unsettled, ignorant and inexpert company in a constant state of nerves.

Mr Metcalfe was of the opinion efficiency manifested itself in proportion to the number of officers disposed about the deck and the orders given. He believed any transgression or failure should be corrected, not by instruction, but by abuse and punishment. Tactful attempts by the mild and sensitive David Gordon to point out the folly of this procedure brought down the wrath of Mr Metcalfe on the unfortunate head of the second lieutenant.

Out of Metcalfe's hearing Moncrieff had shrewdly observed it a matter of prudence to 'keep the weather gauge of Mr Metcalfe. He wants at least one of you Johnnies betwixt himself and trouble.' And failing to see the light of any comprehension in his messmates' eyes in the aftermath of Metcalfe's humiliation of Gordon, he had added, 'to keep his own yard-arm clear, d'you see, and the smell of himself sweet in his own nostrils.'

The quaintness of Moncrieff's assertion had imprinted itself on the minds of his listeners and Mr Wyatt had affirmed the opinion as sound by a loud and conspicuous hawking into the cuspidor.

Sadly, the first lieutenant had had his way, for the mysteries of 'official business' had kept Captain Drinkwater ashore almost continuously until this evening and Frey had not enjoyed his commander's absence.

'Frey?' The peremptory and haughty tone of Metcalfe's voice cut aptly into Frey's train of thought.

'Sir?' He looked round.

'You heard the Captain, Frey. You and Belchambers are to take the launch and scour the town for seamen. Try the village there,' Metcalfe said, in his arch tone, nodding at Cawsand where the first faint lights were beginning to show in the cottage windows.

'Aye, aye, sir.' Frey's acknowledgement was flat, formal and expressionless. There were no seamen to be had in Cawsand, nor within a night's march into Cornwall. They might pick up a few drink-sodden wretches in the dens of Dock Town, but he was not optimistic and was disappointed in Drinkwater's suggestion that anything practical might be achieved. He was about to walk away when Metcalfe spoke again.

'And Frey . . .'

'Sir?'

'Let me know', Metcalfe said with a pained and put-upon look, 'when the Captain is coming aboard next time.'

'The midshipman reported the boat's approach to you in the wardroom.'

'Don't be insolent, Frey, you don't have the charm for it and it ill befits you.'

Frey bit off a hot retort and held his tongue, though he was quite unable to stop the colour mounting to his cheeks. Beyond Metcalfe's shoulder he could see Captain Drinkwater had returned to the quarterdeck.

'I know you served in the ship's last commission,' Metcalfe went on, oblivious of the captain's approach, 'but it don't signify with me, d'you see?'

'Mr Frey.' Drinkwater's curt voice came as a relief to Frey.

'Sir?'

Metcalfe swung round and saw Drinkwater. 'Ah, sir, I was just directing Mr Frey to take command of the press . . .'

'I told you to deal with that, Mr Metcalfe. Mr Frey has another duty to perform.'

'Indeed, sir, may I ask what?'

Drinkwater ignored Metcalfe, addressing Frey directly, over the head of his first lieutenant. 'The launch has, in addition to Mr Vansittart's personal effects and two servants, a large quantity of cabbages, Mr Frey. See they are got aboard and stowed carefully in nets. I want them exposed to the air.'

'Cabbages, sir?' said the first lieutenant, his face registering exaggerated astonishment, 'Are they your personal stores?'

'No, Mister,' Drinkwater said, a note of asperity creeping into his voice, 'they are for the ship's company.'

The captain swung on his heel; Metcalfe stared after him until he was out of earshot.

'Rum old devil, ain't he, Mr Frey?' and the remark shocked Frey for its shift of ground, betraying the inconsistency he had already noted in Metcalfe, but striking him now as deeper than mere pig-headedness.

Frey did his best to keep his voice non-committal. 'Excuse me, sir, I've my duty to attend to.'

'Ah, yes, the cabbages,' Metcalfe said, as though the earlier invitation to complicity had never passed his lips. Lapsing into an almost absent tone he muttered, 'Two servants, damme,' then, raising his voice he bellowed, 'Mr Belchambers! Lay aft here at the double!'

Chapter One *August 1811*

The King's Messenger

Captain Nathaniel Drinkwater hauled himself up the companionway against the heel of the ship and stepped on to the quarterdeck. Clapping one hand to his hat he took a quick reef in his billowing cloak with the other and made his way into the partial shelter of the mizen rigging.

'Morning, sir.' The third lieutenant approached, touched the fore-cock of his hat and added, quite unnecessarily, 'A stiff breeze, sir.'

'Indeed, Mr Frey.' Drinkwater stared aloft, at the whip of the topgallant masts and the flexing of the yards. The wind had veered a touch during the night and had hauled round into the northwest quarter. He knew from the tell-tale compass in his cabin that they were making a good course, but he knew also that the shift of wind would bring bright, squally weather. The first rays of the sun breaking above the cloud banks astern of them promised just such a day.

'Let's hope we've seen the last of that damned rain and sea fret,' Drinkwater said, turning his attention forward again, where the bow swooped, curtseying to the oncoming grey seas.

Two days west of the Scillies, clear of soundings and with a fine easterly wind giving them the prospect of a quick passage, the weather had turned sour on them, closed in and assailed them with a head wind and sleeting rain.

'Treacherous month, August,' Mr Wyatt the master had said obscurely. In the breaks between the rain, a thick mist permeated the ship, filling the gun and berth decks with the unmistakable stink of damp timber, bilge, fungus and human misery. The landsmen, yokels and town labourers, petty felons and vagrants swept up by either the press or the corruption of the quota system which allowed substitutes to be bought and sold like slaves, spewed up their guts and were bullied and beaten into the stations where even their puny weight was necessary to work the heavy frigate to windward.

In his desperation to man the ship, Drinkwater had written to his old friend, Vice-Admiral Sir Richard White, bemoaning his situation. *You have no idea the Extremities to which we are driven in Manning the Fleet Nowadays. It matches the worst Excesses of the American War. We have every Class of Person, with hardly a Seaman amongst them and a large proportion of Men straight from Gaol . . .*

Sir Richard, quietly farming his Norfolk acres and making the occasional appearance in the House of Commons on behalf of a pocket borough, had written in reply, *My Dear Nathaniel, I send you Two Men whom you may find useful. Though both should be in Gaol, the one for Poaching, the other for Something Worse. I received your letter the Morning they came before the Bench. Knowing you to be a confirmed Democrat you can attempt their Reformation. I thus console my Guilt and Dereliction of Duty in not having them Punished Properly according to the due forms, &c, &c, in sending them to Serve their King and Country . . .*

Drinkwater grinned at the recollection. One of the men, Thurston, a former cobbler and of whom White had insinuated guilt of a great crime, was just then helping to hang a heavy coil of rope on a fife-rail pin at the base of the main mast. About thirty, the man had a lively and intelligent face. He must have felt Drinkwater's scrutiny, for he looked up, regarding Drinkwater unobsequiously but without a trace of boldness. He smiled, and Drinkwater felt a compulsion to smile back. Thurston touched his forelock respectfully and moved away. Drinkwater was left with the clear conviction that, in other circumstances, they might have been friends.

As to the crime for which Thurston had been condemned, it was said to be sedition. Drinkwater's enquiries had elicited no more information beyond the fact that Thurston had been taken in a tavern in Fakenham, reading aloud from a Paineite broadsheet.

Sir Richard, not otherwise noted for his leniency, had not regarded the offence as meriting a prison sentence, though conditions in the berth deck were, Drinkwater knew, currently little better than those in a gaol house. Thurston's natural charm and the charge imputed to him would earn the man a certain esteem from his messmates. Prudence dictated Drinkwater keep a weather eye on him.

Drinkwater watched the bow of his ship rise and shrug aside a breaking wave. The impact made *Patrician* shudder and throw spray high into the air where the wind caught it and drove it across the deck to form a dark patch, drenching Thurston and the party of men with whom he went forward.

Frey crossed the deck to check the course at the binnacle then returned to Drinkwater's side

'She's holding sou'west three-quarters west, sir, and I think another haul on the fore and main tacks will give us a further quarter point to the westward.'

'Very well, Mr Frey, see to it.'

Drinkwater left to Frey the mustering of the watch to hitch another fathom in the lee braces and haul down the leading tacks of the huge fore and mainsails. He looked over the ship and saw, despite eight months in dockyard hands, the ravages of time and long service. His Britannic Majesty's frigate *Patrician* was a cut-down sixty-four-gun ship, a class considered too weak to stand in the line of battle. Instead, she had been *razéed*, deprived of a deck, and turned into a heavy frigate.

A powerful cruiser when first modified, she had since completed an arduous circumnavigation under Drinkwater's command. During this voyage she had doubled Cape Horn to the westward, fought a Russian seventy-four to a standstill and survived a typhoon in the China Seas. A winter spent in home waters under another post-captain had further tested her when she had grounded in the Baie de la Seine. Refloated with some difficulty she had subsequently languished in dock at Plymouth until recommissioned for special service. Her prime qualification for this selection was her newly coppered bottom which, it was thought, would give her the fast passages Government desired.

'Well, we shall see,' Drinkwater thought, watching the sunlight break through the cloud bank astern and suddenly transform the scene with its radiance, for nothing could mar the beauty of the morning.

The grey waves sparkled, a rainbow danced in the shower of spray streaming away from the lee bow, the wave-crests shone with white and fleeting brilliance, and the details of the deck, the breeched guns, the racks of round shot, the halliards and clewlines coiled on the fife-rails, the standing rigging, all stood out with peculiar clarity, throwing their shadows across the planking.

The sails arched above them, patched and dulled from service, adding their own shadows to the play of light and shade swinging back and forth across the wet deck, which itself already steamed under the sun's influence.

Drinkwater felt the warmth of the sunshine reach him through the thickness of his cloak, and with it the sharp aroma of coffee floated up from below. A feeling of contentment filled him, a feeling he had thought he would not, *could* not, experience again after the months of family life. He wished Elizabeth could be with him at that moment, to experience something of its magic. All she knew was the potency of its lure, manifested in the frequent abstraction of her husband. He sighed at the mild sensation of guilt, and at the fact that it came to him now to mar the perfection of the day, then dismissed it. A great deal had happened, he reflected reasonably, since he had last paced this deck and been summoned so peremptorily to London, what, a year ago?

Then he had been in the spiritual doldrums, worn out with long service, seeing himself as the scapegoat of government secrecy and hag-ridden with guilt over the death of his old servant Tregembo in the mangrove swamps of Borneo. He had thought at the time that he could never surmount the guilt he had felt, and had accepted the mission to Helgoland in the autumn of 1809 with a grim, fatalistic resignation.

But fate, in all things capricious, had brought him through the ordeal and, quite providentially, made him if not wealthy, then at least a man of comfortable means. True, he had been ill for some months afterwards, so reduced in spirits that the doctors of Petersfield feared for him; but the care of his wife, Elizabeth, and the kindness of old Tregembo's widow Susan, their housekeeper, finally won their fight with the combination of the blue devils, exposure and old wounds.

With the onset of summer Drinkwater and Elizabeth left the children in the care of Susan Tregembo and travelled, spending Christmas at Sir Richard and Lady White's home in Norfolk where their children, Charlotte-Amelia and their own Richard, had joined them. It had been a memorable few months at the end of which Drinkwater's convalescence was complete. It was from the Whites' house that Drinkwater wrote to the Admiralty soliciting further employment. Nothing came of his application, however, and he was not much concerned. The short, cold winter days of walking or riding, of wildfowling along the frozen salt-marsh, were pleasant enough, but the luxury of the long, pleasurable evenings with Elizabeth and the Whites was not lightly to be forsaken for the dubious honour of a quarterdeck in winter.

'You'll only get some damned seventy-four blockading Brest with the Black Rocks under your lee, and some damn fool sending you signals all day,' White had mistakenly consoled him. For although Drinkwater did not have the means for an indefinite stay ashore, nor the inclination to consider his career over and to be superseded by the back-benches of the House of Commons, life was too pleasant not to submit, at least for the time being, to the whim of fate.

Games of bezique and whist, the sound of his daughter's voice singing to Elizabeth's accompaniment, the warmth of White's stable and the smell of fresh meat from the kitchen had served to keep him content. Elizabeth was happy, and that alone was reward enough. He had played with Richard, Montcalm to his son's Wolfe as they refought the capture of Quebec above a low clay cliff under-cut by the River Glaven. Richard, a year senior to White's boy Johnnie, died spectacularly in his young friend's arms with victory assured as Drinkwater himself expired uncomfortably among the crackling stalks of long-dead bracken.

He had led his daughter out at the New Year ball and seen her eyed by the local bloods, flinging her head up and laughing, some-times catching her lower lip in her teeth as he had first seen Elizabeth do in an apple orchard in Cornwall thirty years earlier. And best of all, he had lain nightly beside his wife, moved to acts of deep affection, a poor acknowledgement of her gentle constancy.

Nor had this idyll been rudely terminated by the intrusion of duty. In the end it had been crowned with an unexpected event, a circumstance of the utmost felicity for them all.

Two days into the new year, as the spectre of reaction began to show its first signs with the planning of arrangements to return the children to their home in Hampshire, White received an unex-pected letter from solicitors in Ipswich. Sir Richard had inherited a small estate betwixt the Deben and the Alde, a remote corner of Suffolk lying east of the main highway north from the county town, within sight of the desolate coast of Hollesley Bay and com-prising one modest house and two farms. The estate had once formed part of the lands of a dispossessed priory, the ruins of which stood romantically in its northwest corner.

'It sounds delightful,' said Elizabeth over breakfast, as Catherine White explained the lie of the land and Sir Richard scratched his head and pulled a face.

'Too damned far, m'dear,' he explained, 'no good to me. Belonged to a cousin o' mine. Eccentric fellow; built the place but never married. House can't be more than three years old.' White picked up the letter again, searching for a fact. 'They found him dead in a coppice, frozen stiff, poor devil.'

They had fallen silent, sipping their chocolate with the spectre of untimely death haunting them.

Later, as Drinkwater and White drew rein atop a low rise that looked west to the Palladian pile of Holkham Hall gilded in the sunshine of the winter morning, Sir Richard had turned in his saddle.

'It's the place for you, Nat . . .'

'What is?' asked Drinkwater, staring about momentarily confused, his mind having been fully occupied with his mount and the need to keep up with his host.

'Gantley Hall. I can't keep the place, damn it; have to sell it. What d'you say? Make me an offer.' And he put spurs to his big hunter and cantered off, leaving Drinkwater staring open-mouthed after him.

And so, after a visit in perfect spring weather when the red-brick façade glowed in the afternoon sun and the young apple trees were dusted with the faint, lambent green of new buds, Elizabeth pronounced herself delighted with the house. Less easily satisfied, Drinkwater had interviewed the sitting tenants in the two farms and voiced his doubts.

'If I return to sea, my dear, how will you manage?'

'Well enough, Nathaniel,' Elizabeth had said, 'as I have always done in your absence.'

'But an estate . . .'

'It is a very modest estate, my dear.'

'But . . .'

His protests were brushed aside and they concluded the treaty of sale. By midsummer they had removed from Hampshire and brought with them Louise Quilhampton, Elizabeth's friend and companion, her son, Lieutenant James Quilhampton and his wife

Catriona migrated with them, renting a house in Woodbridge, content to enjoy married life until, like Drinkwater himself, necessity drove James to petition the Admiralty for another posting.

For Drinkwater the summons had come too early, but the letter was a personal one, penned by John Barrow, their Lordships' Second Secretary, whose attitude to Captain Drinkwater had, hitherto, been cool.

It transpired that Drinkwater's success in Hamburg and Helgoland* had rehabilitated his reputation with Barrow. Behind the Second Secretary's phrasing Drinkwater perceived the shadow of Lord Dungarth, head of the Admiralty's Secret Department, and although his new posting did not derive from Dungarth but from the Foreign Office, he was not insensible to his Lordship's backstairs influence:

. . . To conduct with all possible Dispatch the Bearer, Mr Henry St John Vansittart, to the shores of Chesapeake Bay, Providing Him with such Comforts and Necessities as may appear Desirable, to Land and Succour Him and Render Him all such as may, in the circumstances, be Appropriate . . .

Thus ran his instructions and thus far his duty had been light, for poor Vansittart proved a miserable sailor and had yet to make a single appearance at Drinkwater's table. Perhaps, mused Drinkwater, stirring himself and beginning a slow promenade between the windward hance and the taffrail, the seductive aroma of coffee would finally tempt the unfortunate man from his cot.

Reaching the after end of his walk Drinkwater nodded at the stiffening marine sentry posted at the quarter to heave the emergency lifebuoy at any sailor unfortunate enough to fall overboard. For a moment he stood watching the sea birds quartering their wake.

Frey pegged the new course on the traverse board and met Drinkwater as he turned forward again.

'West sou'west, sir,' Frey announced with an air of triumph.

'Very well,' Drinkwater nodded, recalled to the present. He wanted a quick passage, not so much to conform to their Lordships' orders as to avoid the equinoctial gales blowing up from Cape Hatteras. After discharging his diplomatic duty he was

*See *Under False Colours*.

under orders to return Mr Vansittart to London and had high hopes of seeing in the new year of 1812 with his family at Gantley Hall, even, perhaps, returning some of Sir Richard White's generous hospitality.

There was also the question of James Quilhampton, who looked to Drinkwater for interest and advancement. They had discussed the possibility of his serving under Drinkwater, but the matter had been compromised by the appointment of Metcalfe to the *Patrician*. Besides, Quilhampton had had independent command of a gun-brig and itched again for his own quarterdeck, no matter how small. The career of His Majesty's gun-brig *Tracker* had terminated suddenly in capture, and though cleared by a court-martial, Quilhampton wanted nothing more than to prove himself.*

Drinkwater could only support his friend's ambition and promise to do what he could, leaving Quilhampton to enjoy the favours of his bride for a little longer.

But there were more immediate and pressing matters to consider, matters upon which all these wild and selfish speculations depended. To these Drinkwater now gave his attention.

'How are the men shaping up in your opinion, Mr Frey?'

'You know how it is, sir. At the moment the old hands delight in showing the landsmen their superiority and in frightening them with their antics aloft.'

'Aye, I've seen the conceit of the t'gallant yard monkeys.'

'In a day or two they'll tire of that and begin to complain that all the labour falls on their shoulders.'

'Once we run out of fresh food, I expect,' Drinkwater added.

'Yes, sir,' Frey thought of the cabbages stowed in the boats on the booms and the rupture they had caused between himself and the first lieutenant. Relations between Mr Metcalfe and himself were not cordial.

'Happily this passage should settle most of them into the ship's routine and teach them their business,' Drinkwater went on, thinking of White's caution. 'Thank heavens we ain't keeping watch and ward off Ushant with the Black Rocks under our lee and the guns at St Matthew contestin' the point every time we stick our nose into Brest Road . . . Good Lord . . .'

*See *Under False Colours*.

Drinkwater broke off, excused himself and walked forward as the pale figure of Vansittart appeared, rising cautiously from the companionway.

'Good mornin', Vansittart. How d'you fare today?'

Vansittart drew a dank lock of hair back from his forehead, looked upwards and caught sight of the swaying mastheads. Frey saw him swallow and seize the rail with white knuckles.

'Stare at the horizon, man,' Drinkwater snapped sharply, catching hold of him. 'Come, sir, walk to the rail. There, 'tis easy once you have the knack of it.'

Beneath their feet the deck bucked as *Patrician* slammed into a wave. Vansittart staggered, but kept his balance and reached the bulwark. Sweat stood in beads upon his face and he slowly shook his distressed head.

'Dear God, Captain, if I had known . . .'

'The horizon, sir, keep your eyes on the horizon.'

The four men at the frigate's double wheel wore broad grins. Two of them, landsmen manning the after wheel, had been in a similar condition a few days earlier. They chuckled with the relish of the relieved.

'Mind your steering there,' Frey growled, suppressing his own amusement. He regarded Vansittart's stained and unbuckled knee breeches, the rumpled stockings, loose stock and revolting shirt. The contrast with his first dandified appearance aboard *Patrician* was most marked, the more so since his ensemble was the same. Such disregard for his person indicated the extremity of his illness.

'You *will* become accustomed to the motion, I promise you,' Drinkwater was saying, 'but you must have some breakfast.'

'Zounds, sir, no breakfast, I beg you . . .'

Drinkwater turned, his eyes twinkling. 'Pass word for my steward,' he ordered, and when the man made his appearance, said, 'Mullender, bring some cushions on deck.'

Solicitous for his guest, Drinkwater had them placed on the inboard end of a quarterdeck gun-truck and helped Vansittart ease himself down on to them.

'An hour sitting in the sunshine and you'll have an appetite like a midshipman, Vansittart. Now heed what I say and keep your eyes on the horizon . . . good man.'

Vansittart mumbled his thanks and Drinkwater left him. One

bell was struck forward as Drinkwater paused at the top of the companionway.

'I'm goin' below to break my fast, Mr Frey. When the watch changes and you're relieved, give Mr Metcalfe my compliments and tell him we'll exercise the guns during the forenoon.'

'Aye, aye, sir.'

'And keep an eye on our guest,' he added in a low voice.

'Beggin' yer pardon, sir,' the quartermaster asked Frey when the captain had gone, 'but who is 'e?' The man jerked his head at the crumpled figure sitting miserably on the gun-truck.

'Mr Vansittart's a King's Messenger,' Frey explained.

'Bloody 'ell! Can't 'is Majesty find someone more fit to the task, sir?' The old man dropped his voice and muttered, for the benefit of his companions at the wheel, 'Reckon 'e's proof the King's bleedin' barmy.'

Chapter Two *August 1811*

Roast Pork and Politics

'Fire!'

Beside him, Drinkwater was aware that Vansittart winced for the eighth time, shocked by the concussion of the starboard battery which was now, after the fourth broadside, almost simultaneous in its discharges.

'Very well, Mr Metcalfe, you may secure the guns and pipe up spirits.' Drinkwater turned to Vansittart who had earlier expressed a wish to 'see the cannon fired'.

'I'm afraid, sir, you'll have little option,' Drinkwater had said at breakfast when he had announced his intention of exercising the gun-crews. 'When we clear for action the bulkheads will be removed and your cabin will cease to exist.'

Vansittart's look of mistrust, of being wary in his nautical inexperience of being mocked, had amused Drinkwater. But so it had proved, and the transformation of the ship had astonished Vansittart. The secluded comfort of his small but neatly appointed cabin was suddenly invaded by a gang of barefoot and grinning seamen even before the bosun's mates had finished their dreadful squealing at the hatchways and while the marine drummer still rattled his snare drum in the ruffle that signalled the ship was beating to quarters.

Volubly protesting, Vansittart's valet Copford had scooped up his master's silver-mounted mirror and brushes, his jade pomade pot and writing-case, together with his books, papers and dispatch box, before the coarse hands of the seamen threw them unceremoniously into a spare chest Mr Gordon, just then officer of the watch, had thoughtfully sent down. The chest of drawers and washstand vanished before Vansittart's eyes and he was left contemplating two huge, 24-pounder cannon of whose existence he had only hitherto been vaguely aware. At that moment, sent from the quarterdeck above, Mr Midshipman Porter had plucked at his sleeve.

'Captain's compliments, sir, and would you care to join him on the quarterdeck.'

It sounded neither complimentary, nor a question; beneath its formal veneer it was a command and it irritated Vansittart. He had only just mastered seasickness; now the wretched comforts of what passed at sea for civilization had been rudely snatched from him and this greasy, red-faced boy was dancing impatiently round like an imp.

'Damn it,' he began, choking the protest off in a masterly effort to retain his *sang froid* before Porter. He had nowhere else to go and he was now being rudely jostled as the powder monkeys ran about the place and the seamen round the guns stretched tackles and hefted rammers and sponges. Mr Gordon appeared, his hanger bouncing belligerently upon his left hip, gesticulating, Vansittart observed, with a hand wanting two fingers. The normally mild officer had a gleam in his eye that lent force to his 'If you please, sir . . .' which dissolved into a shout at his gunners. 'Clear away there, starbowlines, look lively and beat those lubbers to larboard.'

'Careful, damn your eyes,' snarled Porter at a passing landsman who slopped water from his pail over Vansittart's feet. 'This way, sir . . .'

And Vansittart bowed to the inevitable and allowed himself to be drawn, squelching miserably in sodden shoes, on to the quarterdeck.

For three-quarters of an hour he wondered what all the fuss had been about. On deck, he could no longer see the main batteries properly, though he caught glimpses of activity beneath the boat booms in the waist. The upperdeck gunners manning the quarterdeck 18-pounders seemed to squat idly round their guns for some time while a tirade of shouted orders in which the clipped voices of Frey and Gordon, each in charge of a 24-pounder battery on the gun deck, were interspersed with shouted exhortations from Mr Metcalfe.

The first lieutenant's most offensive weapon was a silver hunter which he consulted with maddening and incomprehensible regularity, dictating numerous time intervals to Porter who ran after him with a slate as he went from waist to quarterdeck and back, pausing now and again to make some remark to Captain Drinkwater.

The captain appeared to take very little interest in the proceedings but stood by what Vansittart was now able to identify with some pride as the mizen weather rigging, addressing the occasional remark to Mr Wyatt, whose face bore a sort of disdain for the present activity. Vansittart knew Wyatt was specifically charged with the frigate's navigation and supposed it was some esoteric point on this to which he and Drinkwater referred.

Periodically there was an awful rumbling from below which Vansittart felt most through the soles of his feet, but it did not appear to affect the men on the upper deck. Quite mystified as to what was happening and ignored by all who might otherwise have enlightened him, Vansittart was compelled to wait foolishly for an explanation.

In the event he was saved the trouble, for after half an hour Metcalfe ran up from the waist, stared at his watch, referred to Porter's slate, muttered something to Drinkwater, and turned his attention to the quarterdeck guns.

Silence was called for and the 18-pounders that had been cleared away earlier were brought to a state of readiness. Metcalfe excitedly called out a stream of orders at which the gunners, with varying degrees of verisimilitude and enthusiasm for so dumb a show, leapt around their pieces. The cause of the rumbling was swiftly revealed as the 18-pounders were run out through their open ports. On the command 'Point!' the gun-captains kneeled beside the breeches of their brute black charges, squinted along the sights and ordered the carriages slewed, adjusting the elevation at the same time. Vansittart looked in vain for a mark, concluded correctly that it was a sham since no boat had put out from the ship, neither had she been manoeuvred, and watched with increasing fascination. Each gun-captain drew away from his gun, raised one hand in signal while the other grasped the lanyard of his fire-lock. When the row of hands had all gone up, Metcalfe yelled 'Fire!' and there was an anti-climactic click as flint sparked ineffectually against steel.

Having repeated this procedure with both quarterdeck batteries and then the half-dozen 42-pounder slide-mounted carronades on the forecastle, Metcalfe trotted back to Drinkwater.

'Very well,' Vansittart overheard the captain say, 'you may load powder.'

For the next few minutes Vansittart's ear-drums were assailed by the battering thunder of the guns. Clouds of acrid grey smoke swept over him and he was dimly aware, through the sudden, bright flashes that pierced the smoke, of dark objects hurled from the guns, first to starboard and then to larboard. At last they fell silent and Drinkwater turned towards him, the infuriatingly amused yet somehow attractive smile playing about his mouth.

'The noise disturbs you, Mr Vansittart?'

'A little, I confess,' Vansittart said, feeling more than a trifle foolish.

'They were only half-charges, don't you know, to conserve powder. I get no allowance from the Navy Board, damn them.'

'And you fired them at no mark?' Vansittart asked in an attempt to appear knowledgeable. 'I mean you did not intend the shot to hit anything?' He thought of the black dots he had seen in the centre of the discharges.

'No, no, no, we fired at no mark and shot off nothing more offensive then the wads . . .'

'But I saw . . .'

'Oakum wadding, nothing more. The only ball you see, they say, is the one heading directly towards you, and I hope it won't come to that, eh?'

'Oh.' Vansittart's tone was crestfallen.

Drinkwater felt sorry for the diplomat. ' 'Tis too lively to try at a target. If the wind falls light I will put out a boat, but the men are untried, a mixture, rough and uncoordinated as is usual at the beginning of a commission. At first it is essential, a moment please . . .'

Drinkwater broke off his explanation to attend to Mr Belchambers. Vansittart could not hear what passed between them, but the midshipman's face was dark and Drinkwater's bore a look of disquiet when he turned back to resume.

'At first it is essential to ensure the gun-crews operate in a disciplined manner and serve their guns correctly. One cannot afford mistakes in the heat of battle. You have doubtless seen an excited sportsman loose off a ramrod at game birds, well the same thing may happen here. Perhaps worse. A new charge thrust hastily into an unsponged gun may result in a premature discharge in which the carriage recoils over a gun-captain engaged in clearing a vent.'

He paused, then added, 'As it is, one man is suffering from crushed fingers.'

'Mr Belchambers . . .?'

Drinkwater nodded. 'Yes, he brought me word of it. I ordered the powder largely to gratify the hands. Prolonged dumb show is useful, but nothing makes 'em concentrate like gunpowder. Now I'm doubting the wisdom of my own action.' A rueful expression crossed the captain's face and he smiled. 'A pity,' he concluded.

Drinkwater turned away. Metcalfe was hovering with his insufferable watch, demanding the captain's attention. Vansittart cast about him. Already the guns were resecured and the pipes twittered at the hatchways with their appalling raucous squealing. Suddenly, as the cry 'Up spirits!' went round the ship, Vansittart was aware of a strange buzz, as of a swarm of bees, and realized it was the ship's company, mustering for their daily issue of grog. For the first time since he had stepped on board, Mr Vansittart felt inexplicably easier about his situation.

He went below. Miraculously his cabin had reappeared. Copford was laying his toiletries on the chest of drawers. He looked white and drawn.

'Where the devil were you?' Vansittart asked.

'With the surgeon, sir. In what's called the cockpit. Full o' knives and saws it were, an' they brought some young cully down with his hand all bloody . . .'

It was not with the intention of holding a post-mortem that Drinkwater invited his officers to dinner that afternoon. It occurred to him that the time was ripe, both on account of the weather and the fact that the gunnery exercise had been a corporate act different from the heaving and hauling, the pumping and sheer drudgery necessary to clear the chops of the Channel. Whatever its failings, it had been the first step in shaking his crew together as the ship's company of a man-o'-war.

Looking at his officers as they silently sipped their soup, nervously adjusting to the unaccustomed luxury of his cabin, Drinkwater wondered what they feared about him, for their lack of chatter was awesome. Frey might have lightened the mood with his familiarity, but Frey had the deck and Drinkwater had not invited any representatives from the gunroom. He would break his fast with the midshipmen tomorrow morning. For the nonce it was his officers with whom he wished to become better acquainted and their present quiescence was vaguely worrying. Did he intimidate them?

It had come upon him, on recent mornings as he shaved, that he was ageing. He had no idea why this sudden realization of the obvious had struck him so forcibly. Perhaps it was the return to the cares and concerns of command after months of indolence, perhaps no more than the half-light that threw his face into stark relief as he peered at his image in the mirror. Whatever the cause, he had had a glimpse of himself as others saw him. Did that grim visage with its scarred cheek and the powder burns tattooed into one eyelid intimidate?

In repose he wondered what expression he habitually wore. Elizabeth had told him that his face brightened when he smiled. Did he not smile enough? Did he wear a perpetual scowl upon the quarterdeck?

He looked down the twin lines of officers, bending over their soup, concentrating on their manners lest it slop into their white-breeched laps. At the far end of the table Metcalfe laid his soup-spoon in his plate and Mullender loomed up at his shoulder. Others followed suit, the chink of silver upon china the only sound in the cabin, if one set aside the wracking groans of the frigate's fabric, the low grind of the rudder and the surge and hiss of the sea beneath the windows.

The handsome Gordon and the thin-faced chaplain Simpson, the ruddy Wyatt, the elegant Moncrieff, the purser and the surgeon remained disappointingly unanimated.

'Well, gentlemen,' Drinkwater said, laying down his own soup-spoon, 'what is your judgement of the temper of the men following our exercise at the guns this morning?'

If he had hoped to bring them from their tongue-tied awkwardness by the question, he was sadly disappointed. He sensed an invisible restraint upon them, a disquieting influence, and looked from one to another for some evidence of its source.

'Come, surely someone has an opinion? I never knew a wardroom where criticism of one sort or another was not lavished upon someone.' His false attempt at levity provoked no wry grins. He tried again. 'Mr Gordon, how did the men at your battery respond?'

'Well, sir,' Gordon faltered, shot a glance at the other end of the table and coloured, coughing. The blond lick of his hair fell forward and he threw it back. 'Well, sir, they were well enough, I believe.' He was oddly nervous. 'Their timing improved. According to the first lieutenant . . .'

'They did well enough, sir, for our first exercise,' broke in Metcalfe stridently. 'The starbowlines were faster than those on the port side and loosed both their broadsides in seventy-nine seconds . . .'

Drinkwater was fascinated. The riddle, if he judged aright, was solved by the presence of Metcalfe. Yet these younger men were not intimidated by the first luff, merely silent in his company, as if to speak invited some response. Belittlement perhaps? A mild but persistent humiliation? Did they simply choose not to speak in Metcalfe's presence? Was the man a tyrant in the wardroom? He was clearly a fussy and fossicking individual. It was interesting too, to hear Metcalfe trot out the word 'port' instead of larboard. True, its usage was gaining ground in the Service, but something in Metcalfe's tone endowed the word with fashionable *éclat*, and more than a little bombast.

'But did you mark any change in their mood, Mr Gordon ?'

'You mean after the exercise as compared with before, sir?'

'Yes, exactly.' Drinkwater was aware of a faint air of frustration in his tone.

'They were . . .'

'A damned sight smarter at the conclusion.' Metcalfe finished the sentence and Drinkwater detected the corporate affront passing through the officers like a gust of wind through dry grass. Moncrieff, resplendent in the scarlet of the marines, threw himself back in his chair. It might have been for the benefit of Mullender, just then serving them all with thick slices of roast pork, but conveyed a different significance to the vigilant Drinkwater.

'I thought them to be much more cheerful, don't you know. As though they enjoyed loosin' oft the cannon.'

Drinkwater turned to the speaker, Henry Vansittart, sitting on his right-hand side and whose presence Drinkwater had ignored in his preoccupation. He might, he thought with sudden guilt, have prompted a conversation with poor Vansittart whom, he knew, felt gauche among these tarpaulin jacks. Vansittart's assessment was exactly what he had hoped Gordon would say, and judging from the mute nods of concurrence, was at least sensed by most of them.

'Oh, they like their bangs, all right, sir.' Wyatt's contribution fell like a brick into a still pool and Drinkwater was glad of it, inappropriate though it was. 'They'll give the Yankees something to remember, never you fear.'

'I do hope it doesn't come to that, Mr . . ., oh dear, forgive me . . .' Vansittart floundered and Drinkwater hoped his diplomatic skills were not demonstrated by his inability to remember the master's name.

'Wyatt, Mr Vansittart, Wyatt.'

'Of course, of course, how foolish . . .'

Wyatt pronounced the name like 'fancy-tart' and thereby brought a smile to the faces of the diners. Drinkwater was sorry for Vansittart, but glad of the joke. 'I agree with Mr Vansittart,' he said, trying not to make the pronounciation of the name too obviously correct. 'As for their fighting ability, we shall see, depending upon our luck. However, we may try them at a mark if we are becalmed, which reminds me, Mr Moncrieff, your marines must be put to some target practice. Tomorrow do you let 'em loose on the bottles we empty today.'

Moncreiff opened his mouth to reply but was prevented.

'Capital idea, sir.'

'I'm glad you approve, Mr Metcalfe,' Drinkwater replied, and was delighted at catching the exchange of hastily suppressed grins between Gordon and Moncrieff. He had certainly learnt more about them than they about him.

'Perhaps, Mr Vansittart, you could enlighten us all as to the current state of relations between ourselves and the United States of America. Do I take it from your reaction to Mr Wyatt's bellicose assertion that we are anxious to avoid a conflict with our quondam cousins?'

'Damme yes, sir. Most emphatically. Whilst I don't doubt for a moment the temper of your men, it would place an insupportable burden on the Ministry to engage in hostilities with them.'

'I think it might place an insupportable burden on His Majesty's Navy,' Drinkwater added, thinking of the difficulties they had experienced manning *Patrician*.

'Aye,' put in Metcalfe, 'we have squadrons in almost every corner of the world in addition to the Channel Fleet. To raise another, or reinforce the ships at Halifax . . .'

'Plans are afoot to send Rear-Admiral York out with four

seventy-fours and a brace of frigates, I believe,' Drinkwater said, 'though I agree that this would be insufficient for a blockade, and if we contemplate war then we must enforce a blockade.'

'What force is the American navy?' Moncrieff derided.

'Small, lad,' said Wyatt, helping himself to more wine 'but they will issue letters-of-marque and have privateers shoaling like herrings.'

'Oh, come Wyatt, privateers . . .'

'Enough of 'em and they'll pick our bones clean, snap up our trade. Don't despise the Yankees. Remember the *Little Belt* . . .'

'That was a damned outrage,' protested Metcalfe vehemently, alluding to the unprovoked attack made by the American frigate *President* upon the smaller British sloop, 'a deliberate provocation . . .'

'What tommy-rot and nonsense, it was a case of mistaken identity . . .'

'The principal aim of British policy', Vansittart broke in, aware that his lecture, hitherto the only means of ascendancy he had gained over the frigate's officers, had been seized by his audience, 'is to avoid provocation. That is why the offence committed by the *President* was allowed to pass . . .'

'To our eternal shame,' interrupted Metcalfe.

'Sometimes it is necessary to swallow a little pride, Mr Metcalfe,' Vansittart said, 'in order to guide the conduct of affairs. Some sea-officers consider themselves so far in the vanguard of matters that they rashly compromise our endeavours. Take Humphries of the *Leopard*, for instance, when he engaged the *Chesapeake*; he scarcely endeared us to the Americans.'

'Oh, damn the Jonathans,' snapped Wyatt, out of patience with the pettifoggings of diplomacy. 'They poach our seamen and must be made to spit 'em out again, given a . . . what the deuce d'ye call it, Bones?' Wyatt turned to the surgeon.

'An expectorant, I think you mean,' Pym answered drily, adding, ' 'tis all very well to take men out of Yankee merchant ships, God knows we do it enough to our own, but to attempt to do so out of a foreign man-o'-war and then fire into her when she won't comply . . .'

The allusion to Captain Humphries' action provoked Wyatt further: 'That's what the buggers deserved! You call 'em foreign, by God! They were no more than damned rebels!' Wyatt protested, dividing the camp. There was a rising tide of argument into which Vansittart plunged.

'They are most certainly not, Mr Wyatt! You'll please to recall they are a legitimately established sovereign state, what ever memories you older gentlemen have of the American War.'

Drinkwater's grin was still-born; he was one of those 'older men'.

The whole business was a shameful affair,' Vansittart went on, 'the *Chesapeake* was not in fighting trim, half her guns were not mounted and she had no cause to expect an attack . . .'

'Beyond the fact that she had British deserters on board,' Wyatt persisted sarcastically.

'Her captain surrendered,' added Metcalfe with a characteristic lack of logic lost in the heat of the dispute.

'He struck, Mr Metcalfe,' Vansittart said, and Drinkwater realized he was more than holding his own; he was enjoying himself. 'He struck, merely to avoid the further effusion of blood. It was a pity Humphries insisted on searching the *Chesapeake* . . .'

'He found *four* men,' Wyatt snapped, 'four deserters.'

Vansittart turned a contemptuous expression on Wyatt. 'The facts, Mr Wyatt,' he said with a cool detachment 'indicate three of those men were Americans pressed into our service. Had Captain Humphries contented himself with accepting the surrender and apologizing for the dishonour he had done the American flag by his unprovoked attack, we might have thus avoided the necessity of eating humble pie in the affair of the *President* and the *Little Belt*.' Vansittart stared round the table, a smile of satisfaction playing round the corners of his mouth which he hid by delicately dabbing at it with his napkin. He had achieved a victory over these rough sea-officers and was justifiably pleased with himself. He caught Drinkwater's eye. 'I know many of you to be vexed by the case of Americans born before Independence and therefore theoretically British subjects ripe for impressment into the British fleet. But I hardly think one of you to be so mean-minded as to admit this a *casus belli*, eh?'

'I do not think the Americans will go to war over the plight of their seamen,' Drinkwater said, breaking the silence of Vansittart's triumph, 'though their politicians may make a deal of noise about it. However, there is always the danger that they may imagine us to be in a position of weakness, as indeed we are, with the army in

Spain to supply. Suppose they did let loose say five hundred privateers, as Mr Wyatt suggests, to tie up our cruisers with the burden of convoys, and suppose then they attempted, as they did in the last war, to conquer Canada. I would venture to suggest the most disloyal conjecture that they might succeed.'

'Ah, sir, that', said Vansittart, holding up a wagging finger to add import to his words, 'is what concerns His Majesty's government . . .'

'Or that of the Prince of Wales,' Metcalfe interjected sententiously.

'No, sir, the Ministry remains the King's; the Prince, in his capacity as Regent, is, as it were, *in loco sui parentis*.' Vansittart's little joke was lost. The King's supposed insanity combined with his son's extravagant and profligate frivolity and the Duke of York's corruption and malpractice at the War Office, served to cast a shadow over most political deliberations.

'We should also remember Russia,' Drinkwater went on. 'She has seized Finland from the Swedes and her fleet is not to be despised . . .'

'Canada is the keystone to it all,' Vansittart said, almost waving away Drinkwater's words. 'It all depends upon whether the hawks prevail over the doves in the Yankee administration.'

'Let us hope', said the chaplain, speaking for the first time, 'that good sense and Christian charity prevail . . .'

'We always *hope* for that, Mr Simpson,' said Pym the surgeon ironically, 'and are so consistently disappointed, that did hope not spring eternal into the human breast, there would be an end to all your piety.'

A small tribute of laughter followed this and a silence fell as Mullender cleared the table. The ruined carcass of the pig lay dismembered before them. The dinner had not been entirely unsuccessful.

'It is the Orders-in-Council prohibiting trade with the French Empire which will provoke a war,' Drinkwater said. 'The Americans believe it to be an unwarranted interference with their right to trade. Their grain saved the Revolution once, in '94, and they are great boys for profit . . . they might yet prove a force to be reckoned with.'

The cloth was drawn and the decanter set before him. He held the lead-crystal glass against the heel of the ship. It had been a present from Elizabeth and he would be most upset if it were lost. He drew the stopper and sent the port on its slow circulation. An anticipatory silence fell upon the company.

When it had completed its circuit he proposed the loyal toast. 'Gentlemen,' he said, solemnly, 'the King.'

'The King,' they chorused.

He raised his glass a second time. 'His Royal Highness, the Prince Regent.'

They mumbled their responses and waited as Drinkwater again lifted his glass. 'And to peace, gentlemen, at least with the Americans.' He bowed towards Vansittart. 'And success to Mr Vansittart's mission.'

'Amen to that,' said the chaplain.

After the officers had left, Drinkwater motioned Vansittart to remain behind. He refilled their glasses while Mullender clattered the dishes in the adjacent pantry.

'I am glad to see you fully recovered from the sickness, Mr Vansittart, and in such good form. I am afraid they are not sophisticates where political matters are concerned.'

'I thought my presence offended them, they seemed so taciturn.'

Drinkwater laughed. 'You marked their odd behaviour then, but discovered the wrong cause.'

'I think not, Captain, though I own to that apprehension initially. It seemed to me they find Metcalfe overbearing.'

'Yes, you are right,' agreed Drinkwater admiringly. Vansittart was no fool, though there was no point in dwelling upon the subject. 'As to their attitude to our present assignment, they have been too closely bred to war and would delight in licking what they consider to be the upstart Yankees.'

'You have reservations, Captain?'

'I am old enough to have served in the last American war and, in a lifetime of service, have found it to be a foolish man who underestimates his adversary.'

Vansittart nodded, his face suddenly wise beyond his years, borne down by the responsibility of his task.

'You are more than a mere messenger.'

Vansittart looked up, his eyes shrewd. He could hold his liquor too, Drinkwater acknowledged.

'Yes. It is likely that we will give ground on the matter of impressment. It will be a great *coup* for John Quincy Adams who has been alleging our perfidious actions are on a par with murder. He claims several thousand such cases and it will set a deal of lawyers pettifogging over the rules governing neutrals but . . .' he shrugged.

'Needs must when the devil drives, eh?'

'It defuses any action mediated towards Canada. You see, Captain, there is a rumour, gathered by persons close to French affairs, which suggests the Americans will claim certain oceanic rights over the Gulf Stream, and that they are approaching France for the means to build seventy-five men-o'-war . . .'

'And John Quincy Adams has been hob-nobbing with Count Rumiantsev in Russia . . .'

'How the devil d'you know about that?' Vansittart's eyebrows rose in astonishment. 'Ah, I collect: Lord Dungarth.'

Drinkwater nodded. 'He has from time to time seen fit to enlighten me.'

'He seeks to draw Russia back to the old Coalition and reaffirm an alliance with Great Britain again.'

'Yes.' Drinkwater thought of the dropsically obese, one-legged man whom he had first known as a dashing young first lieutenant in the war with the American rebels a generation earlier. 'He has devoted his life to the defeat of the French.'

'It is not entirely that which prompts this appeasement of the Americans, nor the news of Adams and the Russians combining against us. The truth is that a halting of trade with America is having a bad effect on our industries. The mercantile lobby is active in Parliament and though the Luddites are hanged when caught, their cause cannot be thus easily suppressed. Public disorder', Vansittart said, leaning forward slightly and lowering his voice confidentially, the exaggeration betraying a degree of insobriety, 'is currently tying down more regiments of light dragoons then the French are in Spain.'

Drinkwater knew of the frame-breaking riots. Skilled unemployed men, deprived of their trades by new-fangled machines, had taken the law into their own hands and the law had fought back with its customary savage reprisals. He thought of the Paineite, Thurston, occupied somewhere about the *Patrician*.

He refilled Vansittart's glass. 'So politics are again guided by expedience, eh, Vansittart?' he said. He raised his own glass and stared at the dark ruby port, then looked directly at his young passenger.

'D'you reckon you can do it?'

'Not a doubt, Captain. They shouted loudest about sailors' rights, whatever their true motives. We'll concede that point and all will be well.'

'But for one thing,' Drinkwater said, squinting at his glass again, 'which I doubt you have taken into account.'

'Oh? And what is that?'

'It will encourage our men to desert.'

Chapter Three *August 1811*

A Capital Shot

In the hermetic life of a ship the smallest matters assume an unreal importance. This is often the case when a voyage has just begun, as with His Majesty's frigate *Patrician*, during the process of shaking down, when men thrown together under the iron rule of naval discipline jostle each other for the means by which to express themselves, to keep and maintain their own sense of identity.

The obligations of duty combined with those of dutifulness to suppress the natural instincts of the officers in a subtler and more dangerous way than among the ratings. The stuffy formalities and the rigid, pretentious hierarchies mixed uneasily with a cultivated and assumed languor in the wardroom. The officers were fortunate in having their cabins. Convention permitted private retreat, but while this was more civilized, it tended to prolong the incubation of trouble.

Elsewhere, on the berth and gun decks, men frequently abused each other and came quickly to blows. Such explosions were usually regulated by the lower deck's own, inimitable ruling, and while fights were swift and decisive, they were rarely bloody or degenerated into brawls. The bosun's mates and other petty officers charged with the maintenance of order knew how far to let things go before intervening.

The midshipmen's berth, by its very proximity and open location in the orlop, generally knew about these disturbances, but a tacit and unspoken agreement existed between the men and the younkers, for the latter too often had recourse to their own fists.

While the officers festered in their differences and disagreements, the fights held in the semi-secret rendezvous of the cable tiers provided a cause for betting and gaming, as much natural releases for men pent up within the stinking confines of one of

His Britannic Majesty's ships of war, as the catharsis felt by the protagonists themselves.

The tiny, insignificant causes of disorder, whether in the wardroom, the gunroom or the berth deck, fuelled the ship's gossip, or scuttlebutt. Their triviality was rarely a measure of their importance. This lay chiefly in their ability to rouse sentiment and cause diversions.

In the case of Mr Frey's dislocation with Mr Metcalfe, it united the wardroom almost unanimously behind the third lieutenant. *Almost* unanimously, because Mr Wyatt refused to take sides, his coarse nature impervious to aesthetic considerations, while Mr Simpson the chaplain pretended a charitable neutrality, though Metcalfe's manner deeply offended him.

It was this strained atmosphere that the officers took with them to dinner with Captain Drinkwater and although they might have left it behind them in their commander's presence, it was Metcalfe's peculiar comments about the captain which prevented this. The cause of the trouble had been nonsensical enough. Mr Frey, during his afternoon watch below, had spread a sheet of paper on the wardroom table upon which he was executing some water-colour sketches. He had brought a large number of pencil drawings back from the *Patrician*'s circumnavigation. Some of these had been of hydrographic interest and had been worked up, overlaid with washes, and submitted to the Admiralty. Their lordships had expressed their approbation and Frey, by way of diversion as much as seeking further approval, had decided to embellish all his folio of drawings, many of which were competent and fascinating records of the frigate's sojourn on the coasts of China and Borneo. They ranged from a spirited representation of an attack on the stronghold of piratical Sea-Dyaks and the horrors of a typhoon to dreamy washes showing the Pearl River under calm, grey skies, the background pierced with the exotic spires of pagodas and the foreground filled with the bat-winged sails of junks tacking up under the high poops of anchored Indiamen.

Returning from some roving inspection, Metcalfe had entered the wardroom and sat without comment in his customary chair. Tipping it back on its rear legs against the heel of the ship he nonchalantly threw both feet upon the table. One heel rested upon, and tore, the corner of a sheet of Frey's cartridge paper. Frey looked up from his work with brush and paints. 'If you please, sir . . .' he said, at which Metcalfe adjusted his feet and succeeded in extending the tear. Instead of the margin of the paper being damaged, the washed-over drawing was ripped still further.

In the argument which followed, Frey was constrained by his subordinate rank and his outrage, which made him almost mute with indignation. Metcalfe protested Frey had no business 'covering the whole damned table with rubbish', and compounded his vandalism by picking up the drawing by a corner. Already old and browned at the edges, the paper tore completely in half as he held it for the inspection of the others. Frey went deathly pale.

'Have a care, sir . . .' he breathed almost inaudibly and Moncrieff, suddenly alerted to the seriousness of a situation which warranted a challenge, rallied to Frey's support. He lamented the first lieutenant's carelessness and when Metcalfe rounded on him, damning his insolence Moncrieff coloured dangerously and put his hand on his empty hip.

'By God, sir, had you done that to me I should have drawn upon you,' he hissed as Simpson came forward to restrain him and Pym emerged from his cabin to stare over his glasses at Metcalfe.

The first lieutenant continued to bluster and Simpson expressed regret that Metcalfe had not the manners to apologize. The consensus of opinion had gathered against Metcalfe. He resorted to a damning of them all for being the captain's lickspittle and reviled Captain Drinkwater for an incompetent tarpaulin officer who, by his very age, was barely fit to command a frigate, had been passed over for a line-of-battle ship and clearly deserved no better than to be commander of the glorified dispatch-boat that the *Patrician* had become. This irrational outburst astounded the officers. They stood silent with disbelief as Metcalfe's bravado ran its erratic course and he finally slammed out of the wardroom.

For a moment nobody moved, then Frey began to put his paints and paper away and, as always, the routine of the ship reasserted itself. The watch was called, and Frey prepared to go on deck.

'Thank you, Moncrieff,' Frey said as the marine officer bent and retrieved half the water-colour sketch, 'I mean for your support.'

'I can't take the measure of the man,' Moncrieff said puzzled and staring at the closed door of the wardroom, 'what does he hope to gain by such conduct?'

Frey shrugged. 'I don't know.'

'You kept your temper very well, Mr Frey,' put in the Reverend

Simpson, 'under somewhat extreme provocation.' The chaplain's thin, soft fingers had reached out for one of the sketches. 'These are really very good . . . but not worth fighting over.'

'I collect Mr Metcalfe's distempered spirit may be something to beware of, gentlemen. Well, we are expected for dinner . . .'

Frey cooled off during his watch, his anger subsiding to mere annoyance. He regretted being unable to dine with Drinkwater but could not have sat at the same table as Metcalfe that afternoon. Nor could he, at the end of his watch, return to the wardroom where Metcalfe, being a creature of predictable habit, would be drinking a glass of wine. At such times, the man was at his most truculent and critical, and habitually found some small matter to complain of, a gun in one's battery untidily lashed, a rusty round-shot in the garlands, or a seaman upon whom some misdemeanour could be pinned but in which his divisional officer was implicated. It was remarkable, Frey reflected how in so short a time Metcalfe has impressed his generally unpleasant character upon the ship.

Resolved not to return to the wardroom, Frey decided instead to visit Midshipman Belchambers in the gunroom on the pretext of giving him some instruction. Immediately upon descending to the gloom of the orlop he realized his mistake. The surprised and furtive looks of men about him, the quick evasive slinking away and the whispered warning of a commissioned presence seemed to Frey's overwrought nerves to echo into the dark recesses of the ship with a sinister significance. Off-duty marines in their berth just forward of the midshipmen's den stopped polishing boots and bayonets. The midshipmen themselves wore expressions of guilt and Frey was just in time to see a book snapped shut, a pencil hurriedly concealed and a stack of promissory notes swept out of sight. He caught Mr Midshipman Porter's eye.

'What are you running a book on, Mr Porter?'

'Er, a book, sir? Er, nothing, sir . . .'

Frey looked about him. The collusion of the midshipmen argued against anything serious being wrong. He had not disturbed a mutinous assembly and would be best advised to turn a blind eye to the matter.

'Mr Belchambers?' he said, affecting a disinterested tone, 'Is he here?'

'First Lieutenant sent for him, sir.'

'Ah . . .' Frey cast a final look round the dark hole. The stale air was thick with the stink of crowded humanity, stores, bilge-water, rust, rot and rat-droppings. He retreated to the ladder.

'Pass word for Sergeant Hudson, will you,' he called mildly to the marine sentry at the companionway. Frey dawdled in the berth deck, wandering forward. Hudson caught up with him as he stood surveying the surviving pigs in the extempore manger just forward of the breakwater set across the ship to stop sea sloshing aft from the plugged hawse-holes.

'Sir, Mr Frey, sir?' The marine sergeant puffed up, buttoning his tunic and jerking his head. Men in the adjacent messes, alerted to something unusual by Frey's presence so far forward, made themselves scarce.

'Hudson, what the devil's going on below?' Frey pretended interest in the pigs and spoke in a low but insistent voice.

'Below, sir? Nothing, sir . . .'

'Don't take me for a fool, Hudson. Something is, or has been going on. When the officers were dining with the captain, I suspect.'

'Ah, well, er, yes, sir . . .'

'Go on.'

'Well, sir, weren't nothing much, sir, only a bit o' fun,

'Gaming, you mean?'

Hudson shrugged. 'Well, a few side bets, sir, you know how it is.'

'On what? Baiting? A fight, a wrestle?'

'Bit of wrestling, sir. Nothing to worry about, sir. If it were I'd be down on it like a cauldron o' coal.'

Frey looked hard at the man. 'If I get wind of an assembly, Hudson, I'll have your hide. We want no combinations aboard here.'

Hudson shook his head and Frey noticed the man had no neck, for his whole body swung, adding emphasis to his indignant refutation of the suggestion. 'No fear o' that, sir, not while Josiah Hudson is sergeant aboard this here man-o'-war.'

'I hope you're right, Hudson.'

'O' course I'm right, sir. 'Tis against regulations in the strictest sense but, well, why don't you place a bet, sir? Won't do no harm and I'll do it for you. You won't be the only officer . . .' Hudson paused, aware he was being indiscreet.

'Really? Who else?' Frey disguised his curiosity.

'Oh, *I* don't know that, sir, but one or two o' the young gennelmen seems to have enough money to be acting as agents.'

The information robbed Frey of the initiative. He turned aft. At the wardroom door he met Mr Belchambers in search of him.

'I believe you were looking for me, sir.'

'Oh, yes, but it don't matter now. Carry on.'

'Aye, aye, sir.'

Belchambers turned for the companionway when intuition caused Frey to call him back.

'What did the First Lieutenant want you for?'

Belchambers stammered uncertainly, his eyes on the wardroom door and the sentry posted there. 'Oh, er, er, a small . . . er, private matter, sir.'

'A private matter between you and the First Lieutenant, Mr Belchambers?' Frey said archly. 'You should be careful your private affairs are not capable of misconstruction . . .'

Belchambers blushed to the roots of his hair. 'I, er, I . . .'

'Did he win?'

'Sir . . .?'

'Did the First Lieutenant win? I assume you had been summoned to tell him whether he had won or lost the bet you had placed for him.'

Belchambers swallowed unhappily. 'Sir, I was unwilling . . .'

'Don't worry,' said Frey, his voice suddenly sympathetic, 'be a good fellow and just let Mr Porter know I am aware of the situation and I've promised a thrashing to anyone I find running a book.' Belchambers caught the twinkle in Frey's eye. He knew Mr Frey, he was a certainty in a shifting world. Mr Belchambers was learning that ships changed as their companies changed and though he respected Captain Drinkwater, the captain was too remote to know the miseries and petty tyrannies that midshipmen endured.

Whilst Captain Drinkwater was unaware of Belchambers' misery and knew nothing of the improper conduct of his first lieutenant as discovered by Mr Frey, he was troubled by the evident bad blood prevailing among his officers. There was little he could do about it, and at heart he was disinclined to make too much of it. They were bound on a specific mission, their cruise was circumscribed by the Admiralty's special instructions and with the Royal Navy pre-eminent in the North Atlantic he privately considered it most unlikely they would see action. Not that he was complacent, it was merely that in weighing up their chances of meeting an enemy, he thought the thing unlikely. Anyway, if he was wrong, *Patrician* was a heavy ship with a weight of metal superior to most enemy cruisers. Only a line-of-battle ship would out-gun her and she had the speed to escape should she encounter one.

Nevertheless he knew that grievances, once they had taken root, inevitably blossomed into some unpleasantness or other. He would have to wait and see what the disaffection between Mr Metcalfe and his fellow officers produced. For himself, the company of Vansittart proved a welcome diversion. The younger man was pleasant enough, and well-informed; close to Government circles he gossiped readily, though Drinkwater formed the opinion that his own connections with Lord Dungarth proved something of a passport to his confidences. Vansittart knew when to hold his tongue; his present indiscretions were harmless enough.

Mr Frey found his discovery of the secret wrestling match preoccupied his thoughts during the middle watch the following night. Metcalfe's involvement was foolish, the more so since he had implicated Belchambers, who was otherwise an honest lad. It was clear there was nothing he himself could do, though Metcalfe's unwise behaviour would, he felt sure, some time or another cause the first lieutenant to regret the impropriety of his conduct. Metcalfe was not easy-going enough to embroil himself with the dubious affairs of the lower deck. He had already had two men flogged for minor misdemeanours, and while Captain Drinkwater had been compelled to support his subordinate he had passed minimum sentences upon the men concerned.

It was, Frey consoled himself, none of his business, but with that peculiar importance events assume in the small hours of the night, he felt a strong compulsion to probe further into the matter. In the end he waited for Belchambers to make his report at six bells. As the bells struck and the lookouts and sentries called 'All's well' from forecastle, quarter and gun deck, the midshipman of the watch came aft, found Frey in the darkness and touched the brim of his hat.

'All's well, sir, and six bells struck.'

'Very well. Tell me,' he added quickly before Belchambers turned away, 'this business of gaming in the cable tier. Are all the midshipmen involved?'

'Well, more or less, sir,' Belchambers replied unhappily.

'That ain't exactly your kettle o' fish, is it, Mr Belchambers?'

'Not strictly speaking, sir, no . . .'

Frey waited in vain for any further amplification. 'Is it Porter or the First Lieutenant?'

'First Lieutenant's pretty keen, sir,' Belchambers began, as though glad of the chance to speak of the matter, then halted, trying to study Frey's expression in the gloom, failing and adding hurriedly, 'though Porter's the devil if he's crossed, sir, and . . .' He trailed off miserably.

'Have there been many of these bouts?'

'Three, sir, since we left Plymouth. There were several before we commissioned properly . . . dockyard entertainments they called them. I think one or two of the hands took the idea . . .'

'Are they always the same men who wrestle?'

'No, sir.'

'Who was it yesterday?'

'Newlyn and Thurston, sir.' The names meant nothing to Frey, neither man was in his division.

'And there are no other officers present?'

'Not present, no, sir.'

'Then other officers place bets?'

'Yes, sir.'

'Who are they, Mr Belchambers?' Frey's voice hardened in its expression and he wondered he had heard nothing of it in the wardroom.

'Mr Wyatt, sir.'

'Interesting,' remarked Frey almost casually. 'Now, there's something I want you to do for me, Mr Belchambers . . .'

'Sir?'

'Be a good fellow and let me know when there is next to be a bout, even if I'm on watch, d'you understand?'

'Yes, sir.'

There was a note of relief in Belchambers' voice, as though he felt happier for Frey's discovery and offer of alliance. Mr Belchambers trusted Frey.

'And don't say a word to a soul, d'you hear me?'
'No, sir, of course not.'

The morning after he had his officers to dinner, Captain Drinkwater invited the midshipmen to breakfast. They seemed a sound enough group of young men. The two master's mates, Davies and Johnson, were a little older, midshipmen waiting for promotion, and not likely to get it, Drinkwater thought, with *Patrician* bound on her run back and forth across the Atlantic and a spell tendering to the Western Squadron at the end of it.

After breakfast he sobered them just as they had begun to unwind with the news that he would inspect their journals within the week. Belchambers, used to Drinkwater's methods, brightened perceptibly. He was clearly the only member of the gunroom who had been keeping his journal up to date. The boy's expression puzzled Drinkwater, and it was not until after they had all gone with their formal and insincere expressions of gratitude that he realized Belchambers had been subdued throughout the meal. He had always been a quiet, sensitive fellow Drinkwater recalled him fainting at the awful spectre of a deserter being hanged at *Patrician*'s fore-yardarm – but he was usually of a cheerful disposition. Had some of the wardroom malaise spilled over into the gunroom?

Drinkwater took his cloak and hat from the hook beside the door and went on deck. Moncrieff was ordering his marines up and the men were falling in for inspection. A basket full of empty green bottles clinked and the frigate rolled and pitched, her grey canvas spread to the topgallant yards as, braced hard up against the starboard catharpings, they drove to the westward with clouds of spray sweeping over her bluff bow.

Drinkwater recalled his order to Moncrieff and watched Sergeant Hudson checking his men while Corporal Bailey issued cartridge and ball for the practice shoot. Metcalfe stood by watching, having directed a pair of grinning topmen to run a flag-halliard up to the lee main topsail yardarm where they rove it through the studding sail boom and brought the end back on deck. The boom was run out, a pair of hitches thrown over the neck of an empty bottle from the basket, and a moment later it twinkled green and provocative at the extremity of the thin spar.

'Very well, Sergeant, you may drill your men. One at a time at the target. It's accuracy we want, not speed of fire, so take your time, my lads. Carry on.'

Moncrieff, having inspected his men in the belief that ineffective pipeclay and polish inhibited the true martial qualities, retreated to the mizen mast, where a knot of curious officers had assembled, forming round Vansittart who was professing himself something of a wildfowler. Frey, Gordon, Wyatt and Metcalfe watched as Hudson gave some inaudible instructions to his men, told them off in order and formed them into a rough line.

Then, one by one, they stepped up to the hammock nettings, rested their muskets on hammocks or against the iron cranes that supported the nets, took their aim and fired upwards.

Far above them the bottle danced impudently. A slight slackness in the halliard, the working of the ship and the whipping of the spar made it an extremely lively target. Of the thirty-seven privates in Moncrieff's detachment, not one succeeded in hitting the mark, though several struck the studding sail boom and one severed the downhaul of the halliard.

Each shot was keenly watched. Men on deck ceased their tasks, the midshipmen off duty emerged to stare. Every miss was met with a chorus of moans, punctuated by outraged shouts from Wyatt or Metcalfe when splinters flew from the boom. There were five misfires, which Moncrieff disallowed, nodding permission to Corporal Bailey to issue fresh cartridges. He turned to Metcalfe.

'D'your men have to stand and gawp, Mr Metcalfe? Have they nothing better to do?'

'They've nothing better to watch, Mr Moncrieff,' Metcalfe chortled facetiously. The marine officer turned away angrily. The first of the five marines given a second chance squinted along the barrel of his Tower musket and took aim with painstaking slowness. The watchers waited, almost holding their breath in anticipation, their good-natured mockery suspended.

'There's no need to worry about breaking this one, Moncrieff,' Metcalfe called, spoiling his aim, 'we've a whole basket of 'em!'

The frustrated marine glared insubordinately at the first lieutenant's wisecrack. At the end of the five shots, the bottle still swung unmolested. Constrained by the presence of the captain and first lieutenant, the marines shuffled disconsolately off and fell into rank and file.

'You'd better let 'em try again, Mr Moncrieff,' Drinkwater called.

'Aye, aye, sir.' Moncrieff had coloured at his men's failure and Drinkwater heard Metcalfe make some comment to which Moncrieff returned a furious look.

'If you can do any better . . .' Drinkwater heard Moncrieff snarl.

As the marines reloaded, Metcalfe went below. Drinkwater had dismissed him from his mind, feeling sorrier for Moncrieff who had detached himself from the officers about Vansittart and occupied a miserable no man's land between his colleagues and his men.

'I might ask you gentlemen to try your hands in a moment,' Drinkwater called in a gesture of support for Moncrieff. The marine officer threw him a grateful glance. 'We could tighten the halliard,' he offered.

Moncrieff shook his head. 'It wouldn't be the same ,sir.'

'Perhaps not, but . . .'

'Thank you, no, sir. It wouldn't be the same.'

'Very well.'

The first marine stepped forward, raised his musket and fired. The snap of the lock and spurt of powder-smoke at the gun's breech transmitted itself to a short, yellow-tipped cough from the muzzle. They stared upwards at the dangling bottle. It spun from the passing wind of the ball, but it remained infuriatingly intact.

'Next!' commanded Moncrieff, superseding Hudson in his anxiety to obtain a hit.

Drinkwater was looking up at the third or fourth shot when Metcalfe reappeared on deck. It was only when these failed and he said in a loud and truculent voice, 'Haven't you succeeded yet?' that Drinkwater saw he was carrying a musket, presumably from the arms rack outside the wardroom.

'With your permission, sir?' he addressed Drinkwater, his expression arch and vaguely offensive.

'Do you ask Moncrieff, Mr Metcalfe.'

'Well, Moncrieff, will you let a fellow have a pot-shot?'

Moncrieff visibly bit off a retort. He had himself been contemplating a shot, but resisted the impulse, for to have missed would have been more irritating and, in any case, the object of the exercise was to train the men. Their shooting had been damned close for Tower muskets with a three-quarter-inch bore and balls whose casting was often more a matter of luck than precision. Let Metcalfe have a shot and damn him. He would be devilish lucky to hit the damned bottle and if he made a fool of himself, then so much the better! He nodded.

Metcalfe walked confidently to the rail, set the musket against his shoulder and raised the barrel. The bottle swung with the wind of the ball's passage and the officers and marines watching let out a hoot of triumph, for he had missed. They were all still laughing at Metcalfe's pride preceding his humiliation, when a second discharge followed. The bottle shattered, its jagged neck left at the boom-end.

Even as a suspicion crossed Drinkwater's mind, the certainty of it had been realized by Moncrieff who was already striding across the deck.

'Let me see that fire-lock,' he cried.

'It ain't a Brown Bess, for sure,' Vansittart opined stridently, moving forward with the others to discover by what malpractice Metcalfe had cheated them.

The speed and accuracy of the second shot had raised all their suspicions. Metcalfe was surrounded by the officers and Drinkwater heard the accusations rain on the first lieutenant.

'It's a damned *rifle* . . .'

'That's a Chaumette breech, damn it . . .'

'Let me see . . . the devil! 'Tis a Ferguson rifle! Where the deuce d'you get this, Metcalfe?' Metcalfe had surrendered the gleaming weapon to their scrutiny and Moncrieff now held it. The question silenced their mild and curious outrage and they stood in a circle, staring at the first lieutenant. A feeling of premonition crept over Drinkwater as he watched these antics, marking the distastefully smug expression on the face of his second-in-command.

He heard Metcalfe utter the words 'a gift from Captain Warburton', and the mention of his predecessor confirmed his hunch.

'Sergeant Hudson,' he called, suddenly bestirring himself, and the crack of his voice stilled the curious officers examining the rifle.

'Sah!' Hudson was ramrod stiff, his body an admonition to the levity on the quarterdeck.

'There are a dozen or more bottles yet to be shivered. Another round for each of your men and try again.'

'Yes, sah!'

Recalled to his duty, Moncrieff gave back the rifle and bustled to muster his men again. The officers broke up, some still admiring the Ferguson rifle in Metcalfe's hands, others waiting and watching the marines, others wearied of the sport now the first bottle had been dispatched.

Drinkwater went below. As he reached his cabin door he growled to the marine sentry, 'Pass the word for my servant.' A minute later Mullender appeared.

'Mullender, you recollect when we were in the Pacific I had a gun, a rifle . . .'

Patiently Drinkwater awaited the slow workings of Mullender's memory.

'Aye, sir, I do. You fetched it back one day from the Californio shore,' Mullender said slowly, his brow furrowed with concentration..

'Yes, exactly. What did we do with it?'

'Well, sir,' Mullender began, stepping forward and wiping his hands on his apron, 'we stowed it in the settee locker, but . . .'

Drinkwater had the squabbed cushion beneath the stern windows off in a trice, long before Mullender could complete his explanation.

'But after you left the ship, sir, in a hurry like you did, sir, and we heard you wasn't to be coming back, sir, well, that's what we was told at the time and then Captain Warburton and his own man came and I was sent forward, sir . . .'

The stern locker was empty, at least of the oiled cloth package Drinkwater now clearly remembered laying there for safe-keeping. He had forgotten all about the rifle, assuming it was lost along with his journals and the polar bearskin he had left in Mr Quilhampton's safe-keeping. When Quilhampton had lost the gun-brig *Tracker* . . .

Above their heads the bangs of the marines' discharges were suddenly followed by a cheer: a second bottle had been hit!

'It was in here, wasn't it, Mullender? You don't recall it being removed when Mr Quilhampton took my personal effects ashore?'

'No, sir,' Mullender hung his head miserably. 'I forgot it, sir, when I packed, like, 'twas in such a hurry and Mr Quilhampton was bursting to get ashore . . .'

'It doesn't matter, Mullender,' Drinkwater said, leaving the puzzled steward staring after him as he took the quarterdeck ladder two at a time. Metcalfe was still on deck, the Ferguson rifle held in the crook of his arm. Drinkwater crossed the deck and confronted Metcalfe.

'That was a capital shot, Mr Metcalfe,' Drinkwater said, 'may I see your gun?'

He knew instantly he had seen the rifle before. It had once belonged to a bearded American mountain-man, a man who spent his life wandering across the vast spaces of North America and who had been shot dead at Drinkwater's feet. 'Captain Mack', he had been called, and the long-barrelled Ferguson rifle had been in his possession since he had captured it from a British officer at the Battle of King's Mountain when the gun's inventor himself suffered defeat at the hands of the American rebels. Odd how things turned out.

'If you turn the trigger guard . . .'

'Yes, I know.' Drinkwater dropped the guard, exposing the breech opening that facilitated the quick loading which had so impressed them all.

'The rifling makes the shot fly true,' Metcalfe tried again, and again Drinkwater quietly said, 'Yes, I know.' In addition to the rifle, Captain Mack had left half a dozen gold nuggets and with the proceeds of their sale, Captain Drinkwater had purchased Gantley Hall.*

'I did not know you were so good a shot, Mr Metcalfe,' he said, handing back the rifle. 'It's a fine piece.'

Metcalfe grinned complacently. 'That is why Captain Warburton kindly presented me with it,' he explained.

'And where did Captain Warburton obtain it?' Drinkwater asked.

'I believe he inherited it, sir.'

'Did he now?'

Above their heads there was the sound of shattering glass and a thin cheer went up from the marines still at their target practice.

*See *In Distant Waters.*

Chapter Four *August 1811*

The Paineite

The last of the daylight faded in the west; ahead the sky seemed pallid with foreboding, Drinkwater thought, drawing his cloak the tighter around him and shifting his attention to the upper yards. There would be a strengthening of the wind before morning.

'Very well, Mr Gordon. You may shorten down. Clew up the main course and let us have the t'garn's off her!'

'Main clew garnets, there! Look lively! Stand by to raise main tacks and sheets!'

A bank of clouds gathered darkly against the vanishing day. The twilight of sunset was always the most poignant hour of the seaman's day and, just as the small hours of the middle watch endowed trivial matters with a terrible gravity, this crepuscular hour invested thoughts with sombre shadows.

What was it, Drinkwater thought, that so troubled him? Did this daily marking of time punctuate the passage of his life? Or was it a gale he feared, rolling towards them from the vicinity of Cape Hatteras, the disaffected mood of his officers, or the poor quality of his crew? Once he would have striven with every fibre of his being to lick them into shape; this evening he felt the task beyond him. He was tired, too old for this young man's game. He should not have come back to sea, but quietly farmed his hundred acres, visited the Woodbridge horse fair and sought a pocket borough.

Damn it, he was not old! He could ascend the rigging with the agility of the topmen now running up to douse the flogging topgallants as they thundered in their buntlines. There were men up there far older than himself!

No, he was disturbed by the vague shadow of a new war, for he sensed it as inevitable as much as it was incomprehensible. No matter the *pros* and *contras* of diplomacy adduced by Vansittart; no matter the crude claims and counter-claims advanced by his fire-brand officers, the fact of a war between the United States and Great Britain being in the interests of neither country was obvious. Only Napoleon Bonaparte could profit. Much might be laid at the door of *his* agents in fomenting the suspicion existing between London and Washington.

Despite these considerations, it piqued him to think he had been placed back in command of *Patrician* precisely because he was ageing. The Ministry wanted no hothead frigate captain with only a score of summers to his credit hanging off the Virginia capes, landing a diplomatic messenger on the one hand and impressing American seamen from American ships on the other. He ought to be flattered, he thought, an ironic and private smile twitching the corners of his mouth. He detested the new breed of sea-officer nurtured on victory and assumptions of invincibility. They had never tasted the bitterness of bloody defeat any more than many of them had participated in a victorious action. This current presumption of superiority was a dangerous delusion, but he had heard it expressed enough while he had been ashore in Plymouth. Thank heaven his own officers seemed relatively free of it.

Shortened down, the frigate rode easier, still standing doggedly to windward. Eight bells struck as the watch changed, and in the gathering darkness Drinkwater saw Gordon hand over to Frey. He caught the simultaneous glance of both their heads and the faint blur of their faces as they looked in his direction. He remembered so well the compound of fear and respect he had felt for most of his own commanders, all of them men with feet of clay; old Hope of the *Cyclops*, Griffiths of the *Kestrel* and the *Hellebore*.

Christ, he was morbid! Was this an onset of the blue devils? It was time to go below. Vansittart had sensibly taken to his cot the moment the weather livened up, now he would do the same. The gale would arrive by dawn, time enough to worry then. For the nonce he could drown his megrims in sleep.

And yet he lingered on, his shoulder braced against the black hemp shrouds that rose to the mizen top, feeling the faint vibration of their tension as *Patrician* harnessed the power of the wind and drove her twelve hundred tons into its teeth.

What an odd thing a ship was, he thought, curious in its component parts: fifteen hundred oaks, several score of pine and spruce trees, tons of iron and copper, miles of hemp and coir, tar, flax and cotton. Full of water and stores to support its living muscles and brains which now in part huddled about the deck and in part slung their hammocks in the corporate misery of the berth deck. Men dreaming of homes, of wives, lovers, children; young men dreaming of prize money, old men dreaming of death. Men troubled by lust or infirmities, men scheming or men hating. Men confined by the power confided by Almighty God in the Sovereign Prince King George III, mad by reputation, puissant by the force of the twin batteries of cannon *Patrician* and a thousand ships like her bore on every ocean of the globe.

And he, Nathaniel Drinkwater, post-captain in His Britannic Majesty's Royal Navy, directed this arm of policy, and took Henry St John Vansittart to *pow-wow* in the lodges of the Yankees in the vain hope of averting a war! Would His Majesty's ministers concede the real point of American objection and lift the ordinances against American trade? Or would the greater preoccupations, the maintaining of a naval blockade of Europe and the supply of a British, a Portuguese *and* a Spanish army in the Iberian peninsula, blind them to the dangers inherent in failing to appease the Americans. And if they did comply with Washington's demands, would the Americans be content to the extent of suppressing their desire for Canada?

Two bells struck; the passing of time surprised him, the watch had been changed an hour earlier. It was quite dark now, the horizon reduced to the white rearing crest of the next wave ahead as it surged out of the gloom. Drinkwater was stiff and cramped, his muscles cracked as he straightened up.

The truth was, he wanted to go home. 'Ah, well,' he muttered, 'I have that in common with most of the fellows aboard.'

His left leg had gone to sleep and he almost fell as he tried to walk. 'Damn,' he swore under his breath, hobbling to peer into the binnacle and check the course. The pain of returning circulation made him wince.

'Course sou'west by west . . .' began the quartermaster.

'Yes, yes, I can see that,' Drinkwater said testily. Frey loomed up alongside. Drinkwater was in no mood for pleasantries. 'Goodnight, Mr Frey,' he said, then called dutifully from the head of the companionway, 'don't hesitate to call me if this wind freshens further.'

'Aye, aye, sir,' the young officer responded confidently. All's right with the world, Drinkwater thought, heartened by Frey's cheerful tone. Mentally cursing the megrims, he descended to the gun deck and the stiffening marine outside his cabin door.

He had no idea afterwards why he paused there. He thought it might have been a lurch of the ship which prevented him momentarily from passing into the sanctuary of his cabin; on the other hand, the marine, a punctilious private named Todd, made a smart showing of his salute and Drinkwater threw back his cloak to free his hand to acknowledge this and open the door. Whatever the cause he was certain it was no more than some practical delay, not premonition or extra-sensory perception.

Yet in that moment of hiatus he knew something was wrong. Quite what, it took him a moment to discover, but the watchful, expectant look in Todd's eyes rang an alarm in Captain Drinkwater's consciousness. He passed into his cabin and stood, his back against the door, listening.

The ship was unusually quiet.

One became accustomed to its myriad creakings and groanings. One heard instead the noises of people, from the soft murmurs of men chatting in their messes, sitting and smoking at the tables suspended between the guns, or idling on the berth deck, through the louder shouts of abuse or jocularity to the bawled orders and shrilling of pipes. The denser concentrations of humanity, like the marines' quarters or the midshipmen's so-called gunroom, produced their own noise, and the low hum generated by a watch below during the daytime was quite different from that produced, as now, when the watches below should have been asleep, or at least turned in.

What had troubled him outside his cabin door was not a total silence, but a curious modulation somewhere that was not *right*, existing alongside an equally curious *lack* of noise to which he could not lay a cause.

Irritated and a little alarmed, still cloaked though he had tossed his hat aside, he threw open the door and stalked outside. The gun deck was quiet. The men who slept there appeared to have turned in, for the few lamps showed bulging hammocks above the faintly gleaming gun breeches.

He turned abruptly and descended to the berth deck. Immediately he knew something *was* wrong. He sensed rather than saw a movement, but clearly heard the hissed caveat that greeted his intrusion. He moved quickly forward, ducking under hammocks and brushing them with his head and shoulders. Many of those slung were full and he provoked the occasional grunted protest from them, but more were empty and, with a mounting sense of apprehension, he dodged forward, aware of someone moving parallel to himself, trying to beat him but, having to move in semi-concealment, not making such light work of it.

He could hear the source of that strange modulation as he drew up beside the bitts and suddenly saw below him a press of men crowded into the cable-tier. Their faces were rapt, lit by the grim light of a brace of battle-lanterns as they listened in silence to a voice which, though it spoke in a low tone, carried with it such a weight of conviction it sounded upon the ears like a shout.

So strong was the impact of this oration that it, as much as astonishment, made Drinkwater pause to listen. In the wings of the berth deck, his shadower paused too.

'The rights of kings might be supported as an argument; nay, friends, adopted as a principle for good government were it not for the fact that it in all cases without exception reduces us to the status of subjects and, moreover, many of us to abject and necessary poverty. For to glorify one requires a court whose purpose is adulatory, if not purely idolatrous, and which, to support itself, requires the extraction of taxes from the subjected.

'Furthermore, it promotes excessive pride amongst those close to the throne. This in turn excites envy among the middling sort who, gaining as they are power in the manufacturies, seek to adopt the manners and privileges of noblemen. Under the heels of this triple despotism are ground the poor, the weak, the hungry, the dispossessed, the homeless and the helpless: men, women and children – free-born Britons every one, God help them!'

Drinkwater drew back in retreat. He had not seen the speaker but knew the man's identity: Thurston, the Paineite, the disaffected seducer of men's minds, a suborner, a canting levelling republican subversive . . .

Drinkwater flew up the ladder and Todd snapped to attention, his face an enigmatic mask. Drinkwater had no idea whether or not the marine knew of the combination gathered in the cable-tier, but he surely must have done. Without pausing, saying nothing, but conveying much to the sentry, he sought the refuge of his cabin, his mind a whirl.

He had suspected something of the sort as he had edged forward under the hammocks. A meeting of Methodists, perhaps, even a mutinous assembly, but this, this was intolerable . . .

Why had he done nothing about it?

The thought brought him up with a round turn. The man keeping *cave* had known of his presence, if not his identity; Todd would soon let them know the captain had been down to the orlop and come up again looking as though he had seen a ghost! Good God, what was the matter with him?

And then the appalling thought struck him that Thurston spoke with an irrefutable logic. What little he knew of the Court of St James and the prancing, perfumed and portentious Regent, struck a note of revulsion in his puritan heart . . .

And yet his duty, his allegiance . . .

'God's bones!' he raged. What was he going to do, flog the lot of them? Suppose the bosun's mates refused? And how could he discover who was in attendance and who had turned in? Could he punish Thurston alone, and for what? Speaking a truth that some called sedition? White had been lenient; had White caught the refreshing breath of truth and let the man escape the horrors of the law's worst excess?

'God damn them!' he snarled, finding himself at the decanter stowed in its fiddle. His hand was already on the stopper when he realized he had no time for such indulgence. He *had* to do something, something which was both everything and nothing, something that would not rouse them to spontaneous and hotheaded mutiny, for what Thurston was undoubtedly ignorant of was the fact that he might ignite something of which he was not master. Yet Drinkwater had to signify his displeasure, his disapproval and his power, in order to dissuade them from ever attempting any mass action. He realized what he faced was not mutiny, not something he could quell by summoning the marines and arming his officers. That would be desperate enough, for God's sake!

What he faced was something infinitely worse: its results would be mass desertion in the United States.

Patrician slammed into a wave and Drinkwater felt her bow thrust into the air as she climbed over it and fell into the trough beyond.

'God damn!' he swore again, with a mindless and futile anger.

Then he snatched up his hat. Out on the gun deck he knew his visit had disturbed them. There was a low murmur of voices as men hurriedly turned in; he knew he had rattled them. Even if they did not know yet it was the captain who had discovered their meeting, they would guess it had been an officer.

He emerged on to the quarterdeck. All was still well there, he consoled himself. They would do nothing until they arrived in American waters. Unless, of course, they decided to seize the ship . . .

'Sir . . .' Frey began, seeing the captain unexpectedly on deck.

'Call all hands,' Drinkwater snapped, 'upon the instant, d'you hear?'

'Aye, sir . . .' An astonished Frey relayed the order and the bosun's mate of the watch piped and shouted at the hatchways.

Drinkwater drew his cloak around him, stood at the windward hance and watched them turn up.

'Sir . . .?'

'Double reef the tops'ls, Mr Frey, and look lively, a watch to each mast.' Drinkwater cut poor Frey off short and watched for Thurston. The men emerged, many of them stumbling uncertainly, torn unceremoniously from their hammocks by the shrilling of the pipes. Drinkwater was not an inhumane commander and worked his crew in three watches. To be turned up like this suggested some disaster in the offing, perhaps an enemy, and to the uncertainty of those aware their political meeting had been discovered was now to be added this element of panic.

Frey and his bosun's mate were already translating Drinkwater's order: 'Way aloft, topmen! Double reef the tops'ls! Hands by the lee braces, halliards and bowlines . . .!'

Drinkwater had no difficulty in singling out Thurston. The man made no effort to merge inconspicuously with the mass of the people, but stood stock still for a moment, at the far end of the starboard gangway. There was no one between them, until a petty officer shoved him roughly into his station with a cut of his starter across Thurston's buttocks.

With a sudden feeling of guilt, Drinkwater turned away. Was he one of Thurston's 'middling sort', apeing the manners and seeking the privileges of a discredited nobility? Was the acquisition of Gantley Hall such an act?

'Is something the matter?'

'Eh, what?'

Vansittart stood beside him, the silk dressing-gown flamboyant even in the darkness of a rising gale.

'Matter, Mr Vansittart?' said Drinkwater, aware of the irony of his situation, 'Why no, we are shortening sail, there's a blow coming on.'

'Oh dear. Then we are to be further delayed.'

'I'm afraid so, but this is one thing we cannot change – the weather, I mean,' he added. Vansittart shuffled away. 'My dear fellow,' Drinkwater said after him in a low, inaudible voice, 'if only you knew by what a slender silken thread the world holds together.'

Far above him men laid out to secure the reef points. Thus far he had the measure of them, and *Deo gratias*, the wind was freshening rapidly!

'Call all hands!'

Drinkwater clapped a hand to his hat as *Patrician* lurched into another wave and the resulting explosion of spray hissed over the weather bow, a fine grey cloud in the first glimmer of dawn. Jamming himself in his familiar station at the mizen rigging he waited for the men to turn up. The bosun's pipes pierced his tired brain and rang in his ears, for he had not slept a wink.

'Another reef, sir?' Lieutenant Gordon struggled up the deck towards him, his cloak flapping wildly in the downdraught from the double reefed main topsail. In the lee of the mizen rigging what passed for shelter enabled the two sea-officers to speak without actually shouting. Gordon's expectant face was visible now as the light grew.

'No, Mr Gordon. All hands to lay aft. And I want the officers and marines drawn up properly. Please make my wishes known.' Drinkwater saw the look of uncertainty at the unusual nature of the instruction cross Gordon's face. 'Do you pass the word, if you please,' Drinkwater prompted. He rasped a fist across his stubbled chin. His eyes were hot and gritty with sleeplessness and he felt a petulant temper hovering. He had spent the night wondering what best to do to stave off the trouble he knew was brewing, trouble far worse than a little bad blood between his officers. He tried to imagine what the wholesale desertion of a British frigate's crew would mean in terms of repercussions. In the United States it would be hailed as a moral victory, evidence of the rottenness and tyranny of monarchy, a sign of the rightness of the emerging cause, perhaps even fuel for the fire of rebellion certain prominent Americans wished to ignite in Canada.

For the Royal Navy itself it would be a dishonour. Already the trickle of deserters from British men-of-war had prompted the stop-and-search policy of cruiser captains, a prime cause of the deterioration in Anglo-American relations. The Americans were justifiably touchy about interference with their ships. The practice of British officers boarding them on the high seas and taking men out of them on the flimsy pretext that they had been British seamen, was a high-handed action, a deliberate dishonour to their flag and a provocation designed to humiliate them. The extent to which this arrogant practice prevailed was uncertain, as was the counter-rumour that trained British seamen made up the gun-crews aboard Yankee frigates; men who would give good account of themselves if it came to a fight, desperate men who resented having been pressed from their homes but who were, nevertheless, traitors.

In this atmosphere of half-truths and exaggeration the defection of *Patrician*'s people would be a death-blow for British hopes of avoiding war. The Ministry in London might be able to overlook the case of 'mistaken identity' which had allegedly occurred the night the USS *President* fired into the inferior *Little Belt*; it would be quite unable to extend this tolerance to the desertion of an entire ship's company. His Majesty's frigate *Patrician* would become notorious, synonymous with the *Hermione*, whose crew had mutinied and carried their frigate into a Spanish-American port, or the *Danae*'s people who had surrendered to the French. Such considerations made Drinkwater's blood run cold, not merely for himself and the helpless, humiliated and shameful state to which he would be reduced, but also for the awful disruption to the mission which would otherwise avert a stupid rupture with the United States.

He had been tortured for hours by this spectre, his mind unable to find any solution, as though he faced an inevitable situation, not something of which luck, or providence, had given him forewarning. His lurking bad temper was as much directed at himself and his lack of an imaginative response, as against the men now emerging into the dawn. In all conscience he could not *blame* them and therein lay the roots of his moral paralysis. He devoutly wished he did not see their side of the coin, that he felt able to haul Thurston out of their grumbling ranks and flog the man senseless as an example to them all. It would tone down the upsurge of their rebelliousness.

Christ, that was no answer!

How could he blame them? Some had been at sea continuously for years. There were faces there, he remembered, who had stayed at sea when the Peace of Amiens had been signed, loyal volunteers to the sea-service, men who had made up the crew of the corvette *Melusine* when war had broken out again. They, poor devils, had had their loyalty well and truly acknowledged when turned over without leave of absence into the newly commissioning frigate *Antigone*, from which, following their captain, they had passed into this very ship in the fall of 1807. Ten years would be the minimum they would have served.

And to them must be added the droves of unwilling pressed men, come aboard in dribs and drabs from the guardships and the press tenders, but who now made up the largest proportion of *Patrician*'s company. Among these came petty criminals, men on the run from creditors or cuckolds, betrayed husbands, men cut loose from the bonds of family, seeking obscurity in the wooden walls of dear old England, fathers of bastards, poxed and spavined wretches and, worst of all, those men of education and expectations whom fate had found wanting in some way or another.

What had they to expect from the Royal Navy? The volunteers had been denied leave, the pressed ripped from their homes, the fugitives and the intelligent found no refuge but the inevitable end of them all, to be worn down by labour, if death by disease or action did not carry them off first.

Nathaniel Drinkwater had faced mutiny before and beaten it, but none of this gave him much confidence, for he had been aware on each of these occasions that he had obtained but a temporary advantage, a battle or a skirmish in a war in which victory was unobtainable. And now, in addition to the catalogue of mismanagement and oppression, the Paineite Thurston had introduced the explosive constituent of something more potent than gunpowder: political logic. Clear, concise and incontrovertible, it had set France afire twenty-two years earlier; it had turned the world on its ears and unleashed a conflict men were already calling the Great War.

Drinkwater found himself again searching for Thurston; the man whom White had sent down in a rare mood of leniency, to stir up the lower deck of the *Patrician* instead of digging turnips on the shores of Botany Bay; Thurston, the man who had smiled and whom Drinkwater conceived might, in vastly different circumstances, have been a friend . . .

And yet the idea still did not seem absurd. He had known one such man before. Perhaps, he thought wildly, they were growing in number, increasing to torture liberally inclined fools like himself until, inexorably, they achieved their aim: the overthrow of monarchy and aristocracy, the reform of Parliament and the introduction of republicanism. That too had happened in England once before, and in English America within his own lifetime.

He recalled the Quaker Derrick, whose fate had been uncertain, lost when the gun-brig *Tracker* had been overwhelmed by Danish gunboats off Tönning and poor James Quilhampton had been compelled to surrender his first command. Derrick had not succeeded because he did not proselytize. Thurston was dangerously different.

God, what a train of gloomy thoughts chased each other through his weary mind! Would Moncrieff never have his infernal marines fallen in? And where the deuce was Metcalfe? Christ Almighty, what a burden *he* was turning out to be!

Why the hell had their Lordships saddled the ship with such a nonentity? He had asked for Fraser, but Fraser, his old first luff, had been ill, and Metcalfe had survived from the last commission when he had served as second lieutenant. It was true he was a good shot, but that did not make him a good officer.

'May I ask . . .?'

'No, you may not!' Drinkwater snapped as the first lieutenant materialized in the disturbingly insinuating way he had. Metcalfe fell back a pace and Drinkwater, meanly gratified at the small humiliation thus inflicted, roused himself and stepped forward. In doing so he appeared to drive the first lieutenant downhill, a sight at once mildly comic, but also threatening. The ship's company, whatever the seductions of Thurston's republican polemic, were more certain of Captain Drinkwater's mettle than he was himself.

'Off hats. Mr Metcalfe,' he said quietly, and Metcalfe's voice cracked with sudden nervous anticipation as he shouted the command.

Drinkwater stared at the ship's company and the ship's company stared back. Some of them were shivering in the cold; some eyed him darkly, well knowing why they had been summoned; others wore the look of blank incomprehension and this was chiefly true of the officers, though one or two made a gallant attempt at pretending they knew why the lower deck had been cleared at so ungodly an hour.

Despite the rising howl of the wind, the hiss of the sea and the creaks and groans of the ship, the waist of the Patrician was silent. Drinkwater withdrew the small book from beneath his cloak, cleared his throat and began to read in a loud voice.

'If any person in or belonging to the Fleet shall make or endeavour to make any mutinous assembly upon any pretence whatsoever, every person offending herein, and being convicted thereof, shall suffer death: And if any person shall utter any words of sedition or mutiny he shall suffer death . . .'

The words were familiar to them all, for on the fourth Sunday of every month, in place of the liturgy of the Anglican Church, the Articles of War were read to every ship's company in commission by their commanding officer. But this morning was not the fourth Sunday in the month, nor did Drinkwater read them all. He excised some of the legal provisos of Articles Nineteen and Twenty, and cut them to their essential bone; he laid heavy emphasis on certain words and punctuated his sentences with pauses and glares at his disaffected flock. He read with peculiar and deliberate slowness, eschewing the normal mumbling run-through to which even the most punctilious captain had succumbed by the end of the routinely morbid catechism.

'If any person shall conceal any traitorous or mutinous practice or design, he shall suffer death . . . or shall conceal any traitorous or mutinous words spoken by any to the prejudice of His Majesty or Government, or any words, practice or design, tending to the hindrance of the service, and shall not forthwith reveal the same to the commanding officer, or being present at any mutiny or sedition, shall not use his utmost endeavours to suppress the same, he shall be punished . . .'

Drinkwater closed the book with a snap. 'That is all, Mr Metcalfe. You may carry on and dismiss the hands.' As Drinkwater stepped towards the companionway Moncrieff called his men to attention and, with some difficulty on the plunging deck, had them present arms.

Drinkwater must remember to thank Moncrieff for that salute; it was quick-witted of him to invest the departure of Captain Drinkwater from the quarterdeck with the full panoply of ceremony. Drinkwater devoutly hoped its effect would not be lost on the men, aware of the theatricality of his own performance. All those who had listened to Thurston's able and seductive sermon would he believed, now be pricked by individual guilt and, as he found himself in the shadows of the gun deck, he wondered how many would report the seditious proceedings.

Not many, he found himself privately hoping. He did not yet wish for the dissolution of his crew. Only an honourable peace could permit that.

'Sir, has something occurred?'

Drinkwater laid down his pen and looked up at Metcalfe. For once the man was flustered, unsure of himself. This was a side of his first lieutenant Drinkwater had not yet observed.

'A very great deal, Mr Metcalfe.'

'But when, sir?'

'When you were asleep, or perhaps taking wine in the wardroom, I imagine.' A slight mockery in the captain's voice alarmed Metcalfe.

'But *what*, sir?' asked Metcalfe desperately and Drinkwater admitted to a certain malicious amusement at his expense.

'Tut-tut, Mr Metcalfe, can you not guess? Surely the Articles I read out were explicit enough. What does the scuttlebutt in the wardroom suggest?'

The question further confused Metcalfe, for the opinion in the wardroom, expressed fully by every officer, was that the captain, perceptive though he was, had got wind of the gaming combination, mistaken it for some sort of mutinous meeting and misconstrued the whole affair. In this conclusion, the debating officers were chiefly concerned to unhorse their overbearing mess-president, and they had succeeded, for a covert conference had been observed between Metcalfe and Midshipman Porter, after which torn pages of a notebook had been seen floating astern. Thoroughly alarmed, Metcalfe had sought this unsuccessful interview with the captain.

'Sir, I must request, as first lieutenant, you take me into your confidence.'

'That I am not prepared to do, Mr Metcalfe,' Drinkwater said carefully, aware that he felt no confidence in the man and could not bare his soul. To admit to his second-in-command that he had discovered a seditious meeting would be an admission to Metcalfe of something he wished to remain between himself and those at whom he had aimed this morning's exercise in intimidation. Besides, strictly speaking, he should report the matter to their Lordships, and to inform Metcalfe of the circumstances and subsequently do nothing would be to lay himself open to charges of dereliction of duty. He would have to tell Metcalfe *something*, of course.

But his refusal to confide in Metcalfe had struck his subordinate's conscience and, unbeknown to Drinkwater, no further explanation was necessary. Metcalfe assumed the worst as far as he, a self-interested man, was concerned. In his guilty retreat he gave up both his chance of a clue that it was not his malpractice of betting on the crew's wrestling which had caused the morning's drama, as well as Captain Drinkwater's rather ingenious explanation of why he had acted so extraordinarily.

It was to Gordon that he spoke about Thurston. The memory of the Quaker Derrick had brought its own solution; what had been done once might be done again. 'The man is in your division and seems a likely character, a man of some education and no seaman.'

'I'm afraid I know little about him, sir,' Gordon admitted.

'You should,' Drinkwater said curtly. 'Anyway, to the point. I have no clerk, and want a writer. You may send him aft eight bells.'

As for an explanation of the morning's events digestible enough for the officers, it was Frey to whom he revealed his fabricated motive.

'It was necessary,' he afterwards told Frey as they paced the quarterdeck together that afternoon when a watery sunshine marked the passing of the gale, 'because as we approach the American coast, I wish to dissuade the men from any thoughts of desertion.'

'But you spoke only of mutiny or sedition, sir,' commented the shrewd Frey.

'I intend to spring the Articles on desertion upon another occasion. This was but a preamble.'

They exchanged glances. Frey was undeceived, and for reasons of his own he passed on this intelligence only to those whom he knew to dislike the unfortunate Metcalfe.

Chapter Five *August-September 1811*

An Invitation

'By the mark thirteen!'

Drinkwater looked at the American chart. 'Very well Mr Wyatt, you may anchor the ship.'

'Aye, aye, sir.' Wyatt raised his speaking trumpet. 'Main braces there, haul all aback!'

The knot of officers on the quarterdeck stared upwards as the main topsail and main topgallant came aback and flattened against the mast and the maintop.

'By the deep twelve!' the leadsman's chant continued. 'A quarter less twelve!'

Patrician lost what way she had been carrying in the fickle breeze blowing off the green river-banks and bringing with it the nostalgic land scents of grass and trees. The hands hauled the fore and mizen yards aback and the frigate glided to a stop, submitting to the rearward thrust of her backed sails and the current of the river. Wyatt and Drinkwater each selected a transit ashore, Drinkwater a lone tree which drifted into line with the corner of a white Palladian mansion standing majestically amid a broad and luscious swathe of grass. The two objects remained in line for a moment and then began to reverse the direction in which they had closed: their drawing apart signified that the frigate was moving astern over the ground. Wyatt caught his eye and he nodded.

'Let go the cat stopper!' Wyatt called and there was a thrumming as the short rope ran out, followed by a splash and then the vibrating rumble as the cable ran out through the hawse-holes.

The ship would take some time to bring up to her cable and Drinkwater pulled his Dollond glass from his tail pocket, levelling it momentarily at the noble house and its beautiful sweep of parkland. It made a mockery of his scrubby Suffolk acres and the homely architecture of Gantley Hall. He watched as a groom, a tall negro, brought a chestnut horse round the corner of the house from what he assumed was a stable block.

'Castle Point, Captain.'

Drinkwater was not certain whether Vansittart, resplendent in plum-coloured velvet, meant this as a statement of fact, or a query as to whether or not they had reached their destination. He swung his glass to the ship ghosting up two cables' lengths distant from them. She too followed the same procedure, backing her sails and letting go her anchor.

'Aloft and stow!'

'Aloft and stow!'

The orders were piped and called simultaneously from each ship and it was clear a race was to be made of it. The topmen leapt into the rigging, setting the shrouds atrembling in their haste to be aloft, urged on by Metcalfe's usual loud, unnecessary exhortations and the active chivvying of the bosun's mates.

Drinkwater watched the other vessel. She was no more than a sloop, a twenty-gun ship, but at her peak, lifting languidly in the light breeze, flew the stars and stripes of the United States of America. She had laid-to athwart their hawse off the Virginia capes, her guns run out, and had sent a lieutenant across by boat demanding to know the reason for their presence in American waters. By his bluster the officer had clearly been expecting a show of arrogant truculence on the part of the British commander. It transpired that within the previous two months a pair of British frigates had been cruising off the capes, stopping and searching American merchantmen for both contraband cargoes bound for Napoleonic Europe and British deserters. Hard-pressed for men, they had inevitably poached a handful of seamen which had infuriated Yankee opinion, disturbed the peaceful prosecution of trade and insulted the sovereignty of the United States. The *Patrician*, it seemed, appeared as another such unwelcome visitor, and this time Mr Madison's administration had seen fit to have a guardship off the capes to ward off such an impertinence, if not to challenge openly any such mooted interference with American affairs upon her own doorstep.

Much of the American officer's bluster was understandable. After the unfortunate incident between the *Chesapeake* and the *Leopard*, the British government had not reacted when the USS *President* fired into the much smaller British sloop, the *Little Belt*.

The British press, however, had made much of the incident, screeching for revenge, and the Ministry's restraint must have seemed to the Americans uncharacteristic, wanting only an opportunity to reverse the odds and hammer the upstart navy of the young republic. The materialization of the *Patrician*, clearly a frigate of the heaviest class possessed by the British navy, could therefore have but one interpretation to the commander of the patrolling sloop. He had sent his first lieutenant to find out.

Drinkwater received the young man with considerable courtesy, invited him below and introduced him to Mr Vansittart, whom he had ensconced in his own cabin. There was, Drinkwater observed, a regrettable air of condescension about Mr Vansittart, trifling enough in itself, but obvious enough to provoke a reaction from the American lieutenant, whose corn-pone homeliness was laid on a little for Vansittart's benefit.

Nevertheless, Lieutenant Jonas Tucker went back to his ship with a request for Vansittart's passport to be honoured. The two ships lay-to together for half an hour within sight of Cape Charles and Cape Henry awaiting the American commander's sanction before Lieutenant Tucker returned with his senior officer's compliments. Drinkwater refused his offer of pilotage as being not consonant with the dignity of the British flag, but diplomatically accepted an escort into Chesapeake Bay.

'If you will follow our motions, sir,' Tucker had drawled, addressing Drinkwater and ignoring Vansittart, who had accompanied him on to the quarterdeck, 'and bring to your anchor here.' He unrolled a chart and Drinkwater bent to study it.

'Off Castle Point?' Drinkwater had asked.

'Just so, sir.'

Drinkwater had looked up, 'Mr Wyatt, do we have Castle Point on our chart?'

'You may have the loan of this one, sir,' said Tucker.

'Thank you.' Drinkwater had accepted the American's offer. 'We will salute the American flag, Lieutenant, immediately upon anchoring, if you will reciprocate.'

'I guess that will be an honour, sir,' Tucker had replied with insincere formality, and had taken his departure.

They had doubled Cape Charles, standing south towards Cape Henry to avoid the Middle Ground before hauling the yards and swinging north-west into the bay. Ahead the American sloop led them in. They cleared the Horse Shoe shoal and The Spit, between which the York river debouched into the bay and where thirty years earlier Cornwallis had surrendered to Washington and Rochambeau, effectively ending the American War and ensuring independence from Great Britain. They steadied on a northward course, forming in line ahead, finally entering the mouth of the Potomac and anchoring two miles below Falmouth township, off Castle Point.

The rumble of the veering cable ceased with the application of the compressor bars. *Patrician* brought up to her anchor and immediately from her forecastle the first boom of the salute reverberated around the anchorage. Clouds of pigeons rose in a clattering of wings from the adjacent woods and a flock of quacking duck and wildfowl flew up from the reedbeds fringing the river. The concussion of the gunfire echoed back and forth, returned by the classical façade of the mansion. The exact, five-second intervals between each explosion were timed by Mr Gordon, so that the twenty-one discharges sounded like a cannonade, only to be repeated and amplified by the gunners of the Yankee sloop they now knew to be the USS *Stingray*.

As the last echoes faded away, Drinkwater turned to Vansittart.

'Well, Vansittart, it's up to you now.' He paused to stare through his glass again at the American ship, continuing to speak. 'I imagine our friend will provide a boat escort, but you can take my barge up to Washington. 'Tis a goodish pull, but unless we can obtain some horses . . .' A solitary figure was staring back at them. Drinkwater lowered his glass and raised his hat by the fore-cock. The American commander ignored the courtesy, but continued to stare through his own telescope.

'Perhaps he didn't see you,' Vansittart consoled.

'Oh, he saw me all right,' Drinkwater replied. The thought of horses made him swivel round and refocus his glass. The Negro was walking away from the mounting block and Drinkwater was just in time to see the big chestnut break into a canter and disappear into the trees to the right of the house. He caught a fleeting glimpse of a woman in grey with a feathered bonnet riding side-saddle. 'I wonder', he remarked, 'why we have been brought to an anchor here . . .?'

'Even I, in my ignorance, know "goodish pull" to be something of a euphemism, Captain,' said Vansittart grinning. 'It must be forty miles to Washington.'

'I'm glad to see our somewhat land-locked surroundings have persuaded you to recover your good humour,' Drinkwater riposted, but both men were interrupted by Midshipman Belchambers reporting the approach of a boat. Ten minutes later Lieutenant Tucker once again stood on the quarterdeck.

'Captain Stewart presents his compliments, gentlemen. He intends to let the Administration know of the arrival of Mr Vansittart himself without delay. He hopes to return shortly with the Administration's response.'

'Would he be kind enough, Lieutenant Tucker, to convey a letter from myself to Mr Foster?'

'Mr Foster, sir?'

'His Britannic Majesty's ambassador to your government,' Vansittart explained.

Tucker shrugged. 'I guess so, sir.'

'If you would give me five minutes.' Vansittart withdrew below.

'Well, sir,' Drinkwater said, attempting to fill the five minutes with polite if meaningless small-talk, 'it is beautiful country hereabouts.'

'It sure is,' said Tucker bluntly, awkwardly adding, lest he seem too abrupt, 'real beautiful . . .'

'Plenty of wildfowl,' said Metcalfe, coming up and joining in with the cool effrontery he often displayed. Drinkwater, irritated at the intrusion but equally relieved to have his burden halved, recalled Metcalfe's expertise with the Ferguson rifle. They were standing staring ashore at the parkland surrounding the Palladian mansion when from the trees whence she had disappeared earlier, Drinkwater saw the lone horsewoman reappear. Her horse was stretched at a gallop and the plumed hat, which he had noticed earlier, was missing. She brought the horse to a rearing halt a pistol-shot short of the river-bank and Drinkwater thought she was waving at them. Beside him Lieutenant Tucker chuckled.

'Reckon Belle Stewart's just had a scare,' he remarked. 'That goddam gelding of hers must've had a rare fright from the salutin' cannon.

'She's shaking her fist and not waving, then,' Drinkwater said.

'She could be doin' either, Cap'n, she could be doin' either. She might be shakin' her fist, 'n' she might not. She might be wavin' at her brother, Cap'n Stewart, Master Commandant of the United

States Sloop o' War *Stingray*, but then again, she might be a-shakin' it at you for a-firing all those guns.'

'I'd say we were both equally guilty,' Metcalfe said, matching Tucker's condescending drawl.

Drinkwater ignored the implied slight. 'Ah, I see. Captain Stewart resides hereabouts, then,' he said, indicating the house.

'Well not exactly resides . . . his sister does the residin', but I guess it was in his mind to get a horse here.'

'I understand. And will that facility be extended to Mr Vansittart, d'you think?'

'I don't know, Cap'n. Matter of fact, I don't know exactly what's in Cap'n Stewart's mind, sir.' Vansittart reappeared with his letter and Lieutenant Tucker took his departure. Drinkwater, Metcalfe and Vansittart lingered, watching the return of the American boat and then, sweeping round the saloop's stern, the departure of a second boat from the *Stingray*. She was a smart gig with white stars picked out along her blue sheerstrake. Red oars with white blades swung and dipped in the dark waters of the Potomac river. Upright in her stern stood a midshipman, hand on tiller, beside whom sat a sea-officer. He was, Drinkwater guessed, the same man who had scrutinized them from the quarterdeck of the *Stingray*. Drinkwater walked aft to the taffrail and stared down as the gig pulled close under *Patrician*'s stern. Vansittart and Metcalfe joined him. Again he lifted his hat.

The midshipman, curious about the heavy British frigate, was looking up at the three men and could not have missed the private salutation. They saw him turn and address a remark to the officer sitting next to him. No flicker of movement came from the immobile figure; he continued to stare straight ahead, just as his oarsmen, bending to their task, stared astern, over the shoulders of their officers, as if the British ship did not exist. The officer must have made some remark to the midshipman, for the boy solemnly raised his own hat.

'That's a gesture of the most sterile courtesy,' Vansittart objected.

'That, I fear, is Master Commandant Stewart,' Drinkwater concluded, 'and I hope he don't exemplify the kind of response you're going to get in Washington, Vansittart.'

Vansittart grunted.

'I collect that we should blow the insolent ass's piddling sloop out of the water while it lies so conveniently under our guns,'

Metcalfe interjected, with such pomposity that Drinkwater understood the motive for his earlier intrusion. Metcalfe was eager to ingratiate himself with Vansittart. Drinkwater wondered how much of this insinuating process had already been accomplished during their crossing of the Atlantic. The idiocracy of the remark was so at variance with the first lieutenant's earlier caution that Drinkwater was compelled to remark upon it. 'I thought, Mr Metcalfe, you were opposed to provokin' hostilities with the United States.'

'Well, I consider . . .' Metcalfe blustered uncomfortably, clearly having abandoned reason in favour of making an impression, but could find nothing further to say.

'I think we may forgive a little rudeness from so young a Service, mayn't we, Mr Vansittart?' Drinkwater said archly, catching the diplomat's eye.

'I think so, Captain Drinkwater. Particularly from the commander of a ship whose company had their sails furled half a minute before our own.'

Metcalfe opened his mouth, thought better of saying anything further and stumped away with a mumbled, 'By y're leave, gentlemen . . .'

'Touché Vansittart,' Drinkwater murmured.

Vansittart and Drinkwater idly watched the *Stingray*'s gig ground on a bright patch of sand lying in a shallow bay. The horsewoman in grey walked her now quietened mount towards the boat and they watched the mysterious Captain Stewart address her, saw her turn her horse and, with Stewart walking beside her, return to the house. She looked back once at the two anchored ships, then both disappeared inside. Shortly afterwards a man rode off on horseback.

'So there goes Captain Stewart, bound for Washington.'

'Is it unusual for a, what d'you call him . . .?'

'Master Commandant,' Drinkwater explained, 'their equivalent of Master and Commander; a sloop-captain, in fact.'

'I see; is it usual then for such a curious beast to be absent from his ship under the circumstances?'

'The circumstances being your arrival, I should say it was essential,' Drinkwater said.

'Might he not be suspicious of your taking men out of his ship?'

'To be truthful, Vansittart, I am more concerned to stop my men deserting to his.'

'D'you think it likely?' asked Vansittart, displaying a mild surprise.

'Certainly 'tis a possibility. Did you not mark the furling of the sails? You noticed we were slower.'

'I, er, assumed it not to be significant . . .'

'The last tucks in the fore t'gallant were deliberately delayed. I conceive that to have been a mark of sympathy with the Yankees.'

'A form of insolence, d'you mean?'

'Something of the kind.' Drinkwater raised his voice, 'Mr Metcalfe! Mr Moncrieff!'

When the two officers had approached he said, 'Gentlemen, I wish you to consider the possibility of desertion to the American ship or', he looked towards the longer distance separating the frigate from the lush greensward sweeping down to the Potomac, 'directly ashore. Mr Moncrieff, your sentries are to be especially alert. They must first challenge but thereafter they may fire. They are to bear loaded weapons.' He turned to the first lieutenant. 'Mr Metcalfe, we will row a guard-boat day and night. The midshipmen to be in command. There will be no communication whatsoever with either the shore or the American ship.' He paused. 'I am sorry for the Draconian measures, gentlemen, but I'm sure you'll understand.'

'Of course, sir,' Moncrieff nodded.

'Yes, sir,' Metcalfe acknowledged.

'You will be pleased to pass on to all the officers that the desertion of a single man in such circumstances', he gestured at their idyllic, land-locked situation, 'may not be a disaster in practical terms for the ship, but it will be a considerable embarrassment to the Service. I therefore require the lieutenants and the master to maintain their watches even though we are anchored. Is that understood?'

'Aye, aye, sir,' Metcalfe said woodenly.

'You *are* taking this seriously,' Vansittart said, after the two officers had been dismissed.

Vansittart's apparent flippancy revealed the maritime naïvety of the man. Vansittart had not been witness to Thurston's oratory; nor would he have been so susceptible, Drinkwater thought, coming as he did from a family long in the public service. Mr Vansittart would have scoffed at Captain Drinkwater's misgivings. Such guilty considerations had kept Drinkwater from revealing anything of his private thoughts. Besides, he did not need to be told his duty and he had at least the satisfaction of knowing that Thurston was kept obedient and under his immediate eye. 'Oh yes, indeed I am,' he said, 'I cannot tolerate a single desertion. The consequences acting upon the remainder of the people would be most unfortunate.'

They passed an uneasy night. The knocking of the guard-boat's oar looms against the thole pins, the routine calls of the sentinels that all was well, and the airless, unaccustomed stillness of the ship after her ocean passage, combined with Drinkwater's anxiety to keep him awake, or half-dozing, until dawn, when sheer exhaustion carried him off.

They estimated that Captain Stewart, at best, would not return until the following evening. The parallel existences of the two ships passed the hours: the trilling of the pipes, the shouting of orders and the regularity of the bells, each chiming just sufficiently asynchronously to remind their companies they each belonged to different navies, lent a suspense to the day. Occasionally a boat put off from the American ship and her midshipmen doffed their hats to those rowing their tedious duty round *Patrician*. The absence of so crude and despotic a routine about the *Stingray* was a permanent reproach to the British and a source of delight to the Americans.

Towards late afternoon, however, the returning American cutter, instead of taking a sweep round the circuit of the guard-boat, cut inside, making for *Patrician*'s side. A midshipman, smart in blue, white and gold, a black cockade in his stovepipe hat, came smartly up the side and, saluting in due form, handed a note to the officer of the watch, Lieutenant Frey. Frey took the missive below to Captain Drinkwater.

'Enter.' The September sunshine slanted into the great cabin, picking up motes of dust in the heavy air. Drinkwater, his shoes kicked off and in his shirt sleeves, was slumped in a chair dozing before the stern windows.

'What is it?' he murmured drowsily, his eyes closed.

'Message from the shore, sir.'

'Read it, then.'

Frey slit the wafer. 'It's an invitation, sir . . . er, Mr Zebulon and Mistress Arabella Shaw of Castle Point request the pleasure of the company of the Captain of the English frigate and his officers, at six of the clock . . .' Frey broke off, a note of excitement testimony to the boredom of his young life. 'There'll be food, sir, and music, and', he added wistfully, 'company.'

'I suppose you'd like me to accept on your behalf, Mr Frey.'

'Well, yes please, sir.' The merest suggestion that Drinkwater might refuse clearly alarmed Frey.

'Zebulon who?' Drinkwater queried in a disinterested voice.

'Er,' Frey studied the invitation again. 'Shaw, sir.'

Drinkwater was silent for a while. 'You were with me on the *Melusine*, weren't you?'

'Yes, sir,' replied Frey, impatiently wondering where this line of questioning was leading them and rather hurt that it was necessary.

'We didn't have much opportunity for social life in the Greenland Sea, did we?'

'Not a great deal, sir.'

'And the natives were not particularly attractive, were they?'

'No, sir, their huts weren't quite like the wigwam ashore there, sir.' Ducking his head Frey could see a white corner of the stables adjoining the classical frontage of Castle Point.

'I wonder why they call it Castle Point . . .?'

'There are some battlements, sir.'

'Are there? Well, well.' Gantley Hall had no battlements. 'You'd better call Thurston . . .'

'I'll write the reply myself, sir, if you like,' Frey said then thinking he was being too forward he added, 'there's a midshipman from the Yankee sloop waiting on deck . . .'

'Is there, by God?' Drinkwater said, sitting up, rubbing his eyes and feeling for his shoes.' Then we'd better jump to it and not keep young Master Jonathan waiting . . .'

'I beg your pardon . . .'

'Don't be a fool, Frey. I know full well you want to stretch your legs, and preferably alongside a rich Virginian belle in the figures of a waltz. It's a damned sight better than takin' the air on the quarterdeck, ain't it?'

Drinkwater gestured for the note; Frey gave it to him. The paper gave off a faint fragrance and was covered in an elegant, feminine script. Presumably the patrician hand of Mistress Shaw. Going to his desk he drew a sheet of paper towards him, lifted the lid of his ink-well and picked up the Mitchell's pen Elizabeth had given him.

'To Mister and Mistress Zebulon Shaw . . .' he murmured as he wrote, wondering what manner of man and wife owned so luxurious a property. The bare untitled names reminded him of the virtues of republicanism. Perhaps it was as well he had not summoned Thurston to pen this acceptance. When he had sanded it dry he gave it to Frey.

'There, Mr Frey, and remember we are ourselves ambassadors in our small way.'

'Aye, aye, sir,' replied Frey, grinning happily and retreating as hurriedly as decency permitted.

Chapter Six *September 1811*

The Widow Shaw

'Lord, Lootenant, you *are* hot!'

Arabella Shaw looked up at the handsome face of the English officer.

'And you, ma'am,' Lieutenant Gordon replied with equal candour, 'are beautiful.'

He smiled down at her, blaming his own goatishness on her soft body and its capacity to arouse. He clasped her waist tighter as they whirled together in the waltz. She judged him to be a year or so short of thirty, at least ten years her junior, but with a chilling absence of two fingers on his left hand. She could feel the lust in him, pliantly urgent. He might have excused his obtrusiveness by claiming an overlong period at sea, but he pretended it did not exist and she acknowledged this intimate flattery by lowering her eyes.

Mr Gordon took this for surrender; not, he realized, of the citadel, but of an outwork, a ravelin. He gathered her closer still, enchanted by the scent of her hair in his nostrils, her exotic perfume and the swell of her breasts against his chest.

Mistress Shaw endured his rough attentions and curtseyed formally as the music stopped. As he returned her to her seat, she quietly cursed her own weakness for suggesting this evening. Her widowhood had begun to irk her and she had felt the impromtu ball an occasion enabling her to cast aside more than a year of mourning, besides helping her father-in-law do what he could to stop the imminent rupture between the United States and Great Britain. He had enthusiastically adopted her suggestion of inviting the officers of both naval ships to a rout.

She had to admit her own motives were far less philanthropic. It had been curiosity which tipped her judgement in favour of making the suggestion; curiosity to see the English officers. She had been a girl at the time of Yorktown when the hated redcoats had surrendered sullenly against overwhelming odds. Defeat had not robbed them of their potent terror to a young mind and the childish impression had remained. She still thought of them as bogey-men inhabiting the dark, threatening spectres to be conjured up when children were disobedient. And once again they were at large, plundering American ships off their own coastline and carrying off innocent sailors like the Barbary pirates with whom her country had already been at war. Tonight she had thought, with a *frisson* of fearful delight, she would see these mythological beings for herself and she was half-disappointed, half-relieved that they were not the pop-eyed, dissolute, viciously indolent exquisites she had expected.

There had been, too, the added inducement to exhibit a new gown, a gay, uninhibited contrast with the black bombazine which for so long had hidden her figure. To this was added a patriotic justification, for the gown had been smuggled from Paris to replace her widow's weeds and she wore it in defiance of the British blockade. The wicked desire to try its effects on English sophisticates (as she imagined them to be) had honed her anticipation. She had had enough of the male society of Virginia. The rich, elderly and often dissolute men who had shown an interest in her had seemed either opportunist or calculating. Their expressions of regard had been too contrived for sincerity, or their desires too obvious for a permanent attachment. None had struck an answering longing in her own heart. For her all men had died with her husband, whose mutilated body they had found already putrefying beside his exhausted horse. They said the stump of an Indian arrow in his back had killed him when mounting, and not the dreadful, nightmare gallop of a terrified mount whose rider had fallen backwards with one foot caught in a stirrup.

They reached the table and Gordon's mangled hand gave her a sharp reminder of the mortality of men. She was suddenly sorry for him and ashamed of her soft breasts that jutted, *à la Marie-Louise*, to tantalize him. She sat and sipped from her glass while Gordon, handsome and eager, hovered uncertainly. She was about to ask him to sit too, since his awkwardness was unsettling her, when he was superseded. A tall, gaunt young Scot in the scarlet and blue facings of her childhood fancy, a glittering gorget and white cravat reflecting on a pugnacious chin, elbowed Gordon aside. She sensed some tacit agreement, for Gordon withdrew unprotesting and bowing. She felt cheap, not wicked, as if the subtleties of wearing the gown were lost on these boors and had merely made of her a whore. The lobsterback officer was bending over her hand.

'Quentin Moncrieff, ma'am, Royal Marines, at your service. The band is about to strike up, I believe, and I would be obliged if you would do me the honour . . .'

The leg he put forward was well muscled, the bow elegant enough, and, as if to emphasize his authority, the music began again, silencing the buzz of chatter. She submitted, Moncrieff led her out and almost at once she regretted Gordon's honest lust as Moncrieff's flattery assaulted her.

Both had the same end in view; she had clearly been pointed out as a widow, perhaps in a moment of weakness by the rather gauche-looking American officers grouped around one table muttering amongst themselves and regarding their visitors with suspicion. She supposed she had upset them by dancing exclusively with the British; it was a good thing her brother was not here, though Lieutenant Tucker would doubtless keep him informed.

Moncrieff's remarks blew into her ear. Oh yes, they knew her for a widow all right, a woman who in their opinion must, by definition, need a man and who, moreover, would be discreet in having one. She did not know a sizeable wager rested upon her virtue.

She was tiring of the evening as a self-satisfied Moncrieff led her back to her table. She tried to recall what she had said to him, but found the intimidating glares of Lieutenant Tucker and his cronies only made her reflect what a pity it was that events always had the contrary result to what had been intended. She was beginning to wish she had not suggested the evening in the first place as much as regretting the *décolletage* of the French gown. Inspiration saved her from surrender to yet another eager young officer who appeared to head a queue of blushing midshipmen.

'Mr Moncrieff,' she asked in her low drawl, 'would you be kind enough to introduce me to your captain?'

She had missed the arrival of the British officers. They had been prompt – some talk of a race between the boats of the two ships, she believed, though where she had learned the fact, unless it was from Moncrieff's panting eagerness to pour his heart's desire into her ear, she could not be sure – and her maid had not done her hair properly so *she* had been late. Her father-in-law had greeted them all and the ballroom was already filled with chatter and the glitter of uniforms by the time she had joined them.

'The Captain, ma'am? Why . . . er, of course.'

She sensed the response to discipline, felt the effect of iron rule even here, in the privacy of Castle Point. Moncrieff ceased to be himself and became merely an officer, correct, precise and formal. She felt a momentary pity for him and his colleagues, a wildly promiscuous desire to touch them all with herself and release them from the thraldom of lust and duty.

Moncrieff surveyed the company as the music began again and Lieutenant Tucker, his arm about the waist of Kate Denbigh of Falmouth township, prepared to out-do the British and show them how a Yankee officer danced the polka.

'This way, ma'am.'

Moncrieff was eager to be rid of her now, eager to slide his own arm round the slender waist of a younger, less worldly woman than the Widow Shaw. He led her to an open French window where a solitary figure stood, half merging with the heavy folds of a long blue velvet curtain.

Moncrieff coughed formally. 'Sir? May I present Mistress Shaw . . .'

The captain did not turn, indeed he did not appear to have heard and she thought the authority of a British captain too elevated to acknowledge an American widow hell-bent on escape from his officers. His indifference riled her far more than their concupiscence and she felt humiliated in front of Moncrieff. She played a final desperate card and dismissed the marine officer.

'Thank you, Mr Moncrieff.'

Lamely Moncrieff carried out the final ritual of his duty: 'Captain Drinkwater . . Mrs Shaw . . .' He bowed, disappointed, and withdrew.

She hung there, flushing, resenting this necessity of suspension between the two men – two Englishmen!

'I was admiring the view, ma'am,' the captain said, almost abstractedly and without turning his head. 'The moonrise on the Potomac . . . yours is a very beautiful country.'

He turned then, catching her wide-mouthed, angry and flushed.

She was, he saw, voluptuously handsome, her black hair a legacy of Spanish or Indian blood, her skin creamy from some Irish settler. Too lovely to contemplate, he thought with a pang, and swung abruptly away, disturbed despite his fifty years.

She saw a stoop-shouldered man, whose epaulettes failed entirely to conceal something odd about his shoulders. He was of middle height with still-profuse and unpomaded hair. The iron-grey mane was drawn back and caught behind his head in an old-fashioned, black-ribboned queue which she longed to tug, to chastise him for his rudeness.

'You are not dancing, Captain?' she said desperately at this infuriating indifference.

He was aware of his ill-manners and turned to face her properly. 'Forgive me, ma'am. No, I am not dancing. Truth to tell, I dare not . . .'

His forehead was high, his nose straight and his face at first seemed to be a boy's grown old, an impression solely due to the twinkle in his grey eyes. But his skin was weathered and lined, and the thin scar of an ancient wound puckered down his left cheek.

She responded to the dry twist of his mouth, her anger melting now she had his attention. 'Dare not, sir? Do I understand a British captain is afraid?'

He grinned, and again there was the suggestion of boyishness, disarming the mild jibe. Drinkwater himself warmed to the gentle mockery which reminded him of his wife, Elizabeth.

'Terrified, ma'am . . .'

'Of what, pray?'

'Of betraying my incompetence before my officers.' They laughed together.

'They sure are a scarifying lot,' she said. 'I have just escaped their clutches.'

'Ah,' said Captain Drinkwater, looking her full in the face and seeing for the first time she was no longer a girl. 'And am I to understand you feel safer here, eh?' He did not wait for a reply, but went on. 'If I attended to my duty I should remonstrate that your gown has an obvious origin, which I disapprove of, but I am not yet too dried up to be so ungallant.'

'I am glad of that,' she said, now strangely irritated by the success of her ploy in wearing it, 'but we conceive it to be no right of yours to blockade our coast.'

'Ma'am, in all seriousness, we have not yet *begun* to blockade your coast.'

His eyes wandered past her bare shoulder as he tried to mask the gall her remark provoked and to forget the terrible cost in British lives that the blockade of Europe was costing. What its extension to the seaboard of the United States would mean could only be guessed at. It was not the roaring glory of death in battle that was corroding the Royal Navy, but the ceaseless wear-and-tear on ships and men condemned, officers and ratings alike, to a life deprived of every prospect of comfort or privacy. It was over a twelvemonth since Collingwood had died at his desk aboard the *Ocean*. Five years after Trafalgar and without leave during the whole of the period, Nelson's heir had followed his own brother, whom Drinkwater had once met, to an early grave. It was a bitter pill to swallow, to be deprived of Elizabeth and yet to see this woman done up in the height of Parisian fashion. He sighed, aware she was no more mistress of her own destiny than he was of his. Providence ruled them all and it was no excuse for discourtesy. There were parsons and squires aplenty in Kent and Sussex who roistered to bed full to their gunwhales with cognac. Had he not seen himself, on the island of Helgoland, the lengths to which men would go to trade in proscribed goods? There were too many transgressors to offend this woman on the far side of the Atlantic. He made amends as best he could.

'I regret I did not catch your name, ma'am.' He made a small bow. 'Nathaniel Drinkwater, Captain in His Britannic Majesty's Navy, at your service.' He recited the formula with a tired ruefulness he hoped would pass in part for apology, in part for explanation.

'Arabella Shaw,' she replied, 'widow . . .' She did not know why she had revealed her status, except perhaps to prick his stiff British pride and ape his own portentousness.

'I'm sorry, ma'am, I had no idea.' He looked gratifyingly confused.

'It seemed common knowledge among your officers.'

'Hence your escape?' he asked and she inclined her head. 'Then I apologize for their conduct and my own failure to render sympathetic assistance.'

'Lord, Captain, you make me feel like a derelict hulk!' She was smiling again and he was feeling an unaccountable relief.

'You are familiar with a nautical metaphor?'

'I am no stranger to boats, Captain, while my brother is a Master Commandant in our *un*-Britannic navy.'

Comprehension dawned upon him and it was Drinkwater's turn to flush. 'Forgive me . . . Mrs Shaw, of course, I am sorry, I had not realized, you are the daughter of the house . . .'

'Daughter-in-law, Captain. Unfortunately I was not here to receive you . . .'

'We were inconsiderately early,' he said quickly and then turned to look round the dancers. His eye fell upon the bald head of their host. 'I thought the tall lady in brown silk with Mr Shaw . . .'

'Oh, she'd like to become Mrs Shaw, but she is actually still Mrs Denbigh, from Falmouth, a widow and a somewhat designing woman with two pretty daughters . . .'

'Ah, and you are the young lady whose horse we startled this morning . . .'

'With your preposterous cannon, yes, I spoke to my brother Charles about that. Why on earth you should have wished to disturb the peace and tranquillity of half Virginia with such nonsense passes my comprehension!'

He remembered Captain Stewart walking at the head of the chestnut and talking to its rider. Righteous indignation lent colour to her cheeks.

'I think a flag of truce is in order, Mistress Shaw, do you not?'

'Is that what you have come here for? A flag of truce, or something more durable? My father-in-law sees no advantage in a war.'

'What about your brother?'

She shrugged. 'He seems to be like most men – eager to fight.'

'He would not be so eager had he spent his lifetime thus.'

The conviction in Drinkwater's tone made her look at him with renewed interest. 'I know you to have brought a diplomatic mission . . .' She looked round the ballroom.

'No, he is not here. He has some notion of propriety that it would not be politic for him to step ashore until he has official approval . . .'

'So you too are against an open breach between our countries?'

'Certainly. And so, I think it is not indiscreet of me to say, is he.'

'I am glad of that. You must meet my father-in-law later. Come, show me the moonlight on the Potomac, Captain Drinkwater.'

She slipped her arm in his with sudden, easy familiarity, and they stepped through the French windows on to a battlemented terrace which crowned the rising ground upon which the house was built.

'My late husband's grandfather intended to build a castle on the hill here, hence its name. It was barely started when he was killed at the Battle of the Brandywine. This terrace is called "The Battery", though it mounts nothing more offensive than a flower urn or two.'

'Your husband's grandfather had a fine eye for landscape, ma'am; it reminds me of an English deer-park.'

'*Your* English deer-park, perhaps?' she asked shrewdly.

He laughed, thinking of Gantley Hall and its two modest farms. 'Lord no, Mrs Shaw, my own house boasts nothing more impressive than a walled garden, a kitchen garden and an orchard which would fit upon the terrace here.'

Mrs Shaw nodded to another couple taking the air. 'And is there a wife, Captain Drinkwater, to go with all this domesticity?'

He looked at her, about to ask if it mattered either way, while she waited, herself annoyed that it did. He nodded turning the knife in the unguessed at and, for her, unexpected wound. 'And a son and daughter. Do you have children, Mrs Shaw?'

She shook her head and digested the fact in silence, comparing it with her own bereavement and catching the wistful note in his voice.

'If you miss them, Captain,' she asked softly, 'why do you come here?' There was a hint of Yankee hostility in the question.

'That is a question I frequently ask myself, Mrs Shaw.'

She sensed his retreat and found it surprisingly hurtful. Silence settled on them again and after a while she shivered.

'Shall we go in?' he asked.

They turned back to the brilliantly lit ballroom. He was already remote again, ready to detach her as they approached the French windows. She stopped short of the light spilling on to the *pavé*.

'Do you ride, Captain?'

He halted, surprised. 'Ride? After a fashion, an indifferent bad fashion, I'm afraid.'

'Would you care to see some more of my beautiful country tomorrow?'

He thought of the enchantment inherent in such an invitation, the release from the isolated and tedious splendour of his command, the surrender to landscape, to fecund greenery after the harsh tones of sea and sky. Then he thought of the ship and the discontent seething between her decks, of men mewed up by force, of the guard-boat and the sentries with their orders, *his* orders to shoot . . .

He had left a disgruntled Metcalfe aboard this evening; how could he leave them again and go gallivanting about on horseback in full view of the ship's company?

She took his hesitation for imminent refusal. She knew her brother's return from Washington was as likely to bring rebuttal to the English peace overtures as acceptance, that the English frigate might overnight become an enemy and be compelled to put to sea. A sense of panic welled up within her, a sudden, overwhelming urge to see this man again; she tried to find something wittily memorable to say to him and compel him to change his mind.

'I promise my habit will be less contentious, Captain,' she said, furious that her voice trembled.

He could not ignore her, or cast her aside. He told himself he had been more than off-hand with her earlier, that her father-in-law wanted peace and was clearly a man of substance and influence, a man to be encouraged; he told himself that such a meeting might aid the peace process just as he told himself a dinner party at Castle Point might include Captain Stewart and therefore open a discussion of potential interest to a British naval officer.

'Have you a mount docile enough for a sailor?'

'Certainly,' she laughed, 'provided you will lead me in to dinner.'

He inclined his head and bowed, grinning widely. 'I'm honoured, ma'am.'

She smiled and dropped him a curtsey, and they re-entered the ballroom to be engulfed in the gaiety of the scene.

The moon was almost at its culmination when they left Castle Point. The early hostility between the officers of the British and American ships had been skilfully averted by Mr Zebulon Shaw. The protestations of peace and amity, the toasts proposed, seconded and swallowed in assurance of the fact, and the fulsome, wine-warmed expressions of mutual goodwill had healed the incipient rift between the two rival factions. A breach of manners towards their host had thus been avoided. Furthermore, Drinkwater's presence had curbed the taunts of the Americans and intimidated his own people. As far as Drinkwater knew, none of his officers had disgraced themselves, the virtue of the local maids remained intact, if intact it was at their landing, and with the exception of Mr Frey whose farewell had been overlong, all had come away merry, but lighthearted.

It would doubtless have warmed Mr Shaw's heart, Drinkwater thought as he waited to board the gig, if he could have seen Frey finally rejoin his companions, for he strode down the path to the water in company with Lieutenant Tucker, apparently the best of friends. It was only later that Drinkwater learned the cause of this unlikely alliance. While Tucker courted Miss Catherine Denbigh, Mr Frey had been smitten with her sister Pauline.

As for his own farewell, it had consisted of the promise of a meeting on the morrow.

And too long a glance between Mrs Shaw and himself.

Chapter Seven *September 1811*

A Riot in the Blood

His acceptance of Mistress Shaw's invitation troubled Drinkwater the following forenoon. He did not advertise his forthcoming absence from the ship, indeed he busied himself with the routine of paperwork to such an extent as almost to convince himself he had no appointment to keep. Mullender guessed something unusual was afoot, since the captain called for his boots to be blacked, but Mullender, being incurious, gave the matter little thought, and although Drinkwater had a coxswain, the man had never replaced Tregembo as a servant and confidant.

Oddly it was Thurston who almost by default came closest to the captain's soul that morning. Called in to make up the ship's books and to assist in the standing routine inspections of the purser's and surgeon's ledgers, Thurston fell into conversation with the captain.

Until then he had kept a respectful silence and attended to his duties, aware of the awful punishment Drinkwater had it in his power to dole out. He was conscious that the captain was neither inhumane nor illiberal, in so far as a post-captain in the Royal Navy could be expected to be either, having been guided in this matter by older heads who were less willing to heed the trumpets of revolution and had pointed out the virtues of service to the common weal. Thurston was intelligent enough and by then experienced enough to know the sea-service was different from life ashore and that, for cogent reasons, libertarian concepts were inimical to survival at sea. He had therefore learned to tread warily where Captain Drinkwater was concerned.

Drinkwater, on the other hand, now regarded Thurston with more interest than suspicion. By keeping the man to hand and working him hard, by altering his status from pressed man to captain's clerk and by making him a party to a measure of the frigate's more open secrets, Drinkwater had sought to seduce the revolutionary by responsibility.

Prompted by his guilty conscience, he addressed Thurston while the clerk cleared away pen, ink and sand.

'Well, Thurston,' he began, 'are you settled in your new employment?'

'Well enough, thank you, sir, under the circumstances

'What circumstances?' asked Drinkwater, puzzled.

'Of being held against my will, sir.'

Drinkwater gave a short cough to mask his surprise at the man's candour. 'I believe you to be luckier than you deserve, Thurston. You could have been transported.'

'That is true, sir, but that would have been a greater injustice. It in no way mollifies my outrage at being carried to sea. Both punishments, if punishments they be, are unjust.'

'Sedition is a serious matter,' said Drinkwater, regretting starting this conversation yet feeling he could not dismiss its subject lightly, despite the increasingly pressing nature of his engagement. 'You do not truly advocate rule by the mob?'

'Of course not, sir, but the mob is a consequence of the ill construction of government. By exalting some men, others are debased, until this distortion is inconsistent with natural order. The vast mass of mankind is consigned to the background of the human picture, to bring forward, with greater glare, the puppet-show of state and aristocracy.'

'A puppet-show, you say,' Drinkwater said, somewhat nonplussed.

'Indeed, sir, there is no class of men who despise monarchy more than courtiers.'

'You have had much experience of courtiers, have you, Thurston?' Drinkwater asked drily.

'My father was in the service of a duke, sir. It amounts to the same thing,' Thurston answered coolly.

'Ah, I see, so you do not want mobocracy?' Drinkwater said, returning to the safer ground of his earlier remark.

'No. Governments arise out of a man's individual weakness. He places himself and his own in the common stock of society. Locke says for the preservation of his property, but also for the security of his family. He becomes a proprietor in society and draws upon its common capital as a right, thus it follows that a civil right flows from a natural right. If all men behaved with equal respect the one to another, then an equilibrium would exist within society. Each man would give and take according to his means and abilities, thus the differences whose abolition is so much feared by those who misunderstand, would themselves be a natural, earned and unenvied consequence of civil rights, a right in themselves; but no man would want, be beggared or dispossessed, for he would by right hold that of the common stock to which he was entitled.'

'And if he failed to gain that stock, or to hold it . . .?'

'He *could* not fail to gain it, it would be his by natural right. You only raise the matter of loss because you have lived under English law and know it to be possible even when a man does not actively break the law. Dispossession by enclosure, by loom and seed-drill and steam-engine, have severally destroyed the hopes of many, because artful men have seized upon this common stock and called it their own; they have then held it by the immoderate use of superstition and power, created a monarchy under which their privileges stand and are upheld by the law.' Thurston paused.

'That is all very well . . .'

'You know the doggerel, sir, I'm sure,' Thurston went on relentlessly:

> 'The law doth punish man or woman
> That steals the goose from off the common,
> But lets the greater felon loose,
> That steals the common off the goose.'

'That is clever, Thurston . . .'

'As it is true, sir. I do not seek to justify the excesses of a mob, even when it is made up of men without hope. But I do not condone the maintenance, at the expense of the unfortunate, of a parasitic court, of a self-perpetuating legislature, an unjust judiciary, the practitioners of sycophancy, nor all the recipients of privilege, those jacks-in-office who extract the last penny from a man in order that he may prove himself a free-born Englishman!'

Drinkwater wondered if, as a post-captain, he was himself included in that awful list as a recipient of privilege? Did Gantley Hall exist in even its moderate freehold at the expense of a dispossessed yeomanry? Yet he knew to what inequities Thurston referred. From the prevarications and vastly tedious pettifoggings of the High Court of Chancery, to the perquisites and bribes recognized as being necessary to further the public service, no area of life seemed exempt. He looked at his desk. If he and Thurston did not attend to their business properly, if these very books were not properly kept, then a mean-minded Admiralty clerk might postpone their clearance at the end of a commission. Such a delay meant his ship's company would not be paid, further exacerbating an already unjust system which failed to pay men for their labour until a commission ended, forcing them to resort to usurers who bought up their 'tickets' at discount rates, advancing the poor devils cash at far less than face value. It was customary for captains to pass a little money over with their books, to expedite the matter.

'How many widows' men have we entered for this morning, Thurston?' Drinkwater referred to the allowed practice of bearing upon a man-o'-war's books a number of non-existent men to provide a sum for relieving the hardships of the dependants of those lost or killed at sea by disease or action.

'The regulation six, sir.'

'I could make it twelve . . . and either pocket the difference myself, or distribute it among the needy.'

'Sir, I had not meant anything personal . . .'

'I had not thought so, but either act would be illegal, within the strict letter of the regulations.'

'You suggest that I should wait for a better life in heaven then, sir?' Thurston asked, with a curious bitter hardening of his face.

'Do you truly think this world is capable of improvement?'

'Most assuredly so, sir.'

'They thought so in France, yet they have ended up with an Emperor Napoleon and have trampled on half the nations of Europe . . .'

Thurston shrugged, apparently undisconcerted by this irrefutable logic. 'They are the French, sir, and have merely trampled upon *courts*,' he said. Drinkwater suppressed a laugh with difficulty. Time was drawing on and he was more anxious than ever to escape the oppressive confine's of the ship. 'They order things very differently hereabouts . . .' Thurston's eyes wandered wistfully through the stern windows to the sweep of green grass and deciduous woodland bordering the river. 'Very differently.'

'Thurston, you know very well why I had you made into my clerk, don't you?'

'I think so, sir.'

'You know so, sir . . . and you know why I cannot tolerate your spreading your creed aboard this ship.'

'I know that, sir, and I pity you.'

'Have a care, Thurston, have a care, you may not find things would fall out quite as you wish even in Utopia. I am aware some men think you dangerous, while others think you mad. I am aware too that cranks are small things which make revolutions . . .' The pun brought a smile back to Thurston's face, 'but the word on shipboard also signifies unstable and top-heavy, so have a care. Do you understand?'

'Oh, I understand, sir.'

They faced each other for a moment, the one, unresponsible and armed with the truth; the other worn down by obligations and compromised by the nature of the world.

'Pass word to call away my barge, if you please.'

On Drinkwater's insistence they rode away from the house directly inland. He had first enquired if there was news of Stewart's return with Vansittart's passport and having thus acquitted himself of the last demands of duty he gave himself up to pleasure with a rare and uncharacteristic enthusiasm.

Vansittart reading his novel and patiently awaiting the acceptance of his credentials; Metcalfe, irritated by his non-participation in the previous evening's rout and further annoyed by Drinkwater's departure this morning; Frey, moonstruck and vacant; even Thurston righting all the world's ills with his honest and impossible creed – all could go hang for an hour or two. He had given them enough to keep them busy. A wood and watering party sent off under adequate guard, a restowing of the hold and a rattling down of the rigging should guard against the devil finding work for idle hands . . .

It did not occur to him as he kicked the roan mare after the spirited chestnut gelding that he was the only one whose hands were, at least metaphorically, empty.

'Do we go alone?' he had asked as she walked the leading horse round the rearward corner of the house and so cut off the view of the river.

She had turned and patted a bulging saddle-bag. 'I have a luncheon here,' she called gaily, 'or do you think me in need of a chaperon?' The notion caused her to burst out into a peal of laughter and spur her horse.

For a moment or two Drinkwater was too preoccupied by the need to stay in the saddle to think of anything else. He was aware his dignity was non-existent as he struggled to get the rhythm of the trotting horse, urging the beast to canter as much to stay in the saddle as to keep up with his hostess. It was only when the mare obliged and Drinkwater recalled the tricks he had learned on a similar horse of Sir Richard White's, that it occurred to him Mistress Shaw was wearing breeches.

The day was fine and sunny, with small puffballs of cumulus clouds trailing downwind under the influence of a fresh breeze which made the leaves of the trees rustle delightfully. He had never fully mastered the skills of horsemanship, unlike his father and his younger brother. The former was long dead but Ned, he supposed, was still at large, somewhere in Russia, an adopted Cossack.

And here *he* was, in Virginia, behaving like a fool in hot pursuit of a delightful rump as it bounced ahead of him and, dear Christ, went over a hedge!

'God's bones,' he swore, recalling his mother's adage that pride invariably preceded a fall. There was no need for fate to be so literal, he thought desperately as the hedge drew rapidly closer. And then with a sense of mounting panic he realized it was not a hedge. This was not enclosed England, but wide and wonderful Virginia. He was confronted by a row of bushes which, he realized with sudden certainly, ran alongside a little brook. He was too late to rein in; he felt the mare gather herself and, at the last moment, remembered to lean forward. The mare crashed through the brushwood and stretched herself for the brook beyond. He saw the bright flash of water and then his whole frame shook as the mare landed and the bony structure of her shoulders steadied and received his weight. The horse stumbled, recovered, and began to pant as it breasted the rising ground beyond the brook. Relieved, Drinkwater took stock of his surroundings. Mistress Shaw had halted her horse on the summit of the hill. He pulled up alongside her.

'You promised me . . .' he panted.

'A docile mount, not an easy ride,' she laughed, cutting him short.

'Thank God your horse knows the lie of the land.'

'Betsy would die rather than throw you,' she said, leaning

forward and affectionately patting his mount on her neck. The mare whinnied softly and the chestnut threw up his own head and jingled a protest at this favouritism.

For a moment they sat on their horses and regarded the view in silence. Drinkwater was surprised how far and how high they had come. He could see the roof of Castle Point, and beyond, on the silver-grey waters of the Potomac, the two ships with the bright spots of their rival ensigns at their sterns.

'They look so insignificant from here, don't they,' she said. It was not a question, nor could he argue with the fact.

'They are,' he said suddenly, and the sense of liberation the words gave amazed him. In a sudden impulsive movement he had jerked Betsy's head round to the west and kicked his unspurred heels into her flanks. Without looking back he worked the mare up to a gallop, dropping down towards more trees on the far side of the hill.

She watched him for a moment, holding her own restively eager horse in check until the foam flew from its mouth. Her heart was hammering inexplicably and she knew her hesitation was useless; yet she felt compelled to wait, not knowing the reason for this foolishness. When she could stand it no longer, she gave a yelp, flicked the reins and let the chestnut have its head.

The two ships were instantly hidden behind the summit.

'You remind me of a magnolia we have at home,' he said. 'It grows against a south-facing wall and produces flowers of a singular loveliness.'

'We have them here in Virginia,' she said, blushing and busying herself with the game pie. 'Do you open this.'

He sat up and took the bottle and corkscrew while she knelt and laid two plates upon the spread cloth.

'You have more than a magnolia at home, Captain,' she said pointedly, after a long pause, her voice strained.

'And still you remind me of it,' he said, placing the uncorked bottle on a level corner of the cloth, 'magnolia, home and beauty.'

'Have you killed, Captain?' she asked suddenly, looking at him squarely, her expression intent.

'In cold blood, or action?' he prevaricated, wondering why she had so cruelly turned his love-making aside.

'Does it matter?'

He shrugged. 'Perhaps not to you . . .'

'You men think by setting such moral questions in grades of dreadfulness to make them acceptable.'

'I am somewhat wearied of moral judgements being made against me today. You are not the first woman to ask that question of me. I am a sea-officer, for better or worse. I have my duty.'

'Does it not bother your conscience that you murder with some proficiency?'

'Of course; but adultery is a sin as proscribed as murder, madam, yet is indulged in with little thought by people who do not conceive themselves as wicked. It has been a matter of amazement to me that one who moralizes about the evils of the latter can so easily practise the former. I am a sinner, but hesitate to throw stones.'

She had coloured and bit her lip, then said, 'I had not expected such flippancy.'

'Would you have me bare my soul to a stranger?'

'Perhaps,' she said, looking at him again, 'the stranger would wish to be otherwise.' She poured the wine into two glasses and handed him one.

'And what would the stranger be? An adulterer, or merely a magnolia?'

'Perhaps both.'

Later she propped herself on an elbow and looked down at him as he stared impassively at the clouds moving slowly above the trees.

'You regret what has happened, don't you, Nathaniel?' He remained silent, staring upwards. 'Do not, I beg you, if only for my sake. For you 'twas but a riot in the blood.'

He turned and looked at her, and saw her eyes were brim full of tears.

'I think we are both too old for such . . . such rioting to be passed over thus easily.'

'It doesn't signify . . .'

'On the contrary,' he said gently, 'even madness has its own place under heaven.'

'Do you feel any different now?'

He smiled sadly. 'Not all men spend in the same manner as they piss, Arabella. Perhaps I wish I did, it would make my infidelity the easier to bear.'

'I do not think', she said, her voice trembling, 'you should reproach yourself. I am not . . .'

He took her hand and smiled at her. The boyish attractiveness had gone, replaced by something she could not describe, but which would, she knew with the certainty of true foreboding, haunt her future loneliness. 'My darling . . .' she breathed.

They arrived back at Castle Point at sunset. As they approached, walking their horses for fear they might arrive too soon, yet both aware their arrival was inevitable, the sound of shots rang out. Seized by a sudden awful thought that his absence had precipitated wholesale desertion, he pushed the mare forward until he saw Moncrieff's scarlet coat floundering through a reedbed waving a duck above his head. Relieved, he watched the wild-fowling party which appeared to consist of Moncrieff, Metcalfe and Davies, one of the master's mates, until Arabella drew level with him.

'They are fowling,' he said, 'I hope with your father-in-law's permission.'

'You are forgetting me already,' she reproached him.

'When I heard those shots I feared for my life,' he remarked grimly, then turned towards her. Her hair was dishevelled and her cheeks were wet with tears. 'My dear,' he said, his voice thick with emotion, 'you make me reproach myself . . . please, do not cry, I am not worth it.'

She sniffed noisily. 'We must ride back to the house. Let us at least look as if the day was enjoyable.' And she drove her spurs into the chestnut's flanks so that the galled horse reared up and then leapt forward into a gallop.

Drinkwater followed as best he could, but she was already dismounting as he drew rein in the gravelled courtyard before the stables. The negro groom was rubbing down a large black stallion and, as the horses whinnied at each other and the stallion stamped, Zebulon Shaw came towards them.

'Bella . . . Captain Drinkwater, I trust you enjoyed your excursion.' He clapped his hands and a little negro stable-boy ran out and took the two bridles. Shaw spoke to his daughter-in-law and she turned to her guest.

'My brother is back and wishes that you and Mr Vansittart join us for dinner. He has brought the answer we wish for.' Her triumph was tempered by the formality about to overlay the day's intimacy.

'It is surely good news, Captain Drinkwater,' Shaw said.

'Surely, sir,' Drinkwater replied, easing himself out of the saddle. He looked at Arabella. 'It is for the best, I think,' he added in a low voice.

She caught his eye and then bit her lip, just as Elizabeth was wont to do, turned away and went into the house.

'Shall we say in two hours, Captain?' asked Shaw looking from the retreating back of his daughter-in-law to the large turnip-watch in his red fist. 'Charles has retreated to his ship refusing the ministrations of our servants to wash the dust off him, but I reckon he'll be ashore again by then.'

'I'll fetch Vansittart, Mr Shaw, and perhaps we can make some travelling arrangements for him . . .'

'Of course, of course,' Shaw waved aside any trifling difficulties of that nature. ' 'Tis in a good cause, Captain, the noble cause of peace.'

'Indeed, sir, it is.'

It was almost dark when he reached the water's edge at the same time as the returning shooting-party.

'Have you had a good bag?' he asked and was caught up in the jocular repartee of their high spirits. Metcalfe seemed to have forgiven Drinkwater his absence and had gathered an impressive bag. Already the events of the afternoon were become a memory.

He paused on the quarterdeck and looked back at the shore. The white façade of Castle Point was grey in the gathering dusk. A few lit windows blazed out, some hid behind curtains. Was Arabella concealed behind one washing him from her voluptuous body and dressing for the evening?

'*Post coitus omnes triste est*,' murmured Drinkwater to himself, and went unhappily below.

Chapter Eight *September 1811*

The Master Commandant

The sudden transition from the company of Arabella Shaw to that of his high-spirited officers with their bag of duck and snipe gave Drinkwater little time to reflect upon the events of the day. Even in the odd moments that followed his return to *Patrician* in which his mind had the opportunity to wander, other, more pressing matters supervened. In any case, the day was not yet over and his subconscious subdued his conscience with the certainty of being in Arabella's company again that evening.

The shots of the wildfowlers which had so alarmed him reawakened his fear of mutiny, tapping the greater guilt of absence from the ship which, in its turn, combined with the knowledge that Captain Stewart had returned to his own ship prior to their meeting over dinner, and made Drinkwater consider his coming encounter with the Yankee. From what he had gleaned of Stewart's character so far, and in particular the American's hostile taciturnity, the evening promised more of confrontation than conviviality. The fact that Drinkwater had already established an intimacy at Castle Point gave him a *frisson* of expectation. Such was his state of mind that he was both ashamed and, less creditably, gratified by this, a feeling of elated excitement further enhanced every time he caught sight of the American sloop through the stern windows of his cabin. It was fading in the twilight, merging with the opposite river-bank, but he remained acutely aware of its presence. Not since he had joined *Patrician* in Cawsand Bay had he felt so full of vigour.

There was a knock at the cabin door. 'Come!'

'Is there anything . . .' Thurston began, but Drinkwater cut him short.

'No, thank you, Thurston. I am dining ashore tonight.' He unrolled his housewife, drew out his razor and began stropping it.

'There is one thing,' he said as Thurston was about to withdraw, 'be so kind as to ask Mr Vansittart to join me for a moment, would you?'

He began to shave. Vansittart entered while he waited for Mullender to prepare his bath. He passed on Zebulon Shaw's invitation, adding, 'We can make all arrangements for your travelling through Shaw; he's a most obligin' fellow.'

The diplomat's self-imposed quarantine, though doubtless proper, seemed a little foolish under the circumstances. Shaw was quite clearly opposed to war and if not an Anglophile, he was worldly enough to regard open hostilities between two countries as in nobody's interests. Vansittart might, Drinkwater reflected, profit much from his conversation by way of a briefing before leaving for Washington and he expressed this opinion while he shaved. Vansittart, his elegant legs crossed and a glass of the captain's Madeira in his hand, lounged on a chair and contemplated the dishevelled Drinkwater.

'But supposing, my dear fellow,' Vansittart said in a superior tone suggesting he was already conducting negotiations on the part of His Majesty's government, 'supposing this fellow Shaw has his own axes to grind.'

'I don't follow . . .' Drinkwater stretched his cheek and drew the razor carefully over the thin scar left by a sword cut.

'Well, let us hypothesize that his pacific intentions are governed by his desire not to have some aspect of his personal economy interrupted by war; or perhaps he has some disagreement with a congressman from New England who is of a contrary opinion . . .'

'Suppose he has?' broke in Drinkwater, sensing the looming prevarications and evasions, the tortuous and meaningless sophistry of political blustering. 'What the devil does it signify? If he serves our purpose in bringin' the weight of his opinion in favour of headin' off a rupture, he serves our cause . . .'

'Ah, but nothing,' Vansittart said smoothly and with a hint of patronizing, 'is quite as simple as that.'

Drinkwater looked at the urbane young man. He had been right about the proximity of the land. It had had its effect upon Vansittart, even though he had yet to step ashore. He was no longer a bewildered ignoramus, lost among the technical mysteries of a man-of-war, but a member of an élite upon whose deliberations the fates of more ordinary mortals depended. Already Vansittart's imagination inhabited the drawing-rooms of the American capital and the success his intervention would achieve.

'We are none of us exempt from our personal entanglements,' said Drinkwater pointedly, a small worm of uneasiness uncoiling itself in his belly, 'and now if you'll excuse me . . .' He wiped his razor clean.

Mullender was pouring the last of the hot water from the galley range into the tin bath and the cabin was filling with steam. Drinkwater began pulling his shirt over his head. Mixed with the smell of his own sweat a sweet fragrance lingered.

Vansittart watched for a moment, saw the scarred lacerations and mutilation of Drinkwater's right shoulder and hurriedly rose, tossing off his glass. 'Well, I shall have the opportunity of judging this Shaw for myself,' he said. 'In any event my bags are packed, so I will leave you to your ablutions.'

'I shall be half an hour at the most.'

Drinkwater sank back into the delicious warmth of the bath. 'Well, Mullender,' he said, 'what news have you?'

'Mr Moncrieff has presented you with a brace of ducks, sir.'

'That's very kind of Mr Moncrieff.' He entertained a brief image of Arabella sitting down to a dinner of roast duck with him in the intimacy of the cabin, then dismissed the notion as dangerously foolish.

'Do you want the boots again today, sir? As they're muddy I'll have to clean them.'

'No, no, full dress . . .'

''Tis already laid out, sir, and I've the sponging of your old coat in hand, sir.'

They had lain upon the old, shabby undress coat he had worn for the expedition. The reminder made him move restlessly, slopping water in his sudden search for the soap.

He stood before the mirror with comb and brush, an uncharacteristic defensive vanity possessing him. He suppressed his conscience by convincing himself it was to make an impression on Stewart that he dressed with such care. Mullender moved one of the lanterns and the silk stockings and silver buckled shoes, the white breeches, waistcoat and stock seemed to glow in the reflected lamp-light. He handed the comb and brush to Mullender who, with a few deft and practised strokes, quickly finished the captain's hair off in a queue.

'I suppose I should have it cut,' Drinkwater said.

'Wouldn't be you, sir,' Mullender said with finality drawing the black ribbon tight and levelling its twin tails. Drinkwater held his arms out and Mullender helped him on with the coat. He felt the weight of the heavy bullion epaulettes, one on each shoulder as befitted a senior post-captain, and his gold cuff lace rasped that on his lapels as he adjusted the set of the garment. Mullender pulled the long queue clear of the collar and flicked at Drinkwater's shoulders before stepping back and picking up sword and belt.

'No sword tonight, Mullender, thank you.'

'Aye, sir,' grunted Mullender, clearly disapproving of Drinkwater's tact.

'Call away my barge, if you please.'

Mullender opened the cabin door and spoke to the marine sentry. Drinkwater took one final look at himself in the mirror and picked up his hat.

'Barge crew called, sir,' Mullender reported, 'and Mr Metcalfe said to tell you what looks like a Yankee schooner has just anchored on the far side o' that Yankee sloop.'

'Very well,' Drinkwater said absently and swung round.

'We must get that bulkhead painted,' he remarked suddenly. Mullender looked up.

'Sir?'

'That bulkhead, get it painted!' snapped Drinkwater, abruptly leaving the cabin.

'What now?' Mullender muttered, and sighed, scratching his head uncomprehendingly. He did not see, as Drinkwater saw, the faint discolourations where once the twin portraits of Elizabeth and his children had hung.

'Sir, the Yankee has just gone over the side, if you hurry . . .'

They could hear the squealing of the pipes floating over the still water from the dark shape of the *Stingray*, her tall masts and yards black against the dark velvet of the night sky with its myriad stars. He could see nothing of the schooner beyond her. Metcalfe's almost childish urgency irritated Drinkwater.

'I don't want to make a damned undignified race of it,' he said curtly. 'Let the bugger go ahead . . .' Metcalfe opened his mouth to say something, but Drinkwater was in no mood now to bandy words with his first lieutenant. 'Do you make sure the sentries present arms as he goes past. We are not at war with the United States, Mr Metcalfe, and I'll see the courtesies extended while we are within American waters.'

Metcalfe's mouth shut like a trap and he spun on his heel, but Moncrieff had already dealt with the matter. The American gig, a chuckle of phosphorescence at her cutwater, the faint flash of her oar blades rising and dipping, approached them in a curve to pass under the *Patrician*'s stern. The dim light of a lantern in her stern-sheets reflected upon the face of Captain Stewart and his attendant midshipman.

Moncrieff called the deck sentinels to attention. 'Present arms!' The American boat swept past, Stewart and the midshipman unmoving.

'Insolent devil,' said Moncrieff in a voice that must have been heard in the still darkness. 'Shoulder arms!'

'Are you ready, Vansittart?' Drinkwater enquired as a grey shape joined them.

'I am indeed, Captain Drinkwater.'

'After you, then.' Drinkwater gestured and Vansittart peered uncertainly over the side. Midshipman Belchambers looked up from the barge.

'Just hold on to the man-ropes, sir, and lean back . . .'

He saw her first, in a full-skirted dress of watered green silk the origin of which was not Parisian. Her raven hair was up and a rope of Bahamian pearls wound round her slender neck. She looked remote, proper, Shaw's daughter-in-law-cum-hostess and not the creature who . . .

'Captain Drinkwater, good of you to come.'

'Your servant, sir. May I present Mr Henry Vansittart . . . Mr Shaw.'

'Mr Vansittart, you are very welcome. Captain Drinkwater, you have met my daughter-in-law. Mr Vansittart, may I present Mrs Arabella Shaw . . .'

Bows and curtsies were exchanged, Vansittart bent solicitously over Arabella's hand and Drinkwater turned away. He found himself face to face with Master Commandant Stewart.

He had his sister's features and the likeness shocked him. Yet there was nothing effeminate in the American officer's handsome face, on the contrary, his dark features conveyed the immediate impression of a boldness and resolution which, as he confronted the Englishman, were unequivocally hostile. Drinkwater had the unnerving sensation that, despite his own superiority in years and rank, the American held himself in all respects the better man. A cooler head than Drinkwater possessed at that instant might have considered this impression as a consequence of underlying guilt on his own part and an overweening pride and youthful contempt on the American's. At that moment, however, the impact was uncanny and overwhelming, and Drinkwater endeavoured to conceal his inner confusion with an over-elaborate greeting that the American attributed to condescension.

'Captain Stewart, I presume. I am your servant, sir, and delighted to make your acquaintance.'

The younger man's face split in a lupine grin. From the moment his topman reported the approach of the British frigate, Stewart had been both affronted by the British man-o'-war's presence in American waters, and hoping for some means by which he, the most junior commander on the American Navy List, might personally tweak the tail of the arrogant British lion. Captain Drinkwater, a greying tarpaulin officer of no particular pretension, offered him a perfect target. Stewart would not have admitted fear of any British naval officer, but he nursed an awkwardness in the presence of those urbane and languid sprigs of good families he had once met in New York. Vansittart was so clearly an example of the class, if not the type. In needling Drinkwater he felt he opened a mine under British conceit, laid under so easy and foolish a target as Captain Drinkwater, the more readily to wound Vansittart. The prospect of this revenge for past humiliations, real or imagined, amused and stimulated him.

'You presume a great deal, Captain. As for being my servant that's fair enough, but your delight concerns me not at all . . .' It was a gauche, clumsy and foolish speech, but made to Drinkwater in his present mood and made loud enough for all the company to hear, it had its desired effect, bolstering Stewart's pride and leaving the witnesses nonplussed as they, in full expectation of a sharp-tongued response, left Captain Drinkwater to defend himself.

But Drinkwater blushed to his hair-roots, dropping his foolishly extended hand. Vansittart's inward hiss of breath, of apprehension rather than outrage, broke the silence.

'Gennelmen, a glass,' Shaw drawled, motioning to a negro

servant in a powdered wig and a ludicrous canary-yellow livery. He bore a salver upon which the touching rims of the glasses tinkled delicately.

'I thought rum appropriate to the occasion,' said Shaw, clearly practising a joke he had rehearsed earlier and which was now quite inappropriate to the occasion.

'Indeed, ' Vansittart waded in, 'almost the *vin du pays*, what? Your health, ma'am, and yours, sir, and yours, Captain Stewart. That's a fine ship you command, by the by.'

'Indeed it is,' replied Stewart, clearly enjoying himself and never taking his eyes off Drinkwater, 'the match of any ship, even one of reputedly superior force.'

The sarcasm brought Drinkwater to himself. He mastered his discomfiture and met the younger man's eyes. 'Let us hope, Captain Stewart, the matter is not put to the test.'

'It wouldn't concern me one damn jot, Captain, were it to be put to the test tomorrow morning.'

'Come, come, gennelmen,' said Shaw, stepping between the two sea-officers and smiling nervously at Vansittart, 'damn me, Vansittart, we will have our work cut out to keep such hotheads from tearing each other to pieces. 'Tis as well they put these fellows under orders, or what would become of the peace of the world?'

Drinkwater caught Arabella's eye. Was it pity he saw there, or some understanding of his humiliation?

'I think it you, Charles, who is the greater hothead,' she scolded, half in jest. 'I don't believe Captain Drinkwater to be a man to underestimate his enemy.'

Was the remark taken as one of mere politeness, or an indiscretion of the most lamentably revealing nature? Drinkwater could not be sure how each of them perceived it, for his prime concern was to seize the lifeline she had flung him, to put the company at their ease, to detach himself from Stewart's sarcastic goading.

'I have held that as a guiding principle throughout my career, ma'am.'

'You have seen a good deal of action, have you not, Captain?' Vansittart rallied to him, equally eager to defuse the atmosphere, but painfully aware of Drinkwater's lack of finesse in such circumstances.

'I believe so,' Drinkwater answered.

'What – Frenchmen?' put in Stewart, unwisely.

'Some Frenchmen, yes, but Dutchmen, Russians – and Americans.' He paused, feeling he had regained some credibility. 'War is not a matter to be entered into lightly, no matter how excellent one's ship, nor the fighting temper of one's people.'

Stewart had swallowed his rum at a gulp and it emboldened him. 'Oh, ship for ship, we'd lick you, Cap'n . . .'

Drinkwater experienced that sudden cool detachment he usually associated with the heat of action, after the period of fear before engagement and the manic rage with which a man worked up his courage and in which most men conquered or perished in hand-to-hand slaughter. For him this remote and singular feeling lent him strength and an acuity of eye and nervous response which had carried him through a dozen fierce actions. He suddenly saw this boorish boy as being unworthy of his temper, and smiled.

'Perhaps, ship for ship, you are quite right, Mr Master Commandant, but I beg you to consider how few ships you have and the inevitable outcome of a concentration of force upon this coast. A blockade, for instance; do you comprehend a blockade, Mister Stewart? No, I think not. Say twelve of the line cruising constantly off Sandy Hook, another dozen off the Delaware, another off the Virginia capes, with frigates patrolling in between, cutters and schooners maintaining communications between the squadrons, ships being relieved regularly, and water and wood being obtained with impunity from your empty and unguarded coastline . . . come, sir, that is not a happy prospect, you'll allow?'

Drinkwater observed with a degree of pleasure how Stewart resented the use of his proper rank and Drinkwater's pointed abandonment of his courtesy title. The added irony of begging his listener's consideration was lost on Stewart in his inflamed state, for while Drinkwater spoke, he snapped his fingers and took another glass of rum.

'You couldn't do it,' he said thickly when Drinkwater finished speaking, 'your men wouldn't stand for it . . .'

'We'd still be damned foolish to put it to the test, Charles,' temporized Shaw, 'hell's bells, you professional gennelmen are a pair of gamecocks to be sure. Arabella, my dear, we'd better fill their bellies with something less inflammatory than firewater . . .'

Vansittart laughed loudly and Mistress Shaw caught the manservant's eye and addressed a few words to him.

'Whether or not you gennelmen trade shot for shot rather

depends upon the efforts of Mr Vansittart here,' Shaw said, taking the diplomat's elbow familiarly, 'and we have concluded all the necessary arrangements for you to proceed to Washington, Mr Vansittart. A schooner has just arrived this evening to convey you up to Baltimore and I understand a chaise is at your disposal thereafter. I, for one, hope the news you bring for Mr Foster enables us to conclude a peaceful settlement of our dispute. Foster's a better man than either Jackson or Erskine were in the subtleties of representing the British government over here, so there's some hope!' Shaw raised his glass and was about to propose a toast to peace when Stewart snorted his objection. Shaw put out a placating hand as Stewart made to protest. 'Oh sure, Charles,' he went on, 'I understand your anger, Great Britain *has* undoubtedly acted the part of the bully and I'm sure Captain Drinkwater, being a fair-minded man, will acknowledge that his country's foreign policies have not always been honourable, whatever justification – mainly expedience, I guess – is advanced, but it don't mean we *have* to fight.'

'Men were taken out of my own ship,' Stewart protested.

'The *Stingray*?' queried Vansittart quickly.

'No,' said Shaw, 'Charles was master of a Baltimore schooner between naval appointments,' he explained. 'We have more officers than ships . . .'

'Naval ships,' Stewart said with a heavy emphasis.

'How many guns do your merchant ships mount?' Vansittart asked, anticipating the question forming at the same instant in Drinkwater's mind. Not for the first time, Drinkwater acknowledged the sharpness of Vansittart's intelligence. Yet he did not want Vansittart to overplay his hand. Such a rapid tattoo of queries might make Stewart clam up and, in his perceptive state, Drinkwater wanted the already mildly intoxicated young man to talk a great deal more. Perhaps he might, with advantage, stir this pot a little.

'They make excellent privateers, Vansittart,' he said, 'I recall during the last American war . . .'

Stewart, who had long since swallowed his third glass of rum, grinned. This British captain was not merely ancient, he was also cautious! 'Cap'n Drinkwater is right,' he said with a hint of mimicry, 'they make *excellent* privateers, and we could have 'em swarming like locusts over the ocean.' Stewart held up his free hand and snapped his fingers. 'And a fig for your blockade! You'd have to convoy *everything*!'

'Well, sir . . .' Vansittart began but was interrupted.

'Gentlemen,' Arabella broke in, the yellow-coated servant at her shoulder, 'dinner is served.'

They sat down to dine in the same room as they had used the previous evening, but now gravity not gaiety was the prevailing mood. Zebulon Shaw remained a gracious host and Vansittart a sociable guest but Stewart sank into a moody contemplation of the man who epitomized his conception of the enemy. As for Drinkwater, he did his best to contribute to the conversation and to maintain a somewhat pathetic contact with Arabella. He was largely unsuccessful, for Vansittart divided his easy attention between Shaw and his daughter-in-law.

Drinkwater could not afterwards recall what they had eaten. A spiced capon, he thought, though his abiding memory was a complex feeling of self-loathing, of irritation that Stewart's slowly increasing drunkenness was accompanied by the man's unceasing scrutiny, and of jealousy that Arabella should flirt so with Vansittart, a boy young enough to be her son.

He was in a foul mood when she rose and declared she would withdraw and leave them to their spirits and cigars. As she swept out with a smiling admonition to her father-in-law not to deprive her for too long of the society of so many gentlemen, Drinkwater felt bereft, unaware of a tender and pointed irony in her words.

'This is a superb house,' Vansittart remarked as he drew on his cigar.

'It was my father's conceit to build a castle, such as an English peer might have. He began in '76, three weeks after the declaration of independence, but', Shaw blew a fragrant cloud of tobacco smoke at the ceiling, 'man proposes and God disposes.'

'I don't follow . . .'

'He was killed at the Battle of the Brandywine a year later,' Shaw explained. 'Although a lieutenant in Wagonner's Virginia regiment in Scotch Willie Maxwell's brigade, he had been sent with a message to Wayne at Chadd's Ford where he stopped a Hessian ball. He died instantly . . .'

'I am sorry to hear it, sir,' Vansittart replied.

Shaw shrugged. 'Oh, I bear no ill-will, time heals all things and he died in good company.'

'He died fighting the English,' slurred Stewart.

Shaw seemed embarrassed at the interruption and addressed Drinkwater. 'You served at the time, Captain, did you not?'

'Aye, sir. I served in Carolina – and lost friends there. It had become a filthy business by then. The circumstances of death were less glorious. There was a midshipman whose end was foul.'

'How so?' Stewart put the decanter down and looked up. His intake of wine had been steady throughout the meal and beads of sweat stood out on his forehead. A prurient curiosity blinked through his blurring eyes and Drinkwater wanted to wound the cocksure fool, to disabuse him of his misconceptions of war.

'He was captured and mutilated, Captain Stewart,' Drinkwater said quietly.

'I think we should join . . .' Shaw began, but Stewart ignored his host.

'Whadya mean – mutilated?'

Vansittart half-rose, but his face was turned expectantly towards Drinkwater. The curiosity of the two younger men sent a sudden shudder of revulsion through Drinkwater. The one sought glory in war, the other thought of the business as a gigantic game in which whole divisions of men might be moved across continents as a matter of birth-right.

'We found him with his own bollocks in his mouth, Captain Stewart.'

'I am sorry about Charles,' Arabella said as they stood once more on the terrace.

'It was nothing.'

'For a moment I thought . . .'

'That I would call him out?' Drinkwater chuckled, 'God's bones, no . . . I am too old for that tomfoolery.'

'I am glad to hear it.' She pressed his arm and they stood in silence. The moon was riding clear of a low bank of cloud and the stridulation of cicadas filled the air. In the room behind them Stewart had fallen asleep; Vansittart and Shaw were deep in discussion.

'I am sorry,' she said suddenly.

'For what?'

'I feel now that I should not have asked you to come this morning.'

'My dear, what has passed between us has passed. We may or may not be judged, I don't know . . .'

'Remorse will turn you against me.'

'I can never be anything more to you than I was today, you know that. But I shall never be anything less.'

'I marked you as a man of constancy.'

'You must have faith in your intuition . . .'

'Nathaniel, suppose there are consequences?'

A cold sensation wrapped itself about his heart. 'Is it likely?'

'It is not impossible,' she whispered fearfully.

'I will give you an address in London. I will not abandon a child.' He paused. Pride cometh before a fall, he recalled. The modest competence, the acquisition of Gantley Hall, his wife and family – how he had jeopardized them by his casual dalliance with this woman. A riot in the blood, she had called it . . .

But looking at her he yearned to kiss her again.

'Arabella . . .' She turned her face towards him when a movement at the end of the terrace caught his eye.

'Who the devil . . .?'

'It's me, sir, Frey.'

Gently he detached himself from her, aware, even in that prescient moment when he knew something was wrong, how reluctant she was to let him go. 'Mr Frey? What the devil do you here?'

'Eight men have run, sir. Made off in the blue cutter left alongside from the watering party.'

'God damn and blast it!'

Chapter Nine *September 1811*

After the Fall

'What's to be done, sir?'

'Quiet, boy!'

Midshipman Belchambers' whispered query was hissed into silence by the first lieutenant. Metcalfe fidgeted, clasping and unclasping his hands, then ran a crooked finger round the inside of his stock. He felt Frey's eyes upon him in the preternatural chiaroscuro of the moonlit quarterdeck and concluded that he did not like Frey: he and Captain Drinkwater were, what was it? Too close, yes, that was it, too close; the bonding of long service affronted Metcalfe's hierarchical sensibilities, disturbed him where it had no right to. He felt the silent reproach in Vansittart's presence among them, conceiving the young diplomat one of Drinkwater's party when, by all the social conventions and familial traditions, Metcalfe knew he should not be so constantly at Drinkwater's side. Belchambers was another, a lesser example of the first. He snapped the eager boy to cringing silence and faced aft, unaware of their rationality of his train of thought, as apparently expectant as all the other officers ranged on deck, awaiting the reaction from the shadowy figure standing right aft at the taffrail.

Captain Drinkwater stared astern, towards the confluence of the Potomac with Chesapeake Bay wherein drained the waters of a dozen rivers. The moon rode high, clear of the clouds, apparently diminished in diameter due to its altitude, yet lending a weird clarity to the dismal scene. Captain Drinkwater had been lost in this contemplation for almost ten minutes, while his officers waited on the quarterdeck and below them the ship seethed. Barely a man slept after the hue and cry had been raised and Metcalfe, Gordon, Frey, Moncrieff and his marines, with drawn swords and hand-held bayonets had called the roll and scoured the ship.

'For God's sake . . .' Metcalfe muttered, much louder than he intended. He met Vansittart's eyes and shrugged

'The buggers could be anywhere,' he said, as if Vansittart had asked him a question, 'anywhere, damn them.'

'Do you search for them tonight?'

Metcalfe jerked his head aft, but still Drinkwater remained motionless, his hands clasped behind his back, his head facing away from them. All decisions waited upon the captain's pleasure now he was back on board.

It had been in Drinkwater's mind to vent his temper upon those responsible for the desertions: Metcalfe as his own deputy, the officer of the watch and his subordinates down to the marine sentries and the men in the guardboat.

But he knew he would be guilty of a grave injustice if he did, and he was already guilty of so much that day that the prospect of adding to the woeful catalogue of folly appalled him.

Standing beneath the pale splendour of the moon he felt himself a victim of all the paradoxes visited upon mankind. And yet his sense of responsibility was too keen to submit to so cosy a justification; the harsh self-condemnation of his puritan soul rejected the libertine's absolution.

In the cool of the night his old wounds ached intrusively, the body sharing the hurt of the mind. Mentally and physically he gave himself no chance of surrender to passion, refused to acknowledge the mutual hunger in, and irresistible attraction between himself and Arabella. Perhaps, had he remained in Arabella's presence, he would not have judged himself so harshly, would have placed events in their perspective. But Frey had been the agent of fate and brought the news of providence's swift retribution.

'Pride', he again and again recalled his mother saying, 'always comes before a fall,' and now he remembered another saw she was fond of, a social pretension in its way, almost an aspiration: 'Remember, you are not born to pleasure, Nathaniel, it is not for us. We are of the middling sort . . .'

He had heard the phrase recently and, in remembering, he confronted his own ineluctable culpability. Thurston had used it only that morning. A sudden anger burst in upon his brain. He should never have let Thurston have his head and spew his republican cant so readily! God, what a damned fool he had been to listen; to listen and to be half-convinced the fellow spoke something akin to the truth!

Well, he had his bellyful of the truth now, to be sure, he thought bitterly, victim of his own stupid, expansive weakness, a weakness doubtless induced by the bewitching prospect of a day in Mistress Shaw's company. God Almighty, he had been gulled by a damned whore!

And supposing he had left her pregnant, or worse, she had left him poxed . . .?

He broke out in a cold sweat at the thought. Fate had an uncanny way of striking a man when his guard was down and it had certainly conspired to strike him today.

Forward the ship's bell tolled two. It was already tomorrow, one o'clock in the morning, two bells into the middle watch, almost the lowest, most debilitating hour of the night.

He looked at the moon. It would be setting over Gantley Hall, already the first pale flush of the morning would be turning the grey North Sea the colour of wet lead, glossing the ploughed furrows of his oh-so-proudly acquired acres.

With an effort he mastered his temper, his dark fears and forebodings. 'I am grown selfish, morbid and gloomy,' he muttered to himself, 'and there is work to do.' There was always work, always duty, always the submission of the self to the common weal. It was the great consolation. The thought steadied him, drove back the gathering megrims and the whimpering self-pity that threatened, for one desperate, lonely moment, to overwhelm him.

No, he could not visit his anger upon men who had been merely neglectful of their duty. Doubtless the deserters had employed a degree of guile, slipping into the moored boat and shoving off as the guard-boat vanished round the far side of the frigate. Davies, the master's mate in charge, had heard nothing, nor seen anything. Yes, he had agreed, his men had been pulling somewhat lethargically and the current had, he admitted, swept them down a little too far from the ship than he would have wished, but he had forgotten how many circuits they had made during his watch . . .

Drinkwater could guess the rest. A distracted or dozing sentry, maybe even a colluding one, and who could blame the poor devils when some men had long been away from the kind of comforts he had so liberally indulged in the preceding day?

But eight men had run . . . He began to think logically again, thrusting aside the earlier train of thought. The ache in his old wounds throbbed into the background of his consciousness.

There must be those among them who remembered hanging a man for desertion before *Patrician* left for the Pacific. There was even less cause for mercy upon the present occasion. At least then the victim had the not unreasonable excuse of running to find out whether the tales of his wife's infidelity were true.

The thought of marital infidelity made Drinkwater sweat again. He had betrayed his wife and been unjust to Arabella, she was no wanton and, he reflected, he was no libertine. He took heart from the thought.

Eight men had run and it was time to tackle the problem, but in such a way as allowed him to control events. Yesterday, for that is how it was now, part of the unalterable past, yesterday had been a day during which he had lost control, been swept up by events, relaxed and forsaken his duty; perhaps for a few hours he had been merely himself, in all the lonely isolation of an individual human soul, but now, today, and from this very minute, he must be what he was: a sea-officer. He squared his shoulders, swung on his heel and strode forward.

'Gentlemen,' he said coolly, 'we are here to see Mr Vansittart lands safely and with every prospect of success in his task. He is to board the schooner which arrived here at sunset and will do so at six bells in the morning watch. That is seven o'clock by your hunter, Vansittart, if you made the last correction for longitude. My barge is to be used for the transfer, Mr Belchambers in command. Do you understand?'

There was a mumbled chorus of comprehension.

'Very well, then I suggest those of us not on duty should get some sleep.' He stepped forward and they drew apart.

'Sir, what about . . .' Metcalfe began.

'Let's deal with that in the morning, shall we? Goodnight, gentlemen, I trust you will sleep well.'

'They will be laughing at us over there this morning,' Drinkwater said and Moncrieff, Gordon, Metcalfe and Frey all looked at the *Stingray*, visible in part through the stern windows. 'More coffee . . .?'

If the officers assumed their invitation to breakfast was an invitation to a council of war, they were disappointed. Their commander's detached and almost negligent approach was reminiscent of the night before.

Indeed, Metcalfe, going below to turn in, had expressed the opinion that Drinkwater seemed about to let the matter slide and to bid good riddance to the eight who had run. Such pusillanimity was, he concluded, quite within the captain's erratic character and would have a bad effect on the men. They could, he asserted with an almost cheerful conviction, look forward to more desertions if he proved correct in his assumption. In the prevailing gloom no one had seen fit to contradict him. He was, in any case, given to extreme expressions of opinion and no one took much notice of him. It was only over the coffee and burgoo that they recalled the matter and thought Metcalfe might, after all, have a point. Close to the land as she was, the ship might well become ungovernable and the thought made them all uneasy.

There was no doubt the Yankees would find the event most amusing.

'What *are* your intentions, sir,' Moncrieff ventured boldly, anxiety plain on his open face, 'now Mr Vansittart has gone?'

Drinkwater sat back and regarded the company. Metcalfe looked his usual indecisive, critical self, an air of mock gravity wrapping his moon face in a cocoon of self-importance. Gordon and Frey looked concerned ready to act upon orders but too junior to have any influence upon events. Only Moncrieff, the ever-resourceful marine lieutenant, had physical difficulty in holding his eager initiative in check.

Drinkwater smiled. 'What do you suggest, Mr Frey?'

Frey's Adam's apple bobbed. 'Well, sir, I should, er, send out a search party . . .'

'Mr Gordon?'

'I agree, sir, perhaps to scour the countryside, check the buildings on the estate here . . .'

'Run downstream, they'd have used the current to put as great a distance between us and them and they know there are towns and villages for miles along the banks of the bay . . .'

'Very good, Mr Moncrieff. Mr Metcalfe?'

'I agree with Moncrieff, sir, and they already have a head start of', he pulled out his watch, 'almost ten and a half hours.'

'Do we know exactly what time they got away?'

'Well no, not exactly, sir, but . . .'

'Very well. The launch, with a corporal's guard and provisions for three days, is to leave for a search along the shore. Mr Frey, you are to command. Mr Gordon, you may run along the Potomac shore in the remaining cutter. Take a file of marines, but contrive to look like a watering party, not a war party. I don't want trouble with the local population. Be certain of that. Under the circumstances I would rather lose the men than have a hornets' nest stirred up to undermine Vansittart's mission. That is an imperative, do you understand?'

'Aye, sir.'

'Aye, sir.'

'Very well, you may carry on.'

Frey and Gordon scraped back their chairs. Metcalfe and Moncrieff made to rise too, but Drinkwater motioned them to remain seated. After the junior lieutenants had gone Drinkwater rose, lifted the decanter of Madeira from its fiddle and, with three glasses, returned to the table.

'I was surprised no one mentioned the *Stingray*,' he said as the rich, dark wine gurgled into the crystal glasses.

'The *Stingray*, sir?' Moncrieff said with quickening interest, 'They wouldn't dare . . . I mean how the deuce . . .?'

'When I went ashore, the blue cutter was alongside the starboard main-chains. Davies, the master's mate rowing guard, said they dropped too far downstream before they rounded the stern, but even then I suspect they were too stupefied by the monotony of their duty to notice immediately the cutter was missing in the darkness. They probably fell downstream *every* circuit they made. But being downstream they commanded a fair view of the larboard side of the ship and, with the light southerly breeze then blowing, the ship was canted across the current sufficient to render the starboard, not the larboard side the more obscured . . .'

'And the *Stingray* was in, as it were, the shadow of the ship, lying to starboard of us, begging your pardon, sir,' Moncrieff added hurriedly. 'God damn it, of course! They pulled directly for the *Stingray*!'

'What makes you so sure, sir?' asked the unconvinced Metcalfe. Drinkwater's clever assessment undermined his own carefully argued case for the captain's general incompetence.

'I've a notion, shall we say, Mr Metcalfe? Nothing more.' But it was more, much more. He did not explain that something in Captain Stewart's over-confident demeanour had laid a suspicion in his mind. He had only just realized that himself, but now it gripped his imagination with the power of conviction.

'What about the boat, though?' persisted Metcalfe, unwilling to give up his theory.

'Oh, I expect Frey will find it downstream somewhere. The current and the wind will probably have grounded it on the Maryland shore.'

'Damn it, I think you're right, sir.' Moncrieff's eyes were glowing with certainty.

'Thank you, Moncrieff,' Drinkwater said drily. 'And now I think I'd better write to Mr Shaw and explain why marines and jacks are likely to be seen trampling over his land this morning. Perhaps you'd pass word for Thurston . . .'

'He was among the eight, sir,' said Metcalfe, his theory bolstered by Drinkwater's forgetfulness. 'I told you last night.'

'Oh yes, I had forgot.' Drinkwater felt a sensation of shock. He had been too self-obsessed last night to assimilate that detail. If Metcalfe's nervously delivered report had contained the information, it had simply not sunk in. It was not Arabella who had gulled him, he thought now, kinder to himself and therefore to her, she had merely let passion run away with her, as he had done himself; but Thurston had most assuredly duped him, lectured him and then pulled wool over his preoccupied eyes!

'But if you are right, sir, what do you intend to do about the Americans?' Metcalfe asked, prompting, aware that if Captain Drinkwater did not do something then he would most assuredly dishonour the flag.

'I am going to dissemble a little, Mr Metcalfe.'

'Dissemble, sir?' It was a policy Metcalfe had neither considered himself, nor thought his superior capable of.

'Yes. They are not going to sail until we do; they will sit as post-guard upon us until we depart. Let us bluster about our searches and, while we can, keep a watch upon her deck. You have a good glass, Mr Metcalfe?'

'Aye, sir, a Dollond, like yours.'

'Very well, busy yourself about the quarterdeck without making your spying too conspicuous. How many of these eight men would you recognize?'

'Well, Thurston, sir, and a man called King, foretopman, one of our best . . .'

'I know Carter, sir,' put in Moncrieff, 'and the Dane Feldbek . . .'

'And there were the two Russians, the fellows from the *Suvorov*, Korolenko and Gerasimov,' Drinkwater added, remembering now how Metcalfe had stumbled over the pronunciation of their names, 'you'd recognize them, surely?'

'Yes, of course, sir,' Metcalfe hurriedly agreed, surprised at Drinkwater's access of memory.

'Well, that is six of them,' Drinkwater said, finishing his wine and rising from the table. 'They cannot keep 'em below indefinitely.'

Moncrieff and Metcalfe rose at this signal of dismissal. Drinkwater turned to stare out through the stern windows at the American ship. Sunlight picked out her masts and yards and the thin, pale lines of her immaculately stowed sails. Her ports were open and her guns run out. There were signs of men at exercise about her decks, the glint of cutlasses and boarding pikes.

'What will you do if and when we spot them, sir?' asked Metcalfe from the doorway.

'Mmmm?' Drinkwater grunted abstractedly, still gazing at the Yankee sloop.

'What will you do, sir, *vis-à-vis* the Yankee?'

'Ain't it a first lieutenant's privilege to lead cutting-out parties, Mr Metcalfe?' Drinkwater replied absently, turning back into the cabin.

Metcalfe had difficulty seeing the captain's expression silhouetted as he was against the sun-dappled water in the background, but Drinkwater stepped forward and Metcalfe was shocked to see a look of implacable resolve fixed upon Drinkwater's face. 'Almost', he said to himself, 'as if he had been staring at an enemy.'

Frey's party found the missing cutter. It had grounded on a spit fifty yards from the Maryland shore.

'I don't know where they landed, sir,' he reported later that day, 'but that boat had been drifting.'

'We know where they landed, Mr Frey,' Drinkwater said, nodding at the sloop they could see through the stern windows.

'The *Stingray*, sir?' queried Frey in astonishment.

Drinkwater nodded. 'We've seen both the Russians using the head,' he said drily. 'I daresay if we wait long enough we'll see all eight of them bare their arses in due course.'

'So, er, what do you intend doing, sir?'

Drinkwater drew in his breath and let it out again. 'Well I believe the Americans call it playing possum, but you've a little time before dark. I want you to go and beat up a bit of shore-line. Pull round a little, let our friends over there think we're hoodwinked.' Drinkwater rose and leaned forward, both hands spread on the table. 'I don't want to do *anything* to jeopardize Vansittart's mission. On the other hand, the ship's company must not be allowed to think we are taking no action, so make no mention of the fact that we know about the presence of the deserters aboard the *Stingray*, do you understand?'

'Perfectly, sir. In fact the men may already know.'

'Good, now be off with you and conduct yourself like a man who's just had a flea in his ear and been told not to come back empty-handed.'

'Aye, aye, sir.'

Frey turned and was about to open the cabin door when Drinkwater added: 'You *can* come back though, Mr Frey, and with all your boat's crew, if you please.'

'Aye, aye, sir,' Frey replied with a grin.

Half an hour before sunset Drinkwater called away his barge. The knowledge that the deserters were aboard the *Stingray* gave him some comfort, for Stewart would keep them closer watched than Metcalfe. Whether or not Stewart would keep his secret until after *Patrician*'s departure or make some demonstration embarrassing to Drinkwater remained to be seen. The man harboured a deep resentment against the British and, it was obvious, saw the *Patrician*'s commander as the embodiment of all he disliked. But there was also an ungovernably passionate streak, a rash impetuosity to offset a deep intelligence; that much Drinkwater had deduced from the man's indiscreet drunkenness. Much might also be read from his sister . . .

However, he must dissemble, to gull as he had been gulled, to convince his people that he would not tolerate desertion.

Shaw received him in his dressing-room.

'I had your note, Captain Drinkwater.'

'I apologize for troubling you and hope that my men have not been over-intrusive upon your land, Mr Shaw.'

'Not *over*-intrusive, no,' Shaw replied, his resentment clearly aroused by the minor invasion of the day.

'I apologise unreservedly, sir, if any damage has been caused . . .'

'No, no,' Shaw waved aside the suggestion that anything more than his sense of propriety had sustained injury.

'And I apologize at the inconvenience of the hour, it is intolerable of me . . .'

'Please sit down, Captain. Will you join us for dinner? Arabella will be delighted to see you; she sure enjoyed your company yesterday.'

'Thank you, no, sir,' Drinkwater said, remaining standing. He longed to see Arabella again, for all the pain and remorse it would cause him. 'My official affairs are, alas, more pressing. Perhaps I may wait upon Mistress Shaw at a later date, but for the nonce I must perforce ask you to convey my felicitations to her. My presence is, er, a matter of some delicacy . . .' Drinkwater shot a glance at Shaw's negro valet.

Shaw dismissed the man. 'Come, sir, you have time to sit and take a glass.'

'Obliged, sir.' Drinkwater was not loathe to comply. Shaw poured from a handy bottle on a side-table. They mutually toasted each other's health. 'The point is', Drinkwater went on, leaning forward in his chair to give his words both urgency and confidentiality, 'this affair of deserters is a damnable nuisance. I must make every effort to regain 'em, for my Service, my reputation and general appearances, not to mention *pour discourager les autres*,' he said in his poor French, 'but I wish to do nothin' which might provoke a suspension of negotiations, Vansittart was most tellin' upon this point. It seems, from your discussions with him last night, there are men in Washington seekin' some new impropriety on our part, like Humphries' cavalier behaviour towards the *Chesapeake*, to make a *casus bellum* . . .'

'That is surely true, Captain. They are mostly from New England, hawks we have styled them, perhaps foolishly, for a hawk has a greater appeal than a dove, I allow. But I don't follow why . . .'

'I know where the men are, Mr Shaw . . .'

'You do?' Shaw's eyebrows rose with astonishment. 'Where?'

'Aboard the United States sloop-of-war *Stingray*.'

'The hell they are!'

'I feel sure they have been given asylum by Captain Stewart . . .'

'Have you sent word to Charles? Asked for them back?'

'Mr Shaw, you saw Captain Stewart's attitude to British interests last night. I am not insensible to the fact that he may be personally justified in all his resentments, but I am convinced he would refuse me the return of my men as a matter of principle. Why, I think he would delight in it.'

'He certainly has a thirst for glory.'

'And took against me personally, I believe.'

Shaw nodded. 'I fear so, Captain. Then you want me to approach him, to persuade him to relinquish your deserters?'

'Yes, if you would. It would be the simplest answer.'

Shaw sighed and rubbed his chin. 'What would you do with them? You would have to punish them, would you not?'

'Aye, sir, but I am not an inhumane man. Whatever I decided I would not carry out in American waters and properly I can do nothing until they have been court-martialed.'

'I don't follow . . . would you act improperly?'

'I could deem them guilty of a lesser crime and hence a lesser punishment . . .'

'And simply flog 'em? Pardon me, but the forces of Great Britain have a certain reputation for brutality. I too lived before the Revolution, Captain.'

'I believe General Washington ordered corporal punishment for breaking ranks and deserting, Mr Shaw. It is a not uncommon, if regrettable thing in war.'

'But my country is not at war and I want no part in precipitating any such misery on another . . .'

'I admire your sensibilities, Mr Shaw, but my country is at war.' Drinkwater mastered his exasperation. Shaw, it seemed, wanted to be all things to all men. He thought of Thurston, the idealist without responsibility. Now this wealthy man could keep his conscience clean by stepping round the problem. I am of the middling sort, he thought ironically, the sort that thrust the affairs of the world along day by day. 'I can only give you my word of honour that I will be lenient . . .'

'Be more specific, sir. To what extent will your leniency diminish your sentence of retribution?'

'I will order them no more than a dozen lashes.'

'Good God, sir, a *dozen*?'

'How many do you give your slaves, Mr Shaw?' Drinkwater was stung to riposte, regretting the turn the conversation had taken.

'That is an entirely different matter,' Shaw snapped. Then, struck by a thought and measuring the English officer, he added, 'Hell! Don't get any ideas about making up your crew from my plantation.'

Drinkwater attempted to defuse the atmosphere with a grin. 'I could promise them a nominal freedom aboard a man-o'-war,' he remarked drily, 'but I would not, you have my word,' he added hurriedly, seeing the colour rising in Shaw's face.

Shaw blew out his cheeks. 'Damn me, sir, this is a pretty kettle o' fish.'

Drinkwater seized this moment of weakness. 'I want only to avoid a collision, Mr Shaw. If you cannot be advocate perhaps you could merely ask; let Stewart know I am aware he is harbouring my men. The burden of conscience will then be upon him, will it not?'

'That is true . . .'

Drinkwater rose, 'I have kept you from your table, sir, and I am sorry for it. Perhaps you might consider consulting Mistress Shaw, in any event please present my compliments; she struck me as a woman of good sense. It is my experience that most women know their own minds and what is best for their menfolk too.'

Shaw rose and held out his hand. Both men smiled the complicit understanding of male confraternity.

'Perhaps I will, Captain, perhaps I will,' Shaw said smiling.

And partially satisfied, Drinkwater walked down towards the boat upon the lush, shadowed and terraced lawn. There existed stronger and more instantaneous bonds than those of chauvinism, bonds whose strength and extent were mysteries but whose existence was undeniable.

Chapter Ten *September 1811*

The Parthian Shot

They lay in this limbo of uncertainty for eight days, one, it seemed to those disposed to seek signs amid the random circumstances of life, for every deserter. The fall of the year came slowly, barely yet touching these low latitudes, so the very air enervated them and the pastoral beauty of the scene was slowly soured by idleness and a lack of communication with the shore.

The Patricians, unpatrician-like, still pulled their miserable guard round themselves, while the Stingrays regularly ferried their commander ashore. It was clear to Drinkwater that although Shaw might have spoken to Stewart about the advantages accruing to an honest, open, apple-pie handover of the British deserters, the appeal had fallen on deaf ears. Since they now caught no more than an occasional glimpse of their men, Drinkwater knew that Stewart was guarding his prizes closer still.

To keep the pot boiling Drinkwater dispatched Frey in the launch for a three-day expedition along the Virginia and Maryland shores and Stewart had, perforce, to send a shadowing boat. As for Arabella, Drinkwater saw her three or four times as she rode out. Once they exchanged greetings, she with a wave, he with a doffing of his hat, but on the other occasions, distance prevented these formalities.

The lack of hospitality on Shaw's part discouraged Drinkwater and, when he sent an invitation to Shaw and his daughter-in-law to dine as his guests aboard *Patrician* (Lieutenant Gordon's questing boat-party having disturbed a covey of game birds), it was declined on the grounds of Mr Shaw's absence.

Drinkwater tried to convince himself all parties awaited the outcome of negotiations before re-establishing amicable relations, but he knew the matter of the deserters had come between them all. As for Arabella herself, he thought she wished to distance herself from him and respected her wishes. Besides, he had no desire to make a fool of himself.

'Why did Vansittart have to go via Baltimore, sir?' Frey asked on his return. He had made his report and he and Drinkwater had been consulting a chart, Frey tracing his aimless track along the shores of Chesapeake Bay. 'The Potomac leads directly up to Washington.'

'A matter of formalities, I suppose,' replied Drinkwater absently, filling two glasses. 'Perhaps they did not wish him to see the defences of Washington, or reconnoitre so obvious an approach.'

'He'll come back the same way, then?'

'I imagine so. I've really no idea.'

'I wish *we* were back, sir,' Frey said suddenly.

'Back? Where?'

'In home waters, off Ushant, in the Mediterranean, the Baltic, anywhere but here. God, we're not liked hereabouts.

'We're an old enemy, Mr Frey . . . Tell me have you executed any watercolours lately? I believe you were working on a folio . . .'

'Oh, those, no, I have abandoned the project.' Something wistfully regretful in Frey's tone prompted Drinkwater to probe.

'Not like you to abandon anything.'

'No, maybe not, sir, but this occasion proved the rule.'

'The wardroom's not the most conducive place, eh? Do 'em in here, I could do with a little society.'

'Begging your pardon, sir, but I don't think that a good idea . . .'

'Oh, why not . . .? Ah, I see, presuming on our previous acquaintance, eh?'

'Something of the sort, sir.'

'Who? Not Moncrieff . . .' He knew already, but wanted to see if Frey's admission would back his hunch.

'No, no, not Moncrieff, sir, he's a good fellow . . .'

'Well, Wyatt then, he's no aesthete, though I'd have baulked at calling him a Philistine.'

'No, old Wyatt's a marline-spike officer, not well-versed, but experienced. I find the first lieutenant . . .'

'A difficult man, eh?'

'An inconsistent man, sir,' Frey admitted tactfully, the wine having its effect.

'Ah, diplomatic, Mr Frey, I must remember your talents in that direction. Perhaps you should have gone to Washington in place of Vansittart. He is certainly a curious fellow.'

'Vansittart, sir?' Frey frowned.

'No,' Drinkwater grinned, 'Metcalfe . . .'

It was good to see Captain Drinkwater smiling, Frey thought as he finished his glass, it reminded him of happier times. There was something sinister about this interminable wait, knowing the deserters were within easy reach of them and that they possessed superior force and could scarcely be condemned for insisting their own be returned to them. Frey had, moreover, heard it expressed in a deliberate lower deck stage whisper meant for his ears, that was it not for Captain Drinkwater himself being in command, there would have been more than a handful of deserters.

Drinkwater, regarding his young protégé, wondered what sort of impositions Frey suffered in the wardroom. He had written Metcalfe off as an adequate but fossicking officer whose chief vice was irritation. It had not occurred to him that he was a contrary influence.

'Well, well, I had no idea.'

'There is something else, sir, something you should know about.'

'What is it?'

'The men are *very* restless, sir. I am concerned about it if we are forced to wait much longer.'

'Be patient, Mr Frey. I like this state of affairs no better than you or the hands, but we are tied to Vansittart's apron strings.'

And with that Frey took his dismissal. So downcast was his mood, he thought Drinkwater merely temporizing and failed to catch the faint intimation of a purpose in the captain's words.

Mr Pym was as new to *Patrician* and her commander as most of the other officers. However, he was not new to the Royal Navy, having been an assistant surgeon at Haslar Naval Hospital when Mr Lallo, the ship's former surgeon, was found dead in his cot. Pym had accepted the vacancy in a frigate ordered on special service with alacrity. He was an indolent, easy-going man who found his wife and seven children as heavy a burden upon his tolerance as his purse. He had subdued his wife's protests with the consolation that he could at last drop the 'assistant' from his title and would receive a small increase in his emolument. Having thus satisfied her social pretensions, he had packed his instruments with his beloved books and contentedly joined *Patrician*.

Mr Pym was a quiet, private man. He possessed a kind heart, though he saw this as a vice since it had trapped him into a late marriage and ensured his broody and doting wife fell pregnant with dismal regularity, a circumstance which surprised and flattered his ageing self. He guarded this soft-heartedness, having learned early in his career not to display it aboard ship. Furthermore, like most easy-going and indolent men he was basically of a selfish disposition. The charm he possessed was used to ward off invasion of his privacy, and this latter he employed chiefly in reading. Books were Pym's secret delight.

He played cards with Wyatt, partly because they were of an age, but also by way of a break, a form, he told himself, of exercise between his voracious bouts of reading. As for his duties, he attended to these easily, holding a morning surgery, after which he spent the day as he pleased. Once a week, for the purpose of presenting the sick-book and discussing the state of the ship's company's health, he waited upon the captain.

Professionally he was not over-taxed. There were the usual crop of diseases: mostly skin complaints and an asthmatic or two, a few rheumatic cases, men with the usual minor venereal infections, coupled with a baker's dozen of the inevitable hernias found aboard any man-of-war. There was nothing, it seemed, of a surgical, nor indeed of a general medical nature to interest Pym, and this rather disappointed him.

He had, as a young man, studied at St Bartholomew's under the lame, scrofulous, supercilious and misanthropic physician Mark Akenside. Under Akenside's influence, he had aspired to greatness at an age when all things seem possible to the young and they have yet to discover the limitations of their energies, gifts and circumstances.

Early in life he had fallen into bad company, a mildly dissolute life and debt. The Royal Navy put distance between himself and his creditors, gave him back his character and kept him out of harm's way; but ambition continued to nag, and believing success came from change rather than effort, he accepted a post at Haslar. Here he found himself relegated to the second class and sought consolation in marriage with its consequent burdensome family.

The appointment to *Patrician* presented him, therefore, with a new opportunity.

As with many unimaginative and idly ambitious men, Pym failed to see any opportunity fate cast in his way. Obsessed with the end itself, he missed anything which might, with a little application, have provided him with the means. His books were too good a diversion, too absorbing a hobby. They tied up his mind, leaving it only room to brood upon his failure.

Until, in the hiatus of lying at anchor in the Potomac, he finished them.

To this disaster was now added a trail of men with imagined complaints. The artificial nature of exercises designed to keep them busy fostered a resentment only fuelled by the desertions. It was common knowledge on the lower deck that Thurston and his companions were aboard the *Stingray*. This, and the continuing useless search parties when each man was tempted from his duty by both the abuse offered when they came into contact with Americans and the healthy prosperity of the local population, combined to keep the pot of discontent simmering. Nor did the weather help. Warm and largely windless, the poorly ventilated berth deck became stifling, despite the burning of gunpowder and sloppings of vinegar solution.

'They are', Pym announced to the dining officers, 'rotten with the corrupting disease of valetudinarianism.'

'What's that?' asked Wyatt, his mouth full.

'Malingering,' Metcalfe explained.

Pym made a mock bow to the first lieutenant for stealing his own thunder which Metcalfe, helping himself to another slice of roast snipe, did not see but which tickled Frey's sense of humour so that he first laughed and then choked.

Metcalfe looked up. 'What's so damned funny?'

Frey spluttered and went purple. 'God, he's not laughing!' Moncrieff rose and slammed a hearty palm between Frey's shoulder blades. The piece of wing dislodged itself and flew across the table on to Metcalfe's plate.

'God damn you for an insolent puppy,' Metcalfe exploded; and in the same instant Pym received inspiration and enlightenment. He knew Metcalfe had not seen his own rudeness for he had been looking at the first lieutenant when he produced his little sarcasm. He knew his own mood was due to his having run out of books. A vague idea was stirring that a sure cure to his problem was to write one of his own, though the thought of the necessary effort bothered him. Parallel with these undercurrents of thought had been a detached observation of the first lieutenant's conduct. In this as in much else, Pym was lazy, blind to the clinical opportunity the concupiscence of a frigate's wardroom gave him. He merely concluded Metcalfe would, like so many other naval officers of his era, end up raving in Haslar.

'Though he don't drink much,' he had observed to Wyatt when they had been gossiping.

'Perhaps he's poxed,' Wyatt had suggested in his own down-to-earth manner.

'Or has incipient mercurial nephritis,' Pym had humbugged elevatingly.

But now, watching Metcalfe while the others stared at Frey recovering his breath and his composure, Pym thought him mad from another source and the seed of an idea finally germinated in his mind.

'I say, Metcalfe,' Moncrieff growled as Frey exchanged near-asphixiation for indignation.

'I . . . ain't . . . a . . . damned . . . puppy!' Frey gasped.

'You even talk like the man,' Metcalfe went on, and Pym realized Metcalfe's train of thought was somehow not normal. Here again was the recurrence of this obsessive disparagement of Captain Drinkwater, and Pym wondered at its root. Metcalfe's condemnation of the captain had become almost a ritual of his wardroom conversation, ignored by the others, tolerated only because he was the first lieutenant. Captains had a right to be eccentric, disobliging even, and first lieutenants an obligation to be unswervingly, silently loyal. That was how the writ ran in Pym's understanding.

Poor Frey, unaware of any irregularity in Metcalfe's personality beyond the generally unpleasant, thought the first lieutenant must have heard something about the confidences he and Drinkwater had exchanged earlier. He resolved to have words with Mullender, forgetting in his anger that Mullender had not been in the pantry, and disgusted that Metcalfe had such spies about the ship.

'Take that back, sir . . .'

'Steady, Frey . . .' Moncrieff advised.

'Stap me, you're all in this.' There was a bewildered wildness in

Metcalfe's eyes. 'Why are you looking at me, Pym? Don't *you* think such insolence is intolerable?'

And so the patient delivered himself to the quack and Pym received the means by which he was to achieve fame. 'To a degree, yes, Mr Metcalfe. I concur you've been badly treated,' Pym went on, mentally rubbing his hands with glee and ignoring the astonishment of his messmates' faces. 'Come, sir, don't let your meat spoil. Afterwards you and I shall take a turn on deck.'

For a moment Metcalfe stared at the surgeon, something akin to disbelief upon his face. Pym, in a rare and perceptive moment, interpreted it as relief. Metcalfe bent to his dinner and over his head Pym winked at the others.

Pym was not objective enough to recognize the crisis Metcalfe had reached. He preened his self-esteem even while planning his therapy and probing his patient's mind. Overall lay a vague image of his discovery in print, a seminal work dislodging Brown's *Elements of Medicine*. He would complement Keil's *Anatomy*, Shaw's *Practice of Physic*; alongside Munro on the bones and Douglas on the muscles, they would set Pym's *On the Mind*. Yet amid this self-conceit and at the moment imperfectly glimpsed, Pym had caught sight of a great paradox. Within Metcalfe he sensed a twin existence . . .

And already the opening words of his treatise came to him: *Just as*, in utero, *a foetus may divide and produce two unique, human beings, so in the skull, twin brains may develop, to dominate the conduct and produce responsive contrariness and a lack of logical direction . . .*

Pleased with the portentious ring of the phrases he abandoned them, setting the composition aside as Metcalfe, unsuspicious, soothed by Pym's solicitude, confirmed the growing certainty in Pym's ecstatic imagination.

'Damn the man, Mr Pym,' Metcalfe was saying, 'what is he about? The men have run and we know where they are.'

'Quite, quite, Mr Metcalfe, what do you propose, that we should take them by force and precipitate a crisis at this delicate juncture?' Their situation had been much rehearsed in the wardroom during the week and Pym laid out the logic to see where Metcalfe diverged from its uncompromising path, for he was familiar with a method used to cure the megrims by first rooting out their source.

'We should beat 'em, Pym', Metcalfe said fervently, 'blow 'em from the water, pound 'em to pieces . . .' The wildness was back in

Metcalfe's eyes now and Pym felt disappointment. This was a normal, naval, fire-eating madness after all.

'Perhaps,' he said disconsolately, 'we are to take our leave without raising the matter.' He paused, seeking to lead Metcalfe's thoughts along a different path. 'It is clear to me and all the others you dislike Captain Drinkwater, though he seems reasonable enough to me . . .'

Metcalfe grunted but offered no more.

'Well, I suppose you require his good opinion for advancement . . .' the surgeon suggested slyly.

'Me, Pym? What the devil for? I may make my own opportunities, damn it.'

'Well,' said Pym shrugging, a sense of failure, of approaching boredom, of finding the task he had set himself too difficult making him lose interest. It had seemed a good idea earlier, but perhaps that was the wine. He failed to recognize Metcalfe's massive self-delusion and reverted to a clinical examination. Stopping his pacing, he compelled Metcalfe to do the same. The two turned inwards and Pym looked deliberately into Metcalfe's eyes, while saying with exaggerated and insincere concern, 'How can you be sure of that, Mr Metcalfe? It seems to me the war is a stalemate. All the opportunities seem to have evaporated.'

'If we were to fight *them*,' Metcalfe replied, jerking his head in the direction of the *Stingray*, 'then things would soon be different.'

'But,' said Pym frowning, suspending his clandestine examination of Metcalfe's pupils and rekindling his theory, 'I thought you once expressed a contrary opinion, or was that', he affected a conspiratorial expression, 'merely a matter of dissembling; of, shall we say, seeking the captain's good opinion?'

Metcalfe stared back at the surgeon. 'Good opinion?' he murmured, almost abstractedly, and Pym's heart leapt with enthusiasm again. 'Oh, yes, perhaps . . . yes, perhaps it was.'

And Metcalfe, like a man who had suddenly remembered a forgotten appointment, abruptly walked away. Pym watched him go. 'It's not going to be easy,' he muttered to himself, but later that afternoon he fashioned a new quill-nib and began to write: *I conducted my first series of clinical observations, engaging my patient in conversation designed to draw out certain convictions, simultaneously examining his eyes for luetic symptoms. He displayed a vehement conviction at first, which yielded to a meeker and contrary opinion when this was suggested, thus exhibiting a predisposition towards influence . . .*

Pym sat back very pleased with himself and at that moment the quarter sentry called out that the schooner aboard which Vansittart had left for Baltimore was in sight.

'It is good news,' Vansittart said, sitting back in the offered chair and taking the glass Drinkwater held out. 'I think we shall simply rescind the Orders-in-Council where the United States are concerned, provided they do not press the matter of sailors' rights. There seems little pressure to do so in Washington, whatever may be said elsewhere.'

'I daresay seamen are as cheaply had here as elsewhere,' Drinkwater observed, marvelling at this change of diplomatic tack. 'Did you meet Mr Madison?'

'Alas, no, Augustus Foster handled all formal negotiations, but I learned something of interest to you.'

'To me? What the devil was that?'

'Captain Stewart is shortly to be relieved of his command.'

'Why? Surely not because of his indiscreet . . .?'

'No, no, nothing to do with that,' Vansittart affirmed, swallowing a draught of Madeira. 'It seems to be Navy Department policy to rotate the commanders of their, how d'you say, ships and vessels? Is that it? Anyway, he won't be allowed the opportunity of quenching his fire-eating ardour one way or another now.'

'Well, there is my consolation for eating humble pie and holdin' my hand.' Drinkwater explained about the location of his deserters. 'And it don't taste so bad either. So we may weigh at first light?'

'No. Stewart left word that we should drop downstream at, how d'you say? Four bells?'

Drinkwater grunted non-committally. It would be unwise to seek a meeting with Arabella. He had existed for eight days without her and he had no right to any expectations there. They both had their bitter-sweet memories. It was enough.

Besides, he was meditating something which would hardly endear him to any American.

An hour before dawn Drinkwater turned all hands from their cots and hammocks. The bosun's mates moved with silent purpose through the berth deck, their pipes quiescent, their starters flicking at the bulging canvas forms, stifling the abusive protests.

'Turn out, show a leg, you buggers, no noise, Cap'n's orders. Turn out, show a leg, no noise . . .'

'What's happening?'

'Man the capstan, afterguard aft to rouse out a spring, gun crews stand to.' Mr Comley, the boatswain, passed the word among the men tumbling out of their hammocks.

'Come on, my bullies, lash up and stow. Look lively.'

'We're gonna fuck the Yankees,' someone said and the echo of the statement ran about the berth deck as the men rolled their hammocks. Whatever their individual resentments, the abrupt and rude awakening shattered the boredom of the routine of a ship at anchor. An expectant excitement infected officers and men alike as they poured up through the hatchways, their bare feet slap-slapping on the decks as they ran to their stations like ghosts.

Wrapped in his cloak against the dawn chill Captain Drinkwater stood by the starboard hance and watched them emerge. Any evolution after a period of comparative idleness was a testing time. Men quickly became slack, lacked that crispness of reaction every commander relied upon. Eight days of riding to an anchor could, Drinkwater knew, have a bad effect.

In the waist Metcalfe leaned over the side as a spring was carried up the larboard side. Drinkwater waited patiently, trying to ignore the hissed instructions and advice offered to the toiling party dragging the heavy hemp over and round the multiplicity of obstructions along the *Patrician*'s side. Finally they worked it forward and dangled it down until it was fished from the hawsehole and dragged inboard to be wracked to the cable. He knew, from the sudden relaxation of the men involved, when they had finished, even before Midshipman Belchambers ran aft with the news.

'Mr Wyatt requests permission to commence veering cable, sir.'

'Very well.'

Aft on the gun deck the spring would have been hove taught and belayed; now the slacking of the anchor cable would cause the ship's head to fall off, some of the weight being taken by the spring.

Drinkwater turned and spoke to the nearest guncaptain. 'Campbell, watch your gun, now, tell me when she bears.'

'Aye, sir,' the man growled, bending his head in concentration.

'Mr Metcalfe, be ready to hold the cable.'

Metcalfe waited to pass the word down the forward companionway .

'Gun's bearing, sir.'

'Hold on,' Drinkwater called in a low voice and bent beside Campbell's 18-pounder. He could see the grey shape of the USS *Stingray* against the darker shore, her tracery of masts, yards and the geometric perfection of her rigging etched against the grey dawn. *Patrician* adjusted her own alignment and settled to her cable.

'She's a mite off now she's brung up, sir,' Campbell said and Drinkwater could smell the sweat on the man.

'Veer two fathoms,' Drinkwater called, straightening up. It would be enough. He turned to Frey. 'Your boat ready, Mr Frey?'

'Aye, sir.'

Drinkwater looked at the growing glow in the east, an ochreous backlighting of the overcast which seeped through it to suffuse the sky with a pale, bilious light.

'We'll give it a minute longer,' Drinkwater said, raising his glass and staring at the American ship upon which details were emerging from the obscurity of the night.

'We'll not want a wind outside,' someone muttered.

'What's happening?' a voice said and a score of shadowy figures shushed the coatless Vansittart to silence. 'For God's sake . . .

'Quiet, sir!' Metcalfe snapped, fidgeting as usual.

'I forbid . . .' Vansittart began, but Frey took his elbow.

'It's a piece of bluff, sir. The Captain wants his men back before he goes.'

'But . . .'

'Shhhh . . .' Drinkwater's figure loomed alongside him and Vansittart subsided into silence.

'Very well.' Drinkwater shut his telescope with an audible snap. 'Off you go, Frey.'

With a flash of white stockings, a whirl of coat-tails and a dull gleam of gilt scabbard mountings, Frey went over the rail into the waiting boat.

Drinkwater returned to the hance and again levelled his Dollond glass. He could see a figure on the *Stingray*'s quarterdeck stretch lazily. 'Any moment now,' he said, for the benefit of the others. The cutter cleared the *Patrician*'s stern and rapidly closed the gap between the two ships.

In the stillness the plash of her oars sounded unnaturally loud to the watching and waiting British. Then the challenge sounded in the strengthening daylight.

'Boat, ahoy!'

'Hey, what the hell . . .?'

'They've noticed our changed aspect,' Drinkwater observed, again peering through his glass. An officer was leaning over the side of the American sloop as the cutter swung to come alongside. Frey was standing up in her stern and they could hear an indistinct exchange. The cutter's oars were tossed, her bow nudged the *Stingray*'s tumblehome and Frey nimbly ran along the thwarts between the oarsmen. A second later he was leaping up the sloop's side.

'It's a master's mate . . . no, there's a lieutenant on deck without his coat . . . looks like Tucker, aye, 'tis, and there are men turning up.' The squeal of pipes came to them, floating across the smooth water.

'What's Frey saying, sir?' Metcalfe asked in an agony of suspense, frustration and resentment, because Drinkwater had briefed the third lieutenant without mentioning anything to his second-in-command, though everyone grasped the gist of Frey's purpose. For Metcalfe it was one more incident in a long series of similar slights.

'Why, to request an escort downstream, Mr Metcalfe,' jested the preoccupied Drinkwater, glass still clapped to his eye.

'Not to demand the return of our men?' Metcalfe's dithering lack of comprehension, or dullness of wit, irritated Drinkwater. 'That as well, Mr Metcalfe,' he added sarcastically.

Metcalfe turned on his heel wounded, his hands outspread, inviting his colleagues to share in his mystification. Drinkwater had ordered him from his bed an hour earlier, told him he wanted the ship's company turned-to at their stations, a spring roused out, run forward and hitched to the cable and thought that sufficient for him to be getting on with. Frey's briefing was a different matter. It had to be precise, exact, not subject to committee approval, besides, there had been no time for such niceties, however desirable. As Metcalfe turned he caught Gordon nudging Moncrieff at the first lieutenant's discomfiture. The ridicule struck Metcalfe like a blow.

'Ah, here's Captain Stewart . . .'

Drinkwater's commentary had them craning over the hammock nettings. A group of pale figures in their shirt-sleeves were grouped round the darker figure of Lieutenant Frey in his full-dress. And as their attention was diverted to the *Stingray*, Metcalfe slipped below.

'Good mornin', sir.'

Lieutenant Frey, unconsciously aping his commander's pronunciation, gave the emerging American commander a half-bow.

'Captain Drinkwater's compliments, sir, and his apologies for disturbing you at this hour. He is aware you had arranged with Mr Vansittart via the master of the schooner that we should weigh and proceed in company at four bells, but he insists upon the immediate return of the British deserters you have been harbouring. Truth is, sir, we have known about their presence aboard your ship for several days; saw 'em, do you see, through our glasses. Captain Drinkwater was particularly desirous of not compromising Mr Vansittart's mission and hoped you'd return 'em yourself, but his patience is now run out to the bitter end and, well, you *will* oblige, sir, won't you? Otherwise . . .'

'Otherwise what?'

Frey had enjoyed himself. He was not sure if he had the message word-perfect, but the gist of it, delivered at the run, as Drinkwater had ordered, had been surprisingly easy. Stewart, clogged with sleep, had twice or thrice tried to interrupt him, but Frey had had the advantage and each successive statement had demanded Stewart's sleep-dulled concentration. In the end, despite himself, he had succumbed to the coercion.

'Otherwise what?' he repeated angrily.

Frey heard Tucker mumble something about a spring and a cable.

'Otherwise, sir, the most unpleasant consequences will arise. You lie under our guns.' Frey, his hat in his hand, stepped aside and, with a theatrical flourish about which he was afterwards overweeningly boastful, he indicated the unnatural angle of the *Patrician* and the ugly, black foreshortening of her gun muzzles.

'Why you goddammed . . .' Stewart's face was flushed and his eyes staring as he transferred them from Frey to the *Patrician* then back to Frey.

'I believe sir,' Frey continued, overriding Stewart's erupting anger, 'your removal from your command might be a consequence of interfering with the speedy return of a British emissary after such a happy accommodation has been reached by our two governments.'

Whether or not Stewart knew he was due to be replaced, or that the matter was a mere possibility, Frey had no idea. It was to be his last card and it appeared to work. The American captain clamped his mouth in a grimace and let his breath hiss out between his teeth. The muscles of his jaw worked furiously and when he spoke his voice cracked with the strain of self-control.

'Turn 'em over, Jonas.' Stewart turned on his heel and made for the companionway. Lieutenant Tucker hesitated, stared after his commander, then shrugged and repeated Stewart's order to the officers and men gathering about them.

'Bring up the King's men,' he sneered and sparked off a chorus of muttered curses and imprecations. Frey's cool affront began to quail before this unrestrained hostility.

'Fuck King George,' someone called out, an Irishman, Frey thought afterwards. As if stiffened by that rebel obscenity, Stewart paused, 'like Achilles at the entrance to his tent', Frey later reported, and addressed the British officer.

'Tell your Captain Drinkwater, Lieutenant,' Stewart said venomously, 'that if ever our two countries *do* find themselves at war, this ship, or another ship, *any* other ship commanded by Charles Stewart will prove itself more than a match for one of His Britannic Majesty's apple-bowed frigates!'

'His gauntlet thrown down, he disappeared like Punch, sir,' Frey reported later, 'though his people thought this a great joke, and then I was involved in receiving the deserters . . .'

The reluctant downcast shambling of the half-comprehending Russians, the fury and abuse and scuffling necessary to get the others down into the boat and the obvious distress of the American seamen in having to carry out so nauseating a duty upset Frey. He was a young man of sensitivity and not yet entirely brutalized by his Service.

'Obliged, sir,' he said at last to Tucker, aware that the moral ascendancy he had so conspicuously flaunted a few moments earlier had now passed to the American officer and the cross-armed men ranked behind him. It was a moment or two before he realized he had only received seven men. He stared down into the boat where recaptured and captors were confronting each other none too happily.

He turned to Tucker. 'Where's Thurston?'

Tucker shrugged and grinned. 'I dunno. Maybe he weren't cut out for the sea-life, mister. Maybe he ran away from us too. Anyway he ain't to be found.'

The men ranged behind Tucker seemed to surge forward. Honour could be satisfied with seven out of eight. Frey knew when he was well-off and clamped his hat on his head.

'I'm obliged, Mr Tucker. Good-day.' And stepping backwards, his hands on the man-ropes, he slid dextrously down to the boat. 'Shove off!' he ordered curtly. 'Down oars! Give way together!'

An hour and a half later His Britannic Majesty's frigate *Patrician* broke her anchor out of the mud of the Potomac river, let fall her topsails, hoisted her jib and fore-topmast staysail and unbrailed her spanker. With her foreyards hauled aback and her main and mizen braced up sharp, her bow fell off and she turned slowly downstream, squaring her foreyards as she steadied on course and gathered way to pass the United States sloop-of-war *Stingray*.

'Good riddance,' Frey breathed with boyish elation after his virtuoso performance of the morning.

Captain Drinkwater crossed the deck and levelled his glass at the sloop. Her crew were spontaneously lining the rail, climbing into the lower rigging.

'Frey,' he suddenly called sharply.

'Sir?' Frey ran up alongside the captain.

'Who's that fellow just abaft the chess-tree?' Drinkwater asked, holding out his glass. Frey peered through the telescope.

'It's Thurston, sir!'

'Yes it is, ain't it . . .' Drinkwater took back the glass and levelled it again. They were almost alongside the American ship; in a moment they would have swept past.

Frey hovered, half-expecting an order. Behind him Moncrieff hissed *'There's Thurston!'* and the man's name passed like wildfire along the deck.

On the *Stingray*'s quarterdeck Lieutenant Tucker, now in his own full-dress uniform, raised a speaking trumpet.

'Captain Stewart desires that you anchor until the appointed time of departure, sir.'

As the two ships drew closer a rising crescendo of abuse rose from the *Stingray*'s people. It seemed to the watching Frey that they pushed Thurston forward, goading the British with his presence and their taunts. For his own part Thurston stood stock-still, aloof, as though wishing to be independent of the demonstration, yet the central figure in it.

'Damned insolent bastard!' Frey heard Wyatt say.

'Cool as a god-damned cucumber, by God,' agreed Moncrieff.

'Silence there!' Drinkwater snapped as a ripple of reaction spread along *Patrician*'s gangway and down into the ship. 'Eyes in the ship!' Men were coming up from below, men who had no business on the upper deck. 'Send those men below, Mr Comley, upon the instant, sir!'

The noise, like a ground-swell gathering before it breaks, echoed back and forth between the two hulls as they drew level.

'Silence there!' he called again and a jeering bellow of mimicry bounced back from the Americans.

Suddenly Thurston fell backwards with a piercing cry. The Americans surrounding him gasped, then their jeering changed to outraged cries as the *Patrician* drew away.

'What the devil . . .?' Drinkwater cried in the silence that fell instantly upon the *Patrician*'s people. He was aware that amid the shouting there had been another noise, heard a split-second before Thurston fell with a scream.

'There! Does that please you, Captain Drinkwater?' a voice cut the air.

Lieutenant Metcalfe straightened up beside the transom of the launch on the boat booms. A wisp of smoke curled up from the muzzle of the Ferguson rifle.

PART TWO
The Commodore

'America certainly cannot pretend to wage war against us; she has no navy to do it with!'

The Statesman,
London,
10 June 1812

Gantley Hall *March 1812*

'What became of him?'

Drinkwater stirred from his reverie and looked at his wife working at her tapestry frame. Between them the fire leapt and crackled, Raring at the updraft in the chimney. Its warmth combined with the rum toddy, a good dinner and the gale raging unregarded outside to induce a detached stupor in Captain Drinkwater. To his wife he seemed to be dozing peacefully; in reality he was on the rack of conscience.

'I'm sorry, my dear, what did you say?'

'What became of him?'

'Who?'

'Mr Metcalfe. You were telling me about him.'

'Of course, how stupid. Forgive me . . ..'

'There is nothing to forgive, you dozed off.'

'Yes,' Drinkwater lied, 'I must have . . .'

A gust of wind slammed against the side of the house and the shutters and sashes of the withdrawing room rattled violently. Between them the fire flared into even greater activity, roaring and subsiding as it consumed the logs before their eyes, a remorseless foretaste of Hell Drinkwater thought uncomfortably.

'God help sailors on a night like this,' he remarked tritely, taking refuge in the cliché as he stirred himself bent forward and threw another brace of logs into the fire-basket. 'Metcalfe is in Haslar, the naval hospital at Gosport.'

'I know, Nathaniel, Elizabeth chid him gently 'Is he mad?'

Drinkwater pulled himself together and determined to make small talk with his wife. Her brown eyes regarded him over her poised needle and he felt uncomfortable under their scrutiny. Had she guessed anything? He had asked himself the same question in the weeks he had been home, examined every facet of his behaviour and concluded she could only have been suspicious because of his solicitude. He cursed himself for his stupidity; he was no dissembler.

'The doctors at Haslar were content to conclude it, yes, but our surgeon, Mr Pym, thought otherwise.'

'And yet the poor man was delivered up . . .'

'We had no alternative and, to be candid, Bess, I fear I agreed with the bulk of medical opinion. The man was quite incapable of any rationality after the incident, his whole posture was preposterous . . .'

Drinkwater recalled the way Metcalfe had stood back, the Ferguson rifle crooked in his left elbow, his right hand extended as though for applause, a curious, expectant look upon his face, an actor upon a stage of his own imagining. His whole attitude had been that of a man who had just achieved a wonder; only his eyes, eyes that stared directly at Drinkwater himself, seemed detached from the awful reality of the act he had just perpetrated.

Like everyone on *Patrician*'s upper deck, Drinkwater was stunned; then a noise of indignation reached them, rolling across the water from the *Stingray*. A moment later it was taken up aboard *Patrician*. Thurston had been popular, his desertion connived at: his murder was resented. The undertones of combination and mutiny implicit in the events of the past days instantly rose up to confront Drinkwater. Metcalfe's action had provided a catalyst for disaffection to become transformed into open rebellion. He was within a whisker of losing control of his ship, of having her seized and possibly handed over to the Americans, her people seeking asylum, her loss to the Royal Navy an ignominious cause of rupture between Great Britain and the United States of America.

It was imperative he acted at once and he bellowed for silence, for the helm and braces to be trimmed and for Moncrieff to place Mr Metcalfe under immediate arrest, he was gratified, in a sweating relief, to see others, the marine officer, Sergeant Hudson, Comley the boatswain and Wyatt the master, move swiftly to divert trouble, to impose the bonds of conditioned discipline and strangle at birth the sudden surge of popular compassion and anger.

The *Stingray* had made no move to drop downstream in their wake as Drinkwater crowded on sail, as much to increase the distance between the two ships as to occupy the Patricians. Thus he had escaped into the Atlantic and set their course for home.

'If you were so certain, why did your surgeon think otherwise?' Elizabeth asked.

'Our opinions did not appear to differ at first. We confined Metcalfe to his cabin, put a guard on him and both of us agreed that insanity was the most humane explanation for his conduct, as much for himself as to avoid trouble with the people. There was, moreover, the possibility of diplomatic repercussions, though after I had discussed it with Vansittart, we concluded Captain Stewart was unlikely to have made a fuss, since it was quite clear Thurston was a deserter from *Patrician* and therefore his sheltering by Stewart could have constituted a provocative act. In the amiable circumstances then prevailing, at least according to Vansittart's account, Stewart would have embarrassed his own government and marred his already meagre chances of advancement.' Drinkwater paused, remembering the darkly handsome American. 'Stewart made a number of rather puerile threats against us if I came to war and doubtless has added the incident to his catalogue of British infamy, but I did not take him for a complete fool . . .'

'But you think, despite this trouble, it will not come to war?'

'No,' Drinkwater shook his head, 'I hope not.'

They relapsed into silence again. The gale lashed the house with a sudden flurry of rain and they both looked up, caught each other's eyes and smiled.

'It is good to have you home, my dear.'

'It is good to be home, Bess.'

He sincerely meant it, yet the gusting wind tugged at him, teasing him away from this domestic cosiness. Up and down the country men and women, even the humblest cottager, would be huddled about their fires of peat driftwood or sea-coal. Why was it he had to suffer this perverse tugging away? In all honesty he wanted to be nowhere else on earth than here, beside his wife. Had he not blessed the severe and sudden leak that had confined *Patrician* to a graving dock in Dock Town, Plymouth, where her sprung garboard had caused the mastershipwright to scratch his head? He sighed, stared into the fire and missed the look his wife threw him.

'So what made your surgeon change his mind?'

Drinkwater wrenched his thoughts back to the present. 'A

theory – a theory he was developing into a thesis. If I understood him aright, it was his contention (and Metcalfe had, apparently, furnished him with evidence over a long period) that Metcalfe was, as it were, two people. No, that ain't right: he considered Metcalfe possessed two individual personalities . . .

'Pym argued we all have a tendency to be two people, a fusion of opposites, of contrary humours. The relationship between weaknesses and strengths, likes and dislikes, the imbalance of these humours and so forth, nevertheless produces an equilibrium which inclines in favour of one or the other, making us predominantly one type of person, or another and hence forming our characters.

'He seemed to think Metcalfe's disparate parts were out of kilter in the sense that they exactly balanced, do you see? Thus, he postulated, if you conceive circumstances acting like the moon upon water, the water being these leanings, or inclinations inherent in us, our response is the vacillation of moods and humours. Because one humour predominates, we remain in character, whereas in Metcalfe's case the swings from one to another were equal, his personality was not weighted in favour of choler or sanguinity or phlegm, for instance, but swung more violently and uncontrollably from one *exclusive* humour to another.

'Therefore he became wholly one half of his complete character, before changing and becoming the other. Pym dignified his hypothesis the Pendular Personality and proposed to publish a treatise about it.'

'But surely such a condition is, nevertheless, a form of madness.'

'Yes, I suppose it is. Though Pym suggested that so rational an explanation made of it a disease, madness being a condition beyond explanation. At all events it does not sit happily upon a sea-officer's shoulders.'

Poor Metcalfe. He had wept with remorse when his accusers confronted him with the enormity of murder, yet a day later, when Drinkwater had visited him again, he had screamed ingratitude, claiming to have done everything and more that his commander wished for and chastising Drinkwater for abandoning a loyal subordinate capable of great distinction. Pym had prescribed laudanum and they had brought him back dopey with the opiate.

There had been nothing more that Drinkwater could have done

for Metcalfe. He waited upon the man's wife in her lodgings at Southsea and expressed his condolences. He gave her a testimonial for the Sick and Hurt Board and twenty guineas to tide her over. She had a snot-nosed brat at her side and another barely off the breast. Drinkwater had been led to believe Metcalfe came from a good family, but the appearance of his wife suggested a life of penurious scrimping and saving, of pretensions beyond means and ambitions beyond ability. The impression left by this sad meeting weighed heavily upon his own troubles as he made his way home.

Was Pym right? His theory had, as far as Drinkwater could judge, a logical attraction. He had himself proved to be two men and had behaved as such in the verdant woodlands of Virginia, so much so that he seemed now to be a different person to the man who had lain with Arabella Shaw. That careless spirit had been younger and wilder than the heat-stupefied, half-soaked, married and middle-aged sea-officer now sprawled before the fire in Gantley Hall. Had he, at least temporarily, suffered from an onset of the same dichotomous insanity which had seized so permanent a hold on Metcalfe? Was he in the grip of Pym's pendular personality?

The ridiculous humour of the alliteration escaped him. One could argue he had done no more than thousands of men had done before him. He had, after all, spent most of his adult life cooped up on ship-board, estranged even from the body of his lawful wedded wife, so that the willing proximity of so enchanting, comely and passionate a woman as Arabella was irresistible. He could cite other encounters, with Doña Ana Maria Conchita Arguello de Salas and Hortense Santhonax, women whose beauty was fabled and yet with whom he had behaved with utter propriety, notwithstanding fate had thrown them together in unusual circumstances. He could invent no end of excuses for his momentary weakness and invent no end of specious proofs as to his probity. But he could think of no justification for his behaviour with Arabella.

He dared not look at his wife, lest she catch his eye and ask, in her acutely intuitive way, what troubled him. The events of that afternoon, the riot in the blood which had ended in their physical commingling, stood as a great sin in Drinkwater's mind.

Yet, God knew, he had committed greater sins. He was a murderer himself, perhaps more so than poor Metcalfe, for he had killed in cold blood, mechanically, under orders, at the behest of his Sovereign. And not once but many times.

He had shot out the brains of a Spanish seaman and hacked down a French officer long before his majority, yet had suffered no remorse, rather, he recollected, the contrary. Had the sanction of war relieved him of the trouble of a conscience over such matters? It was not logical to suppose that he suffered now merely because he loved his wife and he had threatened her with his mindless infidelity. Conscience should, if he understood it aright, prick him for every sin, not just the one that threatened his domestic security.

No, he had loved Arabella Shaw that afternoon, loved her as completely and consumingly as he had loved his wife and it was the diminution of the latter that wounded him most.

Arabella too had been driven by more than the demand of physical release, he was certain. She could have had the pick of those eager young officers, yet had chosen him, and as surely as he had recoiled after their wild fling, she had made no move to renew their passion, as if she too half-regretted it. She too harboured another love: that for her dead husband

The moment he seized upon the thought, he doubted it.

'Could you still love me after my death?' he found himself blurting out, so introverted had his train of thought become.

Elizabeth looked up, hand poised above the circular frame, the candlelight playing upon the needle with its trail of scarlet thread.

'Why do you ask?'

He shrugged, colouring, wishing he had guarded his tongue and seized by a sudden conviction that Elizabeth knew all about his affair, that he had spoken in his sleep and had called Arabella's name in his dreams. 'A fancy I have,' he said lamely, 'a self-conceit . . .'

'I love you when you are not here,' she replied, 'it is as bad sometimes as being a widow.'

The phrases struck him as confirmation of his fears, yet it might be mere foolishness on his part. He felt her eyes upon him almost quizzically.

'You are exhausted with this war,' she said, watching her husband with concern, thinking him much older since he returned from America in a way she had not previously noticed.

'I am perverted by this war,' he wanted to say, but he nodded his weariness and thrust himself to his feet. He could not apportion blame elsewhere but within himself. 'I'll take a turn outside before we go up, Bess,' he said instead, 'to see all's well.' He bent over her head and kissed her hair. The strands of grey caught the yellow light and looked almost golden.

'Don't be long,' she said, and the catch in her voice articulated her desire. He squeezed her shoulder. Yes, he would drown his senses in the all-encompassing warmth of her body, but first he must excoriate his soul.

The soughing of the wind in the trees was like the wild hiss of the sea when it leaps high alongside a running ship. The chill of the night and the gale pained him with a heartless mortification which he welcomed. The snorting and stamping from the stables told where the horses were distracted by the wild night and, as he struck the edge of the wood behind the house, he caught a glimpse of the lighthouses at Orfordness. Standing still he thought he could hear, just below the roar of the gale, the sussuration of shingle on the foreshore of Hollesley Bay. Turning his back to the wind and the sea, he headed inland.

The ruins of the old priory had seemed a fashionable embellishment to the acquisition of the hall, a Gothic fantasy within which to indulge his wife and daughter with picnics, not to mention his son to whom the ivy ruins had become a private kingdom. And while he loved the simple modernity of the house, these rambling ecclesiastical remnants had assumed an entirely different character in his mind.

This was the place he came when he was torn by the estrangement assailing all seamen, even when in the bosom of their families. Man returns always and most happily to the familiar, even when it pains him, for from there he can contemplate what he most desires in its most ideal, anticipatory state. For Drinkwater the ruined priory was the place where he came closest to the spiritual, and hence to what he conceived as God. His faith in the timeless wisdom of an omnipotent providence had been shaken by his riotous passion for Arabella. Intellectually he knew the thing to have been a temporary, if overpowering aberration, but he was rocked by its violence, by his own loss of control, by its pointlessness in a universe he imagined ordered. And then it struck him as a terrible self-delusion, this assumption. Either all was indeed vanity or all had a hidden purpose. If the former then every endeavour was destined to a redundancy comparable to the consecrated ruins about him; if the latter then every act was of unperceived, incomprehensible significance. Not only his adultery, but also Metcalfe's Parthian shot.

The enormous significance of this disarmingly simple choice rocked him to the very edge of sanity. He stood alone on the few flags that graced the roofless chancel, unconsciously spread his arms apart and howled at the magnificently merciless sky.

Chapter Eleven *April–June 1812*

A Crossing of Rubicons

When the assassination occurred, Captain and Mrs Nathaniel Drinkwater were in London as guests of Lord Dungarth, no more than a few hundred yards from the lobby of Parliament where the Prime Minister was shot. Spencer Perceval's policy of non-conciliation with the Americans, maintained against a vociferous opposition led by the liberal Whitbread and the banker Baring, also flew in the face of Canning's advice. His calm leadership through the Regency crisis was unappreciated in the country, where the Prince Regent was unpopular, and by retaining his former post as Chancellor of the Exchequer he attracted obloquy, for he controlled the nation's purse-strings. He was widely blamed for the economic chaos prevailing in the country. The middle classes held him responsible for the widespread bankruptcies among themselves, while the town labourers, who had been driven to loom- and machine-smashing in a spate of desperate vandalism, thought him an agent of the devil.

The authorities ruthlessly hanged sixteen Luddite frame-breakers, but failed to quell the widespread discontent resulting from inflation, the depreciation of the pound sterling, bad harvests and a consequent depression. Perceval's name was inseparable from these misfortunes. Starvation, vagrancy and the ills of unemployment in the crowded industrial wens tied down regiments of light horse, while the drain of gold in support of the Portuguese and Spanish in their fight against the French invader further exacerbated the situation.

But Great Britain was not alone. France herself was in the grip of depression and the Tsar of Russia had withdrawn from Napoleon's Continental System sixteen months earlier in an attempt to repair the damage it had done to his own country's economy. Lord Dungarth had been sanguine that open hostilities between Russia and France would follow. For years the efforts of his Secret Department had been largely devoted to promoting this breach, but time had passed and although rumour rebounded, particularly from a Parisian bookseller in British pay who reported the ordering of all available books about Russia by the Tuileries, nothing concrete happened.

Closer to home Perceval was as intransigent as the Admiralty were devoid of instructions for His Britannic Majesty's frigate *Patrician*. He refused any revocation of Britain's Orders-in-Council, even to reopen trade with the United States. Although both the French and British issued special licences to beat their own embargoes by the back door, it was insufficient to relieve the general distress. On 11 May, four days after the Drinkwaters had come up to town, Perceval was shot by a Lancastrian bankrupt named Bellingham. The assassin was declared mad, a diagnosis uncomfortably close to Drinkwater's own solution of the dilemma of Metcalfe.

It was to be the first in a series of events which were to make the year 1812, already heavy with astrological portents, so memorable. Even the inactivity of his frigate seemed to the susceptible Drinkwater to be but a hiatus, a calm presaging a storm.

For Drinkwater and Elizabeth, his Lordship's invitation was a mark of both favour and condescension. Elizabeth was openly flattered but worried about her wardrobe, certain that her own homespun was quite inappropriate and that even the best efforts of the self-styled couturiers of Ipswich were equally unsuitable. She need not have worried. Dungarth was an ageing, peg-legged widower, his house in Lord North Street chilly and without a trace of feminine frippery. The bachelor establishment was, he declared on their arrival, entirely at Elizabeth's disposal and she was to consider herself its mistress. For himself, he required only two meals a day and the more or less constant company of her husband.

Drinkwater was reluctant to tell his wife of their private conversations. She correctly deduced they had some bearing upon affairs of state. In any case the earl redeemed himself by his society during the evenings. Drinkwater knew the effort it cost him, but he held his peace; Elizabeth was enchanted and flattered, and blossomed under Dungarth's generous patronage. They visited a number of distinguished houses, which gratified Elizabeth's curiosity and her desire to sample society, though she continued to suffer agonies over her lack of fashionable attire. Conscience compelled Drinkwater to remedy this deficiency to some extent, but she nevertheless felt her provincial awkwardness acutely. Her ignorance of affairs of the world, by which was meant not what she read in the broadsheets (about which she was exceedingly well-informed) but the gossip and innuendo of the *ton*, provoked sufficient *faux pas* to spoil several evenings. It was an experience she soon tired of.

As for Dungarth, Drinkwater was appalled by his appearance. He had marked the earl's decline at their last meeting, but Dungarth's obesity was dropsical in its extent and his corpulent figure distressed him for its awkwardness as much as it stirred the pity of his friends.

'I am told it is fashionable,' he grumbled, putting a brave face on it, 'that the friends of Holland House all eat like hogs to put on the kind of weight borne by the Prince of Wales, imitation being the sincerest form of flattery. But, by God, I'd sell my soul to the devil if it went with a stone or two of this gross avoirdupois. Forgive me, m'dear,' he apologized to Elizabeth.

'Please, my Lord . . ..' She waved aside his embarrassment, moved by the brave and gallant twinkle in his hazel eyes.

'For God's sake, call me John.' Dungarth dropped into a creaking chair and waved Drinkwater to sit. 'They tell me your ship's held up, Nat.'

'Aye, dockyard delays, a shortage of almost everything . . .'

'Including orders . . .'

'So,' Drinkwater grinned, scratching his scarred cheek, 'you *do* have a hand in her inactivity.'

Dungarth shrugged. 'Interruption of the Baltic trade confounds the dockyards, I suppose, despite *our* best efforts', this with significance and a heavy emphasis on the plural pronoun, 'and the Tsar's declared intention of abandoning the dictates of Paris.'

'And lack of men, of course,' Drinkwater added, suddenly gloomy, 'always a want of them. I understand from Lieutenant Frey that every cruiser putting into the Sound poaches a handful despite my orders and those of the Port Admiral. They have even taken my coxswain.'

'Your worst enemies are always your own cloth, Nat.'

'I hope, my Lord,' put in Elizabeth, 'that that is not too enigmatic a response.'

'Ah-ha, ma'am, you're shrewd, but in this case mistaken. I have nothing to do with the felonious practices of cruiser captains.'

'Since I am so out of tune with you, then, my Lord,' Elizabeth said with mock severity, rising to draw the gentlemen after her and waving a relieved Dungarth back into his sagging chair, 'and since you are so lately come in, I shall leave you to your gossip and decanters.'

'You are cross with me, ma'am . . .'

'Incensed, my Lord . . .'

'But too gentle to tell me; you have an angel for a wife, Nathaniel.'

The men settled to their port and sat for a few moments in companionable silence.

'You're ready to go to sea again, aren't you, Nat?' Dungarth said at last.

'I've no need to argue the circumstances, my Lord . . .'

'John, for heaven's sake . . .'

'You know the tug of one thing when the other is at hand.'

'This damned war has ruined us as men, though only God alone knows what it will do to us as a nation.'

'You want me for the Baltic?'

'If and when.'

'I loathe waiting.'

'If you commanded a ship of the line, you would be doing nothing other than waiting and watching off La Rochelle, or L'Orient, or Ushant . . .'

'The reflection does not stopper off my impatience.'

Dungarth looked at his friend with a shrewd eye. 'Something's amiss, Nat; what the devil's eating you?'

Drinkwater met Dungarth's gaze. He had no need of pretence with so old and trusted a colleague. 'Unfinished business,' he replied.

'In the Baltic?'

'In America.'

'Not a woman like Hortense Santhonax? A temptress? No, a siren?'

'Not entirely, though I am not blameless in that quarter; more a feeling, an intuition.'

Dungarth's look changed to one of admiration and he slapped his good knee. 'My dear fellow, I *knew* you were the man for the task after I'm gone. 'Tis the *feeling* you need for the game, to be sure, and you have it in abundance. You'll suffer for it, as I warrant you already have done – are doing, by the look of you, but 'tis an indispensable ingredient for the puppet-master.'

Drinkwater shook his head at the use of this phrase, 'No, my Lord,' he said with firm formality, 'not that.'

'There is quite simply no one else,' Dungarth expostulated, waving this protest aside, 'but there is a little time. I'm not called to answer for my sins just yet.'

'You've heard news today, haven't you?' Drinkwater asked directly. 'Is it from the Baltic?'

'No, America. I've asked Moira to dinner tomorrow. He has correspondents in the southern states which in general are hostile to us but where he left a few friends. I think Vansittart's mission was, after all, a failure.'

Drinkwater went gloomily to bed. Elizabeth was reading one of Miss Austen's novels by candlelight, Drinkwater noticed, but closed it upon her finger and looked up at her husband who added his own candelabra to the one illuminating the bed. 'May one ask what you two find to talk about?'

Drinkwater knew the question to be arch, that its bluntness hid a pent-up and justifiable curiosity. Elizabeth, with her talent for divination, had sensed from the very length and earnestness of the men's deliberations that something more than mere idle male gossip about politics was in the air. He knew too, with some relief, that she had concluded his own preoccupations were bound up with these almost hermetic discussions.

He took off his coat and sat on the bed to kick off his shoes.

'He knows himself to be dying, Bess, and is concerned for his life's work. Did I ever tell you he was once, when I knew him as the first lieutenant of the *Cyclops*, the most liberal of men? He was largely sympathetic with the American rebels at one time. His implacable hatred of the French derives from the mischief done to the body of his wife. She died in Florence shortly after the outbreak of the revolution. He was bringing her back through France when the revolutionaries, seeing the arms on his coach, tore the coffin open . . .'

'How awful . . .'

'You have seen Romney's portrait of her?'

'Yes, yes. She was extraordinarily beautiful.' Elizabeth paused, looked down at her book and set it aside. 'And . . .?'

'Dungarth has become', Drinkwater said with a sigh, 'the Admiralty's chief intelligencer, the repository and digest of a thousand titbits and snippets, reports of facts and rumours; in short a puppet-master pulling strings across half Europe, even as far as the steppes of Asia . . .'

'And you are to succeed him?'

Drinkwater looked at his wife full-face. 'How the deuce . . .?'

She shrugged. 'I guessed. You have done nothing but closet yourselves and I know he is not a man to show prejudice to a woman merely because of her sex.'

Drinkwater nodded. 'Of course, I am quite inadequate to the task,' he said earnestly, 'but it appears no one else is fitter and I am slightly acquainted with something of the business, being known to agents in France and Russia . . .'

'Spies, you mean,' Elizabeth said flatly and Drinkwater bridled at the implicit disapproval. He opened his mouth to explain, thought better of it and shifted tack.

'Anyway, Dungarth has invited Lord Moira to dinner tomorrow . . .'

'And shall I be allowed to . . .?'

'Oh, come, Elizabeth,' Drinkwater said irritably, hooking a finger in his stock, 'I like this whole situation no better than you . . .'

Elizabeth leaned forward and placed a finger on his lips.

'Tell me who this Lord Moira is.'

'Better I tell you who he was. The Yankees knew him as Lord Rawdon, and he gave them hell through the pinebarrens of Georgia and the Carolinas in the American War. Of late his occupations have been more sedentary. He went into politics alongside Fox and the Whig party in opposition, and is an intimate of the Prince Regent, being numbered among the Holland House set . . .'

Elizabeth seemed bucked by this piece of news. 'Is he married?' she asked.

'To the Countess of Loudoun, his equal in her own right. He is also considered to be a man of singular ugliness,' he added waspishly.

'Oh,' said Elizabeth smiling, 'how fascinating.'

General Francis Rawdon Hastings, Earl of Moira, proved far from ugly, though bushy black eyebrows, a pair of sharply observant eyes and a dark complexion marked his appearance as unfashionable. He was, moreover, a man of strong opinions and frank speech. His oft-quoted opinion as to the virtue of American women expressed while a young man serving in North America had brought him a degree of wholly unmerited notoriety. His more solid achievements included distinguishing himself at the Battle of Bunker Hill and later defeating Washington's most able general, Nathaniel Greene, in the long and hard-fought campaign of the Carolinas. Such talents might have marked him out for command in the peninsula but, like Tarleton vegetating in County Cork, he was out to grass, though talked of as the next governor-general of India.

'Frank has news of a determined war-party in the Congress,' Dungarth said as he carved the beef with its oyster stuffing.

'War *hawks*, they style themselves,' Moira said, sipping the glass of burgundy Dungarth's man Williams poured for him. 'Your health, ma'am,' he added, inclining his head in Elizabeth's direction. 'We shan't bore you with our political clap-trap? '

'Mrs Drinkwater is better informed than most of your subalterns, Frank,' Dungarth said.

'That ain't difficult,' replied Moira, smiling engagingly, 'though I mean that as no slight to you, ma'am.'

'And what are the designs of these hawks, my Lord; my husband tells me the Americans have no navy to speak of.'

'Canada, ma'am, they covet Canada. They tried for it in the late rebellion and failed, they'll try for it again. As for their navy, I can't answer for it. I understand they've a deal of gunboats and such, much like the *radeaux* they had on Lake Champlain, I imagine, but as to a regular navy, well, I don't know.' Moira shrugged dismissively.

'They've some fine ships,' said Dungarth, 'but too few in commission and a fierce competition for them.'

'And some determined men to command them,' Drinkwater agreed, thinking of Captain Stewart.

'So,' said Moira, between mouthfuls, 'we may have the upper hand at sea, but with half the army marching and counter-marching in Spain', Moira paused to allow his opinion of Wellesley's generalship to pervade the atmosphere of the dining-room, 'and the other half aiding the civil power in the north, they have the advantage on land. I'm damned if I know what, begging your pardon, Mistress Drinkwater, will transpire if they do decide on war and advance on Canada.'

'Is it that much a matter of chance, then?' Drinkwater asked. 'I mean to say, will Madison blow like a weather-cock to the prevailing breeze?'

'So my correspondents in the southern states write, and they, needless to say, are opposed to this madness. Everywhere they are surrounded by men intent upon it.' This gloomy assessment laid a silence on them. 'I suppose we'll drum up sufficient ruffians to hold Canada. There are enough loyalists in New Brunswick to form a division, I daresay, and the Six Nations of Mohawks are more inclined to favour us than the perfidious Yankees. With the navy blockading the coast, I daresay things will turn out to our advantage in the end.'

'If we can afford it,' put in Elizabeth shrewdly.

'You *are* well informed, ma'am, my compliments.' Moira downed another glass of the burgundy. 'The India trade will sustain us, though I don't doubt but it'll be a close-run thing.'

'There is one matter we have not considered,' Drinkwater said, an uncomfortable thought striking him with a growing foreboding. He realized that for months he had been subconsciously brooding on Stewart's last remarks. The American officer's allusion to the bluff-bowed British frigates was a criticism that had stuck in Drinkwater's craw if only for its very accuracy. The memory, thirty years old, of being prize-master aboard the Yankee privateer schooner *Algonquin* when a young midshipman had been all the evidence he needed to realize Stewart had been indiscreet; that, and the knowledge Stewart had himself commanded a schooner.

They were all looking at him expectantly.

'The Americans will use privateers, my Lords, if it comes to war; scores of 'em, schooners mostly, manned with the most energetic young officers they can muster from their mercantile and naval stock . . .'

He was gratified by the exchange of appreciative looks between Moira and Dungarth. He sensed, in a moment of self-esteem, he had divined the passing of a test.

'They will attack our trade wherever they are able, just as they did in the last war. Moreover, their success will tempt out the more active of the French commanders and corsairs who would not need to rely on the blockaded ports of Europe, but could shift their operations to American bases where there will be no dearth of support and sympathy, reviving the old alliance of '79 in the name of the twin republics . . .'

'Do you have any more horrors for us, Captain?' Moira asked mockingly.

'Do you want any more, my Lord?' Drinkwater asked seriously. 'They will ambush the India trade, attack our fishing fleets and whalers, ravage the West Indies . . .'

'And how do you know all this, Captain?' Moira asked drily.

'It is what he would do in Madison's place, ain't it, Nathaniel?'

'It is certainly what I would do if I were Secretary of Madison's navy, my Lords, and wanted to compensate for its weaknesses. When it cannot achieve something itself, the state encourages its more rapacious citizenry to do it on its behalf.'

'And will it come to this?' Elizabeth asked. 'You are all talking as if the matter were a *fait accompli*.'

'If Napoleon don't invade Russia, Elizabeth,' Dungarth said with solemn intimacy, 'then he will surely not miss the opportunity to capitalize on a breach between London and Washington which he has for months now been so assiduously encouraging.' And then he snicked his fingers with such violence that the sudden noise made them jump and the candle-flames flickered, adding, as if it had just occurred to him, 'By God! It's what he has been waiting for!'

And for a moment they stared at the puffy face of the once-handsome man, transfigured as it was by realization.

And so it proved, despite a stone-walling by the so-called doves. The hawks, roaring into the Congress chamber banging cuspidors, startled a tedious orator into sitting and conceding the floor. Thus provoked, Speaker Clay put the question which was carried almost two to one in favour of war with Great Britain. Later the Senate agreed and within two days the *National Intelligencer* of Washington, the *Freeman's Journal and Mercantile Advertiser* of Philadelphia and every other broadsheet in the United States repeated the text of the Act opening hostilities. Even the news that the British had finally set aside the infamous Orders-in-Council, anxious to protect the American supplies vital to Wellington's advancing army, failed to stem the headlong dash to war.

Madison's intention of issuing letters-of-marque and of general reprisal against the goods, vessels and effects of the government and subjects of the United Kingdom of Great Britain and Ireland was quoted alongside the declaration.

'America, having obtained her independence from Great Britain, is going to engage her old enemy to prove the young eagle is ready to supersede the old lion,' Drinkwater explained later to his children as they watched in silence while he ordered the packing of his sea-chest.

Within days Napoleon's *Grande Armée* began to cross the River Nieman and invade Russia. Half a million men. French, Austrians, Prussians, Saxons, Wurttemburgers, Italians, Poles, marched, as Marshal Marmont was long afterwards to recall, 'surrounded by a kind of radiance'.

'Now we shall see, Nat,' said Dungarth, the warmth of final achievement mixed with the excitement of a vast gamble, 'what this clash of Titans will decide.'

For Captain and Mrs Drinkwater there were less euphoric considerations. He waited upon their Lordships at the Admiralty immediately and within two days had received his orders. Indeed, the presence of Captain Drinkwater in the capital was considered 'most fortuitous'. While the focus of Dungarth's apprehensions lay to the east, Drinkwater shared Moira's concern for the outcome of events upon the Western Ocean and beyond. At the end of June the Drinkwaters returned home to Suffolk and their children. He was impatient, his heart beating at a faster pace. *Patrician* was to be hurried to sea again, her lack of men notwithstanding.

Drinkwater's last days at Gantley Hall were spent writing letters which Richard, his son, took into Woodbridge for the post. Drinkwater dismissed Richard's pleas to be rated captain's servant aboard the *Patrician*. Instead he roused Lieutenant Quilhampton from his connubial bliss, thundering upon his cottage door on a wet evening when the sun set behind yellow cloud.

'My dear sir,' said Quilhampton, stepping backwards and beckoning Drinkwater indoors. 'We heard you had gone up to town . . .'

'You've heard of the outbreak of war with America?' Drinkwater snapped, cutting short his host's pleasantries.

'Well, yes, yesterday. I meant to try for a ship . . .'

'My dear James, I have no time, forgive me . . . ma'am,' he

bowed curtly to Catriona who had come into the room from the kitchen beyond, with an offer of tea, 'can you spare your husband?'

'You have a ship for me?' broke in Quilhampton, nodding to his wife and ignoring her silent protest.

'Not exactly, James. As a lieutenant I can get you a cutter – or a gun-brig, but nothing more. I am, however, desperate for a first luff in *Patrician*.' He paused, watching the disappointment clear in Quilhampton's expression. 'It ain't what you want, I know, but nor is it as bad as you think, James. I am to be the senior captain of a flying squadron . . .'

'A commodore, sir?'

'Aye, but only of the second class. They will not let me have a post-captain under me, but I can promise you advancement at the first opportunity, to Master and Commander at the very least . . .'

'I'll come, sir, of course I will.' Quilhampton held out his remaining hand.

'That's handsome of you, James, damned handsome,' Drinkwater grinned, seizing the outstretched paw. 'God bless you, my friend.'

'He was mortified you sailed for America without him last autumn, Captain Drinkwater,' Catriona said quietly in her Scots accent, pouring the bohea. Drinkwater noticed her thickening waist and recalled Elizabeth telling him the Quilhamptons were expecting.

'My dear, I am an insensitive dullard, forgive me, my congratulations to you both . . .'

Catriona handed him a cup. The delicate scent of the tea filled the room, but cup and saucer chattered slightly from the shaking of her hand. She caught his eye, her own fierce and tearful beneath the mop of tawny hair. 'My child needs a father, Captain. Even a one-armed one is better than none.

'Ma'am . . .' Drinkwater stammered, 'I am, I mean, I, er . . .

'Take him,' she said and withdrew, retiring to her kitchen .

Drinkwater looked at Quilhampton who shrugged.

'When can you be ready?'

'Tomorrow?'

'We'll post. Time is of the essence.'

'Talking of which, I have something . . .' Quilhampton turned aside and opened the door of a long-case clock that ticked majestically in a corner. He lifted a dark, dusty bottle from its base.

'Cognac, James?' Drinkwater asked, raising an eyebrow. 'How reprehensible.' Quilhampton smiled at Drinkwater's ill-disguised expression of appreciation.

'It is usually Hollands on this coast, but I can't stand the stuff. This', he held up the bottle after lacing both their cups of tea, 'the rector of Waldringfield mysteriously acquires.'

'Here's to the confinement, James. Tell her to stay with Elizabeth when her time comes.'

'I will, and thank you. Here's to the ship.'

Chapter Twelve *July-November 1812*

David and Goliath

'What is it, Mr Gordon?' Drinkwater emerged on to the quarter-deck and clapped his hand to his hat as a gust of wind tore at his cloak.

'*Hasty*, sir; she's just fired a gun and thrown out the signal for a sail in sight.'

'Very well. Make *Hasty*'s number and tell him to investigate.'

'Aye, aye, sir.'

Fishing for his Dollond glass Drinkwater levelled it at the small twenty-eight gun frigate bobbing on the rim of the horizon as they exchanged signals with her over the five miles of heaving grey Atlantic. Then he cast a quick look round the circumscribed circle of their visible horizon at the other ships of the squadron.

The little schooner *Sprite* clung to *Patrician* like a child to a parent, while two miles to leeward he could make out the thirty-eight gun, 18-pounder frigate *Cymbeline*, and beyond her the topsails of *Icarus*, a thirty-two, mounting 12-pounders on her gun deck.

'*Hasty* acknowledges, sir.'

Drinkwater swung back to Gordon and nodded. 'Very well. And now I think 'tis time we hoisted French colours with a gun to loo'ard, if you please, Mr Gordon.'

Midshipman Belchambers had anticipated the order, for it had long been known that they would close the American coast under an equivocal disguise. The red, white and blue bunting spilled from his arms as the assisting yeoman tugged at the halliards. Clear of the wind eddies about the deck, the tricolour snapped out clear of the bunt of the spanker and rose, stiff as a board, to the peak. The trio of officers watched the curiosity for a moment, then Drinkwater held his pocket-glass out to the midshipman.

'Up you go, Mr Belchambers. Keep me informed. We should

sight land before sunset.' He hoped he sounded confident, instead of merely optimistic, for they had not obtained a single sight during the week the gale had prevailed.

The boom of the signal gun drowned Belchambers' reply, but he scampered away, tucking the precious spy-glass in his trousers and reaching for the main shrouds. Drinkwater stared at *Hasty* again as she shook out her topgallants. Captain Tyrell was very young, younger than poor Quilhampton, and he was inordinately proud of his command which, by contrast, was grown old, though of a class universally acknowledged as pretty. Drinkwater suspected a multitude of defects lurked beneath the paint, whitewash and gilded brightwork of her dandified appearance. Yet the young man in command seemed efficient enough, had understood the signals thrown out on their tedious passage across the Atlantic and handled his ship with every sign of competence. Perhaps he had a good sailing-master, Drinkwater thought, again turning his attention to the *Sprite*: they must be damnably uncomfortable aboard the schooner.

Sprite's commander was a different kettle of fish, a man of middle age whose commission as lieutenant was but two years old. Lieutenant Sundercombe had come up the hard way, pressed into the Royal Navy from a Guinea slaver whose mate he had been. He had languished on the lower deck for five years before winning recognition and being rated master's mate. There was both a resentment and a burning passion in the man, Drinkwater had concluded, which was doubtless due to his enforced service as a seaman. Maybe contact with the helpless human cargo carried on the middle passage had made him philosophical about the whims and vagaries of fate, maybe not. His most significant attribute as far as Drinkwater was concerned was his skill as a fore-and-aft sailor. His Majesty's armed schooner *Sprite* had been built in the Bahamas to an American design and attached to the squadron as a dispatch vessel.

As for the other frigates and their captains, the bluff and hearty Thorowgood of the *Cymbeline* and the stooped and consumptive Ashby of the *Icarus*, though as different as chalk from cheese in appearance, were typical of their generation. With the exception of Sundercombe and his schooner, in whose selection Drinkwater had enlisted Dungarth's influence, the histories of the younger men were unremarkable, their appointment to join his so-called 'flying squadron' uninfluenced by anything other than the Admiralty's sudden fright at the depredations of Yankee privateers. None of them had seen action of any real kind, rising quickly through patronage or influence, and had been either cruising uneventfully in home waters or employed on convoy duties. Tyrell on the Irish coast where in the Cove of Cork, he had been able to titivate his ship to his heart's content; and Thorowgood in the West Indies, where rum and women of colour seemed to have made a deep impression upon him. Ashby looked too frail to remain long in this world, though he possessed an admirable doggedness if his conduct in the recent gale was anything to go by, for *Icarus* had carried away her fore topmast shortly before sunset a few days earlier and had been separated from the rest of the squadron. The last that had been seen of her as she disappeared behind a grey curtain of rain was not encouraging. The violent line squall had dragged waterspouts from the surface of the sea and the wild sweep of lowering cloud had compelled them all to look to their own ships and shorten sail with alacrity. *Patrician*'s raw crew, once more decimated by idleness and filled from every available and unsuitable source, had been hard-pressed for an hour.

Captain Ashby had fired guns to disperse a spout that threatened his frigate and these had been taken for distress signals. When the weather cleared, however, there was no sign of the *Icarus*, and though the squadron reversed course until darkness and then hove-to for the night, the dawn showed the three remaining frigates and the schooner alone.

'I suppose', Drinkwater had remarked as David Gordon returned to the deck shaking his head after sweeping the horizon from the masthead, '*our* still being in company is a small miracle.'

But two days later Ashby's *Icarus* had hove over the eastern horizon, her damage repaired and a cloud of canvas rashly set, proving at least that she was a fast sailer and Ashby a resourceful man with a competent ship's company. Now as the gale blew itself out and they closed the lee of the American coast, Drinkwater chewed over their prospects of success and the risky means by which he hoped to achieve it. His orders gave him wide discretion; the problem with such latitude was that his judgement was proportionately open to criticism.

'A sail, I hear, sir,' said Quilhampton, coming on deck and touching the fore-cock of his hat at the lonely figure jammed at the foot of the weather mizen rigging.

Drinkwater stirred out of his brown study. 'Ah, James, yes; Tyrell's gone to investigate and Belchambers is aloft keeping an eye on the chase.'

'I see we've the frog ensign at the peak . . .'

'You disapprove?'

Quilhampton shrugged and cast his eyes upwards. 'I comprehend your reasoning, sir, it just feels damned odd . . .'

'Any ruse that allows us time to gather intelligence is worth adopting.'

'Has *Icarus* gone off flying the thing, sir?'

'If he obeyed orders he has, yes.'

'Deck there!' Both officers broke off to stare upwards to where Belchambers swung against the monotone grey of the overcast, his arm outstretched. 'Land, sir, four points on the starboard bow!'

'What of the chase?' Drinkwater bellowed back.

'Looks like a schooner, sir, to the sou'westward. *Hasty*'s hull down but I don't think he's gaining.'

'He won't against a Yankee schooner,' Drinkwater grumbled to his first lieutenant. 'Though Belchambers can't see it yet, she'll be tucked under the lee of the land there with a beam wind, damn it.' Drinkwater sighed, and made a hopeless gesture with his hand. 'I really don't know how best to achieve success . . .'

'I heard scores of Yankee merchantmen left New York on the eve of the declaration with clearances for the Tagus,' remarked Quilhampton.

'Aye, and we'll buy their cargoes, just to keep Wellington's army in the field, and issue licences for more, I daresay.' He thought of the boasting finality he had threatened Captain Stewart with, calling up the iron ring of blockade to confound the American's airy theories of maritime war. Now the government in London showed every sign of pusillanimity in their desire not to interfere with supplies to the army in Spain. 'I wish to God the government would order a full blockade and bring the Americans to their senses quickly.'

'They misjudged the Yankee's temper,' agreed Quilhampton, 'thinking they would be content with the eventual rescinding of the Orders-in-Council.'

'Too little too late,' grumbled Drinkwater, 'and then David struck Goliath right betwixt the eyes . . .'

No further reference was necessary between the two men to

conjure up in their minds the humiliations the despised Yankee navy had visited upon the proud might of the British. Before leaving Plymouth they had heard that Commodore Rodgers' squadron had sailed from New York on the outbreak of war and, though the commodore had missed the West India convoy, his ships had chased the British frigate *Belvidera* and taken seven merchantmen before returning to Boston. Furthermore the *Essex* had seized the troop transport *Alert* and ten other ships. They knew, too, that the USS *Constitution* had escaped a British squadron by kedging in a calm, and finally, a week or two later, she had brought His Britannic Majesty's frigate *Guerrière* to battle and hammered her into submission with devastating broadsides.

The latest edition of *The Times* they had brought with them from England was full of outrage and unanswered questions at this blow to Britannia's prestige. The defeat of a single British frigate was considered incomprehensible, outweighed Wellington's defeat of the French at Salamanca and obscured the news that Napoleon had entered Moscow. On their passage westward, Drinkwater had plenty of time to mull over the problems his discretionary orders had brought him. They contained a caution about single cruisers engaging 'the unusually heavily armed and built frigates of the enemy', and the desirability of 'drawing them down upon a ship-of-the-line', an admission of weakness that Drinkwater found shocking, if sensible, had a ship-of-the-line been within hail. Yet he had been under no illusion that with 'so powerful a force as four frigates' great things were expected of him, and was conscious that he sailed on detached service, not under the direct command of either Sawyer at Halifax or his successor, Sir John Borlase Warren, even then proceeding westwards like themselves.

Drinkwater had been close enough to Admiralty thinking in those last weeks before he sailed, when he cast about desperately for men to make up his ship's company again and the Admiralty dithered, to know of their Lordships' concern over Commodore Rodgers. The news that Rodgers had sailed with a squadron and had not dispersed his ships added to the rumour that he had been after the West India convoy and had sailed almost within sight of the Scillies, had caused consternation at the Admiralty. To defend so many interests, the convoy routes from the West Indies, from India and the Baltic, the coastal trades and the distant fisheries and, by far the most important, the supply route to Lisbon and

Wellington's Anglo-Portuguese army, meant the deployment of a disproportionate number of ships spread over a quarter of the world's oceans. Until Warren reached Halifax and organized some offensive operations with the inadequate resources in that theatre, Captain Drinkwater's scratch squadron was the *only* force able to mount offensive operations against the Americans. With a thousand men-of-war at sea the irony of the situation was overwhelming.

Drinkwater had twice posted up to London for consultations, briefings and last-minute modifications to his orders. Suddenly the fact that he was a senior captain fortuitously on hand to combat the alarming situation was not so flattering. Imbued with a sense of urgency, the difficulties the Admiralty experienced in scraping together the exigous collection of ships they had at last dignified with the name of 'flying squadron' seemed trivial; Drinkwater was more concerned with his lack of manpower.

Now, however, after the most pressing problem had been at least partially solved, the Admiralty's concern was understandable.

Byron of the *Belvidera* had reported well of the American squadron's abilities, though outraged he had been attacked without a warning that hostilities had commenced. His escape he had attributed to superior sailing, not knowing the true cause was the explosion of a gun in which Rodgers himself had been wounded. Drinkwater did not share the overweening assumption of superiority nursed by young bloods like Tyrell and Thorowgood. He was too old or too honest with himself not to harbour doubts. Even ship for ship, *his* squadron matched against a squadron of Yankees could, he admitted privately to himself, be bested.

If Stewart was anything to go by, the American navy did not lack men of temper and determination, young men, too, men with experience of waging war in the Mediterranean, three thousand miles from their nearest base.

'I think we should not regard the Americans with too much contempt, James,' he said, in summation of his thoughts.

But any concurrence from Quilhampton was cut short by Belchambers hailing the deck again.

'*Hasty*'s broken off the chase, sir!'

'Where away is the chase herself ?' Drinkwater shouted.

'Can't see her, sir.'

'He's lost her, by God,' snapped Quilhampton.

'She's fast, James,' Drinkwater said consolingly, 'don't blame Tyrell; I tell you these damned Yankees are going to give us all a confounded headache before we're through.'

Quilhampton's sigh of resignation was audible even above the noise of the wind in the rigging, though whether it was submission to Drinkwater's argument or his excuse for Tyrell's failure, Drinkwater did not know. He felt a twinge of pity for his friend, perhaps Quilhampton himself should be in command of *Patrician*, perhaps he would make a better job of the task ahead . . .

'Well,' Quilhampton said, breaking into Drinkwater's gloom, 'at least we've got Warren taking over from that old fart Sawyer at Halifax.'

'Yes. I knew Sir John once, when I was master's mate in the cutter *Kestrel*. He had command of a flying squadron just after the outbreak of war with France . . .'

Odd he made that distinction between war with France and war with the United States, when he knew it was all part of the same, interminable struggle.

'Warren had some of the finest frigates in the navy with him, the *Flora*, the *Melampus*, the *Diamond* under Sir Sydney Smith, Nagle's *Artois* and the *Arethusa* under Pellew . . .'

'And look what we've got,' grumbled Quilhampton, watching *Hasty* approach. 'Not a bloody Pellew in sight . . .'

The little sixth-rate bore down towards them. They could see the French ensign at *Hasty*'s gaff, before losing sight of it behind the bellying bunt of her topsails. As she surged past, to lodge under *Sprite*'s stern and come round again in *Patrician*'s wake, Captain Tyrell stood on her rail and raised his hat. Drinkwater acknowledged the salute and felt the wind nearly carry his own into the sea running in marbled green and white between the two frigates.

'Too fast for us, sir!' he heard Tyrell hail, 'A privateer schooner by the look of her. She ran like smoke!'

Drinkwater waved his hat in acknowledgement. It was no more, nor anything less than he had expected.

'The problem is, where to start,' Drinkwater said, leaning over the chart. 'It would be a simple matter if my orders were to blockade the *Chesapeake* . . .'

'I'm damned if I know why they aren't, sir,' Quilhampton fizzed.

'It isn't government policy, James, at least not yet. Warren has a damnably difficult job, but he *must* maintain American supplies to the Tagus. Such a policy may, if we are lucky, promote sentiments of opposition to President Madison who has to maintain at least the illusion of not coming in on the French side in the peninsula. Warren will do his best to foment this discord by appealing to American mercantile avarice and issuing licences.'

'I see,' said Quilhampton, looking at his commander and thinking him unusually well-informed and then remembering the summonses, post-haste, to London from Plymouth. 'On the other hand Yankee avarice will be fired by the vision of plundering our trade,' protested Quilhampton, coming to terms with the enormous complexities Madison's declaration of war had caused. 'And we know the Americans have skilful seamen aplenty, men trained in the mercantile marine . . ?'

'Who know exactly where to intercept our trade.' Drinkwater overrode Quilhampton's exposition. 'And our task is to sweep – an apt verb for a copying clerk to apply, if impossible to obey in practice – to sweep the seas for American privateers . . .'

'With a handful of elderly frigates that can't catch a cold in a squall of rain, let alone a Baltimore schooner on or off the wind.' Quilhampton's protesting asides were meant to be signals of sympathy; they only served to irritate Drinkwater. Or was he annoyed because, all unbidden, his eyes were drawn to the legend *Potomac* on the chart. He fell silent and, watching his face, Quilhampton knew from experience that his expression presaged an idea which, in its turn, would father a plan. He shifted tack, moved to noises of positive encouragement.

'Of course with good visibility we can form a line abreast to cover fifty miles of sea and if we conduct such a sweep, at a focal point of trade, a point at which these smart Yankee skippers will reason they can best intercept a homeward convoy . . .'

'Yes, but which homeward convoy, James?' Drinkwater snapped, his voice suddenly vibrant with determination.

'Well, the West India trade, sir,' Quilhampton said, riffling through the other charts on the table and drawing out a second one. 'Now the hurricane season is over, I suggest – here.' He stabbed his finger at the northern end of the Florida Strait, where the Gulf Stream favoured homeward ships, but where the channel between the coast and the Great Bahama Banks narrowed to less than sixty miles. 'With the *Sprite* to increase our scouting front,' went on Quilhampton, 'we could almost completely cover the strait.' He paused, then added, 'Though I suppose we need her in the centre of the line to let slip like a hound and tie down any privateers until we can come up in the frigates.' Pleased with himself, he looked up at Drinkwater.

The captain's face was clouded and he was not looking at the chart of the Florida Strait. Instead he seemed abstracted, as though he had not been listening, obsessed with the chart of the Chesapeake. Quilhampton coughed discreetly, drawing attention to his presence, if not his expressed opinion. Drinkwater looked up.

'Er . . yes. Yes. I applaud your tactics, James, but not your strategy.'

'Oh,' Quilhampton bridled, puzzled.

'No offence, but what would *you* do?'

'As I say, the Florida Strait . . .'

'No, no, forgive me, I haven't made myself clear. Suppose, well perhaps for you it is not so much a supposition, for you may sympathize with my hypothesis, but suppose you are a bold, resolute American officer – an ambitious man, but not one who gained distinction in the quasi-war with France, or the Tripolitan adventure and, as a result, out of favour denied a naval ship but, being still a man of influence, one who could command a letter-of-marque, perhaps a small squadron of them . . .'

'It would make no difference . . .'

'Bear with me, James,' Drinkwater said tolerantly. 'Now you know perfectly well that every other privateer commander will make his station either the Florida Strait, or the Windward Passage, or some other focal point to intercept the West India ships . . .'

'Yes, but there'll be rich enough pickings for all,' insisted Quilhampton, knowing the way Drinkwater thought, 'and it'll rouse the sugar lobby, bring pressure to bear in Parliament and win the successful privateersman a reputation quicker perhaps than command of a Yankee frigate.'

'D'you rest your case?' Drinkwater asked drily.

Quilhampton blushed, aware that he had presumed on friendship at the cost of respect for rank.

'I beg your pardon, sir.'

'There's no need for that; you're my first lieutenant, such considerations must be encouraged, but think bigger, James. You're *very* ambitious, ambitious enough to attempt the single-handed destruction of the British government at a stroke, not merely stirring up an opposition lobby.' Quilhampton looked blank. 'Come on, you know how parlous a state our country's in . . .' Drinkwater paused, expectant. 'No?'

'I'm afraid not, sir . . .'

'Look; we need American wheat to supply Wellington; with what do we pay for it?'

'Gold, sir.'

'Or maybe a trifling amount of manufactures, to be sure, but principally gold. It is what the American masters want to take home with them. We need a Portuguese army in the field; with what do we pay them? And what do we pay the Spaniards with for fighting to free their own country?'

'Gold again . . .'

'And our troops do not live off the land but pay the Spaniards for their provisions in . . .?'

'Gold.'

'Quite so. A privateersman could stop the advance of Wellington for six weeks if he took a cargo of boots, or greatcoats, or cartridges. But there's precious little profit in a prize containing anything so prosaic. So the death-or-glory Yankee skipper will go for the source of our wealth, James . . .'

'You mean the India fleet, sir?'

'Exactly,' Drinkwater said triumphantly, 'the East Indiamen. They'll be leaving the factories now, catching the north-east monsoon down through the Indian seas, a convoy of 'em. Richer pickings than their West India cousins, by far.'

'So where would you intercept them, sir, St Helena?' Drinkwater could tell by Quilhampton's tone that he was sceptical, suggesting the British outpost as some remote, almost ridiculous area.

'I think so,' he said with perfect gravity, amused by the sharp look Quilhampton threw him. 'But first we'll blockade the Chesapeake, show our noses to the enemy. Let it be known there are detached flying squadrons at sea, it may deter them a little. I'll shift to the *Sprite* for a day or two.' Drinkwater grinned at the look of surprise spreading on Quilhampton's face. 'You'll be in command, James.'

'But why, sir? I mean, why shift to the *Sprite*?'

'Because I intend paying a visit to the Potomac. There is something I wish to know.'

Chapter Thirteen *October 1812*

The Intruder

'Do we have much further to go, sir?' Sundercombe asked, looming out of the darkness. 'The wind is dying.'

'Bring her to an anchor, Mr Sundercombe, then haul the cutter alongside and I'll continue by boat. You'll be all right lying hereabouts and I'll be back by dawn. If I'm not, keep the American colours hoisted and lie quiet.'

'If I'm attacked, sir, or challenged?'

'Get out to sea.'

Drinkwater sensed the relief in Sundercombe's voice. They were seventy miles from the Atlantic, though only sixty from *Hasty*, ordered inside the Virginia capes to flaunt French colours in an attempt to keep inquisitive Americans guessing. They had left *Hasty* before noon, ignored the merchant ships anchored in Mockjack Bay and the James and York rivers, and headed north, exchanging innocent waves with passing fishing boats and coasters. Sundercombe's was an unenviable task, and Drinkwater had given him no opportunity to ask questions, nor offered him an explanation. The fewer people who knew what he was doing, the better. If he was wrong in his hunch, the sooner they got out to sea the better, though their presence under either French or British colours would confuse the enemy. If he had guessed correctly, confirmation would give him the confidence he needed, though he could not deny a powerful ulterior motive: the chance of seeing Arabella Shaw again swelled a bubble of anticipation in his belly. Either way, if he lost *Hasty* or the schooner in the Chesapeake, he would be hard put to offer an explanation. Assuming he survived any such engagement, of course. He thrust such megrimish thoughts roughly aside.

'Pass word for Caldecott.'

Drinkwater's new coxswain rolled aft, a small, wiry figure, even in the darkness.

'I'm going on in the cutter, Caldecott. I have to make a rendezvous, with an informer,' he added, lest the man thought otherwise. 'I want perfect silence in the boat, particularly when and where I tell you to beach her. You must then stand by the place until I return. The slightest noise will raise the alarm and if any of your bullies think of desertin', dissuade them. They might have got away with it a twelve-month ago, but no one loves an Englishman hereabouts now. D'you understand me?'

'Aye, sir. No one'll desert, an' I'll swing if a single noise escapes their bleedin' mouths.' The raw Cockney accent cut the night.

'Good. There'll be a bottle or two for good conduct when we get back.'

'Beg pardon, sir . . .'

'What is it?'

' 'Ow long'll you be?'

'An hour or two at the most. Now make ready. It's almost midnight.'

'Aye, aye, sir.'

Moonrise was at about two, but they were two days after the new moon and the thin sliver of the distant satellite would scarcely betray them. Besides, it was clouding over.

The *Sprite*'s gaffs came down, the mast hoops rattling in their descent, and from forward came the splash of the anchor and the low rumble of cable. The schooner's crew moved in disciplined silence about the deck and Drinkwater marked the fact, reminding himself to advance Sundercombe, if it came into his power.

'Your cutter's alongside, sir. I've had a barricoe of water and a bag of biscuit put in it,' Sundercombe paused, as if weighing up his superior. 'I did not think it would be appropriate to add any liquor though . . .' His voice tailed off, inviting praise or condemnation.

'You acted quite properly, Mr Sundercombe. We can enjoy a glass later, when this business is over.' Drinkwater had explained to Caldecott, he ought at the very least to confide now in Mr Sundercombe. 'I intend to meet an informer, d'you see, Mr Sundercombe?'

'You have a rendezvous arranged, sir?' The question was shrewd.

'No, but I know the person's house.' Drinkwater made a move, a signal the confidence was over. 'I shall be back by dawn.'

'Good fortune, sir.'

Sundercombe watched as Drinkwater threw his leg over the schooner's rail and clambered down into the waiting boat. A few moments later it pulled into the darkness, the dim, pale splashes of the oar blades gradually fading with the soft noise of their movement.

'What's he up to?' A man in the plain blue of master's mate asked Sundercombe after reporting the *Sprite* brought to her anchor.

'Damned if I know,' growled the lieutenant.

Caldecott's men pulled silently upstream for an hour before Drinkwater began to recognize features in the landscape that betokened the confluence of the Potomac with the Chesapeake. He ordered the tiller over and they inclined their course more to the westward, entering the Potomac itself, a grey swathe between the darker shadows of the wooded banks up which they worked their way.

'Inshore now,' he murmured at last, and Caldecott swung the boat's head. 'Easy now, lads.'

The men no longer pulled, merely dipped their oar blades in the rhythm which had become almost hypnotic while the cutter carried her way. A roosting heron rose, startled, with a heavy flapping of its large wings. Drinkwater caught sight of the outline of Castle Point against the sky.

'Here's the place,' whispered Drinkwater.

'Oars,' hissed Caldecott. 'Toss oars. Boat your oars.' The knock and rumble of the oars as they were stowed were terminated in the sharp crunch and lurch as the boat grounded. Drinkwater stood up. He could see the eastern wing of the house clearly now, pale in the darkness, the surrounding trees gathered like protective wood spirits guarding it against incursions like his own. Before him the lawns came to the water's edge. He bent towards Caldecott's ear.

'Remember what I said.'

'No fear of forgettin', sir.'

'Keep quiet, you men,' he said in a low voice as he stepped from thwart to thwart. A moment later his boots landed on the gravel and he was ashore on enemy territory. He pulled his cloak closely round him and checked the seaman's knife lodged in its sheath in the small of his back. Taking a backward glance at the boat, he began to walk boldly up towards the house.

'Where's 'e gone, Bill?' someone asked.

'For a fuck, I shouldn't wonder, lucky bastard.'

'Stow it,' growled Caldecott, 'or it'll be you that's fucked.'

Immediately upon leaving the boat Drinkwater knew he had allowed himself insufficient time. The information he wanted had seemed vital in the security of *Patrician*'s cabin, vital to the scenario he had conjured out of Dungarth's intelligence reports, Moira's correspondence, the Admiralty's fears and his own peculiar brand of intuition, guesswork and faith in providence. Others would call it luck, no doubt, but to Drinkwater it was the hunch upon which he gambled his reputation.

Within minutes he reached the trees surrounding the stables forming the eastern wing of the house. He tried to recall where old Zebulon Shaw kept his hounds and thanked heaven for a windless night. He paused to catch his breath, looking back and seeing no sign of the boat or her crew tucked under the low river-bank. Noises came from the kitchen wing, a few bars of a song and the clatter of dishes, suggesting the servants were about late. He moved off, round the front of the house, traversing it in the shelter of the battlemented terrace until he reached the steps. Below the balustrade where he and Arabella had first traded the repartee which had had such fateful consequences, he stepped back and looked up at the façade.

There were lights still burning behind the heavy, brocade curtains. He tried to recall the plan of the house, located the withdrawing room and moved cautiously on to the terrace. An attack of nerves made him look down at the deserted lawns and the glimmer of the Potomac, empty now, where once, an age ago it seemed, the *Patrician* and the *Stingray* had lain uneasily together.

A fissure in the curtains revealed Shaw seated at an escritoire, his wig abandoned, the candlelight shining on his bald pate and a pen in his hand. A variety of papers were scattered on the small area of boards visible to Drinkwater.

With a thumping heart he stepped back and looked up again at the black windows whose glazed panes stared out indifferently at the night. Her bedroom was on the first floor, one of the rooms he had seen lit the evening before he had dined at Castle Point. A drain-pipe led directly up beside the shallow balcony upon which tall casements opened. Throwing back his cloak Drinkwater drew a deep breath and began to climb.

It was fortunate the house was not old, nor that the drain-pipe's fastenings had been skimped, for he struggled manfully in his effort to be silent. The climb was no more than fifteen feet, yet it took all his strength to claw his way up the wall and get his footing on the balcony's stone rail.

He stopped to catch his breath again, ruminating on the ruinous effects of age and short-windedness, aware that *here*, this close to her, he could not stop the terrible pounding of his heart. He strained his ears, but could hear nothing beyond the curtains. Putting his hand behind his back he drew the seaman's sheath knife, inserting the steel blade between the edges of the windows. With infinite care he located the latch and increased the pressure. To his relief it gave way easily, but he could afford no further delay, not knowing the noise its release had made within. He thrust aside the drapery and stepped inside the bedroom.

She was not alone, but sitting before a mirror, bathed in golden candlelight while her maid brushed out her hair. The unexpected presence of another person surprised him, instantly putting him on his guard, and drove the carefully prepared speech from his head. The unexpected, however, made him cautious not reckless. He drew the door to behind him and faced the astonished pair.

Both women had turned as he burst in. The maid, a white woman of uncertain years and not the negress Drinkwater might have thought likely had he anticipated her being there, dropped the hairbrush and squealed, putting her hands to her face as she backed away. Arabella, deathly pale, her face like wax, her eyes fixed upon the cloaked figure of the intruder, put out a hand to silence the frightened woman.

'There is no cause for alarm,' he said, a catch in his voice.

With a slow majesty Arabella rose to her feet and confronted the intruder. Her recently removed dress lay across her bed and she wore a fine silk negligée over her chemise. Her disarray twisted Drinkwater's gut with a tortuous spasm of desire and she caught this flickering regard of herself, sensed her mastery of his passion at the instant of knowing she might as easily lose it if he meditated rape.

'You! What is it you want?' Her voice trembled with emotion and the maid, pressed back against the wall, watched in terrified fascination, aware of a tension existing in the room extending beyond the mere fact of the stranger's burglarous entry. She too recognized the man, though he did not know her.

Drinkwater suppressed the goading of desire, aware she had divined the effect of her *déshabille*, and annoyed by it. The reflection steadied him again, reminded him of his purpose, of the enormity of his gamble.

'Only a word, ma'am. I shall not detain you long, nor do I offer you any harm.' He shot a look at the maid. 'Will she hold her tongue?'

Arabella looked round at the quailing yet immobile figure. 'Tell me something of your purpose,' she said, addressing Drinkwater again.

'To speak with you,' he said simply, with a lover's implication, gratified that she lowered her eyes, momentarily confused. She remained silent, struggling with his dramatic and violent appearance. Again she turned to her maid and, in a low voice, murmured something. Drinkwater recognized the language and his words arrested the woman's trembling retreat towards the door.

'She is French?' he asked, his voice suddenly harsh.

Arabella nodded. 'Yes, but she can be trusted. She will say nothing about your being here.'

Drinkwater fixed the woman with his most balefully intimidating glare. He was not unduly worried. He had *Patrician*'s red cutter's crew of nine men within hail, men who would delight in rescuing him if it meant they might also make free with the contents of Castle Point while they were about it.

'I am not alone,' he warned, 'there are others outside.'

His stare made the poor woman cringe, her hand desperately reaching for the door-knob.

'She understands, Nathaniel,' Arabella insisted, lowering the tension between the three of them.

'Very well.'

Arabella nodded, the maid fled and they were alone in the perfumed intimacy of her boudoir.

'Why have you come back?' she whispered, her face contorted with anguish as she sat back upon the chair and her right hand drew the silk wrap defensively about her breast.

'Are you in health, Arabella?' he asked, keeping his distance, hardening his painfully thumping heart at her plight.

'Yes,' she nodded, seizing the proprieties he offered, ignoring the incongruity of their situation, 'and you?'

'Yes,' he paused and she saw the struggle in his own face.

'You have nothing to fear,' she said more firmly, looking at him, 'I miscarried in the second month.'

She had conceived! The shock of it struck Drinkwater like a whiplash. It brought him no goatish pleasure, only an appalling regret and a piteous compassion which was out of kilter with his present purpose. 'My dear . . .' he made a move towards her, then stopped at the precise moment she held up her hand to arrest him.

'No! It is over, and it is for the best!'

He avoided her eyes. 'Yes,' he mumbled, 'the war . . .'

'I did not mean the war, Nathaniel, though that too is an impediment now.' She paused, then added, 'You found your wife well?'

'Arabella,' he protested, utterly confused, desperately hanging on to the reason for his unceremonious arrival. In his heart he had no real wish to revive their liaison and her continuing assumption piqued him.

'No blame attaches to you,' she said, sensing his mood, 'but why have you come back?'

He sighed, ashamed of himself now the moment of truth had come. 'I need some information, Arabella, information I thought our former intimacy might entitle me at least to ask of you.'

'You wish me to turn traitor?' she enquired, that lilting, bantering tone on which they had first established their friendship back in her voice, 'just as I once turned whore.'

'No,' he replied levelly, pleased he had at least anticipated *this* question. 'I merely wish to know if the *Stingray* is at sea under your brother's command. Such a question may easily be discovered from other sources; it is rumoured that a Yankee comes cheaper than Judas Iscariot.'

She opened her mouth to protest and then a curiously reticent look crossed her face. Her eyes searched his for some clue, as though he had said something implicit and she was gauging the extent of his knowledge. Then, as soon as the expression appeared it had faded and he was mystified, almost uncertain whether or not he had read it aright, merely left staring at her singular beauty.

'Why should you wish to know this? And why come all the

way from England and up the Chesapeake if it may be bought from some fisherman for a few dollars?'

'Because I wished for an excuse to see you,' he replied, voicing a gallant half-truth, 'and because it might stop your brother and I from trying to kill each other,' he lied. He watched the words sink in, hoping she might recall the respective attitudes he and Stewart had professed when the possibility of war between their two countries had been discussed. He hoped, too, she might not begin to guess how large was the ocean and how unlikely they were to meet. Unless . . .

'The *Stingray*, Captain Drinkwater, is undergoing repairs at the Washington Navy Yard,' she said with a cool and dismissive air. 'My brother is unemployed by the Navy Department . . . out of your reach . . .'

He admired her quick intelligence, her guessing of his dissimulation, and was now only mildly offended at her assumption of motive.

'Madam,' he said with a wry smile that savaged her with its attractiveness, 'I do not meditate any revenge, I assure you.'

The formality had evaporated the passion between them He was no longer a slave to their concupiscence; his imagination ran in a contrary direction.

'He is at sea, though, ma'am, is he not?'

She inclined her head. 'Perhaps.'

'In a Baltimore clipper schooner . . .' He flattened his tone, kept the interrogative out of his voice, made of the question a statement of fact and watched like a falcon the tiny reactive muscles about her lovely eyes.

'You knew,' she said before perceiving his trap and clenching her fist in her anger. 'You . . . you . . .' She stammered her outrage and he stepped forward and put a hand upon her shoulder. The white silk was warmed by the soft flesh beneath.

'Arabella . . .' She looked up, her eyes bright with fury. 'I truly mean no harm to either of you, but I have my obligations as you have yours. Please do not be angry with me. The web we find ourselves caught in is not of our making.'

She put her hand on his and it felt like a talon as it clawed at him. 'Why do you help weave it, then? You men are all the same! Why, you knew all along,' she whispered. Her fingers dug into the back of his hand, bearing it down upon her own shoulder as though she wanted to mutilate herself for her treachery. As he bent to kiss her hair the door was flung open with a crash of the handle upon the plaster.

Drinkwater looked round. Zebulon Shaw stood in the doorway with a scatter gun levelled at Drinkwater's belly.

Behind him, the dull gleam of a musket barrel in his hands, was the dark presence of the negro groom and the pale face of the maid.

'Take your hands off!' Shaw roared.

Shaw's misreading of the situation in thinking the moment of anguished intimacy one of imminent violence, moved Drinkwater to fury. Arabella, too, reacted.

'Father . . .' she expostulated, but Drinkwater seized her shoulders, drew her to her feet, jerked her round and pulled her to him. Whipping the knife from his belt he held it to her neck, hissing a reassurance in her ear.

He had no idea to what extent and in what detail the French maid had betrayed her mistress; he hoped she had acted protectively with some discretion, concerned only for Arabella's safety in the presence of a man who, once her lover was now at the very least an enemy. Whatever the niceties, he could, he realized, avoid compromising Arabella further while at the same time facilitating his escape. Zebulon Shaw's next remark gave him grounds for thinking he had guessed right.

'Drinkwater? Is it you? What in hell's name d'you mean by . . ?'

'I wished to know the whereabouts of the USS *Stingray*, Mr Shaw, and if you'll stand aside, I'll trouble your home no further. I have armed men outside and I have no need to remind you we are at war.'

Shaw's tongue flicked out over dry lips and his face lost its resolute expression. Drinkwater pressed his advantage.

'I apologize for my method,' he went on, sensing Shaw's indecision, 'and it would distress me even more if I had to add mutilation or murder to a trifling burglary.' As he spoke he moved the knife menacingly across Arabella's white throat.

'Damn you!' Shaw growled, drawing back.

'Very well, Mrs Shaw,' Drinkwater said with a calm insolence, 'precede me and no harm will come to you.' He pressed her gently forward, passed into the passage and ran the gauntlet of Shaw and the negro, glaring at the maid as she held up a wildly flickering candelabra in a shaking hand. 'No tricks, sir . . .'

They were convinced by his show of bravado in which Arabella played her part submissively.

'Go, sir,' Shaw called after them, 'go and be damned to you if this is how you treat our hospitality . . .'

'Needs must, sir, when the devil drives,' Drinkwater flung over his shoulder as they reached the head of the staircase. 'Careful, m'dear,' he muttered to Arabella as they descended to the darkened hall.

Shaw and the negro covered their descent and Drinkwater was aware of open doors closing on their approach as inquisitive servants, roused by noises on the floor above, retreated before the sight of the cloaked intruder with their mistress a hostage. He paused at the main door and turned.

'Remain here, Shaw. I shall take your daughter-in-law a pistol shot from the house and release her. I trust you to wait here.'

'Be damned, Captain . . .'

'Do you agree?'

Shaw grunted. 'Under protest, yes, I agree.'

'I bid you farewell, Mr Shaw, and I repeat my apologies that the harsh necessities of war compel me to this action. Perhaps in happier times . . .'

He had the door open and thrust Arabella through, followed her and pulled the door to behind them, then seized her hand.

'Beyond the trees,' he ordered, walking quickly down the wide steps and across the gravel. 'And hurry, I pray you. I do not want you to catch a fever. I am sorry for what has happened. No blame attaches to you and if your maid was at least loyal to *you*, then I think no great harm can have been done. Tell your father-in-law you confessed only that your brother no longer had command of the *Stingray*'.

They reached the trees as he finished this monologue and he let go her wrist. She turned and faced him.

'I am sorry we must part like this,' he ran on, 'as sorry as I was by the manner of our last parting.'

'Sir,' she said, drawing her breath with difficulty, 'I should hate you for this humiliation, but I cannot pretend . . . no, it is no matter. It was guilt the last time, guilt and shame and the confusion of love, but it was better than this!' She almost spat the last word at him. 'God,' her voice rose, exasperation and hurt charging it with a desperate vehemence, 'had I not . . . damn you! Go, for God's sake, go quickly.'

'God bless you, Arabella.'

'Go!'

He turned and ran, not hearing her poor, strangled cry, wondering why on earth he had invoked the Deity. A moment later he cannoned into Caldecott.

'Damn you, Caldecott – is the boat ready?'

'Beg pardon. Aye, sir.'

Drinkwater looked back. There was a brief flash of pale silk and then only the trees and their shadows stood between him and Castle Point.

'Everything all right, sir?'

In answer to Caldecott's query the wild barking of dogs, the gleam of lanterns and shouts of men filled the night. Then came the sharp crack of a musket.

'Not exactly. Come on, let's go.'

Chapter Fourteen *October–November 1812*

Cry Havoc . . .

'What d'you make of her, Mr Sundercombe?'

'I'm not sure, sir, beyond the fact she's a native and determined to pass close.'

Sundercombe handed Drinkwater his telescope. The American brig had trimmed her yards and laid a course to intercept the *Sprite* as the schooner ran south to pass the Virginia capes and reach the open Atlantic. It was midmorning and Drinkwater was bleary-eyed from insufficient sleep. He had trouble focusing and passed the glass back to Sundercombe.

'Send your gun's crews quietly to their stations, load canister on ball, but don't run 'em out. Tell them when they get word, to aim high and cut up her riggin.' You handle the ship, I'll give the order to open fire.' Drinkwater looked up at the stars and bars rippling at the main peak. 'Better pass word for my coxswain.'

'I'm 'ere, sir, an' I've got some coffee.'

'Obliged, Caldecott . . .' Drinkwater took the hot mug.

Sundercombe was already issuing orders, turning up the watch below and giving instructions quietly to his gunners. The *Sprite* mounted six 6-pounders a side, enough to startle the stranger if Drinkwater timed his bird-scaring broadside correctly. He sipped gratefully at the scalding coffee which tasted of acorns.

'Caldecott,' he said, 'I want you to stand by the ensign halliards with one of our cutter's crew. The moment I give you the word, that ensign aloft must come down and our own be hoisted, d'you understand? 'Tis a matter of extreme punctilio.'

'Punctilio – aye, aye, sir.'

Drinkwater grinned after the retreating seaman. He seemed suitably imbued with *gravitas*. Quilhampton had discovered him and sent him aft for approval, concerned that Drinkwater had himself found no substitute for old Tregembo. 'You must have a cox'n, sir. I can't spare a midshipman every time you want a boat,' Quilhampton had protested.

'Can't, or won't?' Drinkwater had enquired.

'You *must* have a cox'n,' Quilhampton repeated doggedly, the flat assertion brooking no protest.

'Oh, very well,' Drinkwater relented, 'have you someone in mind?' Half an hour later the stunted form of Caldecott stood before him. 'Have you acted in a personal capacity before, Caldecott?' Drinkwater had asked, watching the man's eyes darting about the cabin and revealing a bright and curious interest.

'I 'ave, sir, to Captings Dawson and Peachey, sir, an' I was bargeman to Lord Collin'wood in the old *Ocean*, sir, an' 'ad lots of occasions to be 'andling 'is Lordship's personal an' diplomatic effects, sir.'

'Matter of punctilio,' Drinkwater now heard Caldecott repeat to his oarsman and, still grinning, he watched the Yankee brig bear down upon them.

The sight combined with the coffee and the invigorating chill of the morning breeze to cheer him, making him forget his fatigue. His brief nap had laid a period of time between this forenoon and the events of the previous night. They might have occurred to a different man. He was filled with a sudden happiness such as he had not felt for many, many months, the inspiriting renewal discovered by the penitent sinner.

Was that why he had called upon God to bless Arabella last night? Did he detect the finger of the Deity or providence in that last encounter; or in the fortuitous natural abortion of the child their helpless lust had made?

It was, he realized, much, much more than that. Certainly their odd, mutual avoidance had been in some strange way a holding back in anticipation of the final parting which had now occurred. They were, he reflected without bitterness, not young, and though their affair had not lacked heat it had not been conducted without a little wisdom. Moreover, she had loved him as he had loved her, with the self-wounding passion of hopeless intensity. Such things happened, rocked the boats of otherwise loyal lives and sent their ripples out to slap the planking of other such boats, God help them all.

But there was also the timely confirmation of his hunch. The drunk and incautious Stewart had opened his mind and had put

Drinkwater in possession of a key, not to the strategic planning of Madison and his colleagues, but to the freebooting aspirations of his commercial warriors, the privateersmen and their backers. Drinkwater was as certain of this as of the breeze itself.

Sundercombe approached and stood beside him. The brig was two miles away, a merchant ship by the look of her.

'There's a brace of sail hull down to the s'uthard,' Sundercombe volunteered.

'*Hasty*?'

'One of 'em perhaps, sir.'

The old sensation of excitement and anxiety wormed in Drinkwater's gut. They had nothing much to fear from the brig, he thought, any more than the brig had to fear from the schooner she was so trustingly running down towards. Unmistakably Yankee in design, the American ensign at her peak and approaching from the direction of Baltimore, the *Sprite* could be nothing other than a privateer putting to sea. He looked along the waist. The gunners crouched at their pieces, waiting.

'We've forgotten something,' Drinkwater said sharply. 'Have your men drop the fore topm'st stays'l. Contrive to have it hang over the starboard rail and cover our trail boards. Have the men fuss about up there, as though dissatisfied with something. Those men yonder may smell a rat if they know there's no *Sprite* out of Baltimore or the Chesapeake.'

With a sharp intake of breath, Sundercombe hurried off. He had large yellow teeth, like an old horse, thought Drinkwater. He suddenly craved the catharsis of action, knowing that in a few moments he would open fire on the defenceless ship. What else was there for him to do? He was a King's officer, bound by his duty. They were all shackled, one way or another, making a nonsense of notions of liberty.

How could a man be free? He was tied to a trade, to a master, to his family, to his land, to his throne if one chased the argument to its summit. Even poor Thurston, exponent of freedom though he was, had been chained to his beliefs, governed to excess by his obsession with democracy. Everything everywhere was either passive in equilibrium, or else active in collision, in the process of transition ending in balance and inertia. In that state of grace men called natural order, equilibrium reigned; the affairs of men were otherwise and ran, for the most part, contrary to natural order.

Shocking though it had been at the hand of a maniac, Thurston's murder was comprehensible if seen as a drawing upon himself, the libertarian extremist, the pistol ball of an extreme agent of repression.

In such a world what was a reasonable man to do? What he was doing now, Drinkwater concluded as he watched an officer mount the brig's quarter rail, clinging to the larboard gaff vang. He must hasten the end of this long, wearisome war. Duty ruled his existence and providence decided the outcome of his acts.

And what of Christian charity? What of compassion, his conscience whispered? He provided for his family; he was not unkind to his friends; he had done his best in those circumstances where his decisions impinged upon the lives of others; he had taken in those lame ducks whose existence depended upon his charity . . .

'Schooner, 'hoy!'

There was a flurry of activity on the deck of the brig as she drew rapidly closer. Sundercombe came aft again, wandering with a studied casualness and impressing Drinkwater with his coolness. Forward, the staysail flapped over the *Sprite*'s name.

'Schooner 'hoy? What ship?'

Drinkwater drew himself up, doffed his hat and waved. 'Tender to the United States ship *Stingray*, out of the Washington Navy Yard,' he hailed.

The brig was a cable distant, trimming her yards as she braced round to run parallel with the schooner.

'Have you had word? There's a British frigate cruising off the capes.'

'Must be *Hasty*,' a perplexed Sundercombe murmured.

'No,' Drinkwater called back. What the devil had induced Tyrell to douse French colours? 'When was she last sighted?'

'Day before yesterday. He took a Norfolk ship prize.'

'The hell he did!' Drinkwater shouted back with unfeigned surprise. 'He can't have seen those two sails to the south,' he muttered in an aside to Sundercombe.

'He's too big for you to take on, Cap'n,' the American continued as the two vessels surged alongside, their crews staring at one another, the *Sprite*'s gunners still crouching out of sight.

'Where are you bound?' Drinkwater pressed.

'The Delaware.'

'I could give you an escort. We could divert the Britisher, hold him off while you got out. I heard there were some French ships in the offing,' Drinkwater drawled.

Drinkwater watched the American officer throw a remark behind him then he nodded. 'I calculate you're correct, Cap'n, and we'd be mightily obliged.'

'I'll take station on your starboard quarter then. Can you make a little more sail?'

'Sure, and thanks.'

'My pleasure.' Drinkwater turned his attention inboard. 'I think we've hooked him, Mr Sundercombe. Keep your gunners well down. Let him draw ahead and then have us range up on his weather side.'

'Ease the foresheet, there,' Sundercombe growled, clearly not trusting himself to imitate an American accent like Drinkwater. The big gaff sail flogged and the schooner lost some way as the brig's crew raced aloft to impress the navy men and shook out their royals. Sundercombe went aft and lent his weight to the helmsman. *Sprite* luffed under the brig's stern and then, with the foresheet retrimmed, slowly overhauled her victim on her starboard side.

'Get your larboard guns ready,' Drinkwater said, aware the Americans could not hear him but anxious lest they might realize they had been deceived.

He thought he detected some such appreciation, someone pointing at them and drawing the attention of the officer he had seen on the brig's rail to something. He realized with a spurt of irritation that he had forgotten their name exposed on the larboard bow.

The *Sprite* was fast overhauling the brig and Drinkwater knew he dared delay no longer if, as the inconvenient discomfort of his conscience prompted, he was to avoid excessive bloodshed.

'Ensign, Caldecott! Run out your guns, Mr Sundercombe!'

They could not fail to see now. The jerky lowering of the American colours and the hand-over-hand ascent of the white ensign brought a howl of rage from the brig, a howl quite audible above the trundle of the 6-pounder carriages over the *Sprite*'s pine decks.

'Strike, sir, or I'll open fire!' Drinkwater hailed.

'God damn you to hell!' came a defiant roar and Drinkwater nodded. The three 6-pounders barked in a ragged broadside. It was point-blank range; even at the maximum elevation originally intended to cripple the brig's rigging and with the schooner heeling to the breeze, the trajectories of the shot could not avoid hitting the brig's rail. What appeared like a burst of lethal splinters exploded over the brig's deck. A moment later, as the gun-captains' hands went up in signal of their readiness to fire again, the American flag came down.

An hour later the brig *Louise* of Norfolk, Virginia, Captain Samuel Bethnal, Master, had been fired. Bethnal and his people hoisted the lugsail of the red cutter lately belonging to His Britannic Majesty's frigate *Patrician* and miserably set course to the south-west and the coast of Virginia. To the east the horizon was broken only by the grey smudges of a pair of British frigates, and the twin jags of a schooner's sails as she slipped over the rim of the world and left the coast of America astern.

'I don't see the sense in it myself,' said Wyatt, burying his nose in a tankard and bracing himself as the *Patrician* shouldered her way through a swell. 'It ain't logical,' he added, surfacing briefly to deliver his final opinion on Captain Drinkwater's conduct in the dank haven of the wardroom.

'I suppose the Commodore has his reasons,' offered Pym with a detached and largely disinterested loyalty.

'I'm sure he has,' Simpson, the chaplain, said cautiously, then affirming, 'of course he has,' with an air of conviction, before destroying the effect by appending in a far from certain tone of voice: 'in fact I'm certain of it.'

Slowly Wyatt raised his face from the tankard. Rum ran from his slack mouth, adding gloss to an already greasy complexion. 'You don't know what you're talking about,' he mouthed with utter contempt.

'Nevertheless, Mr Wyatt,' the hitherto silent Frey piped up, 'I agree with Simpson and the surgeon.'

Wyatt turned his red eyes on the junior lieutenant. 'An' you know bugger all,' he said offensively.

Frey was about to leap to his feet when he felt Simpson's restraining hand on his sleeve. 'Hold hard, young man, he doesn't know what he's saying.'

'Don't know what I'm saying, d'you say? Is that what you said, you God-bothering bastard?' Wyatt rose unsteadily to his feet, instinctively bracing himself against *Patrician*'s motion. 'With hundreds of bloody privateers shipping out of every creek and runnel on the coast of North America, we, we,' Wyatt slammed his now empty tankard on the table top with a dull, emphatic thud, 'we go waltzing off into the wide Atlantic with the strongest frigate squadron south of Halifax . . .'

'We're going to rendezvous with the homeward Indiamen . . .' Frey began, but was choked in mid-sentence.

'Indiamen be buggered. If we were going to do that why did we go all the way to America?'

'Why *did* we go to America then, Wyatt?' Pym asked provocatively.

Wyatt swung a pitying look on Pym. 'So he', Wyatt gestured a thumb at the deck above, 'could lay with his lady love again.'

'Mr Wyatt, hold your tongue!' Frey snapped, leaping to his feet and this time avoiding Simpson's tardy hand.

'Ah, be buggered,' Wyatt sneered, 'Caldecott saw the woman; half naked she was, in her shift . . .'

'Are you drunk again, Mr Wyatt?'

Quilhampton stood just inside the doorway, his one hand grasping a stanchion. The creaking of the ship and the gloom of the day had allowed him to enter unobserved. Wyatt swung ponderously on his accuser as the other officers heaved a sigh of collective relief. As the frigate lurched and rolled to leeward, the master lost his already unsteady balance and reached for the back of his chair which he only succeeded in knocking over. The motion of the frigate accelerated their fall and Wyatt stretched full length on the deck. He made no move to recover himself and for a long, expectant moment no one in the wardroom moved. Then a snore broke what passed for silence between decks.

'I see you are,' said Quilhampton drily. Looking round the table, he continued, 'Let us avoid complete dishonour, gentlemen, and get the old soak into his cot without the benefit of the messman.'

They rallied round the one-armed lieutenant and, shuffling awkwardly with the dead weight of the big man between them, squeezed into his cabin and manhandled Wyatt into his swinging cot.

Catching their breath they regarded their late burden for a moment.

'Sad when you see drink consume an otherwise able man, ain't it?' Quilhampton asked in a general way. 'I presume he was running the Captain down again.'

'Yes,' Frey said, 'like Metcalfe used to, and in a particularly personal manner, too.'

'It was disgraceful,' said Simpson.

'This story about the woman again, was it?' asked Quilhampton.

'Indeed it was, Mr Q,' said Simpson.

'Well, gentlemen, let me tell you something,' Quilhampton said, herding them back into the common area of the wardroom where they resumed their places at the battered table. 'I have been acquainted with Captain Drinkwater for many years and in that time I have not known him to act improperly. Moreover, I do know him to have the confidence of government, and that if he claims this mysterious woman was an agent, or a spy, then that is very likely what she was. Now I think we can cease speculatin' on the matter and assume the Captain knows what he is doin', eh?' Quilhampton looked round the table as Moncrieff came in.

'Don't you think, Mr Q,' Simpson said, his neat, rosebud mouth pursed primly, 'that you should properly refer to Drinkwater as the Commodore?'

'I daresay I should, Mr Simpson,' Quilhampton said laconically, helping himself to a biscuit, 'what is it, Moncrieff?'

'I am a messenger, James. The Captain, I beg your pardon, Mr Simpson, the Commodore,' Moncrieff said, with ironic emphasis, desires a word with you.'

Quilhampton brushed his coat, rose and bowed to the company. 'Gentlemen, excuse me . . .'

'I suppose they think I'm mad in the wardroom?' Drinkwater said flatly, not expecting contradiction. He remained bent over the chart as Quilhampton replied, 'Something like that, sir.'

Drinkwater looked up at his first lieutenant. 'You're damnably cheerful.'

'The weather's to my taste, sir.'

'You're perverse, James.'

'My wife says something similar, sir.' They grinned at each other.

'What is it they say?' Drinkwater asked, now he had Quilhampton's full attention. He saw Quilhampton drop his eyes, saw the evasive, non-committal shrug and listened to the half-truth.

'Oh, that damned fool Wyatt thinks we should stay on the American coast. I've tried to explain, but . . .'

Again the shrug and then Quilhampton looked up and caught a bleak look of utter loneliness on Drinkwater's face, a look which vanished as Drinkwater recovered himself, cast adrift his abstracted train of thought and fixed his eyes upon his friend.

'I'll admit to it being a long shot, James; perhaps a *very* long shot, and certainly a risky one. I appreciate too, that twenty-two days out of the Chesapeake with nothing to our account beyond a fired brig don't amount to much but . . .'

Quilhampton watched now, saw the inward glance take ignition from the conviction lurking somewhere inside this man he respected and loved, but could never understand.

'You have explained to me, sir, at least in part, but may I presume?'

'Of course.'

'We are on the defensive now. Even our blockading squadrons keep watch and ward off the French ports as the first line of defence against invasion. To some extent I share Wyatt's misgivings. We are a long way from home. Our present passage to the South Atlantic exposes our rear when every ship should be sealing home waters against the enemy. That is where, I have heard you yourself say, American privateers struck hardest during the last war. I fear, sir, for what may happen if you have miscalculated . . .'

Drinkwater gave a short bark of a laugh. 'So do I, James,' he interrupted.

'How *are* you so sure?'

'Because if I were in the same position this is what I would do.'

'And you really think it is him? This man Stewart?'

'Yes.'

'How?'

'I don't really know . . .'

'Then how can you be sure of his mind?'

'I can't be entirely sure of it, James . . .'

'But,' Quilhampton expostulated vainly, frustrated at Drinkwater's failure to see where the decision to sail south might lead them, 'a month ago you were in doubt as to how to proceed . . .'

'But we reasoned here, in this very cabin, the interception of the East India fleet was the most likely thing,' Drinkwater paused.

'Come, James, have faith; stick like a limpet to your decision.' There was a vehemence, a wildness in Drinkwater's voice, almost a passion that disturbed Quilhampton. It just then occurred to him with a vivid awfulness that Drinkwater might indeed be on the verge of madness. He stared at his friend and tried again: 'But how . . .?'

'By the prickin' of my thumbs,' Drinkwater said, looking down at the chart again, and Quilhampton withdrew, a cold and chilling sensation laying siege to his heart.

'What do you think, damn it?' Quilhampton asked Pym as the surgeon, spectacles perched on the end of his nose, looked up from the candlelit pages that he held before him against the roll of the ship. 'They're your confounded theories, ain't they? All this bloody obsession and conviction and what-not. Damn it, Pym, I've known the man since I was a boy. He's brilliant, but dogged like so many of us with never quite bein' in the right place at the right time. He got me out of Hamburg in terrible circumstances, all the way down the Elbe in the winter in a blasted duck-punt . . .'

'Yes, I heard about that.'

'D'you think the ordeal might have turned his mind?'

Pym shrugged. 'This', he tapped the notes he had abandoned when Quilhampton sought him out, 'is no more than a theory, based on a single case, that of your predecessor. I don't know about Drinkwater . . . You say he's changed?'

The use of Drinkwater's unqualified surname shocked Quilhampton. It almost smacked of mutiny, as if Pym, in his detached, objectively professional way, had actually committed a preliminary act by divesting Drinkwater of his rank. Quilhampton shied away from committing himself.

'Certainly,' Pym rumbled on, 'there are signs of obsession in his conduct, but I have to say we are not party to his orders and, as you yourself suggested, these may be of a clandestine nature. Wasn't he in Hamburg on some such mission?'

'Yes,' Quilhampton agreed, worried at the direction the conversation was taking.

'Perhaps,' Pym suggested with an air of slyness, removing his spectacles and leaning back in his chair to clean them on his neckcloth, 'there is something else the matter.'

'What the deuce d'you mean?' Quilhampton asked sharply.

'You've heard the stories of the woman. Perhaps it isn't obsession he suffers from, but remorse . . .'

'Preposterous!' snapped Quilhampton dismissively, starting to his feet and looking down at the surgeon.

'If you say so, Mr Q.' Pym replaced the spectacles and picked up his pen

'I most emphatically do say so, Mr Pym.' Quilhampton turned the handle on the surgeon's cabin door, then paused in his exit. 'This conversation, Mr Pym, must be regarded as confidential.'

'We can regard it as never having happened if you wish, Mr Q.'

Quilhampton expelled his breath. 'It would be best, I think.'

'I think so too.'

'Obliged. Good-night, Mr Pym.'

Pym bent to his manuscript and picked up his pen. The ship's motion was easier now and the lantern gyrated less, so he was able to write without the flying shadows distracting his failing sight.

It seems to me from a long observation of commanders in His Majesty's navy that unopposed command may distort the reasoning powers of a clever man, that the balance of his rational, thinking mind may be warped by lack of good counter-argument and his imagination seized by obsession.

Pym paused, tapping his pen on the broken teeth of his lower jaw. 'The trouble is,' he puzzled to himself, 'this is quite the reverse of a man vacillating between two distinct manners of thought. And if I am to identify the one, I needs must also consider the other.'

A warm glow of ambitious satisfaction welled in his stomach. Perhaps, unlike his subjects, he *was* in the right place at the right time. He dipped his pen and bent to his task.

Chapter Fifteen *December 1812–January 1813*

The Whaler

'The rendezvous, gentlemen.' Drinkwater tapped the spread chart with the closed points of the dividers and watched as they leaned forward to study the tiny, isolated archipelago a few miles north of the Equator and already far astern of them as they ran down the latitude of Ascension Island. 'St Paul's Rocks, as likely a spot for the Americans to use too, so ensure you approach them with caution, should you become detached, and that you use the private signals . . .'

He looked round at them. Ashby was still studying the chart but Thorowgood's florid face, evidence, Drinkwater suspected, of a self-indulgent Christmas, hung on his every word, while Sundercombe, a mere lieutenant in the company of four post-captains, regarded him thoughtfully from the rear.

'Now as for our cruising station, you will observe the rhumb-line from Ascension to St Helena as being exactly contrary to the south-east trade wind . . .'

They would, he explained, sweep in extended line abreast, the frigates just in sight of one another, tacking at dawn and dusk, in the hope of intercepting the East India convoy before any American privateers.

'We know the Indiamen will have at least one frigate as escort, but Yankee clipper-schooners will have no trouble outmanoeuvring her and cutting out the choicest victims at their will. News of hostilities with America will have reached the Cape by now and it may be that a second cruiser will have been attached; not that that will make very much difference. However, four additional frigates plus a schooner to match Yankee nimbleness', he paused and smiled at Sundercombe, 'should bring the convoy home safely. Any questions?'

'Sir,' said Ashby, 'may I enquire whether your orders were to escort the East Indiamen, or remain on the American coast? I mean no criticism, but had we proceeded directly to the Cape we would have met with the India fleet for a certainty.'

A groundswell of concurrence rose from the other post-captains. Drinkwater had no way of knowing that the news of the silk petticoat had spread round the squadron by that mysterious telegraphy which exists among ships in company. *Sprite*'s tendering and message-bearing had much to do with it, and the breath of intrigue had engendered a note of misgiving into the minds of Drinkwater's young and ambitious juniors.

For himself, his own sense of guilt had been superseded by the conviction that he had picked up a vital trail at Castle Point, and he saw in Ashby's mildly impertinent question, full of the criticism he denied, the arrogance of young bucks seeking the downfall of an old bull. He lacked in their eyes, he knew, the bold dash expected of a frigate captain, and was, moreover, a tarpaulin officer of an older school than they cared to associate with. He knew, too, they had objected to his burning of the *Louise*. Tyrell, by being in sight in *Hasty*, would have had a legitimate claim to the prize money her sale might have realized, while the general principle of burning valuable prizes appealed to none of them. Ashby's question invited a snub; he decided to administer a lecture. Signalling Sullender to offer wine and sweet-treacle biscuits to his guests, he stared out of the stern windows. Only the lightest of breezes ruffled the sea and *Patrician* ghosted along, the other frigates' boats towing in the slight ripples of her wake. He knew from the silence, broken only by the soft chink of decanter on glass, that they waited for his reply. He swung on them with a sudden, unexpected ferocity.

'You cannot *buy* yourself into the sea-service, gentlemen, as you can into the army. A ship-of-the-line is not to be had like a regiment or a whore. Oh, to be sure, interest, be it parliamentary or petticoat, sees many a fool up the quarterdeck ladder. But that does not *prevent* an able man getting there, though it stops many. Fortunately for the sea-service that peculiarly snobbish genius of the English, that of giving the greater glory to what costs 'em most, is absent in principle from naval promotion.'

He paused, glaring at them, gratified to see in their eyes the expressions of the midshipmen they once had been.

'Nevertheless, a deal of useless articles have arrived on quarterdecks. Since Lord Nelson's apotheosis at Trafalgar, the Royal

Navy has appealed to the second of England's vices after snobbery: that of fashion. How a service which accepts boys to be sodomized or killed at twelve or thirteen, poxed at eighteen and shot or knighted by their majority should become fashionable, is a matter for philosophers more objective than myself. All I know is that those of us who remember the last war with the Americans, if we aren't rotting ashore, dead, or been promoted to flags or dockyards, have been consigned to the living entombment of blockade, whilst injudiciously *fashionable* young men command our cruisers and risk destruction at the hands of the Americans. . . .'

'Excuse me, sir.'

'What the devil d'you want?' Drinkwater broke off his diatribe, aware that Belchambers had been hovering by the door for some time. 'Excuse me a moment, gentlemen,' Drinkwater said, secretly delighted that Thorowgood was nearly purple with fury and Ashby's eyes glittered dangerously. Tyrell was studying his nails.

'The wind's freshening a trifle, sir, and Mr Quilhampton says there's a strange sail coming up from the south'ard. She's carrying a wind and looks to be a whaler.'

The news transformed the gathering, the whiff of a prize, a Yankee whaler, affected them all, with the exception of their commodore.

'Shall we go on deck, gentlemen, and see what we make of this newcomer before you return to your ships?'

The notion of waiting aboard *Patrician* while the whaler closed the squadron obviously irritated them still further. Coolly Drinkwater led the way past the ramrod figure of the marine sentry and up the quarterdeck ladder.

'British colours, sir.'

Quilhampton, who had the deck, lowered his glass and offered it to Drinkwater. Behind them the knot of frustrated frigate commanders and Lieutenant Sundercombe, who stood slightly apart and gravitated towards Mr Wyatt beside the binnacle, drew pocket-glasses from their tail pockets. With irritable snaps the telescopes were raised.

'Maybe a ruse,' growled Thorowgood in a stage whisper.

'Indeed it might,' Ashby added archly.

The whaler, her low rig extended laterally by studding sails, came up from the south with a bone in her teeth. Gradually her sails fell slack as she closed the British frigates and her way fell off.

'I think not, gentlemen, she's losing the wind and lowering a boat.'

They watched as the whaleboat danced over the wavelets towards *Patrician*, the most advanced of the squadron.

'He's pulling pell-mell. Ain't he afraid we might press such active fellows?' Drinkwater asked in an aside to Quilhampton.

'D'you want me to, sir?'

'I think we should see what he has to say, Mr Q,' Drinkwater replied.

The whaleboat swung parallel to the *Patrician*'s side, half a pistol-shot to starboard.

'Good-day, sir,' Drinkwater called, standing conspicuously beside the hance. 'You seem in a damned hurry.'

'Aye, sir, I've news, damnable news. Do I have to shout it out, or may I come aboard with the promise that you won't molest my men?'

'Come aboard. You have my word on the matter of your men.' Drinkwater's heart was suddenly thumping excitedly in his breast. A sense of anticipation filled him, a sense of luck and providence conspiring to bring him at last the news he so desired.

The whaling master clambered over the rail. He was a big, bluff, elderly man, dressed in an old-fashioned brown coat with grey breeches and red woollen stockings, despite the warmth of the day. He drew off his hat and revealed a bald pate and a fringe of long, lank hair.

'I'm Cap'n Hugh Orwig, master of the whaling barque *Altair* homeward bound towards Milford,' the man said in a rush, waving aside any introductions Drinkwater might have felt propriety compelled him to offer, 'you'll be after news of the Yankee frigate.'

'What Yankee frigate?' Drinkwater asked sharply.

'You ain't chasing a Yankee frigate?'

'Not specifically, but if you've news of one at large . . ..'

'News, Cap'n? Bloody hell, I've news for you, aye, all of you,' he nodded at the semi-circle of gold epaulettes that caught the sunshine as they drew closer.

'I heard yesterday, from a Portuguese brig, that a big Yankee frigate has taken the *Java*, British frigate . . .'

'Stap me . . .' An explosion of incredulity behind him caused Drinkwater to turn and glare at his subordinates.

'The *Java*, you say . . .?' He could not place the ship.

'A former Frenchman, sir,' Ashby said smoothly, 'formerly the *Renommée*, taken off Madagascar in May, the year before last, by Captain Schomberg's squadron. I believe Lambert to have been in command.'

'Thank you, Captain Ashby.' Drinkwater returned to Orwig. 'D'you know the name of the American frigate?'

'No, sir, but I don't think she was the same as took the *Macedonian*.'

'What's that you say? The *Macedonian*'s been taken too?'

'Aye, Cap'n, didn't you know? I fell in with another Milford ship, the *Martha*, Cap'n Raynes; cruising for Sperm we were, off Martin Vaz, and he told me the *Macedonian* had been knocked to pieces by the *United States*, said the alarm had gone out there was a Yankee squadron at large . . .'

'God's bones!'

The sense of having been caught out laid its cold fingers round Drinkwater's heart. The American ships must have left from New York or Boston; they could have slipped past within a few miles of his own vessels! It was quite possible the Americans would attempt to combine their heavy frigates with a swarm of privateers, privateers with trained but surplus naval officers like Stewart and, perhaps, Lieutenant Tucker, to command them. It struck him that if such a thing occurred, the United States navy might quadruple itself at a stroke, greatly reducing the assumed superiority of the Royal Navy! The thought made his blood run cold and about him it had precipitated a buzz of angry reaction.

'When did this happen?' he heard Ashby asking Orwig.

'Sometime in October, I think. Off the Canaries, Raynes said,' Orwig replied, adding in a surprised tone, 'I thought you gennelmen would have knowed.'

'No, sir, we did not know.' Ashby's tone was icily accusatory, levelled at Drinkwater as though, in condemning his superior officer for glaring into one crystal ball, he had failed to divine the truth in another, and taking Drinkwater's silence for bewilderment.

'Well, we know now,' Drinkwater said, rounding on them, 'and the India fleet is all the more in need of our protection.'

Quilhampton caught his attention; the first lieutenant's face was twisted with anxiety and apprehension.

'You'll be seekin' convoy, Captain Orwig?' Drinkwater enquired.

Orwig nodded, then shook his head. 'You'll not be able to spare it, Cap'n, not if the Yankees are as good as they seem and you've the India fleet to consider. Leadenhall Street will not forgive you if you lose them their annual profit.'

Drinkwater had no need to contemplate the consequences of the displeasure of the Court of Directors of the Honourable East India Company. 'And you, Captain,' he said, warming to the elderly man's consideration, 'how long did it take *you* to fill your barrels?'

'Three years, sir, an' in all three oceans.'

'Then you shall have convoy, sir, and my hand upon it. I would not have you or your company end a three-year voyage in American hands. Captain Tyrell . . .'

'Sir?' Tyrell stepped forward.

'I will write you out orders in a few moments, the sense of which will be to take Captain Orwig, and such other British merchantmen as you may sight, under your protection and convoy them to Milford Haven and then Plymouth. You will take also my dispatches and there await the instructions of their Lordships. Please take this opportunity to discuss details with Captain Orwig.' Drinkwater ignored the astonished look on Tyrell's face and addressed Ashby, Thorowgood and Sundercombe. 'Return to your ships, if you please, gentlemen. We will proceed as we agreed the moment I have written Captain Tyrell's orders. Your servant, gentlemen; Captain Orwig, a safe passage; Captain Tyrell, I'd be obliged if you'd wait upon me when you have concluded your business with Orwig.'

In his cabin Drinkwater drew pen, ink and paper towards him and wrote furiously for twenty minutes. He first addressed a brief report of proceedings to the Admiralty, stating he had reason to believe a force of privateers was loose in the South Atlantic. That much, insubstantial as it was in fact, yet justified the detachment of *Hasty*. Next he wrote to his wife, enclosing the missive with his private letter to Lord Dungarth to whom he gave vent to his concern over an American frigate squadron supported by private auxiliaries operating on the British trade routes. He was completing this last when Tyrell knocked and came in.

'Sit down, Tyrell, help yourself to another glass, I shall be with you directly.'

'Captain Drinkwater, I don't wish to appear importunate . . .'

'Then don't, my dear fellow,' said Drinkwater, looking up as he sanded the last sheet and stifling Tyrell's protest. 'Now listen, I want you to deliver this letter to Lord Dungarth when you call on the Admiralty. It is for his hand only, and if you fail to find his Lordship at the Admiralty, you are to wait upon him at his residence in Lord North Street; d'you understand?'

'Yes.'

'Good.' Drinkwater rose, handed over the papers and extended his right hand. 'Good luck, and don't get yourself taken if you can help it.'

Drinkwater saw, from the sudden widening of Tyrell's eyes, that he had not, until that moment, considered the possibility.

'Well, Wyatt, what d'you make of the news?' Frey asked as the officers sat over their wine and the *Patrician* heeled to the gathering south-easterly breeze which promised to be the long-sought trade wind.

'The American ships were lucky. I expect their gunners were British deserters. It wouldn't have happened ten years ago . . .'

'I don't mean the American victories, Wyatt, I mean the effect their being at sea has on the safety of the East Indiamen, something you were prepared to regard as . . .'

'Don't resurrect old arguments, Mr Frey,' Simpson cautioned. 'Let sleeping dogs lie.'

'Oh ye of little faith,' Frey said, throwing the remark at the master, who buried his nose in his slopping tankard.

On the deck above Drinkwater dozed in his cot. Orwig's news was worrying. He had felt as though someone had punched him in the belly earlier, such was its impact. The latitude allowed in discretionary orders could hang an officer if he made the wrong decision more certainly than it could bring him success. There were so many options open, but only one which could be taken up. He dulled his anxiety with half a bottle of blackstrap and then settled to think the matter over. Yet the more he worried at the problem, the more convinced he was of the rightness of his decision, despite its unorthodox roots.

The logic of the thing was inescapable; as he had said to Quilhampton and repeated in substance to Dungarth, it was not only what he would have done himself had he been in Stewart's shoes, but what he would do if given President Madison's choices. Over and over he turned the thing until he dozed off in his chair. After some fifteen minutes the empty wine glass slipped from his fingers and the crash of its breaking woke him with a start.

The sudden shock made his heart pound, the wine made his head ache and his mouth felt foul. He rubbed his face, grinding his knuckles into his eyes. Bright scarlet and yellow flashes danced before him.

'God's bones!' he exclaimed, leaping to his feet and striking his head a numbing blow on the deck beams above. He sank back into his chair, his hands over his skull, feeling the bruise rising. 'God damn and blast it,' he muttered through clenched teeth, 'was I dreaming, or not?'

Mullender looked in from the pantry and smartly withdrew. Captain Drinkwater's antics seemed scarcely normal, but Mullender knew personal survival for men in his station largely depended on feigned indifference.

'I *was* dreaming,' Drinkwater continued to himself, 'but it wasn't a phantasm.' He sat up, dropping his hands from his head and staring straight before him, seeing not the bulkhead, but a glimpse of a room through a gap in heavy brocaded curtains and a litter of papers spread about an escritoire.

Had Mullender chosen this moment to enquire after the well-being of his master, he would have thought him stark, staring mad, but Captain Nathaniel Drinkwater had never been saner in his life.

PART THREE
A Furious Aside

'O miserable advocates! In the name of God, what was done with this immense superiority of force?'

'Oh, what a charm is hereby dissolved! What hopes, will be excited in the breasts of our enemies!'

The Times,
London,
27 and 29 December 1812

The Admiralty *December 1812*

Lord Dungarth set down the stained paper he had been reading and rose from the desk, heaving himself on to the crutch which bent under his weight. The reflection of his gross figure in the uncurtained window disgusted him momentarily, until he was close enough to the glass to peer through.

Below, the carriage lights in Whitehall threw their glimmering illumination on streaks of sleeting rain that threatened to turn to snow before the night had ended. He raised his eyes above the roof-tops and gazed at the night sky. Dark clouds streaked across, permitting the occasional glimpse of a pair of stars.

The vision of his long-dead wife's face formed itself around the distant stars, then cloud obscured her image and he saw only the pale hemisphere of his own bald and reflected head. The onset of the pain overwhelmed him; the attacks were more frequent now, more intense, like the pains of labour as the moment of crisis approached. He seemed to shrink on his crutch, diminished in size as death sapped at his very being.

The pain ebbed and ceased to be an overwhelming preoccupation, he was aware of the stink of his own fearful sweat. Slowly he turned and began the long haul back to his desk. He slumped into his creaking chair and with a shaking hand, reached for the decanter. He had given up hiding the laudanum and, with a carelessly shaking hand, added half a dozen drops to the *oporto*.

Sipping the concoction, he half-closed his eyes, trying to recapture the vision of his countess, but instead there came before his mind's eye a picture of gunfire and dismasted ships: the *Guerrière*, the *Macedonian*, with more to follow, he felt certain, the imminence of death and the opiate lending him prescience, an awareness of approaching bad tidings.

And yet . . .

His hand reached out tremulously, seeking the travelstained dispatch in its curious, runic cipher. He had thought, too, that disaster and defeat were inevitable from that quarter after the news of the Russians' abandonment of Moscow following the battle at Borodino.

But now . . .

He frowned with the effort of focusing on the piece of paper. He was so used to the cryptography, he needed no key to decode it, but read the words as if they headlined a broadsheet: *French army have abandoned Moscow. Line of retreat dictated by Russian pursuit. Attacks to be mounted at their crossing of the Beresina . . .*

Lord Dungarth looked up at the dark window. The sleet had turned to snow. The secret dispatch was already a month old.

'At last,' he whispered as the pain gathered itself again and he drained the glass.

Chapter Sixteen *January–February 1813*

The Dogs of War

It was high summer in the southern hemisphere, day after day of blue skies dusted with fair-weather cumulus. Sunlight sparkled off the sapphire seas and the wavecaps broke into rainbows as they tumbled. For a week the squadron tacked wearily to windward. Gulls, petrels and frigate birds rode the invisible air currents disturbed by their passage, amusing the bored lookouts who saw nothing beyond the topgallants of the ships on either flank, though the visibility was as far as the eye could see. A sense of futility was borne in upon them all with their growing comprehension of the vastness of the ocean.

In the wardroom, grumbling and criticism accompanied every meal and even the inhabitants of the lower deck, whose burden was at its lightest in such prime sailing conditions, were permeated by a gloom begun by the news of the three British frigate defeats, and daily worsened with their frustration at discovering no sail upon the broad bosom of the South Atlantic.

As for Drinkwater himself, he endured the loneliness and isolation of his position by withdrawing into himself. Even Quilhampton's diligent and loyal support seemed less enthusiastic, a remnant of past friendship, rather than the whole-hearted support of the present. Quilhampton was friendly with Frey, Drinkwater noted, supposing them both to be presuming on long acquaintanceship and discussing his own descent into madness.

Perhaps he was going mad. The thought occurred to him repeatedly. Loneliness and guilt combined to make his mood vacillate so that he might, had Pym known it, be set fair to become a subject for the worthy surgeon's treatise on the pendular personality. On the one hand his metaphysical preoccupations saw the quest he had set the squadron upon as a cogent consequence of all that had occurred at Castle Point. On the other loomed the awful spectre of a mighty misjudgement, a spectre made more terrible by the ominous threat explicit in the wording of his commission: *you may fail as you will answer at your peril.*

He became unable to sleep properly, his cabin a prison, so that he preferred to doze on deck, wrapped in his cloak and jammed in the familiar place by the weather mizen rigging. As the watches changed, the officers merely nodded at the solitary figure whose very presence betrayed his anxiety and further amplified the depression of their own spirits.

And yet they knew, for all its interminable nature, that such a state of affairs could not go on for ever. One morning, an hour after dawn when the squadron had tacked, reversed the consequent echelon of its advance, and sent the lookouts aloft, the hail from the masthead swept aside the prevailing mood:

'Deck there! *Icarus*'s let fly her t'garn sheets!'

'A fleet in sight!' Frey said with unnatural loudness, rounding on the figure standing by the larboard mizen pinrail. 'The India fleet?'

'Pray to God it is,' someone muttered.

'Mr Belchambers,' Frey said curtly, 'get a long glass aloft. Mr Davies, rouse the watch, stand by the main t'gallant sheets and let 'em fly, and Mr Belchambers . . .'

The midshipman paused in the lower riggin. 'Sir?'

'Make sure *Cymbeline* has seen and acknowledged our repetition.'

'Aye, aye, sir,' Belchambers acknowledged, his reply verging on the irritated, as though weary of being told how to suck eggs. Frey ignored the insubordinate tone and approached Drinkwater, who had detached himself from support and, dopey with fatigue, his face grey, stubbled and red-eyed, stumbled before the circulation returned properly to his legs.

'Thorowgood may have trouble seeing us, sir, in this light.'

'You have a talent for stating the obvious this morning,' snapped Drinkwater testily, 'let us see what Ashby does.'

Frey bit his lip and raised his speaking trumpet. 'Mr Belchambers!' he roared at the midshipman who paused, hanging down at the main upper futtocks. 'Get a move on, boy!'

As the morning advanced ship after ship hove over the southern horizon, the unmistakable sight of laden Indiamen running before the favourable trade wind. Far ahead of them they watched as Ashby's *Icarus* beat up towards a small, brig-rigged sloop-of-war, which was crowding on sail to intercept and identify the first of what must have seemed to her commander to be a naval squadron of potentially overwhelming force.

From aloft Belchambers passed a running commentary to the quarterdeck. 'Eighteen sail, sir . . . The escort's a brig-sloop, sir . . . looks to have a jury main topmast. No other escort in sight, but I can see *Sprite* coming up from the south-west, sir . . .'

'What of *Cymbeline*?' Frey roared.

They saw Belchambers swivel round. 'She's coming up fast, sir, stun's'ls set alow and aloft!'

'I can see her from the deck, Mr Frey,' Drinkwater remarked.

After the private signals had been exchanged, the *Icarus* wore round in the brig's wake and the two men-of-war ran alongside each other. The brig then veered away from the thirty-two and the men now crowding *Patrician*'s deck saw her run down towards them.

'Heave to, if you please, Mr Frey,' Drinkwater ordered, rubbing his chin. 'I'm going below for a shave.'

'Aye, aye, sir,' Frey replied, grinning at the captain's retreating back. The sight of the East Indiamen, splendid symbols of their country's maritime might, transformed the morale of the *Patrician*. Idlers and men of the watch below had turned out to see the marvellous panorama; Frey could forgive the cross-patch Drinkwater, even provoke a grudging acknowledgement of his misjudgement from Mr Wyatt.

'Told you so, Wyatt,' Frey muttered, reaching for the speaking trumpet beside the master.

'You're right – for once.'

Frey grinned and raised the megaphone: 'Stand by the chess trees and catheads! Clew garnets and buntlines there! Rise tacks and sheets!'

'Three ships, you say, Lieutenant?' Drinkwater handed a glass to the young officer from the brig-of-war *Sparrowhawk*.

'Aye, sir, in two attacks . . .'

'And the last when?'

'The day before yesterday, sir. If the wind had been lighter we would have lost more, sir. As it was the India Johnnies gave a good account of themselves. We did our best but . . .' The young officer gestured hopelessly.

'You were outsailed by Yankee schooners.'

'Exactly so. Beg pardon, but how did you know, sir?'

'Intuition, Lieutenant . . .'

'Wykeham, sir.'

'Well, Lieutenant Wykeham, return to Captain Sudbury and tell him we shall do our best to assist you. Your ship is wounded?'

'Aye, sir, we lost the main topmast. One of those confounded Americans had a long gun, barbette-mounted amidships on a traversing carriage. She shot the stick clean out of us and hulled us badly. We lost four men with that one shot alone.'

'How many of them, enemy schooners, I mean?' Drinkwater wiped a hand across his face as if to remove his weariness.

'Six, sir,'

'Any sign of a frigate?'

'An American frigate? No, sir.'

Drinkwater grunted. 'Does Captain Sudbury anticipate another attack?'

'I don't think so, sir. We gave them a bloody nose last time. One of them was definitely hulled and with her rigging knocked about.'

'It doesn't occur to you that the hiatus may be due solely to their effecting repairs to that schooner?'

It had clearly not occurred to either Lieutenant Wykeham or his young commander, Sudbury.

'Young men are too often optimists, Mr Wykeham.' Drinkwater paused, letting this piece of homespun wisdom sink in. 'I have already given my squadron written orders as to their dispositions upon meeting with you. I think you had better cover the van of the convoy. Tell Captain Sudbury to act as he sees fit in the event of another attack, to throw out his routine convoy signals as has been his practice to date. My squadron will act according to their orders. However, I shall not condemn him if he gets his ship into action with one of these fellows. Tell him to aim high, langridge and bar shot, I think, if you have it, otherwise the galley pots and the carpenter's best nails, cripple' em, clip their confounded wings, Lieutenant, for they are better flyers then we.'

'Very well, sir.'

'By-the-by, in which direction did they retire?'

'To the east, sir, that is why we were . . .'

'To the east of the convoy, yes, yes, I understand. You had better return to your ship. Tell Captain Sudbury he is under my orders now and I relieve him of the chief responsibility, but I expect him to carry on as normal, entirely as normal, d'you see? Perhaps we may deceive the enemy, if he returns, into not noticing our presence until it is too late. D'you understand me?'

'Very well, sir.'

After the young man had gone, Drinkwater turned and stared astern. The sea, so lately empty of anything but his own squadron, was crowded with the black hulls and towering white sails of the Honourable East India Company's ships. Craning round, he could just see *Cymbeline* making her way to the windward station. Ashby should be doing the same on the other wing. Once Wykeham's boat had gone, *Patrician* must take up her own position.

There was no American frigate; not yet, anyway, Drinkwater mused. On the other hand, Wykeham had informed him that the last ship to be lost was the Indiaman *Kenilworth Castle* and she had been carrying a fortune in specie.

It cost Drinkwater no great effort to imagine Captain Sudbury's mortification at losing three such valuable ships to the enemy; he had once been in the same position himself.*

In the right circumstances Indiamen could, and had, given the enemy a thrashing. An unescorted convoy of them under Commodore Nathaniel Dance had manoeuvred like men-of-war and driven off a marauding squadron of French ships under Admiral Linois eight years earlier. Their batteries of cannon were effective enough, if well handled, but they could not outmanoeuvre swift gaff-schooners stuffed with men spoiling to tweak the lion's tail and seize rich prizes to boot. During the following day Drinkwater pored over his charts, trying to divine what Stewart intended, for he was convinced Stewart commanded this aggressive group of letters-of-marque.

Stewart would come back, that much was certain, like a pack of hounds baying for more meat once the smell of blood was in their nostrils, but with one of his vessels damaged and three rich prizes to shepherd to safety.

*See *A Private Revenge*.

Drinkwater considered the alternatives open to the enemy. Manning the prizes would not prove a problem. The privateers would have a surplus of men, indeed they signed on extra hands for the purpose, engaging prizemasters in anticipation of a profitable cruise. In all likelihood Stewart would gamble on another attack, cut out what he could, and then return triumphantly to the Chesapeake.

Drinkwater could recapture the *Kenilworth Castle* off the Virginia capes, but to act on that assumption would be dangerous. Now that he had encountered the convoy he could not so easily abandon it. Yet he was prepared to wager that if another attack was mounted it would argue cogently in favour of his theory; and if events fell out in this fashion a spirited pursuit had a good chance of recovering the lost ships.

It was true Baltimore clippers could outsail a heavy frigate, but the same frigate could outsail a laden Indiaman, and even a two-day start would make little difference.

'Sentry!' The marine's head peered round the door. 'Pass word for the midshipman of the watch.'

When Porter's red face appeared, Drinkwater said, 'Make *Sprite*'s number and have her close us.'

'Messages, sir?'

'Just so, Mr Porter.'

'Aye, aye, sir.'

Drawing pen, paper and ink towards him he began to draft new orders to his squadron.

Drinkwater's judgement proved uncannily accurate. Five jagged pairs of sails broke the eastern horizon two hours before sunset, an hour and a half after *Sprite* had delivered the last packet to *Cymbeline*. Thorowgood threw out the alarm signal without firing a warning gun, which proved he had digested his orders on receipt. *Patrician* had not yet made the acknowledgement before her marine drummer was beating to quarters and she was edging out of line, skittering laterally across the rear of the convoy, as, far ahead, Sudbury's little *Sparrowhawk* fired a warning gun and signalled the convoy to turn away from the threat. With luck, Drinkwater calculated, he could close the distance between himself and the point of attack as he had outlined to Wykeham. If he could trap any of the privateers within the convoy, hamper their manoeuvrability, he might . . .

He felt his heart thump uncomfortably in his chest. Already the sun was westering. He hoped the Americans could not see too well against the brilliant path it laid upon the sea . . .

'Steady, steady as you go,' Wyatt intoned, standing beside the men at the wheel, gauging distances as they lifted to a scending sea and threatened to overrun the plodding Indiaman, the *Indus*, upon whose quarter they sought to hide until the privateers singled out their quarry and struck. Two officers on the Indiaman's quarter-deck were regarding them, their attention clearly divided between the following frigate and the predatory Americans on their opposite bow. Wyatt turned to Drinkwater: 'We're overhauling, sir . . .'

'Let fly a weather sheet, or two. I want to cross under this fellow's stern in a moment, not across his bow.'

'Aye, aye, sir. Ease the fore an' main tops'l sheets there!'

'And start the foresheet . . .'

'Aye, aye, sir.'

It took a few moments for the adjustments to take effect, then *Patrician* slowed appreciably.

'What's Thorowgood doing, James, can you see him?'

Quilhampton was up on the rail, telescope levelled and braced against a shroud. 'Aye, sir. He's tucked in behind the *Lord Mornington* . . .' With his one hand Quilhampton deftly swivelled his glass at the schooners. 'They don't suspect a damned thing yet.'

'Perhaps they can't count.' Drinkwater looked at the setting sun. The privateers' strategy of attacking from the east allowed them to escape into the darkness, and silhouetted their victims against the sunset, but it made precise identification tricky. He hoped his frigates might be lost amid the convoy and thus steal a march upon the brash predators. The sooner they were occupied by the business of capture, the sooner he could attack.

From somewhere ahead a ragged broadside rumbled out.

'Deck there,' Belchambers hailed from his action station in the main-top, 'Indiaman has opened fire.'

'Can you see the *Sparrowhawk*?' Drinkwater called, levelling his own glass at the mass of sails ahead of them. Sudbury's little brig must be five or six miles away.

'Yes, sir, she's on the wind, starboard tack, just ahead of the eastern column.'

It was this column which was under attack and Sudbury was doing what was expected of him, attempting to cover his flank. His puny aggression was, however, being ignored by the Americans. The two leading schooners, the stars and bars streaming from their main peaks, huge pennants bearing the words *Free trade and sailors' rights* flying from their mastheads, were coming down fast upon the third ship in the column, the *Lady Lennox*.

All the Indiamen in the eastern column were firing now, filling the air with dense clouds of powder smoke which trailed along with the ships, driven, like them, by the following wind. The approaching schooners shortened the range with the rapidity of swooping falcons, leaving alongside their respective wakes an impotent colonnade of water-plumes from plunging shot.

'Down helm, Mr Wyatt, let us try to keep those fellows in sight.'

In obedience to Drinkwater's order *Patrician*'s head swung slowly to starboard. From the quarterdeck the end of her jib boom seemed to rake the taffrail of the *Indus* as the heavy frigate edged out from the column of Indiamen.

'Haul aft those sheets,' Wyatt was calling. 'Steady there, steady . . .'

'Set stuns'ls, if you please, Mr Wyatt, and bring us back to the convoy's course,' Drinkwater ordered, keeping his voice measured, fighting the rising tension within.

With all her sails drawing again, *Patrician* increased her speed and began to overhaul the *Indus* on a parallel heading. Beyond the Indiamen and taking his cue from Drinkwater, Captain Thorowgood followed suit. *Cymbeline* made sail past the *Lord Mornington*, which ceased her own fire, and both frigates, in line ahead, the *Cymbeline* leading, bore down upon the enemy schooners, partially hidden in the pall of smoke drifting in dense wraiths about the convoy .

This smoke, which half-concealed their approach, also masked their quarry from them. The last glimpse Drinkwater had caught of the privateers had revealed the most advanced of the pair slipping under their chosen victim's stern preparatory to ranging up on the *Lady Lennox*'s port side, while her confederate did the same on the starboard beam.

The boom of a heavy gun floated over the water and Drinkwater recalled Wykeham's report of a traversing cannon mounted amidships in one of the schooners. The moment to press his carefully planned counter-attack had arrived.

He swung around. The remaining three corsairs were in the clear air to windward and astern of them, working round to the southward of the convoy.

'Where's *Sprite*?' he asked Quilhampton.

'There, sir!' Quilhampton pointed. In a gap between two Indiamen Drinkwater caught a glimpse of the British schooner beating up to place herself between three ships and the convoy. Sundercombe carried his little vessel into action with an apparent contempt for the odds against him.

'And there's *Icarus*!' Ashby's frigate was in silhouette. Only her foreshortening against the sunset as she swung identified her as a warship. Even as Drinkwater watched, the bulk of the *Lord Mornington* interposed itself as they swept past. He would have to depend upon Ashby's steadiness in support of Sundercombe to guard the convoy's rear.

'*Cymbeline*'s coming up alongside the outboard schooner, sir!' Quilhampton reported, his voice shrill with excitement, and Drinkwater whirled round.

They had dropped the *Lord Mornington* astern and were almost up with the *Windsor*, the East India Company ship next ahead of her and directly astern of the *Lady Lennox*. The *Windsor* was hauling her yards, a row of white-shirted lascars straining at the braces clearly visible, as she pulled to port to avoid the fracas erupting under her bow. She was also still firing her guns and these presented a greater threat to the overtaking *Patrician* than to the low, rakish schooners grappling her sister-ship ahead.

'Cease fire, damn you!' Drinkwater roared at the offending Company officers who turned in astonishment at the apparition looming out of the smoke astern. They must have been aware of *Cymbeline* overtaking them, but had clearly not seen *Patrician* coming up hand over fist in her wake.

'God damn, we've got 'em!' shouted Quilhampton jubilantly, dancing a jig on the rail and bringing a laugh from the men at the wheel and the quarterdeck guns whose comprehension of events was as confused as that of the officers of the *Windsor*. Drinkwater drew himself up in the mizen rigging to get a better view. The pall of smoke rolled slowly along with them, lifting like fog, but at sea-level it was clear and he could see the hull of yet another Indiaman, her name blazoned in gold letters across her stern below the windows of the great cabin which reflected the glory of the sunset: *Lady Lennox*. A schooner was fast to either of her sides like hounds on a stag's flanks, except that the privateer on the Indiaman's starboard beam was crushed between *Cymbeline*'s hull, and boarders were pouring down the frigate's tumblehome like a human torrent, the air full of their shouts and the spitfire flashes of small arms.

Even as Thorowgood's men scrambled down the side of their frigate to board the schooner, men from the second schooner to port were boarding the Indiaman.

'Mr Moncrieff!'

'Sir?'

'Your men to open fire on those boarders.'

'Aye, aye sir!'

'What is it?' Drinkwater addressed Midshipman Porter, redder than usual from his run up from below.

'Mr Frey says the guns won't depress enough to hit the enemy, sir.

'Boarders, Mr Porter, through the gun ports as soon as we're alongside.'

Beside him Moncrieff's marines jostled, levelling their muskets on the hammocks in the nettings, drawing back the hammers and flicking the frizzens. The air crackled with the vicious sputter of musketry and the solider boom of cannon as somewhere forward, in defiance of the laws of ballistics, several guns were fired. Amid the smoke and racket, Wyatt, Quilhampton, Moncrieff and Drinkwater bawled their orders as *Patrician* ranged up alongside her quarry.

'Douse the stuns'ls . . . rig in the booms and look lively there!'

'Steady, steady as you go . . .'

'Another point to starboard, Mr Wyatt, if you please. Crush 'em, damn it, and don't overrun her!'

'Aye, aye, sir!'

Drinkwater looked up, gauging the diminishing distance, before *Patrician*'s bulk sandwiched the Yankee schooner against the *Lady Lennox*. At the Indiamen's stern an American officer was hacking at the ensign halliards, the last rays of the sun flashing on the sword blade. He looked up, suddenly aware the ship bearing down on them from astern was not another Indiaman, as he had supposed, but a second British frigate. Drinkwater could clearly see him turn and bellow something, he even thought he caught the noise of his order above the shouts and screams and clash of steel. Moncrieff had seen the man too.

'Marine!' he bellowed, his face distorted by excitement, 'Hit that bastard beside the ensign halliards!'

'Yessir!'

There was a crash which sent a tremor through the *Patrician* as the big frigate's starboard bow drove into the larboard quarter of the American schooner and she ground her way past. The ebb and flow of men upon the *Lady Lennox* where American, Briton, Lascar and Chinaman contended for the deck in a dozen desperate fights, seemed to freeze for a brief moment as the impact of the *Patrician*'s arrival made them stagger.

Into this mêlée Moncrieff's marines poured a withering fire. Drinkwater saw the man at the Indiaman's ensign halliards drop his sword, spin round and fall from sight. Men began sliding down the *Lady Lennox*'s side, Americans, Drinkwater guessed, trying to regain their own ship. Beyond the *Lady Lennox*'s farther rail, the bulk of the *Cymbeline* dominated the second schooner, invisible to Drinkwater's summary gaze. He looked down. The deck of the crushed schooner lay exposed, the caulking worming from her sprung deck planking, the long gun on its traversing mounting jammed as its crew fought to swing it round at the *Patrician*. With a thunderous crash the main and fore chain-whales gave way under the compression of the *Patrician*'s hull and the schooner's masts came down, a mass of spars, sails and cordage which obscured the marines' targets and hid the unfortunate Americans from their vengeful enemies.

From the gun ports below, like imps of hell intent on some terrible harvest, dark shapes in the gathering shadows, the gun-crews squeezed through, dropping on to the schooner's decks. They rooted under the canvas with their pikes, savagely pitch forking at every movement in a wild catharsis of relief after weeks of fruitless cruising, venting pent-up emotions and repressed urges in an orgy of licensed butchery so that the schooner's deck assumed the bloody aspect of an ampitheatre of death.

The sight revolted Drinkwater and he picked up a speaking trumpet.

'D'you strike there?' he shouted, 'Strike, sir, and put an end to this madness!'

A man, an officer by his torn blue coat and brass buttons that gleamed dully in the fading light, fought his way clear of the encumbering bunt of the huge mainsail and waved his hand. It was covered with blood which fell upon the canvas beside him. Drinkwater recognized him as the man who had, a few moments earlier, been on the point of hauling down the *Lady Lennox*'s ensign. Somehow he had regained his own deck under Moncrieff's murderous fire.

'Hold your fire, Moncrieff. Cease fire there, cease fire!'

The officer on the deck below him staggered and Drinkwater realized the schooner was sinking beneath his feet.

'Mr Q,' he called, 'have a boat lowered. Mr Davies is to take the survivors off, and pass word to the surgeon to expect some badly wounded. Mr Porter, recall your gunners before they lose their heads completely.' He raised the speaking trumpet again. '*Lady Lennox* 'hoy!'

An officer in the panoply of the Honourable East India Company appeared at the rail. 'Have you suffered much?' Drinkwater enquired.

'A score or so killed and twice as many wounded, mostly lascars and coolies, sir,' the officer said dismissively. 'We took round shot through the hull, but we can plug the holes.' Drinkwater recalled the heavy traversing cannon now hidden under the wrecked top-hamper of the schooner.

'What's the news from the starboard side?' Drinkwater called.

'Much the same. Your frigate's hauling off with the enemy secured alongside. My commander, Captain Barnard, presents his compliments and his deepest sense of obligation to you, sir, and desires to know your name.'

'My respects to Captain Barnard, sir,' Drinkwater replied. 'My name is Drinkwater, Nathaniel Drinkwater, and I am glad to be of service.'

'You have saved the Company a fortune, Captain Drinkwater.'

'I am glad to hear it .

'I know that man,' Moncrieff's voice suddenly announced, cutting through the calm that followed the surrender and the exchange between Drinkwater and the *Lady Lennox*'s officer. 'That fellow staring up at us; he was in the Potomac.'

Distracted, Drinkwater looked down again. The officer with the shattered hand was swaying, the stain of blood on the canvas beside him spreading darkly.

'God's bones,' Drinkwater blasphemed, 'get him aboard at once. It's Tucker!'

Chapter Seventeen *February 1813*

The Flying Squadron

'Who commands you?' Drinkwater asked. Ashen-faced, Lieutenant Tucker lolled in the chair, eyes closed, panting with pain. His roughly bandaged hand with a tourniquet above the wrist lay across his breast. Quilhampton stood anxiously at his shoulder.

It was growing dark in the cabin and other matters clamoured for attention as night fell. 'Come, sir, answer. You may see the surgeon the moment you have told me what I want to know. Who commands you?'

Eyes closed, Tucker shook his head. Drinkwater and Quilhampton exchanged glances. 'It's Stewart, isn't it, eh? Captain Stewart?' Drinkwater raised his voice, cutting through the fog of agony clouding Tucker's consciousness, 'late of the *Stingray*.'

Tucker's eyes flickered open; the small affirmative was enough for Drinkwater. 'Is there a frigate with you?'

There was no doubt, even in his befuddled state, of Tucker's surprise. 'Frigate . . .' he murmured, adding a second word that Drinkwater failed to catch.

'What did he say?'

'Didn't hear, sir, answered Quilhampton, bending over the prisoner.

'Come, sir, you're a damned pirate. You ain't a naval officer and can't expect exchange in a cartel. Answer me and I'll do my best to see you aren't thrown into Dartmoor Gaol. In the meantime you need the services of my surgeon. Is there a frigate in the offing? An American frigate?'

Something like comprehension passed a shadow over Tucker's face, he moved on the chair, tried to draw himself upright, shook his head and muttered, 'Not an American . . .'

'He said, "Not an American . . ."'

'I heard him, James . . . A French frigate, then? Is that it? There's a French frigate to the eastward?'

Tucker's face crumpled, he closed his eyes tightly, and sank into the chair. The bandages wrapped around his stump were sodden with blood.

'Good God!' Drinkwater ran a hand through his hair, ' 'Tis worse than I thought . . .' He looked up at Quilhampton. 'James, I'll stake my hat the lost Indiamen and a French frigate are to the eastward . . . I'll have to explain later. Be a good fellow and see to Tucker here.'

'I'll get him below, sir . . .'

'No, he's a brave fellow, we'll spare him the indignity of Pym's cockpit. Have Pym operate on him here.'

Drinkwater stood for a moment beside the wounded American and put a hand on his shoulder. 'You've betrayed nothing, Mr Tucker, I assure you, merely confirmed my suspicions. Mr Quilhampton will attend to you, he knows what it's like to lose a hand. Give him some laudanum, James, I fear I've used him barbarously.'

Running on deck Drinkwater cast a quick look about him. Night was upon them. The convoy was to the north-north-west, etched black against the last gleam of twilight. Both *Patrician* and *Cymbeline* had detached themselves from the convoy and lay hove-to in its wake. All that remained of the schooner *Patrician* had crushed was some wreckage, dark debris on the grey surface of the ocean. Thorowgood was busy putting a prize-crew aboard the other which, a master's mate in one of *Cymbeline*'s boats was just then reporting to Lieutenant Gordon, had proved to be the *Shark* of Baltimore.

'Tell Captain Thorowgood to rejoin the convoy with *Sprite* and his prize,' Drinkwater called down to the boat, 'I'm going in pursuit.'

Ashby and Sundercombe had ably covered the convoy's rear. Discovering the force against them, the remaining privateers had not pressed their attack. They were making off in the darkness to windward as fast as they could with *Icarus* in lagging pursuit and *Sprite* hard on their heels, white blurs in the gathering night. Drinkwater waved the boat off and rounded on Wyatt.

'Set the stuns'ls, Mr Wyatt, and lay me a course to the eastward.'

'The eastward, sir?' Wyatt stared at the dull gleam of *Icarus*'s battle lantern to the southward.

'Yes, damn you, the *eastward*. Mr Gordon, make to *Icarus* and *Sprite*: discontinue the chase. The night signal, if you please.'

'Aye, aye, sir.'

Quilhampton hauled himself wearily up the quarterdeck ladder. He was aware he had misjudged Drinkwater.

'Well, James,' Drinkwater said briskly, 'I'm setting the kites.'

'You're going in pursuit, sir?' Quilhampton threw a bewildered look at the disparate heading of the schooners and *Patrician*. Wyatt gave a mighty shrug. Drinkwater laughed. His spirits were soaring. 'I'm after bigger fish than those minnows, James . . .'

'Tucker's frigate?'

'Tucker's frigate.'

'You're certain of her being there?'

'As certain of anything in this perilous life, James.'

'Sometime, sir, you might oblige me with an explanation.'

Drinkwater laughed again. 'The moment I'm proved right.' Tiredness and then the exhilaration of the last hours had raised Drinkwater's morale to a pitch of almost unbearable anticipation. 'Is Tucker being attended to?' he asked, in an attempt to recapture the dignity consonant with his rank.

'He's under Pym's knife at the moment, sir.'

'Pym's a good surgeon and Tucker looked to have the constitution of an ox.'

'Very well.'

The formal, non-commital response might have described them all. They had done very well. He was ridiculously pleased he had harangued his captains. It was perhaps fortunate that their gunnery had not been tested, that they had confronted nothing more than privateers, but they had manoeuvred like veterans and he must remember to say so in his report to their Lordships. The escaping schooners were unlikely to return to harry the convoy; they had been thoroughly frightened. Guile and skilful ship-handling had brought the British a local ascendancy. Now, Drinkwater mused, they must hold the advantage surprise had conferred.

'Mr Wyatt!' Drinkwater beckoned to the master and he crossed the deck, expecting a rebuke. 'You did very well, Mr Wyatt. The ship was handled with perfect precision.'

'Thank you, sir,' Wyatt said smugly.

'I may need your skill again before dawn, Mr Wyatt. I am in quest of a frigate . . .'

'A frigate . . .?' Wyatt's tone was incredulous in the dark.

'Not an American frigate, you'll be pleased to hear,' Drinkwater said ironically, 'at least, I hope not . . .' He was interrupted by a hail from the maintop:

'Deck there! I can see fire, fire on the larboard bow!'

'Ah,' sighed Drinkwater, 'ease the helm a half-point, Mr Wyatt. James, pipe up spirits, and then send the men back to their stations.'

An hour later they were approaching the source of the fire with every man at his station, and under fighting sails.

'Ease the helm another point, Mr Wyatt. Let us drop a little to loo'ard and cut off their retreat.' The dull glow of the fire opened on the starboard bow, allowing a better view from the quarterdeck. Their approach, concealed by darkness, was slow enough for Drinkwater, studying the dispositions of a number of vessels clustered about and illuminated by the burning Indiaman, to deduce the gist of what was happening.

'They have very likely spent the day transhipping what they wanted out of the Indiaman they have fired,' he explained to Quilhampton, as both men stood side by side, their telescopes braced against the mizen rigging. 'You can see the schooner which was mauled by *Sparrowhawk* . . .'

'She's lying alongside another East India Company ship,' observed Quilhampton.

'It looks as though they used her mainyard as mast-sheers, they've got what looks like two handy spars back in that schooner already,' he said admiringly.

'There's another ship, looks like an Indiaman, though she could be your frigate, just to the left; d'you see?'

Drinkwater shifted his glass. 'Yes. They're waiting for the schooners to come back with another prize, I think. One of those two will be the *Kenilworth Castle*. She's carrying specie.'

'Didn't that Company Johnnie indicate the *Lennox* was similarly loaded?' Quilhampton asked, catching something of his commander's excitement.

'Indeed he did,' Drinkwater said with a sudden, tense deliberation which made Quilhampton lower his glass, look at Drinkwater and then smartly raise it again.

There was no mistaking the ship that now came into view. Hidden from them at first by the glow of the burning Indiaman, her lower hull was concealed, her tall masts indistinguishable behind the mass of the Indiaman's top-hamper up which the flames were now racing as the fire took a hold. The sudden flaring of the gigantic torch lit up all within its illuminating circle.

Quilhampton gave a low whistle. 'There's your French frigate, sir.'

Patrician was directly downwind of the group now, and a wave of warm air drifted towards them. A dull crackling roar could be heard, borne on the trade wind. The French frigate was hove to, like the Indiamen, under a backed main topsail, drifting slowly past the burning ship from which a cloud of sparks suddenly shot upwards. Concealed from the American and French allies busy at their mid-ocean rendezvous by the utter darkness beyond the range of their bonfire, *Patrician* slipped past unobserved, a mile to the north of them.

'I'm going about in a moment or two, gentlemen,' Drinkwater announced to the officers assembled on the quarterdeck. 'When I have done so we will engage the Frenchman from windward. Starboard battery to open fire. We shall have to watch that burning Indiaman, but his windage is being fast consumed and the others are making greater leeway, increasing the distance between them. I will then attempt to rake . . .'

'Sir!' Gordon was pointing; a moment later the concussion of cannon-fire rolled over the water.

'They've seen us . . .' someone said.

'No they haven't,' shouted Moncrieff, 'they're firing away from us . . .'

'What the devil . . .?'

'It isn't them firing, it's *Icarus*!'

'Hands to tack ship!' Drinkwater roared, 'By God we've got 'em! Take post, gentlemen, upon the instant if you please!'

There was a bustling aboard the *Patrician*, as the officers dispersed to their stations. The men, watching the conflagration in ordered silence, suddenly tensed. They were no longer observers, now they were to participate.

'Mainsail haul!' Wyatt shouted, 'Leggo and haul . . . haul aft the lee sheets, stretch those bowlines forrard now! Keep your eyes inboard and attend to your business!'

'*Icarus* must have mistaken your signal, sir.'

'Aye, we never thought to look astern in our conceit, did we?'

'I doubt we'd have seen her . . . there she is . . . she's got *Sprite* under her lee bow. Ashby must have assumed he was to follow us.'

'Perhaps it was no bad assumption and, damn it, I bet it fooled the buggers – the two of 'em look like a Yankee clipper and a captured Indiaman!'

Icarus could be seen clearly now looming on the edge of the firelit circle, hauling up her fore and mainsail, shortening down to fighting sail as she came up with less caution than Drinkwater's *Patrician*. A broadside rippled along her side, the brilliance of the gun's discharges bright points in the night, though they could see nothing of the fall of the shot.

'Bring her round a little more to starboard, Mr Wyatt. Let us see if we can add to the confusion.'

Slowly *Patrician* swung and gathered way as she came off the wind. With the burning Indiaman, now almost reduced to a hulk, the other ships were drifting away fast. At any moment *Patrician* herself would come between them and the blaze, revealing her presence.

Midshipman Porter bobbed close to Drinkwater, his red face ruddier in the glow. 'Mr Gordon's compliments and the starboard chase guns will bear.'

'Very well, Mr Porter you may tell Mr Gordon to fire at will, but to have every gun-captain lay his piece carefully. I want no noisy, ineffectual broadsides.'

'Aye, aye, sir.'

'The frog's making sail, sir.' They were too late for complete surprise. Someone aboard the French frigate had seen *Patrician* and she was hauling her backed main yards and letting fall her lower canvas. Just then the first of Gordon's 24-pounders roared, followed by a second and a third. A cheer went up from the waist and Quilhampton bellowed for silence.

'He's going to rake Ashby, by God!' Moncrieff called, but Drinkwater had already seen Ashby's dilemma and watched as he threw his helm over, attempting to swing round on to a parallel course to the Frenchman and trade broadside for broadside.

'He's no fool,' Drinkwater muttered admiringly of the French commander. The broadside itself was hidden from them, but they saw the impact clearly on the *Icarus*, even in the dark, for she rolled in the swell as she turned and the pale rectangle of her fore topsail became first a triangle, then ceased to exist as her foremast crashed to the deck.

'Firing high, by God, he's goin' to run!'

Bright pin-points, like two blinking cat's eyes, sparked from the Frenchman's stern. A column of water rose up close to *Patrician*'s starboard bow and a crash from forward, followed by the murderous whirr of flying splinters, told where a shot had struck home.

'He's firing his stern chasers, sir.'

'I can see that, Mr Q. Mr Wyatt, lay me a course to pass close to *Icarus*, I wish to speak to Ashby and it will at least give us a chance to get a broadside in at that fellow.'

The blazing Indiaman was broad on their larboard beam and dropping astern. The French frigate was making off to the north, leaving the remaining Indiaman and the schooner to their fate. *Sprite* had worn round under *Icarus*'s stern and was engaging the jury-rigged schooner.

'Good man, Sundercombe,' Drinkwater muttered, seizing the speaking trumpet as they bore down on the *Icarus*. Men were swarming on her forecastle and he could see the glimmer of lanterns as they sought to clear away the tangle of fallen gear. Drinkwater leapt up on the rail, clasping the mizen rigging with one hand and the speaking trumpet with the other.

'*Icarus* ahoy Captain Ashby . . .'

'Sir?'

'Secure what you can here. Those are two captured Indiamen, by the way, with prize-crews aboard. Then rejoin the convoy. Keep *Sprite* under your orders. I'm going in pursuit of that frigate.'

'He's a Frenchman, Captain Drinkwater, did you know?'

'Yes. Are you manageable?'

'Aye, I've a forecourse, I think . . .'

'Good luck.'

'And you.'

They waved, their ships rolling in the swell, and Wyatt brought *Patrician* on to a course parallel with the retiring French frigate. She was ahead and to starboard of the British ship and both had the fresh trade wind blowing on their starboard quarters.

'It's going to be a long night, James,' Drinkwater remarked.

'It's already nearly ten,' Quilhampton said after consulting his watch.

'Moonrise in three hours.'

They set every stitch of canvas the spars could stand, started the mast wedges and ran preventer stays up to the topmast caps, setting them up with luff tackles. Never had the *Patrician*'s crew been so hard driven since, those who remembered it afterwards claimed, they had been in the Pacific. There was, Drinkwater knew, little doubt of the outcome if the masts and spars and canvas and cordage stood the strain. The French frigate was a fast ship, but slightly smaller than the British, of a lighter build and, though well handled, unable to match the hardiness of her pursuer. *Patrician* was a *razée*, a cut-down sixty-four gun line-of-battle ship, heavy, but able to stand punishment and, in a strengthening wind, in her element with a quartering sea. Moonrise found the distance between the two ships significantly lessened. Patches of cloud came and went across the face of the full moon, adding to the drama and excitement of the night, and periodically Lieutenant Gordon, pointing the guns himself, tried a shot at the enemy's top-hamper, seeking to cripple him as he fled.

And periodically too, the enemy fired back, though both commanders knew the issue would not be so easily settled, that their scudding ships, heeling and scending under their press of sail, were uncertain gun-platforms, that the angle between them was too fine for more than a lucky shot to tell, and that either luck on the part of one, or disaster for the other, would bring the matter to a conclusion before daylight.

Luck, it seemed, first favoured the French. A shot from a quarter gun struck *Patrician*'s waist, felling an entire gun's crew with a burst of lacerating splinters, sending men screaming like lunatics in antic dances of pain and killing three men outright. A second shot struck *Patrician* just below the starboard fore chains, carrying away a stay-rod. But for the preventer rigged an hour earlier, the shroud above might have parted and the entire foremast gone by the board. As it was the carpenter was able to effect repairs of a kind. Half an hour later a third shot hulled the pursuing British frigate and she began taking water. Once again the carpenter and his mates were summoned. They plugged the shot hole and the pumps were manned, but it shook the Patricians' confidence and the men murmured at their inability to hit back.

'I wonder if Metcalfe would have managed anything?' Moncrieff superciliously asked no one in particular. 'He was a damned good shot . . .'

The remark provoked in Drinkwater's mind's eye an image of Thurston falling from the rigging, which was so vivid he started and became aware he had been half-asleep on his feet. 'Metcalfe . . .?' he said, stupidly and shaken, 'Oh, yes, he was, wasn't he . . .'

'He's done it!' Quilhampton's cry was echoed round the ship. Gordon had fired his foremost gun, loaded with bar shot, as the *Patrician*'s stern had fallen into a trough. The rising bow had thrown the shot high, almost too high. But the crazy, eccentric hemispheres had, with the aid of centrifugal force, extended the sliding bars and the spinning projectile had struck the enemy's fore topgallant mast. For a moment the pallid oblongs of its two sails leaned, suspended in a web of rigging, flogging as the wind caught their underbellies, and then they sagged slowly downwards.

Patrician closed on her quarry; after hours of seeming inactivity her quarterdeck was again seething with officers bawling orders.

'Lay her alongside, Mr Wyatt, and shorten sail. Don't overshoot.'

They were too late for such precise niceties of manoeuvring, the night had grown too wild and they were too tired for fine judgement. *Patrician* overran the French ship, loosing off a rolling broadside and receiving fire in return. The British gunners, so long inactive, with news of the fallen topgallant to cheer them, poured more fire into the enemy. On board the Frenchman, the gunners served their cannon gallantly, but the chaos of fallen spars which just then broke free of the restraints of the upper rigging and crashed down through the boat booms, caused their rate of response to slacken as they confronted blazing gun-muzzles forty yards from their ports.

'Let fly sheets! Let her head fall to starboard! Stand by, boarders!'

The two ships closed, the *Patrician* slightly ahead. Between them the water ran black and silver where the moonlight caught it. The slop and hiss as the outward curling bow waves met and intermingled threw spray upwards to reflect the stabbing glare of the gunfire. The night was full of noise, of wind in rigging, of rushing water, of the cheers and shrieks and shouts of four hundred men, the concussions of their brutal cannon and the stutter of Moncrieff's marines as their muskets cleared the way for the mustering boarders.

'He shows no inclination to edge away,' Quilhampton called, drawing his sword, and then the night was split by a man's voice, a bull-roar of defiance:

'What ship is that?'

'That's no frog . . .' Quilhampton began.

'No, I know,' Drinkwater moved to the rail and leaned over the hammock netting.

'His Britannic Majesty's frigate *Patrician*, Nathaniel Drinkwater commanding. Is that you, Captain Stewart?'

'Aye . . . how in hell's name . . .?'

Stewart's voice was drowned in the discharge of Gordon's starboard battery. 'Fate,' Drinkwater muttered as he turned. 'Pass word to Frey to have his larbowlines ready to board. Now, Mr Wyatt, lay us alongside.'

'Aye, aye, sir!'

'Come, James, death or glory, eh?' Drinkwater said, sensing the puzzlement in Quilhampton by the odd stance of the one-armed officer. He drew his sword. The gap between the two ships closed and then they collided. Drinkwater clambered up on the rail, fighting to get his legs over the hammock nettings and gauge when to leap. He dropped into the mizen chains. Below him the bulging topsides of the ships ground together, their rails separated only by the extent of the rounded tumblehome. A quarterdeck 18-pounder went off beside him. He was deafened and the heat seared his stockings. He remembered he had forgotten to change his clothes before going into action, as was customary. It he was wounded, his dirty linen might infect him.

The two ships rolled inwards, the gap narrowed and he flung himself across. A hemp shroud struck him, he grabbed it with his left hand, felt his right foot land on something solid and he steadied. Momentarily he paused, balancing, then gathered himself and leapt down on to the enemy's deck. Off balance he stumbled, a lunging pike missed him and he recovered his footing in time to parry a cutlass slash. He seemed surrounded by figures menacing him in a terrible surreal silence. The moonlight gleamed on naked steel, a pistol flashed noiselessly, then another and he was surrounded by struggling men. Slowly his hearing returned as he hacked and slithered, hardly knowing friend from foe. A sword blade struck his right epaulette and sent half a dozen heavy gold threads past his ear. He cut savagely at his assailant and felt his sword blade bite. A cry, distinct now, struck his ears. He heard again shouts and whoops, the bitter supplications of the dying and the raving of men engaged in murder. He felt the weight of his anonymous attacker roll against his legs. In a split-second of detachment he thought: 'Christ, this is a sin mightier than lying with Mistress Shaw,' and then he heard the bull-roar again.

'Captain Drinkwater. Where in the devil's name are you?'

'Here, damn you! Here!'

Why had he not held his tongue? Why had he identified himself so that, it seemed to him, even in the confusion the contending parties drew apart, exposing him to Stewart?

But Stewart had seen Drinkwater jump aboard and had kicked or thrust aside those of his friends obstructing his passage. He bore a cavalry sabre and whirled it down in a slashing cut. Drinkwater drew back and lunged over the top of Stewart's extended arm. The tip of his hanger caught the American's right bicep, though it failed to penetrate. Stewart recovered and sought to riposte, but the darkness and the confusion helped neither man. Drinkwater was jostled aside. A small, wiry man advanced on Stewart. He was inside the American officer's guard in a second, his tomahawk raised. The weapon caught the moonlight as it fell.

'No!' Drinkwater roared, but he was too late. The sabre fell to the deck and Stewart stood swaying, the dark blood gushing from his neck. 'Caldecott,' Drinkwater cried in recognition, and his coxswain turned. Just then the moon came clear of the clouds and illuminated the baleful scene. Caldecott's face was a mask of hatred. His teeth were drawn back in a snarl, his eyes glittered with a feral madness as he sought another victim. Appalled, Drinkwater stepped aside, let him pass, and then with a groan Stewart fell against him. Drinkwater let go his hanger and it dangled from its martingale. He grabbed the falling Stewart, felt the dead weight of him as his head lolled back, the mouth agape.

Drinkwater stood in the moonlight and held Stewart in his arms as the American died. His mind was filled with the thoughts of the likeness Stewart bore to his sister, and he was sickened to his soul.

Mercifully a cloud obscured the moon and the noise of fighting drowned the howl of his anguish.

'How are you, sir?'

'Oh, well enough, James. It was only a scratch or two, you know.'

'Pym said you were lucky . . .'

'Pym talks a lot of nonsense. How's Tucker?'

'The fever broke last night. He's weak, but will mend.'

'For God's sake, tell Pym not to bleed the poor devil.'

'I doubt he'll take my advice . . .'

'Pour yourself a glass and sit down. I'll have one too, if you please.'

Drinkwater swung round and stared astern. The convoy was in good order, the recaptured Indiamen in their places, the prizes secure in the centre of the mass of ships. He had left a brace of Yankee schooners at large in the South Atlantic, but, under the circumstances, he did not think they would pose a great threat now the East India convoy was safe. He took the glass Quilhampton handed him. 'I believe I owe you an explanation . . .' Drinkwater smiled over the rim of his glass.

'I confess to still being a little mystified, particularly about *Sybille* and this fellow Stewart you mentioned . . .'

'I didn't *know* about *Sybille*, James, I guessed. Oh, I had some clues, some evidence to suppose, were I in the same position, I would do the same thing . . .'

'I understand about the privateers seeking to waylay the East India fleet. The French have done it before, it is an obvious move, but there was something else, wasn't there?'

'You may have heard stories, James, about my excursion in *Sprite* to the Potomac. I went to contact a woman, a potential source of intelligence. Ah, I see by your face you have heard . . .'

'Well, there *were* some rumours, sir.'

'There are always rumours aboard ship,' Drinkwater went on, unaware of Quilhampton's relief at learning his friend's liaison with the American lady had so rational an explanation after the innuendoes he had heard. 'She was able to give me certain information about Captain Stewart which confirmed what I had already guessed and deduced from information I had gleaned from Stewart and what I had been told in London.

'There was something about Stewart, whom I had met earlier, when *Patrician* was in the Potomac, before you joined us. I had a feeling about him; he practically challenged me, an odd notion unless one nursed a secret in which one had a great deal of confidence. Then luck threw something my way, quite by chance and so circumstantial that I did not know what it was until I recalled the matter much later. The woman dwelt in her father-in-law's house. His name was Shaw. When I first met him, Shaw was a veritable cooing dove, opposed to war. A day later, when we met in different circumstances and I needed his help, he seemed to have cooled. When I left you and shipped in the *Sprite*, I returned as you now know to contact the woman, Captain Stewart's sister and Shaw's daughter-in-law. I saw old Shaw working on some papers. I was at the time apprehensive at the prospect of shinning up a drain pipe at my time of life and chiefly concerned with avoiding detection. I think, having been rebuffed by Shaw, I was instinctively suspicious of him. I didn't take much notice at the time and it was only weeks afterwards that I remembered what I had seen through a crack in the curtains . . .'

'Well, sir?'

'One draught of a sheer-plan, one chart and three or four sheets of paper that looked like accounts. I was quite unaware that Shaw had an intimate knowledge of nautical matters and it suddenly struck me the chart was of Brest.'

Quilhampton was frowning, then he shrugged and waited for Drinkwater to supply the explanation.

'You see, James, the Americans have plenty of men, trained naval officers like Stewart and Tucker plus their own considerable mercantile marine to draw from. Their problem is insufficient naval vessels. I stumbled on the first part of their strategy after we encountered the whaler, *Altair*. The news her master, Orwig, brought of an American frigate at large made me realize the Americans could increase the size of their fleet at a stroke by operating their own flying squadrons of a heavy frigate and a swarm of Baltimore schooners, d'you see?'

'Aye, by heaven, I do . . .'

'Then, when we interrogated Tucker, he mentioned a *French* frigate in the offing and I began to consider the implications of a revival of the old alliance, a combination of American seamen manning French-built ships. You may not be aware, James, but the

French and their allies, in every suitable port between the Baltic and the Mediterranean, have been building men-o'-war of every class, including ships-of-the-line. If such ships ever got to sea and combined with additional flying squadrons of these damnable frigates and schooners . . .'

'They would have had us by the throat,' Quilhampton said in a tone of appalled wonder and growing comprehension. 'And was this all to be paid for by John Company's profits from India and China?'

Drinkwater nodded, 'I believe so . . .'

'It's a diabolically clever notion,' Quilhampton said appreciatively, then frowned. 'What was Shaw's part in all this?'

'No more than a hook upon which my suspicions were obstinately pegged. Like Stewart, I couldn't get rid of the notion of the fellow. Shaw was obviously tied up with American diplomacy and foreign policy by his very solicitude for Vansittart and the fact that Stewart had us anchor in the Potomac. Then there were those papers and so forth. Finally . . .' Drinkwater tapped a sheaf of documents lying on the table behind him, 'there was Stewart aboard a French frigate in the South Atlantic after a mid-ocean rendezvous, with this bundle weighted about his waist. No wonder the poor fellow succumbed to Caldecott's tomahawk.'

'The papers implicate Shaw?'

'Yes, he was, as it were, the broker between the French and the Americans. In concert with the French invasion of Russia the consequences of the success of this joint venture are not to be contemplated.'

'It would have compelled us to raise the blockade of Europe and let the French fleet out . . .'

'It really doesn't do to think of such an eventuality,' said Drinkwater, suppressing a shudder. 'Come, fill your glass again.'

He had not told Quilhampton the whole story, but enough of it to make sense. Besides, how could he tell his friend of what he had learned from Arabella in her boudoir, another Parisian dress discarded on her bed, that curious moment of reticence followed by her wholesale condemnation of men and their scheming? Was that why providence had made them lovers, so he might divine these things? He threw aside the thought, discarded it with the sense of relief flooding through him. He smiled at Quilhampton.

'I make you a toast, James: to the ladies.'

'God bless 'em!'

'Johnnie? Can you hear me?'

Lord Moira bent over the man in the sick-bed. The grossness had fallen away, leaving a face that seemed twenty years younger but for the yellow pallor of approaching death.

'Frank, is that you?' Lord Dungarth opened his eyes.

'Yes. How are you today?'

'As you see, failing fast . . .'

'Come, you mustn't give up hope.'

'Damn it, Frank, don't cozen me. The quacks will kill me with their nostrums and leeches quicker than this damned distemper. I'm as good as dead.' Dungarth paused, catching his breath. 'Listen, there's something I want you to do for me.' He raised a trembling hand to his throat. The skin was translucent, the blood vessels below, ribbed and dark, writhing over the stretched tendons. Parting his nightshirt, Lord Dungarth withdrew a key, suspended from his neck by a thin black ribbon. 'Help . . . me.' He gasped with the effort.

Moira assisted Dungarth to raise his head and eased the ribbon over the bald skull.

'It is the key to my desk at the Admiralty. You are to make sure Captain Drinkwater receives it. Upon your word of honour, d'you understand?'

'Upon my word, Johnnie, I promise.'

Dungarth sighed and sank back on to his pillow. 'What news of the French?'

'The Russians are approaching the Rhine and Wellington the Pyrenees.'

'And from America?'

'Not so good . . .'

'Is there news of Drinkwater yet?' Dungarth broke in feebly.

'We shall learn something in a few days,' Moira disembled.

'I shan't last a few days, but he's the man, Frank. He has the ability . . . the *nous*.'

Despite himself, Moira smiled at the use of the Greek word, then wondered if the man Drinkwater, in whom Dungarth had such faith, really had the intuition his friend thought. A diseased man was, in Moira's experience, no very reliable Judge.

'Tell him about the bookseller in the Rue de'laaah . . .' Pain distorted Dungarth's face. Moira reached for the bottle beside the bed and poured the neat laudanum drops into a tumbler of water.

'Here, old fellow,' he said, putting an arm about Dungarth and lifting his shoulders. With his other hand he held the glass to his friend's lips.

'You still pull strings, then?' Moira said admiringly.

'To the end, *mon ami*, to the end the puppet-master. Don't forget Drinkwater . . .' Dungarth whispered as his eyes closed. 'Your word upon it, Frank, your word . . .'

Author's Note

The depredations of privateers are largely unrecorded in purely naval histories, but 'letters-of-marque and reprisal' were issued in copious numbers by both the French and American governments at this time. Indeed, most American merchant ships carried them, so the distinction between the dedicated privateer and the opportunist cargo-carrier is somewhat blurred. However, the astonishing successes of the corsairs in the war against British trade were far from insignificant and the most interesting of the vessels used by the Americans was the Baltimore clipper schooner which possessed a revolutionary new hull form, with hollow entry and run, the antithesis of the frigates and sloops sent against them. Nevertheless, many were captured and, like the fast French frigates before them, adopted and copied by the Royal Navy.

The lengths to which the British went to keep Wellington's army in the Iberian peninsula supplied were often devious. American traders were quite happy to supply both sides, no matter their government was at war with one of them. Much of the investment available for the later expansion of nineteenth-century America originally came from this source.

Napoleon assiduously worked on an American rupture with Great Britain, seeking to embroil his implacable enemy with an opponent who had designs on Canada and posed a very real threat at sea.

Henry Vansittart is my own invention, though a King's messenger was sent to Washington at the time Drinkwater first arrived in the Potomac. The surplus of American naval officers is also a fact; many brilliant young men were unable to find employment in naval vessels and were driven, like Stewart, to find other ways of demonstrating the fervour of their patriotism.

The value of the frigate actions between the Royal and United

States navies was much exaggerated and had little real effect. In America they provided the foundation for a tradition of glory; in Britain they were taken as a sign that the Royal Navy was in decline. The Americans assumed that, like schoolboys with a triumphant conker, the victor accrued to itself the triumphs of its victim. This was plainly nonsense. The value of a navy rests on its strategic power and the fate of its individual parts is only significant if it materially affects this. The Royal Navy suffered such damage in the early years of the Second World War, not between 1812 and 1814. The defeat of a handful of British cruisers did not diminish the great and wearying achievement of continental blockade and when this was extended to America, the balance swung back in favour of the British. Nevertheless, it rattled the British public at the time, and was thought to be of greater importance than the destruction of the Grand Army in the cold of a Russian winter.

Beneath the Aurora

For Rozelle and Dick Raynes and their ships *Martha McGilda* and *Roskilde*

Contents

PART ONE
A Distant Treachery

'We may pick up a Marshal or two, but nothing worth a damn.'

WELLINGTON

A Person of Some Importance

September 1813

Lieutenant Sparkman eased off the second of his mud-spattered boots with a relieved grunt, and kicked it beside its companion. Leaning back in the chair he wriggled his toes, picked up the tankard beside him and gulped the hot rum flip with greedy satisfaction. The heat of the fire drew steam from the neglected boots and a faintly distasteful aroma from his own feet. The woollen stockings were damp, damned near as damp as the Essex salt-marsh alongside which he had ridden that afternoon. Boots were no attire for a sea-officer, he reflected, though he had heard hessians were increasingly fashionable among the young blades that inhabited His Majesty's quarterdecks nowadays. But as an Inspector of Fencibles, Sparkman was no longer what might, with justice, be called a 'sea-officer'. His sore arse testified to the time he spent in the saddle and he promptly set the thought aside. He avoided disquieting recollections, having learnt the wisdom of jettisoning them before they took root and corroded a man's good temper.

True he had been disappointed in his expectations in the naval service, but he had little to complain about since swallowing the anchor. After all, the path of duty was not arduous: the Red Lion at Kirby-le-Soken was a comfortable enough house and the landlord a convivial fellow, having once been at sea himself. They would doubtless share a glass or two before the night was out. Sparkman stretched himself again and swallowed more rum; he should reach Harwich before noon next day, which was time enough; he had no intention of starting early, for the weather had turned foul and there was little improvement expected. He half cocked an ear at the wind blustering against the Red Lion's sturdy walls and the faint rattling of tiles above his head. Periodically the fire sizzled and smoked as, through some vagary of the chimney, a spatter of rain was driven down against the updraught.

He wriggled his toes again, content: in Harwich there was a chambermaid in the Three Cups who was worth the effort, despite the weather, for Annie Davis had taken a shine to him on a previous visit and would share his bed for a florin.

The easterly gale which had begun that morning threatened to blow for a week, a wind which, despite its ferocity, would once have had every Tom, Dick and Harry on the coast fearing invasion. Those days were over, thank heaven. The French were on the defensive now, hard pressed by Great Britain's Continental allies. News had arrived of the check administered by the Emperor Napoleon to Schwarzenburg's Austrians; but the two Prussian armies had achieved success. One under Blücher, had surprised Marshal Macdonald on the Katzbach River and had routed him with the loss of 20,000 Frenchmen and over 100 cannon; while the second, commanded by von Bülow, had caught Marshal Oudinot south of Potsdam, and had defeated him at Gross Beeren. Moreover, all the while, knocking at the back door of France Lord Wellington's Anglo-Portuguese army steadily advanced across the Pyrenees out of Spain.

Sparkman yawned and cast a glance at the dank leather satchels hung across the back of the room's other chair, dripping darkly over the floorboards. He thought of the report he should have been writing on the sea defences along the coast of the Wallet. It seemed a rather small and trivial task, set against this vast ebb and flow of soldiers marching and counter-marching across war-weary Europe.

Well, so be it. To the devil with his report! He would write it when he arrived at Harwich, after he had had a look at the redoubt there (and taken his pleasure on the plump but enthusiastic body of Annie Davis). The Martello towers from Point Clear to Clacton were sound enough, even if their garrisons were tucked up in Weeley barracks, a good hour or two's march from their posts.

'There's a manned battery at Chevaux-de-Frise Point,' Sparkman muttered to himself, easing his conscience, 'and no damned radeaux will put to sea without the free-trade fraternity knowing about it, never mind an invasion fleet.'

The wind boomed in the chimney and rattled the small window, emphasizing the drowsy snugness of his room under the thatch. He recalled an old woman who had passed the time of day with him in a lane that morning. Pointing to the proliferation of wayside berries, she had croaked that it would be a hard winter; perhaps the crone had been right. He continued to toast his feet and look forward to a chat with the landlord, a beef pie and clean sheets all in due time, teasing himself with anticipation at parting Annie's white thighs.

He was dozing when the landlord burst in. An uncivil clatter of boots followed him on the wooden stair. It was clear his host's abrupt entry had precious little social about it.

'Mr Sparkman, sir, Cap'n Clarke is here demanding to speak with you.'

For a moment the tired Sparkman was confused, the rum having drugged him. He woke fully to an ill-tempered resentment, irritated that men such as Clarke should call themselves 'Captain'. The upstart was no more than Master of a smuggling lugger.

'I don't know a *Captain* Clarke . . .' he began, and then Clarke himself was crowding into the room, with two ruffianly seamen in tarpaulins and a fantastically bewhiskered and cloaked officer whose moustaches curled extravagantly beneath a long nose. The quartet were soaked, their clothes running with water, which rapidly darkened the floor, mixing with the mud from their boots.

'Oh, yes you do, Sparkman,' Clarke said grinning, 'we need no introductions. But I have brought someone you haven't met yet.' Clarke drew off his low beaver and threw out an arm with a mock theatrical gesture. 'Colonel . . .'

The grotesque apparition threw back his cloak with a flourish that showered Sparkman with water, to reveal a scarlet plastron fronting a white tunic laced with silver.

'Colonel Bardolini, Captain,' the stranger announced in good English, shrugging himself free of the restraining seamen and flicking his extended wrist at Clarke in dismissal. 'I am come on an embassy to the English government. You are a naval officer, yes?'

'Rummest cargo I ever lifted, Mr Sparkman,' Clarke put in, ignoring the foreign officer.

'I daresay he paid you well,' retorted Sparkman, who had recovered something of his wits at this damp invasion. With wry amusement he observed that this Bardolini shared his own opinion of Clarke. 'You were ever one to drive a hard bargain,' he added obliquely, referring to a past transaction over some bottles of genever.

'This is different,' Clarke said darkly, ''e ain't French, 'e's Italian.'

'I am Neapolitan,' said Bardolini, firing his sentences like shot.

'I am in the service of King Joachim. I have papers for your government. I am a person of some importance.'

'Are you now,' said Sparkman 'and what proof . . .?'

But Bardolini had anticipated resistance and whipped a heavily sealed paper from the ample cuff of his white leather gauntlet.

'My passport.' He held the document out. 'I have plenipotentiary powers,' he declared impressively.

Sparkman had only the vaguest understanding of the Neapolitan's claim, but a respect for the panoply of administrative office bade him be cautious. He slit the seal and with a crackle opened the paper.

'Signor, please, these men . . .'

Sparkman looked up and nodded to the smuggler. 'Tell your men to be off, Clarke,' he ordered and then, as the seamen retreated, clumping down the stairs, he asked, 'Where did you pick this fellow up?'

'At Flushing. I was told take a passenger . . .'

'Told?' Sparkman asked. 'By whom?' and, seeing Clarke's hesitation, 'Come on, Clarke, you've no need to haver. If I read you aright, you've brought live cargo over before, have you not?'

'A man has to feed his family, Sparkman, and these are hard times . . .'

'Never mind your damned excuses. Who approached you?'

'A man who has arranged this kind of business before.'

'Very well. And what were you contracted to do with this fine gentleman?' Sparkman indicated the Neapolitan who was about to speak. 'A moment, sir,' Sparkman cut him short. 'Go on, Clarke.'

'To deliver him to a government officer. When I heard you had been inspecting the coast . . .'

'You were damned lucky I was about, then, and that it wasn't an Exciseman or a Riding Officer you bumped into.'

'I wouldn't call it luck, Sparkman,' Clarke countered darkly, alluding to the intelligence system the so-called 'free-traders' possessed.

'I suppose you'd have left him to walk the Gunfleet Sands until the tide covered him?'

'I usually do what I'm told in these circumstances, Sparkman . . .'

'Aye, and avoid the gallows by it!'

'I'd advise you to do the same, Sparkman. The gentlemen at

Colchester are in my pocket too,' Clarke said, his grin sinister with implication.

'Why you impertinent . . .' The reference to the army officers of the local garrison irritated him.

'Are you a naval officer?' Bardolini snapped, breaking into the row fomenting between the two men, which it was clear he understood perfectly. 'You have my passport. Please be good enough to read it.'

Sparkman turned his attention on the colonel. He was about to retort, but the gleam in Bardolini's eye persuaded him otherwise. He shrugged and looked at the paper the Neapolitan held out. It was in French and English, that much he could see, but his sight was poor and with only the light of the fire he could make out little more than the formula 'allow to pass without let or hindrance, the bearer, Colonel Umberto Bardolini of the Neapolitan Service on a mission to the Court of St James's'. There was a string of legal mumbo-jumbo in which the words 'plenipotentiary. . . . authorized to act on behalf of . . . is of my mind and fully conversant with my innermost thoughts', seemed sufficiently portentous to confirm Lieutenant Sparkman in the wisdom of his caution. At the bottom, above another seal, was a scrawl that may or may not have spelled out the name 'Joachim', but in fact used the Italian form 'Giacomo'.

Sparkman looked up at the bristling moustaches. 'Colonel, my apologies. Welcome to Great Britain.' He held out his hand, but Bardolini ignored it and bowed stiffly from the waist.

Sparkman was aware of Clarke grinning diabolically in the firelight at this slight.

'Who are you?' Bardolini asked peremptorily and for the third time.

'Shall I get you some vittals, Lieutenant Sparkman?' put in the landlord who had remained silent until a commercial opportunity offered.

'No, damn you,' Sparkman snapped, 'tell your boy I want my horse again, and get me another for this fellow to ride.' He handed the passport back to Bardolini. 'I am Lieutenant Sparkman of His Britannic Majesty's Royal Navy, Colonel.' Then he sat and pulled on his boots.

'What are you going to do with him?' asked Clarke.

'I shan't be taking any chances, God rot you,' said Sparkman, standing and stamping his feet into the boots, then casting about the room for his belongings, muttering about the lack of candles.

'D'you wish for a candle, sir?' enquired the landlord. 'It will take but a moment . . .'

'I want a quiet evening before the fire,' Sparkman muttered through clenched teeth.

'Aye, sir, 'tis a bad night, and . . .'

'Be so good as to stand aside!' Sparkman exploded.

'What about payment for the room?'

Bardolini shuffled round as Sparkman seized his damp cloak from the bed and drew it about his shoulders. The wet collar rasped against his neck, reminding him of the weather outside and the comfort he was forsaking. He threw the landlord a handful of silver.

'You will take me to see the General Officer commanding at Colchester?' the Neapolitan asked, obviously well-informed.

'No, sir, 'tis too far. I will take you to Harwich for tonight. Tomorrow we will see about Colchester.' Sparkman turned on Clarke who barred his exit. 'You must have had a bad passage, Clarke.'

Clarke grinned and jerked his head at Bardolini, at the same time holding out his hand and preventing anyone from leaving the room. 'He certainly did.'

With an extravagant sigh, Bardolini drew a purse from his belt. Sparkman heard the chink of coin as he passed it to the smuggler.

'I wish you good-night, gentlemen,' said Clarke, standing aside and bowing with an ironic exaggeration.

Sparkman threw the wet satchel over his shoulder and picked up a pair of pistol holsters. 'Be so kind as to bring my baggage, landlord,' he ordered, nodding at his portmanteau, then he stepped forward, through the slime his visitors had left by the door.

As he passed, Clarke muttered sarcastically, 'I took his pistols while he was vomiting over the rail. He won't give you too much trouble.'

'I am much obliged to you, Clarke,' Sparkman retorted with equal incivility.

'*Captain* Clarke, Mr Sparkman.'

'Damn you for an insolent dog, Clarke . . .'

Clarke laughed and held up the jingling purse under Sparkman's nose. 'There's more than you make in a year in here, Sparkman . . .'

'God help England when money purchases rank, Clarke! You're a dog and always will be a dog, and no amount of gold, no, nor putting your betters in your pocket, can make you a gentleman! Come, Colonel.'

'What pretty notions you do have, Sparkman,' Clarke called after them, laughing as they clattered down the stairs.

Sparkman had to put his shoulder to the outer door as a gust of wind eddied round the yard. Rain lashed him in the twilight as Bardolini emerged, attempting to put a crazy, square-topped shako on to his head. Then Sparkman was struggling with his reluctant horse and taking the reins from a wretched little stable-boy. Satchel, portmanteau and saddle-bags were finally settled on the fractious animal and then Sparkman hoisted himself aloft.

Bardolini was already mounted, smoothing his curvetting horse's neck with a gloved and practised hand. The sight irritated Sparkman; but for this effete Italian he might, at that moment, be tucking into a beef pie.

'Come on, then, damn you!' he roared and put spurs to his tired horse, which jerked him forward into the rain and wind.

Chapter One *September 1813*

A Lucky Chance

Captain Nathaniel Drinkwater read the paragraph for the fourth time, aware that he had not understood a word of it. The handwriting was crabbed, the spelling idiosyncratic and the ink smudged. He began again. The lines forming the words seemed to uncoil from the paper into a thin trail of smoke. He was aware he had fallen asleep, his mind dulled with a torpor he found difficult to shake off.

'God's bones,' he muttered, tossing the paper on to the pile which covered the green baize on the desk-top and standing up with such violence that his chair overturned and, for a moment, he had to clutch at the desk to stop himself from falling.

The dizziness passed, but left his brow clammy with sweat. He ran a forefinger round his neck, tugging at the constriction of his stock, swearing beneath his breath with forceful eloquence. He went to the window and leaned his head upon the cool glass. The sash vibrated slightly to the gale blowing outside, and rain fell upon the glass panes with a patter which occasionally grew to a vicious tattoo in the gusts. It was almost dark and he told himself it was the dusk which had brought on his tiredness, nothing more.

He turned and, leaning against the shutter, stared back into the room. It was small, containing the baize-covered desk, his chair and a wicker basket which stood on a square of carpet to keep his feet from the draught that blew between the wide deal floorboards. The window was flanked on one side by a tall cabinet whose glazed doors covered shelves of guard books, on the other by a low chest whose upper surface was a plane table. It had a trough for pencil and dividers, beneath which a series of shallow drawers contained several folios of charts. On its top was a long wooden box containing a single deep and narrow drawer.

The only other article of furniture in the room was a small, rickety, half-moon table set against the wall beside the door. Upon it were a pair of decanters, a biscuit barrel and four glasses. One contained a residual teaspoonful of madeira.

On the wall opposite the window, above the grate and mantelpiece, hung a gilt-framed canvas depicting a moonlit frigate action. It had been commissioned by Drinkwater and painted by the ageing Nicholas Pocock, whose house in Great George Street was hard by Storey's Gate into St James's Park. The painting showed the frigate *Patrician* overhauling and engaging the French National frigate *Sybille* and Drinkwater had described the canvas to his wife Elizabeth as 'a last vanity, m'dear. I shan't fight again, now that I've swallowed the anchor.'

The recollection made him turn to the window again, and stare down into the darkening street. Despite the weather, Whitehall was full of the evening's traffic: a foot patrol of guardsmen, a pair of doxies in a doorway cozening the grenadiers, whose bearskins lost their military air in the rain, a dog pissing against a porter's rest, and a handful of pathetic loiterers huddling out of the rain in the sparse and inadequate clothing of the indigent. Carriages came and went across his field of view, but he saw none of this. It depressed him; after the broad sweep of the distant horizon seen from the pristine standpoint of a frigate's quarterdeck, the horse turds and grime of Whitehall were a mockery.

He turned and, as abruptly as he had risen, closed the shutters against the night. Then he righted his capsized Windsor chair and sat in it. Picking up the paper he twisted round, held it to the flickering firelight and began to read out loud, as if by enunciating the ill-written words he would keep himself awake enough to assimilate their content.

'Sir, further to my communications of December last and May of this year, in which there was little of an unusual nature to report, it is now common knowledge here . . .' Drinkwater had forgotten the origin of the paper and looked at the heading. 'Ah, yes,' he murmured, 'from Helgoland . . . last month, no, July . . .'

He read on, 'that a considerable quantity of arms for equipping troops have lately arrived in Hamburg and in expectation of their shipment, have been placed in a warehouse which is guarded by . . .'

There was a knock at the door and Drinkwater paused. 'Enter,' he called.

A slim, pinch-faced man with prematurely thinning hair appeared. He wore a black, waisted and high-collared coat. The points of his shirt poked up either side of his face, and a tight cravat in dark, watered silk frothed beneath a sharp, blue chin. The figure was elegant and, though daylight would have betrayed the threadbare nature of his dress, the candelabra he bore only enhanced the ascetic architecture of his skull.

'Ah, Templeton, about time you brought candles.'

'My apologies, Captain, I was delayed in the copy room . . .'

'Scuttlebutt, I suppose.'

'I wish it were only gossip, sir, but I fear the worst.' Templeton's words were so full of foreboding that Drinkwater was compelled to look up. Templeton's head was bent askew in such a way that, though he stood, his eyes must of necessity look under his brow so that his whole demeanour bespoke grave concern.

'Which touches me, Mr Templeton?'

'Indeed, sir, I fear so.' A brief smirk passed across Templeton's features, the merest hint of satisfaction at having conveyed the full import of his meaning with such admirable economy. It would have passed a less intuitive man than Drinkwater unnoticed.

'Is this a secret of state, or merely one which is denied the Secret Department, Mr Templeton?' Drinkwater asked with heavy irony.

'The latter, Captain Drinkwater,' Templeton replied, the corners of his thin mouth creeping outwards in a smile, hinting at the possession of superior knowledge.

'Well, then, I am waiting. What is this gossip in the clerks' office?'

'I am afraid, sir, 'tis said this department is to be discontinued.'

A feeling of something akin to relief flooded through Drinkwater. There were times in a man's life when to submit to the inevitable meant avoiding disagreeable concomitances. He could never have explained to Elizabeth how constricted his soul was, cooped up in this tiny Admiralty office. He had accepted his appointment, half out of loyalty to his late predecessor, Lord Dungarth, half out of a sense of necessity.

This necessity was harder to define, exposing as it did the infirmities of his character. A believer in Providence, he knew his posting to this obscure office was only partly the result of

Dungarth's dying wish. Fate had consigned him to it in expiation of his unfaithfulness to his wife, for his *affaire* with the Widow Shaw.*

Now Templeton, his obsequious but able cipher clerk, a man steeped in the clandestine doings of the Secret Department, who possessed encyclopaedic knowledge of the letters pasted in the guard books resting behind the glass doors of the cabinet, brought him release from this imprisonment.

'I see you are shocked, Captain Drinkwater.'

'I am certainly surprised,' Drinkwater dissimulated. 'Upon what logic is this based?'

'Cost, I believe,' Templeton replied and added, rolling his eyes with lugubrious emphasis and pointing his right index finger upwards, though Drinkwater knew nothing but the attics were there, 'and a certain feeling among those whose business it is to attend to such matters, that our continued existence is no longer necessary.'

'The war is not yet over, Templeton.'

'I entirely agree, sir.'

Drinkwater realized Templeton awaited his reply as a matter of some importance. Indeed the clerk had confided in Drinkwater in order to rouse him to a defence of the Secret Department, not so much to contribute to ending the war by its continued existence, but to preserve Templeton's unique position within the Admiralty's bureaucratic hierarchy. Templeton was not the first to assume, quite wrongly, that Nathaniel Drinkwater was a man of influence. How else had he inherited this post of Head of the Secret Department?

How indeed? It was a conundrum which obsessed Drinkwater himself. He knew no more than that he had received a letter signed by the Second Secretary to the Board of Admiralty, John Barrow, appointing him, and a visit from the Earl of Moira explaining that it had been the dying wish of Lord Dungarth that Drinkwater should take over the office.

'Johnnie said you were the only man capable of doin' the job, Captain, the only man with the *nous*. He was emphatic upon the point, wanted me to tell you about a bookseller fellow in Paris, and

*See *The Flying Squadron*.

a Madame de Santon, or some such, but he slipped away, poor devil. He was in a deuce of a lot of pain at the end, despite the paregoric.'

Moira had given him the key to the desk at which he now sat, striving for some temporizing reaction to Templeton's news.

'Barrow has not mentioned the matter . . .'

'It was only decided at Board this morning . . .'

'You're damned quick with your intelligence,' Drinkwater snapped sharply. 'So much for the confidentiality of the copy room!'

'I believe Mr Barrow wished it to be known, sir, in this round-about way.'

'How obligin' of him,' Drinkwater muttered, knowing that in the past he had once crossed the Second Secretary and done him-self no favour thereby. 'You had better pour us both a glass, Templeton.'

Drinkwater rose, aware that he had still not thoroughly read the dispatch from Helgoland. He moved towards the little half-moon table where the clerk poured the rich madeira. He caught sight of himself reflected in the glass doors of the cabinet. The bottle-green coat did not suit him, and was at odd variance with his old-fashioned queue with its clump of black ribbon nestling at the nape of his neck. He looked a damn fool!

Templeton handed him the glass. 'What are we to do, Templeton?' he asked. 'D'you have any bright ideas? If they want for money, we've no means of raisin' revenue, and if they want value for what little they allow us, how in heaven's name do we give it to 'em?'

He was half-hearted in his complaint, but Templeton did not seem to notice. The truth was, the intelligence reports processed by the two of them contained little of significance now that the naval war on the coast of Europe was reduced to the tedious matter of blockade. There were the lists of Yankee ships slip-ping in and out of French ports, but as many were doing the same in Spain and the British were purchasing the supplies they brought to keep Wellington's Anglo-Portuguese army in the field. As for the matter of their own funds, Drinkwater had learned that Dungarth had himself underwritten most of the department's expenses, squandering his modest inheritance to the distress of his Irish tenants. His own finances would not extend so far.

In so far as the Secret Department had achieved anything recently, Drinkwater could recollect only his pressing the Board to increase the strength of the blockade on the eastern coast of the United States. He had written an appreciation of the matter born out of his own experience of Yankee privateers rather than the coded missives of spies.

'We appear to be redundant, Mr Templeton,' he said with an air of finality.

'I fear that may well be the case, Captain Drinkwater,' Templeton said, sipping his wine unhappily.

'You will retain a position within the Admiralty, surely.'

'Oh, I daresay, sir, but not one of such gravity, sir, not one with such, er, such opportunities.'

The emphasis on the last word reminded Drinkwater of the vital perquisites of office among these black-garbed jobbers. There were expenses to be written off, bribes to be paid and spies to be funded. Everything was reduced to money and everyone had their price, women as well as men.

He thought of Moira's 'Madame de Santon, or some such'. Drinkwater knew her better as Hortense Santhonax, née Montholon. Dungarth's key had revealed his secret dossier on Hortense and the small pension she received to keep open communications with the Emperor Napoleon's former Foreign Minister, Talleyrand. He concentrated on the present. There was Liepmann in Hamburg, Van Ouden in Flushing and Vlieghere at Antwerp.

'Well, Templeton, what have we received recently? There was the letter from Carlscrona reporting eleven of the line in ordinary . . .'

'From the Master of the *Lady Erskine*, sir.'

'Quite so . . .'

'And the message from Antwerp about the current state of new building there, four ships and a frigate. A routine report, to be sure, but one which demonstrates the continuing ability and determination of the French and their allies to build men o' war.'

'Yes, and the encrypted dispatch from Helgoland spoke of arms being stored at Hamburg. There does not seem much of significance in that.'

'No, no,' Templeton agreed quickly, 'Hamburg is a French fortress. Cavalry remounts, recruits, stores and so forth are all assembled there. The French Army Corps in North Germany draw their reinforcements from the Hamburg depot.'

'And yet Liepmann thought it worth letting them know in Helgoland,' Drinkwater reflected, adding, 'Liepmann is in our pay, not that of the Foreign Office.'

'You have great faith in Herr Liepmann, sir,' said Templeton obliquely, knowing that Drinkwater had once met the Jewish merchant.

'It would not surprise me if these arms are locked away in one of our Hebrew friend's warehouses, Templeton. If so, he has probably learned of their purpose. Don't you think it odd they may be secured in a warehouse, rather than in the possession of the French military authorities?'

'That is mere conjecture,' Templeton said dismissively.

'True.' Drinkwater was content to leave the matter there. He knew Templeton set great store by the intelligence from Antwerp. It was a regular dispatch, a long message in the cipher it was Templeton's peculiar skill to disentangle and he had a proprietorial air towards it.

But Templeton had become wary of his new master. The ageing post captain with his outmoded queue, lopsided shoulders and thin sword scar down his left cheek was a contrast after the huge, dropsical bulk of the one-legged Lord Dungarth. But, Templeton had come to learn, both had an uncanny knack of nosing out the obscure from the obfusc. The talent made Templeton nervous.

'Your meaning is unclear, sir,' Templeton prompted.

'Mmm? You mean the significance of my conjecture is unclear?' Drinkwater asked wryly.

'Exactly so.'

'Well, you are right. It is only conjecture, but Liepmann finds it necessary to tell us a quantity of arms has arrived at Hamburg. There is nothing unusual in that, we conclude, except that Herr Liepmann knows of it. Now I'll warrant that there is nothin' significant in replacement equipment arriving in Hamburg in the normal run of things, eh? Nor would one expect Liepmann to know of it. But Liepmann does know, and considers it worth lettin' us know.'

'But if the fact was of real significance then surely he would have amplified the matter. The message is in cipher. If these arms, whatever they consist of, are in his own warehouses, he would have given us more details. I don't see it signifies anything.'

'You have a point, Templeton. Perhaps my assumption was foolish. But suppose they are in the custody of a friend, an associate. Liepmann perhaps smells a rat. He sends us the information thinking it may be a piece of a larger puzzle.'

'Well, it isn't.'

'You are not convinced.' Drinkwater's tone was flat, a statement, not a question. He shrugged, drained his glass and sighed. 'So be it. Come, it is gettin' late. It is time you went home.'

Templeton put his empty glass down on the half-moon table. 'Good-night, sir,' he said, but he seemed reluctant to leave.

'Good-night.' Drinkwater turned to his desk, gathering the scattered papers, waiting for Templeton to go. When the clerk had finally gone, he locked them away. He turned then to the shutters and opened them. Throughout his interview with Templeton he had been aware of their faint but persistent rattle.

He peered again through the window. For a moment, the full moon appeared from behind flying cloud and he thought of the strong spring tides its influence would produce and the ferocious seas which would be running in the Channel.

'God help sailors on a night like this,' he muttered to himself in a pious incantation. The brilliant moonlight and a clatter below briefly attracted his attention. He caught a glimpse of a horseman turning in off the street and entering through Nash's screen wall, his mount striking sparks off the wet cobbles. Messengers were something of a rarity nowadays, he reflected, so sophisticated had the semaphore telegraph system become. It was capable of transmitting news with great speed from the standard on the Admiralty roof, along half a dozen arteries to the great seaports of Britain, even to such exposed outposts as Yarmouth Road, on the coast of East Anglia. He wondered idly where the rider's dispatches originated, then dismissed the thought and closed the shutters.

Drinkwater succumbed to the temptation to pour another glass and sat again, turning his chair so that it faced the dying fire. He was in no mood to return to a house empty of all except its staff. Bending, he stoked the fire into a final flaring, listening awhile to the boom of the gale across the massed chimney pots on the roof above while the tiny flames licked round the glowing coals, then subsided into a dull, ruby coruscation.

He brooded on his predicament. He was supposed to be a puppet-master, pulling strings at the extremities of which several score of agents danced, ceaselessly gleaning information for the British Admiralty. Templeton, his confidential cipher clerk, decoded their messages and entered their dispatches in the guard books. He was a genius of sorts, a man whose mind could disinter a hidden fact, cross-refer it to some other seemingly unrelated circumstance and draw a thread of logic from the process. Except, of course, when he disagreed, as at present. Then he could be monstrously stubborn. Drinkwater sometimes marvelled at the obscure man's abilities, quite oblivious of his own part in these deliberations and the confidence his personal imprimatur gave Templeton. He was more likely to see himself as a fish out of water, an ageing and foppish extravagant in his bottle-green coat and his increasingly affected mode of speaking. It seemed to him that he had reached this point in his life without quite knowing how he had got there, carried, like a piece of wood on the tide, into some shallow backwater and left grounded in a creek.

He had fondly supposed that he would see something of his wife, but Elizabeth and the children were almost a hundred miles away, in Suffolk, while he vegetated in the capital, choking on smoke and falling victim to the blue devils and every quinsy and ague coughed over him by London's denizens! Moira had implied he might mastermind a *coup*, insisting Dungarth knew him capable of executing some brilliant feat. But while Drinkwater had pored in fascination over the papers pasted in the guard books, prompted by a natural curiosity concerning the fate of Madame Santhonax, whose husband Drinkwater had killed in action, he had come to realize all such opportunities seemed to reside firmly in the past, and the distant past at that.*

His present duties seemed to entail nothing more than reading endless reports and dispatches, many of no apparent meaning, still less of significance, until he dozed over them, half asleep with inertia.

*See *Baltic Mission*.

'God's bones,' he had snapped at Templeton one morning, 'what am I to make of this catalogue of stupefying facts? If they conceal some great truth then it passes over my head.'

'Patience, sir,' Templeton had soothed, 'gold is never found in great quantities.'

'Damn you for your philosophical cant, Templeton! Did Lord Dungarth never venture abroad, eh? Send himself on some mission to rouse his blood?'

'Yes, sir, indeed he did, and lost a leg if you recall, when his carriage was mined by Bonaparte's police.'

'You are altogether too *reasonable* for your own good, Templeton. If you were on my quarterdeck I should mast-head you for your impudence.'

'You are not on your quarterdeck, Captain Drinkwater,' Templeton had replied coolly, with that fastidious detachment which could either annoy or amuse Drinkwater.

'More's the damned pity,' Drinkwater had flung back, irritated on this occasion and aware that here, in the Admiralty, he was bereft of the trappings of pomp he had become so used to. It reduced the bottle-green coat to the uniform of a kind of servitude and his clipped speech to a pompous mannerism acquired at sea through the isolation of command. Neither consideration brought him much comfort, for the one reminded him of what he had relinquished, the other of what he had become.

Nevertheless, Drinkwater mused, leaning back in his chair and staring into the fire's dying embers, it seemed enough for Templeton methodically to unscramble the reports of spies while Drinkwater himself ached for something useful to do, instead of this tedious seeking of windmills to tilt at.

He was fast asleep when Templeton knocked on the door and he woke with a start as the clerk urgently shook his shoulder. Templeton's thin visage hung over him like a spectre.

'Captain Drinkwater, sir, wake up!'

'What the devil . . .?' Drinkwater's heart pounded with alarm, for there was something wild in Templeton's eye.

'I have just received a message from Harwich, sir. Sent up post-haste by a Lieutenant Sparkman.'

'Who the devil is he?' Drinkwater asked testily, his eye catching sight of a folded paper in Templeton's hand.

'An Inspector of Fencibles . . .'

'Well?'

'He is holding a prisoner there, sir, a man claiming to be a colonel in the service of the King of Naples.'

'The King of Naples? Marshal Murat?'

'The same . . .'

'Let me see, damn it!' Drinkwater shot out his hand, took the hurriedly offered note and read:

Sir, I have the Honour to Acquaint Their Lordships that I am just Arrived at Harwich and have in My Custody a Man just lately Arrived upon the Coast and claiming to be a Colonel Bardolini, in the Service of the King of Naples and Invested with Special Powers. I have Lodged him in the Redoubt here and Await your Instructions at the Three Cups Inn.

Sparkman, Lieutenant and Inspector of Sea Fencibles

Drinkwater turned the letter over and read the superscription with a frown.

'This is addressed to the Secretary . . .'

'Mr Croker is at Downing Street, Captain Drinkwater, and Mr Barrow is paying his respects to Mr Murray, the publisher.'

A wry and rather mischievous expression crossed Templeton's face. 'And it is getting rather late.' Templeton paused. 'I was alone in the copy room when the messenger was brought in . . .' The clerk let the sentence hang unfinished between them.

'A *coup de hasard*, is it, Mr Templeton?'

'Better than the *coup de grâce* for the Department, sir.'

'Perhaps.' Drinkwater paused. 'What d'you think it means? I recollect it was Murat's men who approached Colonel . . . damn me, what was his name . . .?'

'Colonel Coffin, sir, he was commanding Ponza and received overtures from Naples to Lord William Bentinck at Palermo,' said Templeton, already moving across the room to the long wooden box on the table from which he pulled an equally long drawer. It contained a well-thumbed card index and Templeton's thin fingers manipulated the contents with practised ease. After a moment he drew out a small, white rectangle covered with his own meticulous script. Holding it up to the candles he read aloud: 'Joachim Murat, born Lot 1767, trooper 1787, commissioned 1792, Italy,

Egypt, assisted Bonaparte in his *coup d'état*, commanded Consular Guard, fought at Marengo and in operations against King Ferdinand of the Two Sicilies . . .'

'Whom he has now despoiled of half his kingdom,' put in Drinkwater, 'and not in the manner of a fairy tale.'

'No, indeed,' Templeton coughed and resumed the card's details. 'Marshal of France 1804, occupied Vienna 1805, Grand Duke of Berg and Cleves 1808, Jena, Eylau, Madrid, King of Naples 1808. Commanded cavalry of Grande Armée in Russia, succeeded Bonaparte as C-in-C. Married to Caroline Bonaparte . . .' Templeton paused, continuing to read in silence for a moment. Then he looked up, smiling.

'In addition to the communication opened with Coffin and Lord William, we have several references to him from captains of men-of-war off the Calabrian coast.'

Drinkwater knew that the card index, with its potted biographies, was but an index to the volumes of guard books, and the references to which Templeton referred were intelligence reports concerning Marshal Murat, husband of Caroline Bonaparte and puppet King of Naples.

'I think we have an emissary of the Emperor's brother-in-law on our hands, sir.'

'Then it is a *coup de main*, is it not, Templeton?' Drinkwater jested, but his clerk wanted none of the pun. 'The question is, does he act on his own or Bonaparte's behalf?'

'Captain Drinkwater,' Templeton said in an urgent whisper as if he feared the very walls would betray him, 'if Mr Croker had received that letter he would pass it to the Foreign Secretary.'

'What letter?' asked Drinkwater, letting the missive go. It fluttered from his hand, slid sideways into the draught drawn into the chimney, hovered a moment above the glowing coals, then began to sink, shrivelling, charring and then touching down in a little upsurge of yellow flame before it turned to black ash, with a curl of grey smoke, and subsided among the clinkers in the grate. Drinkwater looked up, expecting outrage at this high-handed action, but was disappointed to see Templeton's face bore a look of such inscrutability that it crossed Drinkwater's mind that the clerk was pleased.

'I shall go to Harwich, Mr Templeton.'

'Tonight, sir?'

'Of course. Be so kind as to pass word for a chaise and let Williams know my portmanteau is to be made ready . . .'

'At once, at once . . .'

Templeton scuttled from the room and Drinkwater had the impression that he was actually running along the corridor outside. 'A rum fellow,' Drinkwater muttered, dismissively.

He rose from his chair, poured himself another glass of wine and took it to the window. He opened the shutters again. The moon had vanished and the night was black. Rain still drove on the panes, and the gusting wind rattled the sash incessantly.

'What a deuced dreadful night to go a-travelling,' he muttered to himself, but the window reflected a lop-sided grin above the rim of the wine glass.

Chapter Two *September 1813*

A Secret from the South

Lieutenant Sparkman dozed over the mulled wine, one booted leg stretched out on the wooden settle. Curled at his feet lay a brindled mongrel cur of menacing size. Periodically it came to frantic life, a hind leg vigorously clawing at a hidden flea, before it subsided again.

Having discommoded himself of the Neapolitan officer, he had not had much sleep in the arms of the energetic Annie. He was no longer a young man and the excesses of the night dissuaded him from taking too much of an interest in his report. He felt as weary that morning in the empty tap-room of the Three Cups at Harwich as he had at the Red Lion at Kirby-le-Soken the previous evening. He looked up as the latch of the door lifted and Annie, smiling at him above her unlaced stays and white breasts, led a stranger into the room.

'Tell your master that I want new horses in three hours and a dinner in two,' the stranger said, turning his back on Sparkman as he took off his tricorn and a heavy cloak and threw them on a wooden chair on the opposite side of the fireplace. The newcomer wore a suit of bottle-green which sat awkwardly on asymmetrical shoulders down which fell his hair in an old-fashioned queue set off with a black ribbon.

'New horses, sir, an' a dinner, aye, sir . . .' Annie bobbed and pouted at the newcomer and Sparkman felt a mean resentment at the intrusion, at the bossing of Annie Davis, at the little whore's attitude.

'Put some more coal on the fire,' Sparkman commanded, 'and get me a pipe and baccy while you're about it.'

Annie flashed him a quick, pleading look which spoke of obligations and priorities not purchased with his single florin.

'A glass of black-strap, if you please,' said the stranger, re-engaging Annie's attention, and she curtsied again, to Sparkman's intense irritation. But before he could add to the catalogue of Annie's chores, the man turned.

He was about fifty with a high forehead from which his grey-brown hair was drawn back severely. His face was lined and weatherbeaten, though a faint, pallid sword scar ran down his left cheek. His mouth, circumscribed by deep furrows, was expressive of contempt as he regarded the dishevelled Sparkman from stern grey eyes.

Sparkman's irritation withered under the stranger's scrutiny. He felt uncomfortably conscious of his dirty neck linen and the mud-stained boot outstretched on the settle seat. He lowered his eyes, raised the tankard to his lips. The fellow had no business with him and could go to the devil!

Drinkwater stared at the slovenly figure, noting the blue coat of naval undress uniform.

'Lieutenant Sparkman?'

Sparkman coughed with surprise, spluttering into his mulled wine in an infuriating indignity which he disguised in anger. 'And who the deuce wants to know?'

'You are Lieutenant Sparkman, Inspector of Sea Fencibles, are you not?' Drinkwater persisted coolly, drawing a paper from his breast pocket and shaking it so that the heavy seal fell, and unfolded it for Sparkman to read.

'I am Captain Nathaniel Drinkwater, from the Admiralty, Mr Sparkman. You wrote to their Lordships about a Colonel Bardolini.'

Sparkman's mouth fell open; he put his tankard down, wiped his hands upon his stained breeches and took Drinkwater's identification paper, looking at Drinkwater as he sat up straight.

'I beg pardon, sir . . .' He read the pass and handed it back. 'I beg pardon, sir, I had no idea . . . I wasn't expectin' . . .'

'No matter, Mr Sparkman, no matter.' Captain Drinkwater took the paper, refolded it and tucked it inside his coat.

'Where is this fellow Bardolini? In the Redoubt, I think you said.'

'Yes, sir, I thought it best . . .'

Annie Davis came back into the room with a glass of black-strap on a tray. 'Here you'm be, sir.'

'Obliged.' Drinkwater swallowed hard. 'No doubt you did think it for the best, Mr Sparkman, but I doubt Colonel Bardolini will be of so sanguine an opinion. Does he speak English?'

'Yes, very well.'

'Good. Where is this Redoubt?'

'You passed it, sir, just before you came to the main gate . . .'

'Ah yes, the glacis, I recollect it. Shall we go then?' Drinkwater tossed off the glass and swept up his cloak and hat. 'A dinner in two hours, my girl, and no later; a hot meat pie will do very well.'

Apart from its flagstaff, the Redoubt was as well hidden from sight as from cannon shot, nestling below a glacis which rose fifty feet above the level of the country. This slope terminated on the edge of a vertical counterscarp, and the brick bulk of the circular fort rose on the far side of a wide ditch. This was crossed by a drawbridge which led directly to the rampart, which was pierced by embrasures each housing a huge, black 24-pounder. Under the iron arch with its empty sconce, which marked the inconspicuous gateway to this military wonder, they were challenged halfheartedly by a blue-coated artilleryman on sentry duty. He had spied them walking out through the town's main gate and he had summoned a lieutenant who hurried up to greet them. For the second time in an hour, Drinkwater produced his identification.

'Your servant, sir,' the artillery officer said with a good deal more *savoir-faire* than Sparkman had mustered, handing back the paper. 'Lieutenant Patmore, sir, at your service. I've made the Italian officer as comfortable as possible, sir . . .' Patmore paused and shot a look at Sparkman, 'but I'm afraid he's frightfully touchy about his honour.'

Drinkwater regarded Sparkman and raised an eyebrow. 'You may announce me, Mr Sparkman. Lead on, Mr Patmore.'

They turned left and for a moment Drinkwater caught a glimpse of the open sea to the south-east, then the opposing salient of Landguard Point with its much older fortification, a shingle distal which formed a breakwater to the Harwich Shelf whereon a dozen merchantmen, collier brigs for the most part, rode out the last of the gale. To the north the River Orwell disappeared beyond a pair of Martello towers, winding through woodland to the port of Ipswich. Somewhere, beyond those treetops, lay Gantley Hall beneath the roof of which dwelt his wife Elizabeth, his children Amelia and Richard, and all his worldly desires.

Closer, behind the roofs of Harwich itself, the River Stour

stretched westward to Manningtree, where he had had his final change of horses prior to traversing its banks that very forenoon.

'Your batteries command the harbour very well, Mr Patmore. Have you been stationed here long?'

'I came with the guns, sir, from Woolwich, three years ago.'

They passed a stiffly rigid bombardier and two gunners, then turned suddenly, out of the wind and down through a stepped tunnel, descending rapidly to the level of the bottom of the dry moat, emerging within the wall's circumference on to a parade ground almost ninety feet across. Walking quickly round its edge they passed a number of wooden doors, some open, betraying a kitchen, a guardroom and the garrison's quarters, then stopped beside one which Sparkman unlocked.

Inside the casemate, wooden stalls formed the fort's prison, and at the opening of the door the inmate of the nearer leapt to his feet and Drinkwater saw the blazing dark eyes and fierce moustaches of the Neapolitan officer.

'This is an outrage! I demand you release me at once! I am invested with plenipotentiary powers by King Joachim Napoleon of Naples! An insult to me is an insult to the King my master! You have taken my sword and with my sword my honour! I wish to be taken to London . . .'

As this tirade burst upon them, Drinkwater turned to Patmore and, putting up a hand to the artillery officer's ear, asked, 'Do you have a room I could use? Somewhere you could serve some bread and meat, and perhaps a conciliatory bottle?'

Patmore nodded.

'Would you oblige me by attending to the matter?'

'Of course, sir. I advised Sparkman against this line of conduct.'

'Leave the matter to me, Mr Patmore.'

'Of course, sir. If you'll excuse me . . .' Patmore turned away, obviously glad to be out of the embarrassing din which echoed about the chamber.

'I give myself up to you, Signor Sparkman, in honour, in friendship, in trust. I have plenipotentiary powers . . .'

'Will you hold your damned tongue!' Sparkman cried, his efforts to expostulate having failed under Bardolini's verbal barrage. Bardolini grew quiet, seeing Drinkwater properly for the first time as he moved away from the door and ceased to be in silhouette to a man who had spent fifteen hours in the dark.

'This is Captain Drinkwater, Colonel, from London . . .'

'A *captain*,' Bardolini sneered, 'a *captain*? I am a colonel in the light cavalry of the Royal Life Guard! Am I to be met by a *captain*?'

'I am a captain in His Britannic Majesty's Royal Navy, Colonel Bardolini,' Drinkwater said, stepping forward and edging Sparkman to one side. 'I believe us to be equal in rank, sir,' he added with a hint of sarcasm which, he noted, was lost on Bardolini. 'Do you release our guest, Mr Sparkman.'

'I, er, I don't have the key, sir. Mr Patmore . . .'

'Then run and get it,' Drinkwater snapped. As soon as they were alone, he turned to Bardolini. 'I beg you to forgive the inconvenience to which you have been put, Colonel. You must appreciate the dangers of accepting everyone arriving from Europe at face value. Our orders are quite specific and to men of Lieutenant Sparkman's stamp, essential. D'you understand?'

'What is *stamp*?'

'Character . . .'

'Ah, *si*. Not so clever, eh?'

'Indeed, yes.' Drinkwater smiled. The untruthful but reassuring little collusion between two senior officers mollified Bardolini, and then Sparkman was back with a key and they led the Neapolitan out into a watery sunshine which showed the breaking up of the scud and foretold a shift in the wind. On the far side of the parade, Patmore stood beside an open door and Drinkwater began to walk towards him.

Behind him Bardolini stopped and looked up at the circle of sky above them, stretching ostentatiously. He ran a finger round his stock, then put on the hat which he had tucked under his arm. Drinkwater was amazed at the splendour of the man. He wore the tight *kurtka* deriving from the Polish lancers of the Grande Armée, a white jacket with a scarlet plastron and silver epaulettes. His long cavalry overalls were scarlet, trimmed with twin rows of silver lace, while his headdress also echoed the Polish fashion, a *czapka* with its peak and tall, square top, braided with silver and magnificently plumed in white. Colonel Bardolini was turned out in *la grande tenue* of parade dress and wanted only a shave to complete the impression of military perfection.

'Come, Colonel. I have ordered some meat and wine for you, and if you wish we can send for hot water for you to shave . . .'

'Good!' snapped Bardolini and crossed the parade.

Patmore led them into another casemate which served as the officers' mess. It was simply furnished with a table, chairs, a sideboard and some plate. Another artillery lieutenant lounged over a glass and bottle, already well down the latter for his welcome was heartily indulgent.

'Please sit down, gentlemen. Henry Courtney *à votre service*. Here, sir,' he said to Bardolini, 'your breakfast.' A gunner in shirt-sleeves brought in a platter of sliced meat and bread. Courtney poured wine into a second glass. Bardolini hesitated, then sat and fell ravenously upon the plate.

'Mr Courtney,' Drinkwater said as Bardolini devoured the food, 'would you do me the courtesy of allowing me a few moments of privacy with our guest?'

'Oh, I say, I've not finished . . .'

'Harry!'

Courtney turned and caught the severe look in Patmore's eye. 'Oh, very well,' he said unconvincingly, and rose with a certain display of languid condescension, 'as you wish.'

Drinkwater helped himself to a glass of wine as the door closed. The shirt-sleeved gunner looked in and Drinkwater dismissed him, closing the door behind him. Then he walked back to the table, drew the identification paper from his breast yet again and laid it before Bardolini. The Neapolitan read it, still chewing vigorously. Then he stopped and looked up.

'My own papers, they are with my sword and sabretache! I do not have them!'

'Calm yourself, my dear Colonel,' Drinkwater said and sat down opposite Bardolini. 'We can attend to the formalities on our way back to London. At the moment I wish only to know the purpose of your visit.'

'I have plenipotentiary powers, Captain. They are, with respect to yourself, for the ears of King George's ministers. I have a letter of introduction to Lord Castlereagh . . .'

'You speak excellent English, Colonel, where did you learn?' Drinkwater adroitly changed the subject.

'I worked for many years in the counting-house of an English merchant in Napoli. He taught it to all his clerks.'

'You were a clerk then, once upon a time?'

'But a republican always,' Bardolini flared.

'Yet you represent a king, and seek the ministers of a king. That is curious, is it not?'

'King Joachim is a soldier. He is a republican at heart, himself the son of an inn-keeper. He is a benevolent monarch, one who wishes to unite Italy and be a new Julius Caesar.'

'I thought Caesar refused a crown . . .'

'King Joachim is not a king as you understand it, Captain. Believe me, I lived under the rule of that despot Ferdinand and his Austrian bitch. They are filth, perhaps as mad as they say your own king is, but certainly filth, not worthy to eat the shit that ran out of the sewers of their own palazzo.'

'And yet I have to ask what King Joachim would say to the mad King George's ministers?'

'I cannot tell you.'

'I cannot take you to London.'

'You would not dare to refuse!' Bardolini's eyes blazed.

'Colonel, the ocean is wide, deep and cold. The men who have seen you today will have forgotten you in a month. Why do you think I have come here today? Do you think I myself do not have special powers, eh?' Drinkwater paused, letting his words sink in. 'Come, sir, telling me what you have come here for is likely to have little effect on matters if I am a man of no account. On the other hand, going forward to London on my recommendation will ensure your mission is swiftly accomplished.'

Bardolini remained silent.

'Let me guess, then. You are here in order to open secret negotiations to preserve the throne of Naples in the name of King Joachim Napoleon. You speak very good English and have plenipotentiary powers in case it becomes possible, in the course of your discussions, to conclude a formal accommodation, or even a full treaty of alliance, in which the British government guarantee Naples for the King your master who, though he remains a Marshal of France and Grand Admiral of the Empire, lost his French citizenship on succeeding to the crown of Naples.' Drinkwater paused, aware that he had Bardolini's full attention.

'You have, moreover, a difficult game to play because, on the one hand, King Joachim does not want his brother-in-law, the Emperor Napoleon, to know of this action. Nor does he wish the Austrians to learn of it, for while they may well toy with King Joachim, his desire to unite the Italian republicans and then the whole peninsula is inimical to their own interests. Moreover, it will cause deep offence to King Ferdinand, whose wife, Queen Maria Carolina, is not only the sister of the late Queen of France, Marie Antoinette, but was also born an Austrian archduchess and who, though ruling still in Sicily, has been deprived of the Italian portion of his kingdom by conquest. King Ferdinand regards your King Joachim as an usurper.

'Nevertheless, Prince Cariati at Vienna is assiduously pressing King Joachim's suit to the Austrian ministry. So your master must play a double game, for the Emperor Napoleon works to detach the Austrian Emperor from his alliance with us, thinking his own new wife, the Empress Marie-Louise, yet another Austrian archduchess, possesses influence to succeed in this endeavour, being daughter to the Emperor Francis himself.'

Drinkwater paused. Bardolini had ceased chewing and his jaw lay unpleasantly open so that half-masticated food was exposed upon his tongue. Drinkwater poured another glass of wine and looked away.

'Now, Colonel, do you have anything to add to this?'

Bardolini shut his mouth, chewed rapidly and swallowed prematurely. He lunged at his glass and gulped at the claret, wiping his mouth on the scarlet turn-back of his cuff.

'*Sympatico*, Captain, we are of one mind!'

'Perhaps. But King George's ministers will be less easy to oblige than you imagine, Colonel. Consider. Your master has already communicated with us through his Minister of Police, the Duke of Campochiaro, who sent one of his agents, a certain Signor Cerculi, to discuss with Colonel Coffin at Ponza matters of trade and an easement of the naval blockade of Calabria. Is that not true? And after these negotiations had been concluded, Cerculi let it be known that King Joachim and his brother-in-law had fallen out, indeed, that they were frequently at odds. King Joachim wants to rule in his own name and Napoleon wants him as no more than a tributary-king, a puppet – a marionette. Is this not so?'

'How do you know all this?' Bardolini looked genuinely puzzled.

'Because', Drinkwater said, leaning forward and lowering his voice, 'Colonel Coffin reported the matter back to the Sicilian court at Palermo, and from there it was passed to London.'

Such a torrent of detail clearly surprised Bardolini. He was astonished at the knowledge possessed by this strange Englishman. He did not know that Coffin had regaled the British frigate captain with the whole story and he, bored with the tedium of blockade, had confided all the details to his routine report of proceedings. This, in turn, had crossed Drinkwater's desk within two months, at the same time that the confidential diplomatic dispatch from Sicily had reached the office of the Foreign Secretary.

'But therein lies our dilemma, Colonel,' Drinkwater continued relentlessly. 'King Ferdinand has been assured that the British government wants to see the King of the Two Sicilies restored to his rightful place in his palace at Naples. How, then, can His Britannic Majesty's government take King Joachim seriously?'

It was, Drinkwater thought wryly, a fair question. Napoleon Bonaparte, having driven Ferdinand across the Strait of Messina, placed his brother Joseph on the vacant throne at Naples, leaving Ferdinand and Maria Carolina to vegetate under British protection at Palermo. Then, when he deceived the King of Spain and took him prisoner, Napoleon transferred Joseph to Madrid, installing him as king there, and sent Marshal Murat to Naples as King Joachim. It was rather a tawdry and expedient proceeding.

'Ferdinand is not important. He fled in English ships to Palermo. You support him there, without English ships he is powerless. Your government can abandon Ferdinand. Lord William Bentinck, your former minister at Palermo, has already been recalled by Lord Castlereagh.'

'But what has King Joachim to offer us in exchange for our protection? Can he guarantee that, if we maintain the dignity of his throne, the people of Naples, let alone of the whole of Italy, will acknowledge him as king?'

'*Si!* Yes! He is most popular! Without your ships, Ferdinand would be lost and Sicily would join all of Italy. Would that not be better for England? To have a friendly power in the Mediterranean? You would like a naval port at Livorno, or La Spezia.'

'Perhaps. Are you empowered to offer us a naval port?'

Bardolini shrugged again and looked about him. 'This is not the place . . .'

Drinkwater grinned. 'You may have to content yourself with such a place, Colonel,' he said dryly, 'you are in my hands now,' and his expression and tone of voice, strained by tiredness, appeared to Bardolini to be full of menace.

In fact Drinkwater was disappointed. The Neapolitan had nothing to offer. Joachim Murat was hedging his bets fantastically. It would be an act of humanity to send this candy-stick officer back to Flushing by the first available boat, but perhaps he would play the charade for just a little longer.

'Well, Colonel,' he said with an air of finality, stirring as though to rise and call Patmore and Sparkman, 'is King Joachim to be trusted? He is married to Caroline Bonaparte, the Emperor's sister. If he commits himself to coming over to the Allied cause like Bernadotte, his position must be unassailable. He courts Austria, which has her own deep interest in Tuscany and the Papal States, and would rather an accommodation with Ferdinand of the Two Sicilies than the adventurer and parvenu King Joachim . . .'

'Captain! You should not call him that! He is brave, and true! And devoted to his people and the Rights of Man!'

The sincerity of Bardolini's florid passion was genuine, though he had looked angry at Drinkwater's reference to Bernadotte. They were getting nowhere. For all the confidence of his exposition, Drinkwater was exhausted. The overnight journey jolting in a chaise, turning over and over in his mind the likely outcome of this queer meeting; the memorizing of the notes he had scribbled from a quick rereading of the guard books; the rehearsal of facts; the guessing at motives and the building in his own mind of a convincing, watertight reason for this singular, strange invasion, had left him weary. He had wanted to rage at the imbecile Sparkman, so obviously raddled by a night of dissolution, yet the lieutenant's inhumane treatment of Bardolini had left the man indignant for his own honour, and unguarded about his master's.

Drinkwater mustered his wits for one last argument. The drink had made him dopey and he forced himself to his feet, leaning forward for emphasis, his hands spread on the table before him. Again he managed a thin smile at Bardolini.

'There is one last point that we must consider, Colonel Bardolini. Where is the King of Naples now?'

The question caught Bardolini off guard. 'He is at Dresden.'

'With his Emperor?'

'With the Emperor of the French, yes.'

'As a Marshal of France, commanding the cavalry of the Grande Armée.'

Bardolini nodded, frowning.

'Yet he must be on the winning side, must he not? And to preserve his integrity it must never be known that he treated with the other. Is that not so?'

'You are an intelligent man, Captain. The King is married to the Emperor's sister. They correspond. There could be no absolute secrets between them . . .'

'No!' snapped Drinkwater with sudden vehemence. 'Bonaparte is a cynic; he will overlook base ingratitude, even treason if it serves his purpose, but do you think the Emperor Francis of Austria will be so tolerant? He is not so *republican* a king.'

Bardolini shrugged, missing the sarcasm. 'The Emperor Francis will bow if England is in alliance with the King of Napoli. A man who will declare war on the husband of his daughter will do anything.'

The cogency of the argument was impressive; and Bardolini's diplomatic ability was clear. Drinkwater fought to retain control of the dialogue.

'But, Colonel Bardolini, even as we speak Marshal Murat is in the field alongside his imperial brother-in-law. At least Bernadotte has repudiated his former master and is at the head of his Swedish troops and in command of an Allied army. His victory over his old friend Marshal Oudinot at Gross Beeren can hardly be called equivocating. Moreover, Colonel, on the sixth of this month, this same *ci-devant* republican soldier of France beat another old friend, Michel Ney, at Dennewitz. You did not know that, eh?' Drinkwater paused to let the import of the news sink in, then added, 'but your master has no such earnest of good faith to offer from his headquarters at Dresden, does he, eh? He behaves as he is, a tributary king, a puppy fawning on the hand that feeds him.'

Drinkwater finished his diatribe. Tiredness lent a menace to his final words and Bardolini was visibly upset by the torrent of logic poured upon him by this apparently scornful Englishman. He remained silent as Drinkwater straightened up, contemplating the evaporation of his hopes.

'Come, sir. We will summon your sword and sabretache. You shall accompany me to an inn where my chaise will be ready. You may shave there while I eat. I can promise you nothing, but we will proceed to London.'

Bardolini looked relieved as he stood and reached for his ornate *czapka*.

'By the way, Colonel, we do not need an Italian port as long as we have Malta. Besides, how long could we trust a king who was married to a Bonaparte princess, eh? Tell me that if you can.'

Suddenly, in the ill-lit casemate, the beplumed Neapolitan looked ridiculously crestfallen.

The wind, which had veered in the night and brought a cold forenoon of bright sunshine, backed against the sun as it westered, so that the sky clouded and it began to rain long before they reached Colchester. Drinkwater was tempted to stop and spend the night there, but the steak-and-kidney pie Annie Davis had served him at the Three Cups put him into a doze so that inertia dissuaded him from making a decision and the chaise rumbled on westward.

He had no thought now but to disencumber himself of Bardolini as soon as they reached London, and when he woke briefly as they changed horses he felt only an intense irritation that he could not have turned north at Manningtree, crossed the Stour and taken the Ipswich road towards Gantley Hall and his wife Elizabeth's bed.

The recent weather had turned the road into a quagmire. Every rut had become a ditch, the horses were muddied to their bellies and the wheels spun arcs of filth behind them. The chaise lurched over this morass and bucked and rocked in the gusts of wind, the rain drummed on the hood and he heard Bardolini cursing, though whether it was the weather or his predicament that most discommoded the Neapolitan, Drinkwater neither knew nor cared. At about eleven that night it stopped raining. On the open road the going improved and they reached Kelvedon before midnight. Both men got out to stretch their legs and visit the necessary at the post-house. A draught of flip restored Drinkwater to a lucid state of mind. The stimulus of the alcohol and the irregular motion of the chaise when they drove forward again continued to make sleep impossible. Bardolini, sitting opposite, was equally unable to doze off and in the intermittent moonlight that peeped from behind the torn and ragged cumulus, Drinkwater was aware of the fierce glitter of the Neapolitan officer's eyes.

Initially Drinkwater expected sudden attack, an instinctive if illogical fear of treacherous assault. But then he realized Bardolini was caught in a reverie and his eyes merely sought the future. Or perhaps the past, Drinkwater mused, which might be full of disappointments, but was at least inhabited by certainties. As he had found so often at sea, the light doze he had enjoyed earlier had restored him, and he felt an indulgence towards his fellow traveller.

'Colonel,' he said, as they passed through a patch of brilliant moonlight and he could see Bardolini's face in stark tones, 'I do not hold out much hope for your mission. *Entre nous*, the idea of a republican king is something of a contradiction in terms. Your reception in London is not likely to be, what do you say? *Sympatico*?'

'I have plenipotentiary powers, Captain. I am on diplomatic service. I expect the normal courtesies . . .'

'I do not wish to alarm you unduly, Colonel, but I am not aware that we recognize the government of King Joachim. Only your uniform prevents your arrest as a spy. That, and my company.'

'But you will take me to Lord Castlereagh, Captain?' Bardolini asked with a plaintive anxiety.

'I will send word to the Foreign Secretary that you are in London, but . . .' Drinkwater left the conjunction hanging in the darkness that now engulfed the two men. The unspoken clause was ominous and, unknown to Drinkwater, had the effect on the Neapolitan of causing him to come to a decision.

Upon landing in England, Colonel Bardolini had expected to be quickly picked up by the police, to be whisked to London with the Napoleonic thoroughness by which such things were managed in the French Empire and those states under its influence. He had not expected to stumble upon the discreditable Sparkman and then be locked up like a common criminal. Protestations about his honour, his plenipotentiary status and offers of his parole had fallen upon deaf ears. Now Drinkwater's assertions clothed this outrage with a chilling logic. The English were, just as he had been led to believe, barbarians.

Notwithstanding these considerations, Bardolini had not anticipated this strange English naval officer would possess such a commanding knowledge of the situation in Napoli; it was uncanny. Indeed, such was the extent of the captain's familiarity with the plight of his master, King Joachim, that Bardolini suspected treachery. His imprisonment was consonant with such a hypothesis and he believed he was, even now, on his way to a more secure incarceration.

The only thing which Bardolini *had* expected was the violence of the sea passage and the weather which now assailed the chaise and deterred him from any rash ideas of escape. Not that he had abandoned them altogether; he carried a stiletto inside his right boot, but to reach it beneath his tight cavalryman's overalls was well-nigh impossible, and his sword was secured to his portmanteau. Besides, there were other considerations. Though he spoke English well, he could hardly melt inconspicuously into the countryside! Besides, if he stole a horse, he would only be returned the faster to the shores of that damnable sea.

As the dismal hours succeeded one another, he resolved on the one course of action he had reserved for Lord Castlereagh alone, in the hope that this naval officer, whose grasp of diplomatic affairs seemed so inexplicably comprehensive, would favourably influence his request for an interview with the British Foreign Minister. Now, as Drinkwater hinted so forbiddingly at the hostility of his reception, Bardolini played his trump card and spoke out of the darkness.

'Captain Drinkwater, I believe you to be a man of honour. You are clearly a person of some influence, your knowledge of affairs of state makes that quite clear. It is possible you are a police agent . . . If that is so, I ask only that what I am about to confide in you, you report to your superiors . . .'

'I am not a police agent, Colonel. We have not yet adopted all your Continental fashions. I am what I told you.'

'Perhaps,' Bardolini acknowledged doubtfully, 'but your word, please, that what I tell you will be treated with the confidence it deserves and be passed to Lord Castlereagh himself.'

'Are you about to give me a pledge of your master's good faith?'

'*Si*.'

'Very well. You have my word.'

'You are at war with the Americans, are you not?'

'You know that very well.'

'I also know that there are men in America who would rule Canada, and Frenchmen in Canada who would welcome American assistance to separate them from your country, even if it meant joining the United States.'

'That is not a very great secret, Colonel.'

'No. But King Joachim wishes to make known to your government that the Americans have negotiated a secret treaty of mutual assistance with the Emperor Napoleon, a treaty which, in exchange for American attacks on British ships and a quantity of gold, guarantees a large shipment of arms, powder and shot. These are to be used for raising a revolution in Quebec. The Quebecois will join up with an American army marching north from New York next spring.'

'Go on, Colonel, you have my full attention.'

'During the winter bad weather, American ships will arrive in the waters of Norway . . .'

'Where in Norway?' Drinkwater cut in.

'A place called the Vikkenfiord.'

'Go on, Colonel.'

'Secretly, the arms and munitions will be taken to them by the Danes. The Americans will also stop supplying your army in the Iberian Peninsula. The Emperor believes that with rebellion in Canada, your government will no longer be able to support the Spanish insurrection, will withdraw Wellington's army and transport it to North America. Great Britain will retreat behind its traditional defence, the sea. It will not be able to expend its treasure on maintaining Austrian, Prussian and Russian armies in the field. Your country's alliance will die and the Emperor of Austria will accept King Joachim as the sovereign of Italy.'

But Drinkwater was no longer listening; he was thinking of Herr Liepmann's dispatch and the shipment of arms lying somewhere in Hamburg.

Chapter Three *September 1813*

Arrivals

There was a clever simplicity in Bardolini's revelations. Not only was their substance of crucial importance to the survival of Great Britain, but the plan was cunning in its construction, satisfying both political and economic needs. For while raising rebellion and absorbing Canada in the Union would placate the war-hawks in the American Congress, it would also compensate the United States' treasury for the loss of British gold now paid for the grain being sent to Wellington's army in Spain. For Britain herself, the loss of American supplies was more important than the saving to her exchequer. It was well known that the Americans were happy to export to both contending parties in the great war in Europe, and that they sold wheat to the British with whom they were themselves at war! But a greater irony existed if the arms they were to buy from the French were paid for with gold sent to the United States by Great Britain in the first place.

This vast and complex circulation wormed its way into Drinkwater's tired brain as the buffeted chaise passed Chelmsford and rumbled on towards London. He mused on the tortuous yet simple logic, aware from his own experience with Yankee privateers that American ambition was as resourceful as it was boundless. There was, moreover, an insidious and personal reflection in his train of thought. In all the weary months he had spent at the Admiralty's Secret Department, he had hoped for some news like Bardolini's. He had not the slightest doubt that the Neapolitan colonel had been delivered into his hands by Providence itself, nor that it was not Joachim Murat's secret overtures that were the most important feature of Bardolini's intelligence.

The fantastical image of Napoleon's great cavalry leader was a tragi-comic figure in Drinkwater's perception, a man raised to such heights of pomp and pride that violent descent could be its only consequence. The very weakness of the parvenu king's position, his desire to maintain friends on both sides of the fence, so that when he tumbled from it there would be waiting arms to save him, was too ridiculous to be treated seriously.

King Joachim's secret earnest of good faith, the revelation of the bargain struck between the French Emperor and the Americans, was clever enough, for it was invaluable to Great Britain, but its defeat, if the British chose to act, left King Joachim untouched and would hurt his brother-in-law enough to incline fate to favour the Allied cause. Nor was its betrayal a serious enough treachery to deprive Murat of his kingdom if Napoleon defeated his enemies in detail. The French Emperor was not a man to deprive the husband of his favourite sister of his crown for a mere peccadillo!

Nor could Drinkwater ignore the consequences of success for Napoleon himself. If the Emperor of the French did succeed in forcing the British to withdraw Wellington's army for service in America or Canada, such a move would not only remove the threat to southern France, it would also release battle-hardened troops under his most experienced marshals to reinforce the ranks of the green 'Marie-Louises' now opposing the combined might of Russia, Prussia and Austria.

As Drinkwater nursed an aching head and the beginnings of yet another quinsy, as he slipped in and out of conscious thought, nodding opposite the now sleeping Bardolini, his resolve hardened round the central thought that this was without doubt the event for which Lord Dungarth had named Nathaniel Drinkwater his successor in the Secret Department of the British Admiralty.

In his tired and half-conscious state, Drinkwater found nothing incongruous in attributing Dungarth with such prescience. The earl had possessed a keen and analytical brain and had been quite capable of sensing some innate ability in his ageing protégé. But for Drinkwater it was to prove a dangerously deluded piece of self-conceit.

Drinkwater was at his desk by three o'clock that afternoon. When they changed horses at Brentwood he had instructed the post boy to take them directly to his home in Lord North Street. Both he and Bardolini were jerked rudely awake when the chaise finally stopped outside the terraced house.

The place had been left to Drinkwater by Lord Dungarth with a pitifully small legacy for its upkeep and the continued maintenance of its staff. It was a modest house, the austere earl's only London establishment, which had become home for Drinkwater now that his new post detained him so much in the capital. Ideas of a convenient *pied-à-terre* for Captain and Mistress Drinkwater had proved impractical. Elizabeth, never entirely at ease in town, had almost conceded defeat, and contented herself with running the small Suffolk estate, while Drinkwater led his own miserable and unhappy existence dragging daily to Whitehall.

He had done nothing to the interior of the house and it remained as it had been when Dungarth occupied it. He had even ordered Williams, Dungarth's manservant, who had performed the joint offices of butler, valet and occasional secretary to the earl, to retain the black crêpe drapes over the full-length portrait of Dungarth's long-dead countess which hung above the fireplace in the withdrawing-room. The gesture had earned Williams's approval and the transfer of loyalty to Captain Drinkwater had thereafter been total.

'He's very like his Lordship in many ways,' Williams had confided to his common-law wife who, as cook and housekeeper, formed the remainder of the staff.

'Yes, he's a gennelman all right,' she agreed.

'Not *quite* in the same way as Lord John was,' Williams added, his notion of the finer distinctions of society more acute than that of his spouse, his terminology uttered with an unassailable familiarity, 'but inclining that way, to be sure.'

'To be sure,' agreed his wife docilely, aware that her own status was as much a matter of delicate uncertainty as Captain Drinkwater's, and always anxious to avoid the slightest disturbance to her husband's tranquillity of mind which, he had long ago assured her, was of the utmost importance in their relationship.

Williams now met Drinkwater and took his instructions. The strange colonel was to be given every comfort; a meal, a bath and, if he wished, an immediate bed after his long and tedious journey.

Williams's long service had conditioned him to odd arrivals and departures. He was well aware of the nature of the business of his employers, past and present, and the moustachioed figure was but one of a succession of ill-assorted 'guests' that he had accommodated. Having instructed Williams, Drinkwater turned to Bardolini.

'My dear Colonel, please accept my hospitality without my presence. Williams here will see to your wants. You must, as we say, make yourself at home.' He smiled at Bardolini who, as he removed his cloak, looked round with an air of curiosity, then gravely bowed a courtly acknowledgement. He looked every inch the plenipotentiary in his scarlet, white and silver.

'Thank you, Captain.'

'I shall leave you for a matter of a few hours. We will dine together tonight, when I hope to have news for you. In the meantime I will announce your arrival.'

'You wish to see my accreditation?' asked Bardolini, recovering his dangling sabretache on its silver-laced straps.

'Indeed, I do.'

'I am trusting you, Captain, with my life,' Bardolini said solemnly, handing over the heavily sealed paper which Drinkwater opened and scanned briefly.

'It is not misplaced, I assure you,' said Drinkwater, turning to Williams. 'See Colonel Bardolini wants for nothing, if you please, Williams. I shall be back for dinner at eight.'

Thus Captain Drinkwater was at the Admiralty before the clock at the Horse Guards struck three hours after noon.

Templeton met him as the Admiralty porter stirred himself from his chair.

'Good to have you return, sir,' said Templeton with a curtness that drew Drinkwater's attention to the fixed and unhappy expression on his face. 'Shall we go up directly?'

'As you please, Templeton,' said Drinkwater, somewhat nonplussed by his clerk's obvious discomfiture.

'What the devil's the matter?' Drinkwater asked, the moment they were inside his room. They had met but one other clerk upon the stairs and he had drawn aside with an unusual display of deference as Templeton had sped past, so that Drinkwater became alarmed at what news had broken in his absence.

'Barrow is the matter, sir. He has closed us down without further ado and in your absence. The matter is most improper.' Templeton fidgeted with an unhappy agitation, his face pale and anxious. 'The guard books are to be transferred to the Second Secretary's office, sir, and I,' Templeton's voice cracked with emotion, 'I am to be returned to the general copy room.'

It was not the worst fate that could befall an Englishman, Drinkwater thought, Templeton could be press-ganged, but he forbore from pointing this out. Nevertheless, it was clear that this humiliation had hurt the clerk, for news of the projected closure had come as no surprise. The thought sowed a seed in Drinkwater's over-stimulated brain but, for the moment, he confined himself to a sympathetic concern.

'My dear fellow, that is bad news, but don't despair, perhaps . . .'

Templeton shook his head. 'I have remonstrated with Barrow, sir. He is adamant that our activities can be subsumed by his own office and that my own personal expertise is of little consequence.' Templeton paused to master his bitterness, adding, with a touch of venom, 'I think he is jealous of our independence.'

'I shouldn't wonder,' Drinkwater temporized, pondering on how best to further matters in so far as Bardolini's news was concerned.

'I assured him that, notwithstanding our lack of recent progress, there were indications that matters of importance would shortly come to a head and that your own absence testified to this.' Templeton fell ominously silent. There was obviously an element of deep and significant drama, at least as far as Templeton was concerned, in this exchange.

'What did Mr Barrow say to that?' Drinkwater prompted with a tolerant patience he was far from feeling.

'He said', Templeton began with an evasive air, as if he found the admission distasteful, 'that it did not seem to much matter these days whether you were in or out, sir, but that on balance your achievements in the past had proved rather more effective in the public service when you were out, preferably at sea, sir.'

Drinkwater suppressed an outburst of laughter with a snort that Templeton construed as indignation. In all justice Drinkwater could not find much flaw in Barrow's decision, given that Barrow knew nothing of the events of the last two days, but in consideration of Templeton's feelings, he kept his face straight.

'It is my fault, I'm afraid, Barrow has never liked me . . .'

'I find it difficult to see why, sir.'

'Thank you, but we disagreed some years ago and I think he has seen my installation here as something to be terminated when the opportunity arose. I do not believe he wanted the department to outlive Lord Dungarth. Anyway, I think it is no matter now . . .'

'Oh, yes . . . forgive me, Captain Drinkwater, I have been so unseated by this unpleasant matter . . .'

'Of course, Templeton, of course. I take it you do not wish to return to the copy room?'

'The loss of emolument, sir . . .' Templeton looked aghast.

'How attached *are* you to my person, Templeton? Sufficient to go a-voyaging?'

'To sea, sir?' Templeton asked incredulously.

'That is the purpose of Admiralty,' Drinkwater replied drily.

'Well yes, sir, I understand, but my widowed mother . . .' Templeton was deathly pale.

'Never mind, then,' Drinkwater said brusquely, 'go at once and inform Mr Barrow of my return and my desire to speak with Mr Croker. Then, if you please, find out for me the ships and vessels currently at anchor in roadsteads on the east coast, from the Downs to Leith. A list of guardships and convoy escorts, that sort of thing, do you understand?'

'Perfectly.' The clerk's voice was not above a whisper.

'Good, then bring that to me, wherever I am in the building.'

Barrow received Drinkwater in his spacious office. Neither man had alluded to their disagreement some six years earlier.* Indeed Drinkwater supposed Barrow had long ago forgotten about it, for it was Drinkwater himself who had been the more angered by their unfortunate encounter. Nevertheless, since his posting to the Secret Department, memory of the matter had disinclined Drinkwater to force his presence on the Second Secretary and he had preferred to rely upon written memoranda to communicate with the Board.

'Pray sit down, Captain Drinkwater. Mr Croker has taken his seat in the House today and I have therefore taken the liberty of asking you to see me. I think I know why you wish to speak with the First Secretary and I apologize for the manner in which you learned of our decision to incorporate Lord Dungarth's old office with my own. I am sure you can see the logic . . .'

'I perfectly understand the logic, Mr Barrow,' Drinkwater broke in, 'and it is *not* what I have come to discuss with either Mr Croker or yourself.'

*See *Baltic Mission*.

'Oh, I see, then what may I ask . . . ?'

'Templeton is somewhat anxious about his future as, I admit, I am for my own.'

Barrow was immediately deceived by Drinkwater's opening. He was used to self-seeking, whether it was that of clerks or sea-officers, but it was crucial to Drinkwater that he should know whether or not the Admiralty had any plans for himself.

'We thought perhaps some furlough; you have not had the opportunity to spend much time on your estate, nor to enjoy the society of your wife and family.'

'You have no plans for me to have a ship?'

'Not immediately, Captain, no. There are Edwardes and Milne both clamouring for release from the American blockade, and when Green returns from the West Indies . . .'

'I am not anxious for a seventy-four.'

'No, quite, blockade is a confoundedly tedious business, I'm told.' Barrow smiled. 'Since you're too old for a frigate,' he added with a laugh, 'it looks as if your Suffolk acres will have to serve you for a quarterdeck.'

Drinkwater ignored the mockery and changed the subject. 'I have been away, Mr Barrow, and I desire you to communicate a matter of some importance to the Foreign Secretary directly.'

'And what is that?' Barrow asked with unfeigned surprise.

'I have, in my custody, a Colonel Bardolini of the household cavalry of King Joachim of Naples. The King, if that is what he is, wishes to secure a guarantee from His Britannic Majesty's government that, irrespective of the fate of the Emperor of the French, Joachim Napoleon will remain King of Naples.'

'But King Ferdinand . . .'

'I have explained *all* the ramifications attaching to the matter,' Drinkwater said wearily, drawing from his breast pocket Bardolini's diplomatic accreditation and laying it on the desk before Barrow. 'Moreover, I am of the opinion that King Joachim is a reed awaiting the stronger breeze. Nevertheless, Bardolini has been invested with plenipotentiary powers and sent here on a mission to the Court of St James's.'

Barrow leaned forward and drew the document towards him. 'Murat,' he murmured, reading the paper, 'well, well.'

'There is another matter, Mr Barrow,' Drinkwater began, but he was interrupted by a knock at the door.

'Come,' Barrow called, without looking up from Bardolini's paper.

Templeton approached across the carpet and held out a sheet of paper. Drinkwater took it and stared at it. Templeton had written: *The Downs, The Nore, Ho'sley Bay, Yarmouth, The Humber, Tyne, Leith,* and under each the names of one or two ships.

'What is that? What do you want, Templeton?' Barrow looked up, frowning at the intrusion.

'My fault, Mr Barrow,' Drinkwater put in quickly, 'I asked Templeton to bring me a list of ships in the ports of the east coast . . .'

'What on earth for . . . ?'

'Thank you, Templeton, kindly wait for me in my room.'

'Very well, sir.' Reluctance was in every step of the clerk's retreat.

'Captain, if you please, explain . . .'

'Of course, Mr Barrow, of course. There is another matter arising out of this approach from Marshal Murat . . .'

'I presume this other matter touches us . . . I mean their Lordships, rather than the Foreign Secretary?'

'You are an astute man, Mr Barrow.'

Drinkwater explained, repeating Bardolini's revelation and adding the corroborative evidence from Herr Liepmann at Hamburg sent through the British-held island of Helgoland. When he had finished, Barrow was silent for a moment. 'I recollect', he said gravely, 'your report on the destruction of the American privateers, and the concomitant matters you raised.' Barrow frowned, deep in thought. 'You are uniquely placed to understand the importance of this intelligence, are you not?'

'Hence this paper, Mr Barrow.'

'The paper?' Barrow frowned again, but this time with incomprehension.

'I want two things, Mr Barrow . . .'

'You *want* . . . ?'

'You give my office a brief stay of execution and you give me', he looked down at the paper Templeton had brought to where his thumb lay adjacent to the note *Leith*, 'the frigate *Andromeda*.'

'But I . . .'

'Come, come, I have been here long enough to know Lord

Melville will put his name to anything you recommend, as will Mr Croker . . .'

Barrow grunted, fell silent, then said, 'But is one frigate enough, Captain? You had a flying squadron at your disposal before.'

'Another thing I have learned is that we have few enough ships to protect our own trade, Mr Barrow. How many can you spare me? The cutter *Kestrel* used to be at Lord Dungarth's disposal, but she has long since . . .'

'No, no, you may have her, if you wish, as a tender or dispatch vessel.'

'And I may write my own orders?'

'You may *draft* your own orders, Captain,' said Barrow smiling, 'and you may retain Templeton to do it . . .'

'I was thinking of taking him to sea.'

'A capital idea.'

'I think their Lordships might permit me the luxury of a secretary.'

'I think they might be persuaded.' Relief at having the problem of Templeton so neatly resolved delighted Barrow.

Drinkwater rose. 'What of Bardolini? He is safe enough with me for a few days and I shall want a week to make my preparations, but after that he will be an encumbrance.'

'Give me a day or two, Captain Drinkwater, and I will let you know – by, say, Thursday?'

Drinkwater nodded. 'What d'you think Castlereagh will do?'

'I would imagine almost anything to string Murat along and prevent him giving his wholehearted support to Bonaparte.'

'So we will send Bardolini back with a diplomatic humbug?'

'It is not for me to say, but I would imagine so.'

'Poor fellow.'

'*C'est la guerre, n'est-ce pas?* You may send him to Helgoland in the *Kestrel*. He may then be landed near Hamburg and rejoin his master at Dresden.'

Drinkwater nodded. 'Very well. I shall hear from you by Thursday?'

'Of course.'

Whether or not Barrow recalled their past disagreement, Drinkwater had forgotten it as he left the room.

Templeton was not in his room when Drinkwater returned to it, and he sat and contemplated the papers on his desk. A dozen dispatches and reports had come in in his absence, an unusual amount for two days and ironic in the light of the imminent demise of his office. The sheets were neatly minuted in Templeton's impeccable script and, where necessary, additional sheets of paper were pinned to the originals, decryptions of enciphered text.

He riffled through them. They were tediously routine: a deciphered message from a Chouan agent in Brittany recounting the numbers of French warships in Brest which would serve merely to corroborate the sightings of the blockading frigates off Ushant; a report from St Helier in the Channel Islands about a small convoy which would have reached its destination by now; and a report from Exeter concerning the escape of a score of American prisoners-of-war from a working detail sent out from Dartmoor prison.

Templeton entered the room at that moment. 'I'm sorry, sir, I . . .'

Drinkwater waved aside the man's apology. 'No matter. How do we come to receive this? This is a matter for the civil authorities.' He indicated the report concerning the American prisoners.

'They were seamen, sir, and therefore we were notified. We usually inform the Regulating Captains . . .'

'And they try and pick them up for service in our own fleet, eh?'

'I believe so, sir. They are more productive serving His Majesty at sea, rather than being detained at His Majesty's pleasure ashore!'

'A vicious habit, Templeton, which don't make the life of a sea-officer at all comfortable, and a pretty extremity to be driven to.' Drinkwater pulled himself up short. Templeton was not to blame for such matters, though it would do him good to see something of life's realities. 'Besides,' he added, 'they were not idle when they escaped, they were building dry-stone walls.'

'Yes, sir,' Templeton said resignedly, leaning forward and drawing a last letter to Drinkwater's attention. 'There is a *post scriptum* to the affair.'

Drinkwater took the letter and read it. 'So they melted into the countryside. Does the fact seem the least remarkable to you, Templeton? Wouldn't you have done the same?'

'It is customary to have a few reports of sightings.'

Drinkwater dropped the letter. 'Pass these to Mr Barrow's people. We have other work to do. Do you draft orders, in the usual form, to the officer commanding HMS *Andromeda* . . .'

'He is not on board, sir, having been lately called to Parliament . . .'

'Then that is his damned bad luck, who is he?'

'Captain Pardoe. He is the Member for Eyesham.'

'Well, so much the better for Eyesham. An order for his replacement, my commission . . . where is *Kestrel*?'

'*Kestrel*, sir? Er, she is a cutter . . .'

'I know *what* she is, I want to know *where* she is.'

'Laid up, I think,' said Templeton frowning, 'at Chatham, I believe.'

'Find out. Let me know. Now I shall write to my wife. We have less than a week before we leave London, Templeton.'

'*We*, sir?'

'Yes. You are appointed my secretary.'

Templeton stared blankly at Drinkwater and opened his mouth to protest. It had gone dry and he found it difficult to speak, managing only a little gasp before Drinkwater's glare dissuaded him from the matter and he fled. To lose all hope of elevation and suffer the ignominy of virtual demotion was enough for one day, but to be a pressed man as well was more than flesh and blood could stand. Templeton reeled out into the corridor dashing the tears from his eyes.

He left behind a chuckling Drinkwater who drew a clean sheet of paper towards him, picked up his pen and flipped open the inkwell.

My Darling Wife . . . he began to write and, for a few moments, all thoughts of the war left him. As he finished the letter he looked up. It was almost dark and the unlit room allowed his eyes to focus on the deep blue of the cloudless evening sky. The first stars twinkled dimly, increasing in brilliance as he watched, marvelling.

He would soon see again not merely those four circumscribed rectangles, but the entire, majestic firmament.

It was almost a cruelty to bring Elizabeth to London for a mere three days, but two in the society of Bardolini, who insisted on continually badgering his host for news, was a trial to Drinkwater for whom the wait, with little to do beyond a brief daily attendance at the Admiralty, was tedious enough.

Difficulties began to crowd him within an hour of his wife's arrival. Bardolini insisted upon paying her elaborate court, depriving her husband of even the chilliest formality of a greeting, but then a more serious arrival in the shape of the young Captain Pardoe threatened to upset Drinkwater's humour still further.

'I understand, sir, that it is largely upon your intervention that I have been deprived of my command,' Pardoe had expostulated on the doorstep.

'Whereas I understand the demands of party expect you in Westminster, sir, where, happily, you are,' Drinkwater replied coolly.

'Damn it, sir, by what right do you . . . ?'

'You are making a fool of yourself, Captain Pardoe, pray come inside . . .' Pardoe was admitted and confronted with the uniformed splendour of Colonel Bardolini. Introductions were effected to both the Neapolitan and Elizabeth, hushing Pardoe. At an opportune moment, Drinkwater was able to draw him aside and whisper, 'Colonel Bardolini is an important diplomatic envoy. Your ship is wanted for a mission of some delicacy, such that an officer of my seniority must assume command. It was thought better all round by the ministry that you should take your seat, I believe you are warm in the government's cause, and I should take command.'

Drinkwater's dark dissimulation appeared to have a swiftly mollifying effect. 'I see,' said Pardoe. 'Of course, if that is the case, I am naturally happy to oblige.'

'We knew you would be, Pardoe,' Drinkwater smiled, hoping Pardoe connected all the insinuations and believed *Andromeda* to be bound for the Mediterranean.

'D'you care for some tea, Captain?' asked Elizabeth soothingly, and the awkward incident passed, dissolving into the inconsequential small-talk of the moment. Elizabeth delighted in talking to a man who seemed to be at the heart of affairs and Drinkwater unobtrusively observed the pleasure she took in the company of Pardoe and Bardolini.

When, at last, they were alone together in their bedroom and Elizabeth had unburdened herself of news of the farms and the well-being of family and tenantry, he asked, 'Have you seen James Quilhampton recently?'

'Yes. He was dandling his son on his knee,' Elizabeth said pointedly.

'But was anxious for employment?'

'He did not say.'

'Bess, I . . .'

'You said you would not be going to sea again, not that it matters much since I think I would rather you were as sea than languishing in this gloomy place.'

'I thought you liked this house?'

'When it was Lord Dungarth's, I did; as your London establishment, I don't care for it at all.

'Johnnie died in this room, didn't he?' His wife's familiar reference to the dead Dungarth discomfited Drinkwater. She had been as fond of him as he of her, and the difference between the sexes had led to an easing of the formalities that bound her husband. He changed the subject.

'I have to go, Bess . . .'

'I know, affairs of state,' she sighed, then resumed, 'though I wonder what important matters demand the presence of so obscure an officer as my husband.'

'Perhaps I am not so obscure,' he said, in a poor attempt to jest, or to boast.

'Try persuading me otherwise, Nathaniel.'

'There is Colonel Bardolini.'

'He is pathetic and rather frightened.'

'Frightened? Why do you say that?' Drinkwater asked with sudden interest.

Elizabeth shrugged. 'I don't know; he just gives that impression.'

'Well, he's safe enough here and, for the few days we have, you can look after him.'

'Thank you, kind sir,' she said. 'But you have changed the subject. I want to know more of this proposed voyage. I suppose you wish me to carry orders to James when I return in the same way that I carried your sea-kit up to London.'

'You rumble me damned easily, Elizabeth.'

'You shouldn't be so transparent. I suppose you cannot or will not confide in me.'

'It is not . . .'

'A woman's business, I know.'

'I was about to say, it is not easy to explain.'

'Try.'

And when he had finished Elizabeth said, 'I hate you going, my darling, but knowing why makes it bearable. I know I shall never have you to myself until this war is over and anything that brings peace nearer is to be welcomed. I can only pray that God will spare you.'

He bent and kissed her, but she yielded only a little, pushing him gently away. 'Must you take James? Catriona has waited so long for him and you summoned him before, then left her to bear the child alone.'

'Bess, you know James has no means of support beyond his half-pay; he yearns for a ship . . .'

'You promised him his swab, Nathaniel, yet he remains on the lieutenants' list.'

'You know I recommended him, but . . .'

'The matter proved only your obscurity,' Elizabeth was quick to point out.

'*Touché*,' he muttered. 'Well, I can't guarantee him his swab, but I can put him in a good position to earn it. He can have the *Kestrel*, d'you remember her?'

'She's only a little cutter, isn't she?'

'Yes, but she provides him with an opportunity,' countered Drinkwater, increasingly desperate. 'You know too damned much about naval affairs, Elizabeth,' he said, rising from the bed and tearing testily at his stock.

And though they lay in each other's arms until dawn, they were unable to find the satisfaction true lovers expect of one another.

Chapter Four *October 1813*

Departures

On the last Thursday in September, Drinkwater rose before dawn. Elizabeth, as used to the regime of the byre as her husband was to that of a ship, was astir equally early. She was to leave for Gantley Hall after breakfast, though without orders for James Quilhampton who had been sent to Chatham the instant Drinkwater learned the cutter *Kestrel* was mastless.

'My dear, I have to go to the Admiralty. I shall have the coach brought round for you.'

'As you wish.'

Bardolini, in shirt and overalls, caught him on the landing as he prepared to leave.

'Captain, please, today . . .'

'Colonel, today I promise. I told you not to expect a response until Thursday, and you shall have your answer today.'

'But I have yet to meet Lord Castlereagh . . .'

'Lord Castlereagh has been informed of your arrival. Now do be a good fellow and be patient. I shall send for you before this evening, rest assured upon the matter.'

'This evening? But, Captain . . .'

Drinkwater hurried on down the stairs and met Williams in the hall. 'Williams, be so kind as to send word for the coach. My wife's portmanteau is almost ready to come down.'

Elizabeth, in grey travelling dress and boots, her bonnet in her hand, joined him for coffee. He nodded at the sunlight streaming in through the window.

'Well, my dear, you should have a pleasant enough run. D'you have something to read?'

'You know I have trouble reading in a coach, Nathaniel.'

'I'm sorry. I had forgotten. You used to . . .'

'We *used* to do a lot of things,' she said quietly, and the words stung him with reproach.

'The Colonel will have to break his fast alone this morning,' she continued. 'It is curious, but I always thought soldiers were early afoot.'

'I think not Neapolitan soldiers,' he said, smiling, grateful for the change of subject and the lifeline she had thrown him.

'He is a strange fellow, though well enough educated. He reads English books. I found him reading your copy of Prince Eugène's *Memoirs* yesterday, but he seemed distracted. Has he been out since his arrival?'

'I cautioned him not to venture far and not to be absent for more than half an hour. His uniform is somewhat distinctive, even when he wears a cloak.'

'At least he doesn't wear his hat.'

'No,' Drinkwater laughed, 'though there are so many foreign corps in our service today that I doubt one more fantastic uniform among so many peacocks will turn any heads. Have you seen what they have done to our light dragoons? They've turned them into hussars with pelisses and more frogging than ratlines on a first-rate's mainmast. How the poor devils are supposed to campaign, let alone fight in such ridiculous clothes, I'm damned if I know.'

Williams looked in to announce the coach.

'Well, my dear, looks like goodbye.' He stood as she dabbed at her lips with a napkin and rose, picking up her bonnet. He took it from her and kissed her. He felt her yield and stirred in reaction to her softness.

'Oh Bess, my darling, don't think too ill of me.'

'I should be used to you by now,' she murmured, but both knew it was the unfamiliar and uncertain future that lay between them.

At the Admiralty Drinkwater called upon Barrow and received the orders he had drafted. 'God speed and good fortune, Captain. Lord Castlereagh will receive Bardolini this evening.'

'Thank you, Mr Barrow.'

In his office he removed Pocock's painting and asked for a porter to take it to Lord North Street, then sent for Templeton.

'D'you have all your dunnage, Templeton?'

'I believe so, sir.' Templeton's tone was, Drinkwater thought, one of miserable and reluctant martyrdom.

'You have done as I asked?'

'To the letter, sir.'

'Good. That is a sound principle.'

'The papers you were anxious about are secured in oilcloth in the corner.' Templeton pointed to a brown parcel secured with string and sealing wax.

'Very well, I shall take them myself.' Drinkwater looked round the room. The bookcase which had contained Templeton's meticulously maintained guard books was empty.

'This is a damnable place,' Drinkwater said curtly. Templeton sniffed disagreement. 'It is better to be pleased to leave a place than to mope over it,' Drinkwater added.

'It is a matter of opinion, sir,' Templeton grumbled.

Drinkwater grunted and picked up the parcel. 'Come, sir, let us be gone.'

The clock at the Horse Guards was chiming eleven as he walked back to Lord North Street to take his final departure. Williams greeted him and Drinkwater asked that his sea-chest be made ready.

'Mrs Williams is ironing the last of the shirts, sir.'

'Very good. Where is the Colonel?'

'He left an hour ago, sir.'

'What, for a walk?'

'No, sir, a gentleman called for him. He seemed to be expected.'

Drinkwater frowned. 'Expected? What d'you mean?'

'The man said he had called for Colonel Bardolini. I asked him to come into the hall and wait. When I brought the Colonel into the hall, he asked the gentleman whether he had come from Lord Castlereagh. The gentleman said he had, and Bardolini left immediately.'

'You are quite certain it was Bardolini who mentioned Lord Castlereagh?'

'Positive upon the point, sir. I could not have been mistaken. If you'll forgive my saying so, sir, I could not . . .'

'No, no, of course not, Williams, I just need to be certain upon the matter.'

'Is something amiss, sir?'

Drinkwater shrugged. 'I'm not sure. Perhaps not . . . Come, I must gather the last of my traps together, or I shall leave something vital behind.' And so, in the pressing needs of the everyday, Drinkwater submerged a primitive foreboding.

At four in the afternoon an under-secretary on Lord Castlereagh's staff arrived in a barouche to convey Bardolini to his Lordship's presence.

Drinkwater met the young man in the withdrawing-room. 'Is the Colonel not with his Lordship already?'

'Not that I am aware of,' said the under-secretary with a degree of hauteur. Drinkwater, in grubby shirt-sleeves as he finished preparing his sea-kit after so long in London, felt a spurt of anger along with a sense of alarm.

'But I understand one of his Lordship's *flunkeys* called for him this morning.'

'Mr Barrow was told that Colonel Bardolini would not be received before noon, very probably not before evening. His Lordship has rearranged his schedule to accommodate the Colonel, not to mention Captain, er, Drink . . .'

'Drinkwater. I am Captain Drinkwater and I am obliged to his Lordship, but I fear the worst. It would appear that the Colonel has been carried off by an impostor.'

'An impostor? How is that?'

'Come, sir,' said Drinkwater sharply, 'there are French agents in London, are there not?'

'I really have no idea.'

'I am sure Lord Castlereagh is aware of their presence.'

'How very unfortunate,' said the under-secretary. 'I had better inform his Lordship.'

'A moment. I'd be obliged if you would take me to the Admiralty.'

Drinkwater was fortunate that Barrow had not yet left. 'This is a damnable business,' he concluded.

'I do not think Lord Castlereagh will trouble himself overmuch, Captain.'

'No, probably not,' Drinkwater said, 'until Canada catches fire.'

Drinkwater returned to Lord North Street for the second time that day. He was in an ill humour and full of a sense of foreboding. He put this down to Bardolini's disappearance and Elizabeth's departure, and these circumstances undoubtedly made him nervously susceptible to a curious sensation of being followed. He could see no one in the gathering darkness and dismissed the idea as ludicrous.

But the moment he turned the corner he knew instinctively that something was wrong. He broke into a run and found his front door ajar. In the hall Williams was distraught; not half an hour earlier a carriage with drawn blinds had pulled up and a heavily cloaked figure had knocked at the door. Williams had opened it and had immediately been dashed aside. Thereafter two masked accomplices had appeared, forcing their way into the house and ransacking it.

'I thought it was the Colonel or yourself coming back, sir,' a shaken Williams confessed, his tranquillity of mind banished.

'Did you hear them speak?' Drinkwater asked, handing Williams a glass of wine.

'No, sir, but they weren't Frenchmen.'

'How d'you know?'

'I'd have smelled them, sir, no doubt about it. Besides, I think I heard one of them say something in English. He was quickly hushed up, but I am almost certain of it.'

'What did he say?'

'Oh, "nothing in here," something to that effect. They had just turned over the withdrawing-room.'

A faint wail came from below stairs. 'Did they molest your wife?'

'No, sir, but she is badly frightened. They were looking for papers . . .'

'Were they, by God!'

'They broke into the strong-room.'

'They took everything?'

'Everything.'

Drinkwater closed his eyes. 'God's bones!' he blasphemed.

He waited upon Mr Barrow at nine the following morning. Curiously, the Second Secretary was not surprised to see him. 'You have heard, then?' he said, waving Drinkwater to a chair.

'Heard?'

'The body of your guest was found in an alley last evening. He had been severely beaten about the head and was unrecognizable but for the remnants of his uniform. Oddly enough I was with

Murray last evening when Canning arrived with the news. It crossed my mind then that it might be our friend and I instituted enquiries.'

'You did not think to send me word . . .'

'Come, come, Captain, the man was an opportunist, like his master. He played for high stakes, and he lost. As for yourself, you would have insisted on viewing the corpse and drawing attention to your connection with the man.'

'Opportunist or not, he had placed himself under my protection.' Drinkwater remembered Elizabeth's assertion that Bardolini was a frightened man. 'Whoever killed Bardolini ransacked my house. I have spent half the night pacifying my housekeeper.'

'Did they, by heaven? D'you know why?'

'I think they were after papers. I have no idea what, apart from his accreditation, Bardolini carried. Whatever it was he did not take it to what he supposed to be a meeting with Lord Castlereagh.'

'Then they left empty-handed?' asked Barrow.

'More or less. I had some private papers . . .'

'Ahhh. How distressing for you . . . Still, someone knew who he was and where he was in London.'

'That argues against your hope of keeping me out of the affair.'

'Damn it, yes,' Barrow frowned. 'And we must also assume they knew why he was here.'

'Exactly so.'

'I should not delay in your own departure, Captain Drinkwater. Would you like me to pass word to the commander of the *Kestrel* to proceed? At least you have no need to divert to Helgoland now.'

'No. I'd be obliged if you would order Lieutenant Quilhampton to Leith without delay.'

'Consider it done.'

After the hectic activity of the past fortnight, there was a vast and wonderful pleasure in the day of the departure of HMS *Andromeda* from Leith Road that early October forenoon. The grey waters of the Firth of Forth were driven ahead of the ship by the fresh westerly breeze, quartered by fulmars and gannets whose colonies had whitened with their droppings the Bass Rock to the southward. Ahead of them lay the greener wedge of the Isle of May with its square stone light-tower and its antediluvian coal chauffer. To the north, clad in dying bracken, lay the dun coast of the ancient kingdom of Fife, a title whose pretentiousness reminded Drinkwater briefly of the sunburnt coast of Calabria and the compromised claims of the pretender to its tottering throne.

He had not realized how much he had missed the independence, even the solitariness, of command, or the sheer unalloyed pleasure of the thing. There was a purposeful simplicity in the way of life, for which, he admitted a little ruefully, his existence had fitted him at the expense of much else. It was, God knew, not the rollicking life of a sailor, or the seductiveness of sea-breezes that the British public thought all their ill-assorted and maltreated tars thrived upon.

If it had been, he would have enjoyed the passage north in the Leith packet which had stormed up the English coast from the Pool of London on the last dregs of the gale. As it was the heavily sparred and over-canvassed cutter with its crowded accommodation and puking passengers contained all the misery of seafaring. True, he had enjoyed the company of Captain McCrindle, a burly and bewhiskered Scot whose sole preoccupations were wind and tide, and who, when asked if he ever feared interception by a French corsair, had replied he 'would be verra much afeared, if there was the slightest chance of being overtaken by one!'

The old seaman's indignation made Drinkwater smile even now, but he threw the recollection aside as quickly as it had occurred for Lieutenant Mosse was claiming his attention.

'If you please, sir, she will lay a course clear of Fife Ness for the Bell Rock.'

'By all means, Mr Mosse, pray carry on.'

'Aye, aye, sir.'

Drinkwater watched the young second lieutenant. He was something of a dandy, a sharp contrast to the first luff, a more seasoned man who, like James Quilhampton aboard the cutter *Kestrel* dancing in their wake, was of an age to be at least a commander, if not made post. Drinkwater had yet to make up his mind about Lieutenant Huke, though he appeared a most competent officer, for there seemed about him a withdrawn quality that concealed a suspicion which made Drinkwater feel uneasy.

As for the other officers, apart from the master, a middle-aged man named Birkbeck, he had seen little of them since coming aboard three days earlier.

The crew seemed willing enough, moving about their duties with quiet purpose and a minimum degree of starting from the bosun's mates. The boat's crew which had met him had been commanded by a dapper midshipman named Fisher who, if he was setting out to make a good impression upon his new captain, had succeeded.

He could have wished for a heavier frigate, his old *Patrician*, perhaps, or at least *Antigone* with her 18-pounders, but *Andromeda* handled well, and if she was not the fastest or most weatherly class of frigate possessed by the Royal Navy, the ageing thirty-six gun, 12-pounder ships were known for their endurance and sea-kindliness.

She bore along now, hurrying before the westerly wind and following sea, her weatherbeaten topgallants set above her deep topsails, the forecourse straining and flogging in its bunt and clew-lines as it was lowered from the yards on the order 'Let fall!'

'Sheet home!'

The ungainly bulging canvas, constrained by the controlling ropes, was now tamed by the sheets which, with the tacks, were secured from its lower corners and transmitted its driving power to the speeding hull. With the low note of the quartering wind sounding in the taut stays, the frigate ran to the east-north-east.

A moment or two later the topmen, left aloft to make up the gaskets after overhauling the gear and ensuring the large sail was set without mishap, lowered themselves hand over hand to the deck by way of the backstays. Standing by the starboard hance, Drinkwater concluded that he had, like those simian jacks, fallen on his feet.

Evening found them passing the Bell Rock lighthouse, a marvel of modern engineering built as it was upon a tide-washed rock. The brilliance of its reflected light far outclassed the obsolete coal chauffer of the Isle of May, and Birkbeck confidently took his departure bearing from it when it bore well astern.

Having assured himself of the presence of *Kestrel*, Drinkwater went below. His quarters were small compared to those he had enjoyed on board *Patrician*, but admirably snug, he told himself, for a voyage to the Norwegian Sea with winter approaching. He settled in his cot with a degree of contentment that might have worried a less elated man. But that day of departure had been, in any case, a day of seduction; if Captain Drinkwater failed to notice any of the many faults that encumbered his command, it was because he had been too long ashore, too long kept from contact with the sea.

And the sea was too indifferent to the fates of men to keep him long in such a placid state of grace.

PART TWO
A Portion of Madness

'A portion of madness is a necessary ingredient in the character of an English seaman.'

Lord Howard of Effingham

Chapter Five *October 1813*

A Most Prejudicial Circumstance

'Pray sit down, Mr Huke.'

Huke threw out his coat-tails and sat on the edge of the chair bolt upright with his hands upon his knees and his elbows inclined slightly outwards. It was not a posture to put either of the two men at ease.

'I was much taken up with the urgency of departure and communicating the purpose of this voyage to Lieutenant Quilhampton of the *Kestrel*.' If Drinkwater had expected Huke to look from his captain to the cutter, which could be glimpsed through the stern windows when both vessels rode the crest of the wave simultaneously, he was mistaken. Mr Huke's eyes remained disconcertingly upon Drinkwater who wondered, in parenthesis, if the man ever blinked.

'Sir,' said Huke in monosyllabic acknowledgement.

'It is proper that I explain something of the matter to you.' Huke merely nodded, which irritated Drinkwater. He felt like the interloper he was, in a borrowed ship and a borrowed cabin, and that this was the light in which this strange man regarded him. He considered offering Huke a glass, but the fellow was so damnably unbending that he would seem to be currying favour if he did. 'Before I do confide in you,' Drinkwater went on pointedly, regretting the necessity of revealing anything to Huke, 'perhaps you will be kind enough to answer a few questions about the ship.'

'Sir.'

'You are up to complement?'

'Within a score of hands, aye.'

'Is that not unusual?'

'We took aboard near twenty men during the last week off Leith. All seamen. Took most of 'em out of a merchantman.'

'Very well. Now the Master reports the stores will hold for three months more . . .'

'And our magazines are full; we have scarce fired a shot.'

'Did Captain Pardoe not exercise the guns?'

'Oh, aye, sir.'

'I don't follow . . .'

'Captain Pardoe was not often aboard, sir.'

'Not often aboard?' Drinkwater frowned; he was genuinely puzzled and Huke's evasive answers, though understandable, were confoundedly irritating.

He rose with a sudden impatience, just as the ship lurched and heaved. A huge sea ran up under her quarter, then on beneath her. As he staggered to maintain his equilibrium, Drinkwater's chair crashed backwards and he scrabbled at the beam above his head. From the adjacent pantry came a crash of crockery and a cry of anger. So violent was the movement of the frigate that the perching Huke tumbled from his seat. For a moment the first lieutenant's arms flailed, then his chair upset and he fell awkwardly, his skinny shanks kicking out incongruously. Hanging over the table, Drinkwater noticed the hole worn in the sole of his first lieutenant's right shoe.

He was round the far side of the table and offering the other his hand the moment the ship steadied. 'Here, let me help . . . there . . . I think a glass to settle us both, eh?'

He was gratified to see a spark of appreciation in Huke's eyes.

'Frampton!'

Pardoe's harassed servant appeared and Drinkwater ordered a bottle and two glasses.

'We'll have a blow by nightfall,' Drinkwater remarked, as they wedged themselves as best they could; and while they waited for Frampton, Drinkwater filled the silence with a reminiscence.

'This is not the first ship I have joined in a hurry, Mr Huke. I took command of the sloop *Melusine* in circumstances not dissimilar to this. The captain had become embroiled in a ridiculous affair of honour and left me to make a voyage to the Greenland Sea in a ship I knew nothing of, with officers I did not know. You can doubtless imagine my sentiments then.'*

*See *The Corvette*.

'When was that?' Huke asked, curiosity about his new commander emerging for the first time.

'At the termination of the last peace, the spring of the year three.'

'I was promoted lieutenant that year.'

'Mr Huke,' Drinkwater began, then Frampton appeared and they concentrated on the wine and glasses. 'Did you lose much just now, in the pantry?'

'Aye, sir, two cups and a glass.'

'Oh, a pity.'

'Aye, sir.'

'You were saying, sir?' Huke prompted expectantly.

Drinkwater felt suddenly meanly disobliging. 'I forget,' he said, ''twas no matter.'

Huke's face fell, relapsing into its disinterested expression. There was a predictability about the man, Drinkwater thought, to say nothing of a dullness.

'Anyway, your health.' Huke mumbled a reply before his beak of a nose dipped into the glass.

'Ah, I recall, I was asking about Captain Pardoe, his exercising of the crew. They seem reasonably proficient.'

'Aye, they are.'

'Thanks to you?'

'Yes, in part.'

'Well come, Mr Huke,' said Drinkwater, a note of asperity creeping into his voice. 'Do I attribute your lack of respect to your not being unduly used to having an officer superior to yourself on board?'

Drinkwater caught the swift appraising glance of Huke's eyes and knew he had struck home. It had not entirely been guesswork, for in addition to Huke's hints had come a somewhat belated realization that it was odd that Pardoe had turned up on his London doorstep so promptly after Barrow had indicated that the *Andromeda* could be made available.

'I thought the regulations were quite specific upon the point, expressly forbidding captains to sleep out of their ships . . .'

Huke gave a great sigh. 'Very well, since you'll not be content, *sir*, until you have dredged the bottom of the matter, Pardoe has no interest in the ship and we are cousins. I made up the ship's books and the rest of the officers and crew thought he was detained on parliamentary business. He is the Member for Eyesham . . .'

'So *you* maintained the fiction?'

'That is right,' Huke said wearily. 'And in return I was allowed an emolument . . .'

'An emolument?'

'A portion of Captain Pardoe's pay went to my sister who lives with my widowed mother and has no other means of subsistence.'

'And will Captain Pardoe continue with this arrangement?'

Huke gave a thin and chilly smile. 'Would you, Captain Drinkwater, if there was no reason to?'

No wonder, thought Drinkwater, Pardoe had been so keen to relinquish his ship once it was clear that the interests of party had been served by his obliging the ministry. The captain's protests had been all sham. He would make an excellent politician, Drinkwater privately concluded.

'If he told you he regretted handing over command, sir, it was a lie. He is a man who seeks ease at all times, and even when aboard never took the conn or put himself to the least trouble. He is a great dissembler; any man would be fooled by him as would be any woman.'

Huke broke off. He did not reveal that his sister had been dishonoured by Pardoe, and had borne him a bastard, acknowledged only because of the ties of blood. The child had died of smallpox eighteen months earlier, so Pardoe could cynically drop the old commitment.

'I'm sorry, Mr Huke. I had no wish to pry. Pray, help yourself.'

'It's been difficult, sir,' Huke said, the wine loosening his tongue. 'It was not in Captain Pardoe's interest to see me advanced . . .'

'No, I can see that,' Drinkwater frowned. 'My presence here is hardly welcome then?'

'I could not expect promotion because of Captain Pardoe's removal, sir, but, yes, at least under the previous arrangements I had a free hand on board and my dependants cared for.'

'Damn it, Huke, 'tis outrageous! We must do something about it!'

Huke looked up sharply. 'No, sir! Thank you, but you would oblige me if you would leave the matter alone. It was inevitable that it would end one day . . .'

'Well, what did Pardoe think would happen when I joined?'

'That I would simply carry on as any first lieutenant.'

'I don't want a resentful first lieutenant, Mr Huke, damn me, I don't, but I'm confounded glad you have told me your circumstances. What's your Christian name?'

'Thomas, sir.'

'D'you answer to Tom?'

Something of a smile appeared on Huke's weatherbeaten face. 'I haven't for some time, sir.'

Drinkwater smiled. This was better; he felt they were making progress. 'Very well, then let us to business.' Drinkwater pulled a rolled chart from a brass tube lashed to the table leg and was gratified that Huke helped spread it and quickly located the lead weights to hold it down upon the table. He indicated its salient points:

'To the west Orkney and Shetland, to the east the Skaw of Denmark, the Naze of Norway and here,' his finger traced the Norwegian coast due east of Orkney, 'Utsira.' Beside the offshore island of Utsira the ragged outline of the coast became more deeply indented, fissured with re-entrant inlets, long tapering fiords that bit far into the mountainous terrain, separating ridge from ridge where the sea exploited every glacial valley to thrust into the interior. Each fiord was guarded by rocks, islets and islands of every conceivable shape and size, their number, like the leaves upon a tree, inconceivable.

The names upon the chart were long and unpronounceable, the headwaters of the inlets faded into dotted conjecture, the hachured mountains rose ever vaguer into the wild hinterland.

'It is a Danish chart, Tom, incomplete and probably poorly surveyed. It is the best the British Admiralty could come up with. The Hydrographer himself, Captain Hurd, sent it . . .'

Huke straightened up and looked Drinkwater squarely in the eye. 'There is something out of the ordinary in this business, then,' he said quietly.

Drinkwater nodded. 'Yes, very. Is it only the chart that has made you think this?'

'And the manner of your arrival, sir.'

'Ah. In what way?'

'I had heard of you, sir. Your name is not unfamiliar.'

'I had no idea,' Drinkwater said, genuinely surprised.

'You mentioned the *Melusine* and a Greenland voyage. And did you not take a Russian seventy-four in the Pacific?' There was a strained tone of bitterness in Huke's words.

'Luck has a great deal to do with success, Tom . . .'

'As does a lack of it with what others are pleased to call failure.'

'Indeed, but look, see that little fellow doing a dido on the quarter?' They stared across the mile of grey, windswept wilderness that separated the diminutive cutter *Kestrel* from her larger consort. 'Her commander is a mere lieutenant, like yourself, an *élève* of mine, God help him, a bold and brave fellow who lost a hand when a mere midshipman before the fortress of Kosseir on the Red Sea.* I have been striving to get a swab for him for years, so do not conceive great expectations; by which I do not mean I will not strive to advance any officer worth his salt.'

'I shall concede him the precedence,' Huke said, adding, 'he has independent command in any case.'

'I shall do my best for both of you, but James Quilhampton is a good fellow.'

'I have not yet met him . . .'

'No, had we had more time, I should have dined all of you. I hope that we shall yet have that pleasure, but for now rest assured that if we are successful in our enterprise, then I will move heaven and earth to have those officers who distinguish themselves given a step in rank.'

'And what *is* this enterprise?'

'Blowin' great guns, sir!'

Lieutenant Mosse was a dark blur in the blackness.

'Indeed it is.' Drinkwater put a hand to his hat and felt the wind tear at his cloak as he leaned into it, seeking the vertical on the wildly gyrating deck. Above his head the wind shrieked in the rigging, its note subtly changing to a booming roar in the gusts which had the almost painful though short-lived effect of applying pressure on the ears. The ship seemed to stagger under these periodic onslaughts, and around them the hiss and thunder of tumbling seas broke in looming chaos beyond the safety of the wooden bulwarks.

As he struggled past the wheel and peeped momentarily into

*See *A Brig of War.*

the dimly lit binnacle, the quartermaster shouted, 'Course dead nor' east, sir.'

He tried looking upwards at the tell-tales in the thrumming shrouds but he could see nothing but the pale blur of a scrap of canvas somewhere forward.

'Wind's sou' by east, sir, more or less, been backing an' filling a bit, but tending to veer all the time.'

'Thank you. What's your name?'

'Collier, sir.'

'Very well, Collier, and thank you.'

He passed from the feeble light of the binnacle into the manic darkness. The moving deck beneath his feet dropped, leaving him weightless. He felt the wild thrust of the storm as *Andromeda* dipped her stern and a sea ran beneath her. Then the next wave was upon them, hissing and roaring at them, its crest tumbling in a pale, sub-luminous glow that lay above the line of the taffrail. The frigate felt the uplifting buoyancy of its front, she pressed her decks insistently against the soles of Drinkwater's shoes and he was saved from blowing overboard. He reached for and grasped the lanyard of an after mizen backstay, pulling himself into the security of the pinrail where he looped a bight of downhaul round his waist and settled his cloak in a warm cocoon, feeling still the forces of nature through the vibrating rigging.

He had not forgotten the knack, though he had certainly lost his sea-legs in his months ashore. It was preferable to be up here than cooped in his cabin, for he could not sleep. He was too restless, his mind too active to compose himself, and even lying in the cot had failed to lull him. The ship was noisy as she strained under the onslaught of the sea. Her complex fabric groaned whilst she alternately hogged and sagged as the following waves lifted her and thrust her forward, then passed under her and she fell back off each crest, into the succeeding trough.

Added to this ceaseless cycle of stresses was the resonance produced in the hull by the deep boom of the storm in the spars and rigging, that terrible noise that lay above the adolescent howl of a mere gale and sounded like nothing so much as the great guns of Mosse's phrase. And for Drinkwater and the officers quartered in the stern of the ship, there was the grind of the rudder stock, the clink of chains, and the curious noise made by the stretching of white hemp under extreme tension as the tiller ropes flexed from the heavy tiller through their sheaves to the wheel above, where Collier and his four helmsmen struggled to keep *Andromeda* on her course.

Secure and familiar now with the pattern of the ship's motion, Drinkwater took stock. They had struck the topgallant masts before sunset, and sent the upper yards down. Only the small triangle of the fore topmast staysail and the clews of the heavy forecourse remained set above the forecastle, yet even this small area of sail, combined as it was with the mighty thrust of the wind in the standing masts, spars and rigging, sent *Andromeda* down wind at a spanking six or seven knots.

This, Drinkwater consoled himself, was what frigates of her class were renowned for, this seaworthiness which, provided everything was done in due and proper form, engendered a sense of security. Then a thought struck him with as much violence as the storm.

'Mr Mosse!' he bellowed, 'Mr Mosse!' He began to unravel himself, but then the lieutenant appeared at his elbow.

'Sir?'

'The lantern! Did I not leave orders for the lantern to be left burning for *Kestrel* to keep station by?'

'Aye, sir. But it has proved impossible to keep it alight. I sent young Pearce below to set a new wick in it. He should be back soon.'

'When did you last see the cutter?'

'I haven't seen her at all, sir, not this watch.' Mosse continued to stand expectantly, waiting for Drinkwater to speak, but there was nothing he could say.

'Very well, Mr Mosse, chase the midshipman up.'

A few minutes later Drinkwater was aware of figures going aft with a gunner's lantern to transfer the light. They knelt in the lee of the taffrail and struggled for a quarter of an hour before, with a muffled cheer, Pearce succeeded in coaxing the flame to burn from the new wick and the stern lantern was shut with a triumphant snap.

Its dim glow, masked forward, threw just enough light for Drinkwater to see the muffled figure of the marine sentry posted by the lifebuoy at the starboard quarter. Neither vigilant sentry nor lifebuoy would do any poor devil the least good if he fell overboard tonight, Drinkwater thought, feeling for poor Quilhampton in his unfamiliar and tiny little ship.

No, that was ridiculous, James was as pleased as punch with his toy command and had made a brilliant passage from the Chapman light to Leith Road in four days, comparable to the best of the Leith packets and certainly faster then the passage Drinkwater had himself made with Captain McCrindle.

'She's a damned sight handier than the old *Tracker*,' Quilhampton had crowed, as he entertained Drinkwater to dinner in the cabin of the cutter aboard which Drinkwater himself had once served. He had proudly related how he had overhauled one of the packets off the Dudgeon light vessel.*

The recollection alarmed Drinkwater. He had so often witnessed pride coming before a fall, and, moreover, he was acutely aware that history had a humiliating habit of repeating itself. He recalled a storm off Helgoland when he had lost contact with his friend aboard the gun-brig *Tracker*. He had later been overwhelmed by Danish gun-boats, wounded and compelled to surrender, and the ship in which Drinkwater sailed had been wrecked upon the reefs off Helgoland itself.†

He discarded the unpleasant memory, choking off the train of reminiscence as it threatened to overwhelm him. The past was past and could not, in truth, be reproduced or resurrected. He stared out into the hideously noisy darkness, aware that the motion of the ship had changed. The sea no longer roared up astern in precipitous and tumbling ridges from which *Andromeda* flew headlong. Now the crests had gone and, as he craned his head round, he felt the stinging impact of sodden air, the dissolution of those very wavetops into an aqueous vapour that filled the air they breathed.

Looking up he saw the night was not so dark: a pallid, spectral mist flew about them, streaming down wind with the velocity of a pistol shot, it seemed, so that the masts and rigging were discernibly black again, yet limned in with a faint and tenuous chiaroscuro. For a moment he thought it was St Elmo's fire, but there was no luminosity in it – it was merely the effect of salt water torn from the surface of the sea and carried along by the extreme violence of the wind.

A man could not face this onslaught, for it excoriated the skin

*See *A King's Cutter.*

†See *Under False Colours.*

and stung even squinting eyes. It not only made manifest the frigate's top-hamper, it also carried moisture into every corner. Running before even so severe a storm, *Andromeda*'s decks had remained dry. Hardly a patter of spray had hissed over the rail, but now, in the back eddies and arabesque fantasies of air rushing over the irregularities of her upperworks and deck fittings, the sodden air flew everywhere. In minutes Drinkwater's cloak was soaked, as though he had been deluged with a green sea; and while hitherto the wind had not seemed excessively cold, there now struck a numbing chill.

He tried to imagine what it would be like for Quilhampton aboard *Kestrel*. The cutter's low freeboard and counter-stern would have made her prey to a pooping sea. If she still swam out there somewhere astern, Quilhampton would have hove her to, he was sure of that. She hove to fairly comfortably, Drinkwater remembered.

Somewhere, distant in the booming night, the ship's bell tolled the passing hours. The incongruity of the faultless practice of naval routine in such primeval conditions struck no one on the deck of the labouring British frigate. Such routine formed their lifeline to sanity, to the world of order and purpose, of politics and war, and so it went on in its own inexorable way as did the watch changes. The blear-eyed, shivering men emerged on to the wet deck to relieve their soaked and tired shipmates who slid below in the futile hope that some small comfort awaited them in their hammocks. Watch change followed watch change as the routine plodded through the appalling night and, in the end, triumphed.

For dawn brought respite, and a steady easing of the wind, and found Drinkwater asleep, unrested, half severed by the downhaul. He staggered and gasped as he woke and Huke gave him his hand.

'God's bones!' he groaned. The furrow caused by the lashing had bruised his ribs and he gasped as he drew breath.

'Are you able to stand, sir?' Huke's expression of concern was clear in the dawn's light. Even as returning circulation caused him a slow agony and brought tears to Drinkwater's eyes, he found some satisfaction in the knowledge. He had won Huke over.

'Damn stupid thing to do,' Drinkwater managed, gradually mastering himself as the pain eased. 'How's the ship?'

'When I heard you had been up all night I came to report. I've had a look round. She's tight enough, four feet of water in the well, but the watch are dealing with that now. One seaman sprained an ankle, but he'll mend.'

'Is the surgeon competent?' Drinkwater asked.

'It would appear so, by all accounts. He's a young fellow, by the name of Kennedy. Scuttlebutt has it that he had to leave Bath in a hurry. Something about a jealous husband. He's full of fashionable cant and thinks himself the equal of a physician, but he does well enough. At least Bath taught him plenty about clap and the lues.' Huke dismissed the world of the *ton* with contempt. Drinkwater liked him the more. He began to pace the deck, Huke falling in alongside of him. Every moment the light grew stronger.

'Odd, ain't it, that hurricane last night knocked the sea down so fast, there'll be little swell today if the wind continues to drop.'

'Did you look at the glass this morning?' Drinkwater asked.

'Steadied up.'

'Good. I'm concerned about the *Kestrel*.'

'She'll fetch the rendezvous at Utsira. We're almost certainly bound to be there before her.'

'Yes, you are very probably right.' There was a reassuring conviction in Huke's words. 'Yes, you're right. Nevertheless . . .'

'Don't concern yourself, sir. I'll have the t'gallant masts sent up again after breakfast and a lookout posted aloft.'

'Very well.' They walked on a little. Then Drinkwater remarked, 'She's a lot easier now.'

It was relative, of course. The ship still scended and the dying sea surged alongside her hurrying hull.

'Shall I let fall the forecourse and set the tops'ls?'

'No, let us wait for full daylight and assure ourselves that *Kestrel* ain't in sight before we crack on sail.'

Drinkwater felt much better with a bellyful of burgoo and a pot of hot coffee inside him. Huke, he had learned during their morning walk, prescribed hot chocolate for the wardroom, said it gave the young layabouts a 'fizzing start to the day'. Apparently the idea originated with Kennedy, but Huke had tried it and endorsed it, to the disgust of several of the younger officers. Drinkwater had promised he would try it himself, but not this morning. After so miserable and worrying a night, he wanted the comfort of the familiar and had, in any case, brought a quantity of good coffee aboard in his otherwise meagre and hastily purchased cabin stores.

Mr Templeton joined him for a cup as he finished breakfast. The poor man looked terrible and stared unhappily at the rapid rise and fall of the sea astern, visible now that Drinkwater had had the shutters lowered. Templeton had been prostrated by sea-sickness before they passed the Isle of May, and last night had reduced him to a shadow.

'If it is any consolation, Mr Templeton,' Drinkwater said, waving him to a chair, 'the storm last night was one of the most severe I have experienced, certainly for the violence of the wind.'

'I scarcely feel much better for the news, sir, but thank you for your encouragement.' And, seeing Drinkwater smile, he added, 'I never imagined . . . never imagined . . .'

'Well, buck up,' Drinkwater said with a cheeriness he did not truly feel. 'We have lost contact with the *Kestrel*, but perhaps we shall have news of her before nightfall. Just thank your lucky stars that it was over so soon; I've known weather like that last for a week. Today promises to be different.' Drinkwater grabbed the table as *Andromeda* heeled to leeward and drove her bowsprit at the sea-bed.

'You mean *this* is a moderation?'

'Oh my goodness, yes! Why, you should have been in the old *Patrician* with me when we fell foul of a typhoon in the China Sea . . .'

But Drinkwater's consoling reminiscence was cut short by a short, sharp rumble that was itself terminated by a shuddering crash.

Drinkwater knew instantly what the noise was, for it was followed by a further rumbling and crash as *Andromeda* rolled easily back to starboard. He was out of his chair and halfway to the door before Templeton had recovered from this further shock.

'Gun adrift!' snapped Drinkwater by way of explanation as he flung open the cabin door and the noise of turmoil flooded in further to assault the already affronted Templeton. Rising unsteadily, he followed the captain, but waited on the cabin threshold. Beside him the marine sentry fidgeted uncomfortably.

'Number seven gun,' he muttered confidentially to the captain's clerk. The significance of the remark, if it had any, was lost on

Templeton. He did not know that the guns in the starboard battery were, by convention, numbered oddly. Moreover, the perspective of the gun deck allowed him to see little. The receding twin rows of bulky black cannon breeches, with their accompanying ropework, blocks, shot garlands and overhead rammers, worms and sponges, looked much as normal. It was always a crowded space, and if there were more men loitering about than usual, a cause was not obvious. His view, it was true, was obscured by the masts, the capstans, stanchions, and so forth, but the marine's confident assertion meant nothing to him and gave him no clue.

And then the tableau before him dissolved. The frigate's lazy counter-roll scattered the group of men. With shouts and cries they spread asunder, leaping clear of something which, Templeton could see now, was indeed a loose cannon. The lashings which normally held it tight, with its muzzle elevated and lodged against the lintel of its gun-port, seemed to have given way and parted.

This had caused the gun to roll inboard, as though recoiling beyond the constraints of its breechings. It had fetched up against one of the stanchions, a heavy vertical timber supporting the deck above. Here it had slewed, perhaps due to one of its training tackles fouling, but this had caused it to swing from right angles to the ship's fore and aft axis, thus giving it greater range to trundle threateningly up and down. Its two tons of avoirdupois had already destroyed a lifted grating, splintered half a dozen mess kids, buckets and benches, and split the heavy vertical timber of the after bitts.

As *Andromeda* heaved over a sea, the malevolent mass began to move aft, gaining a steady momentum that caused Templeton, well out of its line of advance, to flinch involuntarily. As the deck rocked, this slowed and then went into reverse, but by now the forces of order were mustered. Templeton could see Captain Drinkwater and Lieutenant Huke (a dour but competent soul, Templeton thought), the marine sergeant and Greer, an active boatswain's mate who had befriended Templeton in an odd kind of way and seemed willing to answer any of Templeton's technical questions. He had asked them at first of Mosse, but that dapper young officer did not conceive his duty to be the instructing of a mere clerk. Greer had overheard the exchange, made in Leith Road before the onset of sea-sickness, and volunteered himself as a 'sea-daddy'.

Templeton watched fascinated as ropes appeared, sinuous lines of seamen running to keep them clear of fouling as, in a moment of temporary equilibrium, someone shouted:

'Now!'

And the errant gun was miraculously and suddenly overwhelmed. A knot of officers remained round the gun, Drinkwater among them. Templeton was childishly gleeful. He felt less queasy, slightly happier with his lot. The swift, corporate response had impressed him. Men drew back grinning with satisfaction, and although the 12-pounder stared the length of the gun deck, it was held unmoving in a web of rope, even when *Andromeda* tested the skill of her company by kicking her stern in the air and then plunging it into the abyss.

'Like Gulliver upon the Lilliputian beach,' he muttered to himself.

'Like 'oo, sir?' the marine beside him asked.

'Like Gulliver . . .' he repeated, before seeing the ludicrous waste of the remark.

From behind him came the crash of crockery. He turned and looked back into the cabin. Coffee pot, cups and saucers lay smashed on the chequer-painted canvas saveall.

'Cap'n's china, sir,' said the marine unnecessarily.

'Oh dear . . .'

Templeton retreated into the cabin and stood irresolute above the slopping mess, then Frampton, the captain's servant, with much clucking of his tongue, appeared with a cloth.

'I don't know what Cap'n Pardoe'll say. We've only the pewter pot left,' he grumbled.

'Get out!' Templeton swung round to find Drinkwater in the doorway. The captain's face was strangely set. He shut the door and strode aft, putting his right hand on the aftermost beam, resting his head on his arm and staring astern. The servant swiftly vanished and Templeton himself hesitated; but it was clear the captain did not mean him. Templeton averted his eyes from the heave and suck of the wake and turned his gaze inboard. He admired again the rather fine painting of Mrs Drinkwater which the captain had hung the previous afternoon. He felt a return of his nausea and fought to occupy his mind with something else.

'Is . . . is something the matter, sir? I, um, thought the taming of the gun accomplished most expertly, sir.'

Drinkwater remained unmoving, braced against the ship's motion. 'Did you now; how very condescending of you.' Templeton considered the captain might have been speaking through clenched teeth. Was this another sea-mystery? Was the captain himself suffering from *mal de mer*?

Templeton had reached this fascinating conclusion when the door opened once more and Huke strode in. He was carrying a short length of thick brown rope.

'Well?' Drinkwater turned. 'What d'you think?'

Huke held the rope out. 'There's no doubt, sir. Cut two-thirds through and the rest left to nature. Thank God it didn't part six hours earlier.'

And it slowly dawned upon Mr Templeton that the breaking adrift of the cannon had been no accident, but a deliberate act of sabotage.

'That is', he said, intruding into the exchange of looks of his two superiors, 'a most prejudicial circumstance, is it not?'

Chapter Six *October 1813*

Typhus

'We must not make our concern too obvious,' Drinkwater said, after a pause during which Templeton blushed in acknowledgement that he had spoken out of turn. 'If the sabotage was merely malicious, a detestation at having been sent so abruptly on foreign service, or some such, vigilance may be all that is necessary. Do you, Mr Huke, have a discreet word with all of the other officers on those lines.'

'Aye, aye, sir. You want any other construction played down, I assume.' Huke looked significantly at the captain's secretary.

'Templeton is party to everything, Mr Huke. He was lately a cipher clerk at the Admiralty.'

'I see,' said Huke, who did nothing of the kind.

'But yes, play it down, just the same,' Drinkwater said, and Huke nodded. 'And I think I will let the marine officer know exactly what is going on. Is he a sound man, Mr Huke?'

'Mr Walsh is reliable enough, but unimaginative and not given to using his initiative. He is somewhat talkative but steady under fire.' Huke paused. 'If I might presume to advise you, sir . . .'

'Yes, of course. You think him liable to be indiscreet?'

Huke nodded again. 'I should tell him only that we are bound upon a special service. It is not necessary to say more. He will be as vigilant as Old Harry if he thinks there's the merest whiff of mutiny attached to this business.'

'So be it.' Drinkwater looked from one to the other. 'Are there any questions?'

'Do you think it is possible to identify the culprits?'

Drinkwater and Huke stared incredulously at the clerk who, for the third time that morning, wished he had kept his mouth shut.

'These things are managed by men who take every precaution

to ensure no officer ever gets to hear how they happen,' Drinkwater explained. 'These men are not stupid, Mr Templeton, even when they lack the advantages of knowledge or education.'

'And one or two', added Huke with heavy emphasis, 'are not wanting in either.'

Drinkwater spoke to Lieutenant Walsh shortly afterwards. 'The gun that broke loose was partially cut adrift, Mr Walsh. Have you had much of this sort of thing in the ship before?'

Walsh whistled through his teeth at the intelligence, then shook his head. He was a thick-set, middle-aged man whose prospects looked exceedingly dim. He should have reached the rank of major long before, and have been commanding the marine detachment aboard a flagship. He had a high colour, and Drinkwater suspected his loquacity might be proportional to his intake of black-strap.

'Nothing, sir, of much significance. The odd outbreak of thievery and so forth, but nothing *organized*.'

'Well, I want you to keep your eyes open – and your mouth shut if you find anything out. I want to be the first to know *anything*; any scuttlebutt, any evidence of combinations, any mutterings in odd corners. D'you understand?'

'Yes, sir.'

'But I don't want a hornet's nest stirred up. I don't want your men ferreting and fossicking through the ship so that even a blind fiddler can see we're concerned.' Walsh frowned. 'The point is, Mr Walsh, and this is strictly confidential, we are engaged upon a special service and delay of any kind would be most unfortunate. Do I make myself clear?'

'You want me to keep my eyes and ears open, sir, but not to let on too much, and to let you know immediately if I get wind of anything.'

'You have it in a nutshell.'

Drinkwater went on deck after terminating his interview with the red-coated marine. The topgallant masts were already aloft again, the order to refid them having just been given. Drinkwater paced the quarterdeck, watching the men as they set up the rigging. From time to time he fished in his tail pocket and levelled his glass at the horizon, sweeping it in arcs, hoping to see the angular peak of *Kestrel*'s mainsail breaking its uniformity.

The wind was down to a stiff breeze from the south-east and

Andromeda bowled along, her topsail yards braced round to catch it, the deep-cut sails straining in their bolt-ropes.

As they went about their tasks under the supervision of Mr Birkbeck, the boatswain and his mates, the men frequently cast their eyes in Drinkwater's direction. If he caught their glance they swiftly looked away. This was no admission of guilt, or even caginess. Their curiosity would have been natural enough in any circumstances, given his recent arrival on board, for the captain of a man-of-war held autocratic powers over his unfortunate crew. Indeed, Drinkwater recalled incidents of flogging for 'dumb insolence' if a man so much as stared fixedly at his commander, so he attached no importance to this phenomenon. There would be no one on the frigate who did not know by now of the incident of the cannon, for it remained where it had been lashed. How their new captain reacted was of general interest. If his restless scourings of the horizon with his glass conveyed the impression of a greater anxiety for Quilhampton's *Kestrel*, it would not have been far from the truth.

At one point he thought he saw her. A blurred image swam past the telescope's lenses. Unaccountably the cutter had somehow worked ahead of them. He moved smartly forward, along the gangway on to the forecastle. Here, the boatswain, Mr Hardy, was about to sway up the fore topgallant yard.

'Carry on, Mr Hardy,' he said as the petty officer touched his hat.

'Aye, aye, sir.'

Reaching the foremast shrouds, Drinkwater levelled his glass. He carefully traversed the horizon. It was blank. He worked carefully backwards from right to left. Again, nothing.

'T'garn yardmen to the top!' Hardy bawled almost in his ear as he conned the horizon yet again, convinced that he had seen something and waiting for the ship to lift to a wave on each small sector again.

'Send down the yard ropes!'

The yard, its sail furled along it, rose from the boat booms and began its journey aloft.

'High enough! Rig the yardarms!'

The men on the forecastle waited for their colleagues aloft to finish their preparatory work.

'Taking their bloody time . . .' a man grumbled quietly.

'Shut up, Hopkins, the cap'n's over there . . .'

'Hold your blethering tongues!' Hardy said as he stared aloft, where some difficulty was being experienced. Drinkwater barely noticed these *sotto voce* remarks. He was concentrating on the business of seeking a second glimpse of that distant sail.

Hardy and the men aloft held a brief exchange. A call came down that all was now well. 'Sway higher . . . avast! Tend lifts and braces!' Men shuffled across the deck, more ropes were cast off belaying pins, their coils flung out for quick running and tailed on to by the seamen, chivvied by Greer.

'That's well there. Stand by! Now . . . sway across!'

Hitched properly the topgallant yard left the vertical and assumed its more natural horizontal position. 'Bend the gear!'

It was secured in its parrel and the mast slushed. Those on deck cleared up, recoiling the ropes and preparing to move aft to the mainmast. If the south-easterly wind continued to fall away, they would be setting those sails before they were piped to dinner.

'Lay down from aloft!'

The topmen swarmed down the backstays, hand over hand, saw the captain and ceased their chaffing with hissed cautions. Drinkwater shut his glass with a snap and walked aft. He must have been mistaken. There was no sign of *Kestrel*.

Halfway along the gangway a thought struck him with such force that he stopped beside the men now mustering round the mainmast. The man who had been called Hopkins caught his eye.

'You there!' he called. 'That man, Mr Hardy, beside the larboard pinrail, d'you know his name?'

The boatswain looked round. 'That's Hopkins, sir.'

'Hopkins, come here.'

The men had stopped work. Lieutenant Huke and the master, Mr Birkbeck, came towards him, uncertain of what was happening. With obvious reluctance the man identified as Hopkins approached and stood before Drinkwater.

'Have I sailed with you before, Hopkins?' Drinkwater asked. His tone of voice was pleasant, deliberately relaxed, as though wanting to make an impression by this mock familiarity.

'No, sir.'

'I'm certain we've sailed together before. D'you have a twin?'

'No, sir.'

'You were on the *Antigone*, or was it the *Patrician*?'

'No, sir.'

'Where are you from, Hopkins, eh?' Drinkwater went on, probing for something longer than these monosyllabic words. Watching his quarry, Drinkwater saw the eyes flicker uncertainly. 'Where were you born?'

'London, sir.'

'What part of London?'

Hopkins shrugged. 'Just London, sir.'

'And you say you've never sailed with me before?' Sweat was standing out on Hopkins's brow.

'No, sir.'

'Well stap me, Hopkins, I'd have laid money on the fact!' Drinkwater smiled. 'Very well, then, carry on. Carry on, Mr Hardy, let's have the men at it again. I want those t'gallants set.'

'Aye, aye, sir.'

Hopkins turned and escaped. Odd looks were exchanged between officers and men alike as they went back to their tasks. Drinkwater continued aft, with Huke and Birkbeck staring after him.

'Odd cove,' remarked the master, looking at Drinkwater who had continued to the taffrail and stood staring astern, his hands clasping the brass tube of the Dollond glass behind his back.

'Yes,' replied Huke doubtfully. 'Carry on, will you, Mr Birkbeck.'

Huke walked aft himself and stood next to Drinkwater. After a moment Drinkwater said, without turning his head, 'That man Hopkins, have you had him aboard long?'

'No, sir. Pressed him out of that merchantman I mentioned.'

'Ah, yes, I recall . . .'

Huke waited for more, but Drinkwater continued to stare astern.

'I cannot imagine what has happened to Quilhampton,' he said with a faint air of abstraction.

'Sir, d'you mind if I ask . . . ?'

'No, Mr Huke, I don't mind you asking.' Drinkwater swung round and looked at his first lieutenant. 'But perhaps you'll answer my question first. How many more men that you pressed from that same merchantman are Yankees?'

It was far from a comforting thought, and it would not leave

Drinkwater alone throughout that worrying day. Huke had hurried off and returned after a few moments with the assurance that, although most of the men out of the merchantmen had American accents, when challenged, all had claimed to have been of loyalist descent.

'Very fine and dandy, if it's true, which I doubt.'

'But why should it not be true? If they had been Americans, they would not have submitted without protesting at being pressed.'

'Indeed. But that doesn't prove they are what they say they are. Did they submit to being placed on board docilely?'

'No, of course not, sir, but they said they were owed money, that they had not received their wages or slops and they were dressed in filthy rags. I ordered them fitted out.' Huke's explanation petered out, then, as if summoning himself, he added, 'Sir, if I might say so, I think you are concerning yourself over-much. You had little sleep last night.' Huke stopped as the spark of anger kindled in Drinkwater's eye.

'Damn it, sir . . .!'

'I mean no impertinence, Captain Drinkwater.' Huke stood his ground. Several thoughts flashed through Drinkwater's mind. He was tired, it was true, but all was far from well and he felt he had touched something. The man Hopkins had been deliberately evasive. Not merely unwilling to answer the captain's questions, but suspecting something when asked, persistently, if he had sailed with Drinkwater before. Moreover, no Londoner would be content not to refer to his natal quarter of the capital.

If Drinkwater was right, doubts had been sowed in Hopkins's mind as much as in Drinkwater's, and he might move again, and soon. The reflections calmed Drinkwater.

'You are right, Tom, forgive me.' He smiled and Huke reciprocated.

'Of course, sir.'

'Just humour an old fool and keep a damned close eye, as unobtrusively as possible, on that man. Make a particular note of his cronies.'

'Very well, sir, I'll see to that.'

'I think I shall take a nap then. Be so good as to see the t'gallants set and have me called at six bells in the afternoon watch.'

'Of course, sir.'

'And round up Walsh, Birkbeck, Templeton and, what did you say the Bones's name was?'

'Kennedy.'

'Him and a couple of the midshipmen, to join me at dinner. I'll tell Frampton to have a pig killed.'

'I'll do that, sir.'

'Very good of you, Tom.'

The wind held steady from the south-east, but continued to fall away during the afternoon so that as the officers assembled for dinner, *Andromeda* slipped easily through the water.

Circulating among them, Drinkwater sought to draw his guests in turn. Walsh proved as talkative a fellow as the first lieutenant had suggested, battering Drinkwater with a torrent of inconsequences he quite failed to understand so that Walsh followed when he stepped forward to meet the two midshipmen, one of whom was no more than a child.

'You are Mr Fisher, are you not?' Drinkwater quizzed, as the boy nervously entered the cabin in the company of a much taller, out-at-elbows young man Drinkwater recognized as Pearce.

'Yes, sir,' the boy squeaked. 'My name is Richard Fisher.'

'How old are you, Mr Fisher?'

'Eleven, sir.'

'That is very young, is it not? And how long have you been aboard this ship?'

'Three months, sir.'

'Ah, quite the old hand, eh? You commanded the gig when I came on board.'

'Yes, sir.'

The similarity of names reminded Drinkwater of his own son Richard who had once implored to be taken to sea. Drinkwater had not even entered him on a ship's books, so little did he want to encourage the lad. Now the youthful Dickon increasingly managed the modest Suffolk estate with its two farms and had forgotten his idea of following his father's footsteps into the Royal Navy.

'There's one born every minute,' Walsh remarked, and Drinkwater let the rubicund marine officer scoop up the younkers and bore them with tales of derring-do when the war and he had been young.

Drinkwater raised an eyebrow at Huke, who gave a slow, tolerant smile and shrugged.

'When will we close Utsira, Mr Birkbeck?' Drinkwater asked conversationally. 'I have somewhat neglected matters today.'

'You had a bad night of it, sir,' said Birkbeck indulgently, 'but I got a squint at the sun and reckon, all being well, noon tomorrow.'

'I think we may be able to take stellar observations at twilight tomorrow morning,' Drinkwater said.

Frampton, the captain's steward, went round and refilled the glasses, Fisher's included, and the air rapidly filled with chatter. Drinkwater looked round with a sense of some satisfaction. It was only a small portion of the complement of the wardroom, of course, but they seemed good enough fellows. He caught Frampton's eye.

'Sir?'

'Five minutes.'

'Aye, aye, sir.'

'And no more wine for Mr Fisher.'

'Aye, aye, sir.'

Drinkwater turned to Huke. 'Damn fool,' he muttered, then, 'Would you introduce me to the surgeon, Tom?'

Huke performed the introduction. 'Mr Kennedy, sir.' The curt half-bows performed, Drinkwater said, 'Glad to make your acquaintance,' and to the company at large, 'I'm sorry, gentlemen, not to have made your acquaintance earlier, but the somewhat irregular circumstances of my joining and the haste of our departure combined with last night's blow to make the matter rather difficult. I hope this evening will set matters to rights.'

'I'm sure, sir,' said Jameson, the third lieutenant, in his thick Scotch burr. ''Twas an infernal night; ha'e ye ever known its like afore, sir?'

'Well, yes,' Drinkwater said, and told briefly of the typhoon and the storm off Helgoland before turning to the surgeon. 'You have not been long at sea, I understand, Mr Kennedy, how did you cope with the motion?'

'Somewhat miserably I fear, sir. When the physician is indisposed, there is little hope for the sick.'

'You are better now?'

'As a matter of fact, sir, I'm ravenous.'

The remark coincided with Frampton's arrival with the meat.

The delicious smell of succulent roast pork filled the cabin, killing the conversation as all swung in happy anticipation to the table. The joint, the fresh vegetables, potatoes, gravy and apple sauce suggested a meal ashore, rather than one aboard a man-of-war upon an urgent cruise.

'Please take your seats, gentlemen.'

The rumble of talk resumed, joining the scraping of chairs as the officers sat and flicked their napkins into their laps. Then they fell silent, leaving only Walsh to remark to Fisher, 'You had better ask the captain, young fella.'

'What had you better ask me, Mr Fisher?'

'Why, sir, where we are going?'

Surprise at the youthful indiscretion was clear on all their faces, though it amused Drinkwater. 'What makes you think we are going anywhere particular, Mr Fisher?'

Midshipman Fisher was flushing with the realization that he was the cynosure of all eyes. 'Well, s . . . s . . . sir,' he stammered, 'I s . . . supposed we might be, sir.'

'Go on, sir,' said Drinkwater, breaking the expectation by beginning to carve.

'Well, sir, we were quietly at anchor with Captain Pardoe away in Parliament and then, sir, here you are and off we go!'

He was in his stride by the end of it and the officers laughed indulgently as Frampton went round filling their glasses.

'Well, Mr Fisher has a point, gentlemen,' Drinkwater said as he finished passing the platters of sliced meat down the table. 'We are engaged on a particular service, as some of you may know. As to what it is, it is difficult at this juncture to be absolutely certain, so shall we say we are engaged on a reconnaissance?' He handed a plate to Huke and looked at Fisher. 'Well now, Mr Fisher, do you know the course?'

'North-east, sir?'

'And what do you suppose lies to the nor' east of Leith Road, eh?'

'Norway, sir?'

'Indeed, Mr Fisher, Norway. In the next few days we shall take a look into a fiord or two and see what we can find . . .'

'In the way of an enemy, sir?' asked Fisher, pot-valiant.

'Possibly, Mr Fisher. Mr Walsh, do see that Mr Fisher has enough potatoes.'

'Oh, yes sir, of course.'

'Tae stop his gob,' Jameson muttered.

The general babble recommenced with indulgent grins bestowed on the blushing midshipman. After the pork, a duff appeared and when the cloth had been drawn and the loyal toast drunk, Walsh lit a cheroot and hogged the decanter.

'A fair wind, if you please, Walsh,' prompted Huke, and the evening passed into a pleasant blur.

When it was over Drinkwater invited Huke to take a turn on deck to clear their heads. It was not quite dark. Thin tendrils of high cloud partially veiled some of the stars, but a dull red glow hung in the northern sky.

'It looks like a misplaced sunset,' Huke remarked, puzzled.

'Aurora borealis,' Drinkwater said, and they paused to stare at it for a moment. The crimson glow seemed to pulse gently, increasing in brilliance, then dying again, like coals that are almost extinguished. 'It can take on the most incredible forms,' Drinkwater remarked, and they began walking again.

Andromeda ghosted through the water, for the wind had gone down with the sun.

'I wish to God we knew the whereabouts of the *Kestrel*.'

'Yes. Perhaps he'll head back to Leith, the wind's been fair.'

'Sir?' A figure loomed in the darkness. It was not Mosse, the officer of the watch.

'Is that you, Mr Kennedy?'

'Yes, sir. I'm afraid I've some rather bad news.'

'Then keep your voice down, man,' hissed Huke.

'We've a case of typhus aboard,' Kennedy whispered.

Chapter Seven *October 1813*

Utsira

At dawn next morning the frigate was stirred to life by the marine drummer beating the ship's company to quarters. It was a grey morning, with a translucent veil of high altitude cloud spread across the sky, robbing them of the stellar observations Drinkwater and Birkbeck had hoped to secure. The horizon had not yet hardened before the stars, like distant lamps, had faded. Extinguished, Drinkwater mused to himself as he came on deck and took stock, by overly frugal angels.

The ship's company knew nothing of this disappointment. The watch on deck cast about in confusion at the sudden appearance of the captain, marine officer and first lieutenant and the rattle of the drummer's snare, for there was no obvious enemy in the offing. The watches below tumbled up, chivvied by thundering hearts and starters, and equally confused for, as they ran to their action stations, the mystified petty officers knew only that the men were to be stopped from clearing for action and casting off the guns' breechings. Instead, they were to fall in in their messes, and the transmission of this unorthodox procedure caused further confusion. This took a few extra moments and in turn provided an adequate time-lapse to breed rumour.

There were two of these speculations forming and they spread by muttered word of mouth faster than a spark along a quick-match. How these incomplete utterances sped round the ship, how one utterly defeated the other so that, by the time the divisional officers each sent their midshipmen aft to report their men mustered, the victorious buzz had convinced thirteen score of men, is a mystery understood only by those who have experienced it.

One theory was that their proximity to the enemy coast was such that standing to in the light of dawn was a precautionary measure. It gained ground among the more experienced, but it swiftly withered when the second overwhelmed it. They had been called to account, it was asserted, for the cutting adrift of the cannon. The absence of punishment at the time had been commented upon. Neither Huke's reputation nor Drinkwater's lack of it seemed to square with inaction on the part of authority, and therefore this postponed corporate muster seemed a logical consequence. Nor did anything that happened in the next few extraordinary moments persuade the ship's company of His Britannic Majesty's frigate *Andromeda* that they were wrong.

Flanked by Huke and Walsh, Drinkwater stalked the groups of men, taking a sinister interest in several, moving close to them so that the more perceptive and less terrified said afterwards that the captain had 'sniffed them like a dog at a bitch's arse'.

This indelicacy was not so very far from the truth and some of those subject to this personal attention were sent sheepishly aft to a waiting Kennedy, watched by the others. From time to time a muttering rose with a mutinous undertone of protest which either Huke or the divisional officer swiftly silenced. When Drinkwater's curious, shifty inspection was complete he returned to the quarterdeck.

'Very well, Mr Huke. The duty watch is to rig the washdeck pumps and the Hales's ventilators. The gunner's party is to prepare powder for burning 'tween decks. The carpenter is to take three hundredweight of sand to the galley and the cook is to have it heated. The purser is to issue one bar of soap to every mess. The watch below is to turn up and be hosed down. After every man has been washed, he is to shift his linen and put on clean clothes. If a single man has on an item he is wearing now, I shall cover him with my cloak and flog him!'

Drinkwater gave his bizarre orders in a loud voice, and those mustered below in the gun deck who failed to hear him soon learned of his intentions. Nor was a single man under the impression that a shred of solicitude attached to Drinkwater's offer of his 'cloak'. All knew the term a euphemism for the ration of lashes permitted a post-captain under the Thirty-Sixth Article of War which he might give without reference to any higher authority. By the time Drinkwater had finished, every man jack knew that what the watch below had to endure, the duty watch would also submit to, that the ship would be scrubbed from orlop to main deck, that the ports would be opened, that a mechanically induced draught via

Dr Stephen Hales's patent ventilator would join the natural air flowing reluctantly through the ship, and that hot sand and burning gunpowder would dry and purify the air between decks.

In the ensuing period the deck of the *Andromeda* assumed the grotesque appearance of a bacchanalia. Had an enemy chanced upon them at that time, it was afterwards remarked, they would have caught the *Andromeda*'s company with more than their defences down. The spurting jets of water plashed upon the naked limbs and bodies of each mess in turn, and the initial misery and humiliation of those first chosen gave way to a whooping glee as group succeeded group and the naked increased and soon outnumbered the clothed.

As each division underwent this strange, humiliating metamorphosis, their officers came aft, grinning at the men's discomfiture, grouping on the quarterdeck to be driven, as their own reserved participation in this spree, to comments of impropriety.

'My word,' rattled a red-faced Walsh, 'young Hughes is rigged like a donkey!'

An acutely embarrassed Midshipman Fisher stared wide-eyed at a small, deformed and excessively hairy man who giggled insanely and was commonly thought to be mad.

'And look at Taylor . . .'

'Good God, what a scar . . .'

Having been stripped and drenched, the ship's fiddler was set upon a forecastle carronade breech to strike up a lively jig, which prompted the most excitable to dance and skylark with even more vigour than the cold sea-water.

When the greater proportion of the watch below cavorted in damp nudity, Drinkwater sprang a second and greater surprise upon the ship.

'Frampton!' he called, and the steward, stark naked, his hands held in front of his chill-shrivelled genitals, approached the officers. Drinkwater turned to the crescent of watching officers.

'Well, gentlemen, rank has its obligations as well as its privileges. I do not know whether it was Epictetus or Marcus Aurelius who claimed the essence of command to be example, but if this performance is to be of any benefit, then we must take part . . .'

Drinkwater stared round at the officers on whom the light of comprehension broke somewhat slowly. He began to take off his coat and held it out to the dripping and shivering Frampton who reluctantly relinquished his protective stance. Several of the officers began to move away, while the midshipmen continued to stare goggle-eyed at their commander. Drinkwater removed his neck linen, stock and shirt, kicked off his shoes and, putting his right foot on a quarterdeck carronade truck, rolled down a stocking.

'Not here, surely, sir?' queried an incredulous Walsh.

'Why not, Mr Walsh, here is as good a place as any, for we must not only take part, but be seen to take part.' Drinkwater unbuttoned his breeches.

'What is the point, sir?'

'The point, Walsh,' offered Kennedy, fast following the Captain's example, 'is prophylaxis, the prevention of disease.'

'What disease?'

'Don't bandy it about, Walsh, but ship fever, camp fever, low, slow, putrid and petechial fever, call it what you will, but do not lay yourself open to its infection . . .'

Walsh was open-mouthed, but the surgeon's words were drowned as the ship's company realized that the captain was naked and that, incredulously, the other officers were following suit, slowly at first but then faster as they were egged on by whoops of rankly insubordinate derision. Drinkwater gasped as an eager party of men turned a hose upon him, the men at the levers of the portable pumps jerking up and down, one wet with tears at the hilarity of the scene and the joy of deluging his captain with icy water.

Within moments even the sluggards were under the pumps and the tide had turned, the entire waist was filled with pink flesh and cascades of water. Buckets were cast overboard and retrieved with lanyards, their contents emptied indiscriminately.

Chaos, it seemed, reigned for a quarter of an hour, until Drinkwater, still naked, leapt up on the rail and roared for silence. Those occupants of the wardroom who afterwards deplored the anarchy were swiftly silenced by others who argued that the immediacy of the response to Drinkwater's summons to order proved them wrong.

'Very well, my lads, we are all more or less alike, I see . . .' A laugh greeted this joke, and Drinkwater, while he awaited their attention, remembered inconsequentially how, long before aboard *Patrician*, he had discovered a woman dressed and thought of for months as a man. The laughter and mutual chaffing subsided.

'Now do you pay attention. It's a change of clothing for every man jack of you, d'you hear? Then the ship is to be stummed before we break our fast. After that, you are all to wash every stitch you have just removed. It looks like a drying day and you will scrub hammocks by watches. If you clear the ship by noon, we'll exercise the guns . . .'

This news raised a cheer which, half-hearted at first, soon grew in modulation, a madcap disorganized noise accompanied by grins and laughter and multiple shiverings.

'Very well, then,' Drinkwater continued after the noise had died away, 'the watches below have twenty minutes to get into fresh clothes. Then they are to relieve the watch on deck. If I see a naked man half an hour from now, he'll be in the bilboes. Pipe down the watch below!'

Drinkwater jumped down from the rail. He was shuddering from the chill and covered with goose-pimples. 'Come, gentlemen, what do you want to make of yourselves, a spectacle?'

The ship had not quite been abandoned to these cavortings, but the calm had made easier this odd business of sanitation. As the officers tumbled below to the partial privacy of the wardroom and shut the door on the berth deck beyond, they reacted according to age and temperament. The paunchy Walsh was outraged, amusingly speechless and spluttering with florid indignation. The others, even the sober Huke, were constrained to laugh, Jameson continuing to leap about, flicking a towel with aggravating accuracy at Walsh's wobbling buttocks.

'Damn you, Jameson! Don't do that, you confounded fool!'

'Come, come, Walsh, don't be an old prude, you enjoyed the bathe, don't deny it!'

The elegant Mosse had been resolutely opposed to undressing, until he realized his pride would take a bigger dent if he refused. The second lieutenant was as elegant without his uniform as when fully attired. It was, he later claimed, untrue to say clothes made the man, but that beauty only needed to be skin deep to make an impression.

In this he was disturbingly right for one member of the officers' mess. A man-of-war lodged many types but all, whether extrovert or introvert, were eventually compelled to surrender in large measure any sense of individual privilege; a mess – whether forward or aft – rubbed along together on consensus, and disagreements were usually things of small moment.

But *Andromeda*'s wardroom sheltered a misfit in Mr Templeton. As long as Templeton could haunt the captain's cabin, nursing his own secrets, he was content. But when he was compelled to associate with these bears, he felt awkward, conspicuous and a figure of ridicule. While being with them, he was not of them.

Much of this self-perception was in his own imagination, but the events of the early morning had shocked him deeply, not just as a matter of spectacle, but as a powerful and unlooked for spur to a hidden, barely acknowledged lust, which distracted him from all his other preoccupations.

Templeton had never acknowledged the proclivity that now overwhelmed him. He had spent his drab, pretentious life of genteel servitude largely occupying his mind. His social life, such as it was, had revolved around that of his ageing mother and her coterie of friends. He had vaguely supposed he would at an appropriate time and when one or other of the matrons had decided the matter for him, take one or other of their plain daughters to wife. To this end, and to satisfy his ambitions, he had sought to improve his place at the Admiralty. Meddling in its intrigues and hoping to advance from lowly copying clerk, he had aspired to and achieved the post of a cipher clerk, a confidential servant of the state, whose opinion was sought first by Lord Dungarth and now by Captain Nathaniel Drinkwater.

In some ways this filled him with a heavy conceit, partially satisfying inner hungers, but from time to time he was moved to acknowledge another stirring, aware that there was about this an air of disgrace. This in turn was sublimated by classical considerations and not held to resemble, in even a distant way, the disgusting soliciting, importuning, love-struck moonings and filthy couplings of his fellow clerks with the doxies who inhabited the purlieus of Whitehall.

The morning's events had, however, brought him perilously close to a terrible exposure, for he had been physically moved by the experience, almost conspicuously aroused. He had consequently suffered the acute fear of discovery together with the agony of frustrated desire caused by the mass propinquity. Nor had it helped to see the odd individual, from an indisputably lower order of society, in a state of abandoned tumescence. That their fellows dismissed them laughingly made his own situation all the more shameful, for where this condition had occurred to him naturally, he had always banished it by occupying his mind with the diversion of a book, or some other study.

Now he hid in his flimsy cabin and wept, for it only added to his burden of fear.

The score or so of men whom Drinkwater had so disreputably sniffed out received Kennedy's especial attention. A perceptive observer would have noticed these unfortunates had in common the most wretched and ragged appearance. The surgeon took their names and ensured their washing was more than a cursory drenching, subjecting them to a thorough examination, then flinging their clothes overboard. Afterwards he sent them to the purser for new slops, brushing aside their protests that they could not afford such luxuries with the assurance that they 'would soon be able to pay out of their prize-money'.

As for the poor fellow who had caused all this to-do, he was brought on deck in a hammock and set in the pale sunshine that finally triumphed over the cloud. By mid-morning a light breeze had sprung up from the west and above the already stuffed hammock nettings, spread in the ratlines and along light lines rigged for the purpose, breeches and trousers, shirts and vests and pantaloons, cravats and neckties, scarves and bandanas, socks and stockings, aprons and breeches fluttered in the breeze.

Amid this gay and unwarlike decoration, Drinkwater paced the deck in deep confabulation with Kennedy.

'Well, sir, we have done what we can . . .'

'I'm told it is very efficacious, that the contagion is spread by the flea and that only extreme cleanliness will extirpate it.'

Kennedy frowned. ''Tis true, sir, that the putrid fever is common to poor conditions, but to attribute it to the flea is somewhat far-fetched.' Kennedy had wanted to say 'preposterous', but in view of the captain's age and rank he forbore. Nevertheless he pressed his argument.

'If your hypothesis was right, sir, then the disease would be as prevalent among people of the better classes as among the poor; but it is the poor who are most afflicted. The flea is common to both, but dirt and misery are not.'

'*Quod erat demonstrandum*, eh, Mr Kennedy?' asked Drinkwater wryly. He was in better humour, glad that matters had passed off as well as they had and that, apart from the surplus bunting, order was now restored to the ship.

'Exactly so, sir.'

'I shall not argue the point with you. I only know what I have observed, or heard others speak of. Not all were ancient tarry-breeks.' Drinkwater smiled at his young colleague. 'Keep that fellow in a fever out of the berth deck and we may yet save others. Ah, Tom, are you better for your bath?'

'I have to say, sir, that for a moment or two, I seriously doubted the wisdom of what you were doing, but', he shrugged and looked about him, 'there seems little sign of ill-effect, beyond the adornments aloft, that is.'

They all laughed at the first lieutenant's allusion to the fluttering disorder about them.

'There'll be none, Tom,' Drinkwater said reassuringly. 'It was all taken humorously and most of 'em will know by now that it was for their own good. As for the officers, it was for their benefit too; besides, 'twas a case of *noblesse oblige*.'

'Perhaps you are right. I certainly feel better now the gunpowder is all doused. Seems a damned dangerous thing to do, to stum the ship like that.'

'But you have to dry her through, Tom; you know how oak sweats and she'd been closed down during the storm. After we've exercised the guns I want the bilges pumped dry and then have salt sprinkled into the wells . . .'

'Aye, aye, sir,' said Huke, with just a faint trace of resignation in his tone to amuse Drinkwater.

More officers joined them, and it occurred to Drinkwater that each felt a compulsion to reappear upon the quarterdeck fully accoutred, to reassert their individual status. Whatever the darker motives, they laughed and smiled, exchanging grins with the men at the wheel.

'Have you heard Jameson's joke, sir?' drawled Mosse.

'No, pray share it, Mr Jameson.'

The third lieutenant blushed, made a face at Mosse and shook his head.

'Come, Roger, or I shall steal it . . .'

'Do as you please, damn you, Stephen.'

Mosse turned insouciantly to Drinkwater and Huke. 'Jameson

has some crack-pot notion that we were ridding ourselves of fleas, sir, and, having due regard to the naked disorder so recently upon our decks, likened it to an event of history, sir.'

'And what was that, Mr Mosse? As I am sure you are about to tell us.'

'Why, the Boston flea party, sir!'

Despite the misgivings of his officers, Drinkwater had known very well what he was doing. By following the mass drenching with a gunnery exercise he achieved that unity in a crew which, with a less active commander, might otherwise have taken months. He had been lucky in Huke, capitalizing on that diligent officer's hard work, but he was pleased that after noon, notwithstanding the ridiculous washing that still blew about above their heads, they had loosed three broadsides from each battery, and shot at a dahn-buoy until their ears rang with the concussions of the guns.

To crown the events of the day Drinkwater cleared the lower deck and summoned the ship's company aft.

'Well, my lads, it has been an eventful day,' he said, pausing long enough to hear a groundswell of good-natured agreement, 'and it is likely to be succeeded by a number of such eventful days. We are not far from the coast of Norway, and we are here to flush out a few privateers who have been reported lurking hereabouts. In a moment or two I am ordering the hoisting of Danish colours and we shall enter Danish waters. Next time you hear the drum beat to quarters the only surprise will be the one we will give to the enemy! Now, Mr Huke, we have disrupted the ship's routine sufficiently for one day and delayed long enough. Be so kind as to pipe up spirits!'

Drinkwater went below to a cheer; if there was opportunism, even sycophancy in it, he was undeceived. He had other matters to concern him. Quilhampton was still missing, and the men who had half-severed the gun-breech were among the mob happily awaiting their daily ration of rum.

'Sir!'

Drinkwater stirred and saw Midshipman Fisher's head peering round the door. 'What is it?'

'Mr Birkbeck's compliments, sir, and we've sighted Utsira.'

'What time is it?'

'Almost six bells, sir.'

'Very well.' The boy vanished. Drinkwater roused himself, swivelled in his chair and stared through the stern windows. It was three o'clock in the afternoon and he must have dozed for over an hour.

'I am growing old,' he muttered to himself. There were not many hours of daylight left and the horizon was depressingly empty. He remembered James Quilhampton's *Kestrel* with a pang of conscience. 'Old and forgetful.' The thought, too, was depressing.

Rising stiffly, he went into his night-cabin, opened the top of his chest and poured some water into the bowl recessed there. He threw water into his face, ran the new-fangled toothbrush round his mouth and stared at himself in the mirror. He was sure there was more of his forehead visible than when he had last looked, then chid himself for a fool, for he had done his hair immediately after the morning's dousing.

On deck he became brisk and eager for a sight of the island. 'Where away, Mr Birkbeck?'

Birkbeck was standing with one of his mates, a man named Ashley. Both men lowered their glasses. 'Two points to starboard, sir.'

'Here, sir.' Ashley offered his telescope.

'Thank you, Mr Ashley.'

Drinkwater focused the lenses upon the low island that appeared blue and insubstantial, then swept the sea around it in the vain hope that the grey-white peak of *Kestrel*'s mainsail would break the bleakness of the scene.

'Not a landfall to stumble across in the dark, or the kind of weather we laboured in the other night,' remarked Birkbeck.

'No, indeed . . .' Drinkwater lowered the telescope and handed it back to the master's mate. 'Obliged, Mr Ashley.' He looked up at the spanker gaff, where the unfamiliar red swallowtail ensign with its white cross flapped bravely in the breeze.

'Handsome flag, ain't it? Last time I saw it fly in anger was at Copenhagen,' Birkbeck said.

'Which ship were you in?' Drinkwater asked attentively.

'I was with Captain Puget in *Goliath*.'

'I don't recall . . .'

'In Gambier's attack, sir, not Nelson's.'

'Ah, yes . . .'

'You were in the earlier action then?'

'Yes. I had the bomb *Virago*.'

They reminisced happily, staring at the distant island as, almost imperceptibly, it took form. Drinkwater forbore from telling Birkbeck the clandestine part he had himself played in the events that led up to the appearance of Dismal Jimmy Gambier's fleet before the spires of the Danish capital in 1807. Instead, Birkbeck wanted to know of his brief meetings with Lord Nelson, which led to the inevitable revelation that Captain Drinkwater had not only been a witness to the battle of Copenhagen in 1801, but had also, 'somewhat ignominiously', been a prisoner aboard the enemy flagship *Bucentaure* at Trafalgar.*

'I had no idea, sir,' said Birkbeck admiringly.

'It was not a post to which much glory accrued,' Drinkwater replied ruefully. 'Fate plays some odd tricks . . . I cannot begin to describe the carnage . . .'

The blue smudge hardened, grew darker and sharper, its outline more defined. Presently Huke joined them as Utsira revealed itself as a rocky, steep-sided, low island, with the surge and suck of a heavy groundswell washing its grim shoreline. Then, as the sun westered, it threw the rough and weathered surface into hostile relief.

'Nasty place,' said Huke with the true instinct of the pelagic seaman.

And then, as they watched, far beyond the island, beyond the horizon itself, the sun gleamed briefly on distant mountain peaks floating above cloud. The sight was over in a numinous moment and left them staring with wonder.

'"To Noroway, to Noroway, to Noroway, o'er the foam,"' quoted Huke in a rare and revealing aside.

'Must be thirty leagues distant,' Birkbeck said.

Drinkwater said nothing. He was reminded of the *nunataks* of Greenland which he had last seen from afar off, remembering the enchantment distance lent them, and the harshness of the landscape in reality. On that occasion he had felt relief, for it had been a moment of departure. This was the opposite, and as the mountain summits

*See *The Bomb Vessel* and *1805*.

faded, he wondered whether they had been revealed as portents and what it was that lay in wait amid their inhospitable fastnesses.

He turned his attention again to Utsira. Gone was any picturesque aspect. It was a rampart of rock, to be avoided at all costs, about which the tide ripped past.

'Put the ship about, Mr Birkbeck, and shorten down for the night. We will see whether daylight brings us the *Kestrel*.'

'Aye, aye, sir.'

Birkbeck tucked his glass away and picked up the speaking trumpet from its hook on the binnacle. He began bawling orders to the watch on deck.

'I wonder how many islands we have passed, Tom, in all our combined travels,' Drinkwater remarked idly as the helm went down and *Andromeda* swung slowly to the west, her high jibboom raking the sky.

'The Lord knows. I'm afraid I never kept count.'

'Nor me . . .' Drinkwater was thinking of the island of Juan Fernandez, with its curious rock formation, a great hole eroded through a small cape. Then he recalled the deserters, and the manhunt, and the fight in a cave below the thunder of a waterfall which had ended in the death of the runaways. One had been a gigantic Irishman, the other his lover, the girl they had all known for months as a young seaman named . . . He had forgotten. Witheredge? Witherspoon? Yes, that was it, Witherspoon.*

How one forgot, Drinkwater mused sadly, how one forgot. Again the spectre of age rose to haunt him. He shook the queer feeling off. He had remembered the girl's shattered and beautiful body earlier that very morning; it had stimulated the coarse joke that had bound his ship's company together. He felt a mood of awful self-loathing sweep over him. He himself had shot the girl, shot her unknowingly it was true, but had nevertheless been the agent of her death. Something of his personal disquiet must have showed on his face, for he sighed and then looked up to see Huke staring at him.

'Are you all right, sir?'

Drinkwater smiled ruefully. 'Well enough, Tom, well enough.' He brightened with an effort. 'An attack of the megrims, nothing more.' He forced a laugh. 'Too many damned islands.'

*See *In Distant Waters*.

Chapter Eight *October 1813*

A Bird of Ill-omen

The morning bore a different aspect. Drinkwater woke to the short, jerking plunges of the creaking frigate as she butted into a young head sea and knew the worst. Dressing hurriedly, he went on deck to find his apprehensions confirmed. As he ascended to the deck, he noticed the hammock of the sick man swinging in isolation beneath the open waist, slung between the boat-booms. Then, as he emerged on to the quarterdeck, the near gale buffeted him, the howl of it low in the rigging. Under topsails and a rag or two of staysails and jibs, *Andromeda* rode a grey sea studded with paler crests which reflected the monotone of the sky. Curtains of rain swept eastwards some two miles away on the lee bow, and the blurred horizon to windward promised more. The decks were already sodden, and much of the good work of the day before was already undone. Staring about him he saw no sign of Utsira.

'Morning, sir.' Lieutenant Jameson touched the forecock of his hat which, Drinkwater noted, dripped from earlier rain as he held his head down against the wind. 'A few squalls ha'e blown through, but she's snug enough under this canvas, sir.'

'Yes.' Drinkwater wanted to ask if they had seen any sign of the *Kestrel*, but it would only have betrayed the extent of his anxiety, for it was obvious there was no sign of the cutter in the grey welter beyond the safety of *Andromeda*'s bulwarks. Instead he asked with almost painful inconsequence, 'Where are you from, Mr Jameson?'

'Montrose, sir.'

'And your family? Do they farm?'

'My father is an apothecary, sir,' Jameson said, with a hint of defiance, as though he was half ashamed and half daring his commander to scoff at his low birth.

'A useful calling, Mr Jameson. I wonder what he would have thought of the event of yesterday?'

'I doubt that he would ha'e seen the amusing side of it, sir.'

'And you? What did you think?'

'I, sir . . . well, I . . . I don't know . . .'

'Come, come, I never knew a lieutenant who had no opinion. I'll warrant you had one in the wardroom last night. Perhaps you did not approve?'

'No! I mean, I don't think I would ha'e done . . . I mean . . .'

'You mean you *could* not have done it, I sense. Is that not so?'

'Well, sir, perhaps,' agreed Jameson, whose chief objection had been having to jump around naked himself, though he had taken his discomfiture out on the embarrassed Walsh.

'Sometimes, Mr Jameson, it is very necessary to do things which seem, at face value, to be ridiculous. Your joke about the flea party was a good one, for, though you may have considered the proposition ridiculous, I am of the opinion that the ship-fever is caused by that annoying little parasite and that he will hop aft along the gangway and nip you as readily as he will nip those men forrard there.'

'You are very probably right, sir,' capitulated Jameson resignedly.

'Well, then, perhaps you are more resolute in what you think we should do today. What would you advise?'

Jameson shrugged. He was not used to having his opinion sought, least of all by the captain. 'Heave to, I suppose, since we are on the rendezvous.' He paused and looked at Drinkwater who said:

'Nothing more?'

'No . . . well, yes, I suppose it would be best to run back towards the island, we ha'e hauled out to the nor' west during the night.'

Drinkwater nodded. 'See to it then,' he ordered curtly and turned away, to begin pacing the deck along the line of the starboard carronades.

'Strange old cove,' Jameson muttered to himself, raising the speaking trumpet to his mouth. 'Stand by the braces, there!' he called, then lowering the trumpet towards the men at the helm, 'Larboard wheel if you please . . .'

In the cabin Drinkwater was studying the spread charts with Birkbeck when Huke knocked and entered.

'Fishing boats in sight, sir. I thought at first it was the cutter. I've told Mosse to drop down towards them.'

'What good will that do, Tom? To maintain the fiction of being Danish we would need to speak . . .'

'We've a Dane on board, sir,' Huke interrupted, 'I meant to tell you earlier. His name is Sommer. I have instructed him to lay aft.'

'Well done. Bring him below.'

Huke disappeared and returned a few moments later with an elderly man who, from his sandy eyebrows, might once have been blond, but whose head was now devoid of hair.

'You are Sommer?'

'Yah. I am Per Sommer.'

'How long have you been in this ship?'

'Oh, long time, Captain. In *Agamemnon* before, and *Ruby* and some other ships. In King George's service long time.'

'You have no wish to go home to Denmark?'

Sommer shrugged. 'I have no family. My mother died when I was born, my father soon after. He was fisherman. I become fisherman. Then one day we have big storm, off the Hoorn's Rev. Later we see ship and I become British seaman. Now *Andromeda* my home. Not go back to Denmark. Too old.'

Drinkwater looked blankly at the elderly man. For a moment or two he was lost in contemplation at the sad biography, moved at the surrender to providence. Had fate compelled Sommer to this comfortless existence just to provide him, Captain Nathaniel Drinkwater, with an interpreter at a crucial moment?

'Lucky for us, sir,' prompted Birkbeck.

'What? Oh, yes. D'you know why we are flying the Danish flag?'

Sommer shrugged. 'Not worry very much about flags.'

'Very well. We want you to speak to the fishing boats ahead, Sommer. I want to ask them if they have seen any strange ships, big ships. American ships, in fact, Sommer. D'you understand?'

'American ships, yah, I understand.'

'What about . . . ?' began Huke, but Drinkwater had already considered the matter.

'I want you to put on my hat and cloak when you speak to them, Sommer, to look like an officer.'

'An officer . . . ?' Sommer grinned, not unwilling to enter the little conspiracy. 'Yah, I can be captain.'

And they bowed him out of the cabin with almost as much ceremony as if he were.

*

The two fishing boats, their grey sails almost indistinguishable against the sea, lay to leeward as the mainyards were swung aback and Sommer hoisted himself up on to the rail. There followed an exchange which, by its very nature, raised Drinkwater's spirits, for it was obvious from the Dane's question and the pointing gestures that followed that it had been positively answered.

'Give them this,' Drinkwater commanded, holding up a knotted handkerchief. Sommer took the small bundle and tossed it into the nearer boat as it wallowed below them. There were expressions of thanks and Sommer dropped down on deck, taking off the captain's cloak and hat. Drinkwater took them and, in doing so, thrust a guinea into Sommer's rough hand.

'Thank you, Sommer. What did they say?'

'Two American ships, sir, sailed into Vikkenfiord three days ago.'

'Very good. If we take them I shall rate you a quartermaster for prize money.'

'Thank you, Captain.' The Dane knuckled his forehead and shuffled forward.

'Haul the mainyards, Mr Mosse! Mr Birkbeck, the chart . . .'

They had located the Vikkenfiord as a long inlet which once, in primeval times, had been formed by the erosion of a mighty glacier. It appeared like a long finger reaching, with a slight crook in it, into the mountainous interior. Its entrance was very narrow.

'For a moment I thought it was not going to be on our chart,' Drinkwater confided.

''Twould have to be well enough known for the Americans to find, sir,' replied Birkbeck.

'Yes,' Drinkwater agreed, feeling a little foolish, for that was an obvious point and the entire ship knew by now that they were seeking Yankee privateers. 'We could do with better visibility before closing the coast, but I fear we are more likely to encounter fog.'

'Aye, I was thinking much the same. This can be a damnable spot . . .'

'Well, there is no point in dwelling on the matter. Lay us a course to Utsira. We can afford a little further delay and if the Americans were anchored three days ago, it seems unlikely they have left already . . .'

'They could have slipped out yesterday,' said Birkbeck.

'True.' Drinkwater could not tell the master why he was certain they had not left, but his own heart quickened, for he was sure they lay within the fastness of the fiord. The weather they had endured would not have encouraged the passage of a ship from Denmark with French arms, having been contrary for a passage out of the Skagerrak, for whereas the Norwegian coast north of Utsira was fissured with sheltered inland passages, the area to the south was not.

'We will pass another night on the rendezvous,' Drinkwater said firmly, 'and then, if the weather serves, we will run into this Vikkenfiord and take a look.'

Drinkwater slept well that night and woke in optimistic mood. To his unutterable joy the wind had hauled south-east and Utsira was dead astern, no more than three or four leagues distant. Such a wind shift seemed like an augury of good luck. He shaved, dressed and hurried on deck. The change in the weather had encouraged more of the local fisherfolk to venture forth, and Drinkwater saw this as additional proof of providential approval.

He had not expected to find *Kestrel* in the offing but such was his mood that he would not have been surprised had she been in sight, and he privately dared to hope that she and her company were safe.

Although it was not his watch, the master was on deck, taking bearings and hurrying below to lay them off on the chart. When he returned to the deck he approached Drinkwater.

'With your permission, sir, a course for the entrance to the fiord?'

'If you please, Mr Birkbeck.'

So they bore up and, with their yards braced to catch the steady beam breeze from the south-east, *Andromeda* headed north-east again, dropping the isolated outcrop of Utsira astern and soon afterwards raising the grey ramparts of the coast of Norway.

It had escaped anyone's notice that Mr Templeton had not quitted his cabin since the morning of the great dousing. Anyone of significance, that is, for the wardroom messman was aware of the captain's secretary's 'indisposition', and catered for him until, on the morning they departed Utsira, he passed word to the surgeon.

Templeton himself had fallen victim to a conflict of emotion. Unaware of the captain's preoccupations, he was somewhat affronted that Drinkwater had not sent for him. He was also concerned, for reasons of his own, as to what Drinkwater now intended to do. On the other hand, he found himself unable to resist submitting to wild and beguiling fantasies which washed over him in waves of sensual anticipation, so that he dared not leave his cabin to confront a world of reality in which, he felt sure, his guilt would be written plain upon his face. He had not counted upon the world of reality visiting him.

Mr Kennedy knocked and immediately opened the cabin's flimsy door unannounced. 'Now what in the world is the matter with you, Templeton?'

Templeton was shocked at the intrusion. He expected his shut door to be respected as if it were that of his home. He had no concept of ship-board manners, or prerogatives, something that Kennedy had quickly assimilated. Caught off guard and guilty, he forgot his 'illness' and was merely outraged.

'How dare you come bursting in like this . . .'

'There's nothing wrong with you,' said Kennedy, well practised in detecting the vapours among the so-called well-to-do. 'Come, turn out! What would become of us if we all lay about in such a manner?'

'I've caught an ague from the cold water . . .'

'Rubbish! Salt water never gave a man an ague! You are malingering, sir!' Kennedy snapped, 'And I have work to do!'

'I didn't summon you,' protested Templeton, adding, as he saw the baleful look in Kennedy's eyes, 'nor has Captain Drinkwater sent for me.'

'I think he is far too busy. Do you know where we are?'

'Off Norway, I shouldn't wonder.'

'Almost *upon* it, in fact. There's talk of American ships and action before the day's done.'

'Action?' Templeton's face grew ashen.

'Aye, Templeton, action. You had better be out of bed by then, cowardice in the face of the enemy's a hanging offence!'

There were a lot of men on deck, Templeton thought, the same men he had last seen naked; men on and off duty, for the vista about them was such as to stun the dullest mind. They ran through a narrow strait in which the sea bore the colour and smoothness of a sword-blade. Upon either side rose precipitous heights, great dark cliffs, deeply fissured, their snow-capped summits wreathed in veils of cloud. As they passed the gorge, the land fell back, to reveal the fiord itself, opening ahead of them. The ground-willow and scrub of the littoral gave way to pines and firs whose dark cladding moved in waves with the breeze, accompanied by gentle susurrations. These trees climbed the slopes, finally dwindling to concede the rising ground to bare rock and, here and there, patches of scree. Above the talus, solitary snow-encrusted crags stood out against the sky, about the peaks of which an occasional eagle could be seen wheeling.

''Tis wonderful, sir,' a voice said, and Templeton turned to see his sea-mentor Greer, the boatswain's mate, standing awe-struck.

'Sublime, Greer, sublime,' Templeton whispered, suddenly aware of an overpowering breathlessness.

'I've never seen nought like it, Mr Templeton, 'cept in a picture-book once, when I was a boy, like.'

The revelation of childhood wonder combined with so manly an appreciation of nature's bounty to make Templeton turn to Greer. Their eyes met and Templeton *knew* for a certainty that Greer had similar inclinations, though not a word passed between them and they regarded again the dark shores of the Vikkenfiord. Templeton felt quite deliriously free of all his cares.

A few yards away Lieutenant Mosse nudged his scarlet-clad colleague Walsh. 'There, sir, I do declare I was right and you owe me a guinea.'

'You may be right, Stephen, but that ain't proof!'

'What proof d'you want?'

'Just proof,' said Walsh enigmatically, leaving Mosse shaking his head, amused.

'You have no need to worry about the depth,' Drinkwater said to Birkbeck, 'though it will not hurt to take an occasional cast of the lead. These fiords are uncommon deep.'

'Aye, sir, but just in case . . .'

'Indeed, by all means.'

And so their progress was punctuated by low orders to the helmsmen which kept the frigate in the centre of the fiord, her yards squared to the following wind, and the desultory and unrewarded call of the labouring leadsmen of 'no botto-o-om'.

Presently the high land fell back and the gradient became less steep on the southern shore. The margins of pine forest widened to great swathes, rounding the contours of the mountains under their dark, luxuriant mantle.

'Something sinister about them damned trees,' said Huke.

'Hiding trolls and what-not, eh, Tom?' grinned Drinkwater, 'I didn't know you had a fancy for the Gothick.'

'Sir! Right ahead!' A hail from the forecastle broke into this inane conversation and Drinkwater raised his glass. Ahead of them the fiord widened considerably, having an appearance more like an English lake in Cumbria. To starboard the mountains retreated further to, perhaps, ten miles distant, while to port they remained closer, their foothills coming down in hummocks and indenting the coast, so that little bays with brief strands alternated with rocky promontories. Ahead, one such headland, more prominent than the others, gave the fiord its crooked shape. Just emerging beyond this small but impressive cape were the masts and yards of two large ships.

They were some distance off and Drinkwater could make out little of them before he was confronted by a more immediate problem. The wind, which had funnelled through the gorge, from which they had run well clear, now assumed its truer direction and swept down from the south-east and the more distant mountains to starboard. Above their heads the squared sails were all a-flutter with a dull, insistent rumble.

'Larboard braces there! Lively now! Cast off your starboard pins!'

In a few moments order was restored and, with a beam wind, *Andromeda* gathered speed. Drinkwater raised his glass again. The strange anchored ships beneath the cape were clearer now. He could see the bright spots of their ensigns and he closed his glass with a snap.

'Beat to quarters, Mr Huke, and clear for action.'

His Britannic Majesty's frigate *Andromeda* bore down upon the anchored ships at a fine clip, the deceitful swallowtail Danish ensign standing stiffly out from the peak of the spanker gaff. A British ensign awaited the order to be run aloft. Boarding parties of seamen and marines, each told off under the command of a midshipman or master's mate, waited by the quarter boats, the red and blue cutters.

It was clear that the only patch of shallow water capable of holding the flukes of an anchor lay close inshore, in the bay that, Drinkwater guessed without looking at the chart, lay just beyond the bluff. A sudden gust of wind laid the frigate over, so that she surged ahead, rapidly drawing closer to the point itself.

Beside him Huke reported the ship cleared for action. Every gun, including the runaway cannon which had been hand-spiked and shoved back into its rightful station, was loaded and shotted and every man stood ready at his post.

'We'll have the t'gallants off her and the courses clewed up. There's enough wind to handle her under the topsails.'

Huke and Birkbeck nodded their understanding. With the ship heeled and moving fast, the gunnery would be inaccurate and wild, and Drinkwater had given specific orders that he wanted little damage done to the enemies' fabric.

'Take 'em quickly by surprise, with as little damage as possible,' he had said. The thought of rich prizes gained this policy a ready co-operation and the word passed along the gun decks. A short and lucrative cruise would be dandy!

The bay beyond the bluff was just beginning to open now. They could see the two ships with boats about them, see too the stars and bars of their hostile nationality.

There was a sudden sound as of rending silk. Aloft three holes appeared in the main topsail and the twanging of parted rigging came to the astonished knot of officers on the quarterdeck. To starboard half a dozen columns of water sprung into the air.

'What the devil . . . ?'

The boom of a battery's fire rolled over the water towards them. Drinkwater saw the little clouds of smoke swiftly torn to shreds by the wind from the gun embrasures that lined the cliff-top of the bluff. Above the half-hidden but unmistakable grey line of a stone parapet, another swallowtail ensign rose upon a flagstaff.

'There's a fort there!' Birkbeck cried in sudden comprehension, with the outraged tone of a cheat outsmarted.

'Aye,' Huke retorted, 'and he knows us for what we are.'

'He certainly ain't fooled by our colours!'

Confronted by this sudden revelation, Drinkwater had to think swiftly. He was reluctant to give up the attempt on the American ships, but the next salvo from the fort hit home, tumbling men from a forecastle gun like rag dolls. Their sudden cries rent the air, as an explosion of splinters erupted from the bulwark. Another shot ploughed up the deck and crashed through the opposite bulwark to fall, spent, into the sea alongside the starbord main-chains.

'Let fall the courses, there! Set the t'gallants!'

He must run on, then work up to windward and return under the lee of the opposite, southern shore, past the fort but out of range of the guns hidden behind those high ramparts. It was the only way he could reconnoitre the enemy position.

The discovery of the fort transformed the situation. The matter would be more difficult than he had at first anticipated, no mere tip-and-run raid, but it could be managed if he kept his head. He felt the hull shudder as more shot struck them. How far did those damned guns in the fort traverse?

Then, with the added momentum of the extra sails and without firing a shot in return, they swept out of range and Drinkwater forced himself to concentrate his attention on the two ships anchored in the bay. Both were frigate-built, large privateers, or possibly worse: perhaps naval frigates.

It was essential, then, that Drinkwater should turn *Andromeda* and move her back to seaward of the enemy ships. At least he could cut them off from escape. Moreover, it was imperative that he find an anchorage, for they could not beat out through the gorge with the wind funnelling through it. The lower appearance of the southern shore suggested the sea-bed extended into the fiord at a similar gradient, affording him the shallow water he sought. He only hoped that whatever bottom the anchor flukes might strike, it would prove soft enough to hold them.

'Full and bye, Mr Birkbeck. Brace the yards sharp up. I want to claw offshore, tack ship and seek an anchorage under the lee of the farther side.' He turned to the first lieutenant. 'Secure the guns, Mr Huke.'

A buzz of disappointment greeted this order. On the gun deck Lieutenant Mosse, commanding the starboard battery, sheathed his sword and addressed his colleague in charge of the port cannon.

'He who turns and runs away, lives to fight another day, eh, Jameson?'

'A flea flees,' returned Jameson.

'You possess a shining wit, Jameson.'

'I'd sooner that than a wicked tongue.'

Andromeda came up into the wind with a clatter as the helm was put over. Her sails bellied aback as she came round and the bead-blocks aloft rattled as she bucked up into the wind.

'Mainsail haul!' The main and mizen yards were trimmed to the new course as the foreyards continued to thrust her head round on to the larboard tack.

'Let go and haul!'

The frigate settled down to claw her way across the fiord. The wind was strong now, augmented by cold katabatic gusts that slid down from the distant high ground. Drinkwater regarded the enemy fort over the starboard quarter.

'The ruse with the ensign didn't pay off then, sir,' Huke said, after reporting the guns secure.

'I think, Tom,' Drinkwater replied, without taking the glass from his eye, 'that as we carried off most of the Danish fleet, what few ships they retain are well known to any Danish officer worth his salt.'

'Even one commanding a remote fort in Norway?'

'Well, I don't think it is any coincidence,' Drinkwater said, counting the embrasures in the distant fort, 'that the Yankee ships are anchored under those guns, do you?'

'No. It's a damnably perfect rendezvous for them.'

'I think, sir,' put in Birkbeck sharply, 'they were expecting something larger!'

An urgency in Birkbeck's voice made Drinkwater lower the glass and look round. 'What the devil . . . ?'

He swung to where Birkbeck pointed. Far down the fiord, her white sails full of the following wind which had so lately wafted *Andromeda* through the narrows and which now mewed her up in the fiord, a large man-of-war was running clear of the gorge.

'Now there', said Drinkwater grimly, raising his glass, 'is a bird of exceeding ill-omen.'

Chapter Nine *October 1813*

The Wings of Nemesis

Captain Drinkwater felt the cold grip of irresolution seize his palpitating heart. Here was the spectre of defeat, of dishonour. Retreat, he knew, merely postponed the inevitable and spawned greater reluctance; honour demanded he fight, if only to defend that of his flag. The white ensign now flew in place of the swallowtail *ruse de guerre*. He considered striking it after a few broadsides in permissible, if disreputable capitulation.

These thoughts coursed through his mind while it was yet clouding with other, more demanding preoccupations, for he saw the approaching enemy not merely as a hostile ship-of-war, but as the manifestation of something more sinister, an agent of fate itself. Here came the punishment for all his self-conceit. Sommer had served not simply his own ends, but also a greater purpose, to accomplish the destruction of Captain Nathaniel Drinkwater and his overweening pride in the obscurity of a remote Norwegian fiord.

How foolish he had been, he thought, to believe in providence as some benign deity which had taken a fancy to himself and which would cosset him personally. Blind faith proved only a blind alley, a trap.

Oh, it had sustained him, to be sure, given him a measure of protection which he, during his brief strutting moment, had transmuted into a gallant confidence, but he had outrun his allotted span, a fact which he now knew with a chilling certainty. He was old and careworn, a dog who had had his day and was masquerading in a young man's post, seduced by what . . . ?

He found, in a wave of mounting panic, that he did not know. The vaguest notion of duty swept through his perception, to be dismissed as cynical nonsense and replaced by damning self-interest. What did he hope to achieve? This enemy ship approaching them had come, undoubtedly, to transfer the arms and munitions to the waiting Yankees, as Bardolini had foretold. And if providence had, in its cosmic wisdom, decided that Canada should, like America itself, be free of King George's government, it would surely engineer the defeat of so petty a player as Nathaniel Drinkwater.

He silently cursed himself. He could have, *should* have, been at home on his Suffolk acres with Elizabeth, expiating his many sins and wickednesses. His great conceit had been to think that fate had delivered Bardolini into his hands for him to accomplish some grandiloquent design and keep Canada as a dominion of the British kingdom. If fate had wanted that, it would never have condoned the revolt of the Thirteen Colonies.

This simplistic and overwrought, though logical conclusion terminated Drinkwater's nervously self-centred train of thought. Huke, Birkbeck, Mosse and Jameson were looking at him expectantly. The hands, many belonging to the watch below, just stood down from their action stations, milled curiously in the waist. They too stared expectantly aft.

Drinkwater raised his Dollond glass again, a charade he enforced upon himself to compel his wits to return to reality. With slow deliberation he lowered the telescope.

'We will attempt to break out to seaward,' he said with what he hoped was a quiet authority. 'Send the hands back to their quarters. Starboard battery to load bar-shot and elevate high. We will exchange broadsides as we pass and do our best to cripple that fellow. Mr Birkbeck, lay me a course to pass, say, seven cables distant from him . . .'

'The wind will be foul in the narrows, sir.'

'When the wind comes ahead we will tow through. He is heavier than we are. That is a small advantage, but an advantage, none the less. You have your orders, gentlemen. We have a chance, let us exploit it!'

Drinkwater raised the glass again. Concentrating on the enemy's image occluded the closer world, left him to master himself, conspicuous upon his quarterdeck but mercifully hidden from all.

She was a big ship, a heavy frigate such as had long ago superseded the class to which *Andromeda* belonged, equal to the large American frigates which had so shocked the Royal Navy by a series of brilliant victories over British cruisers at the outbreak of the present war with the United States.

To counter this, the British had reacted by cutting down some smaller line-of-battle ships, producing *razées*, such as the *Patrician*, which Drinkwater himself had lately commanded. Had he had her at his disposal now, he would have been confident of taking on this powerful enemy, for with her he had shot to pieces the Russian seventy-four *Suvorov*. That, he reproached himself bitterly, was a past conceit, and it was for past conceits and victories that he was now to receive due retribution.

The Danish frigate, for he could tell she was such by her ensign, bore down towards them as they in turn, yards braced up, racing through the comparatively still waters of the fiord, rapidly closed the distance. Doubtless the Dane would seek to cripple *Andromeda* and, as the leeward ship, her guns would be pointing much higher. Drinkwater considered edging downwind, to give himself that advantage, but he dismissed the thought. It was just possible that the Danish commander did not know who, or what, they were, that their own ensign was masked by the mizen topsail, and he would think they were one of the American ships bearing down in welcome. No, the sooner they rushed past, the better.

At all events, the Dane stood stolidly on.

Huke came aft, his face grim. 'All ready, sir.'

'Very well.'

The first lieutenant contemplated the Danish ship. 'She's a heavy bugger.'

'Yes. Must be a new ship. I thought we'd destroyed all their power.'

'They've had time to build new. We left them numerous gun-vessels for their islands, I suppose they've built this fellow to defend the coast of Norway.'

'In which case he's doing a damnably good job. You know, once we work ourselves past him, we could blockade those narrows . . .'

'Let us get out first,' Huke cautioned. 'Hullo, he's shortening down; the cat's fairly out of the bag now!'

Critically they watched the topgallant yards lowered and the black dots of topmen running aloft. *Andromeda* had been eight or nine miles from the Dane when they first sighted the enemy. Now less than four miles separated the two frigates as they closed at a combined speed of sixteen or seventeen knots. They would be abeam of each other in a quarter of an hour. It seemed an age.

Mr Templeton was as confused about what was happening as he was about his own, private emotions. The ship's company had run to their battle stations and the internal appearance of *Andromeda* had been transformed; bulkheads were folded up under the deckhead, and the officers' quarters on the gun deck seemed suddenly to vanish. It had all been explained to him, but he still found the reality disquieting. Then, on passing the anchorage where, it was plain even to Templeton's untutored eye, two American ships lay, they had turned away and the men had been stood easy. After what seemed to Templeton so long a voyage, with their objective at last in sight, Captain Drinkwater's present action was incomprehensible. Templeton felt a certain relief that the air was not about to be filled with cannon-balls. Some days previously, Greer had picked one out of the garlands and thrown it to him. The sudden dead weight had almost broken his wrists and Greer had explained the crude technicalities of their brutal artillery with a morbid delight.

The very obvious reversal of orders, with the men chattering excitedly as they resumed their positions, now puzzled him and he ventured to ask Lieutenant Mosse what was going on.

'There's an enemy frigate approaching,' said Mosse obliquely, drawing his hanger with a wicked rasp. 'I suggest you might go on deck and watch.' Templeton hesitated and Mosse added, 'Much safer than staying here.'

Only half-believing this lie, Templeton reluctantly made for the forward companionway. Mosse winked at Jameson.

Thus Mr Templeton made to ascend the ladder normally reserved for the crew.

'Steady there, as she goes, Mr Birkbeck.'

Drinkwater watched the approaching ship. Both frigates ran on almost exactly reciprocal courses. Birkbeck and Ashley stood beside the binnacle where three helmsmen and a quartermaster held *Andromeda* to her track. Along the bulwarks the stubby barrelled carronades of the quarterdeck battery were surrounded by their crews, the gun-captains holding the taut lanyards to the cocked flintlocks. On the forecastle a lesser number of carronades supported the long bow-chasers. Below them, a similar scene was enacted, with the larger gun-crews gathered round the heavy 12-pounders of the main batteries. At key points aboard *Andromeda* the lesser and petty officers mustered groups of men ready to board or repel the enemy, bring ammunition or fire hoses, or work the ship if she was to be manoeuvred. Other groups clustered in the tops, marines among them, to act as sharpshooters, man the light swivel guns or lay out along the yards to shorten sail.

Upon the quarterdeck Huke, the first lieutenant, assisted the captain. A trio of midshipmen waited to act as messengers or attend to signals with the yeoman and his party. Lieutenant Walsh commanded the main detachment of marines who, interspersed with the carronades, laid their long muskets on the hammocks in the nettings and drew beads on the dark heads of the approaching enemy officers.

'You may fire when your guns bear!' Drinkwater's voice rang out, clear and crisp. The moment of fearful anticipation had passed and he was as cold and as purposeful as a sword-blade. Matters would fall out as they would, come what may.

'Pass word to the lieutenants on the gun deck, Mr Fisher,' Huke said, relaying Drinkwater's instruction. The boy ran off unobserved as every man concentrated upon the enemy ship. She was much closer than the seven cables Drinkwater had intended, but Mosse had drawn all the quoins and was sanguine that his guns would elevate. Periodically Drinkwater would quiz the gun-captain at the nearest carronade whose breech-screw fulfilled the same function.

'How is she now?'

'She'll do, sir . . .'

There was a last expectant hiatus which all knew would be broken by the eruption of the first gun, the starboard bow-chaser whose position commanded a field of fire closer aligned to the *Andromeda*'s line of advance than any other. The air was filled with the subdued hiss of the sea as it curled back from *Andromeda*'s apple-bow, the steady thrum of wind in the rigging, the creak of the ship, of her hemp and canvas, of the long tiller ropes, the straining sheets and tacks, the lifts, halliards and braces that converted the energy of the wind into the advance of the frigate and her iron armament.

Then came the report of the bow-chaser, the bright flash from its muzzle and the puff of cloudy smoke which hung for a second under the lee bow before being shredded by the wind. A second report, that of the enemy's reply, coincided with the flat echo, followed by the general reverberations of a furious exchange of shots. Drinkwater marked the quickening succession of flashes rolling aft towards him as each gun bore.

Then something went terribly awry. Instead of the bearing of the enemy opening with inexorable precision as the two frigates passed each other on reciprocal courses, there was a sudden, inexplicable acceleration. The Danish ship drew aft with miraculous speed and the British guns threw their shot not at the enemy, but at the empty sea on their own starboard beam.

'What in the devil's name . . . ?'

'What the hell . . . ?'

A dozen fouler exclamatory questions stabbed the air. Drinkwater spun round, momentarily confounded and utterly confused. All he knew was that from passing the beam, the enemy was now, against all reason, crossing their stern.

'Oh, my God!'

'For what we are about to receive . . .'

Inexplicably, *Andromeda* lay in the ideal position to be raked.

Mr Templeton saw exactly what happened, though he did not understand it at the time. He was, however, aware that the sudden movement of a group of seamen a few moments earlier had nothing to do with the business in hand, for he had heard no orders to stimulate men who, throughout the ship, were so manifestly poised but immobile with expectation. He was ascending the forward companionway as the two ships made their final approach and before the sudden and disorientating event which so perplexed all but a few on the upper deck, when he was abruptly shoved aside. As he spun round, expecting some jibe from Mosse, he caught sight of both lieutenants bent and staring out of gun-ports at the enemy, as were most of the men clustered about the guns, oblivious to this sudden rush of others to the upper deck.

Templeton had forgotten what Greer had told him, that when the ship cleared for action, marine sentries were posted at each of the companionways throughout the ship to prevent any man from leaving his post. Thus dissuading cowardice, these sentinels let only approved persons pass them: the ship's boys, the powder-monkeys, with cartridges for the cannon, midshipmen acting as messengers, officers, stretcher parties and the walking wounded.

Now he was reminded of that rude instruction, for the marine sentry at the forward companionway had fallen almost at his feet, stretched upon the ladder, the handle of a long butcher's knife protruding from his chest. Templeton saw the man's face white with shock, his hands pulling futilely at the yellow horn handle even as death took possession of him.

So quickly and silently had the thing happened that the sentry's musket had not clattered to the deck, but had been seized and taken by one of the men running past him. Templeton was no man of action, yet he felt shock and outrage at what had happened, knew it was impermissible, rebellious, contrary to those draconian Articles of War he had read abstractedly at the Admiralty and heard uttered by Captain Drinkwater on a windswept Sunday a few days earlier. It was this outraged impropriety, this affront to established order that propelled him upwards, after the running men; this and a horrified dread of the marine who twitched his last and had just attracted the notice of the crew of an adjacent gun.

So small a space of time had been occupied by this event that he arrived on the forecastle hard on the heels of the rebels, quite unaware that he was lucky to have escaped with his own life. He saw, looming above him and, it seemed, just beyond the stuffed hammock nettings, the rushing bowsprit, jibs, figurehead and forefoot of the passing Danish frigate.

Andromeda's starboard bow-chaser fired, the gun carriage rolled inboard and her crew leapt round it with sponge and worm, cartridge, ball and rammer. The next gun fired, and the next. Concussion was answered by concussion. The air seemed thick with great gusts of roaring wind and heated blasts that made him gasp. He was spun round, confused; he breathed with difficulty, his quarry had vanished, seemingly swallowed up in this smoky and explosive hell.

Then he saw them, clustered above the port sheet anchor lashed in the larboard forechains. A second later he also saw the fluke and stock disappear overboard. To the buzzings and roars, cries and thumps was added an undertone he was unfamiliar with.

Unbeknown to Mr Templeton, just beneath his feet and in preparation for anchoring in the fiord if it had been necessary, the sheet anchor drew its heavy hemp cable rumbling after it to the sea-bed. In the stunning confusion of the noise and smoke, it suddenly struck him what was happening and he hesitated.

Drinkwater knew what had happened the moment he realized that the sudden acceleration of the enemy was apparent, not real, motion.

As he looked round he saw that it was the sudden swing of *Andromeda's* bow to port, manifested by the rake of the bowsprit across the distant hills, that had caused this disorientation. In the instant of comprehension, cause was of less moment than effect. From having a sporting chance at inflicting damage upon her enemy, *Andromeda* was suddenly laid helplessly supine under the enemy guns, her vulnerable stern exposed as she swung.

The Danes were not slow to exploit this chance, for the British frigate continued to turn slowly, obligingly, caught by her treacherously released larboard sheet anchor. The rebels had put wracking stoppers on the cable so that, when some fifty fathoms had run out, it jerked at the anchor, and the flukes far below bit at the deposits of moraine on the sea-bed.

Circumstances had conspired in their favour, for it so happened that, having worked across to the opposite shore, *Andromeda* was, as her captain had supposed she would be, in far shallower water than prevailed in the main body of the fiord. Her anchor, after plucking at the bottom, bit effectively. But such was her speed that, although the swinging moment was applied at her bow and she turned to expose her narrow stern to the surprised Danes, she swung through more than a neat right angle. In fact she continued to swing, turning almost back the way she had come and exposing her whole port side. Moreover, this wild turn had flung her sails aback and this caused her to slow, almost to follow her enemy as she floundered and bucked in response to the powerful tug of her hemp cable.

'Bloody anchor's shot away!' Drinkwater roared. 'We've clubhauled! Let go t'gallant halliards! Clew up tops'ls! Main and fore clew garnets!'

They scarcely felt the crash and thump of the Danish shot as it flew about. The air was full of the wind of its passing and men who had been standing one moment had vanished the next, to become a bloody pulp and then a slime as others, their eyes and attention aloft, slithered and stumbled through their remains.

Drinkwater felt a smart blow on the shoulder and the sting of something sharp across his face. His hat was torn from his head and he was vaguely aware, though he remembered this only afterwards, of something gold spinning away from him.

Walsh ran towards Drinkwater as he was consumed with anxiety for the main topgallant mast. It swayed gracefully out of the vertical, halted and swung in a web of rigging, then its broken foot pulled away from the upper hounds and it began to fall, bringing the topgallant yard and sail down with it. About twenty feet above the boats on the booms, its descent was arrested by more rigging and wreckage and it hung, suspended, like the sword of Damocles above their heads, gently swaying.

Huke was already rallying men to get it lowered down on deck to salvage what they could. Drinkwater turned his attention to the departing enemy. He could not suppose the Danes would not come back and finish what they had already begun. He felt someone tugging at his clothing. It was Walsh.

'Oh, my!' the marine officer gasped, 'oh, my!' He knelt at Drinkwater's feet in a ridiculous posture, and Drinkwater looked down at him. The florid face was suffused with hurt and pain and anger, the eyes ablaze, and then the light went out of it, the shadow of death moved swiftly across it and Walsh fell full length at Drinkwater's feet. Afterwards, Drinkwater could not understand how the ball had hit the marine officer, or where it had gone, for its imprint was clear in Walsh's wrecked back.

Drinkwater stared at the mangled man for a moment, felt his gorge rise and turned away, fishing frantically in his tail pocket for the Dollond glass so that he could shut out this madness and concentrate on the neat, ordered image of the enemy frigate again.

'She's the *Odin*, sir, must be new tonnage, we burnt everything on the stocks, but I do recall timbers on the ways being marked *Odin*.' The voice of Birkbeck, calmly professional, steadied him, corroborating his earlier asides to Huke and referring to the great act of licensed arson which had followed Admiral Lord Gambier's action and the military operations of General Lord Cathcart which had culminated in the occupation of Copenhagen six years earlier.

'Thank you, Mr Birkbeck,' Drinkwater said, and the master turned to an elderly master's mate named Beavis and remarked on the captain's coolness. 'Look at him; one epaulette shot away and taken half his cheek with it, no hat and not a word of alarm.'

Birkbeck shook his head. 'I thought him half-mad t'other day when he had us all bollock naked under the pumps, now I know he is.'

'He'll need to be,' replied Beavis, 'if we're to get out of this festering mess.'

The Danish frigate had swept past them and she too was now taking in sail. Already her topgallant yards were down and the men were aloft laying out along them to furl the sails, and her main course and forecourse were swagged up in their buntlines and clew garnets. As Drinkwater watched, he saw her turn slowly into the wind, tack neatly under topsails, spanker and jibs, and head back towards them.

On *Andromeda*'s deck order was reasserting itself. Despite being badly cut up both by the fort and the *Odin*, *Andromeda* was capable of resistance. Huke appeared at his elbow.

'Are you all right, sir?' the first lieutenant asked solicitously, seeing the blood on Drinkwater's cheek.

'Not a good moment for you to step into my shoes, Tom,' Drinkwater joked grimly.

'I meant your face.'

Drinkwater put up his hand and brought it away sticky with blood. 'Well, I'm damned; I had no idea – it's no more than a scratch.'

'You've lost your swab.'

'Ah,' Drinkwater put up his hand, 'confounded thing must have carried away. It's happened before.'

'Aye, and lacerated your cheek. Anyway, I've been forward. I found Templeton up there, he saw what happened.'

'What, with the anchor?'

'Aye, it was cut away – deliberately,' Huke added, aware that Drinkwater was only half-listening, that he was concerned about the Danish frigate a mile away. He beckoned Templeton. 'Tell the Captain, Templeton.'

Templeton's face was uncertain, struggling to comprehend what had transpired.

'Go on, man! Get on with it . . . Oh, for God's sake!' Huke fumed impatiently. 'The shank painter was sliced through like that damned gun-breeching. This,' Huke gestured wildly round, 'this is no accident!'

'The devil it ain't!' Drinkwater experienced a constriction about his throat. He felt a clear sensation of being strangled and as he fought off this weakness, Templeton's expression looked oddly equivocal.

'Would you know the men who did this?' Drinkwater asked desperately.

'I don't know,' Templeton answered evasively, avoiding Drinkwater's scrutiny, 'it was all rather confusing. I could try.'

'Yes, you could,' Drinkwater snapped, his eyes cold. 'Take Walsh and a file of his men . . .' Drinkwater remembered. 'Oh, Walsh is dead.' He looked down at the red corpse. Templeton's eyes followed and saw the horror at his feet for the first time. 'Damnation!' The clerk's eyes glazed over and he crumpled in a swoon at Drinkwater's feet. 'Damnation!' Drinkwater swore again.

'Sir!' The first lieutenant's cry of warning recalled Drinkwater's attention to the *Odin*. He looked out to larboard. The Danish frigate was bearing down on them in a second attempt to rake *Andromeda* from astern. But in her approach, just for a few minutes of opportunity, she was head on to them.

'Messenger!'

'Sir?' Midshipman Fisher stood beside him. The boy was pale and fidgeted with his coat lapels.

'Are you all right, son?'

'Perfectly, sir.'

'Good, go below to the gun deck and tell . . .'

But Huke had anticipated the order and was shouting to Mosse on the gun deck below. The roar of the larboard broadside bellowed defiance at the approaching *Odin*. *Andromeda* rocked with the recoil. The men sponged and loaded and rammed, and again, then again, flung bar-shot high at the enemy's foremast. This was what Huke had trained his crew for, and if Pardoe's absence had been reprehensible, Huke had taken full advantage of the breach of regulations. The bar-shot, each comprising two hemispheres of iron joined by a rod, were flung from the gun muzzles and flailed wildly during their inaccurate, short-ranged trajectory.

The noise brought Templeton to. Drinkwater bent and shook him roughly. 'Get up!' he commanded. 'Get up and pull yourself together. I want those men rounded up.' He turned and bellowed, 'Sergeant Danks!'

'Sir?'

'A file of your men, we've work to do on board! Follow me! Quickly now!'

Drinkwater helped Templeton to his unsteady feet and thrust him forward.

'Shall I come too, sir?' It was little Fisher, still waiting for orders. Another broadside interrupted them.

'No. Do you stand by Mr Huke,' and turning to Huke, Drinkwater shouted, 'Tom, take command on the quarterdeck, d'you hear?'

'Aye, aye, sir!'

'Come, Templeton, Sergeant Danks . . .'

As he led them along the starboard gangway, Drinkwater was aware that it was already dusk, that the shadows of the surrounding mountains threw most of the water into a mysterious darkness from which the first stars were reflected. Night was almost upon them. Damnably odd that he had hardly noticed.

Since their treachery, and in anticipation of *Andromeda* being raked, the rebels had gone over the bow and concealed themselves on the heads. There, beside the pink nakedness of the carved representation of Andromeda chained to her rock, half a dozen men awaited the outcome of the battle, furiously debating their course of action, secure only for the time being, they assumed, because of the demands of the fight with the Danish ship.

As Danks's marines prodded them on to the forecastle at the point of the bayonet, they were greeted by cheers. Drinkwater forgot the matter in hand; he looked round to see the *Odin's* foremast totter and then fall sideways.

'Secure those men in irons, Sergeant,' shouted Drinkwater, ignoring Templeton and hurrying aft towards the first lieutenant, anxiously staring at the *Odin*.

'I think we've scored a point!' Huke shouted, his words drowned in yet another discharge of Jameson's cannon.

'Well done, Tom . . .'

Both officers looked at the Dane. The *Odin* had fallen off the wind and only her bow-chasers bore; after two shots, they too fell silent. As the two men watched, the main and mizen yards were braced round; gradually the *Odin* began to make a stern-board.

'A tactical withdrawal for the night, I think,' offered Huke.

'Yes. And we shall do the same.' Drinkwater looked about him. 'God, what a shambles!' Even in the twilight, *Andromeda*'s deck bore the appearance of a slaughter-house.

Another broadside thundered out, the gun-flashes bright in the gathering gloom. 'You may cease fire now. Pipe up spirits and have the cooks get some burgoo into all hands. The men can mess at their guns, then we have work to do.' He turned to the sailing master. 'What o'clock is moonrise, Mr Birkbeck?'

'Not before three, sir.'

'We shall be gone by then.'

No one paid any attention to Templeton as he hung back until Danks had had time to secure his prisoners in the bilboes. Then he made his way hurriedly below.

Chapter Ten *October 1813*

Friends and Enemies

The dismasting of the *Odin* brought them more than a respite, it brought them a sense of accomplishment. They had not achieved a victory, but they *had* beaten off an enemy with a superior weight of metal. In his cabin, or in the after section of the gun deck which had formerly been his cabin, by the light of a pair of horn-glazed battle lanterns, Drinkwater outlined his plan to his officers. His right cheek was dark and pocked with clotted blood.

'It is going to be a long night, gentlemen,' he concluded, 'but most of us will be able to sleep a little easier when we do turn in. Any questions?'

The officers shook their heads and rose from where they squatted on the deck or the trucks of the adjacent guns, exchanging brief remarks with one another. All wore grim expressions and none were under any false illusions about their chances. Further forward the buzz of the men eating at their action stations swelled at this sudden, conspicuous activity aft.

Huke hung back. 'What about these damned prisoners, sir?'

'I'll see them in a minute. Get a screen put up, will you? A canvas will do, just enough to discourage prying eyes. Ah, and post a marine sentry on its far side.'

Huke nodded. 'I've taken command of the marines myself, I hope you approve?'

'Yes, of course. I'm going to see the wounded first. Get the screen rigged and we'll find what's at the bottom of all this.'

In the cockpit Kennedy was finishing the last of his dressings. 'Twenty-three wounded, sir, five seriously.'

'How seriously?'

'Very. Two are mortal, maybe three. Deep penetration of the abdomen, vital organs in shreds, severe blood loss.'

'Bloody business.'

'Very.'

'You look tired.'

'Not used to naval surgery. Noisy business. Most of the poor devils are dead drunk. Used a lot of rum.'

'Go and get something to eat. I'm afraid we're going to start getting the ship out of this predicament.'

'Ah,' replied Kennedy. He had no idea what the captain was talking about, but was too tired to ask.

'By the bye, how is the man with typhus? I had quite forgotten him. I take it we sent him below?'

'He's here . . .'

Drinkwater followed Kennedy through the Stygian gloom. The low space, usually the mess and living quarters of the midshipmen and marines, was filled with the mutilated wounded who groaned where they lay. Kennedy's assistants were clearing away the blood-soaked cloth from the 'table' upon which the surgeon had wielded scalpel and catling, saw and suture needle. The stink of bilge, blood and fear hung heavy in the stale air. Snores and low moans punctuated the sounds of deep breathing, and the grey bundles moved occasionally as the fumes of oblivion cleared momentarily. In a corner a hammock was slung.

'How are you?' Drinkwater asked the pale blur that regarded him.

'Better than those poor bastards.'

The man's manner was abrupt, discourteous even, his accent American. Abruptly Drinkwater turned about and made for the gun deck. The canvas screen was almost rigged. When it was finished, Drinkwater, in the presence of Huke and Templeton, summoned the first of the prisoners aft.

He could not imagine why he had not realized it before, but it was impossible to conceal and it took little time to unravel, once the first tongue wagged. He was glad he had ordered the issue of spirits for, although prisoners were forbidden this privilege, such was the solidarity of the lower deck that some sympathetic souls would go to considerable lengths to supply men in the bilboes with rum, if only to help them endure the flogging all must have felt was inevitable.

In rousing sympathy, it did not much matter what a man was charged with, unless it was thieving from his shipmates. In this case few knew what had happened beyond the fact that these men had stabbed a marine and run and hidden. Cowards they might be, but a measure of sympathy had been extended by a couple of radical souls, enough to loosen a tongue or two, to the point of indiscretion, for the marines, the ship's police, could count enemies among the thirteen score of men whom they regulated.

When the interrogation of the prisoners was over, Drinkwater ordered the men taken away and returned to the bilboes. 'They are to be securely chained for tonight.'

Sergeant Danks took them off with a smart salute and an about-turn. Drinkwater turned to Huke. 'Well, Tom, here's a pretty kettle of fish.'

Even in the poor light of the battle lanterns, Huke's pallor was evident.

'I had no idea, sir.'

'And there's one missing. The ringleader, of course.'

'Malaburn.'

'An ominous name, by the sound of it,' offered Templeton nervously.

'It wasn't your fault, Tom,' said Drinkwater, ignoring the clerk. 'The truth is, there is a great deal more to this than you know. I blame myself that I didn't smell a rat the moment I heard Hopkins's Boston accent. Then, when we had the case of typhus, I should have realized that the infected man came aboard with the draft you pressed out of that merchant ship and that he was also American . . .'

'It's the damned war, sir. We've such a polyglot mob aboard here, what with Irish, Yankees, Negroes, Arabs, Russians, Finns, Swedes and that Dane, Sommer.'

'That may well be the case, but you don't know the whole story. Those Americans had only recently joined that merchantman at Leith because they had just come out of gaol. It was only just now that I recalled typhus ain't only called ship, low or putrid fever, but is also called *gaol* fever. You said yourself they offered little resistance. I think the reason they were so compliant was that they wanted to be pressed.'

'*Wanted* to be pressed?' Huke repeated incredulously, 'I don't follow; why in God's name would they *want* to be pressed?'

'To get aboard a man-o'-war destined to attempt the seizure of a large arms shipment to America to support an insurrection in Canada.'

Huke whistled. 'You mean with the intention of thwarting that seizure?' He frowned and added, 'Then getting a passage home? Is that your meaning?'

Drinkwater nodded.

'But how d'you know?'

'Don't ask me how, Tom, not now; but I'm damned certain they were sprung from Dartmoor gaol for the purpose.'

'The devil they were, and how the bloody hell did they spirit themselves from Dartmoor to Leith?' Huke asked, perplexed.

'By a carter, it seems, or maybe a whole host of carters. Such men move easily about the country and for all I know belong to some Corresponding Society or seditious, republican fraternity, though I grant the thing appears impossible.'

Huke scratched his head, then shook it. 'Perhaps not.' He spoke abstractedly and then looked up sharply, as though the consideration had led him to some pricking anxiety. 'We still have to take Malaburn.'

'He will be in the hold, and every exit is barred, is it not?'

'Aye, Danks has seen to that . . .'

'Well, let him rot there for a while. At least until we've concluded this business.'

'It's true he'll not get out, sir, there's a sentry on each hatchway, but I don't like the idea, sir.'

'Perhaps not, Tom – but leave him, just the same.'

They relapsed into silence for a moment, the constrained silence of disagreement, then Drinkwater said, 'Poor Walsh. We shall have to bury them all when we get outside.'

And '*if*,' Huke added privately to himself, while Templeton, an increasingly nervous witness to these proceedings, nursed his own feelings.

'Look!'

'What is it?'

By the dim light of the stars the working parties had lowered the wreckage of the main topgallant mast, but unravelling the intricate web of tangled rigging that it had pulled down with it properly required daylight. Then, about four bells in the first watch, about ten o'clock by a landsman's time-piece, the high mountains to the north-west seemed to loom above them, closer than they remembered, a gigantic theatrical backcloth dragged forward by trolls. It was the second and more disquieting illusion of the day. A milky glow filled the sky above the mountain peaks, an ethereal and pulsing luminescence that made them all stand stock-still in amazement.

'Aurora borealis,' explained Birkbeck. 'Get back to work there! You can see what you're doing now.'

It was as though that strange phenomenon had been produced not merely for their wonder but also for their convenience. Tired though they were, the ship's company laboured with scarcely a grumble, until, long before midnight, the main was shorn of its upper spar, the broken stump drawn from the doublings and sent down to be split for kindling in the galley stove, and the lines tidied away. By the light of his lantern, the carpenter had declared it was no great thing to fish a new heel on to the old spar, and the men had been stood easy for half an hour, while spirits, biscuit and treacle were issued.

'Playing the deuce with my stores,' the purser complained.

'As you play the devil wiv our'n,' retorted a seaman within earshot, but he made no further complaint, having heard that Captain Drinkwater was no friend of speculating jobbers. Things had been somewhat different in Captain Pardoe's day . . .

At midnight the hands were sent to the capstan. The wind had fallen light after dark, though it was still foul for a passage of the narrows. Even a light breeze, funnelled between those rock buttresses, gained strength enough to prevent them making any attempt to work through under sail. The boats were hoisted out and manned. The carpenter had first had to put a tingle on the red cutter, and the launch required more extensive repairs before she could be lowered into the water again.

Ranging up under the bow, a rope was passed down into each and the boat officers, the second and third lieutenants and Beavis, the senior master's mate, fanned their charges out ahead of the frigate.

There was a faint outward current to carry them seaward, produced by streams and freshets further up the fiord, and they made slow but steady progress. By moonrise they were below the beetling crags of the narrows. After four hours Midshipman Fisher was dispatched in the white cutter with a relief crew for the first boat. Having run alongside Mr Jameson's boat and transferred his oarsmen, Fisher had the tired men of the third lieutenant's boat pull ahead, before he swung clear of the others, advancing in line abreast. Then his eye was caught by something irregular etched against the night sky. Under the black loom of the cliffs, no light came from the fading aurora. The sea beyond the gutway was a slightly less dark plane, its presence guessed at, rather than actually perceived. And Fisher was certain, as only the young can be, that something lay upon it.

'Oars,' he whispered to his men, though the grunting and straining of the men in the boats behind were plain enough. The oarsmen, eager for food and drink, ceased rowing and leaned on their oar looms. The curious craned round impatiently. 'What is it young 'un?' a voice enquired as the boat glided through the still water.

'There's a ship out there!'

'Well, why don't we just pull over an' capture it, an' make your bleedin' fortune, cully, eh?' The anonymous voice from forward was weary with sarcasm.

'Oi ain't following no little bugger whose bollocks are still up 'is arse,' another countered.

'Be quiet! Stand by! Give way together!'

With a knocking of oars, the boat forged ahead again, but Fisher did not put the tiller over.

'He's taken your advice, Harry, you stupid sod.'

'He would, the little turd.'

'Be quiet, damn you,' Fisher squeaked, uncertain whether to react to this blatant insubordination or to let it pass, since the men pulled on, seemingly willing enough.

''E won't live long enough to be a Hadmiral.'

'It's that cutter!' hissed Fisher excitedly, meaning not another pulling boat but a small, man-of-war cruiser. Older heads in the boat were less eager to share the midshipman's certainty. Men stopped pulling, missed their stroke and, for a moment or two, the discipline in the boat broke down as they craned round to see where the headstrong child was taking them.

'Boat ahoy!' came to them out of the darkness, the accents unmistakably, imperiously English. 'Lie to upon the instant or I shall blow you to Kingdom Come!'

'It's that one-handed bean-pole . . .'

'It *is* the *Kestrel*!'

'I told you it was,' Fisher exclaimed gleefully.

'Well, tell that bloody lieutenant, before he shoots us!'

'Boat from *Andromeda*, permission to come aboard!'

'Come under my lee!'

They could see the irregular quadrilateral shape of the cutter's mainsail and the two fore triangles of her jib and staysail as she ghosted in towards the narrows and the Vikkenfiord.

'Put about, sir,' called Fisher, '*Andromeda's* towing out astern of us! There's a big Danish frigate and all sorts inside . . .'

They were alongside now, a rope snaked out of the cutter's chains to take their painter, and the next moment they were towing alongside.

'Come aboard and report.'

Fisher scrambled up and over the cutter's side. 'Midshipman Richard Fisher, sir, from the frigate *Andromeda*, Nathaniel Drinkwater commanding.'

'He's right enough, Mr Quil'ampton, there's a frigate comin' up ahead.'

'Put her about, Mr Frey . . .'

'What's all that noise there?' The voice of Lieutenant Huke boomed into their deliberations as he shouted from *Andromeda*'s knightheads, his voice amplified by a speaking trumpet and echoing about in the stillness.

Quilhampton cupped his good hand about his mouth: 'Cutter *Kestrel*, Lieutenant Quilhampton commanding!'

'Follow me out, Mr Q, and come aboard for orders.'

'That's Captain Drinkwater's voice,' advised Fisher.

'I know that.'

'We lay to under the trys'l, and when the weather moderated we made a good stellar observation and laid a course for the rendezvous. I guessed you couldn't afford to linger and that you had pressed on when we saw a man-o'-war's t'gallants away to the eastward, so we cracked on, thinking it was you.'

'That must have been the *Odin*,' observed Huke.

'Yes. Well, anyway, it was lucky we saw her, for it was just a question of watching her vanish. Frey, my first luff,' he explained for Huke's benefit, 'took a bearing. We ran down it and here we are. I thought we were heading for a wall of rock and was just about to put about when your young midshipmite hove out of the darkness.'

'Well, I am damnably glad to see you, James. Forgive my lack of hospitality, but we've been cleared for action for some time now. To be truthful, I didn't expect to see you again, first on your own account, and then on ours. We've just taken a drubbing.'

Drinkwater explained the day's events.

'So we've the goods, the Dane who brought them, and the Yankees who are going to tranship them to North America all boxed up in the Vikkenfiord, eh?' Quilhampton said with an air of satisfaction, when Drinkwater had finished.

'That's certainly an optimistic view of the tactical situation,' remarked Drinkwater drily.

'Well, they might think they've the measure of you, but they don't know I'm here yet.' Quilhampton grinned enthusiastically.

'True, James, true.'

'It's certainly food for thought,' said Huke. 'Will you be able to beat out behind us?'

'Yes. She ghosts in light airs and she's fitted with centre-plates. She can point much closer to the wind than you.'

'Gentlemen,' said Drinkwater, 'we will lie to now, until daylight. Recover the boats, Mr Huke, as soon as we are clear of danger. Then let us get an hour or two's sleep. Tomorrow we will see what we can accomplish. It will be the first of the month, I believe.'

''Tis already that, sir.'

Lieutenant Huke had conceived a liking for his odd and unorthodox captain. During the crazy interlude of the great dousing Huke had noticed, as had many others, that in addition to the faint facial scar and the powder burns on one eyelid, Captain Drinkwater was disfigured by a lop-sided right shoulder and a mass of scar tissue which ran down his right arm. These were the legacy of two wounds, one acquired in a dark alleyway in the year 1797, at the time of the great mutiny, the other the result of an enemy shell-burst off Boulogne, four years later. Such marks earned their bearer a measure of respect, irrespective of rank. In a post-captain they bespoke a seasoned man.

But, on that night and for the first time, Thomas Huke

considered Captain Drinkwater's conduct to be, if not reprehensible, at the very least most unwise, an error of judgement. The first lieutenant felt that the matter of Malaburn could not be left until the morning.

He excused the captain on the grounds that Drinkwater did not know the man, despite the claims he had made about their escape from gaol and extraordinary migration north. Drinkwater had not had his suspicions aroused as had Huke. As an experienced first lieutenant Huke had acquired an instinct for trouble-makers, sea-lawyers and the disobedient. There were attitudes such men struck, inflections they used when spoken to, places in which they appeared unaccountably and times when they were late in mustering. A man might do such things once or twice in all innocence, but persistent offenders were almost always revealed as falling into one or other of these troublesome categories. Malaburn had been one such, conspicuous from the first day he had come aboard at Leith.

'Provoked me,' Mr Beavis had reported back in Leith Road. The master's mate had been in charge of one of the ship's three press-gangs sent to comb the ale-houses and brothels of Leith and Granton for extra hands a few days before Huke struck 'lucky' and obtained what he wanted from the merchantman. 'Almost dared me to take him,' Beavis had expanded, 'but, like most braggarts, gave in the moment we got a-hold of him.'

There seemed little enough in the remark at the time, except to draw Lieutenant Huke's attention to the man as he was sworn in. And although Malaburn had overplayed his hand a trifle in his eagerness to get himself aboard His Majesty's frigate *Andromeda*, he had succeeded in fooling them all. Until, that is, Captain Drinkwater made his mysterious revelation, alluding to the curious desire of the Americans to be pressed. The assertion fitted not just the group lifted from the merchantman, but also Malaburn.

Thus it was that Lieutenant Thomas Huke decided not to allow Malaburn to elude his just deserts an hour longer and why he passed word to Sergeant Danks to muster half a dozen of his men at the main capstan.

Drinkwater had not wished to raise a hue and cry for the one member of the ship's company unaccounted for after the action with the *Odin* for a number of reasons. The first was that, as far as he could determine, few people as yet realized that the letting go of the anchor had been a deliberate act, rather than an accidental misfortune. The anchor had been cleared away ready for use as they closed the land, a cable bent and seized on to it. It was possible that a chance shot had carried away the lashing and it had fallen from the fore-chains. Old seamen could tell countless tales of odder circumstances; of balls hitting cannon muzzles with such exactitude that they opened them like the petals of flowers; of a shot which had destroyed the single remaining live pig being fattened for an unpopular captain, and so forth.

More important, the conspicuous arrest of the handful of men hiding on the heads had looked like the rounding up of a group of yellow-bellies, an untruth given credibility by the fact that the men were newcomers who had kept themselves to themselves and failed to court popularity with their shipmates. Their reason for doing so was now apparent to those in the know, but had not yet permeated through the ship. Doubtless the truth would get out in due course, but Drinkwater wanted his men rested, not seething with vengeful discontent that the men now clapped in the bilboes as cowards had tried to deliver them all into the hands of the enemy.

From what he could glean, his prisoners, having done what they could to incommode the British frigate, were to have escaped to the American ships in the fiord. When the Danish ship appeared, Malaburn had changed the plan, seeing a greater chance of success in the overwhelming of the *Andromeda* by the *Odin*. Drinkwater also wondered whether Malaburn had thought the British ship was retreating, that she had given up hope of cutting out the Yankees from under the Danish guns in the fort, and that the sudden appearance of the *Odin* gave him an opportunity both to destroy the British ship and to secure the escape of himself and his fellow conspirators before it was too late. It was, after all, a risky and uncertain business, being pressed into the service of King George.

If that was how Malaburn's mind had construed the day's events, he had demonstrated a commendable adaptability. Once the *Andromeda* had been brought to her anchor, confusion reigned upon her decks and her officers were distracted with the business of resisting the attack of the *Odin*. Drinkwater imagined Malaburn's party were hoping they could soon escape by getting aboard the Danish ship as she dropped alongside to board, and giving themselves up.

Whatever their expectations, and fear of a return to incarceration in Dartmoor must have been a powerful motive, their leader had been a man of determination, and if Drinkwater did not wish to stir his ship up that night, he did not wish to lose her either. What he feared most was an incendiary attack. A lone man with flint and steel could set fire to the frigate. For all her mildewed damp, there were combustibles enough to set *Andromeda* ablaze like a torch. Drinkwater had seen the fearful sight of ships burning and exploding and the thought made him shudder.

Malaburn, languishing in the dark recesses of the hold, was unlikely to cut his own throat with two of his countrymen's privateers in the offing. Why else had he preserved himself? In the morning they would winkle him out. With that thought, Drinkwater heaved himself into his cot and pulled the sheet and blankets over his shoulders. Let Malaburn stew in his own juice, believing, perhaps, that no one had noticed his absence.

Drinkwater's face was already scabbed, a thick crust which rasped uncomfortably on the pillow. The last thing he saw in his mind's eye was a spinning epaulette which diminished in size as it faded into the far, far distance.

'Pistols and bayonets,' Huke whispered, 'there's no room for muskets. Cold steel unless he fires, and only shoot if you are sure of hitting him. Take my word he's not just a mutinous dog, he's an enemy, a Yankee. He is aboard to make mischief and ensure this ship strikes to either those privateers we saw at anchor or that blasted Dane. So, if you can't seize him, and he resists . . .' Huke made an unpleasant, terminal squawk and drew his forefinger across his throat. 'D'you understand?'

A murmur of assent went round the little group of marines. They had a comrade to avenge. Four lanterns stood on the deck at their feet, lighting their white shirts and breeches. With their braces over their shoulders in place of cross-belts the pale ghostly figures had appeared in the gloom of the orlop to arouse the curiosity of the lesser officers quartered there. Huke had sent the inquisitive back into their tiny cabins with a sharp word to discourage their interest.

'Very well. You two go with Sar'nt Danks up the larboard side, you and you, with me to starboard.' Huke nodded and Danks bent to the padlock holding the securing bar over the aftermost grating which led down into the hold. Huke drew his own hanger, laid it on the deck and quickly rid himself of his baldric and coat. Then he recovered his sword, drew a pistol from his belt and, as Danks lifted the grating, led the party down the ladder into the hold.

On the quarterdeck, Lieutenant Mosse had the watch. He was dog-tired and would be glad to get below at midnight, but he was not insensible to the fact that, even under the easy pressure of the main and fore topsail, and a single jib, the *Andromeda* had edged closer inshore than he liked. With an effort he bestirred himself, ordered the helm put over and the yards trimmed.

As the order was passed, he was aware of groans of reluctance, but the watch mustered at their posts, the yards swung in their slings, trusses and parrels, and *Andromeda* headed out to sea.

Shortly before the watch below was due to be called, when the minutes dragged and it seemed that the march of time had slowed beyond human endurance, the tired Mosse and his somnolent watch were jerked wide-awake. What sounded like a muffled cry came to them. Its source seemed to be some way away and someone said it sounded as though it had come from the *Kestrel*, which had last showed the pale shape of her sail two miles to the south-east. Then a jacketless marine arose from the after companion with the shocking speed of a jack-in-the-box.

'Sir! Mr Huke's hurt! In the hold! There's bloody hell on down there!'

As he had raced up from the hold, the distraught soldier had raised the alarm throughout the ship. The curious officers quartered in the orlop, led by Mr Beavis, had not gone quietly to bed, but had remained clustered by the open grating. The sudden cry had stunned them, then there was a brief hiatus and the marines emerged, with Danks throwing the grating down behind him and thrusting the padlock through the hasp on the securing bar. The sudden volley of questions wakened the midshipmen and the other soldiers nearby. One of the marines nursed a badly gashed leg, another was sent into the berth deck to find Kennedy, a third to the quarterdeck. This man raised the alarm at each sentinel post, including the one outside the captain's cabin, and this sentry, aware only that the frigate was suddenly buzzing with an almost palpable anxiety, called the captain.

Drinkwater had fallen into the deep sleep of exhaustion from which he was unnaturally wrenched. Instinctively he pulled on his coat and went on deck. After five minutes of total confusion he learned that Huke had taken a party of marines into the hold to 'deal with Malaburn'.

With great difficulty he suppressed the oath welling in his throat. He was ready to damn Huke for an interfering fool, to set aside any merit the man might possess, for this contravention of orders, this unwanted display of initiative. His body ached for rest, but his heart had taken flight and hammered in his breast. He silenced the hubbub around him. 'Mr Mosse, send the off-duty watch below and stop this babble.'

'Beg pardon, sir, but 'tis almost eight bells . . .'

'Very well,' snapped Drinkwater, 'have the men relieved in the normal way.' He turned to the marine. 'What's your name?'

'Private Leslie, sir.'

'Well, Leslie, what happened? Tell us in your own words. You went into the hold to arrest Malaburn. By which hatchway?'

'The after one, sir, in the cockpit . . .'

'Go on.'

'Well, sir, we was in two parties, I was wiv Mr Huke, like, and Sar'nt Danks led the other up the larboard chippy's walk. We 'ad lanterns, like, an' bayonets and a brace of pistols. Orders was to apprehend, but to shoot if the bugger – beg pardon, sir – if 'e tried anything clever . . .'

'You were going up the starboard carpenter's walk, is that right?' Drinkwater tried to visualize the scene. The carpenter's walks were two passages inside the fabric of the ship's side enabling the carpenter and his party to get at the frigate's timbers quickly and plug shot holes. The multifarious stores stowed in the hold were inboard of these narrow walkways. The men would have started outboard of and abaft the cable tiers, then edged forward past barrels of water, beef and pork, and sacks of dried peas and lentils.

They would have been walking on gratings. Below their feet the lower hold contained barrels of water stowed on shingle ballast, and the shot rooms. It was a hellish hole, inhabited by rats and awash with bilge water, the air thick and mephitic, the lanterns barely burning.

'I was the last man in my file, sir. I could jus' see Lieutenant 'Uke, sir, wiv 'is lantern, like, when 'e gives this God Almighty screech and the light goes out. Then the bloke in front of me shouts out, turns round an' says, "Christ, Hughie, the bastard's got me, get out!" He bumps into me an' I ain't got no way out but the way I come in, and Sarn't Danks is shoutin' out from the uvver side, "What's wrong?" an' I don't know, 'cept Lieutenant 'Uke's copped it, and my mate wot's pushing me shouts out "Get back in the orlop, Sar'nt!" So out we comes.'

'And Lieutenant Huke is still down there?'

'Well, yes, sir . . .'

'Damn and blast the man!' Drinkwater muttered, inveighing against the idiocy of the first lieutenant, but now doubting the wisdom of his own passive policy. Private Leslie thought he himself was the object of this damnation.

'I'll go back, sir, jus' give us another lantern, an' I'll go right back.'

'Yes,' snapped Drinkwater, 'you will. Give me a moment to dress. Wait outside my cabin, pass word for Danks to report to me.'

He dressed quickly, thinking while Danks stood in the darkness of the day cabin and repeated, in less detail, for he had been on the far side of the ship, what Leslie had already related.

'You didn't think of going to Mr Huke's assistance?'

A short silence followed, then Danks said, 'I wasn't sure what to do, sir. I didn't really know what had happened, except that Lieutenant Huke's dead, sir.'

'Dead? Who said he's dead?'

'Well, sir, I . . . I don't know.' The puzzlement was clear in Danks's voice. It was not fair to imply Danks was a coward. Huke's ill-conceived stratagem was too prone to confusion to blame poor humiliated Danks.

'Very well, Sergeant. Have your men remustered, all of them. In the orlop. I'll be with you directly. Send in a light.'

When Danks had gone Drinkwater finished dressing. He could do this in the dark, but he wanted light to complete his preparations. Frampton, attired in a long night-shirt, appeared with a lantern.

'Will you be wanting anything else, sir?'

'Not at the moment, Frampton, thank you,' Drinkwater said. The steady normality of Captain Pardoe's steward stilled the racing of his own heart. He could never think of Frampton as his own man.

He went to the stern settee, lifted the seat and drew out the case of pistols. Then he sat down and, placing the case beside him, opened it, lifted out the weapons and checked their flints. Having done that he carefully loaded both weapons. He had had a double-barrelled pistol aboard *Patrician*, but these were a new pair and he thrust them through his belt. Then he stood for a moment in the centre of the cabin and retied his hair. When he had finished he drew his hanger and passed the door on to the gun deck.

A garrulous crowd had gathered in the orlop and the appearance of the captain silenced them. 'This is a damned Dovercourt, be off with you! Marines, stand fast. You there, Mr Fisher! Pass word to have the surgeon standing by. Oh, and please to lend me your dirk, young man. Here,' Drinkwater turned aside to Beavis, 'be so kind as to look after this for me.' He handed his hanger to the master's mate.

Before scuttling off on his mission, Fisher had darted to his mess and taken his dirk from its nail in the deck-beam above his sleeping place. It was a small, straight and handy weapon.

'Here, sir.' He held the toy weapon out; its short blade gleamed dully in the lantern light. Drinkwater's fist more than encompassed the hilt.

'Right, Danks,' Drinkwater dropped his voice, beckoning the marines to draw closer. 'This is what I intend to do.'

Chapter Eleven *November 1813*

The Enemy Within

Drinkwater led them below. At the bottom of the ladder he moved aside and let the marines file silently down into the hold. Then he directed Sergeant Danks and his senior corporal, Wilson, to lift the after gratings and descend into the lower hold, and as they did so the foul stench of bilge rose up to assail them. Both Wilson and Danks were armed with muskets. Behind them went two other marines, each with a lantern, followed by two men armed with bayonets. When Danks had moved out to the larboard wing, and Wilson to the starboard, Drinkwater gestured to the remaining men to fan out. Then he called:

'Malaburn! This is the captain. We know you are down here and you have until I have counted to ten to give yourself up. If you hail at that time you will be given a fair trial. If not I regard you as beyond the law, and the safety of my ship demands that I exert myself to take you at any cost. That may well be your own life.' He paused, then began to count.

'One. Two. Three . . .'

In the silence between each number he heard nothing beyond the laboured breathing of the marines still behind him.

'Five. Six. Seven . . .'

He turned. Holding a third lantern, Private Leslie was ready behind him with another marine in support, and Corporal Smyth made to take his two men up the larboard carpenter's walk to flush Malaburn from his hiding place. Drinkwater now had four groups of marines ready to move forward, two at the level of the carpenter's walk, two below, floundering their way over the shingle ballast and the casks of water in the lower hold, for Drinkwater was convinced Malaburn had taken refuge in that most evil and remote part of the ship.

'Eight. Nine. Ten. Proceed!'

Drinkwater had enjoined Smyth, advancing on the higher larboard level, not to move faster than Danks's party below him who would have far more trouble moving over the shingle ballast than those above walking on the level gratings of the carpenter's walk. Both upper and lower parties had to search each stow of stores inboard of them as they edged forward and it was five long minutes before those with Drinkwater, creeping up the starboard side, discovered the bloodstains marking the place where Huke had been wounded. The absence of Huke was both a hopeful and a desperately worrying sign. Malaburn had done exactly what Drinkwater would have done in his place: he had dragged the first lieutenant off as a hostage.

'Smyth, Danks! Mr Huke's been taken hostage!' he called, to let those on the far side of the ship know what had happened.

'Aye, sir, understood!' Danks's voice came back from beyond a large stow of sacked and dried peas.

They shuffled forward again. The shadows thrown by the lantern behind Drinkwater projected his own form in grotesque silhouette on the uneven surfaces of futtocks and footwaling. He held the little dirk in his outsize hand. It was a pathetic and inadequate weapon, but he had brought it in place of his hanger which, he had realized, would have been an encumbrance in the restricted space of this narrow catwalk.

'Nothin' yet!' shouted Smyth, and Wilson and Danks echoed the call. The stink of effluvia, bilge, dried stores, rot, fungus, rust and God knew what beside made breathing difficult. The lanterns guttered yellow, their flames sinking as they moved forward. The whining squeak of rats accompanied their scuttering retreat from this unwonted incursion into their private domain and added a quickening to the tired, low groans of the ship as she rolled on the swell.

Drinkwater's heart hammered painfully. He saw a score of phantasmagorical Malaburns, the swinging, hand-held lantern light throwing maddening shadows which moved as they did. Sweat poured off him, and he stopped to wipe it from his brow.

And then, quite suddenly, without any violent reaction of either party, he found himself staring at Malaburn. In a recess, where a large stow of barrels gave way to more sacks and these fell back, showing signs of recent removal, the American lay at bay, holding the pale form of Huke hostage. Drinkwater stopped and, without taking his eyes off the white mask of Malaburn's face, beckoned behind him with the dirk. Leslie thrust the lantern over his shoulder.

Huke lay oddly, his feet no more than a yard from Drinkwater, his legs splayed slightly apart so that Drinkwater could see, amid the pitch-black shadows, the dark trail of blood that smeared the white knee-breeches and revealed the deep thrust of the wound in Huke's groin. Malaburn had been in the lower hold, the head of a pike through a hole in a grating waiting for the advance of the impetuous lieutenant. The wound was hideous, the pain must have been excruciating and the bleeding Huke was insensible, his face averted, lolled backwards as he lay in Malaburn's malevolent embrace.

The American had one arm across Huke's chest but the first lieutenant still breathed in shallow rasping gasps. Malaburn's other hand held a long-bladed knife at Huke's throat. In the sharp contrast of the lanternlight, Drinkwater could see the taut tendons in Huke's neck standing out like rope. Beneath them lay the vulnerable carotid artery and the jugular vein.

Drinkwater said in a low voice, 'Put your knife down.'

The blade wavered, a faint reflection of lantern-light revealing Malaburn's hesitation.

'Put your knife down, Malaburn.'

'No. I will let the first lieutenant go only if you give me your word that you will put me aboard one of those Yankee ships.'

'You know that is impossible . . .'

'You could do it, if you wanted to, Captain Drinkwater. If you gave me your word and called your men off. I trust you, d'you see.'

'Malaburn, Lieutenant Huke is bleeding to death,' Drinkwater began, trying to sound reasonable, knowing that a move of his left hand which held a pistol would cause Malaburn to react with his knife. But Malaburn was unmoved by Drinkwater's logic.

'Your word, Captain Drinkwater,' he hissed urgently, 'your word!'

A dark suspicion crossed Drinkwater's mind. Malaburn's presumption was no quixotic plea, there was too much certainty in the man's voice. He knew Drinkwater could not give his word, dare not give it.

'Who the devil are you, Malaburn?'

'Are you all right, sir?' Danks's voice, muffled by the contents of the hold, reminded Drinkwater of the other men. Beneath his own feet, Drinkwater realized now, Wilson had stopped, aware of something happening above him.

'Stay where you are, Danks, you lobster-backed bastard,' shouted Malaburn, 'and you others, wherever you . . . !'

He never finished his threat. There was a flash of light and, when Drinkwater's retinae had adjusted themselves, Malaburn's face had vanished. The long-bladed knife was lowered almost gently on to Huke's chest by the nerveless hand, and the sacks which had cradled Malaburn's head as he awaited his hunters were stained with its shattered remains.

The explosion of the musket deafened them momentarily, and the brilliance of its flash blinded them. Stunned, Drinkwater was uncertain where the shot had come from, or who had fired it. He thought himself shouting with anger, though no one seemed to hear him, and he suddenly heard Sergeant Danks's voice, no longer muffled, say with savage satisfaction:

'Got the bugger!'

Danks's disembodied face appeared above Huke's. He was casting aside sacks as he fought his way through from the far side of the ship, the long barrel of his still smoking musket visible beside him.

'I gave no orders . . .' Drinkwater began, but the words did not seem to be heard and he thought afterwards that he had only imagined them. Leslie was gently squeezing past him with a 'Beg pardon, sir . . .'

And then Drinkwater heard his own voice astonishingly loud, uttering the fact before he had apparently absorbed it. 'It's too late. He's already dead.'

He must have seen the shallow respirations cease, known when he saw that terrible, gaping wound, that Huke was dying. The vicious pike thrust was mortal, not the work of a man acting in self-defence, but the cold act of a murderer. And Drinkwater knew that it was not Danks he was angry with for so precipitately killing Malaburn, but himself, for not having dispatched him for killing a man whom Drinkwater counted a friend.

'Bring both of them out,' he ordered, desperate for fresh air and afraid he might vomit at any moment. He turned and thrust back past the other marine. 'Give 'em a hand,' he muttered through clenched teeth.

As he approached the foot of the ladder to the orlop deck he paused. He could see someone at the bottom peering forward and waving a lantern, hear a babble of curious men pressed about the coaming of the hatchway. He wiped his face and drew several slow and deliberate breaths. Then he strode out of the darkness.

'Here's the Captain . . .'

'Sir? Is that you?'

'Stand aside, if you please. They will be bringing out the first lieutenant's body in a moment, along with that of Malaburn. Pass word to have both prepared for burial.'

Then he went straight to his cabin and flung himself on his cot.

Drinkwater woke at dawn. He was cold and cramped, gritty with dried sweat and foul exertion. The stink of the hold and the discharge of black powder clung to him. He rubbed his eyes and the colours leapt before him and dissolved into the deep red of blood. Drawing his cloak about him he went stiffly on deck.

He had given no thought to the fate of the ship in the aftermath of Huke's terrible, unnecessary death. It seemed almost miraculous that this neglect had been ameliorated by the regular rhythm of the ship's inexorable routine. The realization steadied him and, as he acknowledged Jameson's salute, he saw it was raining.

'Ah'm verra sorry about Tom Huke, sir.'

'Yes. He should never . . .' He caught himself in time. He could not possibly blame Huke for his own death. 'He should never have been so zealous,' he managed.

'He was a guid first luff, sir.'

Jameson's almost pleading tone, as though explaining Tom's character for this Johnny-come-lately of a captain, was the last act of the night. It reminded Drinkwater that the junior lieutenant sought his, Drinkwater's good opinion. 'I know, Mr Jameson, I had already learned that.'

'He has dependants . . .'

'I know that, too.' Drinkwater shouldered the burden of command again and could almost feel the mood of the third lieutenant lighten.

'Will you gi'e Mr Beavis a temporary commission, sir?'

And with that remark the sun rose yellow behind a distant

mountain, shining pallidly through the cloud and throwing a rainbow against the purple islands to the westward. The ship's routine had sustained them through the hours of darkness, and now the rigours of the naval service demanded their attention again.

'I expect so, Mr Jameson.'

Jameson seemed satisfied. The preoccupations of uncertainty were at an end. He and, Drinkwater supposed, Mr Mosse, could rest easy. He realized suddenly that he might have brought Quilhampton across from the cutter and that the fact had not escaped the two lieutenants.

'Do you think Mr Mosse is likely to be as good a first luff as Tom Huke?'

'Well, sir,' Jameson began, but then the impropriety of the thing occurred to him, as did Captain Drinkwater's arch condescension. Jameson felt put in his place and Drinkwater strode off in search of Frampton and hot water, savagely indulging in his rank.

The ship's routine, which had seen *Andromeda* safely through the night, had not proceeded smoothly. News of the irregular events in the hold had spread like wildfire and the berth deck had buzzed with claim and counter-claim, rumour and inaccuracy. What emerged as fact was that a group consisting of the pressed American merchant seamen had, by an act of what was popularly regarded as 'treachery', attempted to cripple the British ship and render her helpless under the guns of an enemy. Whatever the private and internecine tribulations which beset the company of the British frigate, it was widely understood that when in the face of the enemy they sank or swam together. Claims of American 'patriotism' were thus easily dismissed, as was any idea that Sommer had acted treacherously. They were united by the white ensign which fluttered above the quarterdeck.

During the minutes that elapsed while Drinkwater and the marines ferreted in the hold, an aimless disorder had reigned above them. In this anarchic state, with all the ship's non-commissioned marine officers in the hold, men milled about, increasingly curious, spilling from hammocks and wandering into places they would not normally visit. Even the officers were affected, waiting round the orlop hatchway, or on the quarterdeck, gossiping intently until Birkbeck began to see the dangers inherent in this general laxity.

Mr Templeton was not exempt from the effects of this electricity.

He was already in a state of high excitement at the revelations of the interrogation and now, in the gloom of the orlop, he came across Greer. Somehow, unaccountably, their hands met and, encouraged by the general dissolution of order, the intensity of a mutual passion overwhelmed them. Unseen, they retreated into the fastnesses of the ship far from the after hold where they stayed throughout the remainder of the night.

An hour after dawn *Andromeda* was hove to and Huke and Malaburn were buried. Then the yards were squared away, the sails filled, and the frigate stood inshore again. When under way, Drinkwater sent for one of the American prisoners. Danks brought the man before him.

'Who was Malaburn?' Drinkwater asked.

The American prisoner shrugged. 'I don't know. A patriot.'

'Had you seen him before you came aboard?' The American remained silent.

'Please believe me,' Drinkwater said quietly, 'I can soon make you talk. Do you know how Malaburn killed the first lieutenant? No? Then I will tell you. He waited beneath the carpenter's walk for Mr Huke to pass overhead, and then he thrust a boarding pike upwards through the grating!'

Drinkwater's words rose in tone. The man winced involuntarily and Drinkwater's voice sank to its former modulation. 'Come now; had you seen Malaburn before you came aboard?'

'I hadn't . . .'

'But others had, is that right? Shall I get one of the others?' The prisoner shrugged.

'I can hang you, you know,' Drinkwater said quietly. 'Have you seen a man hanged? The victim dances and then, when he cannot draw breath, he evacuates himself. It is not a pretty sight, but I shall do it if you do not talk.' Beads of sweat stood out upon the prisoner's pallid brow.

'Did Malaburn have anything to do with your escape from Dartmoor?'

The prisoner swallowed and nodded. He had to cough to find his voice; then he admitted, 'I'm told he did, but, honestly Cap'n, I don't know how. I didn't see him when we got away.'

'Got away? You mean from Dartmoor?' The American nodded. 'How did you get away?'

'We were a stone-breaking gang, on our way back from the quarry. The guards were bribed, I guess; we were told to stop and then our leg-irons were struck off by the guards. We left them – the guards – trussed beside the road. I didn't think of anything much at the time, except being free of going back to that gaol. I didn't see anyone at the time except the guards. I guess the whole thing was arranged. Others in the gang said they'd been told something might happen, but I hadn't. Happen I was just in the right place at the right time. It was only when we came aboard that Malaburn was pointed out to me and I was told to do what he said. When I asked why, I was told it was he who freed us from the chain-gang and that I was to obey his orders and he would see us safe back to Boston.'

'Who told you all this?'

'Hopkins, a Boston man like myself. We were taken out of a merchant schooner by one of your damned British cruisers more than a year ago. He seemed to know we were going to be released that day and what to do. The guards were quite friendly towards him and it was Hopkins who made us lash them together.'

'Hopkins is one of the others in the bilboes, sir,' put in Beavis who, with Sergeant Danks and a marine, was part of this impromptu, drum-head court martial. 'D'you want to see him?'

Drinkwater shook his head and continued his interrogation. 'You didn't see Malaburn until you came aboard this ship?'

'No.'

'And how did you get to Leith?'

'We didn't know we was going to Leith, and I daresay had we known how far it was we'd have refused. Hopkins said Bristol was closer, but orders were to lie low . . .'

'But how did you get across country?'

'We moved at night, slept rough, under the stars – that's kinda natural for us, Cap'n, if we're used to trapping . . .'

'Go on.'

'After about a week, Hopkins orders us to lie low for a day, then he comes back one afternoon with a carter, orders us into the back and tells us all is well. I don't recall where we stopped, though we stopped many times, but it was always at night in a town, and we were taken care of in a barn, or a byre, or once in a house.' The prisoner paused and seemed to be making up his mind before saying, 'We were kindly treated, Cap'n, people were mighty well disposed to us.'

'And when you arrived in Leith, you were shipped directly aboard a merchantman?'

'The brig *Ada Louise* of Hull, aye.' The American paused, then added, 'We seemed to be expected, though we had no issue of clothes.'

Drinkwater knew enough now from this and the earlier interrogation. 'Take this fellow forward again, Danks, and make sure he is secure.'

'Aye, aye, sir.'

'Mr Beavis, signal *Kestrel* for Mr Quilhampton to come aboard.'

'Ah, James, come in, a glass?'

Drinkwater was light-headed with a perverse and inexplicable exhilaration. Lack of sleep and the death of Thomas Huke had strung his nerves to a high and restless pitch, for he had woken with the thoughts tumbling over and over in his mind, and the short encounter with Jameson had been merely a symptom of his mental turbulence. From the interrogation of the American he had added substantially to his mental jigsaw puzzle.

He poured two glasses and felt the wine hit his empty stomach. It was, he knew, unwise to take drink in such circumstances, but such was the state of his excitement and so intense was his desire to seize those small opportunities he saw before him that he shunned the path of reason. Something of Drinkwater's state of mind communicated itself to Quilhampton.

The younger man had seen these moods of deliberate endeavour before and wondered then, as he wondered now, why he did not consider them reckless. He was certain that, in any other officer, he would have considered them so and was tempted, for an instant, to marvel at his own faith in Captain Drinkwater, but then fell victim to his professional obligation to listen and understand what was being said.

At their meeting in Leith Road, Drinkwater had told James Quilhampton the background of their mission. Now he expatiated, rationalizing the cascade of ideas that had occurred to him in the turmoil of the night.

'Something about the man Malaburn, the way he spoke to me, the coolness of his actions, bespoke *purpose*, James. Don't ask me how I know, one simply forms convictions about such things. He *knew* why *Andromeda* left Leith for Norwegian waters; he sprang a group of Yankee prisoners from Dartmoor and trepanned them to Leith to help him in the business of stopping us from thwarting the American rendezvous here in the Vikkenfiord. Suborning a carter who must have been a republican accomplice, and a host of republicans *en route*, to deliver and succour them is the work of no ordinary man. Then he bribes a boarding-house crimp and spirits them aboard a ship he knows to be short of men, or pretends to be, thereby arranging for their concealment at Leith. The master or mate of the *Ada Louise* must have been in his pocket and 'tis fairly certain they were in the plot, for they issued no slops to the new hands and merely put up with their presence until the press arrived.'

'So they appeared to be brought aboard *Andromeda* in the usual manner?'

'Yes, I imagine so. Tom Huke suggested the matter had been easy.'

'Too damned easy,' Quilhampton said slowly. He paused, then went on, 'And this Malaburn knew about that Neapolitan business?'

'*Yes!* I'm damned certain he did. He knew Leith was the point of departure . . . Damn it, he must have known from the start, mark you!'

'The devil!'

'He planned to cause us to anchor and deliver us to the guns of the two American ships. Whether they are national men-o'-war or privateers matters little. Combined, they mount enough weight of metal to outgun us. Make no mistake about it, Mr Malaburn knew all about them, and us. He must have been overjoyed to see that Dane appear just as I thought we had beaten a timely retreat.'

'You knew nothing of the fort, then?'

Drinkwater shook his head. 'No. Nothing.'

'Your escaping serious damage and towing through the passage must have been what persuaded him to hide, then.'

'Yes. He had only the one chance with the men he had sprung from gaol. He could not confer much with them on board for fear of arousing suspicions and, when he appeared to have lost his opportunity, he sought to cause us maximum embarrassment. Between you and me, James, when we got clear of that confounded Dane, I was exhausted. I wanted Malaburn left until morning, but Huke . . . well, no good will come of raking the matter over again.'

'You risked him doing something desperate like setting fire to the ship,' Quilhampton said in defence of the dead Huke. 'I would probably have done what Huke did.'

Drinkwater looked at his friend, but said nothing. 'Huke has dependants,' he heard Jameson saying, as a wave of weariness again swept over him.

'But why take Huke? Why not just hide and lie low?' Quilhampton asked. 'He could, in all probability, have evaded capture and slipped overboard at any later opportunity.'

Drinkwater sighed. 'He was desperate. He did not know what other opportunities might offer. I will pay him the compliment of saying he was a determined man. Huke's appearance was fortuitous; a bad blow for Malaburn. I don't suppose he meant to kill Huke, merely to wound him in the leg, to take him hostage. He could then negotiate with me . . .' Drinkwater frowned, still puzzling over those few brief words he had exchanged with Malaburn.

'The one thing that makes no sense, James, or at least I can make no sense of it, is the fact that *he knew me*, knew my character well enough to know that if he extracted some form of parole, he thought I would honour it. That is uncanny.'

'Perhaps you imagined it, sir.' Quilhampton's face was full of solicitude. 'I don't imagine holding a hostage binds one to a parole.'

Drinkwater was touched. He managed a wan smile. 'Perhaps. Anyway it is too late now. I shall never know.' He refilled their glasses. 'Besides, we have other work to attend to.' They drank and Drinkwater added, 'I am glad you brought Frey with you.'

'That was luck. I received a letter from him the very day I left Woodbridge. Catriona brought it to me as I was in the act of strapping my chest. I wrote to him and told him to come at once. It was just as well. The lieutenant in charge of *Kestrel* at Chatham had the energy of a wallowing pig. I had his bags packed too!'

'Well,' Drinkwater cut in, a hint of impatience in his tone, 'he'll do splendidly in *Kestrel*. I want you aboard here, in command in my absence.'

'Your absence, sir?'

'You are the senior lieutenant and I must have a man here who knows my mind. I'm taking *Kestrel* back into the fiord under a flag of truce . . .'

'But, sir, I can do that! It's my job!'

'Of course you can do it, James, but I've already a good idea of what the lie of the land is in the Vikkenfiord, and there's no purpose in your taking risks, what with Catriona and the child . . .'

'But, sir . . .'

'But me no buts, James, you've already shaken my confidence in you by admitting you'd have done as Tom Huke did . . .' Drinkwater smiled and Quilhampton shrugged resignedly.

'If you insist.'

'I do. It occurs to me that the appearance of *Kestrel* might persuade our friends that we have been reinforced out here. I may be able to wring some advantage out of the situation. At the very least it will provide an opportunity for reconnaissance.'

'Time spent in which is seldom wasted,' Quilhampton quoted with a grin. 'I had thought for a while that you intended to withdraw.'

'I cannot with honour do that. Besides, we have an objective still to achieve, and Tom Huke to avenge.'

'Welcome aboard, sir!'

Lieutenant Frey touched the forecock of his bicorn hat and grinned broadly as Drinkwater scrambled up on to *Kestrel*'s low bulwark.

'My dear Frey, how good to see you.' Drinkwater clambered stiffly down from the cutter's rail and shook Frey's hand.

'You damn nearly left without me, sir,' the younger man said lightly, the joke concealing a sense of affront.

'Not having my own command and occupying a rather difficult position at the Admiralty has left me somewhat bereft of influence,' Drinkwater conceded, and Frey caught a gentle reproach in his voice. He opened his mouth to apologize, but Drinkwater beat him to it. 'But I've made amends by giving you command for the day. Be so kind as to pass my gig astern under tow and, by the by, d'you have a sheet or a tablecloth on board?'

'We boast a tablecloth, sir, but why . . . ?'

'Hoist it at the lee tops'l yardarm and proceed into the Vikkenfiord. A flag of truce,' Drinkwater added by way of explanation at Frey's quizzical frown.

'Aye, aye, sir.'

Frey acknowledged the order and turned away to execute it. Drinkwater stared curiously about him. The cutter had not been new when he joined her at Tilbury in the winter of 1792 and she had undergone radical structural alterations some years later. She bore the marks of age and hurried restoration: scuffed timbers, peeling paintwork, worn ropes, patched sails and dull brass-work.

'We've been attacking the binnacle with brick-dust and lamp-oil,' Frey said apologetically, 'but we were waist-deep in water on the passage and it's been a bit difficult . . .'

'It don't signify,' Drinkwater said pensively, his hand rubbing the edge of the companionway to the after accommodation from which, he noticed standing aside, the officers' tablecloth was being brought on deck by the steward. 'If you can manoeuvre under sail and fire your cannon at an enemy . . .' He looked at Frey. 'I commanded her at Camperdown, you know.' He remembered being cold and sodden as they beat about the gatways behind the Haak Sand off the Texel in the days before the battle, while Admiral Duncan's fleet mutinied off Yarmouth.*

'I didn't know that, sir.'

'It was a long time ago.'

He had known Frey for ten years; the lieutenant had been a midshipman aboard the sloop *Melusine* when he had last ventured north. The boy was a man now, growing grizzled in the sea service as this long war rumbled interminably on.

'She still sails well?'

'She leaks like a sieve. She had her keel and kelson pierced for centre-plates which make her claw up to windward like a witch, but the boxes let in water and she needs regular pumping.'

'I recall them being fitted,' Drinkwater mused, then asked, 'Did you bring your paint-box?'

'Never go anywhere without it, sir,' Frey said, waving an enthusiastic hand about him. On either side the steep, dark sides of the gorge closed about them, and beyond, its surface pale and cold, the fiord lay bordered by the dark forest. 'Imagine being here, amid this splendour, without the means to record it.'

*See *A King's Cutter.*

'I cannot', said Drinkwater ruefully, 'imagine what it must be like.'

And he grinned as the shadow of the gorge fell across the deck, and they entered the Vikkenfiord.

Chapter Twelve *November 1813*

The Flag of Truce

The twelve-gun cutter *Kestrel* ran up the Vikkenfiord with a quartering wind, her huge main boom guyed out to larboard, obscuring the lie of the land and the bluff upon which lay the guns of the Danish fort. Though the British ensign flew from the peak of her gaff, the white tablecloth flapped languidly in the eddies emptying from the leeward leech of the square topsail set above the hounds. Astern, Drinkwater's gig towed in their wake.

The rain had passed and, though the threat of more lay banked up in engorged clouds beyond the mountains to the south and west, the sun blazed upon the blue waters of the fiord and the breeze set white-capped waves dancing across its surface. The low, black-hulled cutter raced downwind. She still sported two long 4-pounders forward, but her ten pop-gun 3-pounders had long ago been replaced by carronades. Frey had had these cleared away and now ordered the square topsail clewed up and furled. *Kestrel* would neither stay nor wear quickly with it still set, and Drinkwater wanted the little cruiser to be as handy as skill and artifice could make her, in case his enterprise collapsed.

Leaving the management of the cutter to Frey, he walked forward and levelled his glass at the bluff, steadying it against a forward shroud. Above the embrasures of the fort, the colours of Denmark proclaimed Norway to be a possession of the Danish crown. Drinkwater could already see the masts of the American and Danish ships, lying at their anchors in the small bay beyond the bluff and under the protection of the fort's guns.

As they drew closer, Drinkwater watched and waited for a response from these cannon. At two miles he saw nothing to indicate the sentries had seen the approaching cutter, then they were within cannon shot.

'Any signs, sir?' asked Frey, coming forward and screwing up his eyes.

'Not a damned thing,' Drinkwater muttered, his glass remaining to his eye. 'Ah, wait . . .'

For a moment he had thought the brief flash to have been the discharge of a cannon, but then the white of an extempore flag like their own appeared to hang down from a gun-embrasure, pressed by the wind against the grey stonework of the rampart.

Drinkwater lowered his glass. 'I think we may stand on with a measure of confidence, Mr Frey.'

'I'll heave to just off the point then.'

'Yes, and get the boat alongside and the crew into it as fast as possible. I don't want them coming to us.'

'Aye, aye, sir.'

Drinkwater raised his glass again and swept the adjacent coast with care. 'Time spent in reconnaissance', he muttered to himself, quoting Quilhampton, 'is seldom wasted.'

So engrossed was he in this task that the sudden righting of *Kestrel*'s heeling deck and the shift of its motion to a gentle upward and downward undulation as she came head to wind took him by surprise. The headsails shook for a moment and then the jib was sheeted down hard and the staysail sheet was carried to windward as Frey hove his charge to on the starboard tack. The bluff, with its granite coping and the dark gun-embrasures, loomed above the cutter's curved taffrail, and on her port quarter where the gig was being quickly brought alongside, the bay beyond was filled with the three ships and its sheltered waters dotted with the oared boats Drinkwater had been so assiduously studying.

Now he went aft, watched as a boathook adorned with a table-napkin was passed to the bowman and, gathering up his sword, eased a foot over the rail, stood awkwardly on the rubbing band, chose his moment and tumbled into the boat.

Barking his shins he stumbled aft with considerable loss of dignity to take his seat beside Captain Pardoe's coxswain, Wells.

'Carry on, cox'n. Make for the Danish ship!'

'Aye, aye, sir.'

They pulled away from the cutter and were soon in the comparatively calmer waters of the bay. Drinkwater coughed to catch the attention of the labouring boat's crew. 'Keep your eyes in the boat, men. No remarks to any enemy boats that may come near and', he turned to the coxswain, 'lie off a little while I am aboard.'

'Aye, sir.'

As they approached the *Odin*, Drinkwater threw back his boat-cloak to reveal the remaining perfect epaulette on his left shoulder. He wore the undress uniform he had worn in the action of the day before. The bullion on his right shoulder was wrecked beyond repair, though Frampton had done his best when he swabbed the blood from the coat. Drinkwater stared woodenly ahead, but allowed his eyes to rove over the scene. The Danes had made good most of the ravages of the action, reinstating the foremast just as Quilhampton was doing at that moment aboard *Andromeda* beyond the entrance to the fiord.

Inshore of the Danish frigate the two American ships lay at anchor. They looked slightly less formidable upon closer inspection: privateers rather than frigates, though well armed. Between them and the Dane all the boats of the combined ships seemed to be waterborne, industriously plying to and fro. Many had stopped, their crews lying on their oars as they watched the bold approach of the enemy. They were quite obviously engaged in the business of transferring stands of arms, barrels of powder and the product of Continental arsenals destined for North America.

'Boat 'hoy!'

'Oars, cox'n.'

'Oars!' ordered Wells and the gig's crew stopped pulling, holding their oar-looms horizontally as the gig gradually lost way some fifty or sixty yards from the bulk of the *Odin*'s dark hull. Officers lined the quarterdeck while the faces of many curious onlookers, Danish sailors and marines, stared down at the approaching gig. Drinkwater stood up and doffed his hat.

'Good morning, gentlemen. Do I have your permission to come aboard?'

There was a brief consultation between the blue and gold figures. English, it appeared, was understood, but the matter seemed to be uncertain, so Drinkwater called out, 'I know you are transferring arms from your ship to the American vessels, gentlemen. I know also they came from France and travelled via Hamburg to Denmark. I think it will be to your advantage if I speak to your captain.'

'One of these boats coming close, sir,' growled Wells, sitting beside him.

'Take no notice,' Drinkwater muttered.

The officers above them came to a conclusion. '*Ja*. You come aboard!'

'Lay her alongside.'

'Aye, aye, sir.'

Drinkwater ascended the frigate's tumblehome, reached the level of the rail, threw his leg over and descended to the deck. With no boats on her booms the frigate's waist was wide open and the contents of her gun deck and berth deck were exposed. The bundles of sabres and muskets, boxes, bales and barrels that she carried could not be disguised. They were being hoisted out and lowered over the farther side where the boats of the combined ships were obviously loading them. His appearance had stopped the labour but, at a command, the watching men returned to work.

A tall man with a blue, red-faced coat and cocked hat stepped forward. He wore hessian boots whose gold tassels caught the sunshine, and dragged what looked like a cavalry sabre on the deck behind him.

'Kaptajn Dahlgaard of de Danske ship *Odin*. We haf met in battle, *ja*? I see you haf a wound.' Dahlgaard gestured to the large, dark scab on Drinkwater's cheek.

'Indeed, sir, a scratch. I am Captain Drinkwater of His Britannic Majesty's frigate *Andromeda*, at your service.' Drinkwater shot a glance at the officers behind Dahlgaard. Most were wearing the blue and red of the Danish sea service. Two were not. They were wearing blue broadcloth and insolent grins. He knew them for Americans. 'And these gentlemen are from the United States, are they not?' he added, side-stepping Dahlgaard and executing an ironic half-bow at the American commanders. He was gratified to see them lose a little of their composure.

He turned his heel on them and confronted Dahlgaard, addressing him so that the Americans could not hear.

'Captain Dahlgaard, you have, I know, no reason to love my country and, from your actions yesterday, I judge you, as I judged your countrymen at Copenhagen in 1801, to be a brave and courageous officer, but I beg you to consider the consequences of what you are doing. These arms are to spread destruction in a country of peace-loving people . . .'

'I haf my orders, Kaptajn. Please not to speak of this.'

Drinkwater shrugged as though unconcerned. 'Very well, then it is necessary that I tell you my admiral will be happy to let your vessel pass, if you permit us to take the American ships as prizes.'

Drinkwater had rehearsed the speech and was watching Dahlgaard carefully. The tiny reactive muscles round the man's eyes betrayed the Dane's understanding. Here before him stood a British captain claiming to be from the frigate he had engaged yesterday. Having extricated his frigate, this man was now back in a small man-of-war cutter, hinting at the presence of an admiral in the offing. The British officer emanated an air of unmistakable confidence. Now he had the effrontery to press Dahlgaard further.

'Come, sir, what do these men mean to you? What do the French mean to you? They have occupied your country and compelled us to make war upon you. They have forced us to destroy your navy . . . would you be known as the officer who lost the last frigate possessed by King Frederick . . . ?'

The King's name seemed to rouse Dahlgaard. 'The King of Denmark is good ally of France. I haf my duty, Kaptajn, like you. You have no reason to be in Danske waters. No right to demand I surrender these American ships which are', Dahlgaard waved a hand above his head as though drawing Drinkwater's attention to the swallowtail ensigns at the fort and at the *Odin*'s stern, 'under the protection of my flag.'

'Please yourself, Captain Dahlgaard,' Drinkwater shrugged, feigning an indifference he did not feel. The Danish commander impressed him as a resolute character, not one to be easily intimidated by Drinkwater's affectation of bombast. He turned to the Americans. 'I shall see you again, gentlemen.'

'I shouldn't be too sure of that if I were you, Captain,' remarked one.

'He's bluffing, Dahlgaard,' added the second. 'There ain't no British ships in the offing.'

Dahlgaard cocked his head, shrewdly weighing up Drinkwater. 'You think no?'

'No. I'm damn certain of it.'

Dahlgaard drew himself up. 'You are not welcome, Kaptajn.'

Aware that his bluff had failed, Drinkwater bowed to Dahlgaard. 'Until we meet again, Captain.' He stared about him, casting his eyes aloft and into the crowded waist. 'A very fine ship, sir. A damn pity to risk losing her.'

'We'll see about that,' drawled one of the Americans, 'there'll be three of us, you know.'

Close-hauled, *Kestrel* beat back down the fiord to meet *Andromeda*. As ordered, Quilhampton had brought the frigate through the narrows an hour after noon, cleared for action and with her upper studding sails set. A mile short of her, Drinkwater transferred to the gig and left Frey to gill about until he had exchanged places with Quilhampton. With considerable skill, Wells manoeuvred the gig under the bow of the advancing frigate so that Quilhampton had only to haul round and shiver his square sails for the gig to dash alongside.

Drinkwater met Quilhampton at the rail. 'She's cleared for action, sir,' Quilhampton said. 'Birkbeck has the con.'

'Did you clap a cable on a bower anchor?'

'Cables on both bowers, sir. And I've led two light springs outside everything.'

'Very good, James, I didn't notice them. Thank you. No dice with the Dane, but she's a formidable ship. The Yankees are privateers and spoiling for a fight, so keep out of their range. There's a deal of lumber about their decks, arms and the like, but they'll make as much trouble as they can. Try and sink their boats, but James, for God's sake keep out of trouble. I need you alive, not covered in death and glory!'

'Don't worry . . .' Quilhampton smiled, his eyes sparkling.

And then he was gone, swung one-handed down into the gig, and Drinkwater was once again absorbed into the business of his own ship.

'Don't wait for the gig, Mr Birkbeck, *Kestrel* will tow her. Let's crack on and surprise 'em. Oh, and keep her close inshore.'

'Aye, aye, sir.'

'I'm going below to shift my linen.'

He stared across the water to where the gig was rounding to under *Kestrel*'s counter. The white table-cloth was fluttering down from the cutter's bare topsail yardarm. The truce was at an end.

Captain Drinkwater was back on deck in fifteen minutes. For the second time within two hours, the bluff loomed above him as

Birkbeck held the frigate's course close under the rocky prominence. This time the battery opened fire as *Andromeda* approached. Shot plunged on either bow, pierced the upper sails and parted a brace of ropes, but did no real damage. The rate of fire was slow but steady, a fact Birkbeck remarked upon.

'I fancy most of the gunners are assisting in transferring cargo out of the *Odin* into the boats,' Drinkwater observed. The next salvo, fired as they drew ever closer, passed overhead.

'Good lord, sir, they're firing *over* us. They can't depress their pieces!'

'Quite,' said Drinkwater smiling, hoping to heaven his confidence in deep water existing up to the foot of the bluff was correct.

A glance astern showed *Kestrel* coming up hand over fist and then they were past the point and the bay was opening up under their lee with the rising pine forest behind, and the muzzles of *Andromeda*'s cannon were pointing at the *Odin*.

'When you bear, Mr Mosse,' Drinkwater called as he studied the bearing of the Danish frigate.

'Fire!'

And the officers on the gun deck passed on the order.

The following wind caused *Andromeda* to carry the smoke of her broadside with her so that it was impossible to gauge the effect of the first shots. The air cleared slowly; glimpses of the enemy's masts and yards were briefly visible in the opening rents, only to be obscured as the larboard battery fired again.

Beside Drinkwater, Birkbeck was bawling orders to the topmen and waisters detailed to handle the frigate's braces and sheets as he slowed *Andromeda*, so that her guns might have the maximum effect upon their targets as she swept across the mouth of the bay and her guns emptied themselves first into the *Odin*, and then successively into the American privateers.

'Take in the stuns'ls, Mr Birkbeck!'

Drinkwater's last words were lost in the concussion of another broadside, but this time it was the enemy's and the air was again full of the buzzing of gigantic bees, of a smack and crack as a ball buried itself in the mizen mast above their heads, and the curious sucking of air as another passed close enough to affect their breathing. There was, too, the twang of ropes parting under load, followed by the whirr and thrap of their unreeving and falling across the deck. Somewhere a man screamed, but that first close broadside from the *Odin* was ragged and their own savage retaliation thundered from *Andromeda*'s side as she swept past and poured her fire into the American ships.

Above the quarterdeck the studding sails flapped like wounded gulls, were tamed by their ropes and drawn into the tops. A half-mile past the bay Birkbeck looked expectantly at Drinkwater who nodded and the helm was put down.

'Hands to tack ship! Stand by the braces, there!' Birkbeck shouted, and *Andromeda* came up into the wind. 'Mains'l haul!'

It was now that Drinkwater played the only card he held after the empty bluster about an admiral's squadron in the offing.

He had deduced that the wind which had prevailed from the south-west and died during the previous night, would very likely do the same today. He could, therefore, bear down swiftly on the anchored ships, but once he was past them, as he was now, he had two choices. He could come about on to the starboard tack and stand across the fiord as he had done the previous day, rapidly passing out of range and working slowly to windward before turning and running back again to renew the attack. By then, however, he would have lost the element of surprise.

His second choice was to come right about on the larboard tack and sail directly into the bay under the guns of an enemy, surrendering all advantages beyond that of hitting all three ships again quickly before they could recover from his first onslaught. But he would risk collision, failure to stay again, and the threat of being raked at pistol shot.

'Haul all!'

He now brought *Andromeda* round on to that potentially fatal tack and bore down into the bay. Despite the hazard of such a move he could cover *Kestrel*'s dash in among the boats by drawing the fire of the *Odin* and the Americans, and continue to inflict damage on the former as fast as his gunners could serve their pieces, for with three potential enemies, this could be no tip-and-run raid.

Puffs of smoke along the topsides of all three ships told where resistance was being organized, and columns of water rose up around them as they crabbed down to leeward, gathering way with the yards braced hard against the catharpings.

Ahead of them, already attracting fire and dividing the concentration of the enemy, *Kestrel* had danced insolently into the bay in the wake of the frigate and Quilhampton had strewn his heavy carronade shot amongst the boats. Drinkwater could see two of them awash to the gunwales, the heads of men swimming round them, then one sank, shortly followed by the other. A moment later *Kestrel's* main boom was swung out and her hull foreshortened as she ran out of the bay towards the approaching *Andromeda* with enemy shot plunging about her.

As *Andromeda* and *Kestrel* passed on opposite courses, Drinkwater could see the little cruiser's bulwarks beaten in where she had taken punishment, but Quilhampton waved his hat jauntily from the quarter where he stood by the great tiller with its carved falcon's head.

'Closing fast, sir,' Birkbeck cautioned, and Drinkwater looked round and nodded.

'This will do very well,' he said, staring at the height of the bluff ahead of them and the hard edge of the fort's rampart against the sky. A ball thumped into *Andromeda*'s hull and another whined overhead. 'I think we should be safe from the fort hereabouts,' he called to the master, 'bring her round now.'

'Down helm,' ordered Birkbeck, picking up his speaking trumpet. 'Hands to the braces!' he roared. Again *Andromeda* came up into the wind like a reined horse, exposing her starboard battery to the enemy.

'Fire!' bellowed Mosse.

'Stand by the larboard cat stopper!' shouted Birkbeck. 'Rise tacks and sheets! Let go!'

The starboard battery now bore on the enemy and its cannon belched fire and smoke at the *Odin* as *Andromeda's* backed yards checked her headway and overcame it, slowly driving her astern. Her anchor bit the sand and dragged the cable out of the ship, just as Malaburn had done the previous day. But now the act was deliberate, placing the British ship not at a supine disadvantage, but with her guns commanding the enemy and strewing the anchorage with her own shot.

'Clew up! Clew up!'

On *Andromeda*'s gun deck the men of the larboard guns now moved over to assist their mates on the opposite side, and the warm cannon poured broadside after relentless broadside into the enemy ships.

But the Danish gunners had overcome their surprise and, with the two vessels now stationary, parallel and head to wind, the odds were rapidly reversed. Nor were the American ships inert and, though slightly less advantageously stationed, with lighter guns and lacking the rigid discipline of regular naval crews, their guns found the range and began punishing the *Andromeda* for her effrontery. The crash and explosion of splinters as enemy balls buried themselves in the British frigate's fabric became regular, and musket shot buzzed dangerously about.

Drinkwater was aware of men falling at their guns, of their being flung back, or thrown aside like dolls in the very act of tending their pieces. He looked up at the fort again. The guns were quiet there and he wondered if the ramparts were pierced for artillery on this side. Whether or not they were, he felt they were again too close under the bluff for carriage guns to depress. Hardly had this satisfactory thought crossed his mind than he found Midshipman Fisher at his side. The boy was shouting and Drinkwater realized that the noise of the action had deafened him. He bent to hear what Fisher had to say.

'Mr Jameson says to tell you that Mr Beavis has been killed, sir. A shot came in through the ship's side . . .' Fisher's voice was distant and Drinkwater had to stare at his mouth to understand him. He could see the tears in the boy's eyes.

'Is it bad below, Mr Fisher?'

'Terrible, sir. Collingwood's dead, sir . . .' The boy's lower lip trembled.

'Collingwood?' Drinkwater said uncertainly.

'The . . . the cockpit cat, sir.'

'Ah, Collingwood, yes . . . I'm sorry. Do you go and give Mr Jameson my compliments and tell him we're giving the enemy a pounding.'

'Giving the enemy a pounding. Aye, aye, sir.'

Drinkwater looked about him through the smoke. 'Mr Birkbeck?'

'Sir!'

'What d'you make of the *Odin?* We've shot away her mizen . . .'

The words were hardly uttered when there came the fatal crack of chain shot aloft. Drinkwater peered upwards and saw the whole of the main topmast tottering.

'Not again,' an anguished Birkbeck called despairingly. Aloft the falling main topgallant brought the fore topgallant with it, and then Drinkwater heard something far more serious. A deep boom came from somewhere to starboard.

'God's bones!' he swore. 'Mortar fire!'

Amid the falling shot, the smoke and confusion, it was impossible to know where that first shell had fallen. It failed to explode, so Drinkwater concluded it had fallen into the sea before its fuse had burnt down, but he knew it had come from the fort.

The second, when it came, proved lethal, exploding twenty feet above the waist, showering the entire upper deck, the tops and even those exposed in the gun deck beneath the boat-booms with shards of splintered iron.

''Tis too hot, sir!' Birkbeck exclaimed, wiping blood from his face.

'Brace the topsails sharp up, starboard tack. And set the sprits'l!'

The fore and mizen topsails, though riddled with shot-holes, were still under the command of their braces. Birkbeck ran forward among the wreckage of fallen spars and ragged sails, dragging men away from the upper-deck guns and thrusting them into line at the braces. Greer was frantically using his starter as they dragged the resisting yards round. Aloft they were encumbered by the dependent mass of the upper spars and broken mast.

Realizing that to wait many moments more would result in the destruction of his ship, Drinkwater ran forward and slipped over the rail on to the fore-chains. Here he quickly found the end of the spring Quilhampton had had prepared and, gathering up a forecastle gun's crew, sent two of them below to the hawse, to draw in the spring and secure it to the cable. Somewhere above and behind him a third shell burst with a dull thump. Drinkwater could hear men screaming, despite his impaired hearing.

Coming aft again he found the wheel shattered, the four helmsmen either dead or dying. Lieutenant Mosse lay across a quarterdeck carronade, his long and elegant legs doing a last feeble dido.

'God's bones!' Drinkwater blasphemed again, desperately casting about him. It seemed in the smoke that he was the only man alive, and then Birkbeck loomed up to report the yards braced.

'Get below and veer cable! I've a spring clapped on it and as soon as the ship's head is cast off the wind, I'll send word to you to cut it!'

Birkbeck vanished. Drinkwater could only hope the master

reached the cable tier without being killed or wounded. He waited, looking up. He could see blue sky above, and the dim geometric pattern of mast, yards and rigging through the smoke. He had to force himself to think, before he worked out it would be the *Odin*.

Behind the Danish man-of-war, the outline of the bluff and the ramparts was visible as though through a swirling fog. A foreshortened faint grey arc rose slowly and gracefully above it. The mathematical precision of the thing struck Drinkwater. He could clearly see the shell that caused it, a black dot, like a meteorite in daylight. The little black sphere grew bigger with an accelerating rapidity that astonished him. He drew back cravenly, behind the insubstantial shelter of the mizen mast. Closing his eyes he rested his forehead against the thick wooden tree. Beneath his feet the ship trembled as the gun carriages recoiled inboard, were serviced and hauled, rumbling, out again. The thunder of the broadsides had broken down now. Every gun was served by its crew individually, the men possessed by the demons of blood lust, slaves to their hot and ravening artillery.

Amid the noise there was a dull thud that Drinkwater felt through the soles of his shoes, and he was aware of a faint susurration. He opened his eyes. The Danish bombardier officer cut his fuses far too erratically. The unexploded mortar shell lay at Drinkwater's feet, half-buried in the decking, its quick-match fizzing and sparking inexorably towards the funnel that carried its contagious fire into the mass of powder packed into its hollow carcass.

Perhaps a quarter of an inch had yet to burn. It puzzled Drinkwater that the unknown artilleryman had made such a mistake. Perhaps the saltpetre with which the fuse was impregnated was of inferior quality. Perhaps . . .

He regarded the thing with a detached curiosity, quite unafraid. He recalled he was supposed to be doing something; that he had initiated a course of action which had had something to do with Birkbeck.

Then smoke blew into his face as Birkbeck veered cable, and he looked up. He could see the mizen topsail above his head filling with wind as *Andromeda* altered her heading, slowly swinging as Birkbeck veered the cable and the weight of the frigate was shared by the spring. Then the wind came over the starboard bow and the ship gathered way, moving ahead.

He felt a sense of overwhelming relief as he remembered what it was he had dispatched the master to attend to. The ship would be all right; she would sail out of danger now. He could die having done his duty. 'Cut!' he yelled, aware that Birkbeck, far below, could not hear him. 'Cut!' he shouted again, and he thought he heard someone below take up the cry, but was not sure. He could do no more.

He looked at the shell again, at the rapidly shortening fuse, waiting for the explosion: then it occurred to him that he might douse it. Bending forward he pinched the hot and spluttering end between thumb and forefinger. He felt the heat sear him and transferred his hand to his mouth. He tasted bitterness, but the thing was extinguished. He bent and, with his sword blade and considerable effort, levered the shell from the splintered and cracked deck planking. Only a heavy deck beam below had prevented it from passing through and blowing up in the crowded confines of the gun deck.

He lifted the black iron sphere and, walking to the rail, put a foot on the slide of a carronade. It had ceased firing and its crew had fallen about it in positions of abandon. Some were obviously dead, their bodies mutilated by the impact of shell fragments. Others looked asleep. He heaved himself up, leant upon the hammock netting and dropped the shell carcass overboard. Then he hung there, hooked by his armpits on the cranes. He longed to shut his eyes and sleep, but he watched the plume of water raised by the splash draw astern as *Andromeda* stood out of the bay.

The butcher's bill was appalling. *Andromeda* lay at anchor on the far side of the Vikkenfiord, not far from where Malaburn had tried to deliver her to the *Odin* the day, or was it a lifetime, before. Kennedy, the surgeon, stood before Drinkwater and read from a crumpled sheet of paper.

'Messrs Mosse and Beavis; Greer, boatswain's mate; Wilson, corporal of marines . . .' Kennedy read on, thirty-seven seamen and thirteen marines dead and the list of the wounded twice as bad, many mortal.

The reproach in Kennedy's eyes was insubordinate. 'Thank you, Mr Kennedy.'

'I did my best, sir, but I cannot work miracles . . .'

'No, of course not. I don't expect that.'

'You expected it of the ship's company.' Kennedy's voice rasped harshly as he made his accusation.

Exhaustion and failure made Drinkwater lose his temper.

He turned upon his tormentor. 'I shared their exposure, damn you!'

'You've the consolation of doing your duty to your king, I suppose,' conceded Kennedy, equally angry.

'Mind your tongue, and keep your Jacobite sympathies to yourself!'

Both men stared at each other. Drinkwater was faint with hunger and exertion. He had had nothing to eat all day and Kennedy was haggard from his foul labours over the operating table. He would, he had confided to his mates, rather have tended the most corrupted fistulae at Bath than hack off the limbs or probe for shards of shell carcass, splinters of wood or grapeshot in the bodies of healthy men.

Abruptly the surgeon turned on his heel and left the cabin. Drinkwater sank into the single chair he had had brought up from the hold. Apart from dropping the cabin bulkhead, the ship remained ready for action. A bitter chill filled the cabin from the breeze that blew in, unimpeded, through the wreck of the starboard quarter gallery, battered into splinters by several cannon shot from the Yankee privateers. Drinkwater drew his cloak closer round him. His head ached and waves of blackness seemed to wash up to him, then recede again. He wanted to sleep but the cloak could no more keep out memories than the cold. He had an overwhelming desire to weep and felt a first shuddering heave.

A knock came at the door and Fisher's smoke-blackened face appeared. It momentarily crossed Drinkwater's overstimulated imagination that this was no mortal visitor but an imp of Satan.

'Beg pardon, sir, but *Kestrel*'s just come alongside.' Such had been the decimation among the officers that the midshipman was keeping the anchor watch.

'Oh, yes.' Drinkwater reproached himself for having momentarily forgotten about the cutter. With an effort he pulled himself together. 'Be so kind as to ask her commander to report aboard.' His voice cracked and he hoped the boy could not see in the gloom the tears filling his eyes.

'Aye, aye, sir . . .'

'By the way, what's the wind doing?'

'Flat calm, sir.'
'Good. Very well, cut along.'
After Kennedy, it would be good to talk to Quilhampton. James understood the brutal and unavoidable priorities of a sea-officer's duty. A few minutes later there was a second knock.
'Come in, James.'
But it was Frey who came into the bare cabin.

Chapter Thirteen *November 1813*

Failure

Drinkwater knew the worst from Frey's expression. The young lieutenant was grimy from powder smoke, his cheeks smeared and pale, his eyes wild.

'How did it happen? Tell me from the beginning.'

Drinkwater hauled himself out of his chair and went to the settee placed below the stern windows. The shutters were pulled and a single battle lantern lit the unfurnished space. Lifting one of the padded settee seats he rummaged and withdrew a half-full bottle. Extracting the cork, he handed the bottle to Frey and gestured to the settee.

'The glasses are all stowed. Please, sit down . . .'

Frey took the bottle and swigged greedily, sat and offered it to Drinkwater who shook his head. Frey took a second draught and then cradled the bottle on his lap.

'We followed you directly into the bay and threw several shots among the boats with some success.' Drinkwater nodded; he remembered seeing this and then *Kestrel* running out towards them as *Andromeda* bore down into the bay to anchor and bombard the enemy ships.

'We sustained some damage from the Americans and lost three men killed and two wounded before we extricated ourselves. Then we tacked in your wake and came back astern of you. From what we saw you achieved complete surprise. The Danes seemed uncharacteristically irresolute.'

'Their decks were cluttered with armaments they were tran-shipping to the Americans and they had many of their men away in the boats.'

'Yes. By the time you had come to your anchor the boats had retreated to their respective ships and I had no specific targets. As we bore down, I went aft to obtain fresh orders. The smoke from your guns drifted into the anchorage and made it difficult to see what was going on. To round your stern would have put us uncomfortably close under the guns of the Americans, so James tacked offshore a little, intending to beat back into the bay across your bow and see if anything advantageous offered.

'We managed to lay a course that not only took us across *Andromeda*'s bow, but also carried us athwart the hawse of the *Odin*. All the recovered boats were lashed alongside her starboard waist in the security of her unengaged side. It was also fair to assume the gunners on that side would be helping their mates on the other, for she was by then putting forth a furious fire.

'"We will cut those boats up, tack and get out before they know what has happened," James ordered, and in we went. I depressed our carronades and James took her in like a yacht. I had time to prime my gun captains and we swept in with terrific effect!

'I'm not certain how many of those boats we smashed but their big launch was definitely sunk, along with two cutters and possibly a third. As soon as we were past, James put the helm over. We could do nothing else and . . .' Frey's voice faltered.

'You put your stern to the enemy.'

Frey nodded. 'They had woken to our presence and we received fire from their quarterdeck cannon. Langridge swept the length of the deck; James, both helmsmen and a dozen others fell. The boat in the stern davits, the binnacle and after companionway – all shot to pieces. The boom's bespattered with the damned stuff and the foot of the mains'l in tatters.'

Frey paused and shuddered at the recollection. He took another swallow from the bottle. 'We missed stays . . .'

Drinkwater could imagine the confusion. With no hand on the tiller, *Kestrel*'s rudder would have swung amidships and the turning moment applied to the cutter would have ceased. She would have sat, a perfect target, at something less than pistol shot, off the *Odin*'s starboard quarter.

'I went aft and put the helm over to make a stern board and we backed the jib, but we were too close under the land to get a true wind and she blew towards the *Odin* and paid off to starboard again, back on our former tack. We took another storm of raking fire . . .'

It was a marvel that Frey had not been hit, Drinkwater thought, watching him take a fourth swig from the nearly emptied bottle.

'Then your shot from *Andromeda* brought down the *Odin*'s fore and main topmasts and her fire slackened perceptibly. Anyway, *Kestrel* paid off fast to starboard and we cleared the *Odin*'s stern, thank God! My next problem was the Americans. The Yankees were doing their best, though their fire was nothing compared to the *Odin*'s. They soon saw us though, coming out of the smoke on the *Odin*'s starboard quarter, and quickly laid their guns upon us. I couldn't risk running under their lee, so I gybed and got her on to a broad, starboard reach . . .'

'You sailed across the bows of the Americans and across their field of fire?'

Frey tensed, nodding unhappily. 'I wanted only to get out of that accursed bay, damn it!'

'I am not judging you, my dear fellow,' Drinkwater said with a gentle resignation.

Frey relaxed visibly. 'We returned fire,' he said with a shred of pride, 'but lost our topmast and were badly hulled . . .'

'And the butcher's bill?'

'Almost half the ship's company killed or wounded, sir.'

'God's bones,' Drinkwater whispered, rubbing his hand across his face. He looked at Frey. 'And what of James?'

'It must have been instant, sir. He was quite shot to pieces . . .'

A heavy silence lay between the two men as they mourned their mutual friend. The bottle dropped from Frey's hand with a thud, recalling Drinkwater to the present. Frey drooped sideways, fast asleep. Drinkwater rose and lifted his legs out along the settee, settling him down. Then he took his cloak and laid it over Frey, tucking it in to prevent him from rolling off the narrow settee. As he took his hands away they were sticky with blood.

Drinkwater paced the quarterdeck. With his officers decimated and his ship requiring a thorough overhaul and reorganization, he had enough on his mind without grief and the presence of an enemy immeasurably stronger than himself not four miles away.

After he had sailed clear of the bay, he had brought *Andromeda* back across the fiord and found the shallows upon which Malaburn had so treacherously anchored the frigate only a day before. Here the ship and her company drew breath beneath the northern stars. A rudimentary anchor watch kept the deck, and most men slept, exhausted by the day's exertions.

Drinkwater walked up and down, up and down. The extreme lethargy that had seized him earlier, that had driven all thought of *Kestrel* and James Quilhampton from his brain, had left him. He felt almost weightless, as though he derived energy from the workings of his mind. He did not question or marvel at this manic activity; it did not occur to him that the news of Quilhampton's death compounded the weight of accuracy of Surgeon Kennedy's insubordinate accusation. This fateful personalization of so terrible a truth drove like a blade into his soul, and his unquiet spirit teetered on the brink of reason.

Up and down, up and down he paced, so that the men on duty, huddled in the warmest corners they could find beneath the wrecked masts, formed their own opinions as they watched the figure of their strange captain. His body was dark against the sky, the relentless scissoring of his white-breeched legs pale against the bulwarks.

'You know he pinched the fuse out of a shell,' a seaman whose battle station had been at a forecastle carronade whispered to a shivering watchmate. 'Bill Whitman told me he was as cool as a cucumber. Just looked at it for a bit, then bent over and squeezed the fuse. Then he dug the bloody thing up with his sword and dropped it over the side.'

'Christ, he's a hard bastard!'

'Makes old Pardoe look like a fart in a colander.'

'Anyway, bugger Drinkwater. I could do with a drink.'

'Couldn't we all . . .'

'He'll have had one.'

'Or two.'

They dozed into envious silence as Drinkwater's restless pacing soothed the fury of his thoughts, ordered their priority and saved him from the descent into insanity.

'Two watches,' he muttered to himself, 'Jameson and Birkbeck. First to clear the rest of the wreckage, then rig topmasts. Birkbeck will accomplish that, if we are left alone. If . . .'

He turned his mind to the problem of the enemy. He was compelled to accept the fact that yesterday's action had been a defeat. He drew no morsel of comfort from anything which Frey had reported. It was perhaps a cold consolation that the *Odin*'s fire had been furious, but Dahlgaard's countrymen had twice before impressed British seamen with their valour and this was mere corroboration. It was a bitter pill for him to swallow, to have come so close, to the point of actually observing the very muskets and sabres which would be used to ravage the peaceful settlements of Canada being lifted from the *Odin*, and to be powerless to stop their transhipment.

Had he been able to fire at the American ships, he might at the very least have reduced them to a state which no prudent commander would take across the Atlantic in winter. But the presence of the *Odin* had transformed the situation, and cost Drinkwater any tactical advantage he might otherwise have possessed.

The irony of it burned into his self-esteem. He shuddered, as much with self-loathing as with cold.

Faced with such reproach how could there be any satisfaction in knowing he had done his duty? He had spent a lifetime doing his duty and what had it availed? The war ground interminably on, the men he had befriended and then led had died beside him. His friendship seemed accursed, a poisoned chalice. He wished he had been wounded himself, killed even . . .

He drew back from the thought. What would Birkbeck do now if he was dead? The thought struck him like a pistol ball, stopping him in his mad pacing. What was *he* to do? He felt bankrupt of ideas, beyond the obvious one of slipping unobtrusively out of the Vikkenfiord. Instinctively he sniffed the air. There was something odd . . .

He had not noticed the creeping chill of dampening air. Now sodden ropes dripped on a deck perceptibly dark with moisture. The fog had come down with a startling suddenness, though its symptoms had encroached gradually.

Fog!

Even in the darkness he could see the pallid wraiths steal in over the bulwarks, wafted by the light breeze that blew the cold air from the distant peaks down over the warmer waters of the fiord.

Fog!

Hated though it was as a restriction on safe navigation, the enfolding vapour was a shroud, hiding them from the enemy. Could he spirit his ship to sea, clear of the gorge? He thought not; the fear of losing her filled his heart with dread.

Fog!

Then, as the fog enveloped them completely, the idea struck Drinkwater. Fate tugged at the cord of his despair and wakened hope.

Templeton had never before experienced so terrible an event as the action in the bay. When he learned that they had anchored to engage the *Odin* he could not understand so deliberate and foolhardy a decision, until Kennedy, up to his elbows in reeking blood, explained that it was expected of a man-of-war that she be carried into battle against all odds and that to shirk such a duty laid her commander open to charges of dereliction of duty and cowardice.

'And they wouldn't scruple to charge him either,' Kennedy said, as he completed the last suture and motioned his patient aside and the table swabbed for the next.

Templeton knew of such things in the abstract, had read a thousand reports in the copy room, but the reality had never struck him with all its terrible implications as the torn and mangled wrecks of what had, shortly before, been men were dragged on to the surgeon's extempore operating table. Convention demanded that a captain's secretary share the risks of the quarterdeck with his commander, but Drinkwater, unused to such an encumbrance, had made it known to his clerk that he expected no such quixotism.

'Besides,' Drinkwater had said, 'only you and I are privy to the exact details of this matter and, if anything happens to me, you will be best able to advise my successor. Stay below, you may be able to assist Mr Kennedy in his duties.'

Thus it was that Templeton found himself in the cockpit, among the gleaming scalpels, saws, clamps, catlings and curettes of Surgeon Kennedy's trade when the wounded began to pour below in ever-increasing numbers.

Templeton's experience of the previous day's action had, if not inured, at least accustomed him to expect the conventional brutalities of naval war. And the unaccustomed harshness of his existence since joining the frigate, the miseries of sea-sickness and the violence of the ocean had begun the ineluctable process of eroding his sensibilities. But the action in the bay produced so severe a drain upon Kennedy's resources that Templeton found himself inexorably drawn into the actual business of assisting.

Whereas on the previous day he had merely tied bandages,

passed words of consolation along with a bottle among the men, and taken and recorded their names and their divisions, today he had actively helped Kennedy and his tiring loblolly 'boys' in the gruesome business of amputation, excision and debriding. He found, after a while, assisted by rum, a savagery that matched the speed of Kennedy's actions.

But nothing had prepared him for the horror of discovering Greer's white and mutilated body stretched upon the sheet spread on the midshipmen's chests, of seeing the mangled stump of Greer's right arm whose hand had so lately transported him; or the shock of the apparent callousness of Kennedy's cursory examination.

'Nothing to be done. Move him over.'

Templeton was incapable, in that awful moment, of understanding that Greer's multiple wounds were mortal, his loss of blood excessive, and that no skill on earth could staunch the haemorrhage or close those dreadful wounds.

'But he's alive!' he protested, staring in outrage at the indifferent Kennedy.

'His wound is mortal.' Kennedy's tone was brutally honest. 'I don't possess the cunning to prevent death.'

And Templeton looked again and saw the blue tint to the lips and the pallor of the formerly weathered features.

'Here.' Kennedy picked up a bottle he kept at his feet and held it out across the body. The loblolly boys dragged Greer from beneath Kennedy's outstretched arm. 'Come, bear up,' Kennedy growled, 'pull yourself together, or men will say you were fond of him!'

Templeton grabbed the bottle and averted his eyes from Kennedy. The accusation implicit in Kennedy's remark did not strike Templeton until later when, he realized, lying awake while the exhausted ship slept around him, none would make any distinction in the nature of his 'crime' as proscribed by the Articles of War. The thought added immeasurably to his burden of guilt.

'What is the time?'

Full daylight glowed through the nacreous fog as Drinkwater woke suddenly from a deep sleep. He was sat against a quarterdeck carronade, sodden from the fog, agonized by a spasm of cramp as he tried to move.

'Eight bells, sir, morning watch just turning out, I took the liberty of mustering all hands and telling them off in two watches.'

'Well done, Mr Birkbeck, I had the same thing in mind. Now, give me your arm . . .' Birkbeck assisted him to his feet.

'Galley range is alight and burgoo, molasses and cheese are to be issued. Mess-cooks have just been piped. Purser kicked up a fuss about the cheese, but I told him to go to the devil.'

Drinkwater nodded his agreement while the blood trickled painfully back into his legs. He sought to invigorate himself by rubbing his face, but his palms rasped at the encrusted scab, which he had momentarily forgotten, and he swiftly desisted.

'You can issue spirits before you turn all hands to, and what about the officers' livestock?' he added as the idea struck him. 'With so few of them left, can I not purchase what remains so that we can get a decent meal into the men at midday? I'll add my own pullets and capons.'

'That'll put heart into the men, sir, and God knows they need it. The wardroom bullock took a cannon-shot, but he's edible. Beef and chicken stew sounds like the elixir of life.'

'Yes, it does. As for the ship herself . . .'

'We can begin to clear this lot, and the carpenter and I reckon we can step topmasts again.'

'By tonight?'

'By tonight.'

'Excellent!'

'And we've a spare tops'l just finished at Leith. Oh, I reckon she'll show enough canvas to handle.'

'Mr Birkbeck, if you achieve that I don't know what I can do for you.'

'Get me home in one piece, sir, and I'll not complain.' The master paused and looked at Drinkwater. He was unshaven and still besmirched with powder grime, the abraded scab bleeding again from one disturbed corner, the undress coat with its missing epaulette emphasizing the cock-eyed set of the captain's shoulders. With his loose hair, strands of which had escaped from the queue, Drinkwater looked like some raffish and outcast beggar.

'You'd feel better after a wash, sir,' Birkbeck offered.

'Yes, yes, I would,' Drinkwater replied, finally stirring.

'I'll pass word to Frampton.'

'I thought I might have lost him too,' Drinkwater said in a low voice, and Birkbeck, taking advantage of this moment of confidentiality, asked:

'What d'you intend to do, sir, when this fog clears?'

'How long d'you think it will hang about? There's no sign of the sou' westerly . . .'

'Glass is rising. I reckon we can guarantee today, that's why I want to crack on with the masts. Can I use *Kestrel*'s men? I've been aboard her this morning and she's very badly hulled. I doubt she can make a passage and we could use her lieutenant . . .'

Drinkwater walked awkwardly to the frigate's side above which he could just discern the cutter's truncated mast, and peered over the rail. Birkbeck drew alongside him.

They could just make out the shattered and splintered state of *Kestrel*'s upperworks.

'I don't think she's fit for much. We could burn her,' Birkbeck suggested.

'Yes, perhaps,' Drinkwater agreed thoughtfully. 'Anyway, you may have as many men as you like after I have two dozen volunteers. Call for them after they have broken their fast and do you see that you feed *Kestrel*'s crew along with our own.'

Birkbeck looked mystified at first and then horror struck. 'You don't mean to attempt something against the enemy, sir?'

'Yes, I do, and if I have not returned by tomorrow morning, Lieutenant Jameson will be in command.'

'But with respect, sir, I think we have done as much . . .'

'Give me half an hour to wash and shave, Mr Birkbeck, then ask Jameson to wait on me. Muster my volunteers at two bells. Come now, there ain't much time.'

Drinkwater left Birkbeck staring after him open-mouthed.

Chapter Fourteen *November 1813*

A Measure of Success

In the event, Drinkwater found his plan to use *Kestrel* quite impracticable. She had been badly hulled and even the plugs put in by her carpenter failed to stem the leaks which proved too copious for the pumps to handle without almost continual manning.

'We can't risk being betrayed by their noise,' Drinkwater remarked to Frey, who had had his wound dressed and insisted he was fit for duty.

'We could fother a sail, sir,' suggested the cutter's boatswain.

'T'would take too long, and there is much else to be done,' replied Drinkwater.

Instead they put the volunteers to emptying the cutter of her powder, and her gunner to preparing some mines, small barricoes filled with tamped powder and fitted with fuses made from slow-match.

It was not so much her waterlogged state that made Drinkwater abandon using *Kestrel* as the difficulty of approaching the enemy anchorage undetected. Although fitted with sweeps, she would be awkward and sluggish to row and difficult to keep on a precise course. The ship's boats were a different matter, but they could not carry the quantities of inflammable material that *Kestrel* could, and Drinkwater had, therefore, to modify his intentions.

When he had exchanged with Quilhampton the previous day, James had departed in Drinkwater's own gig, and had left it towing astern throughout the action. Though it had received damage in the way of splintered gunwales and a few holes in the planking, these were soon repaired with tingles, lead rectangles lined with grease-soaked canvas patches that were nailed over holes or splits.

Kestrel herself bore two boats, one slung in stern davits which had been rendered useless, but another on deck amidships which, though damaged about the transom, and with one large chunk out of her larboard gunwale, remained seaworthy. These, with an additional serviceable pulling cutter from *Andromeda*, provided Drinkwater with what he needed.

'We can't man an armada, Mr Frey,' he explained as he outlined his plan, 'but if we take advantage of this fog and do our work coolly, there is a chance, just a chance, that we may yet achieve a measure of success.'

Frey had nodded.

'Are you fit enough for this enterprise, Mr Frey? I would not have you risk your life unnecessarily . . .' Drinkwater broke off, remembering the blood on his own hand and attributing the unnatural glitter in Frey's eyes to grief and pain. He was, after all, of a sensitive, artistic bent.

Frey cleared his throat. 'I am quite all right, sir.'

'Very well, then. Do you take *Kestrel*'s boat. We know the course and will compare our compasses when we have drawn clear of *Andromeda*. I will follow in *Andromeda*'s cutter and tow the gig. The rest you already know.'

'Aye, aye, sir.'

The interview with Jameson had been more difficult. However sanguine Jameson's ambition, he had not dreamed of such rapid promotion. To find himself elevated to first and only lieutenant was bad enough, but to have command, however temporary, devolved upon him so suddenly was clearly beyond the computations of his ambition.

'But, sir, if I went in the boats . . .'

'If you went in the boats I would have no one to take *Andromeda* home, Mr Jameson. And if I am not back by midnight that is exactly what I wish you to do. Here is my written order.' He handed the reluctant Jameson a scribbled paper. 'Captain Pardoe would never forgive me for losing *all* his officers.' The bitter joke twitched a responsive smile out of the young officer. 'This is a desperate matter, Mr Jameson, one that I cannot, in all conscience, delegate to you. Should I not return on time, I wish you good luck.'

Jameson accepted the inevitable with a nod. In reality Drinkwater had abandoned reasons of state in prosecuting this last attack personally. Rather, a desire for vengeance inspired him – that, or a wish to die himself.

He had thought vaguely of Elizabeth and the children and the handful of Suffolk acres that gave him the status of a country gentleman, but they were so far away, existing in another world, that he doubted their reality at all. They were a sham, an illusion, a carrot to dangle before him. Besides, return meant also the assumption of responsibility for Huke's mother and sister, Catriona Quilhampton and her child . . .

He thrust such considerations aside. He had forfeited all claim upon the smiles of providence when, in a storm of passion, he had lain with the American widow. He had proved himself no better than the next man and could claim no especial privilege. All he could do now was to stake his own life as a tribute to the dead. They left almost unnoticed, clambering down into the boats while Birkbeck supervised *Andromeda*'s toiling company as they disentangled the shot-away spars, cleared away the raffle of fallen gear and salvaged what could be reused.

The men who had volunteered for Drinkwater's forlorn hope took their places at the oars. The looms were wrapped in rags and slushed with tallow or grease where they passed the crutches and thole pins. In every spare space the small barricoes of powder, jars of oil and impregnated rags lay in baskets. In the stern sheets, alongside the boat compasses and in two tinplate boxes in which officers usually kept their best hats, slow matches glowed. The tin boxes bore the names *Huke* and *Mosse*.

'Give way.'

'Give way.'

The boats drew away from the ship, paused while Drinkwater and Frey conferred over their respective compass headings, and then settled down to the rhythmic labours of the oarsmen.

Drinkwater had no intention of trying to run straight into the anchorage. The vagaries of the compasses, particularly in these high latitudes, and the risks of being detected dissuaded him. He knew this was a last chance, knew too that once Captain Dahlgaard had discharged the remainder of his cargo and the fog had cleared, *Odin* would set off in pursuit of the British frigate.

Instead, he had laid off a course which would take them beyond the bay, striking the coast north of the anchorage. This would allow them to drop back along the shore towards the enemy, encountering the American ships first. Dahlgaard, he argued, would be as exhausted as he was himself and preoccupied by completing the transfer of the shipment of arms and equipment, refitting his ship and preparing for sea. At the very least, Drinkwater's attack of the previous afternoon must have incommoded this plan to a degree. Frey had mentioned the *Odin*'s loss of her fore and mainmasts, and he himself thought the mizen had been shot away earlier.

As the boats glided over the still waters of the fiord, these considerations obsessed Drinkwater. Beside him Wells sat attentively, watching the man in the bow who held the end of a length of spun yarn. The other end was held in the hand of a bowman in Frey's boat, so that, paying out and heaving in, as the boats made small variations from their rhumb-lines, they kept in contact. At first it proved awkward and cumbersome, but after ten minutes or so, the men settled to their strokes and, just in sight of each other most of the time, they pulled along in line abreast.

Drinkwater had given orders for the strictest silence to be maintained in the boats and after an hour's hard work, in a brief clearing in the fog, he waved at Frey. Both boats ceased rowing and, with the oars drawn across the gunwales, they ran alongside, willing hands preventing them from coming into contact. Astern of Drinkwater's boat the empty gig ran up under their transom and Wells put out a hand to prevent it colliding.

'Rum, I think, Mr Frey,' Drinkwater murmured in a low voice, and was gratified to see the men grin. Volunteers they might be, but they brought with them no guarantee of success.

'No more than another mile, by my reckoning.'

Frey nodded, and Drinkwater noted the high colour of his cheeks. It was probably the effect of the damp chill, he concluded, munching on a biscuit and sipping at a small pewter beaker of rum.

Resting in silence they all heard the noise, a regular knock-knock, as of oars.

'Guard-boat,' whispered Drinkwater, hoping to Almighty God it was not an expedition bound on a reciprocal mission to their own ships. They listened a little longer. Drinkwater thought he heard background noises of men speaking, and of them labouring at some task, but dismissed them as wishful thinking. They sat still as the sound died away, the men shivering as the fog chilled their sweat-sodden bodies.

'Let's be getting on, then,' he ordered quietly, and the boats were shoved apart, the oars pushed out and the first strokes taken.

A few minutes later, with the spun-yarn umbilical between them, they had taken up their former stations. Only the chuckle of water under the bows of the three boats and the dip and gentle splash of the oars marked their progress.

Their arrival was less well organized, for the loom of smooth boulders ahead of Frey's boat caused her coxswain to put his tiller over and she ran aboard her sister with a clatter and an outbreak of muffled invective. Then the towed cutter ran up astern and struck Drinkwater's boat with a second thud, so that the ensuing confusion took a moment or two to subside.

Frey's boat edged ahead and found a second boulder and then a steep shingle beach which rose swiftly to a gloomy forest of pine and fir. They ran the boats aground and Drinkwater ordered them all ashore. While the men relieved themselves, Drinkwater checked the slow matches. The foggy damp and the need for silence had dissuaded him from any ideas of striking flint and steel. Happily, the matches still burned.

Satisfied that he could do no more, Drinkwater strode off to ease himself. Above the smooth stones of the beach, the ground grew soft with fallen needles and the air smelt deliciously of resin. Outcrops of rock broke through here and there, and were fronded with ferns, but an awesome and sinister stillness pervaded the forest, and he was glad to retreat to the water's edge, where the men talked in low voices.

'Silence now.' The babble died down and, when all were reassembled, Drinkwater asked quietly, 'Any questions?' There was a general shaking of heads.

'Back into the boats. Line ahead, Mr Frey.'

Frey's boat led, out beyond the rocks then turning to starboard, edging along the shoreline. From time to time they had to shorten oars, even trail them, as they glided between the massive boulders that, smoothed by ice and water, had been cast aside as glacial moraine thousands of years before.

As they worked their way south-west, Drinkwater gradually became aware that he could see the shore and the dark shapes of the trees more and more clearly. Their tops moved languidly in the beginnings of a breeze, no longer grey monotones, but assuming the dark and variegated greens of which he knew them to be composed. The fog was lifting.

Then, almost it seemed in the sky itself, the topgallant yards of the first ship appeared above them. It was the American privateer anchored closest inshore.

Ahead of them Frey, whose boat still ghosted through the clammy vapour, had seen this apparition and altered course towards it. With a surge of jubilation, Drinkwater realized that though the fog was dispersing, the shift of wind which caused it had merely altered the relative balance of nature. He had seen sea-smoke in the Arctic years before, and now his boat pulled happily through it as it clung to the surface, rising no more than ten or fifteen feet, exposing the top-hamper of the enemy while concealing their own approach.

He made a gesture to Wells and the coxswain leaned on the tiller. Drinkwater's boat pulled out to pass Frey and edge round the enemy, clear of her and obscured by the low fog. They could see the grey loom of the American ship and then lost sight of Frey as his boat dropped alongside and merged with her.

From on board he could distinctly hear a voice sing out, 'Lower all, handsomely! Avast! Come up!' The accent was unmistakably American and Drinkwater was immeasurably encouraged by this, for they were clearly still loading cargo.

Drinkwater felt his own sleeve being plucked and swung round. Wells was pointing ahead, to where the next ship was looming. Her hull seemed more distinct, the sea-smoke less dense. An empty boat lay under her stern davits, and a rope ladder dangled invitingly down from an open stern window. As they closed it, they could see the boat was picked out in white and blue, with some fancy gold gingerbread work along her quarters. Beneath the windows the privateer's name was carved, gold letters on a blue background: *General Wayne.*

Without a word, the coxswain ran alongside, the bowman caught the painter round a thwart on the enemy boat and several oarsmen manoeuvred the trailing cutter alongside their own unengaged side.

A moment later two men were swarming up the ladder, the first signalled the cabin was empty and then there was a general scramble as men clambered aboard, helped to lower lines and hoisted the combustible stores they had brought with them. They lifted the inflammables in through the cabin windows. Drinkwater motioned for the barricoes of powder which would form the explosive mines to be rolled towards him and flung back the rich carpet that was spread across the deck of the cabin to reveal the hatchway to the lazarette below. He was crouched beside it when the cabin door suddenly opened. The American commander Drinkwater had last seen aboard the *Odin* stood transfixed in the doorway. The look of insolence he had shown on the former occasion was gone, and now he wore an expression of incomprehension which turned rapidly to alarm.

Drinkwater had had his back to the door as he inspected the hatch. Fitted with a bar and hasp, this would have been padlocked under normal circumstances. But the ship had been in action and the padlock had not been replaced. The carpet, however, had been roughly pulled back over the hatchway with its loose bar and Drinkwater had been in the act of lifting the bar clear when the American had appeared.

Even as the Yankee commander opened his mouth, Drinkwater struck. Twisting with all his strength he straightened his legs, swinging upwards from his crouching position, the bar in his hand. The blunt edge struck the American violently, winding him so that he buckled forward. One of the seamen grabbed him, drew him into the cabin and shut the door.

For a moment not a man moved, but no alarm was raised outside and Drinkwater had his hanger at the man's throat as he gasped for breath.

'Get on with it!' Drinkwater hissed, and the tableau dissolved, the men tearing off the lazarette hatchway and stuffing it and the cabin full with the mines, powder and oil-soaked rags.

Drinkwater bent to the American. 'I'm going to save your life and I'm going to gag you, then you go down into my boat. One false move and you are dead. Do you understand?'

The American commander was still gasping for his breath, but he nodded and Drinkwater grabbed a passing seaman. 'Give me your kerchief. Now, you are to take this man back to the boat . . .'

From somewhere beyond the window a dull thud sounded: Frey's party had either been discovered or had begun their work of destruction.

'Out, you men!'

They seemed to take an interminable time to scramble back through the open stern window. Drinkwater could hear cries of alarm on deck and the pad-pad of running feet. Any moment now and there would be someone reporting to the privateer's commander.

'Ready, sir.' Wells had the hat-box open and the slow-match in his hand. Drinkwater nodded and the match was touched to the first of the three mines. When its fuse was alight, Drinkwater dropped it into the lazarette. 'Get out!' he ordered. 'Get back to the boat!'

The shouting on deck had increased. He took the slow-match and touched it to the protruding fuse of the second mine and rolled it into a mass of rags. The third he had just ignited when the door opened for the second time:

'Cap'n Hughes . . . what the hell . . . ?'

Drinkwater's pistol ball smashed into the man's chest, flinging him backwards, his breastbone broken. Drinkwater threw the weapon after it and made for the window. Below him the men were tumbling into the boat and beyond them there was an orange glow which leached through the last of the fog and grew as he watched. Frey's party had been successful and the American privateer astern of the *General Wayne* was well ablaze.

'Hey! Look!'

The voice came from above, where the *General Wayne*'s people had run aft to see what had happened to their consort and who now, staring down, saw the British seamen climbing out of their own ship and into the strange boats trailing astern.

'The bastards have been aboard of us!' The voices were outraged, surprised and affronted.

'They've been in the bloody cabin!'

'Here, get me a rifle!' Above Drinkwater's head the urgent sound of hurrying footsteps passed to and fro.

'Pass some muskets, quick!'

Drinkwater could see the men settle at their thwarts and Wells looked up at him, his face anxious and expectant. Drinkwater waved his boat away, unwilling to shout and betray his own presence. The coxswain looked nonplussed and Drinkwater made violent, swimming motions. Wells understood; the initial oar strokes of the boat's crew coincided with the report of a musket from the quarterdeck above.

'Another shot and your cap'n's a dead duck!' Wells roared defiantly, his arm round the wild-eyed figure gagged beside him.

'Christ! They've got the cap'n!' an American voice warned.

This last confusion gave Drinkwater the momentary respite he needed. He glanced back into the cabin. The fuses on the mines sizzled, that on the first he had lit must almost have burned through. The last thing he noticed, as he turned back to the window, was the tin hat-box and the name *Thos. Huke* executed in white upon its black-japanned surface.

Climbing on to the window ledge, he dived into the sea.

The water was shockingly, numbingly cold. He surfaced, gasping, and drew a great, reflexive breath. A ball smacked into the water close by, and he struck out wildly. Another raised a short, vicious spurt of water alongside his head and he felt a sharp blow to his arm, but no pain as he plunged on.

Then his tormentors stopped, blown upwards as the first powder-packed barrico exploded and counter-mined the others with a terrific roar, setting the whole after part of the *General Wayne* ablaze. Dully, he realized what had happened and rolled over on to his back.

The stern of the American privateer appeared in black silhouette against the blaze. He could see the apertures of the stern windows within which the fire rapidly became an inferno. The mines had blown the decks upwards and flames shot skywards, licking hungrily at the mizen rigging, taking hold, then racing aloft. Around the stern dark objects of debris, animate and inanimate, fell into the cold and crystal waters of the fiord.

He turned away. To his left the other privateer was on fire, sparks and cinders rising rapidly from her as the flames, little yellow flickers at first, grew redder in their intensity as they rose up her rigging. It was like some over-blown and monstrous firework display. The neat and ordered lines of the rigging were displayed to perfection by the racing flames, holding their accustomed pattern for one brilliant, incandescent instant, and then falling away in ashen dissolution.

He no longer felt cold. Somewhere to his right he could hear English voices. One of them called his name. He shouted back.

It was with considerable difficulty that they dragged him shivering into the boat.

He was still shuddering so badly three hours later that he could not level his glass at the burning ships, but fumbled and dropped the telescope. The cold water had struck deep into his body. The damaged muscles of his old shoulder wound ached with breath-taking pain, the scab on his cheek had softened and partly sloughed off. As he warmed through, the enlarging capillaries began to bleed again. Oddly, he felt nothing of the slight flesh wound, where the Yankee musket-ball had galled his arm.

It was almost dark and the fog had gone, but he needed no lens to watch as the two privateers blazed against the sombre background of the forest behind them. He derived no satisfaction from the sight; only a loathing for what he had accomplished.

'You *must* go below, sir,' Kennedy insisted, almost manhandling Drinkwater from his position by the mizen rigging. 'Frey has a rare fever from his wound, and if you don't take care of yourself upon the instant, I cannot answer for the consequences.'

Drinkwater submitted, and allowed himself to be led off.

'We have neither the men nor the boats to tow out through the narrows,' he heard Birkbeck saying as he stumbled below, leaning on Kennedy's shoulder.

And the words mocked his success as Kennedy and Templeton wrapped him in warmed blankets and plied him with hot molasses.

Chapter Fifteen *November 1813*

The Fortune of War

Drinkwater had no idea how long he slept, only that when he was woken he regretted it, that Jameson's face was strange to him, and he wished to be left alone. He closed his eyes, seeking again the oblivion of sleep.

'Sir, you must wake up! Sir!'

Jameson shook the cot. It made Drinkwater's head ache and with the acknowledgement of pain came memory. He shook off the luxury of oblivion.

'What is the matter?'

'The Danish frigate, sir, the *Odin*, she is under weigh!'

Drinkwater frowned. 'Where is the wind?'

'In the north, sir.'

'The north!' Drinkwater flung his legs over the edge of the cot and realized he was completely naked. Jameson averted his eyes.

'What o'clock is it?'

'Four bells, morning watch.'

Ten in the morning! He had slept the clock round and more! Why had they not woken him? What had they been doing? 'Pass word for my servant and then you had better beat to quarters. We shall have a battle this morning.'

But Jameson had gone and he was talking to himself.

The two frigates presented an odd sight as they stood down the fiord, both heading for the narrows and the open sea beyond. But this was a deceit, for neither could leave the other behind; the honour of their respective flags denied them this escape, so their almost parallel courses converged slightly, to a point of intersection some half a mile before the gorge, where the matter between them must be decided.

Their unusual aspect was caused by the mutual damage they

had suffered and inflicted. It was some consolation to the watching Drinkwater that he had cut up his opponent so badly, for she bore no mizen topsail, her aftermost mast supporting a much-reduced and extemporized spanker, and although her main and foremasts bore topsails, that on the foremost was a diminutive, a former topgallant. Clearly the *Odin* possessed insufficient spars to replace all her losses. Drinkwater shut his glass with a decisive snap and summoned Jameson and Birkbeck. They conferred in a huddle beside the starboard hance.

'We have one opportunity, gentlemen. Our lack of manpower . . . well, I have no need to emphasize our disadvantages. I shall exchange fire and run directly aboard him. He has the weather gauge, but with that rig he will find it impossible to draw ahead of us. Mr Birkbeck, you will remain on the quarterdeck and handle the ship. Mr Jameson the starboard battery. I will lead the boarders. The topmen are to grapple, then seize us yard-arm to yard-arm. The matter will be decided on her deck. Very good. To your posts and good fortune.'

Drinkwater turned away. 'Sergeant Danks?'

The marine sergeant hurried over and Drinkwater explained his intentions. 'Volley fire as we approach, then, when we close, let the men fire independently. When I give the order to board, half your fellows are to follow me, you are to remain on board in command of the rest and cover our retreat if we are driven back. Understand?'

'Aye, sir. Odds will follow you, evens stay with me.'

'And tell the men in the tops to mind their aim. Fire ahead of us, not into our backs!'

'Aye, aye, sir.'

Danks went off and Drinkwater studied his enemy again. His fears on waking had been unjustified, for he had come on deck flurried and anxious to find Birkbeck had the matter in hand, his re-rigging as complete as skill and artifice could make it and the anchor a-trip.

'I told you, sir,' Birkbeck had said when Drinkwater complimented him, 'I am quite keen to get home all in one piece.'

They had been under weigh within moments of Drinkwater's appearance on deck and now the two frigates were running neck and neck, *Andromeda* drawing slightly ahead.

'That'll change when we fall under her lee,' Drinkwater muttered to himself.

'What will? Our speed?'

He looked round to find Frey beside him. The young lieutenant had been at some pains to repair the ravages of battle to his uniform.

'I heard there was to be an action, sir.'

'Yes, but you are not fit . . . What about your wound? Your fever?'

'I'm as fit as you, sir,' Frey said quietly. He looked astern. 'What happened to *Kestrel*?'

Drinkwater regarded his young colleague and their eyes met. There was the glitter of resolution in Frey's and Drinkwater sighed, then smiled.

'A master's mate named Ashley volunteered to bring her in with a prize crew. He's on our larboard beam.'

Frey craned round and saw the man-of-war cutter. 'Ah, yes. I wonder what their chances are?'

'Less than fifty-fifty.'

Drinkwater did not say that he would never have let Ashley go had not the odds against their own survival been considerably shorter. Ashley carried a hurriedly written report of proceedings and a secret, enciphered dispatch. Both had been prepared by Templeton at Drinkwater's dictation while he had dressed.

Drinkwater looked at Frey. 'Very well. Do you keep an eye on things here. I'm going to take a turn below.'

He descended to the gloom of the gun deck. The gunners were, to a man, gathered about their cannon, staring at the enemy through the open ports. Behind the guns the powder-monkeys crouched, trying to see between the men. Standing at the bottom of the ladder, Drinkwater was struck by the lack of numbers. The larboard guns were almost unmanned. Shackled amidships were the chained American prisoners. Drinkwater had quite forgotten them. His memory seemed, these days, to be fickle in the extreme.

Further forward, beside the mainmast, Lieutenant Jameson was studying the enemy and haranguing his men.

'He's going to open fire any moment, my lads. When he does I want him to feel the weight of our metal in one blow.'

A murmur of appreciation greeted this speech. Someone forward, in the eyes of the ship, cracked a joke, and Drinkwater heard the expressions of mirth roll aft.

'Make 'em eat shit, Jamie!' another called, and a good-natured laugh broke out again.

'No, no,' Jameson called, never taking his eyes off the enemy. ''Tis too soft.'

The filthy jests went on, bolstering their courage. This was a Jameson Drinkwater had never met, but would be glad of in the coming hour. He abandoned any thought of addressing these men and made to return to the quarterdeck. The sudden movement attracted attention. Midshipman Fisher saw him and touched the brim of his ridiculous hat. Others caught sight of their captain and the whisper of his presence passed along the line of guns like a gust of wind through the tops of fir trees. Jameson became aware of it and straightened up.

'Don't let me distract you, Mr Jameson, I merely came to satisfy myself that you were ready,' he called.

'We're ready, sir, aren't we, my lads?'

'Aye, we're ready!' They broke out into a cheer. It was foolish; it was utterly beyond reason and it was pitifully affecting. Drinkwater stood stupid with emotion and, although stoop-shouldered beneath the beams, he raised his damaged hat in solemn salutation. Then he turned and ascended into sunshine as the cheers of the gunners below followed him.

The noise was taken up on the upper deck. The men at the forecastle guns, those mustered at the mast and pinrails and stationed on the quarterdeck at the carronades and the wheel, began to cheer.

He let them be, let their enthusiasm subside naturally and, walking to the ship's side, wiped the moisture from his eyes as unobtrusively as possible. He was a damned ninny to be seduced by such stupidity, but he could not prevent himself from feeling moved.

Sniffing, he looked again at the enemy; she was much closer now.

The line of the *Odin*'s opened gun-ports suddenly sparkled, then faded from view, obscured by the smoke from her broadside. Shot whined overhead, fell short or thudded into their side before the sound rolled down upon them.

He heard Jameson's order and *Andromeda* shook to the simultaneous discharge of her own battery. Plumes of spray rose up along *Odin*'s waterline and a cannonade which was to last for twenty long minutes began.

Shot smacked home, the faint trembling of the hull betraying a ball burying itself in the frigate's stout oak sides; ropes parted aloft; more holes appeared in the already tattered sails with an odd, sucking plop; explosions of splinters lanced the deck and the hot breath of cannon shot made them gasp. The business of dying began again; men screamed and were taken below.

'I believe you're boarding, sir.'

'What?' Distracted, Drinkwater looked round to see Templeton beside him.

'I understand it is your intention to board the *Odin*.'

'Yes.'

'It is my intention to accompany you.'

'The devil it is . . .'

Drinkwater looked at the clerk. Was he pot-valiant? Drinkwater could smell no liquor on his breath, and Templeton winced as the starboard battery fired again. Templeton had not occupied much of Drinkwater's time or attention during the last fortnight. He had been summoned when required, which had not proved often, and for the most part had been left to his own devices and desires. He looked somehow strange, different from the man who had stood in his room in the Admiralty, but then Quilhampton was dead and Frey was a changed man; so, he supposed, was he. If Templeton wished to prove himself it was his own affair, and who was Drinkwater to judge him for taking a nip to fortify his nerves?

'Very well, Mr Templeton, if that is what you wish. I should have sent you with Ashley in the *Kestrel*, but I shall be glad of all the support I can get.'

'Thank you.' Templeton moved away and stood by the mizen mast, selecting a boarding pike from the rack. Six feet away a ball from the *Odin* crashed into the bulwark between two larboard carronades and a spray of musketry spattered aboard, killing a marine and wounding a gunner. Drinkwater saw Templeton jerk with involuntary reaction.

The distance between the two ships was closing rapidly now. It must have been obvious to Dahlgaard what Drinkwater intended, but the Danish captain made no attempt to draw off and pound his weaker opponent.

'Edge closer, Mr Birkbeck, then go at her with a run, we're falling under her lee!'

Shot thumped into *Andromeda*'s planking and the enemy's

upperdeck cannon belched langridge at them. The iron hail swept whistling aboard, taking Drinkwater's second hat from his head. He drew his hanger. He was conscious now of only one burning desire, to end this madness in the catharsis of a greater insanity.

'Now, Birkbeck! Now!'

Andromeda was losing ground quickly as the *Odin* masked her from the wind, but Birkbeck had the measure of the situation and put the helm up the instant the guns had fired a broadside. The British ship swung to starboard with a slow and magnificent grace. Her bowsprit rode over the Dane's waist and the dolphin striker lodged itself in the *Odin*'s main chains. The impetus of the *Odin* caught the lighter ship and drew her alongside, so the first impact of the collision was followed by a slewing of the deck; then the two ships ground together, locked in mortal combat, a tangle of yards and hooked braces aloft, their guns muzzle to muzzle below.

From the corner of his eye Drinkwater caught a glimpse of a grapnel snaking out as he clambered up on the rail and stepped over the hammock netting. Other men were gathering, anticipating his order:

'Boarders away!'

He could never afterwards remember those few vulnerable seconds as he scrambled aboard the *Odin*, beyond realizing that the Danish frigate had two feet more freeboard than her adversary and he had to climb upwards. It was always something of a mystery as to why the defenders of a ship did not find it easy to repel attackers coming aboard in so haphazard a manner. A mystery, that is, until one considered the encumbrance of the hammock netting which was designed to form a breastwork behind which sharpshooters could be stationed, but which almost perfectly masked an attack made up the ship's side.

Sometimes a ship would hoist boarding nettings, but neither had done so, perhaps each to facilitate their own attacks. Astride the *Odin*'s hammock netting Drinkwater discharged his pistol into the face of a Danish marine, then leaned down and thrust his hanger at a gunner waving a pike. The pike ripped his sleeve and, gripping the hammocks with his legs as though on horseback, he jabbed the discharged pistol barrel into the man's eye. As his victim fell back, Drinkwater stood, swung both legs over the netting and, grabbing a mizen shroud with his left hand, slashed a swathe with his sword and jumped down on to the *Odin*'s deck in the space thus provided.

Other men tumbled all about him, a 'veritable cascade of seamen and marines', he afterwards wrote in his full report of proceedings, Templeton among them, keening in a curious, high-pitched squeal as he cut dangerously left and right with his sword.

''Ere, watch it, Mr Templeton,' somebody sung out, clear above the howls of rage and the screams of the dying.

Drinkwater engaged a second Danish marine, cut at the man's forearm and winged him, advanced a half step and grasped the musket's muzzle, ducking under the bayonet and jabbing his hanger at the soldier's stomach. The man cried out, though his voice was lost in the general bedlam and Drinkwater was conscious only of the gape of his mouth. The musket dropped between them, Drinkwater withdrew and slashed down at the marine's shoulder as he fell, parried a pike and felt the flat of a cutlass across his back.

He half-turned as the weapon was thrust again, flicked his own hanger and pricked the seaman's hand as he lunged with the clumsy cutlass. The severed tendons cost the man his grip. Drinkwater grunted with the speed of his response, raised his sword-point and, as though with a foil, extended and withdrew. Blood ran down the hapless sailor's face and his breath whistled through his perforated cheek as he fell back.

A musket or pistol was discharged close to him. Drinkwater felt the fierce heat from its muzzle and a stinging sensation in his ear. He cut right, parried a sword thrust and bound the blade; bellowed as he thrust it aside and slid forward, driving his sword home to the hilt in the soft abdomen of a man he had barely seen in the press of bodies.

He was conscious of an officer, of two officers, threatening him from the front in defiant postures. He was running short of wind, but Templeton was on his right and he shrieked, 'Here, Templeton, to me!'

Drinkwater engaged, crossed swords and felt the Danish officer press his blade. Drinkwater disengaged with a smart cutover, but was thwarted as the Danish officer changed his guard. Drinkwater dropped his point and reverted to his original line, extending without lunging. The Dane grinned as he parried high and extended himself. Drinkwater was drawing his breath with difficulty now, he ducked clumsily and fell back, expecting a swift *reprise*, but the Dane would not be drawn and stood grinning at the panting Drinkwater.

Drinkwater's puzzlement was brief. On his flank Templeton was whirring his blade with such fanatic energy that his opponent was confused, or would not be drawn, and maintained a defensive position.

Then, in the hubbub and confusion, Drinkwater realized, drawing breath in the brief and timely lull, that the two officers were defending a man seated behind them in a chair.

It was Dahlgaard and he was pale as death, a pair of pistols in his lap.

'Captain Dahlgaard!' Drinkwater shouted, 'I see you are wounded! You can do no more! Surrender, sir! Strike your flag and stop this madness!'

'No!'

The officer from whom Drinkwater had just escaped howled his commander's defiance.

Drinkwater fell back a step. Templeton had drawn off and suddenly pulled a pistol from his belt. He fired at the officer he had been fighting and, as the Danish lieutenant fell, he stepped quickly forward and thrust savagely at Dahlgaard.

The officer who had defied Drinkwater's call to surrender, seeing what was happening, made to strike Templeton but lost his balance.

Drinkwater was on him, lunging forward with such speed that he, too, lost his footing and slammed into the Dane, his hanger blade snapping as he drove it home.

As Drinkwater fell to his knees something struck him on the shoulder. The blow was not hard. He sat back on his haunches and looked up into Dahlgaard's face. The Danish captain's eyes were cloudy with pain, his face wet with perspiration. Blood ran from the new wound Templeton had inflicted in his upper arm. Between these two men, instigators of the carnage all about them, Dahlgaard's young lieutenant was pinioned to the deck by Drinkwater's broken sword-blade.

Breathing in gulps, Drinkwater realized the injured Dahlgaard had struck him with one of his pistols. It had already been fired.

'I strike my flag,' Dahlgaard called, his voice rasping with agony.

'You surrender?' Drinkwater gasped, uncertain.

Dahlgaard nodded. '*Ja, ja*, I strike.' The Dane closed his eyes.

'They strike!' shrieked Templeton. 'They strike! They strike!' And heady with victory Templeton ran aft to cut the halliard of the Danish ensign.

Wearily Drinkwater heaved himself to his feet. He felt the madness ebb, heard the cheering as though it came from a great way away. He was sodden with sweat and breathing with difficulty. Lightly he placed his hand on Dahlgaard's shoulder.

' 'Tis the fortune of war, Captain Dahlgaard, the fortune of war.'

Dahlgaard opened his eyes and stared up at Drinkwater, blinking. 'He was my sister's son, Kaptajn Drinkwater, my sister's only son . . .'

And Drinkwater looked down at the body which lay between them, oblivious of Templeton who bent over the *Odin*'s taffrail, the blood-red and white Danish colours draped about him, vomiting into the sea below and weeping in a rage at his own survival.

Chapter Sixteen *November 1813*

To the Victor, the Spoils

Lieutenant Frey climbed wearily out of the boat, up the frigate's tumblehome and over the rail on to Andromeda's quarterdeck.

'The Captain's in the cabin, Frey, and asked if you would report when you arrived.'

Frey nodded to Lieutenant Jameson and went below. He found Drinkwater sitting having a dressing changed on his arm by the surgeon.

'Help yourself to a glass, Mr Frey, you look quite done in.'

'He still has a fever,' put in Kennedy.

'I'm fine, Kennedy, just a little tired.'

'Who isn't . . . ?'

'I didn't know you had been hit, sir,' Frey said quickly, restoppering the decanter.

'It's nothing. A scratch. A Yankee galled me as I swam away from the *General Wayne*. My exertions yesterday reopened it . . .'

'It needed debriding', said Kennedy severely, 'before it became gangrenous. Your face is a mess, too; you'll likely have a scar.'

'Stop clucking, Mr Kennedy. Thanks to your superlative skill, I will mend,' said Drinkwater, silencing the surgeon. 'Now, Frey, tell me about your expedition, what of the two Americans?'

'The *General Wayne* burned to the waterline and settled where she lay. The other, the *Hyacinthe* – a French-built corvette – drifted ashore after her cable burnt through and then blew up. Her remains continued to burn until there was little left of her, or her contents. As for the matter of the truce, I had no trouble in landing my party. The commandant of the fort, a Captain Nilsen, or some such, is making ready to receive the wounded from the *Odin*. He was especially solicitous for Captain Dahlgaard. I understand they are related in some way.'

Drinkwater recalled Dahlgaard's dead nephew and dismissed the morbid thought. 'And you mentioned the *Kestrel*?'

'Yes. They seemed relieved not to have been entirely deprived of a means of communication with Bergen, or Copenhagen for that matter. I formed the impression that the Americans are an acute embarrassment to them.'

'I am truly sorry for the Danes,' Drinkwater said. 'Captain Dahlgaard was a most gallant officer . . .'

Kennedy sniffed disparagingly at this assertion. Drinkwater ignored the man's infuriating importunity.

'And what arrangements have you concluded?'

'That all the Danes are to be landed and that we hand over the *Kestrel* immediately prior to our departure. A truce is to obtain until we are seaward of the narrows, thereafter they may communicate with Bergen.'

'Very well. In the circumstances we must count that as satisfactory. Captain Dahlgaard may be sent ashore as soon as is possible.'

'I took the liberty of permitting the one launch left to the Americans to pull out immediately and take off the worst of the wounded.'

Drinkwater nodded. 'That was well done. Birkbeck has completed his survey of *Kestrel* and has condemned her as totally unfit for further service. Properly we should destroy her, but I do not think their Lordships will judge us too harshly for leaving this place with a measure of magnanimity towards our beaten foe.'

Kennedy sniffed again as he completed his work.

'Physician, I suggest you heal yourself', said Drinkwater, 'instead of making that ridiculous noise.' Kennedy scowled as he added, 'Thank you for your solicitude.'

Frey watched the surgeon leave and turned to Drinkwater. 'Sir, there is a matter of considerable importance I have to discuss with you . . .'

'If it is to do with a prize-crew . . .'

'No, no! Though I should like to know what arrangements you are intending.'

'You will take the *Odin* home. We will stay in company and make for Rattray Head, thereafter I will signal Leith, or London, depending upon the circumstances. But come, what is this matter of such importance?'

'Gold specie, sir.'

Frey breathed the words with a quiet satisfaction, as though not daring to frighten them away. Comprehension dawned slowly on Drinkwater.

'Aboard the *Odin*?'

Frey nodded conspiratorially. 'I was in a lather of apprehension whilst I was away, but it is quite safe. Captain Dahlgaard had made especial provision for it and I do not think many of his people knew. It was in a small lazarette below his cabin . . .'

'And had, I think, come out of a similar lazarette in the *General Wayne*,' said Drinkwater, remembering the empty space into which he had rolled the little barrels with their lethal filling of fine-milled black powder. 'But how did you come by it?'

'When we boarded and you attacked aft,' Frey explained, 'my party went for the wheel and then the gun deck. I had hoped to take the gunners in the rear, but too few of our fellows followed me. Most of the Danes on the upper deck fell back on their quarterdeck and we got below without encountering much resistance. The gun deck was reeking with smoke and we got the hatches down amidships and aft before, I think, anyone was aware of our presence. When I secured the after hatch to prevent anyone coming up from below, we were seen and set on by the aftermost gun crews. There were about a dozen men with me at that time including Fisher and we had a hard few moments of it, being hopelessly outnumbered and totally unsupported.' Drinkwater could imagine the scene: the noise and confusion; the Danish gunners blazing away, half-deafened, the gun deck full of smoke and then someone spotting the strange intruders.

'Go on,' he said.

'It was curious, but the Danes had left the after bulkhead down. Fisher got the cabin door open and we retreated into Dahlgaard's quarters, leaving four of our number outside. None of the after guns in there were manned . . .'

'Well I'm damned! I never noticed, but forgive me; do go on.'

'Dahlgaard had emptied the cabin space of furniture, though, and it struck me that there was a reason why he had not completely cleared the after part of the ship for action. At the time I gave it no further thought, beyond welcoming the respite, expecting the Danes to burst through the flimsy door at any moment. In fact the fire beyond the bulkhead slackened and then ceased. A few minutes later, things having fallen silent, we ventured out to find the ship had struck her colours. I think those men who were not still at the guns had been called away to defend the upper deck just at the point when you gained the upper hand.'

'Go on.'

'After you left me prize-master I posted guards and went back into the cabin to seize the ship's papers. Dahlgaard had left a bunch of keys, a pair of pistols, a telescope and a number of other articles one would have supposed he ought to have had disposed about his person. I found them on the stern settee. I tried the keys and found they fitted the usual lockers and also a lazarette hatch. I think Dahlgaard underestimated us, sir, thought he could dispense with the aftermost guns in order to preserve intact what lay below his cabin.'

'The specie?'

'Yes. A dozen chests of it. Gold ingots . . . I have no idea how many.'

'And you placed a guard on it?'

'Mr Fisher. I locked the poor fellow in. I have just been aboard, before reporting to you. He is all right; he stuck to his post after I impressed the importance of it upon him, though he is very hungry.'

'Does he know what he is guarding?'

Frey shook his head. 'No, not exactly; only that it is important.'

'Twelve-year-old boys take much for granted, including the presumed wisdom of their elders, I'm glad to say. And the Danes made no attempt to regain it, not even during your negotiations?'

Frey shook his head. 'No. I thought better than to draw their attention to it.'

'Quite.' Drinkwater frowned, then said, 'Perhaps Dahlgaard and his lieutenants were the only ones to know of it, and I suppose the Americans themselves may well have physically shifted the stuff. The fact that it was concealed in wooden boxes would have prevented all but a few officers from knowing its true nature. It would also explain the protracted length of time taken to tranship that cargo. I imagine Dahlgaard insisted the Americans surrender the gold before he released the arms. There was certainly much toing and froing between the ships, and the *Odin* would have been stuffed with the arms shipment. Her crew must have been heartily sick of having their freedom impeded by so much cargo.'

Frey looked puzzled. 'I'm sorry, Frey,' Drinkwater added, 'you ain't party to all the ramifications of this business. I will tell you all about it when we anchor in British waters.' Drinkwater smiled wanly. 'You'll have to possess your soul in patience until then, but suffice it to say the Danes were only acting as carriers, which may explain their indifference to the gold's fate. It was destined for Paris, not Copenhagen.'

'Ah, I see. Payment from the Yankees to the French for the arms being shipped into the American privateers.'

'Exactly so.'

'And kept damn quiet by those Danish officers in the know.'

'Yes.'

'I imagine there can be few of them left,' Frey said, 'judging by the carnage on deck.'

'No.' Both men were briefly silent, then Drinkwater returned to the matter in hand. 'You had better take Danks and four marines with you as a special guard. Keep Fisher, take Ashley and pick your prize crew, sixty men. We will weigh as soon as possible. Rattray Head is to be the rendezvous.'

'You don't wish to tranship the specie aboard here, sir?'

Drinkwater shook his head again. 'No. The fewer people who know about it the better. It is safe enough in your hands. Besides, I don't want to wait a moment longer.' His last sentence was an excuse. The truth was, there was something obscene about the thought of tucking the gold under his own wing.

'I rather think you have made your fortune, sir.'

Drinkwater shook his head again. 'I doubt it. I'll lay a guinea on it becoming a droit of Admiralty, Mr Frey, but you may at least have the commission for carrying it.'

And a brief gleam of avarice came into Frey's eyes, the first manifestation of mundane emotion since he had announced the death of James Quilhampton.

Mr Templeton looked up at the figure silhouetted against the battered remains of the stern windows. The seated clerk was shivering with cold and persistently glanced at the blanket forming an inadequate barrier to the open air which whistled with a mournful moan through the shot-holes in *Andromeda*'s starboard quarter.

Captain Drinkwater's silence grew longer, past the point of mere reflection and into an admission of abstraction. Templeton coughed intrusively. Drinkwater started and looked round.

'Ah . . . yes . . . Read what you have written, Templeton,' Drinkwater commanded.

'To the Secretary, and so on and so forth,' Templeton began, then settled to read: 'Sir, I have the honour to report . . .'

Head bent and stoop-shouldered beneath the deckhead beams, his hands clasped behind his back, Drinkwater paced ruminatively up and down the shattered cabin as Templeton's voice droned on through the account of the past weeks. He was compelled to live through those last hours in Quilhampton's company and forced to recreate from the spare words of his report the frightful minutes crawling through the hold in search of Malaburn. Finally Templeton concluded the details of the final action which culminated in the capture of the *Odin* as a prize of war.

'. . . And having, subsequent to a survey by Mr Jonathan Birkbeck, Master, condemned the *Kestrel*, cutter, as unfit for further service, her stores and guns having been removed out of her, she was, by my order, turned over to the enemy as an act of humanity in order that communication might be opened with Bergen and the removal of the wounded to that place be effected.

'Having taken in my charge the former Danish frigate *Odin* and placed on board a prize crew, Lieutenant Frey in command, the said *Odin* did weigh and proceed in company with HBM Frigate *Andromeda*, leaving the Vikkenfiord shortly before dark . . .'

'Very well. Add the date.' Drinkwater paused while Templeton scratched.

'Is that all for the time being, sir?'

Drinkwater had yet to account for the dead, to write their collective and official epitaph.

'Yes, for the time being. It is getting dark.'

'The evenings draw in swiftly in these high latitudes, sir.'

'Yes,' Drinkwater replied abstractedly. 'It is time we were gone, while this favourable breeze holds.'

'Mr Birkbeck says the glass stands very high and the northerly wind will persist for many days.'

'Does he now?' Drinkwater looked at Templeton as if seeing him for the first time in weeks. Templeton was not usually prone to such abject ingratiation. 'You are taking an uncommon interest in nautical matters, Mr Templeton.'

'Sir?'

The sarcasm struck Templeton like a whip and he turned his

face away, but not before Drinkwater had seen the unaccountable effect his words had had. Nor could Templeton disguise the withdrawing from his sleeve of a pocket handkerchief.

Drinkwater was about to speak, then held his peace. He had been too hard on a man not inured to the fatigue of battle. A man of Templeton's sensibilities might receive hidden wounds, wounds of the mind, from the events of the last few days. For a moment Drinkwater looked at his clerk, remembering the rather supercilious man who had brought the news of Bardolini's landing that night at the Admiralty. Drinkwater felt the stirrings of guilt for, had he not insisted that Templeton sail aboard *Andromeda*, the wretched fellow might never have been subjected to the rigours of active service.

They had gone through much since, much that should have brought them closer, but Drinkwater felt a constraint between them; they no longer enjoyed that intimacy of communication which had marked their relationship in London. Something between them had diminished and failed to withstand the manifold pressures of life at sea. Perhaps it was merely the distance imposed by the isolation of his rank, and yet Drinkwater felt it was something more subtle. And with the thought, Drinkwater realized he felt an intuitive dislike of Templeton.

The dull boom of a gun, followed by another, echoed across the water. It was the agreed signal that Frey was ready to weigh, though it made Templeton start with a jerk.

'That is all for now, Mr Templeton.' Drinkwater watched the clerk shuffle unhappily forward, blowing his nose, bearing his own weight of guilt and grief.

Drinkwater threw his cloak about his shoulders, clamped his damaged hat upon his head and went on deck. He could not dismiss the unease he felt about Templeton, aware of his own part in the clerk's transformation. Something had altered the man himself, and Drinkwater felt an instinctive wariness towards him. It was a conviction that was to grow stronger in the following days.

The two ships stood down the fiord in line ahead, the symmetry of their sail-plans wrecked by battle. *Andromeda*'s jibboom was shortened from her impact with the *Odin*, and both frigates bore an odd assortment of topsails on a variegated jumble of jury-rigged spars.

Already the high bluff with its fort and the burnt-out wrecks of the two American privateers had faded in the distance. They seemed now to have no existence except in the memory, though Drinkwater wondered how the Danish garrison were coping with the influx of wounded and the encumbrance of numerous Yankee privateersmen. He wondered, too, whether Dahlgaard had survived his wounds, or whether death had claimed him as well as so many others.

On either hand the mountains and forests merged into a dusky monotone, and the waters of the fiord, though stirred by the breeze, were the colour of lead. Even the pale strakes of their gun decks, yellow on *Andromeda* and buff on *Odin*, were leached of any hue; nor were the white ensigns more than fluttering grey shapes at the peaks of the twin spankers, for Drinkwater had forbidden *Odin* to fly her colours superior to those of Denmark while they remained in Norwegian waters.

'I dislike gloating, Mr Frey. You may play that fanfare when in a British roadstead, but not before.'

They could judge him superstitious if they liked, but he had tempted fate enough and they had yet many leagues to make good before crowing a triumph.

The shadow of the narrows engulfed them. In the twilight, they moved through an ethereal world; the cliffs seemed insubstantial, dim, almost as though seen in a fog, except that beyond them lay the distant horizon hard against a sky pale with the washed-out afterglow of sunset.

Then, as they cleared the strait and left the Vikkenfiord behind them, as the grey and forbidding coast began to fall back on either side and the vast ocean opened about them, they saw the last rays of the setting sun strike the mountain summits astern. It was, Drinkwater recalled, how they had first spied them. For a moment it seemed as though the very sky had caught fire, for the jagged, snow-encrusted peaks flashed against the coming night, then vanished, as the western rim of the world threw its shadow into the firmament.

Drinkwater turned from contemplating this marvel and swallowed hard. Birkbeck came towards him.

'Course set sou'west by south, sir. Should take us clear of Utsira before dawn.'

'I hope so, Mr Birkbeck, I hope so.'

' 'Tis a damnable coast, sir, but we've been lucky with the fog. Just the one day.'

'Yes. We've been lucky.'

They stood for a moment, then Birkbeck said, 'I hope you don't mind my saying, sir, but Pardoe would never have done what you did.'

Drinkwater stared blankly at the master. Then he frowned. 'What's that?'

'He'd have drawn off after the first encounter . . .' Seeing the bleak look on Drinkwater's face, Birkbeck faltered.

'Perhaps he would have been the wiser man, Mr Birkbeck,' Drinkwater replied coldly. Had it all been worth it? So many dead: Quilhampton, Mosse, that marine corporal – Wilson, the boatswain's mate Greer and so many, many more: Dahlgaard, his sister's son, and the Americans. He was reminded of the fact that he still had American prisoners, though he had returned the Yankee privateer commander to the fort under Frey's flag of truce.

Birkbeck looked nonplussed, then said, 'Beg pardon, sir, I meant no offence . . .'

'There was none taken.'

'Well, I'll . . .'

'Go below, Mr Birkbeck. You have done your utmost and I shall remember your services. Is there anything in my gift that I might oblige you with?'

Even in the gloom, Drinkwater could see Birkbeck brighten. 'I should like a dockyard post, sir, if it ain't asking too much.'

'I will see what I can do. Now, do you go below and I will keep the deck until midnight.'

'There's no need . . .'

'Yes there is. I have much to think about.'

Time seemed of no account as the ship, even under her patchwork sailplan, leaned to the breeze and seemed to take wing for the horizon. The northerly wind was light but steady, and bitterly cold, fogging their exhalations and laying a thin white rime on the hemp ropes as the night progressed.

Drinkwater paced the windward quarterdeck, no longer unsteady on his legs, but with the ease of long practice and the nervous energy of the sleepless. The sky was studded with stars, the great northern constellations of Ursa Major and Cassiopeia,

Cygnus, Lyra, Perseus, Auriga and, portentously, Andromeda, rolled about Polaris, beneath which lay the terrestrial pole. Across the heavens blazed the great swathe of the Milky Way. Such was the cold that their twinkling seemed to the watching Drinkwater to be of greater vigour than was customary.

About four bells in the first watch he became aware of the faint luminosity to the northward that marked an auroral glow. It was so faint that he thought at first he had imagined it, but then he became aware that it was pulsing, a grey and pallid light that came and then faded. Slowly it grew more intense and concentrated, turning in colour from a deathly pallor to a lucent green, appearing not as a nebulous glow but as a defined series of rays that seemed to diffuse from a distant, invisible and mysterious polar source.

For some fifteen or twenty minutes this display persisted and then the rays subsided and consolidated into a low, green arc. This in turn began to undulate and extend vertically towards the zenith so that it hung like some gigantic and diaphanous veil, stirred by a monstrous cosmic wind which blew noiselessly through the very heavens themselves. To men whose lives were spent in thrall to the winds of the oceans, this silence possessed an immense and horrible power before which they felt puny and insubstantial.

The sight overwhelmed the watch on deck; they stared open-mouthed, gaping at the northern sky, their faces illuminated by the unearthly light, while the frigate *Andromeda* and her prize stood south-east beneath the aurora.

Chapter Seventeen *December 1813–January 1814*

The Return

'So, you bring home a prize at last, Captain Drinkwater.'

Barrow peeled off his spectacles and waved Drinkwater to a chair. A fire of sea-coal blazed cheerily in the grate of the Second Secretary's capacious office, but failed to take the chill out of the air. Outside the Admiralty, thick snow lay in Whitehall, churned into a filthy slush by the wheels of passing carriages. Icicles hung from every drainpipe and rime froze on the upper lips of the downcast pedestrians trudging miserably along.

Drinkwater sat stiffly, feeling the piercing cold in his aching shoulder, and placed his battered hat on the table in front of him.

'Is that a shot hole?' Barrow asked inquisitively, leaning forward and poking at the cocked hat.

'A musket ball,' Drinkwater said flatly, finding the Second Secretary's curiosity distasteful. 'I fear my prize is equally knocked about,' he added lest his true sentiments be too obvious.

'I hear the Master Shipwright at Chatham is much impressed with the *Odin*; a new ship in fact. There seems little doubt she will be purchased into the Service. I don't need to tell you we need heavy frigates as cruisers on the North American station.'

Drinkwater nodded. 'Quite.'

'You do not seem very pleased, Captain.'

'She has already been purchased at a price, Mr Barrow.'

'Ah, yes. I recollect your losses. Some friends among them, no doubt?'

'Yes. And their widows yet to face.'

'I see.'

Drinkwater forbore to enlarge. He was filled with a sense of anti-climax and a yet more unpleasant duty to attend to than confronting Catriona Quilhampton, or Tom Huke's dependent womenfolk.

'Coming from Norway,' Barrow continued, 'you will not feel the cold as we do! The Thames is frozen, don't you know. It has become such a curiosity that there is a frost fair upon it in the Pool.'

'I saw something of it as I came across London Bridge.'

'Indeed. Well, Captain, the First Lord desired that I send for you and present the compliments of the Board to you. Whatever the cost it is better than losing Canada; imagine that in burnt farmsteads and settlements, the depredations of Indians and the augmentation of American power.' Barrow smiled and replaced his spectacles. One hand played subconsciously with a pile of papers awaiting his attention. The profit and loss account of the Admiralty was, it seemed, firmly in credit and John Barrow, fascinated by a hole in a sea-officer's hat, was satisfied.

'You will not have heard all the news, I fancy, though it is run somewhat stale by now.' Barrow's high good humour was so buoyant that it threatened to become infectious.

'News, Mr Barrow? No, I have heard nothing.'

'Dear me, Captain, we must put that right at once. Boney was trounced at Leipzig in mid-October,' Barrow explained. 'Schwarzenburg's Austrians refused battle with the Emperor, but attacked his marshals in detail and forced the French to concentrate on Leipzig. With Blücher attacking from the north, Schwarzenburg pushed up from the south, leaving Bernadotte to advance from the east. *He* dallied, as usual, waiting to see which way the wind would blow, but Bonaparte sent a flag of truce to discuss terms. The delay allowed the Russians to reinforce the Allies and the attack was resumed next day with the odds two to one in the Allies' favour. At the height of the battle the Saxons and Württembergers deserted Boney and, with the game up, he began to withdraw across the River Elster. He might have got away, but the single bridge was prematurely blown up, and in the ensuing chaos the French losses were gargantuan – over two hundred and fifty guns alone! Since then thousands of men have straggled, conscripts have deserted in droves and the French garrisons in Germany are isolated. The 26,000 men at Dresden have surrendered and typhus is said to be raging in the camps of the Grand Army!'

Drinkwater suppressed a shudder at the mention of that fearful disease, but was unable to restrain his interest. 'And what is the news from Spain?'

'Wellington is across the Pyrenees,' Barrow declared, his eyes shining, 'he deceived Soult by crossing an "impassable" but shallow channel of the River Bidassoa. He entered France and forced the Nivelle in November, a month after Leipzig! I tell you, Captain, it is now only a matter of time.'

'And what of Marshal Murat?'

Barrow barked a short, derisive laugh. 'King Joachim has retired to Naples to raise troops, but is, in fact, in contact with the Austrians.' Barrow paused and smiled. 'So you see, Captain, we have not entirely lost the services of a Secret Department in your absence.'

There was a sleek complacency in Barrow's patronizing which irritated Drinkwater after the rigours of his short but violent voyage. Nor had the Second Secretary yet finished the catalogue of Allied triumphs.

'And you will be interested to know that King Joachim', Barrow pronounced the title with sonorous irony, 'has not only concluded a treaty with Vienna, but also one with His Majesty's government, as recently as last week.'

'I see. Colonel Bardolini would have been pleased.'

'Bardolini?' Barrow frowned. 'Oh, yes, I recollect; the Neapolitan envoy. Well, at all events, Captain Drinkwater, the Board are most gratified with the success of your cruise, and not displeased that you have enjoyed a measure of personal success.'

'That is very civil of the Board, Mr Barrow.' Drinkwater bestirred himself; much had happened in his absence. 'Please be so kind as to convey my thanks to Lord Melville and their Lordships.'

Barrow inclined his head. 'Of course.'

Drinkwater rose and reached for his hat. The inferred message in Barrow's complimentary speech was less subtle than Barrow imagined. Drinkwater was not to expect a knighthood for taking the *Odin*; moreover, the Admiralty Board considered he should be satisfied with his prize-money. The gold was indeed a droit of Admiralty, having originated in Britain in the first place, as payment for wheat sent to Wellington's army in Spain two years earlier.

Drinkwater cleared his throat. 'I should like to ask for a dockyard post for Birkbeck, my sailing master, Mr Barrow, and a step for Mr Frey,' he said.

Barrow frowned. 'He is getting his percentage for carrying the specie as you requested in your report.'

'He is an excellent officer, Mr Barrow, a competent surveyor and first-rate water-colourist. Please don't forget', he added, with an edge to his voice, 'that several officers have died upon this service.'

Barrow opened his mouth, saw the harshness in the eyes of the sea-officer before him and cleared his throat. 'Frey, d'you say?' He made a note of the name. 'Then perhaps I might find something for him.'

'I should be obliged.' Drinkwater was satisfied, unaware of the effect his expression had had on Barrow. His time at the Admiralty had not been entirely wasted. He would not otherwise have known of Barrow's predilection for exploration. 'Good-day to you.'

'Good-day.' Drinkwater had reached the door when Barrow called after him, 'Oh, by the way, what happened to that clerk Templeton? I did not see his name among the dead or wounded.'

'He is well,' Drinkwater replied, adding evasively, 'he has taken furlough.'

'He has lodgings off the Strand, if I recall aright. Lived there with his mother in some decayed style, I believe.'

'Indeed.'

Drinkwater did not wish to pursue the matter and was in the act of passing through the door when Barrow went on, 'You may tell him there is still a place for him in the copy room. We still need a good cipher clerk – though not so often now.'

'I will tell him,' replied Drinkwater, 'though I am not certain he wishes to return to the copy room.'

'Very well. That is his affair. Good-day to you, Captain.'

'Good-day.'

Drinkwater walked down Whitehall towards the Abbey. He was deeply depressed, for Templeton was no guest of his, but had been held at the house in Lord North Street against his will under the close guard of Mr Frey.

The fate of Mr Templeton had been the last strand in the splice. And, ironically, he had been the means by which the rope's end had come unravelled in the first place, with his news of Bardolini's arrival at Harwich. And, Drinkwater thought savagely, pursuing his nautical metaphor, the last strand had been the most difficult to tuck.

He had attended to all the incidental details of the affair. He had buried Quilhampton as he had buried Huke, along with all the dead that had not been unceremoniously hurled overboard during the action fought with the *Odin*, sending their weighted bodies to the deep bed of the Vikkenfiord as he read the burial service, culminating with the psalm, 'I will lift up mine eyes unto the hills: from whence cometh my help . . .'

The cold and distant mountain summits had mocked him in his grief.

And he had dutifully written to Mosse's father, and to Huke's sister and asked permission to wait upon her and her mother; he had discharged into the hands of the military the American prisoners who had been Malaburn's confederates. They, in due process, would be returned to Dartmoor gaol.

And still there was Templeton.

The vague unease which Drinkwater had felt towards his confidential clerk had, he now knew, been founded on half-realized facts and circumstantial evidence that the preoccupations of those desperate days in the Vikkenfiord had driven from his immediate consideration.

When, however, the light northerly winds persisted and promised them a cold but steady southward passage, Drinkwater had had more leisure to mull over the events of recent weeks. The high pressure of the polar regions extended the length of the North Sea, bringing to England a bitter, snow-girt Christmas and to London the novelty of a frozen Thames.

Ice settled, too, about Drinkwater's heart.

He had wondered who had murdered Bardolini, attributing the crime to one of the many spies Napoleon maintained in London, as he had suggested to Castlereagh's under-secretary, but the cunning and co-ordination of Malaburn's actions, the appearance, compliance and ready impressment of those Americans, the sabotaged gun breeching, the certainties inherent in Malaburn's conduct in that last, fatal encounter, all argued something more sinister, more organized. He became obsessed with the notion of a conspiracy.

Drinkwater could not evade the question of what he would have done had Danks not so peremptorily shot Malaburn. With Huke dead, Malaburn had overplayed his hand, but with Huke still alive, Drinkwater did not truly know what he might have done.

These events, isolated in themselves, were but elements in the desolation of the last weeks. Their linkage was circumstantial, no more part of a conspiracy, in fact, than Herr Liepmann's report of a quantity of arms arriving at Hamburg. And yet, for so fatalistic a man as Nathaniel Drinkwater, the train of isolated occurrences wanted only a catalyst to link them as certainly as Bardolini's intelligence had led *Andromeda* to the American privateers anchored in the Vikkenfiord.

Two days south from Utsira, Mr Birkbeck had placed the catalyst in his hand.

'I'm afraid I opened it, sir. I had no idea what it was, but I think you should see it.'

Drinkwater knew what it was the instant he saw the package in Birkbeck's grasp. It had been in his office at the Admiralty, then in the house in Lord North Street. Now . . .

'Where did you find it, Mr Birkbeck?' he had asked quietly.

'In the hold, sir.'

'Malaburn.'

'It has an Admiralty seal . . .'

'Yes, yes, I'm much obliged to you.' Birkbeck had relinquished the canvas parcel and retreated, his curiosity unsated.

Drinkwater knew Malaburn had seized the papers from his London house, but how had this American known of the house, of Bardolini's presence there, or of the Neapolitan's significance? And while the contents of the package had no direct bearing upon the business of King Joachim or the shipment of arms to the Americans for the invasion of Canada, they contained information which, in the hands of Napoleon's chief of police, Savary, the Duke of Rovigo, could betray those persons in France well disposed to the cause of Great Britain, among whom was Madame Hortense Santhonax.

Holding the package after Birkbeck's departure, Drinkwater was almost shaking with relief at having nipped the betrayal of Hortense and her network in the bud, and then he found the answer to the half-formed question which had plagued him.

Apart from Drinkwater himself, only one person existed who could have drawn so fine a thread through this mystery: Templeton.

It came to him then, aside from the formal, everyday loyalty, those tiny fragmented clues, invisible to all but the suspicious and even then almost imperceptible.

He remembered Templeton's subtle attempt to play down the value of Liepmann's intelligence report from Hamburg; remembered Templeton had not broadcast the news of Sparkman's letter concerning Bardolini to the copy room, and had had difficulty concealing his satisfaction when Drinkwater himself, in an act of uncharacteristic high-handedness, had burnt Sparkman's letter. Finally he remembered Templeton's consternation when he learned he was to sail with Drinkwater. He must have been sick with anxiety as to the outcome of events throughout the whole passage, Drinkwater concluded.

It was true that Templeton had witnessed the Americans letting go the anchor to deliver *Andromeda* to the guns of the *Odin*, but that had been a somewhat circumstantial occurrence, Drinkwater concluded. Moreover, in the aftermath of that event, Templeton had been singularly unhelpful in identifying the culprits. Only their own hiding on the knightheads where Huke had discovered them had revealed who they were.

It was clear they knew very little of what was going on, and had acted according to Malaburn's instructions, as well they might, for he had spirited them out of prison and seemed set fair to get them aboard homeward-bound American ships! Malaburn himself had taken pains to keep out of trouble during that first action. Drinkwater had no doubt now that Malaburn had been below throughout the event with the dual objective of avoiding the Danish fire and compressing the cable when sufficient had run out. Why his absence at his battle station had not been reported, Drinkwater would never know, but some dilatoriness on the part of, say, the twelve-year-old Mr Fisher, would seem to provide an answer.

It was not difficult in a man-of-war for a seaman of experience, as Malaburn clearly was, to avoid Templeton, who was himself penned up with the officers. Templeton had given no hint of any foreknowledge of an acquaintanceship with one of the crew, but God knew what anxieties, hopes and fears had made Templeton act the way he did. Templeton's presence may have given the American agent a great deal of anxiety, but Malaburn could not expect events to fall out too pat. He had had the greatest run of luck in collecting his chain-gang from Dartmoor and shipping it so neatly to Scotland to be pressed promptly by the assiduous Huke!

Moreover, Drinkwater remembered angrily, Malaburn had so nearly been successful.

He had not arrested Templeton immediately, but waited until *Andromeda* anchored at the Nore, observing his clerk for any clues of apprehension. On their arrival he had instructed Templeton to accompany him to London, implying his service aboard the frigate was at an end. With the crippled *Odin* sent up the Medway to the dockyard, Drinkwater made out a written order to Frey to turn the prize over to the master-shipwright and join him. Leaving Birkbeck in charge of *Andromeda*, Drinkwater had prepared to post to London, intending to take Frey and Templeton. There was nothing remarkable in the arrangement.

Frey had joined Drinkwater as he emerged from the fine red-brick residence of the Dockyard Commissioner where he had been finalizing details for the reception of the two ships. A post-chaise awaited the three men.

'Ah, Frey, you are on time.'

'Good afternoon, sir. It's damnably cold.'

They shook hands and Drinkwater turned to Templeton. 'I appear to have left my gloves, would you mind . . . ?'

'Of course.' Templeton had returned towards the house.

'Frey,' Drinkwater had said in a low and urgent voice, 'I want you to accompany me to London. I've made the necessary arrangements for the *Odin*.'

'Is it the *Kestrel*, sir?' Frey had asked anxiously. As the senior surviving officer of the cutter, Frey was naturally concerned with their justification for handing over the little ship. He feared a court-martial.

'No, no. Listen . . .' but Templeton was already returning, holding Drinkwater's full-dress white gloves.

'Just do exactly what I say!' he had hissed vehemently, then swung round to Templeton. 'Ah, Templeton, obliged, thank you.'

'You had dropped them in the hall.'

Drinkwater had grunted. Now they were ashore again Templeton had resumed his old familiarity. It bespoke his confidence. Drinkwater clambered aboard and was followed by the others. A moment later the chaise swung through the Lion Gate and on towards Rochester and London.

Drinkwater had waited until it was almost dark before he

struck. He affected to doze, killing off all chance of conversation as the chaise lurched along, passing through a succession of villages. Frey, though consumed with curiosity, obediently held his tongue.

Templeton had stared out over the snow-covered countryside. Surreptitiously watching him, Drinkwater sought to read the man, but Templeton remained inscrutable, unsuspecting.

As a grey twilight spread over the land and the chaise rocked on towards Blackheath, Drinkwater stirred from his mock stupor. He could no longer endure the sharp angularities of the pistol in the small of his back and drew it with slow deliberation.

Templeton, himself half asleep by then, was unaware of anything amiss until Drinkwater, having given Frey's foot a sharp kick, pulled the hammer back to full cock with a loud click.

'Mr Templeton,' Drinkwater said, 'consider yourself under arrest.'

'What the devil . . . ?' Templeton made to move, but Frey seized his arm and held it while the clerk ceased struggling and subsided. Drinkwater watched Templeton's eyes close in resignation and saw his Adam's apple bob nervously above his stock.

'You deceived me, Mr Templeton,' Drinkwater said, 'you were in contact with Malaburn, were you not? You informed him of the purpose and whereabouts of Bardolini, and you are an accessory to the man's murder. You told Malaburn of the purpose of our voyage, you were aware that the package of papers was removed from my office and secreted at my house . . .

'Well, have you nothing to say?'

Templeton shook his head. His mouth had gone dry and he could not speak.

'Is this how you served Lord Dungarth? Leaking secrets to the enemy? Is that how Dungarth was blown up and lost his leg? Did you betray him to the French?'

'No! No, never!'

'So when did you start this?'

'I . . .' Templeton licked his lips, 'I never betrayed Lord Dungarth. I never trafficked with the French.'

'Only with the Americans, eh? Is that right?'

Templeton said nothing.

'Your silence is eloquent, Templeton, and enough to condemn you.'

'Sir . . . Captain Drinkwater, I know you for a man of sensibility, my intention was not murder, I meant only . . .'

'Meant only what?'

Templeton's features worked distressfully in the gloom. He breathed heavily and wiped the back of a hand across his mouth.

'Sir . . . sir, I beg you . . . my mother . . .'

He had looked desperately at Frey and then lapsed into a sobbing quiescence from which Drinkwater had been unable to rouse him. In the end he had abandoned the attempt.

'I am taking you to my house,' he had said. 'You will be held there for the time being.'

'Is that a good idea, sir?' Frey had asked, speaking for the first time, his face bleak with suppressed emotion.

Drinkwater had nodded. 'For the time being, yes. You will look after him until after I have decided what is to be done.'

Night had fallen when they crossed the Thames. The light of a young moon and the gleam of the lamps mounted on the parapet of London Bridge to illuminate the carriageway shone on the white expanse of the frozen river.

'Stap me,' Frey had said, breaking the dolorous silence, 'I wish I'd my paint-box!'

On arrival at the house in Lord North Street they had hustled Templeton quickly inside and upstairs to the bedroom which Bardolini had once used.

'Leave us a moment,' Drinkwater had said to Frey, after he had dismissed the impassive Williams, and Frey, with a glance at the trembling Templeton, had done as he was bid.

Downstairs, the manservant had ushered Frey into the withdrawing-room. Frey settled before a roaring fire quickly conjured by Williams, who poured him a glass of oporto. The young lieutenant sat and stared at the magnificent portrait above the fireplace, marvelling at the skill of the artist. The lady was fair and beautiful and her lovely face seemed to glow in the imperfect candlelight. He had no idea who she was, nor what her relationship had been with Captain Drinkwater. He had had no idea, either, that Drinkwater possessed such a house; the knowledge seemed another mystery to add to the sum of extraordinary occurrences of recent weeks. He wondered whether Drinkwater would vouchsafe him some further explanation when he came downstairs. He knew that

Captain Drinkwater had, from time to time, some connections with secret operations and felt that the death of James Quilhampton had elevated Frey himself to the post of confidant. For the moment he was lost in admiration of the work of Mr George Romney.

So abandoned to contemplation had he been, that Drinkwater startled him. 'She was the Countess of Dungarth,' Drinkwater had explained, helping himself from the decanter. 'The wife of the former head of the Admiralty's Secret Department. This was formerly his house. Your health, Mr Frey. Now tell me what is troubling you.'

Frey had been recalled to the present. 'That man, sir.'

'Templeton? What about him?'

'Shouldn't we turn him over to the constables? If what you say is true, he is guilty of treason, of trafficking with the enemy . . .'

'You are concerned he might escape, that the bedroom is no Newgate cell, is that what's troubling you?'

'Yes it is, in part.'

Drinkwater had sighed. 'I owe you something of an explanation, my dear Frey. You are the only man I can trust in this matter and it must be settled quietly. Forgive me, it is an imposition I would rather not have laid upon you.'

Drinkwater had then related to Frey an account of the arrival of secret intelligence from Naples and of the subsequent disappearance of Bardolini. He told of the sabotage in the Vikkenfiord, of his belated suspicions, of the too pat pressing of the Americans and the mischief they had wrought under Malaburn.

'It was an assumed name, I think, and a flash one, a punning which might have spelled the end for all of us.'

'What do you think he intended to do, if he had not let go your anchor?'

'To set us on fire when we were conveniently close to the American ships and he and his accomplices could escape in a boat. Had he lain low in the hold, he might just have achieved it. He was a resourceful fellow, this Mal-a-burn, he staked a great deal on chance and he nearly won . . .'

Drinkwater did not wish to dwell on how close his own laxity had come to promoting this course of events, nor on what he owed to Thomas Huke whose unnecessary death would reproach him for the rest of his life. The two men were lost in silence for a moment, contemplating what might have happened.

'And Templeton?' Frey had prompted at last. It did not seem to be over until Templeton was dealt with.

Drinkwater stirred and poured another glass for both of them.

'There has been enough blood spilled in this whole wretched business. We have both lost a friend in James, and only you and I know of Templeton's guilt. Let us sleep on it.'

'But he might escape from that room.'

'He might murder us in our beds, it's true, and if he does escape,' Drinkwater shrugged, 'well, what does it matter? It's over now.'

'But *why*, sir? I don't understand.'

' 'Twas a temptation more than he could bear. Consider the matter.' Drinkwater sighed; his conversation alone with Templeton had borne out all his suspicions and answered most of his questions. 'Templeton is an intelligent fellow,' Drinkwater went on, 'skilled, dedicated. For years he toils miserably upwards in the sequestered corridors of the Admiralty, a world of internecine jealousies between pettifogging minds. He finds himself close to secrets of state, unlocks some of them with his ability to decrypt reports at speed. He learns from Lord Dungarth, and later myself, of his true worth, yet he is paid a pittance. He is surrounded by glory and yet not one iota is reflected upon him. You are an artist, Frey, a man of, what did he call me? Of sensibility; surely you can see how such a life could corrode a proud spirit and leave him vulnerable to seduction?'

Frey had stirred uncomfortably, but held his tongue.

'Templeton, I suspect,' Drinkwater went on, 'was as much led astray by Malaburn's gold as Malaburn's promise of a new life. D'you think Templeton was a high Tory or the member of a Corresponding Society, a secret republican? For him America means opportunity, another chance away from our world of privilege and patronage, of jobbing and perquisites, of the eternal English *kow-tow*. I didn't have to ask him if this is true, though I have spoken to him of it. I know it myself; I feel it in my bones, and so, if you're honest, do you.

'No, leave Templeton to his conscience, and the workings of providence. He can do no harm now.' Drinkwater had paused, then said, 'This is a damnable war. It has lasted all my adult life. Quilhampton joined me as a midshipman and was shot to pieces. Now we have a new generation, boys like little Fisher weeping over cats, but bred to war, inured to war like me. I am weary of it, sick to my very soul, Frey, and I am burdening you unreasonably with my confession.' Drinkwater smiled, and his face was oddly boyish.

'Not at all,' Frey said uncertainly, 'not at all. I recall something Pope wrote . . .'

'What is that?'

'"Sir, I have lived a courtier all my days, And studied men, their manners and their ways; And have observed this useful maxim still, To let my betters always have their will."'

'So, you feel something of it too, eh?' Drinkwater smiled again. 'Anyway, my dear fellow,' he said, rising and stretching stiffly, 'I have asked for you to be given a step in rank. You will be a Commander before too long.'

'Is that to purchase my silence in the matter?' Frey had asked quickly, looking up.

Drinkwater laughed. 'Only incidentally. But yes, it binds you to the system and compromises you. Like marriage and family, it makes you a hostage to fortune.'

Drinkwater crossed the room and drew back the curtains. 'Good Lord, I thought it had grown warmer and blamed the wine, but it is raining outside.'

Frey became aware of the hiss of the deluge, then Drinkwater closed the curtains and faced him. 'I think it is time for bed.'

Frey tossed off his glass and stood up. 'Good-night, sir.'

'Good-night. I hope you sleep well.'

'I'll try.'

'Lock your door,' Drinkwater said with a laugh.

When Frey had gone, Drinkwater poured another glass and sat again, to stare into the dying fire as the candles burned low. It was already long past midnight and he would confront Mr Barrow later that day. Finally, after about an hour, he rose, went into the hall and opened the front door. In the street a cold rain fell in torrents; peering out into the hissing darkness, Drinkwater smiled to himself. Turning back into the house he left the door ajar and went quietly upstairs.

Outside Templeton's room he drew a key from his pocket and unlocked the door. He stepped inside; rain beat upon the uncurtained window and he could faintly see Templeton, still dressed, lying upon the bed.

'Captain Drinkwater . . .?' Templeton's voice faltered uncertainly. 'Captain Drinkwater, is that you?'

It suddenly struck Drinkwater that Templeton expected to be executed for his crime of treason, murdered perhaps by Drinkwater himself as Bardolini had been assassinated. Instead, he stood motionless and silent beside the open door.

'I tried to get myself killed in the boarding of the *Odin*,' Templeton said desperately.

'I know,' Drinkwater replied quietly.

'What . . . what do you intend to do?'

'Nothing,' Drinkwater murmured, stepping aside from the doorway, 'now be gone.'

The Frost Fair *26 January 1814*

Upon the frozen Thames in the Pool of London, between London Bridge and the Tower, there had been a great frost fair for some six weeks. Tents containing circus curiosities and human freaks had been set up, stalls selling everything from patent nostrums and articles of cheap haberdashery to roasted chestnuts were laid out in regular 'streets'. Open spaces were cleared for skating and the populace displayed every scale of talent from the inept to the expert. An *émigré* fencing master gave lessons with épée or foil to ambitious counting-house clerks, while rustics exercised at single-stick. Bloods rode their hacks on the ice, caracoling their slithering mounts in extravagant daring for the admiring benefit of credulous belles. Fashion rubbed shoulders with the indigent upon the slippery surface, and many a dainty lady lost her dignity with her footing, to the merciless merriment of her acknowledged inferiors.

Whores and pick-pockets abounded, preying on the foolish. Silly young blades were helped to their feet and simultaneously deprived of their purses.

Good ales were served from barrels set upon stands on the ice, whole sheep were spit-roasted and consumed with the relish that only cold weather can endow. London was entranced, captivated by the spectacle.

On the night of 25 January, the night Templeton was released, the warmth of an approaching depression brought heavy rain. This raised freshets in the Thames valley to the west of the capital. The following day the thaw set the frozen river in sudden motion. Tents and stalls were swept away, along with their customers and the curious promenaders whom even six weeks' revelry could not deter.

In the days that followed, far downstream, amid the samphire bordering the salt-marshes of the Kent and Essex shores, the bloated bodies of the drowned washed ashore.

Among them was the unrecognizable corpse of Templeton. He had been quite drunk when the ice melted.

Author's Note

In 1813 Norway was a possession of King Frederick of Denmark, and occasional raids on its coast were made by British cruisers operating in northern waters.

As a result of the second expedition against Copenhagen in 1807, the Danish navy had been very largely destroyed by the British, though a fleet of gun-vessels and one or two men-of-war remained in commission, along with a large and effective fleet of Danish privateers. Subsequent actions between the British and the Danes became notorious for their ferocity.

The Danes also lost the island of Helgoland which, at the entrance of the Elbe, became a forward observation post for the British, and an entrepôt for British goods destined for the Continent to break the embargo imposed by Napoleon (a fact I have used as the basis for *Under False Colours)*. The island remained in British hands for a century.

After the French Emperor's disastrous Russian campaign, the loyalty of his marshalate was severely shaken. Several of these men, who owed their fortunes to Napoleon, made overtures to the Allies. One, Marshal Bernadotte, became heir presumptive to the Swedish crown and, as a result of his joining the Allied camp, was later ceded Norway, afterwards becoming king of the entire Scandinavian peninsula.

Less successfully, Joachim Murat, King of Naples and Marshal of France, 'the most complete vulgarian and poseur', according to Carola Oman, but an inspired if vainglorious leader of cavalry, opened a secret communication with the British government in the autumn of 1813 with a view to retaining his throne in the event of the fall of his brother-in-law, Napoleon. His rival, the Bourbon King Ferdinand of the 'Two Sicilies', retained the insular portion of his dual kingdom under British protection. Murat's overtures resulted in a treaty with London signed on 11 January 1814. It availed him little; he was shot by his 'subjects' in the following year, and the odious Ferdinand returned to his palace in Naples.

The ambivalent posture of the Americans in their brief war with Great Britain was at odds with their single-minded ambitions towards Canada. Thirty thousand Loyalists had settled in New Brunswick after the War of Independence, a living reproach to the claims of the patriot party, and it was the avowed aim of the war-hawks in Congress to assimilate these and simultaneously liberate the French Canadians from the yoke of British tyranny, to the considerable advantage of the United States.

Between the new and the old worlds lay the Atlantic Ocean, dominated by the Royal Navy which, despite receiving a bloody nose from the young United States' Navy, was by 1813 reasserting its paramountcy. Nevertheless, American privateers continued to operate with impunity and the British were equally equivocal in their attitude to American trade, particularly when it affected the supply of Wellington's army in the Iberian peninsula.

Napoleon, moreover, took an interest in American affairs (his youngest brother Jerome married an American and their grandson was later Secretary of the US Navy, though the lady herself was later repudiated in favour of a Württemburg princess). Napoleon had sold Louisiana and the Mississippi valley as far west as the Rockies to the United States in 1803 with the prescient remark that the Americans would 'fight the English again'. His secret diplomacy thereafter applied pressure to bring about this highly desirable state of affairs.

With Britain contributing 124,000 muskets, 18.5 million cartridges, 34,500 swords, 218 cannon, 176,600 pairs of boots, 150,000 uniforms and an additional 187,000 yards of uniform cloth to the Allied armies for the Leipzig campaign, a similar arrangement between the French and the Americans in exchange for wheat does not seem improbable.

That knowledge of such a deal should form the 'guarantee' of Joachim Murat's good faith and a pledge of his suitability for a throne forms the basis of this story.

Both the British and the American governments were quite indifferent to the fate of merchant seamen, and those Americans lodged in Dartmoor remained incarcerated until long after the signing of the Peace of Ghent ended the war. On 6 April 1815 a riot broke out which left seven American prisoners dead and fifty-four wounded. It is believed that among the dead were a handful that had earlier escaped and been recaptured.